St. Patrick's Training College
All Hallow's College
GRIFFITH AVENUE
RIVER TOLKA
St. Vincent's Asylum
St. Alphonsus Convent
DRUMCONDRA ROAD
DRUMCONDRA
RICHMOND ROAD
BRIAN ROAD
PHILIPSBURG AVENUE
Holy Cross College
CLONLIFFE ROAD
FAIRVIEW STRAND
Croke Park
PORTLAND PLACE
RUSSEL PLACE
BALLYBOUGH ROAD
STRAND
NORTH
RICHMOND PLACE
GARDENER STREET
TEMPLE
Mountjoy Square
SUMMER HILL
SEVILLE
DENMARK STREET
CHURCH ROAD
EAST ROAD
PLACE
Parnell Square
GLOUCESTER STREET
RAILWAY STREET
MARLBOROUGH
Nelson Pillar
Model School
BRITAIN STREET
Pro-Cathedral
TALBOT
STREET
SHERIFF STREET
MAYOR STREET
Custom House
NORTH WALL
River Liffey
CITY QUAY
SIR JOHN ROGERSONS QUAY
TOWNSEND STREET
HANOVER STREET
MISERY HILL
HANOVER QUAY
Bank of Ireland
DAME STREET
Trinity College
NASSAU STREET
GRAND CANAL QUAY
GRAFTON STREET
DAWSON STREET
KILDARE STREET
Leinster House
Marrion Sq.
College of Surgeons
NORTH
SOUTH
Government Building
LOWER MOUNT STREET
MOUNT STREET
BAGGOT STREET LR.
St. Stephen's Green
YORK STREET
SOUTH
HARCOURT STREET
LOWER LEESON STREET
HADDINGTON ROAD
Beggar's Bush
University College
HATCH STREET
CAMDEN STREET
Map by S. T. Palmer

THE END OF THE HUNT

ALSO BY THOMAS FLANAGAN

The Year of the French

The Tenants of Time

The Irish Novelists: 1800–1850

THE END OF THE HUNT

Thomas Flanagan

SINCLAIR-STEVENSON

First published in Great Britain in 1995
by Sinclair-Stevenson
an imprint of Reed Consumer Books Ltd
Michelin House, 81 Fulham Road, London SW3 6RB
and Auckland, Melbourne, Singapore and Toronto

First published in the United States of America by Dutton,
an imprint of Dutton Signet, a division of Penguin Books USA Inc

A CIP catalogue record for this book
is available at the British Library

ISBN 1 85619 520 1

Printed and bound in Great Britain by Clays Ltd, St Ives plc

For Jean, always.
And for Billy, Seamus, Darcy.

THE END OF THE HUNT

I

PATRICK PRENTISS

I came home to Dublin's soft, welcoming sunlight in the spring of 1919, an Irishman discharged from the British Army with the rank of captain, the empty right sleeve pinned neatly into its pocket. For a week I stayed by myself in the tall, echoing house, alone save for Mrs. Haggerty the housekeeper and Lily the remaining maidservant, putting off the invitations of friends who telephoned to welcome me back and leaving their thoughtful notes unanswered on the hall table. Then Myles Keough telephoned, a friend and fellow barrister, a man of cheerful, bottomless ironies, and we agreed to have lunch at the Shelbourne.

I walked into town through that sunlight, the pale skies scoured clean by early-morning rain, the garden hedges green and glistening behind spruce iron railings painted white or black. Beyond the hedges, beyond small, well-tended gardens of spring flowers, stood houses like the one that I had just left, substantial houses a half-century old, Dublin's claret-colored brick, hall doors surmounted by elaborate reproductions of Regency fanlights. Dublin, indeed Ireland, had three years before been transformed by the Easter Rising, but there were no traces of this in Palmerston Park nor Rathgar nor Rathmines, secure worlds of barristers, solicitors, surgeons, chartered accountants. Throughout the Rising, those houses had stood safe, almost beyond the sounds of artillery fire.

"How did you manage without me?" I asked Mrs. Haggerty that morning, before I set out for town, but there had been no need to ask. Every month, the household accounts had come to me in France and then, toward the end, first to the base hospital and then to the convalescent hospital in England. Laboring over them at the kitchen table, as once she had labored before presenting them to my mother, pen dipped in cheap blue ink, tongue slightly protruding.

"Far better than with you," she said, as I had expected. She stood beside my chair at the breakfast table, an old woman now, stout and starchy, pinned above her voluminous bosom the gold chatelaine watch which had been a Christmas gift from my parents. "You have no call to be taking a walk of an hour or more," she said. "Not in the condition that you have come home to us in." "I am all healed now, Mrs. Haggerty," I said, "as good as new, almost." To prove the point, with my newfound dexterity, practiced in the convalescent hospital, I cracked my boiled egg single-handed, tap tap against the shell.

With one month's accounts, in May of 1916, she wrote to tell me, "There has been terrible death and destruction here in Dublin, and all has been anarchy here for a week. It was awful beyond all telling, and the center of our lovely Dublin has been destroyed and the dead are to be numbered in their thousands. I have not ventured down there myself, although it is said to be safe enough now, with the army back in control, but I know those who have and there have been fearful pictures in the *Freeman's Journal.*" Now, three years later, it was likely that she had contrived to forget that letter, now that much of Ireland, our Ireland, Catholic and nationalist Ireland, had come to agree that Ireland's true battle had been fought not at the Somme, but in the streets of Dublin, in buildings held for almost a week against artillery fire. It had not seemed so at the time.

Hanging from a wall in the kitchen now, behind glass, framed by bog oak, were small oval photographs of the fifteen rebel leaders who had been executed by firing squad in the stonebreakers' yard at Kilmainham. Someone, Mrs. Haggerty or Lily, had tacked palm fronds to the frame, pale and brittle. Mrs. Haggerty seemed briefly embarrassed when I discovered it, but Lily glared at me with respectful defiance. "Not at all," I assured Mrs. Haggerty, "I knew two or three of them. One of them was my friend." "He was indeed," Mrs. Haggerty said, looking over toward Lily as though repeating a lesson. "Many's an evening Mr. MacDonagh has spent in this house." Thomas MacDonagh looked out at me from his oval, a poet's face, incongruous Volunteer's tunic, Sam Browne belt, cap. "And others," I said. An unlikely soldier. Like myself. "Yez both had your tasks," Mrs. Haggerty said, as though summarizing the lesson for Lily, "yourself out there in the trenches, saving poor Catholic little Belgium, and Thomas MacDonagh and the lads saving the soul of Ireland here at home." Lily looked docile but unpersuaded.

From Palmerston down the length of the Rathmines Road to the small, humped bridge across the canal I walked through the unchanged, untouched suburb, to where the road ends at the canal, and there, briefly and abruptly, the scene shifted, because the wide laneway into the Portobello barracks was under heavy guard, and with a heavy wooden gate, barbed-wire-entwined. The soldiers guarding it looked negligent and at ease, two of them puffing at cigarettes shielded from view by cupped hands. It had been a far more tense scene three years ago, on the Tuesday of Easter Week, with the bridge astride one of the main southern routes into the center of the city. On that night, a man perfectly innocent of involvement in the rebellion, another friend of mine as it happened, a pacifist and a much-loved eccentric, had been seized at the bridge with two other men, and shot dead by firing squad in the yard of the barracks. The officer who ordered it had been adjudged insane, and rightly in my judgment, but the rumor of Frank Skeffington's murder had traveled through the city that week, ugly and grotesque. Now there was only the barbed wire, the slouching soldiers. Once, walking just here, along the Rathmines Road, Frank had lectured me on women's suffrage, bearded and spectacled, in homespun tweeds, humorless and impassioned, all Dublin knew him.

We are a provincial people when all is said and done, we Dubliners. Standing on the bridge, between the barracks and the road to Stephen's Green, I could see a loaded barge carrying turf to us from the bogland, and imagined a smell of distant countryside. The little bridges dated back to the cutting of the canal itself, at the close of the eighteenth century, bridges at once elegant and unassertive. Leaning on one of them toward evening, one could look toward mountains at the city's doorstep almost, an hour's ride by motorcar, pale greens and dark browns, gorse-covered, stretching toward bogs. And yet a half-hour's walk brought one to hotels, theaters, restaurants, fashionable squares, slums, shops, dinner parties. One could imagine countryside beyond the mountains, pasturelands upon which cattle grazed.

Had I turned right at Portobello Bridge, a ten-minute walk past Leeson Street Bridge and Baggot Street Bridge, along the tree-shaded towpath, would have taken me to Mount Street, where, in Easter Week, rebels held houses which commanded that bridge, and fought off British troops being marched to the city from Kingstown. Instead, I walked along Harcourt Street to Stephen's Green, which the rebels had also held, before falling back to the College of Surgeons, whose neo-Georgian front would stand pockmarked, forever no doubt, by rifle and machine-gun fire, and through the Green, which that week had been gouged by hasty trenches, to the Shelbourne. But three years is a long time, and the trenches had vanished, and all was as it had been. Lawns, winding paths, artful beds of flowers, crimson, yellow, white, a pond small and comely with ducks. Elderly gentlemen strolled the paths or else sunned themselves in low-slung canvas chairs, handkerchiefs spread across faces, hands joined upon paunches. Nursemaids wheeled perambulators, their dark skirts and jackets assertions of their places in the fixed hierarchies of the servants' hall. Someday, perhaps, the cratered moonscapes of Ypres and Passchendaele, even, will be smoothed away, grasses will grow again, hedges.

At the door of the Shelbourne's dining room, Pat, the headwaiter, spied me, and walked nimbly forward, a tall, stoop-shouldered man, long lined face; he had been in this room for as long as I could remember, waiter and then headwaiter. "Now then," he said, "you are most welcome back. Mr. Keough told me that we would be seeing you today, Captain." "Mister," I corrected him, shoving aside, forever I trusted, the Captain Prentiss who had claimed my surname, a strange, unconvincing fellow, tunic, swagger stick. The waiter's practiced eye flickered across the empty sleeve. Someday it would be a habitual, unregarded part of the Dublin scene, like Adams the barrister, my colleague and Myles Keough's, with the black, built-up boot housing a foot shrunken from birth.

Or like Myles's waistcoat. I could not remember what sort he had been wearing when last we had dined in this room, there was a vivid one, persimmon and lime stripes, but today's was white, a watered silk, with small, vivid primroses scattered across it. The suit was a pale, soft gray flannel, to suit the season, and a dark bow tie. "My dear fellow," he said, "my dear, dear fellow," and, as though it were the most natural thing in the world, he seized my left hand in his two. We were at a table close to the window, and midday sunlight fell upon us. Beyond the window, the Green sparkled, paths between lawns and a bit of a flowerbed. It was as though today had been stitched to a day three years earlier, as though the fire from machine guns on the roof of the hotel had not slashed at the trenches, as though shells had not turned the Somme into the landscape of desolation.

"I took the liberty of ordering for us both," Myles said, when our whiskies had been brought to us. "I remembered your favorites, consommé and sole. Off the bone, you used to like it." But I had not liked it off the bone, that I could remember, although from now on I would; manageable for the one-armed.

His face was long, equine, firm-jawed, and eyes blue as cornflowers beneath hair the color of oak, but what one best remembered was the mouth, the lips full and red, and with a constant half-smile trembling between courtesy and banter. He was a marvel in the courtroom, wig perched at a slight angle, almost jaunty, thumbs hooked into a waistcoat decorously black or gray-striped, leaning forward across his brief, the eyes mischievous.

It was as well that he had booked our table, because the room was full. Barristers, solicitors, prosperous farmers in town for the day, gentlemen in heavy tweeds and the fierce look of elderly retired soldiers, a party of four with the somber dress of civil servants, and at a window table beyond us, facing me, a party of three, a uniformed lieutenant with his mother and, as I supposed, his sister or his fiancée. The room was lime-green with white curtains at the windows, and, at the wall facing the windows, a long table at which the roasts were carved. The Shelbourne was the hotel for families of the gentry in town for balls or for the horse show, but middle-class Dublin was attached to it for lunch or for a long, leisurely dinner. As a boy home from Clongowes Wood I would be taken here by my parents as a Christmas treat.

"Now those four," Myles said, as he pretended to study a wine list which he knew by heart, "have strolled up from Dublin Castle to visit us. I know one of them, Tony Powers, an Irishman, he's on their legal staff, a decent fellow. We have clashed in court. Do you know him, no, he is since your time."

As he was telling Pat that we would have the Moselle, I looked out across the Green, toward the College of Surgeons. The rebels had held it for the full of Easter Week, despite the machine-gun and rifle fire from the Shelbourne and the roofs to either side of it. Here, above our heads, above wood and plaster, wardrobes and beds, gunners kneeling behind sandbags. But for all of that week, the rebels who held the College had been unable to fight their way out to link with Kent at the South Dublin Union nor with MacDonagh. Three years before. History. But already there were books of a sort, by British journalists, and by the publicists of Sinn Féin.

"After Pearse surrendered at the Post Office," Myles said, "he sent a message to the outlying commands. A British captain and his company carried it to the College over there, and one of the rebel nurses was with him to swear that it was true."

"The Green was Con Markievicz's command?" I said.

"It might as well have been," he said, "but a young fellow named Mallin commanded. All eyes were on Con though. She was second-in-command, wearing that Citizens' Army outfit she had, do you remember it, with the great slouch hat, and carrying an immense bloody revolver that would have done credit to Buffalo Bill. The *Irish Times* said that she kissed the pistol before handing it over to the captain." He gave a swift glance to the bottle, linen-cradled, which Pat held to him, and nodded. "Uncork it now, and pour away when the fish comes, Pat. And in the meantime, have the lad bring a drop more of the Jameson's to Mr. Prentiss and myself."

"A young fellow named Mallin," I said.

"He is one of the ones they executed by firing squad," Myles said. "The two Pearses, Connolly, Clarke, MacDonagh, Plunkett, fifteen of them in all. If the British had shot every one of them then and there, on the day of the surrender, they might have got away with it. Dublin was boiling with rage. The shawlies jeered them when they were being marched away to the Rotunda. Then General Maxwell arrived with his plans for pacification. Court-martialing them in secret and shooting them in twos and threes, stretching it out over weeks. Every morning, it seemed, two or three names in the morning papers. Chaps we knew, some of them. Like blood seeping from under a locked door. MacDonagh was a friend of yours, was he not?"

"Yes," I said. "We were friends."

Before turning to his consommé, Myles addressed his second Jameson's. "She kissed the great bloody revolver," Myles said, "a gesture which would be of interest to the loony-bin doctors in Vienna. The army captain was Irish himself, Irish in a way, do you follow me? Very brusque with Mallin and the others, but he offered Con a seat in his command car. 'I shall walk,' says the bold Con, 'at the head of my troops.' 'Of course,' the captain says, 'quite right, quite as it should be.' And salutes her! He was a Wheeler, one of the Sligo Wheelers, and when the Gore-Booths speak, the Wheelers jump."

He paused to taste the consommé.

"And yet," he said, "not a month had gone by, less than a month, and those shawlies who had done the spitting had pictures of the martyred leaders on their walls. Very Irish, in its way. And not shawlies alone, Patrick. I came to feel differently myself, we all did. It is a different Ireland from the one you left." His tone was still light, but he had caught me with his blue gaze, as though instructing me.

When Patrick the waiter was next with us, I said, "We were talking about . . ." I nodded toward the Green without finishing the sentence. Dublin is a city of half-sentences.

"To be sure, Mr. Prentiss," he said, bland croupier's face. "A dreadful business." He might have been referring either to the insurrection or to the executions.

"What do you make of it yourself?" Myles asked with affectionate malice.

"About what you do yourself, sir," Pat said, in a masterly countermove, which Myles acknowledged with a smile.

With serving silver, Pat lifted one of the soles, brown and fragrant.

"Were you here yourself through that week, Pat?" I asked him.

"Was I here! Begod, I was here on the Monday when they seized the Green, and the next day when the soldiers moved in with the machine guns, but by Wednesday all of us were gone, all the staff. The soldiers left the top floor a terrible mess."

"Had you no thought to join the fellows in the Green?"

"To dig trenches in the flower beds and then hunker down to wait for machine-gun bullets?" He allowed himself a commentating smile.

The lieutenant and his guests were ready to leave, and Pat hurried to them. The lieutenant looked remarkably young, twenty perhaps; his pips were bright. The girl, who must surely have been fiancée and not sister, was smiling at him, dark eyes and half-parted lips, an unconscious sensuality, as though his mere presence caressed her. Pat escorted them to the dining room door, the boy nodding to him, the girl not listening. The mother walked behind them, tall and unsmiling; she wore an elaborate yet dowdy hat of brown silk.

"A very nice young fellow," Pat said when he returned, "himself and his mother. I have often served the family in this room. The Talbots of Talbot's Bridge below in Kilkenny. Is the fish done to satisfaction, gentlemen?"

"Entirely," Myles said, "eminently satisfactory." His own had been left on the bone, and he was delicately removing its skeleton.

"And the young lady?" I asked.

"Smithson," Pat said. Bare Miss Smithson, no Smithson's Bridge to her name, poor dear. "They are to be married in a week's time, and then he goes back to his regiment, over there." He nodded in what he imagined was the direction of the Rhine. "They are an old army family, the father was killed at the outset of things, at the retreat from Mons." A flickering glance touched my sleeve again.

The Shelbourne was part of a world in which young Talbots took the King's commission, married young girls like Miss Smithson, then rejoined their regiment, on the Rhine or in India, or wherever, depending upon the decade. Never imagining that things could be otherwise, never imagining the retreat from Mons, the mooncraters of the Somme. Never imagining Dublin in flames, the execution wall at Kilmainham. A Protestant Talbot in all likelihood, although there were Talbots on either side of the sectarian divide. But surely a Papist Smithson was unlikely. Was she from Kilkenny herself? I imagined a church in one of the old Ascendancy towns along the Nore, gray dressed stone, and on the inner walls brass memorials to parishioners who had fallen in the Crimea, at Spion Kop. Young Lieutenant Talbot would walk down the aisle of his history, wedded not only to a lovely girl with half-parted lips but to a landscape, a gentle, twisting river, to plaques bearing the names of dead soldiers.

"Damned lucky for you," Myles said, holding the skeleton of

glistening, delicate bone between fork and knife, "that you were tucked safely away on the western front, with nothing to bother you save mustard gas and howitzers and mortars. Had you been with one of the regiments here you might have been sent into action against the rebels." He smiled. "It was a close call for some of our pals, you know. Your great pal Tom Kettle was in Dublin that spring, wearing the uniform of the Dublin Fusiliers, a British officer. And there were your other great pals, Tom MacDonagh and Christopher Blake, rebels in arms against the Crown. A strange moment, Patrick, a strange week, splitting Ireland apart like an orange, the old and the new."

A copy of the *Irish Times*, carrying the text of the rebel Proclamation, had reached Paddy Finucane and myself, in our command hut in Flanders, about a week after the surrender.

"Irishmen and Irishwomen," it began. "In the name of God and of the dead generations from which she receives her old traditions of nationhood, Ireland, through us, summons her children to her flag and strikes for her freedom." Paddy read it aloud, in tones of savage sarcasm. Paddy's father was a judge, as was one of his uncles. His family, like my own, were bulwarks of the old party of constitutional nationalists. We had been at Clongowes Wood together, Paddy and Tom Kettle and myself. Paddy had been prominent in dramatics at school. When, in his reading of the Proclamation by the shielded light of our field bull's-eye, he came to the language about "having patiently perfected her discipline, having waited for the right moment . . . ," there, at the word "moment," he broke into angry and incredulous laughter. "The right moment," he repeated, "when our backs are to the wall is what they mean. Bloody bastards. Stabbing our lads, our Irish lads as well as the others, stabbing them in the back. Pack of Dublin jackeens." He jabbed at the paper, which he had flung down on the sector map. "Dublin. Did you notice that, Patrick? The countryside stayed sound, Patrick. The country is still behind us, thank God."

"At the moment," I said, "I would not recommend standing unarmed Irishmen against a wall to be shot down by British bullets. That does not go down well in Ireland." The Proclamation closed with the names of its signatories. Clarke . . . Mac Diarmada . . . Pearse . . . Connolly . . . Ceannt . . . Plunkett . . . MacDonagh.

A few evenings later, before darkness fell, medical orderlies brought one of our lads in on a stretcher. He was legless; a blanket had been flung across his torso. His helmet was gone, and wide blue eyes rolled within a mud-streaked face. "Jesus Christ," Finucane said. He knelt beside the boy, took out his rosary and began to pray. Then the blue eyes lost focus, and a mouth, shockingly red, dropped open. "Where?" I said to one of the orderlies. "At the angle of the road," he said, "where there are bits of an old shop." Once, this had been a small village. "A present," Finucane said nastily, "from our friends in Dublin." But the artillery shells which pounded Sackville Street and the quays along the Liffey had been as lethal, had torn flesh as savagely.

"How did you spend the week yourself, Myles?" I asked him.

He shrugged. "Like everyone else. Heavy guns were firing on Thursday morning, and I went up on the roof. There was pitched warfare in Dublin, no doubt of it, and I could make out gunfire along the entire line that ran from the Green through Trinity, down Westmoreland to the river. Our city was being destroyed before us, it was terrifying and heartbreaking, slashed through with bits of comedy, as often happens, or so they say. On Friday, I took a chance that my motorcar would not be commandeered, and drove out to Billy Dinneen in Rathfarnham. I ran into a rebel patrol, of course, only one of them in uniform, their lieutenant, but the others had Mausers and bandoliers. The lieutenant and I exchanged a few halting words of Gaelic, and then he waved me on. We had best brush up our Gaelic, by the way, the language of the future. Billy and Rosemary persuaded me to spend the weekend, and I was nothing loath. Where safer than with a member of Parliament?"

William Dinneen was a man nearer our fathers' generation than our own, a heavyset, ponderous man, given to orotund utterance, and, with John Redmond and John Dillon, a ruler of the Home Rule party to which, before the Rising, almost all nationalists had given their loyalty.

"Billy was raging," Myles said, "raging the entire weekend. 'Mark my words,' he said more than once. 'This is not a blow struck against England, it is a blow struck against Home Rule. It is our lads fighting in the trenches and blood of Flanders who are earning Home Rule for us, and these hooligans and corner boys have stabbed them in the back.' Things were made worse on the Saturday, when Timothy Coogan joined us for dinner. Somewhere he had managed to find a copy of the Proclamation, and he had carried it down to us, where he spread it out on the long table in the drawing room. 'Keep it, Billy,' he said to Dinneen, 'it will be a picturesque curio, like the bonds the Fenians used to issue in the old days, payable upon the establishment of the Irish Republic.' 'God Almighty,' Billy said, pointing with a heavy forefinger to the names of the signatories. 'What did I tell you? Worse than corner boys, a superannuated Fenian and a pack of second-rate poets, and they have contrived to destroy Dublin and to destroy Home Rule for another full generation.' 'They have contrived the first of those, by God,' Coogan said. 'The center of Dublin is in flames and ruins, and the army is drawing a tight net. A day more of artillery shelling will end it.' 'Please God,' Billy said."

Midday sunlight sparkled upon window glass, and beyond it, the flower beds of spring. Myles finished his last bit of sole, put down knife and fork, and patted his lips.

"A world ending," he said, "the world of our fathers that seemed as though it would last forever. Poor John Redmond, sinking defeated and rejected into the grave, as decent a man as ever walked, and Dillon brooding over the past up there in Great Georges Street, and Billy Dinneen looking after his 'legal concerns,' as he calls them. Tim Coogan keeps busy though, he is at work on his memoirs. *Memories of an Old Parliamentarian,* he will call it, something like that. A world swept away. But that Saturday night in Rathfarnham, the night before the rebels surrendered, we had no sense of that. It was General Maxwell and his firing squads who turned things around."

Pat took Myles's flourished damask as a signal and was beside us. "And now, gentlemen, what is it to be? There is a nice cheese board today."

"The traditional Irish cheese board," Myles said with a flat neutrality that contrived to be derisive. It was an effective trick in the courtroom: juries admired Myles, and so did some of the judges.

"Ah now, Mr. Keough. There is Stilton and a nice bit of double Gloucester."

It was our new, received wisdom that feelings about the Rising had begun to turn with General Maxwell's firing squads, and so they had, no doubt. "The fools," people said. "It was the first rebellion that ever had the people against it, and they turned the people round in a week." Reading the speech which John Dillon made in Commons while the executions were still in progress, one felt the fury rising from the column of newsprint. "You are turning loose a torrent of blood, a river of blood," he told an infuriated House, and when they began to howl him down, he said—snarled, one suspects would be a more precise word—that "it would have been a damned good thing for you if your soldiers were able to put up as good a fight as those men did in Dublin."

"He has a point there, of course," Paddy Finucane said to me, still in the same command hut, to be reached by walking across duckboards which sank into mud. The newspaper came to us early in June, less than a month before the great offensive was launched on the Somme. "He had his nerve, though," Paddy said, "defending rebellion in time of war."

I could hear Dillon's voice, almost, remembered him sitting at dinner with other leaders of the old Home Rule party, at our own house or at his, myself a fledgling historian just back from Oxford, not yet a barrister, no thought of the law, and history was there for me at those dinner tables, had I thought to notice it, Redmond red and full of face, heavy in well-tailored clothes, smoothing the heavy, downturning mustache.

"Now in the House last week," he would say, "I spoke directly to Asquith. 'Will not the right honorable member,' I began," and as he spoke my father would look down the table toward me, eyes aglint, eyes which said, "Mark this."

And later, after the last guests had left, bundled up against winter chill, my father would take me into his library for a small, final brandy. He was an abstemious man, but every occasion should be rounded off with a small, final brandy.

"There we all are, you see, leaders of a powerful party, more than seventy of us over there in London, the emissaries of our people, doing battle in a foreign land. Impressive, are we not?"

He was not himself a member of Parliament, although he easily could have been, as he could easily have been a judge. The final brandy was precisely that, small and final, measured with great exactness into Waterford glasses held against the light shaded by its bowl of green glass. "There we are, you see."

We sat thus one evening, after guests had driven off into a light snow, the curtains of the library's two tall, narrow windows drawn closed, sat facing each other in the two massive wing chairs on either side of the fireplace.

"You must think us a small army of graybeards, waistcoats and tall hats, oiling and tending the machine of politics. But the people trust us, Patrick, the people trust us to bring the ship of Home Rule safely into port one of these years. And we will. They trust us, Patrick, because we were not always sleek and comfortable. No, by George, you should have seen us twenty years ago. Not one who hasn't spent time in one of His Majesty's prisons, Her Majesty it was in those days. Dillon was a firebrand in those days, a fierce young fellow, savage in his oratory, savage in his invective. Johnny Redmond is a different matter, old gentry stock, Catholic gentry, and he has fallen in love with the House of Commons, it suits him. But never forget, it was young John Redmond who stood by Parnell, when all the world had cast him aside, abandoned by Dillon, abandoned by O'Brien, and worse than abandoned by Tim Healy, betrayed by him."

And there we sat, in the green-shaded study, our brandies warming in our hands, as once, years before, between Clongowes Wood and Oxford, he had shown me how to savor brandy. History sat with us in that room, books, framed maps and estate charts, the massive gold-plated key which had been presented to him by the Irish of Lancaster, Pennsylvania, when Parnell sent the two of them, Dillon and Father, off to the States to raise funds. And the sword, its hilt handsomely restored, which my father's father had as a young man discovered in Meath, our ancestral county, buried beneath the coarse grasses of a field that sloped downwards to the Boyne.

"Swept clean off the board," Myles said. "Mind you, by the war's end, by the time of the general election, everyone knew that Sinn Féin would carry the day. The martyrs of 1916 would carry the day, the dead of Easter Week. In this country, you cannot argue against the dead. The old party was tagged forever as the lot who had dragged us into the war, sent off Irish lads to fight by England's side."

Letters and newspapers reached us, of course, even at the front, irregularly, in great clumps, and then nothing for weeks. But in England, in the convalescent hospital, we had all of the newspapers, and, if we ordered them, two or three days late, the *Irish Times* and the *Freeman's Journal.*

Myles balanced a thick dab of Stilton on a biscuit. "And a small brandy would not go amiss. Am I right, Patrick?" His voice, unlike my father's, was a rich, musical tenor. Once he had terrified his own father by talk of abandoning the law for a career in light opera.

"Swept clean off the board," he said again, savoring the phrase, as though he could see the hand of history brushing away green-painted rooks, bishops, pawns. "Seventy-three seats! A clean sweep! And do you know what seems to me the unkindest cut of all? Poor Dillon losing his seat to De Valera, one of the 1916 rebels. The old order changeth, Patrick."

The hospital, set upon grounds deep in Sussex woods, had a solarium, from whose tall, well-scoured windows I could look out upon bare winter branches, waiting for early buds. I would stretch out there, wool-blanketed, as though aboard an ocean liner, and read the news from the world, from Ireland, or else read in the books from the library's small miscellany, Victorian explorers in Central Asia, an Englishwoman who had lived in Paris during the Terror, Parkman's account of Pontiac's conspiracy. Sinn Féin had done far more than win an election in Ireland: it was pledged not to take its seats in London, but rather to assemble in Dublin, declare itself "the supreme national authority to speak and act in the name of the Irish people," and deny "the right of the British Government to legislate for Ireland."

Soames Hendricks, an artillery officer who used to sit beside me in the solarium, was either amused or infuriated, he was not certain which. "Deny the right of the British Government! How the devil do they plan to accomplish that?" I was not certain myself, and said something about sending a delegation to the Peace Conference. "Peace Conference," Hendricks snarled, and returned to his thriller; he was an Edgar Wallace fan.

By mid-March, the trees were budding, and the hedges which

lined the road down into the village were looking alive after the long winter.

"An extraordinary situation," Myles said. "Tony Powers and his pals over there a bit earlier have hurried back to Dublin Castle, under the impression that they are still governing us, the law courts are still in operation, the Royal Irish Constabulary is at full strength and the British Army is still with us, as strong as ever. And yet, every few weeks, Sinn Féin meets in the Mansion House, passing laws, appointing ministers, sending out messages to the world."

"And what of you, Myles?" I asked. "How have you been faring in the midst of all this?"

With a delicate economy of motion, Pat lifted the brandies from the salver, and placed them by our cups.

"We are fortunate in our profession," Myles said, "this disputatious world of ours is always in need of lawyers."

But as he spoke, he waved his hand in a broad, encompassing gesture, as though summoning the room, the hotel itself, to the witness stand, and his gesture was more eloquent than his words. The Shelbourne Hotel survives regimes, its bricks sturdier than bones, its headwaiters and hall porters swift to sweep away the rubble left by squads of machine-gunners. And of course he was right. Because three years later, after a revolution had been fought and won, a revolution which that spring, without our knowing it, was in preparation, a revolution which would be fought in distant hills and in the streets outside the windows, three years later, the constitution of the Irish Free State would be drafted in a suite of rooms directly above our heads. The Constitution Room, it would be called in time, and it would be shown to tourists.

He rested his hand on the table. "There is more to it than that, though, Patrick. Sinn Féin has claimed the loyalty of the people. There is nothing to choose but Sinn Féin or British rule. They are not a bad sort, you know, a bit rough-hewn, perhaps. And a few of them polished enough. Your great pal Christopher Blake is one of them, you know. A genuine veteran of Easter Week, a veteran of the Post Office." He smiled. "A veteran of two of their prisons. They will be wearing their jail terms as medals."

"Once they have taken power, and thrown out the English," I said. "How do they propose to do that?"

"That," Myles said, running his forefinger along the rim of his glass, "is an excellent question. What do *we* propose, you mean, surely. Surely now that you are back you will be throwing in your lot with us."

It was done so dexterously that I could but marvel at it, a shift of pronouns to proclaim a new allegiance. He was quite right, of course, there was nothing to choose save Sinn Féin or the English, but it was all done like a conjuror's trick, hands moving above coffee cups.

"For you, perhaps, Myles," I said, to test him, "but ex-soldiers in the British Army might be less welcome."

"Not a bit of it," he said. "You poor devils had persuaded yourselves that you were fighting Ireland's battle, how did poor old Redmond put it, wherever the firing line extends, in defense of right and freedom." He sipped cooling coffee. "Discharged British soldiers have been joining Sinn Féin, and they are welcomed." He nodded, and looked across the table at me with those startling eyes, which were always at once friendly and mischievous. It was almost as though he were offering a post in the legal department of the future Sinn Féin republic. But in fact, as I half-surmised, Myles was thus far on the edges of Sinn Féin, a barrister whose talents were useful. Later, of course, matters would be far different.

"My great wish for the moment," I said, "is to do nothing at all."

He shook his head. "You have had a bad time of it, Patrick, four years of a bad time, and then those hospitals. But you mustn't lock yourself away. We are in for exciting times."

"How fortunate," I said, "that I will be here to watch them."

Because I almost had not been, and he must have caught my meaning. He dropped his eyes. The shell which had torn away my arm had driven fragments deep into my chest, ripping away at bone and flesh, grazing an artery. "Bloody" was the first word I heard in the field hospital. "You're bloody lucky to be alive," the surgeon said to me, when he heard my terrified shout. He was tending another patient, and he spoke without turning around, when he heard me. It was my second day in the field hospital, and my first of undrugged consciousness. "Bloody lucky," he said again. While he worked, head bent, a medical orderly beside him with a white tray, he hummed tunelessly. "By tomorrow we'll have you out of here and into a proper bed." After a bit, he said, "There," to the patient, and to me, "Luck of the Irish, eh Paddy?" By then, by the late autumn of 1918, I had been transferred out of the Irish Division, and was serving with Seventeen Corps, south of Cambrai. It was the generic "Paddy," an impersonal affability.

Of the Home Rulers who had signed up to fight for Ireland or for Belgium or for whatever it was, I was one of the last to be struck down. Tom Kettle had been one of the first, killed at Ginchy in September of 1916. Willie Redmond, our leader's brother, was killed the year following, at Messines, at fifty-six the oldest junior officer in the division. And, a week after him, Paddy Finucane, who was in command of the column next to mine.

After lunch, as Myles and I stood in the portico, Cornelius, the doorman, touched his cap to us, and said, "You are welcome home, Captain." "Mister," I said. "Mr. Prentiss it is," he said, with a doorman's practiced agreeability, "as in the old days, am I right, Mr. Keough?" He was a tall, barrel-chested man, tight red curls beneath the gray cap. "A taxi, gentlemen?" "No no," Keough said, "we will be strolling down into the city, what is left of it, God save us all." His tone was bantering. "By God," Cornelius said, "what is the world coming to? I'll tell you a good one, Mr. Prentiss. I heard it from Sammy Fuller, the porter at the United Services. On the Monday afternoon of Easter Week, two young officers were leaving, none the worse for wear, and were looking with bewilderment at what was happening in the Green, fellows with rifles on patrol and other fellows digging up trenches, ruining the flower beds. 'There's the woman who can tell us,' one of the young English soldiers says to the other, 'there's Countess Markievicz.' And at that moment, the countess catches sight of him, lifts up an enormous pistol and begins blazing away. You can still see a brick at the United Services that has been knocked to smithereens. The two of them leapt back inside and ordered large brandies. Isn't that a good one?" "The countess's revolver has passed into folk memory," Myles said.

At the northwest corner of the Green, at the turning into Grafton Street, stood the triumphal arch which commemorated Dublin Fusiliers fallen in the South African war. "Traitors' Gate," we nationalists sometimes called it, but perhaps I no longer could, having taken the King's shilling, worn his uniform. Someday, perhaps, there would be a second arch at the Green's far corner, closer to the bullet-pocked College of Surgeons, closer to where the slim, absurd statue of Robert Emmet stared with blind eyes upon his supposed birthplace. In Dublin, pasts are not canceled but accumulated. Corpulent George II still rode his stone charger in the Green, had looked down upon rebel snipers. William of Orange still rode, so far as I knew, his charger in College Green, and Victoria herself, heavy and capacious-skirted, sat in state in the forecourt of Leinster House. And in Sackville Street, our chief thoroughfare, outside the General Post Office, Nelson stood atop his tall column, its base inscribed, the lettering elegant, chaste, with the names of his great victories, statue and monument erected by a committee of merchants, bankers, lords mayor, grateful that the admiral had swept the seas for Britain, that he had preserved the Empire. But in the GPO, three years before, in 1916, a few hundred men had barricaded themselves to wage war against that empire. Someday, perhaps, an arch would carry names of those who had fallen not on veldt and mountainside beneath African sun, but in our own streets, against a wall in Kilmainham Prison.

The names of the fallen Fusiliers were inscribed on the arch—Kelly, O'Brien, Spellacy, Gilmartin. "Will you do their dirty killing, Brian Og?" sang one of the antirecruiting songs at the time of the African war. But Kettle and Redmond and Finucane and Prentiss had gone on, years later, to do killing on behalf of whatever. On behalf of Ireland, so we had persuaded ourselves, or civilization.

"We are great in this city when it comes to statues," I said, as we turned down into Grafton Street.

"A history to be read in stone," Myles said. In honor of spring, he was wearing his wide-brimmed Panama, cream-colored. "Nelson was spared, a bit chipped off the end of his nose, but no worse. O'Connell fared even better, entirely untouched, with the battle waging fierce to either side of him, but one of his bronze attendant angels took a rifle bullet square in the left bub—one of the four abstractions—Fortitude or Shrewdness or whatever they are intended to represent. And Parnell was spared, up at the top of Sackville Street, gesticulating toward the worst slums west of Belgrade, as poor Tom Kettle used to say. It was just beyond the

Parnell monument, in the lawns of the Rotunda, that the rebels were herded after the surrender."

"Parnell, Nelson, O'Connell," Tom Kettle had said to me once, speaking of the three statues that dominated Sackville Street. "Dublin, chaste and Catholic, her purity protected by three notorious adulterers." "Not proven in O'Connell's case," I said. "Not proven," Tom Kettle said, his voice light, glamorous with wit, whiskey-laden, a Clongowian, like Myles and myself, fellow barrister, fellow scion of one Home Rule dynasty and married into another. "The Scotch verdict. It could be used to advantage in our courts over here. Not proven, meaning not guilty but don't do it again."

We met one last time, Tom Kettle and I, at a base camp which was being used by the Dublin Fusiliers, close to a half-ruined village. It was a month before they were ordered up into the line on the Somme, a month before Tom was killed at Ginchy. "I would have given my life for Thomas MacDonagh," he said, "poor Tom MacDonagh, shot down by their bloody firing squad." He was very drunk.

We were sitting together in the village's bleak café, with two bottles of wine before us, but Tom had managed to procure a bottle of Jameson's. You will hear it said in Dublin in these later days that after the Easter Rising, after the executions, he did not care whether he lived or not, whether he died in a British uniform. And so you might have thought that night, but he would veer around, witty and drunk, from grief to fantasy. "They shot John MacBride as well," he said to me. "Magnificent in death. 'No bandage for me,' he said to the firing squad officer, the bold rebel, 'I have been looking down barrels all my life.' And so he had. Barrels of porter. Poor MacBride, poor MacDonagh. Poor mad Pearse." And his hand, a slight shake to it, added whiskey to our glasses. But an hour earlier, sober and relaxed on respectable wine, he had waved away the Rising, an incident only. "We will come out of this, Patrick, with Colonial Home Rule, earned for us on the battlefields of France and Flanders. A bright future awaits poor old Ireland, Patrick, a free people living freely within the Empire." "A bright future," I said, because one does not argue with whiskey, but I no longer believed that anything bright could come out of mud, bloody limbs, corpses caught upon barbed wire, mustard gas. And the word "empire" now had for me the stench of bloody flux, bloody excrement. Perhaps, who knows, at the very end it may have stunk for Tom as well, for in a sonnet, two days before his death, writing to his small daughter as one already dead, he says, "We fools, now with the foolish dead."

We turned down Grafton Street, the most English of all our streets, narrow, fashionable, and winding, tailors, tobacconists, a cinema, banks built of solid Victorian Gothic, teashops and coffeeshops, a gallery, solicitors' offices above saddlemakers, oculists. And, at the far end, the Bank of Ireland and Trinity College facing each other, splendid with eighteenth-century flourishes of stone, massive assertions gesturing like oratory, like Burke, Grattan, Sheridan. Before the war, and during it, of course, the fronts along Grafton Street, upon any occasion, upon the least provocation, blazed with Union Jacks, red, white and blue flags reaching out and almost touching each other above the heads of pedestrians. There were none today, and had not been, I assumed, for some time.

Combridge's windows offered, in frames of elaborate gilded scrollwork, oil paintings of cattle by quiet ponds, shepherd and herd moving down snowy roads, shattered Norman towers by moonlight; watercolors of Connemara and Kerry. At an earlier time, late in 1914 and into the new year, in the months before I left for France, one of the windows had displayed a vivid poster. A young woman, fair type of Irish maidenhood, half colleen, half Cathleen ni Houlihan, delicate, defenseless, heroic, looked at one directly, but her gesturing hand drew the eye to where a cowering girl stood pressed against a low wall. Soldiers, gray-clad, spike-helmeted, walked toward her. "Protect me by avenging her," the legend said. Against the side display wall, at right angles to the colleen, a young country lad in khaki, cap pushed back from tight curls, a Lee-Enfield slung over one shoulder, stood before a romantic Connemara landscape, blue pool, green pasturelands, a mist-shrouded mountain. "Where there is fighting to be done, send for the Irish." At least, I thought, I had not made recruiting speeches, recruiting tours, as Kettle had done. That world of recruiting speeches, inspiriting posters, lay at the far end of some echoing corridor.

But Myles, imagining that I was studying the oils and watercolors on present display, said, "The standards of art have not been raised, I fear." He had a good eye and was a friend of painters, of Sarah Purser and Jack Yeats.

It was a busy afternoon on Grafton Street. Women shepherded children into Switzer's, or into Bewley's for tea and currant buns. A pair of young women swept past us, chattering in accents which were our own, the faintly metallic accents of educated, middle-class Dublin. I saw them reflected in Combridge's window, ghostly but vivid against snowy roads, moonlit towers. "And since then," one of them said to the other, "she has had exactly one letter from him. In five weeks, one letter!" Her tones were indignant. Once, in that world which had been mine, "he" might have been at the front, or in Egypt. But now, he could have been one of the Sinn Féiners caught up in the most recent sweep, and sent off to a prison in England, or else serving a term here, in Kilmainham or Mountjoy.

"Rip van Winkle," I said, and Myles caught my meaning at once. He put a friendly hand on my elbow. "My dear fellow," he said, "you are most welcome home. We have been waiting for you, all your friends have been waiting for you."

Combridge's stood at the corner of Grafton and Duke streets, and once, on one of the last mornings of peace in 1914, I had turned down Duke Street to have coffee at the Bailey. It was a late-July morning of brilliant sunlight, a bit too warm perhaps, and I was not looking foward to a day's work in the Law Library of the Four Courts.

My friend Christopher Blake had been having coffee with Dennis Ross, but Ross had risen up to leave and I walked over to the table. "Patrick!" Christopher said with delight. "A surprise! Dennis here and yourself know each other, I am certain." "We have met together over the years," Ross said, polite but distant, "on this committee and that." He was a man close to forty, pale cheeks and heavy dark mustache, in one of the dark, heavy suits that he wore without sweat, summer or winter. Dublin was that kind of town in 1914, and the Bailey that kind of public house, in which a respectable Redmondite barrister could encounter an officer of the Irish Republican Brotherhood. We stood smiling at each other without cordiality, and then Ross nodded to the two of us and left. Two years later, in that fatal Easter, he would be shot dead leading a sortie out of Jacob's factory, where Thomas MacDonagh, Christopher's friend and mine, was in command.

"You are keeping dangerous company," I said, but Christopher smiled and changed the subject. I said it thoughtlessly, to tease him. As late as then, as late as 1914, it was difficult to take the Republican Brotherhood seriously, a handful of devout separatists, with dreams of an armed rebellion, Gaelic-language enthusiasts, dark intense humorless men like Dennis Ross, or like old Tom Clarke, who kept a tobacco and newspaper shop off Parnell Square. They were the Fenians, or what was left of them, the heirs of the rebels of 1867 and of the dynamite campaign of the eighties, but quiet enough now, or so we thought.

It was to the book that he had just now finished that Christopher had turned the subject, a history of those Irish families who had supplied regiments to the French Army in the eighteenth century. The task brought him over often to Dublin and to Paris from his work in a London publisher's office, and we had talked about it often and at length. But his talk that morning was distracted, as though he were making conversation, and his eyes kept turning to the windows which looked out upon Duke Street. "Will there be a war, do you think?" I asked him. The day before, Austria-Hungary had delivered its ultimatum to Serbia. Christopher turned suddenly from the window to stare at me, and then, after a moment, he smiled. He had a lean, handsome face, and a memorable smile. Then, in 1914, he was in his mid-twenties, a few years out of our National University. "Did I pull you away from the eighteenth century?" I asked him, and we talked idly, the talk of newspaper readers, about the Kaiser and the Tsar and a murder in Sarajevo, an obscure provincial town which now was known to everyone.

What was known to Christopher, though, and unknown to me and to almost everyone in Dublin, was that on that Friday morning, July the twenty-fifth, while most of Europe was waiting for a reply from Serbia, a fifty-foot gaff-rigged ketch called the *Asgard* was on its way to the Irish coast with a cargo of 900 Mauser rifles and 26,000 rounds of ammunition. Two mornings later, on a bright Sunday, the *Asgard* would land them at Howth harbor, north of Dublin, and Christopher would help distribute them to the waiting companies of Volunteers. These were the rifles which two years later held the GPO and Boland's Mill and the Four Courts and the bridge across the canal at Mount Street.

Once, on a night in 1921, when there was a warrant out against Christopher and he was staying in my house, I reminded him of that morning in the Bailey, and he said that he had almost been tempted to tell me about the *Asgard*. "Your talent," he said, "was for keeping everything orderly, keeping hotheads like myself under John Redmond's control." But it seemed extraordinary to the two of us, that night in 1921, that the two events should be superimposed one upon the other, the Austrian ultimatum which spun Europe into its cataclysm, and Erskine Childers guiding the *Asgard* to Howth harbor with the cargo of secondhand Mausers that he and Darrell Figgis had bargained for in Hamburg. On the night of the sixteenth, off the Devonshire coast, the yacht had sailed straight into the Grand Fleet, on what was to prove its final review before the war, on maneuver out of Spithead. Great searchlights blazed to the northeast.

In College Green, beyond the foot of Grafton Street, Dublin's eighteenth century at its most suave and powerful confronted itself, the magnificent bank, which once, in that century, had been the Parliament of Ireland, Lords to one side, Commons to the other, facing the gates of Trinity College, and the gates flanked by Foley's two serene and seductive statues, one of Burke, one of Goldsmith. As we stood there, at Grafton Street's edge, suddenly two armored cars appeared from Dame Street, from the direction of Dublin Castle. In each of them, a bored Tommy stood leaning against a machine gun. Myles Keough turned toward me and nodded, as though making a point, as though telling me that Dublin had changed, for all that Trinity gates looked the same, and Goldsmith and Burke.

"During the Rising," Myles said, "Trinity kept her gates locked against the rebels. A bit embarrassing, but what could you expect?" Christopher Blake, like most respectable Catholics, had studied at the National University, the son of a respectable Catholic surgeon, but Myles, like my own father, had followed socially aspiring Papists into Trinity, a bastion of Protestantism, of loyalty to the Crown. As for me, I had been schooled by the Jesuits, but then had gone off to Oxford, which put me beyond the pale entirely. "Trinity," Myles said, in mock-tragic tones. "The British gunners housed their weapons inside Trinity gates, in Library Square, their eighteen-pounders. They wheeled them out beside the walls, in Brunswick Street, to shell our lads beyond Aston Quay." Rocking lightly on his heels, outside Trinity gates, bathed in Dublin's soft, familiar light, Myles looked splendid, impervious to history, a buoyant islander.

But from Westmoreland Street, as we walked down it toward the Liffey, we could see, stretched out, the city's ravaged heart, gutted and fire-charred, shelled by artillery, strafed by machine-gun fire, still, three war years later, only patchily repaired. "And above it all," James Stephens the poet was to say to me in a few weeks' time, a gnome of a man bristling with energy of language, "there was Dublin, burning down, burning down, above it all, in the night sky, above flames, was the planet Venus, closer than ever in history."

We stood on Aston Quay, leaning upon the low stone parapet. Below us, the green, soiled waters of the river moved toward O'Connell Bridge, toward Butt Bridge, toward the Alexandra docks and beyond them the Irish Sea. Flung to our either hand, across the river, were the crowning achievements in stone of our eighteenth century, grander than Parliament House and the College, at once serene and bullying, the Custom House to our right, and to our left, its great dome catching afternoon sun, the Four Courts, which once, ten years before, Myles and I had entered as newly hatched barristers, but where the name "Prentiss" would always mean not myself, but my father, Dominick Sarsfield Prentiss, King's Counsel, who could have been, had he chosen, Sir Dominick, but good Irish nationalists did not accept knighthoods.

Directly across the river from us lay the ruins of what Dublin had learned to call Kelly's Fort. "The rebels held it for most of the week," Myles Keough said. "At the end, it took artillery and machine guns playing on it hour after hour. Brave bloody bastards, were they not, when all is said and done." From Trinity, artillerymen would have had a clear shot down D'Olier Street, and the

GPO, farther up Sackville Street, would have been almost in range of eighteen-pounders. Between the two, charred ruins now, lay the Imperial Hotel, where once, long ago, by tall windows, my mother and I had had tea, while in the street outside, an angry crowd of his supporters shouted, "Par-nell! Par-nell! Par-nell!" Myself, a schoolboy home from Clongowes, said to her, in the cab on our way home, "It is bad luck when soldiers turn against their chief," but my mother said, "It is all very complicated, Patrick, so your father says." But she was crying. A part of my life, of all our lives, lay in ruins.

As though gifted with powers of divination, Myles slapped his hand against the cool stone, grayish black, of the parapet. "All of our calculations, Patrick, the counting of votes, the managing of constituencies, the bills carefully guided through Westminster, all of the alliances, all of our frock coats and silk hats on platforms in Ballina and Ballinasloe while cornet bands played 'A Nation Once Again,' all of it blown away by a handful of poets and fanatics. Small wonder that you abandoned history as a profession, the law is safer by far. There stands the Four Courts below there, serene and impregnable, the fountain of order and civic decency."

A handful. Indeed, a small handful. From what we on the outside of things had been able to learn by the middle of 1919, the Rising had been the work of a half-dozen or so determined men, men like Christopher Blake's friend Dennis Ross on the Council of the Republican Brotherhood, men written off as out of style. And, in particular, the work of young Sean MacDermott, handsome, crippled, a cheerful and good-natured fanatic, and MacDermott's mentor, old Tom Clarke, a man in his mid-fifties and looking much older, bald, stoop-shouldered, mustached. In the photographs of the fifteen leaders shot by firing squad, Clarke looks out of place among the young men, high celluloid collar and natty white necktie, looking in fact like what he was, the proprietor of a small tobacconist's shop. Then one sees the eyes behind the thin-rimmed spectacles, implacable. But perhaps that is hindsight.

Once I had gone into the shop. Perhaps he knew me by reputation, as I knew him: it is a small city, but he did not reveal this by a flicker of the steady, nearsighted eyes. Two young fellows were leaving the shop as I entered. A small shop—a few jars of tobacco, tobacco in packets, packets of cigarettes, open boxes of cigars. The varnish on the counter had worn through in places; the bare wood was dark and liverish. Along one wall were ranged the papers and journals I had expected—*Irish Freedom,* the *Irish Review, An Claidheamh Soluis,* the *United Irishman.* Ranged along the back beside the jars of tobacco, Fenian songbooks, a series of thin, paperbound "lives"—Robert Emmet, Wolfe Tone, "Dark and Evil Days: The Martyrs of 1798." "Can I help you, sir?" he asked in flat, reedy tones. "You have Bristol's Mixture there in packets," I said. A short man, he had to reach to his top shelf for it, straining a bit.

In June of 1883, in London's Old Bailey, young Tom Clarke had been convicted before Lord Chief Justice Coleridge of "feloniously and unlawfully compassing, imagining, and devising and intending to depose the Queen from the Imperial Crown of Great Britain and Ireland and to levy war upon the Queen in order by force and constraint, to compel her to change her measures and counsels." In language less stately, Clarke had been a member of one of the dynamite teams sent over from America by the Clan na Gael to blow up London Bridge, Parliament, the Bank of England, and whatever else provided a majestic target. He was a member of what newspapers called "the Gallagher team," but Dr. Gallagher took his orders from a Fenian veteran of terror named Ned Nolan.

Clarke was not turned loose from prison until 1898, the last of the dynamiters to be released, and Portland, a gray penal fortress looking beyond gray shingles to a cheerless ocean, had bitten into his soul; the Irish rebels in Portland had been kept in the strictest of solitary confinement. Ned Nolan, in his day, had been a graduate of Portland, a fighter in the Rising of 1867, and Clarke was a Republican of the same school. As I walked away from his shop that day in early autumn, I imagined he nursed memories of a life before Portland, tattered dreams, faded, once-gaudy like the colors on his penny-dreadful lives of Irish patriots, green banners, swords of freedom. Perhaps I had misjudged him.

"The fountain of order and decency," Myles Keough repeated, pleased with the phrase, and still beaming toward the Four Courts, which did indeed look solid, graceful, gulls swooped above its dome. But during the Rising, the Four Courts had been held by Edward Daly, another of the executed leaders, and only surrendered on the last day, when the order of surrender reached the quays. "They kept the place in order," Myles said, "rebels with a sense of decency when all is said." It was a formula which in Ireland saw service as a law of history.

We stood at the heart of a historied city. History folded and refolded itself, layer upon layer of the same pattern. Once, a century earlier, Robert Emmet, short and meager-framed, had led his dwindling band of rebels, a hundred or a half-hundred, up Thomas Street toward Dublin Castle, making their way past brawling Saturday-night drunkards. After his trial and grandiloquent speech from the dock, "Let no man write my epitaph," and his public hanging, after that, transformed, he had passed into memory. In time, the memory, "bold Robert Emmet, the darling of Erin," had drifted into Tom Clarke's newsagent's shop, a sixpenny pamphlet, the darling of Erin in a coarsely colored version of the uniform, self-designed, which he had worn into Thomas Street, green, with massy epaulets. Now Tom Clarke—weak-eyed, slope-shouldered, shoved against a Kilmainham wall, hammered to the ground by a firing squad's bullets—now *his* portrait hung on kitchen walls, staring across a deal table, chairs, across a century, at the picture, on the facing wall, of Robert Emmet.

And yet I had a sense, I was later to swear to myself that that spring afternoon I had a sense, as I looked down ruined Sackville Street, the Four Courts to my left and the Custom House to my right, across the sluggish, bile-green river, that this time, the chain of repetition and futility might have been broken at last. But I could not have known, surely, guessed, prophesied, that in three years' time, the Custom House would be a scene of battle, set afire, the enormous copper dome melted down by fierce heats. And, a year beyond that, Irishmen would be holding the Four Courts in defiance, not this time of the English Crown, but of other Irishmen in uniforms of green, shelling the Four Courts rebels with artillery pieces borrowed from the British. For that spring afternoon in 1919, history was Sackville Street in ruins, and, behind us in Dawson Street's Mansion House, was a pretend parliament, Dáil Éireann, its orators gesticulating like Robert Emmet in the dock, arm upflung, "Let no man write my epitaph." Of the Easter Week rebels, no speeches from the dock of their military trials had come forward, and Clarke, as we now know, had been shot while wearing too-large trousers not his own. The war of independence, as we have agreed to name what was about to happen, would come in unanticipated forms.

The next morning, at breakfast, as I read the newspapers, I marked, without paying it too much attention, a murder which had taken place a few hours after Myles and I stood together at the Liffey. In the town of Ballina, near the Mayo coast, a resident magistrate named Newton, until recently an inspector of the constabulary, was shot dead in his drawing room. The gunmen had fired through a tall window which had been opened against the mild spring evening. I paid little attention to it. Every few months or so for as far back as I could remember, and well before that, before the Land War and the boycotting, back into the remote days of what was called "agrarian outrage," there would be a story of this sort. An aggrieved tenant, an evicted peasant, a drunken tavern boaster—I had defended one such prisoner in the year of the war. And yet, even as I was reading the story, I was remembering an earlier one, earlier by a month at most, of an inspector shot dead in Newport, which is also in Mayo.

On the very day when Dáil Éireann met for the first time, to proclaim the independence of Ireland, on that day, at a place in Tipperary called Soloheadbeg, two policemen escorting a cartload of gelignite to a quarry were ambushed and killed, and the gelignite carried away. In May, two RIC constables were shot dead in a raid which rescued a rebel prisoner from a railway carriage at Knocklong. A month or so later, in Fermoy, masked men attacked a party of British soldiers and carried off their arms; trees had been felled and laid across the roads to prevent pursuit. RIC men on patrol in the country were stripped of their weapons and on occasion killed. A detective sergeant with intelligence responsibilities was shot dead outside his house in a Dublin suburb. Country houses and the houses of resident magistrates were raided for arms. Stories of this sort had been appearing in the English as well as the Irish papers, but not at great length, and never, not yet that is, placed together to form a pattern. Not even when, in February, Eamon De Valera, one of the heroes of Easter Week, the commander at Boland's Mill and now "president" of the metaphysical "Republic," was rescued from Lincoln Prison in a daring action by two other veterans of 1916 whose names were not yet famous, Harry Boland and Michael Collins.

The inspector who had been shot down in Newport, an elderly man close to retirement, named Ferguson, had a small house on a hill high above the island-studded bay, and the tall, narrow windows of his front room looked out upon the gray waters. He had been well liked "by all persuasions," as the saying went, and the *Irish Times* had reported the event in angry detail. It was through one of the windows, as with the killing of Newton a month earlier, that the gunmen had fired. Ferguson had stepped into the room to wind the clock, "an ormolu clock which had been in the family for several generations." It lay shattered beside his body.

When, in time, a few years later, I had occasion to read that account, I wondered whether the journalist was an accumulator of details or whether he had an eye for a prophetic symbol.

II

JANICE NUGENT

It was late in the winter of 1919, moving on toward spring, that I decided, if that is the right word, to go back to Ireland, to Galway, for an extended visit. I would be welcome, I knew, for Betty had been writing that they missed me, and it was never the same without me, and we could be two sisters together, and more important than that, Father was, not failing certainly, and with his hands steady on the reins, but moving a bit more slowly, a bit less ready to come to decisions about things large and small, and decisions were in order, with the wretched war over at last which had had its impact upon agricultural prices at home. There was much else in her letters, about county neighbors and weddings (but these I knew about because I had been sent cards and had sent off useless things, fish slices were always safe) and news about chaps coming home from France and Mesopotamia, but this was the same news, really, for they made the weddings possible. But if there were local troubles, she said not a word about them, and she would have, I am certain, because she is of a melodramatic turn of mind. It was still our ordered Coolater world that she wrote about, the world of our mother's time, soothing as haymaking, as long green evenings.

It was as though, so I decided after I had arrived, she had organized a strenuous imaginative effort to persuade herself, me, all of us, that if life had changed this was only a slow, pillowing move back to the way it had been before the war. The fields where the Galway rebels had made their forlorn encampments in 1916, if she thought of them at all, were at best an entertaining tale for visitors, had receded into the convenient cradle of the romantic Irish past. In this she was quite wrong, of course, or quite unperceptive it would be closer to say, but we all take comfort from the familiar and the unravished, landscapes, faces, gardens.

At a dinner party the month before I left London, Will Landers, an earnest and awkwardly amorous young man from the Foreign Office, did his best to dissuade me. He had been at Versailles, attached to our delegation at the Peace Conference—the English delegation, I should say—and had more recently been in Berlin as a more or less unofficial observer. "It is very dreadful there, dear Mrs. Nugent," he said, leaning toward me, leaning toward my dramatic opal pendant, "civil war, and no hope really of anything getting itself sorted out." Government troops but they really were not a government; the monarchist thugs who were organized in the Free Corps; revolutionists of several kinds; and armed bands of revolutionary ex-soldiers and sailors. Armored cars with mounted machine guns, screams, executions, the spattering of rifle shots against walls. And the palace of the abdicated Kaiser looted, revealing the most appalling royal taste in decoration, but the looters were not finicky: all this, Will Landers poured out to me with, I am certain, a less than thorough understanding of these events. He seemed intent chiefly upon presenting himself against them in tableau—emerging from his hotel to a rattle of machine-gun fire, German sailors with rifles at the ready rushing upon barricades hastily thrown across the street's end.

I said, "But why, dear Mr. Landers, do you caution me? I am not going to Germany but to Ireland, a far different place."

"Ah, but is it?" he asked. "Is it? There are reports of arms raids there as well, policemen beaten—"

"I am going to Ireland because, you will remember my telling you, because I am Irish."

"Yes," he said, "of course. But there are Irish and then there are Irish, if you take my meaning. There is loyal Ireland and there is disloyal Ireland. What I fear, Mrs. Nugent, goes beyond Ireland or Germany or even the terrible chaos into which Russia has tumbled. I fear for Europe itself. Have you been reading the newspaper reports that have been coming out to us from Hungary, from Poland, from the Balkans? You have not, I suggest."

I had heard about them, read about them, I said with a show of indifference. The downfall of Europe did not seem an inviting subject, nor Mr. Landers a reliable guide through its ruined chancelleries. When we talked, he leaned toward me a bit too closely; his eyes were pale blue and questing.

"I don't profess to know it well," he said, "but I've been there any number of times. Before the war, and during it, for that matter. A lovely country. Between Connemara and our own Highlands I would find it hard to choose."

"I am glad it has your approval," I said, with what I feared was too heavy an irony, but he never noticed, of course. Down the table, Jimmy Hartsdale, as he talked, made shapes in the air with his two hands, and the two young women listening to him were laughing without control, but Jimmy was impassive, pretending even a faint puzzlement. I wished that I were down there with Jimmy; we were great pals, he had had a play which had just now gone off after a good run.

"Is that your county by any chance, Connemara?" he asked. "It is *in* my county, I said. "In Galway. Once my father had a fishing lodge there, beyond Clifden. But we live in East Galway. Outside Loughrea. Or rather, my father does, the O'Gormans do. My husband was a Nugent. Westmeath people. Lake country. The cattle are famous. Of a good hefty girl, the country people will say, 'Beef to the heel like a Mullingar heifer.' Mullingar was our market town."

"Something they could never say of you, Mrs. Nugent," he said. He was quite awful, really. "But to give you a word of caution, if I may. Serious caution. Not my desk at all, of course, but one listens. The Shinners have swept the old constitutional party off the board, you must know that. Not that they were bargains, but there were a few gentlemen among them. Poor John Redmond, and his brother, a gallant man, gallant officer. Died holding the King's commission, out there in Flanders, just as your husband did."

"Charlie was killed in the Dardanelles," I said. "At Suvla Bay." Why did I so dislike Mr. Landers? But to my right, Bobby Wickham, down from Oxford, was boring his partner—a young woman whose rounded bosoms would have driven Mr. Landers mad—with stories of a Viking gold hoard discovered in some unlikely place. I rested my hand on his forearm and it stayed there, unnoticed. By him, not by Mr. Landers, who looked at it, a bit enviously.

"And while they were fighting in France and on the beaches of Gallipoli, the Shinners in Dublin were stabbing us in the back. Now they have set up their own talk shop in Dublin. Don't want anything to do with us. And they mean business, Mrs. Nugent. They had dealings with the Germans straight on to the end. They have arms cached away. They have been drilling. Oh, mind you, I am certain things will be quiet enough around your place, but you should know what you might be walking into."

"I know what my country is," I said.

"I wonder," he said, and there was a change in his tone. "I wonder. If you know what your country is. Galway, you say, and Westmeath. But you seem very much at home here, in London, in Chelsea, at this table. With your hand resting on Professor Wickham's sleeve."

There is this to be said for furtive, timorous lechers: they turn to their advantage the most unlikely moments, gestures, words.

"If the Shinners have their way," he said, "they will give us an Ireland very remote from all this. Ignorant, priest-ridden, Bolshevik for all we know."

"Priest-ridden and Bolshevik at once! That would be an accomplishment."

"Priest-ridden at any rate. 'Home Rule is Rome Rule' is more than a slogan, you know."

"Do you know, Mr. Landers, that I am myself a Catholic? A slave to Rome."

"I did know that you were a Catholic. And you know perfectly well what I am talking about. There is a very considerable difference between yourself and illiterate peasants taking their orders from a parish priest who is himself half-risen from their ranks."

"Dear Mr. Landers," I said, and taking my hand away from the unnoticing Bobby Wickham, I placed it over Mr. Landers's hand as it rested beside his wineglass. "As we say at home, we cannot change the country, let us change the subject." No one could say that *he* left my hand unnoticed. I let it rest there a minute, and then drew it away slowly, my fingers trailing toward his wrist. It was wicked of me, really. Ireland's revenge.

Of course he was keen to see me home, but instead I insisted on sharing a taxi with George and Helen Miller. George sat between us. "Did you see that awful man I was stuck with?" I asked. "No," Helen said, and for some reason I gave them a full account. "I'd rather not know these things," George said, but he was smiling. "The poor fellow must be in a terrible state. I wonder if he might not be right, though. A bit right." "What!" I said, "that I am priest-ridden? Do you find me priest-ridden, George? Whatever that means." "About Ireland," he said, "but I don't expect it will concern you. Your people have always been decent, have they not? No boycotting or anything of that sort." "We don't really have 'people' anymore," I said, "neither in Galway nor at Charlie's. Sold off up to the demesne gates. But no, you're right. Charlie's father was quite patriotic, in fact. An MP for a time, under Parnell. All for Home Rule." "There you are then," George said, relieved, and now he took my hand, which I did not at all mind. It was comforting in the darkness of the cab, and Helen smiled at the two of us. George was a great flirt. "This time they want more than Home Rule. This time they want the country. Their country. Our country." "But that's Home Rule, isn't it? What Parnell wanted." He stroked my arm, as though it held the answer. "Not quite," I said.

It was a lovely night, the air cool and fresh and made fragrant by the gardens of the park. There was a good moon. London seemed suddenly enormous, a world, the great buildings of government and the Palaces of Westminster, the great streets of shops, Mayfair and our own Chelsea, the towns south of the river and the city stretching away, away to the north, to the west, until it dwindled away past suburbs into open country. And I imagined it peopled in its millions, anonymous, its newspapers and the great rivers. I was suddenly aware of its depth of texture and being. And as George moved his hand gently, without threat, up my arm, comforting, fraternal—or so were the terms we had set upon the instant, all three of us—I was thinking how much Charlie and I had loved London, its comforts and certitudes and risks, its theaters and concerts and little parties, its little flirtations. The houses which presently we passed, after we had left the park, had still their lighted drawing rooms, as one could tell by the chinks of light that escaped through the heavy curtains, and two times or three they would be drawn back, so that I saw once a portly gentleman, in evening dress, seated in a high-winged chair and looking toward a young woman who crossed the room to carry him a tray on which was a low, squat bottle. His daughter, I have no doubt, or perhaps she was like myself young and widowed, her husband in a French or Belgian grave or like poor Charlie somewhere on a barbarous shore in Near Asia. Or perhaps, I thought idly and wickedly, as George stroked my upper arm, perhaps she was his young mistress, bought and paid for.

When we stopped before my block of flats, the heel of George's hand moved up and down, by accident, he was not of course aware of it, along the side of my breast. It felt odd, exciting, but only mildly so; it was a faint, diffuse feeling, as though being reminded that I was a woman. I asked them in for a nightcap, but they declined, it was late and there was an early meeting for George with a difficult and lazy novelist, declined decisively, both of them, but you could hear the curlicues of regret in George's voice. It was all for the best, of course, but it might have been fun to see what George might contrive to do. He was a much nicer person than the awful Mr. Landers. They both kissed me good-night, Helen almost on the lips but not quite, although I could taste her lip-rouge.

In the small drawing room, to which I had made few changes in the last years, I turned on two lamps, one on either side of the cheerful sofa with its fabric inspired by Bakst, of which Charlie and I had been so secretly proud. Then I poured myself a brandy, a good stiff one with a brief splash in it, and sat down beside one of the lamps looking toward the empty fireplace with its white, virginal moldings and above it, the Paolo and Francesca engraving which Blake did for *The Divine Comedy.* It is so lovely and sweeping and sad. All swirls, lovers in those too-strenuous Blakean bodies, muscles and cords, but poor Paolo, poor Francesca apart from the others, talking to the fainting poet, and their sin so natural, so human, but that is Dante's point, Charlie used to say. What the hell, I used to say, and Charlie would go into those intricate explanations with theology never far distant. But then he would catch me smiling at him, and say, what the hell. Yes, I thought, surveying the evening and awful Mr. Landers and the touch of George Miller's hand, by accident of course, it has been so long and I miss Charlie so and a life shared.

Everything in the flat, even in the small kitchen, reminded me of a shared design and texture. Our books, and the gramophone records which scratchily carried to us Ravel and Saint-Saëns. The sunlight which fell on Sunday mornings upon the carpet was the same, with its promise of long urban felicities, but I would look alone now on those shafts of mote-crowded light and plan the day, a concert or a visit to a friend. It wasn't so much that I missed the love, the making of love together with Charlie—the sex, as they call it nowadays in Bloomsbury—and indeed I have great difficulty remembering us together in bed, not that I don't try. And not that my life has been so lurid—a brief early time with Patrick Prentiss and the times with those other two fellows—but it was only Charlie that I truly loved, and now surely and certainly I knew that that was fading, as the sunlight was fading the Bokhara carpet.

I hated, truly hated, the thought that I was one in a generation of widows created by that abominable war, which now it is suddenly all right and fashionable to describe as abominable. Hundreds and hundreds of thousands of young fellows, millions of them—English and German and French and Russian and Turk and Italian. And Irish.

But even that was too large a thought. I was resolute against involving my life, my fate, my feelings with those of others, with any others. I was entitled to my grief, and now that had faded to a private emptiness decorated by such feelings and small hopes and cruelties as I had shopped for.

And so I sat there, sipping the brandy which Charlie had always called the only one worth drinking, and its complex taste a touch of his remembered tongue upon my tongue. Perhaps. And thought for a moment of how even reality was a creature of shifting fashion, and Europe was so monstrous, gem-encrusted, cannon-guarded, emperors and kaisers and tsars in their coaches of state, all that Europe had now gone out of fashion, replaced by mobs machine-gunned on the steps of ministries, horrid boys back from the trenches and lurking, leather-coated, at rainy street corners. Patrick Prentiss would call it history, but I call it fashion and I expect we mean the same thing.

Once, before the war, Charlie and I had visited Mr. Yeats in his rooms in Woburn Buildings on one of his evenings, all dark, curtains drawn, tall candles strategically placed, and, of all things, Paolo and Francesca and two other Blake prints of the series. There were other visitors, I cannot remember them. "Another phase," I remember him saying, not to me but to someone else and I overheard, a dark, theatrical voice which the English find very Irish, and the Irish find the very essence of decent respectable middle-class Dublin Protestant, a chartered accountant's voice lowered for effect. "We are entering another phase, murderous, bloody, innocent, pitiless, stone and bronze." "The world is," someone else said. "Ireland is," Mr. Yeats said. "The world has been there for years. In Ireland, things come to us belatedly." People put up with Mr. Yeats's airs and prophecies for the sake of his poetry, but perhaps it should be the other way round. I told Charlie that, in bed, and he accused me of cultivating an unsuitable style of paradox. But no one denies his magnificence as a poet, and those are the very words he used. That had been in the spring of 1914, and three years later he had bought himself his tower in Galway, near Gort, near his Egeria, that awful Gregory woman.

On the Thursday following, I took the mailboat to Kingstown, and stayed the day in Dublin, putting up at the Shelbourne, before crossing the country on the morning train from Kingsbridge. In Dublin, I saw no one and that by choice. Or, almost by choice. I phoned Patrick at the Four Courts, but he was in court, and taking that as an omen I left no message. But I looked up none of my chums, Dolly McMasters in Merrion Square, nor Ronan Joyce and his wife in Rathfarnham, Ireland's only Protestant Joyce, as he used to boast, and so would his children be when in due course they followed along, and be damned to *ne temere*. Nora, his wife, would smile, the smile unreadable.

I lunched in the hotel, faintly not a proper thing to do, alone, but Pat, the headwaiter, recognized me, and we organized a salad and a chop and fresh vegetables. "Mr. Nugent," he said, "terrible news. He was well liked in this house." "Almost everywhere," I said, "a likable man. Three years ago, Pat. A healthy bit of scar tissue now." "Yes, Mrs. Nugent," he said, and came back in ten or fifteen minutes with my meal. "There now," he said. "And what else?" "Nothing," I said, "no, wait, a glass of wine. You choose it for me, Pat." "The gardens in the Green look lovely," I said when he returned. I had taken a small table by the window. "A beautiful job of restoration," he said, with commendable reserve. "They were knocked about a bit, were they not?" I said. "Three years ago? Were they not!" "And what are we at now?" I asked, as he stood by my side, unbidden to leave, hands joined across the small paunch which tall men sometimes acquire.

There are certain kinds of Irish face which, confronted by a direct question, can come suddenly to look almost Chinese, inscrutable. But in Pat's present case, I saw this warring with a simpler, nobler, a positively un-Irish wish to tell me what he thought. He chose to be indirect, the usual compromise.

"The Dáil, you must surely have heard, is meeting five minutes or less from here, in the Mansion House. In Dawson Street."

"The Dáil?"

"The government of Ireland, as it calls itself. The fellows who were elected to Parliament at the general election, but chose to stay here, set up shop. Those of them who aren't in prisons, over in England. Mr. De Valera is in one of the prisons over there, the president of the Republic."

"Of the Republic!" I repeated, and involuntarily I raised my voice.

"They dine in here often," he said, with a cautioning frown. "I wonder they are not yet here. Very well-mannered, well-spoken gentlemen they are, the ones who dine at the Shelbourne at any rate. Count Plunkett, Professor MacNeill, a dozen others that I could name."

"Indeed," I said, with an indifference which I did not entirely feign, and addressed the succulent chop. But later, as he served me my coffee, he said, in a more serious tone, soft and direct, "The one thing that I know for certain, Mrs. Nugent, is that these have become times to be on guard as to what one says and to whom one says it." "Pat!" I said. "You astonish me. That has always been the rule for Dublin conversation, high or low." Which was no more than the truth: Dublin was always a notorious whispering gallery of rumor, malice, speculation, spiced always and made palatable, such was the claim, by wit and vivacity. Or bad manners passing as such.

But the Kingsbridge station, like as much of Dublin as I had seen, was as it had always been. Country people, their transactions in the city completed, on their way back to the west, a few priests, two Protestant clergymen, commercial travelers, an imperious, buttressed matron and her two gawky daughters accompanied by a small flotilla of boxes and cases, and a half-dozen Tommies quite at their ease, joking and gesturing, a London regiment to judge by their accents. Three or four pals in early middle age had managed to do themselves well for such an hour of the morning, and looked as though they had not been to bed, stubbles of beard, and one of them with a damp stain on his trouser leg. Home, I thought, and poor widow or not, I splurged upon a first-class ticket, and to my pleasure discovered that one of the clergymen and myself had the carriage to ourselves.

He was a Grigg, but the name had originally been Gregg, as he explained to me, and he was rector of the church in Athlone. There was a Mrs. Grigg, of course, and a younger son at Trinity and an older one, a lieutenant in the Inniskillings, who had not yet been demobbed; "demobbed" was his word, and he seemed to savor it. He was a pleasant old chap, and as politeness required I told him that Charlie had been with the Connaughts, and had died in the Dardanelles. "So many," he said softly, "so many." And so of course there were, it was like a plague, like an epidemic, like the influenza, it was being said that no other war had destroyed so many—not the wars of Napoleon, not any of them. You could hear it said, on occasion, with a kind of pride, as though this were yet another accomplishment of the twentieth century, along with motorcars and the factory system. But nice Mr. Grigg meant it as simply as he said it—so many.

And then he rather spoiled it a bit by going on. "Young lads like yours and like my Howard were the hardest hit, you know, the chaps from Oxford and Cambridge and Trinity, some had not even seen a university, straight from Charterhouse and Wellington and Portora. First over the trenches, cut down by machine-gun fire. *Their* young officers as well, of course, young German subalterns, Austrians. The best of all our nations. A great tragedy. We must pray for them all."

And perhaps it was true, had its truth, rather. You heard it often enough. "We" had lost a generation, a generation of young leaders, prophets, the golden hair of Rupert Brooke, young Asquith. I even, once, heard it propounded, at a very sound and sober evening, the very opposite of a Bloomsbury evening, that what was happening in Germany, in Berlin, happened because so many young officers had been left behind in the mud, beneath simple crosses, and the returned officers, screaming their command cars across Berlin, holding their automatics in their laps, on the prowl for socialists and profiteers and "politicians" alike, were the tough lads, the hard cases. And what of us, what were all of our young hard-case officers to do—settle back happily into Balliol and Magdalen and construe Euripides or whatever was done to him, and discuss Plato and the Forms?

Even before we had reached Kinnegad, where the boy brought tea round to us, and small sandwiches, the talk had moved, of course and properly, to where we were, to our own country, to Ireland.

"It is quite worrisome, Mrs. Nugent," Mr. Grigg said, as I poured the strong tea into our cups. "It is an absurd situation, a situation which in simple logic cannot last, but there you are, there at this moment we are, and it is capable of breeding the formless bloody misery of which in the past this country has proved itself all too capable. For all purposes, we, all of Ireland, are represented at Westminster only by the loyalists elected out of Ulster. Everyone else, every elected Papist rebel"—he swept a brief, grateful glance about the dusty-windowed privacy of the carriage—"is staying at home, if you please, and declaring himself the legitimate government of Ireland. It cannot last, of course, it is farce. This is Great Britain, not Pomerania or Croatia or Poland. We are the victors in the greatest conflict in recorded history, not the vanquished. And we won that victory at the cost of our best. Our best. As we have reason to know, you and I, Mrs. Nugent." He turned away abruptly, and looked out the window, beyond which, despite the streaks, stretched before us the pastures and low hills of Leinster, with every now and then a ruined keep, the trim spire of a Protestant church, a plantation of oaks sheltering a manor house from view.

Suddenly he said, still staring out, not looking back toward me, "Do you know, Mrs. Nugent, that despite my cloth, or because of it, perhaps, I sometimes have taken pride that I am immune to the bigotry and the sectarianism at work in this country? I have preached from my pulpit and indeed in the public prints, against the mean horror of Orangeism; I refused and refused publicly to make that journey up to Belfast to sign their Solemn League and Covenant. I have once or twice gone so far as to suggest that Home Rule might not be the worst of all fates, a Home Rule brought into being by responsible men like poor Redmond, or even Dillon, even O'Brien. But we have surged past that, and have surged downward, down the slope. I can see only bloodshed ahead, and great humiliations for our church, Mrs. Nugent."

He turned then, and I handed him his tea, which I had been holding for him. He accepted it with gratitude. He had a thin, kindly, worried face.

"Is there no way they can be brought to understand," he said, "that it is our country as well as theirs, that we love it as they do, that we are all Irish?"

Poor decent Mr. Grigg, I thought, as I resigned myself to the railway tea.

"All of us Irish," he said again. "My father was a rector before me, the Griggs are a clerical family. He was rector at Frenchpark after Douglas Hyde's father. I would go out shooting with the gamekeeper, a Papist, a fine old man, I learned a bit of Gaelic from him, have a bit of it yet, phrases, sentences, rhymes, a few songs. My boys used to like to hear them, when they were little. Jolly songs about tinkers and poachers. But why am I telling you, dear Mrs. Nugent? You are Irish yourself. We are all Irish."

"All of us?" I said. "Are we? I would hear talk in London, a bit of talk, not too much, about people who planned to sell out, move over to England, if things were to get really nasty here."

"Ah, but that is the thing, do you see. That is the thing. If you hear a bit of such talk in London, you hear far more of it here. And it happened, some years ago, after the Wyndham Act, people selling out, moving to England. But this would be different, this would be people forced out because events themselves, history itself would be telling them that they have no place here, that they are not—that *we* are not Irish, Mrs. Nugent. That to be Irish you must be Catholic, there is the long and the short of it. A dreadful pronouncement. We have been here, most of us, for centuries."

"That is nonsense," I said, trusting that he knew that I spoke not of him but of unnamed others. "I have seen a copy of the Proclamation which the rebels posted up in 1916. I am certain you have. Everyone has. 'Cherishing all the children of the nation equally,' it says."

"I know," he sighed. "A noble document. No, no, I am not using sarcasm, it is a noble document, shaped by poets who pledged their lives to their words. 'The Republic guarantees religious and civil liberties,' or words to that effect. I accept that. But 1916 was for all that a Catholic uprising, the leaders Catholics, every one of them, and ninety percent at least of the lads who followed them. It was Catholic Ireland rising up in 1916, and it is Catholic Ireland which claims now to be ruling us all through their rump parliament. We are here all right, and welcome to stay. But we are here on sufferance, and must prove ourselves, as it were. It won't do. It will lead to suffering."

His tone was calm, melancholy perhaps, a bit nostalgic for times when this had not been so. I imagined that he had had time to think it all through and come to his gloomy conclusions.

Decent Mr. Grigg had made one mistake at least, and it was a revealing one. He had assumed that I was myself a member of his community, and it was now too late to disabuse him without discourtesy. A revealing mistake: how had he made it? Because we were chatting together in a first-class carriage which in all likelihood he could not afford—rural rectors were poor as church mice, appropriately—but which propriety demanded, first or third my father always said but avoid the second, crawly little solicitors' clerks and school inspectors—and because of how we addressed each other, because of accent, because no doubt of the way in which I poured the horrid tea, because Charlie had been in the army. Because, in short, I was a lady, as Mr. Grigg was a gentleman. And if one met a lady on an Irish train, one assumed that she was a Protestant. As simple as that. There were exceptions, of course, hundreds of them: Protestant bank managers' wives as awful as anything out of Kipling, vulgar country cousins, mere subscription to the Thirty-nine Articles did not confer gentility, but even there, just as in Kipling, there was an assumption of kinship to the raj, however distant, however humble. And on the other side there were people like—well, like me. And Charlie. And Patrick Prentiss. Well, perhaps. Patrick in fact was one up on Mr. Grigg, not Trinity but Oxford, but then he was a lawyer after all, not landed, and to pull the thing off properly, one needed land. The weird and awful thing was that England was thought to be class-ridden, and yet in England we rarely thought about such things, in terms of whether one was a Catholic or a Protestant. There, it was rather dashing to be a Catholic, exotic and yet very English, great hidden recusant families and priests' holes in remote manor houses, and houses which had sheltered Charles II. Although in England Charlie was agnostic whatever that is and I didn't give a damn, but once aboard the mailboat everything changed.

"Suffering," I echoed, so that he would not think I had been woolgathering.

"Yes," he said, "I foresee terrible suffering, Mrs. Nugent." And Charlie's name, of course. Nugent was one of those cozy interdenominational names, not like poor Father with his O'Gorman.

"In the past," he said, "in the past we have been arrogant enough, God knows. And there are those who think us aliens—in thought and creed and blood. It is a dreadful way to think of people." Decent Mr. Grigg: hopeless. Men may perhaps fight if their houses are burned, their gods defiled, their mistresses seduced, but they will always, if snubbed or if their wives are snubbed, carry resentments festering to murderous hatreds.

At Mullingar, the great cattle town, bustling and sprawling, or as much bustle as Ireland can provide, we halted for ten minutes or more. It is also a great railway junction for Cavan, for Sligo, Galway. It is lovely lake country. And it is—was—our market town as well. Charlie's town, Castle Nugent a mile or so away on the far side of the lake, an unusable, battered keep, and beside it a fortified house of the early eighteenth century, not lovely at all, but grim and imposing. There in those difficult decades, hemmed in by penal legislation, the hostility of plantation neighbors, the Nugents, Charlie's great-great-greats, had contrived to hold on to the several hundreds of acres which had remained to them. The miracle of course is that they had not been shipped off a half-century before, with the other Papist gentry, beyond the Shannon, there to scramble and scuffle for land with the native Papists, our own O'Gormans among them. Charlie's father and older brother had once described the means to me at tedious length, involving in one generation a friendly Protestant "front" and in another a timely, transient conversion. However did we survive, we exotic flowers, the remnants of the old, vain, defeated Catholic gentry, faded deeds and charters on the walls, a portrait of some great-great-great-great-uncle, lace at coat collar and sleeve and, above the lace, a journeyman portraitist's desperate efforts to smooth into fashion a red, beefy face, the long upper lip of the Gael. If Mr. Grigg and his congregation were in need of instruction upon how to comport oneself on the back shelf peopled by history's offcasts, they had only to look to us.

"Do you know Mullingar?" I asked Mr. Grigg. "Our—my husband's people live just on Lough Ennell, beyond the town in that direction, the house is splendidly sited." For there was in fact that to be said for it, those lovely lawns moving down, past a gazebo, to the reed-fringed lake, where swans nested.

But Mr. Grigg smiled and shook his head. With a gesture of inquiry, apology, he unfolded his *Irish Times,* and began to read. I caught a glimpse of a one-column headline: "Outrage in Kilkenny. Police Barracks Burned by Arsonists." Arsonists. Throughout the months, the few years into which we had moved, the *Irish Times,* and for that matter the nationalist press, for a time at least were scrupulous in their use of appellations: *arsonists . . . brigands . . . bandits . . . murderers.* Only toward the end did they say, first Volunteers, then Irish Republican Army. Something was happening surely, and yet I could not measure it, when a newspaper could report, as casually as a sailing accident, the destruction of a police barracks.

I saw now why we were delayed. For a squad, some six, of the RIC, with a sergeant in command, came along the platform, having climbed down from a motorvan, and with them a civilian, a middle-aged man, gray lounge suit, neat and respectable, soft gray hat, lean face and downward-turned mustaches. An inspector out of uniform, I thought, or a resident magistrate. They moved past us, as Mr. Grigg and I sat watching, past all the first-class carriages, and we could just, by craning our necks, see them climb aboard a second-class carriage. "A fine body of men," my father almost invariably said when we encountered the RIC, sometimes affectionately, sometimes in sarcasm when they had done something foolish, but most often as a simple statement of fact. However justified might be the feelings of the most extreme of the nationalists, the Kilkenny "arsonists" for example, the constables were for most of us the most familiar and homely of sights, despite their rifles and belted truncheons, Catholics for the most part, of rural stock as we were ourselves, big, hearty men, looking forward to their pensions, and their sergeants in the smaller towns were known for their gardening skills, their roses vying with those of the stationmaster and his wife. It was nevertheless a mildly unusual scene, and the rector and I looked at each other inquiringly, and then shrugged, he returning to his paper.

He was a slow, careful, pondering, masticating reader, and I could tell, so ritualized is the *Irish Times*'s order of presentation, that he had marched forward through national news and the news from "our correspondents" in London and Vienna, and the "Church News," which of course was the news of Mr. Grigg's own church, plans for the synod, a new pastor for the church in Newbridge, and had at last reached the half-page of social and personal news which is for most of its readers the special savor of the *Irish Times*—a strawberry festival in the garden of Colonel and Mrs. Saurin, "The Laurels," Newtownmountkennedy, and Captain Desmond Mullins, late of the Inniskillings, is visiting his parents, the Reverend Mr. Oliver Mullins and Mrs. Mullins, the Rectory, Ballina, Mayo.

And I, who had not thought to bring a book with me, had the countryside to study as we moved across the midlands. In childhood, and in the years when I was away to school in Roehampton, at the Sacred Heart, the train journey across Ireland had seemed to me endless and exciting, like a trip across the far west of America, and it still had not lost a bit of that feel, although the flat midlands were never, for me, the territory to which I was returning. That began, for me, with the river, with the Shannon, at Athlone. Not that our place, outside Loughrea, would count as picturesque, for all that it was in Galway. For that we too, in summer, would move westward, to the far edge of Galway, to Connemara. But there was nevertheless an excitement, and I would imagine almost that the landscape was changing subtly, with each mile that we traveled westward, becoming a bit less tame, a bit more disordered.

But this was not true of Moate, the next stop after Mullingar of any consequence, nor of the countryside around it. I had never set foot in Moate, and yet it had always seemed the dullest of Irish towns. From train windows, one can just make out the wide main street which is its only claim to a visitor's attention, and in which, so I was assured first by my father and then by Charlie's father, important cattle fairs were held.

In the station at Moate, Mr. Grigg put down his newspaper, and, as I was about to tell him something of what I had been thinking, the corridor door swung open, and the conductor looked in to say, "Well, by God, sir, madam, today we will not be long in Moate, I wonder that we bothered at all, for the sake of two half-drunken laborers in third class. Did you take a look at what came aboard us in Mullingar? The times that are in it, sir, madam—" But as he said it, he broke off, and was staring past us, beyond the window. "Jesus, Mary and Joseph," he said as though in simple astonishment, and then said it again in a voice now half-strangled.

I turned toward the window. Out from behind the station had come six or eight or nine men, I was so startled that I had no thought to count them, but three at least, all of them I thought at first, were carrying rifles, and two of them, the two in front, held large revolvers. They were running at an angle to us, but then beside us, past the first-class carriage. The conductor was standing as though rooted, but then he began a slow movement backwards out of the carriage, and as he did so, he raised a hand above his head.

The knot of men was brought up at the rear by another fellow carrying a revolver. Something in our carriage, perhaps the slowly, purposefully moving conductor, drew his attention, and with what seemed a single, swinging movement, he stepped upon the footrest, opened the outside carriage door, came in with us, and sat down abruptly. The door he left gaping open. "Take your hand away from that, now," he said to the conductor, who stood motionless, petrified or baffled, with his hand still raised. "Put your hand down. Don't be an eejut. Take your hand down and come in here and sit down beside the others." He had now a bit of time for us, the conductor moving heavily back into the carriage. I could understand now that his hand had been raised to pull the communicating cord to the engineer. "It would serve no purpose, but why take a chance? If all is going well, the engineer is sitting quiet as an altar boy, with one of these shoved under his ear." We looked at his great revolver, the four of us, and suddenly he said, "I am sorry, ma'am, sir. We'll be gone before you know we are here, there is no way in which harm can come to you. I am sorry indeed." And in truth he was, or at least seemed so. He could scarcely have been more than twenty-three or -four, cloth cap, wool jacket, a muffler about his throat, an ordinary country lad, polite and soft-spoken. "I believe that you do not mean any harm, to us at least," Mr. Grigg said, in a remarkably calm and almost courteous voice. "I trust as much can be said of your leaders here." The fellow grinned, and revealed a missing front tooth, then rubbed the back of his hand across his mouth, a coarse, casual gesture. "I think I am the leader," he said, "God help us." "If it is our valuables you want—" Mr. Grigg began, and at that the fellow lost much of his courtesy. "What the bloody hell do you think we are," he said, and then remembered Mr. Grigg's cloth and my presence. "This is a military action," he said. "It will be accomplished straightaway, and you'll be off to Athlone. I am sorry about this." It was a country man's soft, coarse speech, simple and yet nuanced.

Then, as the four of us watched, the fellows with him led from his carriage the gray-suited, mustached man who had boarded at Mullingar with the constables. Our lad's revolver and his phrase "military action" seemed to serve him as a uniform. "No," he shouted as he jumped up, and climbed out from our carriage. "Move the damned police out with you." His men looked toward him, uncertain, and he walked toward them. It was a quiet, airless day, there seemed not even distant sounds, a cart on a road, birdsong, the shouts of children. But as he spoke, there was a shot from the carriage, it struck the ground near one of the men, and raised a small cloud of dust. "Dear Jesus," he said, and running toward them shouted, "Never mind now, move back behind the station. Bring him with you." There were other shots, and then, almost casually, he swung his revolver toward the carriage, and fired twice. The shots from within the carriage ceased for a time.

Our fellow and the lads with him moved to the safety of the station, one of them holding the inspector—as I thought him—by the arm. He seemed puzzled, quiet, and very frightened. Once, for a moment, I caught his eye. "You can pull the signal cord now," Mr. Grigg said. " 'Tis beyond that now," the conductor said.

Presently, our fellow shouted out from behind the gable wall of the station, "We have taken Mr. Bowers prisoner. That was our purpose. You can move off, the lot of yez. You can do nothing here."

I heard a constable, their sergeant I expect, shout out to him, "Mr. Bowers is traveling under police protection. We intend to protect him."

"A fine bloody job you are doing," our fellow called.

"We intend to do our duty. We will fight you."

"There is nothing you can bloody do. Where you got that rifle from I cannot imagine, but we have your other arms."

There was a long pause, and then they came out together, my fellow—whose name, I was shortly to learn, was Dinny Lawlor—and Bowers. Bowers was quiet and still looked very frightened. Twice, a shudder ran through him convulsively. Lawlor was holding him by the arm, but lightly, and now he dropped his hand, and spoke quietly into his ear. Bowers looked at him, a look which, even from the distance, I found terrifying, hopeless, fearful, perhaps angry as well, I could not tell. He walked slowly away from Lawlor, toward the open door of his carriage, and when he was about ten feet from Lawlor, he paused for a moment as if uncertainly, his foot raised, and at this, almost as upon a signal, Lawlor raised the revolver, and shot him in the head. The noise seemed to fill the air, the universe, more deafening than rifle fire. Then Lawlor stepped forward, to where Bowers had fallen, fired a second time, and then moved back to his line of safety.

I screamed without being aware that I was screaming, it was as though I believed myself to be saying something vital, necessary, but it came out warped and strangled into a scream. I climbed down from the carriage and ran toward where Bowers lay. Mr. Grigg, clenching my arm, tried to hold me back, but I pulled myself free. "Wait, wait," he shouted, "I will come with you."

"Keep clear of him," I heard voices from the carriage shouting. "Be careful."

He lay with his face pressed sideways against the dusty wooden platform. Below the shoulders, the suit of gray tweed was still neat and pressed, his black boots polished, with a faint film now of dust upon them. But above the shoulders, he was all blood, and blood was still pouring from two wounds. The one bullet had struck his head, the other his neck. The long but neatly trimmed mustache was blood-soaked. Mr. Grigg was beside me now, kneeling, and, taking a large square handkerchief from his pocket, placed it over Bowers's face. "Shouldn't we—" I began, but he shook his head.

While we were kneeling beside him, his murderers, it appears, were making their retreat. Perhaps I should have heard the start of their motors, there had been two motorcars parked beyond the platform, others heard them, or claimed to, but I can swear to nothing which I saw or heard, for all seemed distortion, and beneath the level sky, within the dusty afternoon, there was no center save what I knew lay beneath Mr. Grigg's handkerchief, the bloody mustache and the shattered throat. Mr. Grigg helped me to my feet, and by now there were many people on the platform, the stationmaster, who had been held within at gunpoint, the constables, other passengers. I looked from one to another of them and could say nothing, but I must have been looking odd, because the constable put his arm, awkwardly, about my shoulders, and held me for a moment.

"Dear God," he said.

The stationmaster was a small man, almost toothless, and bald save for a fringe of gray hair. "They cut the wires," he said. "The telephone and the telegraph alike. They have been waiting here, in the house, for a half hour or more, an hour perhaps."

"Where is there a phone?" the sergeant said.

It took him a few moments to think it out. "At Dr. O'Malley's," he said. "At the rise of the hill. You can see his house from here."

"What am I to do now, Sergeant?" the conductor said.

The sergeant smiled, as though welcoming a fresh problem with sardonic satisfaction. "You can get your passengers back on board, and make for Athlone. When I am at the doctor's, I will phone ahead."

"They made off like bats from hell," the stationmaster said. " 'Tis the Kilbeggan road they took."

"I am not getting back inside that thing," a country woman shouted to him. Her woman friend, standing beside her, nodded vigorously.

"Please yourself," the sergeant said. " 'Tis a free country."

"Not by the looks of it," she said.

Her friend said, "Sinn Féin is needed to bring safety to the railway stations of this country."

But no one, not even her companion, was inclined toward politics.

The sergeant tilted back his hat and rubbed his forehead with the back of his hand, a homely gesture which put me in mind of the gunman.

"Get back on board," he said, "that's an order now." Suddenly I realized that in all likelihood this was for him, as much as for the rest of us, a first encounter with death by gunfire. He stood so close to the fallen man that by bending down he might have touched him.

Mr. Grigg touched my arm, and I turned with him to go back to our carriage, but then paused. "Sergeant," I said, "who was he?"

Startled, he looked at me a moment before answering. "His name is—his name was Bowers, ma'am. John Harrison Bowers." I was hearing that day, for the first time, a name that would be repeated, again and again, in the years that followed.

"He was an inspector?" Mr. Grigg asked.

"Not of the constabulary," the sergeant said. "He was a bank inspector, a chartered accountant." It seemed neither more nor less strange than anything else happening that a bank inspector should be traveling with police escort, or that he should be shot down in cold blood by armed men attacking a railway train.

"There was nothing you could have done, Sergeant," Mr. Grigg said.

"That is kind of you, sir," the sergeant said, but his eyes denied his words, or rather, Mr. Grigg's words. Bowers had been traveling under police protection, and the sergeant had allowed himself and his men to be overpowered. As Mr. Grigg and I turned away, the sergeant said, "I don't know what the country is coming to, I declare to God I do not."

We traveled half the distance from Moate to Athlone without speaking, Mr. Grigg and I, but rather looking at one another, from time to time, and then out the window. It was strange to be in the same carriage, which looked exactly as it had before, the same rip at the edge of one of the seats, near the door. Then he said, "You were the first to run to that poor man, Mrs. Nugent. The very first." "I don't know why," I answered, truthfully; "it was so awful, to see a life destroyed." And by a fellow who had sat there facing me, a country boy, desperate but courteous. It had all been as though he were acting a part, until that last awful moment, when he bade Bowers walk forward, and then raised his revolver and opened fire. The noise and the sight of Bowers, not falling so much as crumbling, it was as though I had been drawn to his fallen body. "I don't know why," I said again.

Charlie was home twice on leave, once to London, and once to Westmeath so that we might visit with his parents. "No good describing," he said; "don't ask. It's very strange." But that was in that first tour his regiment had, in Flanders. After that, it was the Dardanelles, and there was no leave from the Dardanelles. His commanding officer wrote a nice letter but I could not make sense of it. Perhaps, unless you have the good luck to die in bed, you die as Bowers did, walking in terror and then bullets slamming into you, and after that you are a parcel, a crumpled parcel of clothes and bones.

"It is so strange," Mr. Grigg said, "coming pat upon what we had been speaking of."

"I loathe guns," I said, who in a year would be in love with a man described by the newspapers as a gunman. There was even once a poster. "Christopher Blake," it said. "Educated, well-spoken, of genteel appearance." I would tease him about that dreadful word. "Not gentry," I would say, "but of genteel appearance. Perhaps not even a gentleman, but of genteel appearance." "Quite right," he would say, "a doctor's son, University College, not even Trinity. Genteel appearance fits the bill." Not quite gunman, perhaps, not a gunman as young Dinny Lawlor was, on the day he shot down Harrison Bowers, nor even Lawlor of a few years later than that afternoon, when he had become Commandant Lawlor, and you would hear his name, like Barry's and O'Malley's and Lacy's. Not a gunman, perhaps, but a man who sent gunmen out upon their tasks, which is as bad, surely, or perhaps worse, as any confessor can tell you.

It was long after Christopher and I had become lovers that I told him of seeing poor Bowers shot down. He looked at me at once, concerned, shocked. "That was terrible," he said. Bowers's murder was something one heard of often at the beginning of the troubles, because like Soloheadbeg and the shooting of the soldiers as they came from religious service in the Fermoy church, it seemed so barren of precedent. It was by then, only two years later, a mere shard of history.

"Poor fellow," I said, "he was so harmless and terrified. Somehow I think he knew that he was going to die, although none of us did, none of the passengers, nor the policemen who had been guarding him. A bank inspector."

"A bank inspector," Christopher said. "Did you not wonder why a bank inspector would need the protection of the police?"

"I did," I said, "of course I did, and I was not the only one. People wondered. Was he a policeman himself? Is that it? I never heard that."

"No," Christopher said, "you would not. No, he had been a

bank inspector, by then he was retired, living somewhere not far from you, Athenry I think. But he had special training, special skills, and so he was brought back."

"By his bank?" I asked.

"By Dublin Castle."

We were staying in the weekend cottage which Patrick's friend Keough had given us the key to, on the Connemara coast beyond Ballyconneely. It was a chill evening, and we had built a fire, the turf burning through red and skeletal. Beyond the uncurtained windows, low, we could see the ocean with, very far off, a coaler moving slowly eastwards, and nearer at hand, the sails of two fishing boats. We faced each other, at ease, in easy chairs by the fire, and we had a kettle heating.

I waited for him to go on, and then he said, "He had been a bank inspector thirty years before, in the Land League days. The League kept funds in this account and that, under this name or that. Bowers's task had been to ferret them out. He was very good at it, a legendary name in the Castle, it seems. We had been doing the same thing with the National Loan. We had a problem, you see, the Loan was the treasury of the Republic, and it was quite substantial. We could not keep it in De Valera's boot."

"But the Loan was quite legal surely," I said. "It was all done out in the open. They collected for it outside the church gates in Loughrea. All the church gates, I should think."

"Indeed it was not," he said. "In this country, Dublin Castle decides what is legal and what is not. By the end of the day, we had a quarter-million pounds in hand, part of it in a gold reserve and the rest in accounts under an assortment of names. The book-keeping has been formidable. Bowers headed an inquiry set up by the Castle under the Crimes Act, and he was calling in books and bank managers. It was fortunate indeed for us that he decided to conduct an inspection in Galway. We couldn't get him at the Castle, and he was living there, to stay under close guard."

He spoke with a curious detachment, as though he were at one remove from what he was saying. How close to what had happened had he been? I was not sure that I wanted to know, and my not wanting to know frightened me. I remembered kneeling beside Bowers at that railway station in Moate, I saw his shattered throat, ugly, no longer human.

"You must understand," Christopher said, as though he saw

what I was seeing. "It is because war is dreadful, and we are fighting a war. They deny that, but it is so."

"It is so ugly," I said.

"He was acting as a spy," Christopher said, "a spy or an informer or both. Spies are shot."

"But someone else would take his place."

"Yes," Christopher said. "Someone did. A man named Bell. They—we—got him too. In Dublin. It took a bit longer."

They, we, people in Dublin, all that mattered little to me. Christopher mattered.

"You must understand," Christopher said. "The work I do is quite different. But I have been a part of it all, of Dinny Lawlor at Moate, of all of it."

"Yes," I said, "that was his name, the young man. He is one of your chieftains, there is a song about him. Imagine, a boy!"

"He is your age," Christopher said, "he is a few years younger than I am myself. He is very skillful, with a flying column, they have come close to fighting a pitched battle with the soldiers. On two occasions. It is only the men with the flying columns that we can write about, the others, you know, the local battalions, those are fellows who go about their ordinary business—farmers, teachers. But fellows like Dinny Lawlor, their names are known and they are on the run—that is how the flying columns came into being."

Across the darkening waters, the coaler seemed almost motionless; the water was slate-gray.

"In Limerick," Christopher said, "the Black and Tans broke into the house of George Clancy, the mayor, and shot him dead. Killing Bowers was no different from that. Clancy was one of our brigade commandants."

"No different," I said, but he took no notice of my irony.

"This is the first time in our history that we have fought effectively," he said, "the first time that we have devised a way to fight. We are fighting an empire, with cannon and regiments and wealth at its disposal. We have handfuls of men, moving across glens, mountains, the streets of our cities. The Empire does not know how to fight that kind of war, we have invented a new kind of war."

"And when the war is over," I said, "what will your Dinny Lawlor do, your boy-commandant with the song written for him?

He had the look of a farm laborer, but that was a year ago, he may have changed. Will he go back to that?"

"I don't know," Christopher said, "I doubt if he does. I doubt if he has thought about it. Are we in an argument, Janice? About what? You told me that you had seen a man shot down, and I said that it must have been dreadful for you. So it must."

"No, my dear," I said. "No argument."

For I was arguing not with Christopher but with history. Charlie had sent me letters from the Dardanelles, and I had read them over and over, not alone the protestations of love and loneliness, but those in which he had tried to re-create for me the world in which he lived, putting into the task all his skill, but it remained foreign and bewildering, distant, cold, that world in which he had traveled without me and about which the newspapers were constantly, I am certain, lying. And now, all that was happening in my own country seemed equally distant, lunar, save for what I had seen, the armed farm boy who for a moment had sat in my railway carriage, the accountant shot down on the railway platform, and his face before Mr. Grigg had covered it. Christopher explained why it had happened, had had to happen, as in the newspapers a few years earlier maps and articles by "experts," retired colonels, had explained to me why the attack on Gallipoli was brilliant and how brave all our men there were, including of course poor soon-to-die Charlie. When Christopher and I had our weekends in Myles Keough's Connemara cottage, Christopher traveled armed, always careful not to confront me with the weapon, but I saw it once, a large heavy automatic pistol in the bottom of his case, beneath his shirts, and beside it the box of heavy cardboard which contained bullets for it.

But after we had had our tea, we walked along the strand. There was one other cottage in sight, a fisherman's cottage a mile or so along the strand, with a single light, soft and consoling. The water raked along the shingle almost to our feet, and a full, pale moon had arisen. The darkening water stretched westward and away forever, with the moon touching it into purple and greenish stretches, immensely quiet, there cannot be anything in the world more quiet than that shore, the shingle, the lapping water of the great sea. Behind us, somewhere, were the mountains which cut Connemara off from the rest of the world, so that even Galway, even my own county seemed far distant, soiled, peopled. A bird's cry broke the silence and Christopher turned toward me.

"We are safe here from your damned history," I said to him presently.

"Yes," he said, but told me later, dry, conclusive, that Clifden, the only town, had its flying column and had been raided by the Black and Tans and burned. A young boy from Clifden had been hanged in Dublin after Bloody Sunday.

"What can there be to quarrel over here?" I asked, "over stones and country roads and ponds. What do they want here?"

But on the strand that night he said only, "Yes," yes that there was no damned history, the history which had taken Charlie from me and now tugged at Christopher.

I remember that afternoon, in 1919, when the train pulled into Loughrea, and everyone in the station seemed to know that something or other had happened somewhere along the line. My father, when he led me toward our motorcar, with a boy beside us to carry my two bags, said, "My God, Janice, what happened? Every second person has a different story. Was the train attacked? Were you under fire?" "Something like that," I said, "but, no, I was not under fire," and told him what had happened. "A bank inspector!" my father said, and then broke off, pointing a significant look toward the boy who was stowing the bags in the elaborate baggage rack of the motor, which I had never seen before, had never seen my father drive one. When we were on the road, and driving eastwards toward Coolater, he said, "Decent little fellow that lad seemed, but you cannot be too careful these days, bloody Shinners." "How did you ever learn to drive, Father?" I asked. "And to drive so well," which wasn't quite true, but it was as though he had not heard me.

"Bloody Shinners," he said again. I had wanted a splendid day for my return to Coolater, but it was gray and sunless, and getting itself ready for rain. "Something is happening, Janice," he said, "make no mistake about it. I see the London papers from time to time. They don't seem to understand that there is a war shaping itself up here. Bloody stupid English. Sorry about my language, dear." "You had best make up your mind, dear," I said to him, "you had best decide who is bloody, the Shinners or the English."

"My own lapse gives you no license for such language," he said, treating me as though I were sixteen, and then, after a bit, said, "Both of them, both of them." He seemed to be speaking neither to me nor to himself, but to the road or perhaps the steering wheel. "The whole bloody lot of them."

"The Land War will be nothing beside this," he said presently. "Mark my words."

I marked them, dutifully, after Moate how could I not, but my mind was on the countryside as it rested before rain, the light greens of spring darkened beneath the lowered sky, and a herd of brown-splashed cattle beneath wide-branched elms. It carried the comforting tones of familiarity, as did a woman standing barefoot beside her cabin, a full bucket weighing down her right arm. As we passed, she raised her other arm in lazy greeting, and my father touched his hat brim.

"People like that woman there," he said, "people whom we've known all our lives. I don't remember the Land War all that well, of course, I was away at school and then the army, but we fared well enough, never any trouble, your grandfather always dealt well with his tenants, and they knew it. Others fared less well."

As he spoke, he kept a wary eye on the twisting road, his gloved hands grasping the wheel tightly.

"Perhaps we will fare well now," I said, but more as soothing noise than as a speculation.

"What do they want?" he asked me, in sudden, abrupt exasperation. "They wanted the land, and now they have it. Wyndham and the government handed it to them on a platter. They wanted Johnny Haslip's land, and the government obligingly bought Johnny out. Johnny lives in London now, very comfortable, thank you, and comes back every year for the cubbing. Stays with Mark Nailor. He tells me that he was at the gaming tables in Biarritz one year, and who should come in but George Wyndham himself. 'Look here, George,' he called out, and ran the chips through his fingers, 'I'm playing with my Wyndhams.' That house of his is owned by a bacon curer from Limerick who comes here for the summer, and the land is with twenty, no thirty farmers."

Pasturelands, hills, trees, the wide and empty boglands are not possessions of the imagination alone. Nothing, anywhere, is unowned, if not owned by Mark Nailor, whom I could not for the life of me remember, then by strong-farmers, by bacon curers from Limerick. The rain was moving quickly toward us now, dark clouds tumbling down from low hills, and in the air a faint expectancy. The cattle stirred beneath the elms, and then were gone from our view, and ahead of us, in another pasture, unmeasurably lovely, two foals stood, their chestnut flanks almost touching, their heads raised, alert, to the coming rain.

"Cubbing!" my father said, as though the word were a wire, tripping off another furious thought. "Do you know that the Shinners put down a ban against hunting? Well, they did, everywhere in the blessed country. There was to be no hunting, here or anywhere. Crowds came out with sticks and pitchforks. And one shotgun, at least. In Wicklow, a horse was killed by gunfire. A horse!"

It seemed bizarre, so bizarre that at first I thought he was joking, making his point by exaggeration.

"It worked," he said, "it worked as well as a boycott might. No hunting until the Shinners were back home, the ones who had been jailed in England, De Valera and that lot. No trouble here, thank God. We have a sensible Master. No trouble, no crowds. Daresay the Shinners locally missed it as much as we did, a day's outing, eh?"

"Yes," I said. "Who is our Master now?"

"Tony Sheares at Gorthevner," he said. "He managed it very ably, no noise, nothing in the newspapers. 'Dan Russell will have a holiday this year,' he told us."

"But it could not have been pleasant for him," I said, "an old soldier like Tony Sheares." I saw him striding through the square on a market day, tweed-clad shoulders thrown back, checked waistcoat, billycock hat. Or, more to the point, I saw him on a crisp autumn morning, astride his bay, the heavy shoulders a blaze of scarlet, the hounds belling, reins held lightly in the confident fingers of one hand, the other hand splayed across the broad, muscular thigh.

"No," Father said, "not pleasant at all, and no need for it, you know, by March they had released all of the Shinners, but the season was over. They don't seem to be troubling themselves about the beagling."

The rain was almost upon us now, the clouds moving swiftly across the glen.

"A police inspector has been shot in Westport, you know," Father said, "and the whole county has got itself proclaimed, passed under martial law, and below in Cork and Tipperary. Not much of a welcome home for you, is it, Janice? But the odd thing is, you know, something quite dreadful will happen, and nothing else talked about for days, and then everything is as it always has been. You'll see, my dear, it will be a glorious spring and summer, wash London out of your system."

The rain fell in a swift, sunless shower, spattering the canvas roof of Father's motorcar.

CHRISTOPHER BLAKE

In the spring of 1919, Christopher Blake was living in a flat in Fitzwilliam Square. His afternoons were spent in an office in Harcourt Street, and his evenings and early nights in the Mansion House, where an assembly calling itself Dáil Éireann had come into being, and his late nights, several nights of the week, in the back rooms of public houses, in flats scattered across the city north and south of the river, in suburban houses, and on occasion in remote farms of County Dublin or Wicklow. In these last, in these late-night meetings, he assisted in the reorganization of the Irish Volunteers, as for a year longer they would be called although gradually that name was replaced by another, the Irish Republican Army.

From his top-floor flat, two windows opened upon the small, closed park. Spring slipped week by week into the park, touched branches, flower beds. By April, he could stand by his window with his morning tea and cigarette, imagining the force which would drive itself, green, imperious, seductive, through close-curled buds. From the square, a ten minutes' walk, at the most, down Pembroke Street and then the south side of Stephen's Green. He had not been near to the Green during the week of fighting. In Dartmoor Gaol its comely image had several times returned to him, an orderly world of small, secure bourgeois satisfactions, sun-dappled; in imagination, he had heard the music the band, in their Graustarkian uniforms, would play in summer, selections from *Maritana* and *The Pirates of Penzance.*

Dartmoor he remembered by music of a different kind. In his

cell, in black night, lying sleepless, hands folded, patient, hopeless across his chest, he would hear, from a distant cell, a clear voice raised in a song in Irish, "Sean O'Dwyer" or "Slievenamon," or, in harsher voice perhaps, firm Dublin accent, a Fenian ballad or one of the ballads of the 1798 Rising. Other voices would join in. The warders, a decent lot most of them save for the occasional bastard, would let them sing away, and the voices would echo and reecho down corridors of iron, steel, stone. The Fenian ballads in English were sorry stuff, boastful or lachrymose with sudden dips into bathos, but the voices sometimes gave them, for the moment of their utterance, a thrilling intensity. The songs in Irish were a different matter. They would be sung, however badly, with an almost sacramental reverence, telling, like Mass Latin, truths which lay couched within secret sounds, gestures.

He had returned to Ireland in June of 1917, with the final batch of convicted rebels and on the same boat with their leader in Dartmoor, Eamon De Valera, who had commanded the garrison at Boland's Mill, a tall, bespectacled teacher of mathematics. Like the larger group who had been released five months before, in time for Christmas, they were welcomed as heroes, with immense crowds to cheer them at the dock and to escort them into the city. But they had been expecting this: news had been smuggled into Dartmoor. The Easter Rising had become a legacy, a political gift of incalculable power, but there was no certainty as to how it might best be put to use.

At first, before finding his rooms in Fitzwilliam Square, Blake had lived with his mother in Sandycove, in a trim house of Victorian brick, suitable to the widow of a Dublin surgeon. From his bedroom window, he could see the bay, and, in the far distance, the lighthouse at Howth. In the evenings, when he was visited by one or another of his "associates," as his mother called them, she would leave the front parlor to them. But often they had the evening together, the two of them. They would leave the drapes undrawn: she liked the feel of the sea that close to hand, the salt-heavy fog pressing against the windows. Blake would read and so too would his mother, although at times, because she knew he liked it, she would play the piano, tunes that he remembered from his father's day, Gounod and Massenet.

"He is out of fashion with your London friends, no doubt," she said, "poor Gounod." "Oh, entirely," Blake said. It was a reminder of how strange life had managed to become for him, that he had left England and his English friends to take up arms against them. In "armed rebellion," as the words in the indictment had it. And stranger still that he should have been sentenced to life imprisonment and yet, a year later, be back in Sandycove, with his mother.

"It is a pity," she said, "that you were not here at Christmas. It was a lonely enough time without either Owen or yourself. But the O'Riordans were very thoughtful. I was in Dalkey with them for Christmas dinner."

"I remember, Mother," he said. "You wrote to me." Owen was his brother, a captain in the Royal Army Medical Corps, in France. He had been with the Fourth Dublin at the landing at Sedd el Barr in Gallipoli.

"It must be terrible over there in the trenches," his mother said, "as terrible as anything that has yet happened to man." She was standing by the piano, and rested a hand, a feather, upon the keyboard, as though summoning back some earlier scene. "But his letters make light of it, all jokes and school days remembered, times here. You are as bad yourself, nothing but good fun reported in your letters from that dreadful prison. It has an evil reputation, Dartmoor. Men take great pride in holding things back, it is childish of them. Your father would have been the same."

Her own final schooling had been in a Benedictine convent in Louvain, close to the great library which the Germans were to destroy in 1914. An innocent vanity, she prided herself upon her delicacy of feeling. The nuns of Louvain, she liked to say, can give a polish to the dullest of us. Which she was not, by clear implication. Solid upper-middle-class Catholic nationalist stock. Eleanor Catherine Ronayne, daughter and granddaughter of lawyers. Sometime in the past, generations earlier, the Ronaynes, like the Blakes, had moved into Dublin from Galway. Beyond the piano was a pier glass, in which Blake saw her reflection, a slender woman, dark hair untouched yet by gray.

"Not bad for me there," Blake said. "Really not. Nothing like poor Owen off there in France. They were severe to be sure, but not savage."

Above the gate at Dartmoor was an inscription from Virgil.

Parcere subjectis et debellare superbos. Spare the submissive and wear down the proud. One morning, as Blake and the other rebels were lined up for morning exercise, they encountered a new convict, Eoin MacNeill, the scholar who had commanded the Volunteers and who had managed, with fatal half-success, to countermand the orders for the Rising. Now he had to face the men who had rebelled in spite of him. It was an awkward moment. De Valera broke the tension. He stepped forward, said, "Eyes left," and saluted MacNeill. He was marched back to his cell, but he had made his point, a complicated one.

Much later, on the boat back to Dublin, released prisoners, Blake had asked De Valera about it. He was a tall, thin man, awkward of gesture and movement, self-contained. He paused before answering. "The Volunteers are still in existence, Mr. Blake. And Professor MacNeill is still our commander. I have heard nothing that would contradict that." De Valera, thanks to his American birth, was almost the only commandant to have escaped execution.

"They set us to work making bags," Blake said to his mother. "Dull work, but nothing to wear down the proud. Better than pulling oakum, like poor Wilde at Reading."

"Poor Wilde indeed!" Eleanor Blake said.

Framed photographs of both sons stood on the piano, a recent one of Owen, in uniform, and one of Christopher on the occasion of his degree conferral at University College, gowned and holding the diploma like a baton. Slightly behind them, a photograph of their father, bearded, formally dressed, a glossy silk hat resting on his knee. On the night table in Eleanor Blake's bedroom was a photograph of Bernard Blake and herself in Venice, taken on their honeymoon, in a pigeon-littered Saint Mark's Square, a café out of focus in the background, the sunlight brilliant. As a boy, his father still alive, distant and formidable, Blake had studied it, astonished at the openness of that version of his father, beardless, tentative smile, his eyes half-shut against the sun. He wore a white shirt and held a soft white hat by his side. Eleanor Blake was dressed in the stiff fashion of the day, and yet seemed to Blake soft, vulnerable; she was looking not into the camera but toward her new husband.

She had said to him, "It is wonderful that all of you have been sent home to us, after all the terrible sentences that were passed out upon you all. It must surely have been Mr. Dillon's doing."

John Redmond was still leader of the party of constitutional nationalists, but the Rising had been a dreadful blow to him, and John Dillon was more and more the spokesman.

"Very likely," Blake had said, hoping that the matter would drift away, but his mother was quick to catch tones, reservations.

"Do you not think so?" she asked.

He sighed. "No," he said. "I do not. I think that the English government is desperate to keep Ireland quiet for so long as the war goes on. And I think they are desperate to extend conscription to Ireland. They are setting up a convention to solve the Irish question, and it would never do to have us locked up in English prisons in our hundreds. Not as ordinary people have come to feel about the rebellion."

Ordinary people. And others as well. While the executions were still under way, Dillon himself had traveled from Dublin to Parliament to speak to an infuriated House. These were men, he said of the rebels, who had fought a clean fight, a good fight. There were now photographs of the executed men from one end of Ireland to the other. It would never be possible to discuss Ireland while pretending that 1916 had not happened.

"No doubt," Eleanor Blake said, "no doubt. But you will find, when all has been said and done, that Mr. Dillon and Mr. Redmond and Mr. Devlin and all the others have the best interests of Ireland at heart. That has long been the case."

Long indeed. She was speaking sensibly enough, speaking as his father would have spoken. There were some seventy-odd of them in the English House of Commons, the Irish Party, the watchdogs of Home Rule. For her generation, for most of those in his own, that was political reality—brass bands, bunting-bedecked platforms, small favors, small deals arranged, party of farmers, auctioneers, publicans, clerks, solicitors, minor civil servants, surgeons. Across Blake's childhood had floated the emblems of nationalism: statues of rebel pikemen, speeches, an iconography of martyrdom, Robert Emmet, Wolfe Tone, the Fenians; tunes heard so often that they had become wedded to nerves.

All this had ended, been burned down in Dublin, shot down against the wall at Kilmainham Gaol. Or earlier perhaps. Blake had been present, in civilian clothes, when Pearse, in the uniform of a Volunteer officer, spoke to an immense crowd at Glasnevin, at the burial of O'Donovan Rossa, the old, battered, hard-drinking Fenian, bitter and unrepentant, who had died in New York. But when Pearse spoke, in the calm of a Dublin August midday, his language had lifted the crowd above that: "Life springs from death; and from the graves of patriot men and women spring living nations. The Defenders of this Realm have worked well in secret and in the open. They think that they have pacified Ireland. They think that they have pacified half of us and intimidated the other half. They think that they have foreseen everything, think that they have provided against everything; but the fools, the fools, the fools!—they have left us our Fenian dead, and while Ireland holds these graves, Ireland unfree shall never be at peace."

In those first June and July weeks of 1917, living with his mother in Sandycove, Christopher Blake had fallen into the habit of walking, late at night, along the coast road, to the abandoned Martello tower beside the bay. In the far distance, across water, the last lights of Howth, the lighthouse, on occasion the running lights of ships. They were already in the long nights of the Irish summer. Until ten, the scene was held in changing, diffuse light. Soft, beyond him, the hill of Killiney, suburban villas, gardens tumbling steeply down, artful splashes of purple, crimson, pale blue. Impossible to hold within single scales of the imagination that tranquil scene and the final violent Saturday hours a year ago in Moore Street, beside the burning Post Office, the air heavy with black, choking smoke; before him the barricade at Great Britain Street, rifles and machine guns, bodies in the rubble-littered streets, laneways, in one of them O'Rahilly's bullet-ridden body.

Now, standing by the tower at Sandycove, Blake was filled with a sense that all had changed and yet he had no sense of the new forms which would rise up. The great sheet of water close at hand, the pinpoint light of the distant lighthouse, darkness upon the water—it was like stone awaiting its inscription, paper its tracery.

He would feel it when he walked into town, if he felt brisk, or else took the train. He had volunteered a day a week to the National Aid Fund with offices at 10 Exchequer Street, a few turnings away from Dublin Castle. A most proper and respectable organization, devoted to the families of those who had died in the Rising, and to the hundreds who were returning from the prisons. They were poor enough, most of them, whether Volunteers or Citizens' Army men, and for most of them their jobs in offices and shops had not been kept waiting. It was becoming fashionable to contribute to the Fund—bishops did it, nationalist members of Parliament, journalists, barristers and doctors, farmers, a few country gentlemen, priests. It signaled a sympathy with Easter Week, discreet, legal. Mrs. Clarke, Tom Clarke's widow, had founded it, and an alderman was its president, but its secretary, at a salary, so he later told Blake, of two pounds ten shillings the week, was Collins, Michael Collins, the captain of Volunteers who had stood beside Blake on the lawn of the Rotunda after the Post Office garrison had surrendered.

Late one July evening, waning light in the Exchequer Street offices, a Volunteer with too much whiskey inside him appeared with a revolver, waving it dangerously in the air. "Boland's Mill," he said, "I'm a fucking veteran of Boland's Mill. I fought for fucking Ireland." Blake stared at him. The three Volunteer girls in charge of the canteen were still as death. Blake caught the eye of one of them, a plain-featured girl with blond hair done up in braids; her mouth was half-opened. Blake could not judge the scene, whether the man was idly threatening, half-drunk, but the revolver was real. Collins, at his desk at the far end of the room, stood up and walked to the man, brisk, businesslike, cuffed him across the face with the flat of a hand, twisted the gun away from him, and said, roughly, "Get the hell out of this." The man looked at him, not frightened, but surprised and angry. "Who the hell are you?" he asked; "where the hell were you when you were needed?" "None of your bloody business," Collins said. "Will you walk through that door, or will I kick you out of it?"

On his way back to his desk, Collins paused beside Blake and broke the cylinder of the revolver. It was empty. "A lovely great Webley," he said. " 'Tis an ill-wind that blows no one good." "How will you enter that in your accounts?" Blake said. "Goods contributed," Collins said. "Value uncertain." "That should satisfy Mrs. Clarke," Blake said. Collins had an extraordinary skill with account books and ledgers. From 1906 almost until the Rising he had been a clerk in London, with the Post Office, with a stockbroking firm, with a Labor Exchange in Whitehall. But he had the look and manner of a young countryman, footballer's trunk, wrestler's shoulders, a handsome, heavy face, light, fierce eyes. Blake thought he had him pegged—West Cork accent, at once coarse and musical, Irish-language enthusiast, Sinn Féin enthusiast. A capable fellow, quick, decisive, uncomplicated.

That evening, after they left the office in Exchequer Street, Collins took him to a public house near the quays. "I have never been in here before," he said, "but I pass it each day, walking to the office or from it. It seems a pleasant enough place." An ordinary sort of pub. Dark, dirt-stained wood, posters for race-meetings; the framed oval photographs of the men executed the year before. Behind the bar, above the rows of whiskey bottles, hung a colored print of Croagh Patrick, the colors garish and improbable. Collins carried the two pints, Blake's and his own, to a table at the far end, near the door which led to the toilet. There was no one sitting nearer to them than an old man, neatly dressed, shabby, nursing a glass of what looked like port. "Pleasant enough place," Collins said again. "Small-fry drink in here, you notice? Elderly clerks in the insurance companies, bookkeepers, old fellows who do this or that in Dublin Castle or for the Corporation." His heavy face, massy-boned, turned suddenly from the room to Blake, who noticed, almost with a shock, the gray, challenging eyes.

"Good luck," Collins said, and lifted the shell of ale. "It must be more convenient for you, to have a small place of your own here in Fitzwilliam Square. Sandycove would have been a long haul for you, although 'tis pleasant there, with the great sea air, and good places to walk."

"You are well informed," Blake said, and let the faint annoyance creep into his voice.

"No, no," Collins said. "I chanced to hear one of the girls talking in the office. You're a rare one, you know. Posh accent and the years in London and a book published."

"Published," Blake said. "But left unnoticed."

"On Ireland is it?" Collins asked. Two men, bowler-hatted, came into the pub. Collins's eyes flickered toward them, lingered, then returned to Blake.

"On Connaught in the eighteenth century," Blake said. "What happened to the last of the Gaelic gentry after the Boyne and Aughrim."

"By God, that's a fine subject," Collins said, with sudden,

fierce delight. "The MacDermotts and the O'Connors and the O'Malleys. By God it is. And poor O'Conor of Belnagare stripped by the heel of the hunt to a few hundred acres and his books. A man who had corresponded with the great Dean Swift."

"As I was saying," Blake said, "you are well informed. Professor MacNeill wants to have a look at it. I saw him last week. Do you know what he said? He said, 'A pity Pearse won't have a chance to see it.' A strange man."

"Pearse was strange enough to satisfy my tastes for the odd," Collins said. "You were in Dartmoor, were you not? I was in Frongoch. I got off easy."

Blake sat facing the framed photographs, but they were too far off for him to see them clearly. Pearse was in half-profile, a handsome puzzling face.

"If I had the management of the universe in my hands," Collins said, "I would keep poets and scholars safely away from the levers of power. They have made a terrible hames of things through the centuries."

"Plato was much of your opinion," Blake said.

"Ach, that one. He would have banished them entirely. No, they are the best that the human race produced, the poets and artists. But they shouldn't be let loose. When poor Ireland is free, we will ask Mr. Yeats to build an Olympus on Croagh Patrick, for Æ and Colum and the rest of them."

"Without poets," Blake said, "there would never have been a Rising. Pearse and MacDonagh and Plunkett."

"True enough," Collins said. "It takes poets to stage an armed rebellion in the middle of a city with no lines of communication or retreat."

"They had no need for them," Blake said. "They did not intend to retreat."

Collins moved his glass in circles on the oak surface of the table. "They intended to die there," he said. "There or by firing squad. And they intended us to die along with them. They didn't explain that to me. Was it explained to you?"

"Don't cite me," Blake said. "I came late, you will recall. I asked myself in, like poor O'Rahilly."

"There was a man," Collins said. "That O'Rahilly. It was O'Rahilly gave me a hand trying to put out that damned fire. And when he made the final rush, I was proud to back him up. Do you know what Pearse did when we made that rush into Moore Street, O'Rahilly on one side of Moore Street and myself on the other? He made a speech to us. His reservoir of speeches was inexhaustible. He told us that we were saving the soul of the Gael. 'You're dead right,' O'Rahilly said, 'Gaelic speakers to the rear.' " Collins laughed and flung his head back, shaking a long strand of hair from his eyes.

"You seem sadly disillusioned," Blake said.

"Not a bit of it," Collins said. "Not a bit of it. And if I were, I would not say so. Look at those photographs. And walk up and down the length of Grafton Street. You will see no more Union Jacks, nor posters telling us to go off to Gallipoli or to die for Belgium. There has not been such a fine morale in this country since the days of Parnell. I don't know how I feel about the Rising, to tell you the truth, Christopher. It made a clearing, it made a possibility. And that is what they intended, perhaps—the fellows on the wall there."

He sat with his chair pushed back from the table, hands upon heavy knees.

A bit later, Blake went up to the counter, and bought the other half, two pints. When he had put them down on the table, Collins said, "I'll be gone after this. I am meeting a few fellows in Clontarf."

In a year's time, most of Collins's conversations with Blake would end that way—he would be off to meet a fellow here, a few fellows there, or he would tell you that he would be at "the other place" later on, or he would tell you to be at "the other place" yourself, and he would send a fellow along to you with a message. His own years in London had given him a few Anglicisms, "a bloke you haven't met yet," he might say, the word dropped like an alien raisin into his West Cork accent. In a year's time—but already, Blake knew, Collins was busy with several things at once, that he was one of the men reorganizing the IRB, reorganizing the Volunteers, that he would come late to meetings of the Gaelic League. He moved from place to place by tram or bicycle, and, once in a great while, by taxi.

" 'Tis very good of you," Collins said to Blake, "to give us an evening of your time each week, without fail."

"It is very little," Blake said, "those fellows are having a hard time of it, no jobs open, and some of them with families."

"But you will have your own job waiting for you back there, once you've rested up," Collins said. "They won't hold your little adventure against you. A very chivalrous people, the English, when they can afford to be."

"Like most people," Blake said.

"Ha!" Collins said. "You have the right of it there. And am I right about yourself?"

"No," Blake said, "not really. Like yourself, I have a sense that there has been a clearing, a pause in time. There are people who praise the Easter Week thing now because it has the shrouds of time upon it, a mist. But I don't at all. I think that something is beginning to happen. I will wait around for a bit."

Collins drank a measure from his glass, then rested it on the table.

Suddenly he smiled. It was the smile of a footballer who has discerned his path, a huntsman's smile, a smile of pure pleasure. "By God, Chris, it is indeed. Something is about to happen. You can smell it upon the air. It will not be like the carry-on at Easter, nor the Fenians, nor those fellows in 1848. The cards have been dealt to us at last, Chris. 'Tis up to us to play them."

"We," Blake said, "us," and he let the monosyllables drift upon the air as questions.

"You are a Volunteer, Chris," Collins said, "dues paid up and all, and Gaelic League, and you are close enough to Sinn Féin."

"Oh yes," Blake said, "I have done all the proper things." And things done easily enough, in those years before the war, before the Rising.

"And a bit more. You were there when you were needed, as the lads say in the pubs. You were in the GPO for the whole of the bloody week—"

"Barring the first few hours," Blake said.

"Granted," Collins said. "Granted, but sure, that could redound to your credit. Yourself and poor O'Rahilly. You came in and joined us once you were certain we would lose. That has a nice reckless air to it. And you did your time in Dartmoor. You have all the credentials needed for a career in Irish public life."

Now the public house door opened again, and Blake felt the

city close at hand, waiting outside. Cobblestones. The oily, foul-smelling river.

"A failed uprising and a spell in an English prison," he said.

"Classical," Collins said. "Classical." He smiled again, and as he smiled his eyes moved to the wall clock.

"And yourself?" Blake said.

It was in those summer and early autumn months of 1917 that the political life of the country was transformed, and Collins was everywhere at once, as Blake was to learn. Already, that February, at a by-election in Roscommon, Joe Plunkett's father, a theatrically patriarchal Papal count, had defeated the Irish Party candidate, and Collins had been a campaign worker on the dusty roads. In May, he had helped Joe MacGuiness, a prisoner in England, win the seat for Sinn Féin at another election in South Longford. When the Supreme Council for the IRB was reestablished, Collins became its secretary. In October, when Sinn Féin met to draft a new constitution and choose a president, Collins used the IRB to back Eamon De Valera against Arthur Griffith, and in the Volunteer convention that followed, he would use the IRB to take the presidency of that for De Valera as well. In those months, he must surely have seemed to most as he did to Blake that evening on the quays, a hurler bursting with energy, with initiatives, with enthusiasm, ready to serve the purposes of men with cooler heads, longer experience, a country fellow with some useful training in the civil service.

"You keep your dues paid up, Chris. You might do a bit more. Report to one of the companies. They have begun training again."

Blake shrugged.

"Waiting around to see what happens isn't good enough, boy," Collins said. "There has been enough of that. I'll tell you now what you should do." He took a small notebook and a fountain pen from his pocket and wrote. "This is a company not far off from where you live, Chris. 'Twill be no inconvenience to go and march up and down for an hour or two once a week. And more to the point, the commander is a chum of mine. I will tell him to be expecting you." Neatly, one hand pressed down firmly, he tore the page from the book and handed it to Blake.

Blake read it before folding it and placing it in a waistcoat pocket.

"You be certain to do that, Chris," Collins said. He tilted back and finished off his pint. "I will be depending on you."

"*You* will?" Blake asked, half-amused, half-puzzled.

"I may need someone like yourself from time to time," Collins said, "and you won't be there if you don't keep your medals polished, keep your ticket punched. Mind what I've said now." He pushed back his chair and stood up, settled his gray respectable hat on his heavy head. But at that moment, Blake saw an entirely different man, wary and resourceful behind the barricades of good fellowship, the bluff banter. He sat quietly as he watched Collins make his way to the door. By the entrance, a fellow with one too many under his belt, a tall beanpole of a man in fawn waterproof, tweed cap, collided with Collins, and Collins, once again the farmer's boy in the city, laughed, steadied him with an absent-minded arm, and then walked out.

A year or two later, Blake would be in the habit, almost in exaggeration, in self-parody, of imagining that evening as the occasion of his recruitment not only into the movement but into Collins's private army, an army which would swell to include policemen, civil servants, gunmen, spies, taxi drivers, importers, country bank managers, fishermen, curates, publicans, librarians, innkeepers. Once, one autumn night, a gaunt fellow in a mud-streaked trench coat turned up at Blake's door with a note: "Keep this fellow for a few days, and then I'll take him off your hands. The coppers want him." The note was unsigned. Blake and the fellow liked each other; he was an ex-seminarian from Waterford named Grimes. "I'm damned if I know," Grimes said one night over tea; "I was training recruits at Enniscorthy in Wexford, and I got a note that I was to pack it in and come up here. I spent a night or two in a miserable kip off Dorset Street, and then he sent me along to you. But in Dorset Street I heard that the cops had come round to my lodgings in Enniscorthy." When Blake came home the next day, Grimes was gone, his blanket and sheet neatly folded and no sign of him in the flat.

By then, Collins had moved—to an office in Bachelors Walk, to Cullenswood House in Rathfarnham, which had once been Pearse's school, to two small rooms in Capel Street. At times, late evening, night, he would meet men in a hotel near the Rotunda or, more often, in a public house near the Four Courts, patronized by solicitors, court attendants, neat, self-consciously respectable men. It was there that once, by arrangement, Blake met with him. Collins looked much like the others, suit of blue serge, white shirt with stiff collar, somber tie. "There is a house that can be let, Chris, in Arklow, right on the strand, an elegant house, and it can be let furnished. You would oblige me were you to take it. It will not be costly, but there will be money paid into your account to cover it." There was less of the fellow up from the country about him now, a mannerism shed because no longer needed. "Why do we need it?" Blake asked, but Collins shrugged.

"You need not stay in the damned place," Collins said. "Spend a week or so there, and get the locals to know you. Tell them you have a brother will be coming over from England, and you are renting it for him." "What is my brother like?" Blake asked. "I don't know," Collins said, "I haven't picked him out yet." He laughed and nudged his elbow into Blake's ribs. "I have a brother," Blake said, "a doctor with the army. On the Somme." "Poor bastard," Collins said. Blake paid regularly into a Dublin bank the rent on the Arklow house until the day in 1921 when detectives from the G Division and a squad of Black and Tans raided it and arrested two Volunteer officers and a German arms dealer.

September 1917: Crowds waiting in the streets outside Mountjoy Prison in early-autumn rain while jailers—enraged, embarrassed, clumsy—forced gruel and warm milk into Thomas Ashe, and contrived to smother him. In the rains of early autumn, women knelt upon the stones, said rosaries. London would never understand Ireland, London nor Dublin Castle. Ashe, tall, light-haired, handsome, had been one of the heroes of Easter Week. At Ashbourne, north of Dublin, with fifty Volunteers at his back, he had captured four barracks, and was still in command of the field when Pearse's order of surrender came to him. Imprisoned he had been butchered in ignominy, choking on his own vomit. Ashe, butchered, would weigh more upon Ireland than Home Rule bills or debates in Westminster. Thousands had filed past the open coffin in which he lay in Volunteer uniform, and the government did not dare to deny the presence at his burial of the Volunteers, uniformed and in arms. A volley was fired, and then Collins stepped forward, although few in Ireland would have known who he was, as powerful in build as Ashe had been, but a different order of strength. His speech was brief: "Nothing additional remains to be said. The volley which we have just heard is the only speech which it is proper to make above the grave of a Fenian."

But it was a speech which said much. By calling Ashe a Fenian, Collins had quietly but pointedly reminded some of those present that he had been a member of the Irish Republican Brotherhood, that with Collins, Ashe had been working to reorganize the Brotherhood. But, equally, Collins had reminded the crowd in the sprawling graveyard that two years before, at the burial of O'Donovan Rossa, Pearse had warned a larger crowd that there would be no peace for Ireland so long as it held the graves of the Fenian dead. Living nations, Pearse had said that day, a day of clear sunlight, sprang from the graves of the dead.

Blake, by now a company commander of Volunteers, but only half-uniformed, leggings fastened around tweed trousers, Volunteer's slouch hat of green felt, had been at Glasnevin that day, facing Collins's back, his company forming part of what the grandiloquent new table of organization called "the Dublin Brigade."

Months later, he had said to Collins, "It is fortunate that the Volunteers were allowed to march armed to Glasnevin. You would not otherwise have had a speech." "I had a Webley buttoned up inside my tunic," Collins said. "One revolver shot would have done the trick. The trick is to let them know that we are not fooling. Let all of them know, let England know and let the Irish know. Speeches are all well and good, we all love a lovely speech. But without steel behind it, it is breath upon the wind." "Pearse was not armed when he stood at the grave of Rossa," Blake said. "Pearse is dead and gone," Collins said.

They were walking along Bachelors Walk. By now, Collins was known by sight to many; their eyes would move across his features, a flicker of recognition. The streetlamps had been lighted, but the Liffey beside them was black, with the bone-chilling cold of winter upon it.

"A wonderful man," Collins said, "very eloquent. 'Tis not enough." Suddenly, he gave one of his explosions of laughter. "But you never know. We have gone far on eloquence, speeches, puff in newspapers. We are an eloquent people. Even the English grant us that." He nodded across the river, toward Dublin Castle. "But those lads over there have managed to rule us without need for eloquence. Policemen and police spies and packed juries and carbines and cavalry in the Curragh. It was artillery that they used against us at the end of the day."

"Artillery is in short supply on our side," Blake said mildly.

"Webley revolvers are in short supply," Collins said. "What we must contrive for ourselves is a different kind of army, without parades and without artillery. A gunman with a Webley can be as good as a battalion, if he knows who to kill and where the fellow can be found." He laughed again and jabbed Blake with his elbow. Now he was the young rowdy from West Cork, ready to turn everything into sport, but Blake had come to know the metal, hard as a Webley, behind the soft country manner.

IV

FRANK LACY

Frank Lacy returned to Ireland in the late summer of 1918. His ship brought him to Queenstown, and from there he took the train to Kilkenny. He had only the two heavy cases of black leather with him, and these he left in the care of the stationmaster, and walked through the small city to the offices of the *Kilkenny Nationalist*. These were beside the bridge across the Nore, and close to the railway station, but he swerved aside and walked up and down the length of High Street. At MacIlhenny's hardware shop, across from the Tholsel, a young fellow whom he recognized as Willie Dunphy was setting up upon the pavement a display of bright-finished pots that glinted in the sun. Lacy slowed down as he watched Dunphy, and as Dunphy stood up, he saw Lacy, squinted a bit, and then said, "Jesus," and crossed the road.

He was ginger-haired, and like Lacy, was in his middle twenties. They had been at school together, at the Christian Brothers, before Lacy was sent away to the school in the midlands.

"Jesus," he said again, "Frank Lacy. The return of the hero."

"The prodigal," Lacy said.

"Small chance of that," Dunphy said. "Small chance of that. The fellow who raised up County Galway when the country otherwise was quiet, save for Dublin."

"There was little enough raising up in the County Galway," Lacy said. "Men marching about this way and that way and then fading away up into the hills. And 'twas not I did the raising up, 'twas Liam Mellowes."

"Perhaps so," Dunphy said, "perhaps so. But you get the

credit for it in Kilkenny." He had an apron tied about his waist but was otherwise respectability itself. Neat coat and wool pullover, and a celluloid collar fastened with a gold stud. He was broad-cheeked and ruddy, affable and faintly wary.

"Not in the *Kilkenny Nationalist*," Lacy said.

The grin held itself in place. "The *Kilkenny Nationalist* marches with the times, Frank. We have a Sinn Féin member of Parliament now, Willie Cosgrave, one of the 1916 men like yourself, one of the men who stood with Pearse and Tom Clarke in the Post Office."

With Pearse and Tom Clarke in the Post Office: it was as though they had been lifted into legend by that week at Easter.

"You'll not tell me, Willie, that my father backed Cosgrave and Sinn Féin. Do you think that Kilkenny newspapers never reach New York?"

"Well, then you know, then," Dunphy said. He looked back across the road at McIlhenny's broad front, windows displaying chairs, a parlor table, pyramids of tins. "Sure, how could he, Frank, with himself and John Maginnis friends for twenty years or more, friends since the days of the Parnell trouble."

"To be sure," Lacy said, "the Da has ever been a great one for standing by friends."

"Are you back now for a look around, Frank?" Dunphy said, drawing his hands in a single smooth gesture which untied the apron, as though he only now remembered it.

"I am back in my own county, Willie. It was too hot for me back in 1916, but now bygones are bygones, as I understand it."

"Back to Kilkenny?" Dunphy said.

Lacy shrugged.

"Have you no wish to know how I voted," Dunphy said, "Cosgrave or Maginnis?"

"I take it, Willie, that John Maginnis was also a friend of your father's."

"He is, and of the father-in-law as well. But I cast my vote for Willie Cosgrave, I cast my vote for Sinn Féin. Times change, Frank."

"The father-in-law?"

"Have you not heard, Frank? I am now a married man. I married Lucy McIlhenny." He looked again toward the sparkling windows, the long sign above them, gilt scrollwork upon red, "McIlhenny and Sons."

And son-in-law, Willie Dunphy.

"I shall be here for a few days at least, Willie. Time to drink your health. And Lucy's."

"At Hartigan's," Dunphy said, nodding. "The same as in the old days. Nothing has changed. You will see."

"Times change," Lacy said. "I have your word on that." But he put his hand on Dunphy's beefy shoulder. "At Hartigan's," he said.

But when he left Dunphy, the weight of double histories pressed upon him, his own and that of the old, past-thick town. His last days in Ireland, save for a day or two in hiding in Limerick, had been in small farms or mountainside cabins, and these had clung to his thoughts, the view from the mountainside cabin, distant hills haze-shrouded, morning wind cutting down from the Atlantic, the taste of sweetened tea as he leaned against the wall looking out across the long, cabin-dotted glen, the coarse, rich grasses, yellow gorse, rain-polished stones. There, fragments of rock, grass, wind-driven cloud, had clustered, icons of the Ireland that he had served in those futile spring days. Here, in Kilkenny, thick-woven life pressed down upon him. The city in which he had been born, an ancient cathedral town where once parliaments had met, in one century or another, in whose cathedral Rory O'More, Gaelic and Catholic, had made his submission to Queen Elizabeth. On the river stood the great castle of the Ormondes, the Butlers who had ruled Leinster for the English. Once, and not too long before, the town had been divided into Irish-town and English-town: the names still clung to stones, lanes, archways.

As a boy, with Willie Dunphy or with friends wilder, less reputable than Willie, a coachman's son from the castle, two red-haired reckless boys of a Thomastown farmer, he had swarmed through the alleys and archways of Irish-town, English-town, playing trappers and Red Indians, but conscious even then, Lacy was at least, that older games had been played here.

He walked along the length of High Street to the river, past centuries-old buildings which had been converted into shops, public houses, and at the foot of the street crossed the road to the bridge, where he could look up along the Nore to the castle. Centuries old, but encrusted now with Victorian medieval embellishments, so that the silvery Nore reflected a dream of feudalism, a Walter Scott fortress wafted to the banks of an Irish river. Once, a boy, before visiting his father in the newspaper offices, he had walked to this bridge, had stood where now he stood. All that had in life seemed grand and unobtainable had been concentrated here, high, wide windows, battlements, gardens, and, as he looked, a gentleman and a lady strolled along the terrace, her hand resting on his gray-clad forearm, her head inclined toward his. "I have no idea who they may be," his father had said to him, sitting before the desk at which he wrote his leaders. "But of one thing you may be certain. They have not come down to visit us, Francis. Nor anyone we know." Lacy had felt the metal in his father's words, and yet they served to set the castle apart from the actual world of Kilkenny, the castle and all those who strolled its terraces, gray-clad gentlemen, and ladies in gowns the color of primroses.

"They are not the worst in the world, the Ormondes. The Butlers, that is. Not the worst. Throughout the centuries they shielded these counties, shielded the city, the towns along the river. But at a price, Francis. At a price. They ruled Ireland for the Crown."

And so, Lacy had thought that autumn afternoon as he sat beside his father at the great, paper-strewn desk, and so it was all true, all that he had imagined, great noblemen who held lands for kings and rulers. Lacy's friend Phil Hogan, son of one of the coachmen at the castle, had told him of castle balls, the carriages drawn up beneath the great portico, and footmen to swing open carriage doors and hand down ladies glistening like princesses in Grimm's tales. On Sundays, in summer, the grounds were open to the public, and all of respectable Kilkenny strolled in them, Protestant and Catholic, loyalist and nationalist.

But today the newspaper offices were closed, and the printshop as well. Lacy stood for a moment to admire the gilt lettering on the window, "The Kilkenny Nationalist, est. 1880, Thomas Francis Lacy, Prop." Once, it had seemed to Lacy—like school, almost like church—a center of being. He would go with his father into the shop, to watch his father's words, written in a huge, particular manner, ten lines to a page, transformed by Mr. Gaffney, the printer, into metal type, and then, again, into words upon paper. He knew now that the *Nationalist* was the smaller of the town's Catholic newspapers, and he knew now that most of the Ormonde lands had been mortgaged or sold off, almost to the river's edge. Inside the castle, which several times he had visited, a picture gallery stretched out; dead, faded gentlemen and ladies.

It took him a half-hour to walk to his house, past eighteenth-century houses and almost into open country before he came upon it, a substantial, undistinguished house standing in its own grounds, and, as good luck would have it, his father was just coming out the front door. Lacy paused with his hand upon the garden gate, and his father, taken by surprise, stood looking for a moment as though bewildered, and then the heavy, red face broke into a smile beneath the thick white mustache, and he half-walked, half-ran to Lacy, who came toward him along the path, and they embraced. "Eileen," his father called out before addressing him, "Eileen, he is here, he is here early." He dropped his arms. "You should have telephoned from Queenstown," he said. "We would have met you at the station. We would have met you in Queenstown, by God. Eileen!" he called again.

They had tea in one of the two parlors facing the road, tea and sandwiches of ham and thick-cut bread, slices of dry, currant-studded cake.

"Well, well," Thomas Lacy said at last. Fragments of polite conversation lay about them, invisible—family friends whom Lacy had visited in New York and in Boston, his work with Devoy and on one of the Irish newspapers in the city. "Well, well, so you have turned to journalism yourself at the end of the day. You could choose a worse life."

"I had a living to make," Lacy said.

"Don't we all," Thomas Lacy said. "Don't we all."

Eileen Lacy stirred with faint unease. She had been looking first at the one of them, then at the other.

"And not a bad living either," Lacy said. "I enjoyed it."

And he had, in a way, at times. He had written, each week, the paper's column in Irish, which there was little reason to suppose was read by more than a dozen—an old man in Hackensack who wrote in weekly to reprove his grammar, another man on Eighth Avenue who sent in letters to describe the old Irish-speakers in his own village of Carna on the Galway coast. And every other issue, a column of commentary on affairs in Ireland. The editor, Matthew Egan, read the copy with scholastic fervor, testing each word. Egan was boundlessly patriotic, an enthusiastic supporter of the "men of 1916," described always as the "inheritors of the rebellious tradition of Wolfe Tone and Parnell and the Fenians." But the presence in his office of an actual "man of 1916," one of the fellows who had attacked the RIC barracks in Oranmore, made him faintly nervous, suspicious. "You understand, do you not, Francis? The Irish in this city have their differences, who knows that better than yourself, but they are all good Irishmen, there is no call to go out of our way to antagonize them. And no need to. Aren't we all working for the good old cause?" "So it would seem," Lacy would say. But the path of the good old cause was strewn with pitfalls. Denunciations of England were safe enough, but no one wanted to be thought a hyphenated American. And there were surely many good Irish lads being blown up in the trenches of France, mistaken but good-hearted, misled by John Redmond and John Dillon and so on. "And a good many more," Lacy said, "if England begins conscripting them." "That's the ticket," Egan said, "denounce conscription. No one likes conscription."

"It was good of you," Thomas Lacy said, "to send us your pieces. We read them religiously. You have a nice touch—a bit perfervid, perhaps."

"You did not read the columns in Irish surely?" Lacy said.

"No, I grant you that. But your mother saved them all. Religiously."

"I did," she said, in a complicated tone that wavered between affection and neutrality.

"Your mother and I"—this was a formula possessing a specific authority, to be distinguished from announcements made by Thomas speaking on his own behalf, or on behalf of respectable Kilkenny or of the world or nation at large; "your mother and I" referred to the family, an entity possessing vague and impressive claims upon the three of them—"your mother and I had thought of a small dinner party to welcome you home. No one with whom you would not feel at ease. Dr. Hickey and his wife; Sim Casey; the Reardons; your friend Willie Dunphy and his wife."

"I met Willie this day, in High Street outside McIlhenny's."

"And he told you," Eileen Lacy said, "that he and Lucy McIlhenny are now married."

"He did," Lacy said. "That is a good thought, Father. A good

Sunday meal at home. I thought of them often away there in New York."

"Did you?" Eileen Lacy said, eagerly. "We thought of you often too, of course, Francis. But you seemed to be doing well on your own. As you always have done."

"Dermot Hickey and Sim Casey would have no qualms about sharing a table with me?"

"No," his father said, and would have left it there, but Lacy would not let it rest.

"There was a time when they did," Lacy said, "or have you forgotten that time?"

"Three years ago," his father said. "There were hot words spoken on both sides. By yourself as well as by Sim. A long time ago. Many things have happened. I have not altered my opinion as to what happened in 1916, what you people did. It was reckless and unprincipled. But—"

"Reckless, perhaps," Lacy said, "but not unprincipled, surely."

"Unprincipled," his father said, but his tone was mild, as though he had no more wish than Lacy himself to pursue the matter. "But that is neither here nor there. There is no talk of any second attempt at insurrection. Your people have taken now the proper course, making your case to the people of Ireland. And with some success. We have now one of the 1916 men as our member of Parliament."

"You do and you don't. I am not up on the legalities of such matters, but I don't think that someone becomes a member of Parliament until he travels over to England and takes the oath of allegiance and loyalty to King George. I doubt if this fellow Cosgrave is about to do that. Sinn Féin stand for an independent republic." The intensity of Lacy's tone capitalized the word "Republic." "That is what 1916 was about. And that is the case which is being presented to the people of Ireland."

"We all want a free Ireland," Lacy's mother said. "We all know that."

"But we don't all mean the same thing by what we want," Lacy said, and he matched his father's mildness.

"Now then," Thomas Lacy said suddenly, and brought down his hands upon his heavy knees. "What is needed in this house, by God, is a proper welcome home, and that is something that cannot be done on tea and buns alone. Am I right, Frank?"

"You are, Father."

He remembered his first glass of whiskey, in this house, in this room. His father had held the bottle against afternoon sunlight, and poured measures into stemmed glasses. "Now then," he had said, "and always with a heavy christening of water. Tell me now how much." He held the small water jug above Lacy's glass. Lacy did not know. His father poured until the glass was almost filled, turning the whiskey to the palest of gold. Then he half-filled his own glass, and raised it to Lacy. "Your health, Francis." Lacy sipped, the taste alien, almost unpleasant. He was sixteen. "A fellow should have his first glass in his own house, Francis. And there are a number of other rules. You can't learn them all at once. Never drink alone, they will tell you. Nonsense. Many is the pleasant jar I have had late at night, with your mother asleep for hours. In there, with a good fire going."

He nodded down the hall to the small room where he kept his books. There was a heavy, leather-cushioned chair in it as well, and a table with new books on it and a glass jar which held a golden pheasant standing on a branch of oak. Somehow, the pheasant had contrived to get itself dusty, and the glass bead for an eye was unconvincing. "Never drink alone when you are feeling rotten is what they really mean, and that *is* good advice. I tried it myself once or twice, years and years ago. All young fellows feel rotten once in a while. No cure for it. Certainly this isn't." He sipped at his glass of darker hue, an amber.

In those days, his father's heaviness had seemed to him a form of power, which later would seem slackening muscle, soft belly. His red, full cheeks had been tokens of health, and the red lips beneath the blond, thick mustaches. At his desk at the newspaper offices, he seemed to have his hands upon the ropes of life, cattle auctions, happenings in Dublin, London, news of shipping out of Queenstown, Belfast, Galway. At home, the sagging shelves of books held sets of Dickens, Bulwer-Lytton, George Eliot. But whenever Lacy visited him in that small room, he would be reading *Punch* or the *Illustrated London News*, and yet it always seemed as if he were about to toss away those slick, flimsy pages, take down a novel by Dickens, or the volume of Newman's sermons.

In fact, Lacy had once seen him rest his hand upon the book of sermons, not to take it down but to make a point. "The finest English prose of our century, Francis. John Henry Cardinal

Newman. A Roman Catholic. Born a Protestant but he saw the error of his ways. He was here in Ireland for years. In Dublin. The English never trusted him. They wouldn't, do you see? A fear of the Church is built into those people. They fear it and they hate it, and that is why they fear us as well. 'Lead, Kindly Light.' You know that hymn. Newman wrote it. Dashed it off between sermons and so forth." Of that century, his father meant, not this one. In this century, one relaxed after work with *Punch* or the *Illustrated London News*. The *News* always had a special Christmas number that the entire house read, his father and mother and himself and Susan in the kitchen.

In Kilkenny at Christmas, as everywhere in Ireland, there would be, in every house, a single lighted candle at a window to guide the Christ Child, and a high Mass that morning, greetings to friends, an immense dinner and afterwards friends might call in for punch and pudding. But to Lacy, when a boy, the true Christmas was the one celebrated in the *Illustrated London News*, not Christmas but Yuletide, with elaborate engravings of robins perched on bare wintry branches, the Embankment after a snowfall, the Houses of Parliament, clear, brittle and brilliant as baroque icicles, colored engravings, watercolors reproduced of English country inns with inglenooks and squires, red-vested like robins, black shiny topboots, steaming bowls of punch, and other squires, at home beneath ceilings of oak, holding long-stemmed clay pipes. Green baize doors had been swung back so that servants, mobcapped or bumblebee-waistcoated, could bring in immense and savory roasts. As though England owned not merely an empire, not merely Ireland, but ways of feeling, sentiments, colors, ways of being.

The dinner party that Sunday afternoon went off well enough, Tom Lacy and Frank Lacy straining to hold intact the bond of affection. Seated round the table of heavy mahogany swathed in damask, suits of black Sunday serge or flannel, and the women dove-gray, subdued magenta, a strand of pearls for Philomena Hickey, the doctor's wife, small-boned and fierce-voiced. "God rest them all," Dr. Hickey said, speaking of the men in the GPO, "they fought a good clean fight." "Indeed," Anthony Reardon, the solicitor, said. "John Dillon has said as much on the floor of the House of Commons, and said it in the May of 1916 when there was neither pleasure nor profit to be derived from the saying of it." "He did indeed," Sim Casey said, another solicitor and a friend of John Maginnis whom Sinn Féin had defeated in the by-election, "did you know that, Frank?" "I did indeed," Lacy said; he was helping himself from the bowl of potatoes which Susan held before him. "It was in all the American papers. Those of the Irish persuasion, that is. John Dillon is not the worst by any means."

"He is a gentleman," Casey said, "by birth, education and family connections. He did not approve of the Rising, but those words of his were a benediction upon it. For many of us."

"And you have come back to us yourself as a hero," Reardon said, "from the wide and windy plains of Galway, Frank Lacy the man from Galway. Have you thoughts toward politics yourself, Frank, or will it satisfy you to join your father in his benevolent bullying of the right-thinking folks of Kilkenny?"

There was an immediate silence. Lacy contrived to avoid his father's eye, but not his mother's, anxious, fathomless, pale gray. "I have been away for a year or two," Lacy said; "I have not had a proper chance to sort matters out." And, improbably, it was his father who diverted the stream. "Francis has the right of it there, by God. Give a fellow a chance, will you? Let him get his bearings."

After their guests had left, after lingering goodbyes on the garden path, even after Lacy's mother had said good-night to husband and son, as the two of them, in the small room of books, had a final whiskey, even then, despite Lacy's misgivings, his father did not return to the question that Reardon had broached. But said instead, as the two of them faced each other beside the dead fire, "John Dillon is not the only gentleman in Ireland. John Maginnis is a decent skin, and so was Patrick O'Brien whom he would have followed, a man who fought for Ireland in Westminster since the nineties. Who is this fellow Cosgrave?"

"A fellow who fought for the Republic in Dublin. That is as much as I know of him. We don't all know each other, you know. 'Tis a movement, not a fraternal organization. He fought for Ireland, and that seems to have been good enough for the voters of Kilkenny."

"That is as may be," his father said, as he measured out final glasses of Midleton's. "As may be. But I can tell you that it was like no election fought in Kilkenny for many's the year. There was sympathy to be sure for the men who fought and died in 1916, and your own name did not go unmentioned. But there was a fair amount of bullying as well before the nationalists of Kilkenny could be swerved from their course. Sinn Féin was all over us from Dublin and God knows where. In cars and lorries and with banners manufactured in advance and brought here. 'Sinn Féin. A Free Land for a Free People.' All that."

"What is the matter with all that? A free land for a free people. That sounds all right."

His father fumbled in his coat pocket for the pipe that he no longer smoked.

"You don't know young Cosgrave, you tell me. Have you ever encountered a fellow named Collins? Mick Collins." "I have. I have met him," Lacy said, "late in the day. He had been working in England. He came over to avoid the conscription there." "He was down here, assisting young Master Cosgrave." Hurler's body, Lacy remembered, heavy handsome face, quick of movement, thick accent of West Cork. He could remember little more. Save that Collins was IRB.

"Buying fellows drinks in every pub in Rose Alley. And taking for drinks into the hotel gobshites who had never ventured into it before, save to scrape up friendships with the skivvies. And the next night he is having dinner with this one and that one, talking about Shelley and Walt Whitman. A fine pair those two were."

"That is how it has always gone in this country, for God's sake, Father. I remember well when Patrick O'Brien stood last for the seat. Rare old times in the hotel, even though Mr. O'Brien had no one to oppose him save the loyalists."

"More than that, Frank. More than that. Mick Collins could put a threat in his voice when he wanted to."

"What sort of threat?"

But his father shrugged and turned the subject.

From that Sunday to the next Lacy would remember in the five years that followed, as though they existed out of time, suspended. On one of the mornings, the Tuesday, he rode to the newspaper with his father, Tom Lacy sitting erect behind the wheel, fingers more familiar with reins, gray gloves and well-brushed bowler. It seemed to Lacy as though every fourth or fifth person on the footpaths would greet them, the men with fingers touched to hat or cap.

"There you are," Thomas Lacy said, as he stopped the motor. "The Lacys have a name in this county, and had one long before my own father founded the *Kilkenny Nationalist*. The *Kilkenny Emancipator* he called it. Long before that, the Lacys were respected in city and county alike and your mother's people as well, the Bolgers. Good stock, no call for pretension, but good stock." Before he swung open the door of the motorcar, he turned to look directly at Lacy. "The world does not begin afresh every twenty years or so, you know. Things jog along."

"Once in a while it begins afresh," Lacy said, "once in a great while."

In the office whose windows seemed never to have been opened from one winter to the next, sunlight fell pale through dust upon a frayed Turkey carpet, faded reds and greens in diamonds and lozenges.

"You could do far worse than settling in here, Francis," his father said. "*The Nationalist* is a going concern, it pays its way; it is not a coiner of money like the *Kilkenny People* but it pays its way. I have a good few years in me, a man in his fifties in rude health as the saying has it, but there is work and to spare for another pair of hands and another brain."

"I know that," Lacy said. "I know that. I have thought about it, knowing that you would put the point to me." They sat in silence, not uncompanionable, and then Lacy said, "There was a time when you would not have suggested that."

"And times change," his father said. "That is the message for 1918. There is a Sinn Féin representative from this very town and one from Longford and where else is it? Sinn Féin and the nationalists have stood upon the same platform to oppose conscription."

"The war is winding down," Lacy said, "and when it has ended there will be a general election. And after that there will no longer be a Nationalist party. Sinn Féin will represent the people of Ireland, and not in London, by God. We are past that stage."

"Even so," Thomas Lacy said, "even so. If that is to be the wish of the Irish people, and a very foolish wish it would be, you could do far worse than have the views of your party represented by the *Kilkenny Nationalist*."

"We are not a party," Lacy said. "I am not certain what we are. We stand for what men died for and killed for in 1916. We stand for the Republic."

It had been there in the offices of the *Nationalist*, in 1916, February of 1916, that father and son had last spoken together, before Lacy took the evening train to Dublin, and he remembered his father's face, fierce and red in his anger, and Lacy himself no better. On one of the walls hung a discolored mirror, and once, for a moment, by chance, Lacy had looked over and caught a glimpse of the two of them confronting each other, locked by a love, by years, by memories, that had curdled into anger. "Get along so," Thomas Lacy had half-said, half-shouted at him. "Get along so, and throw your lot in with that lousy crew."

Now, two years later, in that same office, Lacy said, "I mean to see it out with those fellows. Until the Republic is won."

"No matter what their chances?" his father asked.

Lacy shrugged. "Whatever happens," he said, aware that the future which he half-apprehended, violent and formless, was without meaning for his father, Sinn Féin merely another party, like William O'Brien's All for Ireland League, eccentric, faddish, transient. For Thomas Lacy, the old Nationalist party was more than a party, it was the shape of his Ireland, its form, texture, color.

"Whatever happens," Lacy said again, and his father, with equal finality, said, "I see."

On Sunday they went together to Mass, the three of them, as they had gone in the past. His parents took communion, and Lacy, kneeling in the pew, watched them walk back to it. His father was a hale man this side of sixty and his wife a good ten, no was it thirteen years younger. There was a wedding photograph on the piano, his father stiff and awkward, but Eileen Lacy, who had hours before been Eileen Bolger, was smiling, at ease in her gown of elaborate white satin, her lips half-parted. Thomas Lacy was looking somewhere beyond the camera, but Eileen looked into it directly, as though welcoming her future. "What was I thinking?" she said once, responding to Lacy's question. "How do I know what I was thinking? Dear God, the questions that child asks." "You did not take communion," his father said afterwards as they walked through summer sunlight to the church gate. "I trust that there is no—no—" They were surrounded by other Massgoers and he kept his voice down. "Good Lord no," Lacy said, "no reason at all." And as though in confirmation of this, Father Daugherty came up to take his hand. "The warrior's return,"

Daugherty said. "He looks well, does he not, Father?" Eileen Lacy said, and rested her white-gloved hand on Lacy's forearm.

On the Tuesday, he had his drink at Hartigan's with Willie Dunphy. It was a mild, clear evening after early rain, the trees along the river rain-laden. Hartigan's was a handsome public house, none like it in the West and few others in Leinster, elaborate wood paneling, clear glass well tended, and a front snug looking out upon the bridge, where Dunphy was waiting for him. The local ale was Smithwick's, a full, sweet taste upon the tongue.

By the time that he was halfway through his second pint, Dunphy had become less stiff, the friend whom Lacy remembered emerged, joky, cynical, uncertain beneath self-confidence. McIlhenny and Sons.

"Mind you," he said, "I have from time to time been sorry that I did not go up to university like yourself. There would have been no difficulties, the old fellow urged it. But why? And hasn't it all worked out? Lucy and I were destined for each other from the start. Kevin and I hold equal shares in the pub. And Lucy has no brothers." Kevin was Dunphy's brother; Lacy remembered a thin, sallow face. He managed Dunphy's, the family enterprise, a public house on Kytler Street with none of Hartigan's elegance, a drinking-shop for drovers, casual laborers. But drovers drank heartily; both Willie and Kevin could have afforded university.

"And there you are then," Lacy said, lifting his glass, "with your life set out before you upon clear straight lines."

"God willing," Dunphy said, and furtively, as though by accident, he rapped for luck the wood of the table. "And yourself?"

Lacy looked beyond the snug, to the bridge and the dark, wide, lovely river. "My father has offered to move over and make room for me on the *Nationalist*. In New York I worked on this paper and that, small-time Irish papers, but they taught me what I would need."

"There you are," Dunphy said. "In ten years we can have Kilkenny at our feet. The merchant prince and the journalist."

"Perhaps," Lacy said. "It is too early to say. There is unfinished business in this country."

"Isn't that the truth? The country is on the march, but where it is going is a mystery to me."

"But not to me, Willie, not to me. In April two years ago, on the steps of the GPO in Dublin, the Irish Republic was declared as a sovereign independent state. The Republic has not been canceled out. It could not be." He finished off his pint, and gave a signal to the barman. "I'm off on the morning train to Dublin, but let's have a short one."

Dunphy smiled; his teeth were broad, faintly discolored. "Your mind is moving too fast for me, Frank. Are you going up to Dublin to declare the Republic again? The GPO is a burned-out shell."

Lacy returned the smile. "No," he said. "Private business only. But there will be little enough business as usual in the months ahead, Willie. Something was begun, not ended, in 1916."

"Clearly," Dunphy said. "If the son of a publican and the son-in-law of McIlhenny and Sons casts his vote for Sinn Féin, abandoning the sacred Nationalist heritage of his tradition, then something has happened. What of the name of your family newspaper, Frank? Will that have to go?"

"Why did you vote Sinn Féin, Willie? I am curious."

But Dunphy put a cautioning face on, and they were quiet until the barman had placed the two whiskies and the water on the table.

"Hartigan is fierce Nationalist party," Dunphy said, "and his barmen as well. Not like our own shop. The fellows who drink in Dunphy's are all Sinn Féin, whatever they take that to mean. Agricultural laborers, the pride of the countryside."

"I wonder you never drink in your own shop, Willie, neither yourself nor Kevin." He held the cruet of water over Dunphy's glass.

"A bad policy," Dunphy said. The lore of the public house, passed down from father to son. When the barman had his back to them, Dunphy said, "Why is the *Kilkenny People* now behind Sinn Féin? The *Kilkenny People*, Frank, that used to make your father seem a red Republican by contrast. The old party is done for, Frank. 'Tis bankrupt, morally bankrupt."

"But not financially," Lacy said.

"I would not assume that, even," Dunphy said. "Man dear, you should have seen that by-election! The old lads never knew what had hit them. And when the general election comes, it will be Sinn Féin all the way, from one end of the country to the other."

"And that is why you yourself voted for the new lads?"

Dunphy smiled, brief, bleak admission. "In part, Frankie. In part. I would have had no stomach for what you lads were about in 1916, but you were about it, and you may have saved us all. I am an Irishman, and 'tis Sinn Féin that speaks for Ireland now."

"And what is Sinn Féin likely to be saying to you after the election? What if Sinn Féin tells you to take up a gun and fight?"

Dunphy took his time before answering. "Sinn Féin has set its face against a new rebellion, Frank. Or so it tells me. You would know better than I."

"I would?"

"I have no wish to pry, Frank. But I have cause to know that you have been meeting with the lads who run the Volunteers in this city and this county."

"How would you know that?"

"Sure, some of the lads who drink in the brother's shop are Volunteers, and they brag a bit when they have a drop taken. You are quite the hero among the agricultural laborers."

"The Volunteers are not a secret organization, Willie. Should you join up yourself, there would be a welcome for you."

Dunphy shrugged.

"If Sinn Féin wins the election and finds itself with a country on its hands and the bloody British Empire to deal with, it will likely find the Volunteers useful."

Dunphy held up his hand, the palm facing Lacy.

"If Sinn Féin wins," he said, "it will be a tribute to your leaders who were shot in 1916, but it will not be a vote for another rebellion. The British had scant difficulty dealing with you in the middle of the war. Later on, they will be able to give you their undivided attention."

"We'll see, Willie," Lacy said. "We'll see."

Not even the Volunteers were ready for another rebellion, not all of them, perhaps not most of them. Lacy had met three times with Paddy Conroy, a 1916 man who had set to work reorganizing them after his release from Frongoch. "When conscription was a hot issue they came to us like shoals of herrings, but when that eased off so did they. The lads who stayed with us are great lads, though, Frank. But we have no arms, damned little at any rate." They were sitting in the large comfortable kitchen of Conroy's farmhouse, and despite the summer weather there was a soft turf fire. They sat at the table of deal, scrubbed so often that it was white, the wood soft and warm to the touch.

"Are the men organized as units?" Lacy said.

"Oh, to be sure. Brigade, battalions, company. I am myself a vice-commandant. A resounding title." Conroy laughed with delight. He was a cigarette smoker, holding the cigarette ash toward his palm, his fingers cupped, drawing in smoke in fierce gasps. It was a farmer's hand, heavy and broad. Dinny, one of his sons, was sitting beside the fire, working at a bit of leather; he was fourteen, fifteen. Conroy nodded toward him. "There are lads in my battalion only two years or so older than Dinny here. Dinny would be enrolled himself if I would let him."

"And Brigade reports directly to Dublin?" Lacy said.

"It does, of course, Frank. When you are up there, would you tell them how hard-pressed for equipment we are should the need for it arise. There are strict orders that have come down about raiding for arms. There is to be none of that, they said. Then where the bloody hell are we to look? There are houses in this county with their seams bursting with all the rifles and shotguns that are in them."

"I have no right to advise you, Paddy, but I think that Dublin has the right of it. Quiet wins the day for the moment."

"Ah well," Conroy said, "that is all well and good. But I have my lads to keep in line and they are rough fellows, some of them. Rough indeed, and with notions of glory and fighting for Ireland."

"Keeping them in line is your task," Lacy said; "that is why you are an officer. Dublin has confidence in you."

"Does it so?" Conroy asked, cynical, still genial. "I have been twice to Dublin in the past two months. Dublin has little notion what it is like down here, much less across in Tipperary and Cork."

"Wait," Lacy said, and drained his cup of tea as he rose to his feet. "Things will begin to move before too long." Conroy's son looked up from his piece of harness; beside the fire's glow, his eyes were a startling blue, pale but fierce.

* * *

And when Lacy and Willie Dunphy had finished their glasses, they walked out into the gathering twilight. Crossing the road, they stood upon the bridge and looked downriver toward the immense, turreted bulk of the castle.

"Mind you," Dunphy said, nodding toward the bullying castle. "Something like that makes one wonder, does anything change?"

"Oh, things change, Willie," Lacy said. "You may be certain of that. Things change."

By ten that night, Eileen Lacy was above in her bedroom and her husband, Tom, was below, moving from front parlor to kitchen to book room and then back to front parlor again. By now, by ten, Frank would be in Dublin, himself and the heavy cases which he had carried with him from New York. In the kitchen, Tom made himself a pot of tea, and sat there for a half-hour, sipping the milked and heavily sugared tea that was his preference.

It was as though Frank had never been back at all, for he had been polite, courteous but distant, initiated into knowledges of which the father wished to know nothing—oath-bound societies, the bright-flaring night streets of Manhattan. The warm family center, for the three of them, a small family by Kilkenny standards, had always been not front or side parlor but rather the kitchen with its warm fire, the smells of turf and of cooking, and on the smoke-darkened walls the framed and glassed prints that had been there for twenty years or more—a blue-cascading waterfall between banks of verdant emerald grass, and above, rainbow-curved, the emblem, "Ireland a Nation," and a sepia-colored photograph of Kilkenny Castle and the Nore beside it, and a photograph, heavily and chalkily colored, of one of the Land League agitators. In the front parlor, in pride of place, protected from smoke and the steam of boiling cabbage, was the photograph of Parnell, taken in the final year of his life, seated at deceptive ease, jacket of tweed and woolen waistcoat, the bearded, deep-eyed face handsome, opaque of expression. Across it was scrawled, "For Thomas Francis Lacy of Kilkenny, Fighter for Ireland's Liberty. Charles S. Parnell."

And in the offices of the *Nationalist*, on the wall, Lacy kept hung, glassed and framed in bog oak, the front page he had run to announce Parnell's death, with its heavy border of black, and the clumsy sketch of Parnell and the brief statement, itself black-framed, which he had written while brushing away tears, embarrassed by them, angry. "He fell in battle," the editorial statement began, "as though struck down by lance or bullet." How long ago that was! And a long time since the embittered wings of the party were at last rejoined, with Redmond as the leader, Parnell's heir. For the years that followed, it was as though the future of the nation had been invested, secure, permanent, in the party. But now, Tom Lacy knew with reluctant certainty, his son had the right of it. The by-election which had won Kilkenny was a straw in the wind. And all because of a crazy fight in Dublin, machine guns and artillery playing upon Sackville Street, and then men stood up against a wall at Kilmainham and shot, where once Parnell had spent a few weeks in comfortable, gentlemanly confinement. There had been a song back then, in the eighties, "For the uncrowned king of Ireland lies in Kilmainham Gaol." But when the men of 1916 were brought to Kilmainham, it had been for the night only before execution, and in the morning led out, stood against the wall, which Lacy imagined now as stained with a red bleached by rain, faded, but to be there, on that wall forever. And his son Francis, wandering about in Galway before sailing off to the United States.

He carefully turned out all the lights before going upstairs to bed, and paused for a moment by the window that looked out upon the road. A clear night with a pale moon, cloud-shrouded.

"He will be up to Dublin by the morning train," Willie Dunphy said as he climbed into bed beside his wife. "And it is my view that he will be there for quite a while. He keeps his own counsel, and always has."

"He is a good-looking fellow," Lucy Dunphy said. "But very intense like."

"A very decent fellow," Dunphy said. "We have always been the very best of friends, from childhood days onwards."

"I know that," his wife said.

"But he is in with a strange crew," Dunphy said, "and you can take my judgment for that."

"Did he tell you as much?" she asked.

"He did not. Very close-mouthed he was. But you can keep nothing secret in a town like this. Or in any town, no doubt. The Volunteers are a decent lot, by and large, but you will get the strange few. Paddy Conroy is a desperate fellow."

"I know no Conroys," Lucy said. "What Conroys are they?" She was combing her long, fair hair, unbound.

"You do indeed," Dunphy said. "A farm on the Thomastown road. And a fair amount of business done in the shop, and credit extended to them. Not that they have not always been good for it."

"And his wife is a nice, quiet woman who was a Quinn?"

"The very one," Dunphy said. "I am surprised that you did not recognize the name Conroy. He holds high rank in the Volunteers, they are decked out with ranks and titles like the British Army, farm boys and casual laborers."

He had turned out the light above their heads, and they lay in the faint moonlight.

"God send that this does not mean more trouble for the poor old country," he said, folding his hands across his chest.

Later, listening to her measured breathing, he remembered Frank Lacy and himself upon the bridge, two figures out of an allegory, the friend who would bide in the town and the friend who would be off upon mysterious errands.

V

FRANK LACY

On a clear, mild late afternoon in the winter of 1919, Frank Lacy cycled into the Claregalway village of Dawson's Cross, two churches, three public houses, a hotel called the Angler's Rest, a few shops, the gates of a demesne. He wore a suit of blue serge, not new but too new to be shiny, the jacket weighed down by the copy of the Loeb edition of Virgil, which he had lately taken to reading. The pack above the rear fender held a folded mackintosh, a canvas case holding a change of linen, a few unimportant letters, and a loaded Parabellum. His white shirt was unironed but freshly washed.

He went into Patrick Hynes's, the largest of the three public houses, and for a minute, after the flat sunlight, it seemed a cave, but then he recognized the counter, its two ends piled with tins and small cardboard boxes, and the center bare, behind it a woman of middle years, plain-featured, graying hair caught up in a bun. Behind her tall cabinets of a handsome wood, age-mellowed, divided into small drawers.

"A fine day," he said.

"It is, thank God," she said.

A moment's pause, the beat of a metronome, and then she said, "Can I be of help to you?"

He smiled, shook his head, and nodded toward the bar, through an open door toward the rear of the shop.

"Is Michael Hynes in the shop?" Lacy asked.

"He is above," she said. "I will go for him. Make yourself comfortable."

Only then did he remember to take off his tweed cap. "Mrs. Hynes, is it?" he asked, and she nodded. "Michael's mother," she said, "Mrs. Patrick Hynes." The sign on the shopfront was elaborate, crimson background and the name in intricate curlicues. "Patrick Hynes. Wines and Spirits. Provision Merchant."

"Frank Lacy. You might tell him my name. He should be expecting me."

She nodded, and turned away from him. To reach the stairs, she had to step outside the shop.

Lacy walked into the bar. It was empty and dark, cool. Bottles ranged the shelves behind the counter, flanking a mirror. Lacy stared at himself and then turned away. On one side wall, below bunting, soiled, in the three national colors—green, white, orange—the framed large cardboard with the oval photographs of the executed signatories of the 1916 Proclamation. On the other wall, facing it, crossed hurleys and the photograph of a team. Beside them, a notice for that summer's Galway races, decorated with a spirited, muscular horse, the jockey wiry, idling in the saddle.

When Michael Hynes came in, he went, as though by instinct, behind the counter, and then, remembering himself, stretched out to Lacy a white, heavy-fleshed hand. He was a fellow in his late twenties, square, heavy shoulders, thick, muscular neck. He could have been one of the athletes in the photograph.

"Captain Lacy," he said in welcome. "It is Captain, is it not?"

Lacy shrugged, and in response to Hynes's question asked for a glass of porter. Neatly, casually, Hynes drew off a glass for each of them, mahogany-colored, seductive on a December afternoon.

"There is no need for a title on you in Claregalway," Hynes said, "we remember 1916. Yourself and Liam Mellowes. A great inspiration." His voice held sincerity flecked by irony.

"I hope not," Lacy said. "Not an example, at any rate. 1916 was a balls-up here in Galway, worse than Dublin and that was bad enough."

"The father was alive then, and I was working in Galway City," Hynes said by way of oblique explanation. "For Galway City 1916 came and went. It will be different this time."

"I hope to God it will be different," Lacy said. He held the glass in faint salutation to Hynes, and took a pull of the cool, dark porter. It cut the dust of the country roads he had been traveling.

"It was the influenza carried him off," Hynes said. "A terrible business. 'Tis said more have died of it than died in Flanders, in uniform. On the two sides."

"I am sorry for your trouble," Lacy said, and out of courtesy sat quietly.

"Ach," Hynes said, "he was in poor health to begin with. A weakness." He touched his chest by way of explanation. He did not look to have inherited it himself.

"Well now, Captain, what can I do for you?"

"Are you on the phone here?" Lacy asked.

Hynes laughed and for a moment the faint, habitual wariness left his eyes. "Indeed we are not. There is no telephone in the village save for the one at the doctor's house. I don't expect you will want to trouble him."

"No," Lacy said. "I do not. I will tell you now, Mr. Hynes—no, you are yourself a battalion commandant by rank, are you not?"

"I am," Hynes said, and smiled a bit sheepishly. "A mighty title for a small task."

"Not so small, perhaps," Lacy said, "not so small. In the brigade's reports that came in last month you gave your strength as twenty-seven. Is that close enough?"

"Close enough," Hynes said, "one or two have dropped away. Twenty-five would be closer a bit. Twenty-five that can be entirely depended upon. It was far different a year ago, to be sure. We had one hundred and fifty-one last November."

Lacy nodded. It had been the same everywhere. The threat of conscription by the English to fight in their war had shoved up enrollment in the Volunteers, what with everyone set to resist it, Sinn Féin and the old soon-to-be discredited national party and the Church itself, the Church in particular. Standing firm at home somehow linked membership in the Volunteers with the martyred leaders of 1916, and with Thomas Ashe dead on a hunger strike. But now there was excitement and puzzlement in the country, with both England and Sinn Féin claiming to rule Ireland, and the Volunteers suddenly become an enigma. Membership had dropped by perhaps three-quarters, and although many deplored this, Lacy was one of those who did not. The ranks had been thinned down to men ready to fight, ready to use guns against the enemy, once guns could be found.

He drained his porter glass, but when Hynes reached for it, he shook his head. "What are they like?" he asked. "Your twenty-five."

"They are good lads," Hynes said, and he pushed aside his own glass, as though in recognition that pleasantries had ended. "Young fellows from small farms the most of them, the farrier's boy, the potboy in this shop. But they're terrible young. In their early twenties and some of them younger than that. I am twenty-eight myself and I feel like a grandfather to them. And they don't know what's to be expected of them. I drill them one evening a week in the wasteland beyond the hill that you likely passed as you rode here, Slattery's Hill 'tis called. But they don't know why. About eleven of them are armed, and I have myself both a rifle and a revolver, but we are low on ammunition. And in a way the lads don't expect ever really to use them. But then they read about the battle against the police at Soloheadbeg and police inspectors shot down in Thurles and in Westport, and the soldiers attacked in Fermoy. They have their heads filled with General Pearse and the other heroes holding Dublin for a week despite shot and shell and the British ships in the bay with their long-range guns."

"They can forget that," Lacy said, and he smiled in a manner which suggested that he and Hynes were master strategists. Catching a glimpse of himself in the mirror, he disliked that smile. "They can forget that. 'Tis another kind of war that we have in mind, am I right, Commandant?"

"It might be," Hynes said, and leaning back from the counter rested his buttocks against the back bar. Lacy discovered, to his satisfaction, a wariness in Hynes's response. "It might be."

"Who is your second-in-command?" Lacy asked.

"A fellow named Liam Trainor. He was in the war, out in France there, with the Munsters. He is a laborer with a strong-farmer. A good man," he added a bit defensively.

"You need not explain him to me," Lacy said. "I wish to God all our lads had seen service with the British. They have a first-rate army. How does the village get along with the RIC?"

"The RIC is it?" Hynes said. "Sure in this village the RIC is a constable named Baldwin, a Donegal man. He would come in here for a pint in the evening."

"Used to," Lacy said.

"Ach, no longer, be damn. Dev's word was passed along to us down the country." The police, De Valera had said in April in the

Dáil, "must not be tolerated socially as if they were clean healthy members of our organized life. They must be made to feel how base are the functions they perform, and how vile is the position they occupy."

"There is not a human soul in Dawson's Cross who will talk to the bugger, not even the servants at Sir Harry Dawson's."

Lacy nodded.

"I am sorry for him in a way," Hynes said. "Do you know what he said once? He came in for a pint, and there was no one in the house save two old fellows below there at the far end, and where you are sitting now, Liam Trainor and a chum of his. This was before the boycott, of course. He was pulling away at his pint, Paddy Baldwin used to love his pint"—Hynes spoke as though Baldwin had died—"and he was looking across the room toward the pictures of General Pearse and the other martyrs, without really seeing them I thought at first, and then of a sudden, he said, 'They were good men, Pearse and that lot,' he said, 'they struck a blow for Ireland.' I had nothing to say to that and neither did Liam, but if Baldwin expected applause he was much mistaken. 'They rose in dark and evil days,' he said, 'like the Fenians and the men of 'ninety-eight.' 'A lucky chance it was they did not get close to you before they could reach the Post Office,' Liam said, in a mild, venomous voice, 'you'd have clubbed them senseless and dragged them to General Maxwell.' It was as though he had flung a glass into Baldwin's face. Baldwin was after all the law in Dawson's Cross, and in uniform or out, I don't think he had ever been spoken to that way. He thought for a moment, and then he said, 'This day a year ago you were wearing the King's uniform yourself,' and with that he turns on his heel, leaving the pint unfinished. There was a dignity to his bearing, when all is said. But before he could reach the door, Liam hawked up a great noisy gob and spat it out, and ground the heel of his heavy boot upon it. Baldwin has not been in this shop since then, and now there is nowhere in the village where he is welcome and none to talk with him."

"But he is not cut off entirely from the world," Lacy said. "What does he make of what has been going on with the Volunteers and all that?"

"He knows damned well that I am the local commandant and that Liam is my seconder. I was in command two years ago when the Volunteers were still legal and we were drilling openly, and last year at the time of the election, when the Volunteers were out in support of Sinn Féin. And he knows that I am not a likely lad to step aside or out of the gap of danger."

True enough, Lacy thought. He had the look of the village strong boy, publican, shopowner. Ten years ago, he would have been turning out the Nationalist vote, photographs of Redmond and Dillon where now Tom Clarke and Tom MacDonagh and Patrick Pearse stared upon their unimaginable futures, suited and necktied but young Daly in his Volunteer's tunic, unimaginable the stone wall at Kilmainham, rain flecking the gray, sunless morning.

"I have no doubt," Hynes said, "that he sends in his reports to Dublin, on the brigade, on me, what he can guess. Not that we have had much to do as yet, save make our presence felt."

"Time to change that," Lacy said, smiling as though he had brought a gift into Dawson's Cross, strapped to his bicycle like the loaded Parabellum. "Time to move the Fourth Claregalway Battalion to active status."

Lacy waited two weeks before he led out the Fourth Claregalway Battalion in the raid on the RIC convoy. On the morning of the first day he rode by himself down roads, and walked his bicycle across fields. There were two barracks, isolated from one another, on the long, narrow, winding bog road between Gort and Portumna, along the range of the Slieve Aughties. Once a week, on a Tuesday, the RIC would set out from Portumna to bring pay and provisions to the two of them, the one at Derrybrien and the other at Arigna, a Crossley tender and a Lancia, the Lancia in the van, probing the empty air. For ten miles or so beyond Gort, the countryside would be thick-carpeted, the farmhouses close together and companionable, but thinning out then as the road rose, and by the time the two vehicles had crested the high hills, they would be in bare country, a few houses and barns, low fences, dry shallow beds which in summer carried freshets. Across pale, faint-clouded skies the birds of winter, purposeful in flight, hawks and kestrels, vigilant for quick movements along the ground. Although this first winter, the winter of 1919, the warfare was sporadic, isolated, the bleak chillness of the road, the loneliness, would prompt the Lancia and the Crossley following to speed up. At Arigna barracks, the police did not swing back to Gort, but drove into Portumna, a market town, larger than Gort.

On the first morning, a Monday, Lacy cycled out on his own, a country fellow on the road, jacket and white shirt slightly soiled, a muffler close-knotted against a chill Atlantic wind. It was a few miles, twenty miles at most, from the towns which he had sought to raise in Easter Week of 1916, Oranmore and Craughwell and Clarinbridge, and he knew the southern slopes well. He had sheltered there for those weeks after the Rising, before he could make his way first to Limerick and then across to America. But this bleak countryside was new to him, not the dramatic emptiness of Connemara, tumbling clouds, great black rocks rain-washed. No one paid heed to him, a farm fellow on a Raleigh, raising a lazy hand in salutation to a fellow with a donkey cart, in clothes as brown and dusty as the cart itself, or pausing to exchange the time of day with one of the farm wives at a cabin door. But this he did warily, because of his telltale accent, the suave, Norman-molded speech of the rich Kilkenny valleys. By preference he sat, that first day, after walking himself into Portumna, a cooling pint in the Castle Arms, at a point where, upon one side, high tumbled rocks looked down upon a sudden swerve of road, moving it westwards, and then, a mile or two farther on, moving it east again. He sat there for two hours of early afternoon, the sun pleasant but not warm upon his shoulders, his hands cupped about his knees. On the ground beside him, in waxed paper, lay a thick slabbed sandwich of butter and lamb which he had carried with him.

On the second day, he rode not alone but with Michael Hynes and Liam Trainor, the three of them on bicycles, Hynes on a borrowed one, a heavy man carrying himself with the aggressive dignity of weight. They had with them a lunch a bit more elaborate, sandwiches of ham and beef, a roast chicken, bottles of lager and of lemonade. They set out very early in the morning, and the three of them drinking down heavy mugs of sweetened tea. By the time the RIC drove past the tall rocks, the three of them were well in place there, and had made a kind of camp, their jackets spread out neatly upon the coarse ground, and themselves all well hidden from the road.

The Crossley was traveling this morning on its own, without the Lancia.

"That is sometimes the way," Hynes whispered, but Lacy put a cautionary hand on his wrist.

And they waited over an hour, into the afternoon, before it returned. They were not so far up that they could not see it clearly, the driver and an armed constable beside him, and in the open body of the Crossley, four constables facing four others, their carbines held loosely, butts resting on the floorboards, hands curled loosely about the barrels. They were close enough to be looked in the face, thin-faced two of them, but the others with the round, heavy-jowled, ageless faces that folk thought associated with the RIC. The uniforms gave them a common identity, a common psychology, habits of mind. Young Trainor began to laugh, but Lacy again took a cautioning hold upon his wrist. Then they were gone, dust upon the road.

"What was there to laugh about?" Lacy said to Liam Trainor.

" 'Twas nothing," Liam said. Faint embarrassment.

"Something," Lacy said. "You are too sensible a fellow to laugh at nothing."

"One of the peelers," Trainor said. "He was on the bench facing us. He is soft on Sarah Heelan. Bob Heelan, her old fellow, has a shop at the Cross."

"Soft on her, is he?" Lacy said, and picked up the paper of sandwiches to hand them round.

"Aye," Trainor said. He and Hynes exchanged mild, lubricious glances.

"Is Bob Heelan in with the Volunteers?" Lacy asked. He bit into his sandwich, and then seasoned it from the paper spill of salt.

Hynes, taking the point of the question if Trainor did not, thought before answering. "He is not in the battalion, if that is what you mean, and I doubt if he is in either of the other two. He would be too old for it. He is forty-five if he is a day, and we are all of us youngsters in the comparison. But he is nationally minded. At the election, the shop was all done up in tricolors and black-framed pictures of Pearse and Ashe and the others. He is nationally minded."

A phrase you heard often these days, Lacy thought. A safe-conduct. There might be something gained by a talk with Sarah Heelan.

The three of them sat together in companionable silence, the rocks obscuring them from the road. The grass had not been fully dried by the weak, clouded sun, and it was moist to the touch; Lacy ran his hand along it.

"Terrible bare country," Hynes said, with a townsman's condescension, idly. "A snipe had best carry her own rations if she flew across it."

"Sherman had much the same to say about Georgia," Lacy said, "when he made his march."

"Sherman?" Trainor asked.

"A Yankee general in their war," Lacy said, "a ferocious great fellow at the burning and the looting and that sort of thing."

Hynes knew, and sang softly, as though offering a course in history to young Trainor, "Then we'll burn the country from Atlanta to the sea, As we go marching through Georgia."

The words stirred a smoke-tendril of memory in Lacy. In 1917 he had been sent by the paper to report on a Grand Army of the Republic encampment in New Jersey. "Sherman's Bummers," they called themselves, grown ancient, toothless, false teeth clacking, and bearded, thin fluffs of beard. But once, if their own boasts could be believed, they had been terrible fierce fellows in blue, marching through Georgia with hens and ducks skewered on bayonet points, knapsacks rattling with booty, silver spoons and baptismal cups, cruets of cut glass. Behind them, as they marched on, mansions burned, fire disclosing the cores of common brick within Corinthian columns.

In one corner of the field, at a table behind which stood crossed the American flag and the flag of the Fenians, gold harp on a green ground, real or self-styled veterans of the Irish brigades signed a petition to the American Congress and the American President, whose photograph hung between the two flags, lantern-jawed Orange face, pince-nez, and behind the clear glass stubborn uncalculating eyes. "IRELAND A NATION AT LAST" read the legend which surmounted all, with its unstated but understood message—that Ireland had her claims upon America, as Belgium did and Montenegro, stronger claims perhaps for there were few Montenegrin voters in the wards of Brooklyn and South Boston. Lacy had been there to write an account of the proceedings, the oratory. But he was undeceived by any of it: there was little that could be gained from the grim-jawed American President. Less than Casement had screwed from the Germans—a steamer loaded with outdated rifles, and in the heel of the hunt scuttled and sunk. Burn the country from Atlanta to the sea, he thought.

The words, unspoken, brought him back to the present. "In two weeks' time," he said. "A fortnight. We will hit them just here, and from the slope across the road. There are rocks on either side that we can use for cover."

"We," Hynes said, keeping the word flat, neutral.

"The battalion, of course," Lacy said. "The Fourth Battalion, your battalion, Commandant. I will be along with you to offer advice and encouragement, although none will be needed." He pulled a tuft of tall damp grass from the earth, and held it, speaking to the grass and not to Hynes or Trainor. "You have a battalion strength of twenty-five or so, you are telling me. We may not need quite so many, but we will need at least twenty. At least twenty. I am counting upon you for that."

"Jesus, now," Hynes said. "Jesus, Captain. That is a fair number to pull together for an operation like." Lacy, without looking up from his grass, knew that Hynes and Trainor were exchanging glances. "There is great spirit in the battalion, mind you, great spirit, but we have never staged an operation like this before."

"Bloody right you have not," Lacy said. He flung away from him all save a single blade of grass. He held it to his lips and blew; the sound was shrill, carrying the comfort of childhood, faintly mocking. "You are bloody right you have not. You have roughed up a few Redmondite shopkeepers and set fire to a lodge of the ancient Britons, and when a soldier was once home on leave you blackened his eyes and tossed him in the Camowen. A bloody unarmed soldier out for a stroll, not carrying so much as a sidearm. There is the glorious history to date of the Fourth Battalion of Claregalway Brigade."

He looked up now at the two of them and smiled, as though a smile could bleed away what had been said.

"Is that how HQ thinks of us?" Hynes said at last, stiffly. "Is that why you were sent down here to us and set upon us? There are battalions, there are entire brigades across the length and the breadth of this country who have done less. And who lack the spirit that we have shown."

"We are not talking about them at the moment," Lacy said, "but about yourselves. The chain of triumphs that I rattled off to you just now is the one that Brigade sent forward to HQ. Little enough to boast about, but sure you had to put something down."

That was the way of it, as though they were a real army, Sherman in Georgia. Hynes and the other two battalion commanders would make their reports to brigade HQ in Loughrea, and in time brigade HQ would make its report to Dublin. Everything noted down in a jargon copied from the British, because they had no other models, "active service units," "made contact with the enemy," "placed the main body of our force in a secure position, and then sent outriders to explore the terrain." But as often as not it would be eight or ten lads, with two rifles and a shotgun amongst the lot of them, and the enemy two RIC fellows riding home to barracks, capes slung over their shoulders against the drizzling rain, lowering sky, a dog, the barracks pet, running before them, dirty and pelt-soaked. Or in Tipperary, the wild battalion, Sean Treacy country, Dan Breen country, an attack on an RIC barracks, this fellow and that one spoken to after Mass, and Brigade, perhaps, kept carefully uninformed because there was no great kindliness of feeling between the two. The barracks would be attacked with Soloheadbeg gelignite, the gelignite which Treacy and Breen had captured back in January, killing two constables to get hold of it, and which had been hidden since then in barns, in shepherds' huts in the hills, in caves in the earth. It was tricky stuff and had to be unfrozen, the fumes from it blinding, eye-choking. There was nothing those two were not able for, Treacy and Breen, already legends, a year after Soloheadbeg, the legend drawing men to them, wild boys, faction fighters with a cause, rapparees born out of their time. Or not out of their time, perhaps; there had always been lads like Treacy and Breen, the British had soaked them up for a century or more, farm lads like Treacy, railway workers like Breen, clever, wild, brave as bulls, best soldiers in the British Army, the tag had it; now they were their own ragbag army. Tom Barry, below in Cork, had in fact been in the British Army in the war off in Mesopotamia, now he was one of the legends, a battalion commander who took chances but was crafty as well, a fox on the prowl, ready to swoop when he saw the chance, and if the odds favored him, so much the better. But the fighting battalions, Cork, Tipperary, Clare, were still the exceptions. Too much of the Volunteer organization was on paper only, fellows who had joined up in 1917 to take a stand against conscription, and had no sense of what was expected of them now, of what kind of war was being shaped.

Lacy was one of the fellows who had been sent out to show them. Now, as he sat with Trainor and Hynes, a stranger in their countryside, looking down at the road which for them as yet held no meaning other than that of any familiar bog road, he wondered a bit at the kind of fellow he was becoming. Once, four months earlier, he had been sent to Connemara, to Clifden, to talk about the organization of the West Connemara, an easier task than he had imagined, with fellows who knew what they were about, farmers, a shopkeeper, two brisk publicans in the town, weighty men whose words had always been taken. In his time with them, two weeks, there was little to do beyond drilling, staging mock operations, going over terrain with them with that new kind of eye which is a soldier's, and sees fields, streams, hills, fences, not as parts of the natural order but as open country for quick movement by night, safe hidey-holes for snipers, roadside trenches within which men could lie prone, watchfully waiting. They would listen to him and nod, ask quick, pointed questions and then nod again when he had explained. He had not expected that. In the midlands county which he had visited before Connemara, the brigade had been sullen, sarcastic, half-mocking Lacy and half on the point of repudiating him entirely, but not quite reaching that point because there was no question but that he carried the proper authorization, signed by Mulcahy and countersigned by Brugha.

The commandant was manager of the local creamery, and staff met either in his office, or at home, sitting about the kitchen table. The commandant's name was Quinlan, two of his first cousins were in the company, and one of them, his adjutant, sat with them. Laboriously, like a schoolboy drawing the rivers of Gaul, Lacy moved his pen across a quick sketch which he had made of the townland upon which the barracks stood, at a crossroads; beyond, to the left, level pastures but on the right, pasturelands rising to low hills, rock-studded. "Here," he said, jabbing with the nib, "part of your lads must hold the boreen into these hills as a line of retreat, if you get flung back."

Jerry Quinlan, the adjutant, said, "There would be a retreat, by Christ, you could depend upon it. Do you know how strong that garrison is, there are fifteen constables in that barracks, and the walls are three feet thick, good solid stuff like a fortress in India. 'Twas built in the days of the Land War, there was a time when it held both constables and an army detachment in comfort. Lucknow is the local joke name for it, but you would not know that, Commandant Lacy, being a stranger to these parts."

"No," Lacy said, with a patience he had no need to feign. "I would not know that Lucknow is the local nickname. But I do know a bit about the rest of it. I know the strength of the garrison, and I know how well it can be defended. It has great steel shutters that can be swung shut from the inside, with loops for rifle fire built into them." "You have the right of it there," a fellow named Mike Farrell said, a chemist who would be in charge of munitions and chemicals if they had had any. "How is it that you know that?" "Two ways," Lacy said, "two different ways. I called in at the barracks on my first day here, to ask directions from the sergeant, a very obliging fellow he was, affable and soft-spoken. Paddy Mullen his name is."

"The hoor," Tom Quinlan, the commandant, said. "The skirt-smelling hoor."

"You would know better than myself," Lacy said, "I am a stranger here, as you may know." Mike Farrell grinned at him. "But I had a good leisurely look about me, the dayroom and the guardroom which leads off from it. And I got a good view of those shutters. Formidable."

"Two ways, you said," Tom Quinlan said.

"Yes," Lacy said. "I have a copy of the builder's plan. I brought it along with me, and I will leave it with you when I go." He opened up the battered imitation leather case between his feet, and took out the plan, unfolded it, and spread it out. It was a builder's elevation, front and side, with the rooms marked and their dimensions. It was a strange-looking object to some of them, but not to others. Tim Murray who had worked once in a valuer's office in Maryborough, said, "Holy Jesus," and ran his hand across it lightly, almost with reverence. "Where in the bloody hell did you get the plans for the barracks?"

"Not this barracks in its every small detail," Lacy said, "and there may have been changes made here and there over the years, but it will serve us well enough."

But Tom Quinlan sat looking at him, knuckles pressed against parted lips. He expected to hear more. Quinlan was not a fool; an unpleasant fellow, not without his vanities, but no fool.

"This is one of the barracks thrown up in the early eighties, during the Land War, as you said yourself, Mike." Draw them in a bit; show that you're impressed a bit by what they know, history, local lore. "There were eight of them scattered across Leinster and South Munster that were built to the same design."

It was a good six months since Lacy himself had first seen the blueprint from which this copy had been made, folded lengthwise, tossed onto the table where he was working in the Parnell Square office, like a Christmas gift. "There you are," Michael Collins said. "The keys to the kingdom. More or less." He was standing by the desk, his coat unbuttoned, and a hat of soft gray felt pushed to the back of his head. From his pockets, all of them, he was emptying out leaflets, envelopes, scraps of paper, scattering them across the surface of the pine desktop.

Lacy unfolded the document, and studied it, holding it flat on one side with a ledger and on the other with the palm of his hand. He half understood what it was, but had a full, immediate certainty as to its value. In the lower left corner, trim and white, was name and date, "Sisson, R., Major, Corps of Engineers, 2 October 1881." And in the opposite corner, faded, stamped upon the blueprint, the acknowledgment seal of the Ministry of War. Collins patted the pockets of his jacket, fished about in his breast pocket and pulled out another note, dropped it atop the others.

Small wonder that he had not yet been picked up, Lacy thought, for all that he walked from one appointment to the next, or rode there on someone's borrowed bicycle, clips neatly fastened to ankles. For all the vividness of Collins's appearance, the heavy-featured, challenging face, for all that there was a bit of the chameleon. That day, at the moment, in the decent but not expensive blue suit, unlit cigarette, always unlit, in the corner of his mouth, hat the badge of clerical respectability itself, he could be a senior clerk in an accountant's office, or a turf accountant, a commercial traveler.

Collins sat down behind the desk, facing Lacy but as though oblivious of him. From the drawer of the desk, he took out a pad of yellow, blue-lined legal paper, and from his breast pocket a fountain pen, which he slowly unscrewed, with the care of a medical man attending to one of his instruments. The office was small and close. Behind Collins, the single window, dirt-smeared, looked out upon weedy back gardens, chimney pots. Collins placed the pen beside the pad of paper, and began, methodically, to go through the pile of scraps and envelopes he had taken from his pocket. On a few of them he scribbled notes, a few he read carefully and then crumpled and tossed into the metal basket beside the desk. Now he looked the industrious and promising postal clerk he had once been in London; his barony in West Cork had been oddly fecund in the production of clerks for Posts and Telegraphs; "God love him," they would say of a newborn, "he has the look of a born sorter." So had Collins now, a superior sorter, of proven intelligence, capable of making a few decisions as to the disposition of documents. And some of them, Lacy knew by experience, were indeed documents, written in farmer's scrawl, schoolmaster's neat copperplate, a few of them typed. These he placed together in a pile to one side. But some were letters requiring reply, and these he left till last, arranging them in the order he preferred, and then drawing to himself the pad and fountain pen. The slovenly litter he had spilled upon the desk had vanished.

Lacy had put aside for a moment the blueprint he had been studying, and was back at work on a report of his own for Mulcahy, the chief of staff, and eventually, Brugha, the minister of defense. He had been down to Waterford to settle a dispute about the authority of the brigades, the two of them, east and west. East Waterford was no problem, inclined a bit to be lazy, lulled by sea breezes no doubt, but not a problem of authority. West Waterford had been a different matter, its borders marching with those of Tipperary—the brigade lending a hand to Breen and Treacy from time to time, or supplying safe houses to the Third Tipperary when things were hotted up. A man named Mickey Gallivan was commandant of the West Waterford, an able, taciturn man, but there was a difficulty: from time out of mind, from the days of the faction fighters and beyond them to the Rockites, from the days almost of the Whiteboys, there had been two fierce fighting families in West Waterford, the Gallivans and the Talbots, separated from each other more or less by the Knockmealdowns; in recent decades, in the present century indeed, they got along together, but tradition dies hard, and now the Talbots bossed a battalion that took its orders from the Gallivans, took them well enough. Tommy Talbot was a man as reasonable as Mickey Gallivan, but there was bad blood for all that, and a way of questioning the wisdom of things down in the Volunteer ranks.

Lacy had spent four days there, two of them in Cappoquin itself and two of them in a village on the slopes of the Knockmealdowns. In the heel of the hunt, on the evening of the fourth day, Lacy had met with the two commandants and their adjutants in a farmhouse two miles outside Cappoquin, and gave them his idea, that he should propose to HQ in Dublin that West Waterford be divided into two brigades, not one, and that Mid Waterford, as no doubt it would be called, be placed under Tommy Talbot's command. There was room enough for two, God knew, and work enough for two. Talbot was delighted by the idea, it went without saying, but so, for that matter, was Gallivan. The two of them grinned at each other across the kitchen table, reached their arms across the ruins of a meal, plates of cabbage and boiled bacon, and shook hands, like dealers at a fair.

After, Talbot drove Lacy across the Knockmealdowns to Clonmel, across the county line in Tipperary, where Lacy had business. It was late afternoon when they set out from Cappoquin, but dark had fallen before they reached Clonmel. It fell during the long drive over the Knockmealdowns. Sullen hills they seemed to Lacy, who had never seen them before, stretching between Cappoquin and Newcastle. North from the bridge at Cappoquin, up Glenafallia, the road passed Mount Mellary, the Cistercian Monastery, which monks expelled from France in the last century had chosen because the mountains were wild and uninhabited, and they were so still. "By God," Tom Talbot said, "it takes but a few miles to leave the lovely Blackwater behind us, and drop us into the midst of this. The Cistercians are welcome to it, they have a taste for natural phenomena." He was a Cappoquin man, and Cappoquin had a lovely siting, a fine wooded countryside where the Glenshelan joined the Blackwater. "Not that they are not doing

God's own work," he said hastily. The first line of a ballad drifted through Lacy's mind, "She was a king's daughter and she came from Cappoquin." Part of God's work consisted, so Lacy recalled, of taking in drunks for the cure. It was an open car, and the chill air traveled across the mountains; a moon, pale and enormous, had risen. The ballad had a bleak ending, as ballads were wont to have. The king's daughter of Cappoquin stands with her babe, cold, outside the castle of Lord Gregory, the babe's father, but they are denied admission. Half-aware, Lacy had been half-singing the few lines he knew, and now Talbot picked them up, in a fine, firm tenor voice, and sang, as they traveled northwards from Cappoquin, the story of the king's sad, abandoned daughter.

The last line, as custom required, he did not sing, but spoke in a rush of words, saying, with self-deprecating flatness, "as though they had ever had kings in Cappoquin, God help us."

But the song had joined itself to the night, the empty mountains, the wind, and it would not leave them, it lingered, no longer spoken, no longer sung, upon the air. "There are few towns so mean that they lack a song, but you will not find a better one than that. Not in English," Talbot added in a second hasty amendment, keeping his orthodoxies on display, pious and Gaelic-loving. The song, the darkening hills which to Lacy were no longer sullen, the night, were more than wedded, they were pregnant with meaning for him, held unspoken, haunted feelings deep and certain beneath articulation.

"You would laugh to know from whom I first heard that version of it," Talbot said, shaking cigarettes from a packet and handing one to Lacy. "'Twas the RIC sergeant, when I was a lad. Sergeant MacGuiness, a Longford man. He had entire dressers full of song stuffed away in his head, Gaelic and English alike. A great love of the music. Great lovers of music, he always said, the MacGuinesses of Longford. In winters he would be visited for weeks at a time by a brother, Donal, a farmer, a very fine fiddler."

Neither Lacy nor Talbot spoke the thought they both held, that they were at work upon the destruction of MacGuiness and the fellows who wore his uniform. Not MacGuiness himself, to be sure, by now dead or long in retirement, under the handsome provisions that were organized for the force that held Ireland for the Crown. In the heel of the hunt, no doubt, they would have the army itself to deal with, but first it would be England's special army in Ireland, the Irish Constabulary; "Royal" had been an adjective bestowed upon them by Queen Victoria herself for the vigor with which they had crushed the Fenian Rising of 1867; by the constables, and by the March snows which blocked the mountain passes, but there was no way to pin a medal on snow.

They had risen to the crest of the hills by now, and Talbot said, gesturing with mock grandiloquence toward a scattering of lights, "There you are now, the bright lights of the metropolis of Newmarket. Now do you know who is buried there? Damned few do, and it is Newmarket's one claim to fame. Sarah Curran, Robert Emmet's beloved. He could have been safe and away after his rebellion, sheltered by Mickey Dwyer in the mountains of Wicklow, mountains as wild as these, but he slipped down into Dublin to see her one last time, and was captured and hanged. Hanged in public, in disgrace, in Thomas Street, and his only sin to fight for Ireland. A fine young fellow."

"Informed upon and then captured, to be precise," Lacy said. Not this time, by God; not this time. In the 'ninety-eight, in Emmet's rebellion, in the Fenian times, clouds of informers, winesses, spies, suborners, perjurers. Not this time.

" 'She is far from the land where her young hero sleeps,' " Talbot sang, as he drove toward Newmarket, Tom Moore's melody about poor languishing Sarah Curran. He broke off and laughed. "A song about Sarah Curran, right enough, but none about Newmarket. 'Tis not worth a song."

"What is it that you have in hand there?" Collins asked suddenly, but without looking up from the letter he was writing, the pen moving easily, quickly across the page. "Is that that notion of yours to divide West Waterford?" It was not by rights Collins's business at all, minister of finance in the Dáil, director of intelligence in the Volunteers; it was Mulcahy's business, or Cathal Brugha's. But Collins would know. It seemed to Lacy, on his visits to Dublin, that Collins knew every file, every brigade, every safe house. " 'Tis a good plan," Collins said; "it makes sense. Mulcahy will go along with it, and Brugha himself most likely. If there is any trouble in that quarter, have a word with Mulcahy, and tell him it is at my suggestion. Everything to be done in an orderly manner, eh?" He suddenly put down the pen and looked up: another Collins now, the hard man from West Cork, a banter, a joke, and somewhere beneath it all, the bully's warning, "Best stand in with me."

"What do you think of them," Collins asked, "the two lads, Gallivan and Talbot."

"They're good men, the two of them," Lacy said. "Gallivan proved that twice over when he was out with Treacy on operations, and Talbot—"

"All that will be in your report," Collins said impatiently. "I can read it. Tell me the sort of thing that doesn't fit tidily into a report."

"I like Talbot much," Lacy said. "I drove back with him from Cappoquin as far as Clonmel. Levelheaded, reliable, his men swear by him. They will take his lead."

"All that will be in the report, so I trust," Collins said.

"He is a witty man in a quiet way," Lacy said, "and he has a fine singing voice. He is very fond of Cappoquin, God knows why. Is that the sort of thing you mean?"

"He went to school in Cappoquin, and lived there with his uncle as a lad," Collins said. Lacy had not known that. "That is the kind of thing I meant."

"I trust him," Lacy said. "Should I put that in the report? It is my instinct to trust him." It had seemed to Lacy at one moment that Talbot, despite a name that had nothing of the Gaelic to it, had come down from those hills, a shrewd, steady man capable of recklessness when it seemed useful; he had liked the way Talbot had handled his motorcar on the single, narrow, twisting road as the air darkened; talking casually, jokes, bits of song, but steady gray eyes on the road.

"Easygoing sort of fellow is he, who likes to take a drink?" Collins asked.

"We called in at the pub in Newmarket, and had each of us a pint to cut our thirst, but he waited for my half of the round until we had reached Clonmel. He's all right on that score."

Collins nodded but did not move his hand to pick up the pen.

"Sarah Curran is buried in Newmarket," Lacy said. "But you knew that as well, no doubt."

Collins paused a moment, and then grinned. The grin was easy, unweighed, natural. "No, Frank, I did not. Poor Sarah Curran. Poor Emmet."

"Poor shopped Emmet," Lacy said. "Sold out by his own crowd, by our own gang of lousers. The barrister who defended him was in the pay of Dublin Castle. Leonard Bloody MacNally."

"He would not be in the times we are coming into now," Collins said. "There would be a bullet waiting for MacNally in the times that we are coming to." He nodded toward the plan spread out on Lacy's table, part curled without Lacy's hand to hold it down. "That plan will not be of use to us now, nor perhaps in six months' time. There is not an organization of the Volunteers in any county with the strength of arms to take a barracks as formidable as those are, the barracks built to those plans, or plans like them. But it will be of use to us in the times that are coming." He picked up the pen now, and said, "Bring that down to Quill, the fellow who has the photoengraving shop on Suffolk Street, up the stairs above the tailoring shop. Talk to Quill himself, mind you, a small, bald-headed man with spectacles. Tell him you need a half-dozen copies. I will have them picked up on Thursday morning early, before the shop opens."

"On your orders, should I tell him?"

"Let him work it out for himself," Collins said. "He is well able for it. He does a fair amount of copying for us. 'Tis convenient that his shop is that close to the Castle." The pen moved across the paper, line by line. "We are getting a fair bit of information from the Castle these days, you know, Frank. Two of the lads in Special Branch are members of the organization, and they are able to get papers out to us for copying, back in the file by morning or on Colonel Anderson's desk, no one the wiser. Not that the plans came from those lads. That was a different source."

"By God," Lacy said, "when they picked a director of intelligence they picked the right man."

But everyone who had business at HQ knew the rumors, that Collins had been chosen for minister of finance in the Dáil right enough, but had bullied his way into control of intelligence, on the military side, over Brugha's objections. And that he took a free-and-easy view of those responsibilities, sending men off on assignments when he chose, and reporting it to Brugha, if he remembered at all, with a scribbled note. When brigade commanders came up from the country to plead their cases for more arms or more explosives, or to settle disputes, it was to Brugha that they reported, out of respect for authority, but it was to Collins that they looked for decision, a hasty ten-minute meeting in pub or coffeeshop or in the dining room of a respectable solicitor's house on Ailesbury Road.

It was his name they would speak of to Lacy, down the country. His and Dev's, who was after all president of Dáil Éireann, and the senior surviving commandant from 1916. But De Valera kept a deliberately austere, withdrawn image, president of the invisible Republic, and in any event had been in the States since June, seeking support for the organization. And Dev too had contributed to the Collins legend. The first military action of all, Treacy and Breen at Soloheadbeg, had been in January, but in February, more spectacularly, Collins and Harry Boland had gone across to England and spirited De Valera out of Lincoln Gaol, and Sean Milroy and Sean McGarry along with him. "There's the lad right enough," the fighting men down country would say to Frank Lacy or to Ernie O'Malley, "do you see much of him? What sort of lad is he? He has West Cork written all over him, 'tis said." Mick. The Big Fellow. "I will tell you now," Proinsais Murphy said one night to O'Malley, and Murphy was a West Cork man himself, from near Gougane Barra, "that fellow has as many guises as Fantôme in the cinema stories, or Sherlock Holmes. A priest when he wants to be, or a British officer, or a turf accountant in a checked suit." "What did you tell Murphy?" Lacy had asked O'Malley. O'Malley, thin of face, clever eyes, ran a hand through thick hair, bright red. " 'There you have it, Proinsais,' " I told him, " 'they'll never take that lad. A veritable Houdini.' " But Lacy and O'Malley both knew that Collins covered Dublin, wherever he needed to be, with no disguise save that chameleon manner, farmer or postal clerk or teller in a bank or demobbed Irish Tommy. "It's all in Chesterton," Collins had told O'Malley once, "in *The Man Who Was Thursday*. If you don't seem to be hiding, nobody tries to hunt you out." O'Malley only half-believed him; Collins was a great reader, like O'Malley and Lacy themselves, but he was unlikely to learn his tactics from a thriller.

"I'll tell why you can never find the fellow half the time," Peader Burke once told Lacy. Burke was a vice-commandant of the Dublin Brigade, and a bit too fond of the glass for a man holding that rank. They were sitting in the public bar of Sherlock's, at the far, quiet corner. "He has two bits of skirt, you know that, do you not? One of them here on the North Side, and the other one to the south, in one of those flats off Northumberland Road. I've seen that one by chance, and it was with him that I saw her, his back was turned mostly to me but there's no mistaking him. A pretty piece she was with a turned-up nose, and lips that could have been rouged, and a collar of gray fur raised up to her cheeks."

"I'd be careful with talk like that, Peader, if I were you," Lacy said; "there is no way you could have been certain."

"Balls," Peader Burke said.

A year later, Burke was shot down in Henry Street by two men wearing mackintoshes, and who may have been Black and Tans in mufti; before that, he had received two warnings about his drinking, and he had been relieved of his command.

No, Lacy knew, as O'Malley did, as O'Connor and Mellowes did, that just as Collins never troubled about disguise, he was always to be found when he was needed. It was the other way round, more often, arriving when no one expected him or needed him, taking stairs always, without fail, two at a time, and always, his shoulder shoved against the door as he turned the knob. Once in a while, if his instinct told him to, he would have himself shadowed for protection by one of his squad, one of his "twelve apostles," as the bitter Austin Stack called them in mild blasphemy, Jim Irwin most often, a small, slim young fellow, whose hand, shoved in mackintosh pocket, gripped a British Army service revolver.

In that midlands county, six months later, Tom Quinlan, its brigade commandant, said, "That has a lovely look to it." He nodded toward the plan for the barracks. "I feel like Ludendorff or the Kaiser or one of those fellows."

"It is of no use to you now," Lacy said, "but hang on to it. It will be, one of these days." They were almost the words which Collins had used to him, they echoed in memory's ear, their intention the same, to build confidence, the sound of an army. "Not next month, next year, perhaps. What else is this about?"

Quinlan looked over at Mike Farrell, who shook his head. "Whether we would ever have the men and the training, that is Tom Quinlan's word to say, Frank. Not mine. But I doubt if we would ever have the men to take that barracks by rushing it. It would have to be blown. With gelignite, most likely. And who knows how to use it? Not I." He smiled. His chemist's eyes, used to measuring paregoric for infants into bottles, shaking powders onto scales and from scales into round paper boxes, were magnified by thick spectacles, a wide, mild blue. "Dear me, no. Not a clue. All I know is that gelignite must be kept cold, and then heated when it is put to use."

"And what if Tom Quinlan here were to send you off to Dublin, where there are classes in explosives held by a fellow of ours who was a sergeant in the army. The other, that is. The British Army." The real army, Lacy had almost said. "Now there is a different matter entirely. Explosives are chemicals. They can be studied, as all chemicals can." Lacy turned to Tom Quinlan. "Mike has a grandmother who lives in Dublin with her daughter. There is no reason why he should not visit her." Quinlan was a reasonable man, when all was said and done. Not a likable man, but a reasonable man, and he had the backing of the fellows in his battalion.

Late that night, the meeting long over, and no one there now but Lacy and the two Quinlans, Tom Quinlan brought out a bottle of Powers and two glasses.

"A strange life you must have of it, Frank, if you will allow me to say so. Kildare yesterday and here today, and the dear Lord knows where tomorrow, Longford or Waterford."

The attack which they planned that morning was carried out a week later, with fifteen men. They made a practice run, three nights before, not there, of course, but on a stretch of road running toward Gort which resembled it. The men had a sense that they were playacting. It was inevitable, but Lacy hadn't liked it. "We will be doing this in the broad sunlight of afternoon," he told them an hour later, when Hynes and Trainor had reassembled them from the two sides of the road, and from the lookout position. "And we will be firing with whatever we have. They will be firing at us. There will be a hell of racket, louder than anything you have ever heard. And the fellows firing at us will be trying to kill us. Remember that. We will have fine cover behind the rocks, first-rate cover. But nothing is ever perfect. Nothing ever goes entirely as you want it." There were nine of them with rifles, Lee-Enfields, and one with a shotgun. It was his own gun, and he held it with casual familiarity, but the weapons on which Lacy would be depending, the Lee-Enfields, were held awkwardly, as though the men who held them knew them to be alien and deadly.

On the day before the raid, Jackie Kelleher, the RIC man who was soft on Sarah Heelan, told her that he might be seeing her the next night. There was to be a social at the Hibernian Hall and he might look in. He would be back in the town that evening, with the lorry from Portumna. "You had best not come round to the Hibernian Hall," Sarah said, "the RIC is not welcome socially in this village, and well you know it." "I could see you, so," Jackie Kelleher said, and named to her a time and place where they would sometimes meet. She did not say that she would not be there, which was always her way of giving assent, but said instead as she did half the time, "It is ashamed you should be to be wearing that uniform and doing the bidding of the foreign crown." "Foreign crown!" Jackie Kelleher said, "what the devil is a foreign crown to me? Is it throw all away, sick pay and pension and all, and go off to Boston or become a laborer on the roads?" The RIC had always been sought-for, a job for brisk, intelligent lads. Not everyone was good enough for the force; there were qualifications and examinations. "It might be better for your soul," Sarah Heelan said, but entirely without conviction. She reported her conversation to her father, as she had been bid to do, and Bob Heelan reported it to Hynes and Lacy. "He is a good young fellow," Heelan said; "he was around to the house for tea several times, before the ban of the boycott was placed on the RIC." Hynes, his eyes fixed upon a corner of the bar, said nothing, but gave a brief nod. "You meet good fellows in all walks of life," Lacy said.

The attack was to take place after the lorry had rounded a sharp bend in the road, and Lacy was depending upon them not using an outrider on bicycle or motorcycle. Later on, in six months' time, that would be standard procedure, for police or soldiers or Black and Tans, but this was to be the first time a lorryful had been brought under the full attack of a unit of the Volunteers. Lacy allowed time, after the two shouts from the lookout, for the young lads who would be coming along with them, four or five lads of the Fianna, to shove the loose rocks and small fallen trees as a block across the road, after which they were to run like hell out of there. So too were the lookouts. If the police were somehow able to reverse and head back toward Portumna, two men would not be able to hold them off. Ambushes in later months would be more practiced but this one worked quite well; with what textbooks always called the "element of surprise" in its favor. Lacy was sometimes known to some unfriendly commandants of the flying columns as "the textbook general."

It was an afternoon of wonderful clarity, a textbook afternoon, and as soon as the shouts were heard from the lookouts, Tom Henchy, who trained them, set the Fianna boys to work. They worked like little heroes modeled upon the stories of Cuchulain and Ossian and Miles the Slasher as these had been handed down to them by the schoolmaster or at Fianna hostings. They had finished their task and were gone from sight before the men waiting behind the rocks heard, from the distance, the half-rumble, half-rattle of the lorry. Degnan—of the two lookouts it had sounded like Degnan—had shouted once, then paused for a count of ten, then shouted once again. The Lorry was traveling from Portumna without the armored Lancia. Lacy stood up and walked with Hynes to check the roadblock. It was good work; it would stop any vehicle. While they were standing, Trainor, on the other side, rose and waved to them, then sank back out of sight. He had seemed to be wearing his usual quizzical half-grin.

Back into position, Lacy listened to the noise of the approaching lorry. "Tell the men to wait and take their cue from us," he told Hynes. For appearance's sake at least, if not for discipline, it was important that Hynes remain formally in command, with Lacy along as his adviser. "We will give them what time they will need," Hynes said to Lacy, "to climb down from the lorry and stack their weapons." It was a flat statement, but with strands of inquiry, nervousness, a slender strand of foreboding all twisted in. "Oh, to be sure," Lacy said. He fed a cartridge into the chamber of his Lee-Enfield, and held it above his head, as a signal to the others. Then he eased out the Parabellum and rested it on a flat stone beside him. Hynes had no sidearm, only his rifle.

Green fields rose away from them toward the distant brown mountains. The mountains hugged their loneliness, and for a moment Lacy in imagination was among them, a brown of wasteland, boulders washed black by the recent rains. There was always wind in the mountains, from the north or from the Atlantic, salt-laden, cleansing.

When the lorry appeared, what first impressed Lacy was its ordinariness, eleven men by his first count, sitting facing each other, the canvas sidings rolled up that they might enjoy the mild afternoon sun. Four or five of them held their rifles across their knees, as all of them should properly have been doing, but the others had placed theirs on the floor, or at least, they were out of sight. Soon enough, he could make out the features of the driver, a hawk-faced fellow with sallow features beneath his visored cap, and the sergeant seated beside him, with the heavy features appropriate to his rank and a thick mustache; he sat with his arms folded, looking neither to left nor right. For all the uniforms and rifles, for all of the stolid-featured sergeant, it was as common a sight upon the road these days as a cart bringing milk to the creamery, or the lorries moving produce eastwards to the railheads. Lacy gave Hynes a sideward glance. His rifle butt was still firm against his shoulder, but he was wiping a hand, as though sweaty, against his trouser legs. "All right now," Lacy said, "about now, in a minute from now or less."

The lorry had just passed them and was still in full sight and range when it took the turn, and driver and sergeant suddenly saw the blockade of fallen rocks and thick, felled trees. Then the still air was broken all at once by the grinding of brakes and the shrill scream of the sergeant's whistle, blown until his lungs were empty and then blown again. "Ambush!" Lacy could hear him shout. "Ambush! Dismount and take up positions." What positions, Lacy thought, what positions, you unlucky hoor.

"Now," Lacy said, scarcely bothering even to lower his voice, "now give him his warning and be bloody quick." The men, a bit bewildered perhaps, a bit panicked perhaps, Lacy could not tell, began clambering out by whatever means seemed to them quickest, over the sides, or through the lowered tailgate, holding their rifles awkwardly. "There you are," Lacy said, thinking of the rifles. "You below there," Hynes suddenly shouted, the heavy voice close to Lacy's ear, "you policemen below there. Stack your arms by the side of the road. Stack your arms or drop them at least. Do that and you are safe enough." There was no response, if only because the policemen were not yet out of their bewilderment. " 'Tis your arms we want," Hynes shouted. "Give us those and you can wheel round and head back to Portumna." He paused, and then, as though answering silence, added, "Your arms are being requisitioned by the Irish Volunteers. Look alive, we have no time to waste." "Fuck you," one of the policemen shouted, but it was an uncertain cry, wavering, uttered to impress his chums and not the ambush. The other policemen were looking toward their sergeant. Lacy's eyes had never left him. He was standing with his legs apart, his cap pushed to the back of close-cropped sandy hair, and he looked cool enough. He dropped his hand to his leather holster, which he unfastened, and then drew out his Webley. "Move to the far side of the vehicle from those bastards," he called, "and take cover there. Prepare to fire." You foolish man, Lacy thought. " 'Tis a last warning now that I am giving you, in God's name," Hynes cried, almost as a plea. The sergeant, when he saw that his men were moving as he had bid them, made ready to follow them, but as he did, he lifted his revolver, and fired off a round in the direction of Hynes's voice. The bullet passed high over Hynes's head and Lacy's. It was the moment that Lacy had been waiting for. He had been keeping his rifle trained upon a point an inch or so above the buckle of the sergeant's belt of heavy black leather, and now he fired twice. The gun's pull moved the barrel upwards, and the sergeant received both shots full in the chest. Lacy thought that he might have heard him scream, but could not be certain, because shouting at once became general, from the rocks to either side of the road and from the stalled lorry. The sergeant lay sprawled upon his back. His leg kicked out once, convulsively, and then he was still.

"Oh Jesus," Hynes said, "oh my dear Jesus." Lacy ignored him and shouted down, "See now what you have done, you stupid bloody bastards. Drop your weapons and come out into the road with your hands over your heads." "That was a warning shot that he fired surely," Hynes said to him; "there is no one of us could have been hit by that shot. It went high over our heads." Lacy looked toward him. His face was working with anger and grief. "You have a body of the RIC pinned down there," Lacy said. "And your duty is to take their surrender. See to it." And as if in answer, from the far side of the lorry, from the cover of the front wheel, two of the policemen opened fire. "Whatever about your friend the sergeant," Lacy said, "those are not warning shots," and then, ignoring the line of command, he shouted to the fellows on their side of the road, "Commence firing," and called across, "Second company commence firing." The sound was deafening. Along the line, he could see Hynes's men fire, pull back the bolts, fire again. Of some, he could see only legs, booted, sprawled behind rocks, but could see their slight jerk as the rifle exploded into shot.

But then suddenly, because, perhaps, he had recognized the voice as Lacy's and not Hynes's, on the far side of the road, Trainor stood up and shouted out, clear and desperate, "Hynes? Michael Hynes, is that you? Commence firing, is it?" "That tears it," Lacy said, "I wonder he did not give your address and next of kin." But Hynes had a grip on himself and needed no instruction now. "Get your head down, you fool," he shouted, "and open fire."

For a long time after that bright afternoon, Lacy would wonder why the police had not considered that the positions on either side of the road would not be held. It was, he decided at last, because they had never seriously considered the possibility, for such things are relative, of a full-scale attack upon a lorryload of RIC. It was a mistake that was never made again, not after what Republican propaganda began at once to call "The Battle of Dawson's Cross." But other newspapers, the paper which Lacy's father published in Kilkenny, called it "Slaughter of Policemen. Murderers still at large." After Dawson's Cross there were outriders, on motorcycle, when possible, and a Lancia armored car.

It was a short, ugly scrap, as such things went. The policemen were caught within a crossfire, and those on the far side of the lorry, Trainor's side, were without cover. They fought gamely enough, for men without practice in such matters, firing up toward Trainor's rock cover. But in all of the scrap, only one of Trainor's men was hit, and that not seriously, and none at all of Hynes's men. Lacy would remember noise, shouts, twice there were screams, stirs of dust as bullets hit the road or the dirt of hedges. He could see clearly, beyond Trainor's low hill, a field beyond in which stood a farmhouse. No one had stirred from within. What must the noise seem like to them, he thought.

Then, suddenly, a figure broke from the cover of the lorry, and ran out into the road and toward Hynes's rock. "Sweet Jesus," Hynes said to Lacy, "I know that lad, 'tis Jackie Kelleher, Sarah's young fellow." Kelleher had dropped his rifle somewhere behind the lorry, and he had lost his cap. His close-cropped ginger hair was bright in the sunlight; sunlight fell upon a broad face, scattered freckles upon fair skin. "Mr. Hynes," he shouted up. "That cannot really be yourself. Do you mean to kill all of us? Dear Jesus, you should—" But even as Lacy turned toward Hynes, a rifle shot rang out from beyond Hynes, and the bullet caught Kelleher full in the forehead. For a moment, an instant in time, or it may have been an illusion, speed beyond the mind's calculation, young Kelleher stood motionless, a neat round hole in his forehead, then he fell over backwards, without life.

It was after that, perhaps after they had seen the unarmed Kelleher shot down, that four policemen, all that could move of those trapped behind the lorry, burst out, as though in concert, moving at a dead run down the road toward the roadblock. They received full fire from both sides of the road, and three of them fell in the road itself, and the fourth, as he had reached the barricade and his rifle dropped, had placed his two hands upon its jagged top. They were hit, the four of them, repeatedly.

Into a long silence, Liam Trainor, having belatedly learned reticence, called over to them, "There is no resistance here. We have a good clear view." Hynes stood up. "Cease fire," he said. He seemed older to Lacy, his heavy shoulders sagging. Lacy rested his rifle and took out his heavy half-hunter watch, a Christmas gift once from his father. From the time the lorry had stopped its motor, four minutes had passed. He picked up his Parabellum from the stone on which he had rested it. Now, from the farmhouse beyond the field, a man had emerged, and was standing before its door, his arms folded.

Lacy clambered down the stony hill to the road, Hynes behind him and the men following. The bodies lay sprawled in the road. A small pool of blood was spreading from beneath Jackie Kelleher's skull. Another of the men lay facedown. He had been one of the last ones fired upon, as he ran down the road, and a volley of bullets had ripped open his shoulders and lower back. Blood and some darker liquid had begun to soak through his trousers. Another man, lying close to the sergeant, who had been the first to fall, was still alive, despite a bullet in his side, and one which had torn away a part of his face. What may have been shout or scream or speech came out as wet, juicy gurgle. Lacy walked close to him, bent slightly, and killed him with a bullet into the skull.

The shot, crisper and more vivid from a Parabellum than from rifles, hung in the air. The men under Trainor's command had been a bit slower in starting their climb down, and when they reached the road, their eyes were on Lacy, as Trainor's were, and Hynes's. Lacy had a sense, perhaps all of them had a sense, that frightful as the moment was, frightful as was each one's own sense of complicity, it was a moment existing within two realms, the one a realm of that moment, actual, with a puzzled man looking toward them across a field, and the other existing within history, deep and unexpungeable, changing something forever, never to be washed away by time, as soon the pool of blood from Kelleher's skull would be washed away, faded first by sunlight, then washed away by rain.

Lacy knew that he had to do or say something, either himself or Hynes, and, straightening, he said, "The bodies of those men must not be allowed to sprawl there at random like felled sheep or calves. They must be placed side by side, in a seemly manner, beside the vehicle which they defended bravely. They were brave men." The others looked at him, as though they could not understand even the literal sense of his words, and so he set to work himself, standing behind the sergeant, and grasping him under the armpits.

When he had seen them safely at work, he climbed on board the lorry, and there, as he had expected, across the length of it, was a narrow wooden box, green-painted, the lid latched but not locked. He opened the box by its latch, and inside they saw at least a dozen rifles, looking to be in first-rate condition, and with the heavy, oddly comforting smell of oil upon them. Beyond was a smaller box of cartridge cartons. He lifted out one of the rifles, handed it to Hynes, then took out a second. "Here we are, lads," he called out to the brigade, interrupting them at their work. "We will have those weapons below to carry off with us, and these as well. The Fourth Brigade will be lending out weapons to the cowboys in Cork and Tipperary by the looks of things."

But the men looked up at him, without any expression save their shock, with the exception of a young fellow who giggled without humor. They were still at their task, moving the bodies into position. Kelleher, who was the one best known to them, had not been touched. Lacy looked at Hynes, who stood beside him, in control of himself now, Lacy was glad to see, and Lacy said, more to himself than to Hynes, "Right," put back the rifle, and clambered back over the tailgate with Hynes following him.

"Give me a hand here," he said to Hynes, and, walking over to Kelleher, he put an arm beneath the shoulders, and one beneath the thighs. Cradling him thus, they carried him to the row of dead policemen. The back of Kelleher's head was a shattered mess of bone and blood through which the matter of his brain had oozed. They left blood and brain behind them on the roadway. Suddenly, as they moved, the head lolled against Hynes's arm. He gave a sudden, girlish scream. The others paused to look at them, then averted their heads. When they had eased Kelleher down into position, Hynes took out a wide handkerchief and scrubbed frantically at the tweed of his jacket sleeve, then flung the handkerchief away from him.

When they had finished, something would have to be said, Lacy knew, and by himself rather than Hynes. What he did was line them up into their two companies, with Trainor standing at the head of his, but Hynes Lacy held beside himself. He must be seen to be speaking for the two of them, for the brigade, for Headquarters, for the Republic. They kept glancing over, first one of them and then another, toward the bodies. These were fellows, these lads, in farm clothes or else in the jackets of clerks and shop assistants, with here and there a Volunteer's hat, a bandolier, fellows who in the ordinary course of things would never have thought to fire off a heavy bullet into the sergeant or into Constable Kelleher. They had seen themselves as men of the hillside and the glen, Fenians, rapparees perhaps, or perhaps Sarsfield's men who had ridden down the valley in their jackets green following the white cockade. More powerfully than this, a heavy weight pressing upon the imagination, they remembered that Pearse and the Volunteers had held the sandbagged Post Office until the blazing roof had begun to fall upon them, that the outer garrisons had at first refused to surrender, that the leaders had been stood up against Kilmainham wall and shot, all save one who, wounded in the fighting, had been shot while strapped to a chair. But even those memories, bestowed a scant three years ago to the imagination, had something of the legendary, of the remote and disembodied. Most powerfully of all, perhaps, they knew that they were fighting for these hills and roads and fields, the landscape of their lives and of their parents' lives, time out of mind. All this, all imagination, all history, all passion, was less real than the dead men lined neatly and properly beside their lorry and the knowledge of how they had died.

"All right now," Lacy said. "Take a good look over there, and then come back to attention. It is a fearful sight, but we have determined to make war, to fight for a Republic which was proclaimed three years ago, when and where you well know and which will never be given to us without our fighting for it. Empires are not in the business of giving freedom to the small nations they hold, and England has held this country for seven hundred years. Not with soldiers in these latter years although these she has in their plenty, stationed here in this land, but with lads like these. Irish lads, given warm uniforms and promises of pensions and truncheons and carbines and pistols and bullets, and told to act as England's army against their own. Well you know that—your fathers and your grandfathers have told you how that was so, in the times of the Fenians and in the times of the great evictions and in the times of the landlords. Remember Mitchelstown. It was not soldiers who fired into that crowd of unarmed country people, it was men wearing the uniform you see there."

There were fellows in the companies still in their teens, a terrible age at which to put a bullet into a man, tear his flesh apart. But now they returned Lacy's look steadily. It was as much as he had hoped for. "There was a beginning made at Soloheadbeg by the Tipperary Brigade, and there has been another beginning here this afternoon at Dawson's Cross. It will be known across Ireland by nightfall or by morning. Dawson's Cross will be remembered."

By God, it will, he thought, stepping back to leave Hynes in command, in song and ballad one day, no doubt, if things went well, but that would be one day, and not today or tomorrow. He could write tomorrow's headlines for them. "Butchery in Claregalway."

"One other thing," Hynes said, "and it is best spoken openly and spoken here and now. In the excitement of battle, my name was sung out, clear as a bell, across the road you all heard it. They heard it. Constable Kelleher heard it and came shouting it as he ran toward my position. When that name was called out, a warrant against each and all of the constables was signed. It was not myself alone, all of Dawson's Cross knows what fellows train under my instruction. There may come a day when this battalion will have to take to the hills like the rapparees of old, but that day is not yet. Three or four of us will store safely the weapons we have won this day in open battle, and we will all of us get to our tasks. And our homes."

Trainor it was who had called out Hynes's name, but standing at attention he stood there saying nothing, though he was biting his lips fiercely.

It was to the room in the back of Hynes's pub, beyond the shop, beyond the bar, that Hynes and Trainor and Lacy went that night. Lacy brought his bicycle inside and rested it against the bar; he had packed his knapsack. The three of them sat about a deal table to which Hynes's mother brought a large pot of tea and a plate of sandwiches, ham and chicken. Other sandwiches she had wrapped in waxed paper, that Lacy could pack beside his shirts and the Parabellum and the book he carried with him, English on one side and Latin on the other. *Armo virumque cano; Troaie qui primus ab oris.*

They sat there without speaking at first, as the tea drew, and then Hynes poured it out for the three of them.

"There are things done and seen," Hynes said, "that will never be forgotten. Not for a long time, at the least."

"Not ever," Lacy said. "Not ever forgotten."

"That scrap out here in 'sixteen," Trainor said, "there was scant blood drawn. A constabulary barracks rushed, and then fellows on the run."

"Lacy knows that, for God's sake," Hynes said. "Lacy was in command here under Mellowes."

"There was spilled blood to go around in Dublin that week," Lacy said, "and against the wall at Kilmainham in the weeks to come. And since then, Thomas Ashe has been murdered in Mountjoy Gaol. Volunteers have taken action against agents of the Crown, constables and magistrates."

"But not a lorryful of policemen shot down in—" Hynes broke off what he was saying, and picked up his cup in two large, white publican's hands.

"Finish off your sentence, Mick," Lacy said. " 'In cold blood,' is that what it would have been? Those fellows were armed. Far better armed than ourselves. That was the object of the operation. If the sergeant was so foolish as to move his men to Liam's side of the lorry, that was his lookout, and he has paid for it."

"Stupid, stupid, bloody stupid," Trainor said, speaking to the others but of himself. "If I had minded my words." If he had not shouted out Hynes's name, the policemen would have handed over their weapons as they had been ordered and driven back to Portumna, shamefaced but alive. Might have done, he amended to himself, realistically.

"They meant to make a fight of it," Lacy said, "and can you blame them? It is a great disgrace for a soldier to report back to barracks without his weapons. And they are soldiers, never forget that. Armed and drilled and holding down the land as soldiers do." He looked first at one of them and then at the other. "Like the West Kents at Fermoy."

At Fermoy, fourteen soldiers, armed and under command of a corporal, had marched to services in the Wesleyan church, and were attacked by Volunteers of the Fermoy company. The soldiers resisted the call upon them to surrender their rifles, and in the scuffle a soldier was killed, and four others wounded. It was a well-planned raid. The leader and some of the men, with all fifteen of the rifles, drove off down the Lismore road, and the pursuit cars which followed, lorries from the barracks, were caught in a trap of felled trees at Carrickabrick, a mile outside the town, and forced to turn back.

"You know what happened after Fermoy, do you not?" Lacy asked, but he knew they did. "The whole countryside was tossed, and people were dragged from their cars and beaten by the soldiers. And the next night, the West Kents fell down upon Fermoy, and bloody well wrecked the town, smashing shops and houses and setting fire to them. Here is your law and order for you."

"That could happen here," Trainor said.

"It could," Lacy said, "but as likely or more likely in Portumna or Loughrea or Athenry. That is why the Dawson's Cross company was used. And that is why no tales were to be carried back to the Portumna barracks."

Hynes smiled at him quizzically, irritation dashed and salted with a reluctant admiration.

"You are a bloody reckless man, Frank. Do you expect the

same class of a coroner's verdict as was handed down after Fermoy?"

After Fermoy, the coroner's jury had found "that the deceased man died from a bullet wound caused by some person unknown," and added "its sincere sympathy with the relatives of the deceased."

"If it is a sensible jury," Lacy said. "They are your countrymen in these acres, not mine."

"After the final shot was fired," Trainor said, "there was a quiet so full that you could feel it, a hush upon all, the hills and the rocks and the road and what lay there in the road." The last shot, although he did not mention this, had come from Lacy's Parabellum, a sudden, unexpected explosive bark.

"There are birds that can be heard that time of day along the road, because of the copses, the larches and the rowans. The gunfire frightened them away," Hynes said.

"Even before the gunfire, there were no birds. I would have taken notice of them, I think," Lacy said.

"A great man for the birds, are you, Frank?" Hynes asked, the same mixture of dislike and admiration in his voice.

"I was noticing whatever I could," Lacy said, "listening for the first sound of the lorry." His smile acknowledged Hynes's tone. "I used to be a great one for the birds, when I was a lad. A chum and myself used be after them, back in Kilkenny."

Four days later, business still held Lacy in Galway. The night before he caught the train back to Dublin he spent at Haydon's Hotel in Ballinasloe, across from the massive RIC barracks, a barracks so strong and so heavily manned that there was not yet in existence anywhere a brigade capable of attacking it. Not yet, but someday, please God: on this he was in agreement with the local battalion commander, a sensible man, hard as brass tacks. He had left the bicycle in the commandant's safekeeping, and was registered in the hotel under the name of Reynolds. He spent the hours before his evening meal in the commercial room, writing out his formal report for Brugha, and a shorter one, quite unofficial, which was intended for Collins only. Two other men, commercial travelers, shared the room with him, sitting each of them, like him, at a small writing table with inkstand and green blotter covered with the tracks, reversed, of other reports. One of the travelers refreshed himself by long pulls at a pint of ale, and, when it was empty, rang the bell for a second. He punctuated his task with grunts and then belches, delicately covering his mouth. A rail-thin man with a downturned mouth.

At his meal, ham and chicken, potatoes almost the size and weight of grenades, Lacy read the *Connaught Tribune.* There had been no reprisals, neither upon Portumna nor Loughrea, even though the coroner's jury had brought in a verdict similar to Fermoy's, "willful murder by persons unknown and theft under arms of Crown property." But it was to be expected that a force like the RIC would show more discipline in their own country than a company of English territorials dropped down amongst savages. The Bishop of Galway had issued a fierce denunciation: "The work of brutish gunmen who do not deserve the name of Irishmen. Apes and anarchists who have dragged into the mud the flag flown in proud purity above the General Post Office, the flag for which Pearse and his comrades cheerfully offered their lives." In 1916, the bishop had thought less kindly of Pearse, and of the gunmen who had sought to emulate him in County Galway. This showed, Lacy decided, what Cardinal Newman called "the development of doctrine," a delicate concept, fraught with possibilities of heresy, capable of examination only within the tracery of Newman's prose. Give the bishops time, Lacy thought, translating Newman's cloistral delicacy, and they will come round. Once they recognize that the Volunteers are articulating the passions and aspirations of a buried people, a hidden culture.

The *Connaught Tribune* quoted the Fermoy coroner in September: that attack was "an act of actual warfare, well thought out. It would take military strategy of the highest order to equal it." A similar, indeed a greater degree of skill was exhibited in this present outrage in Galway. "An ambush was set at a point in the Portumna road across the Slieve Aughties, a barren terrain which offers good visibility, yet a point at which a lorry traveling without outriders would certainly be checked, and the policemen were then ruthlessly cut down by crossfire. It was a sordid enterprise, but a professional one."

Not so, Lacy thought, angry not with the *Tribune,* but with himself. Luck had been with him, and the execution had been satisfactory but no more than that. Fermoy now, that was a different matter, Fermoy had been the work of Liam Lynch, the commandant of the Cork No. 2 Brigade, a field commander of proven skills, superior even to Barry, a man in a class with Treacy. He had already taken Araglin police barracks, and Fermoy, a different kind of operation, had been carried out meticulously, with enforcements brought in from outlying companies, motorcars laid, lines of retreat prepared and held under guard. Cool in action, not until he was being driven past the Lismore barricade did he reveal that he had been wounded, unbuttoning coat and shirt. It was always to Lacy a matter of surprised exhilaration, the way in which such commanders seemed to spring up, almost from the earth itself—Lynch, Barry, MacKeon, Treacy. More of them were needed, and spread over a wider territory. England would not wait about obligingly while her garrison in Ireland was being boycotted, immobilized, shunned, slaughtered on lonely roads across wastelands.

That night before sleep, he read for an hour. His room was on the top floor, but noises from the street carried to him, fellows shouting to each other as they left the pubs, a careless joviality fired by pints and short ones knocked back before closing time. Once he heard the rumble and grinding gears of a lorry driving through the gates of the barracks. Tauntingly, the words seemed to come more from high spirits than from treason, three or four voices, young, began singing "The Peeler and the Goat," but then the words dwindled, silenced, and the voices commenced afresh, "Soldiers are we, whose lives are pledged to Ireland . . ." Or soon would be, he thought.

VI

JANICE NUGENT

The autumn of 1920—the autumn of the Black and Tans and Terence MacSwiney dead on a hunger strike in Brixton Prison and young Kevin Barry hanged in Dublin—was raw and damp, winds shaking the bare-branched trees in the orchard, shaking the roadside hedges, ice gray and brittle covering our small lake. There had been a time, only a year before, when the Troubles were young, when weeks could pass by without our thinking of them, save when we read a newspaper report of a police inspector shot somewhere else, a resident magistrate shot somewhere else, a raid for arms. But this was no longer the case, and for most of us, in my part of Galway, the change had begun the winter before, the winter of 1919, when the policemen traveling by lorry along the Portumna-Gort road had been ambushed and slain by the Shinners, as my father's friends still called them, or the Irish Republican Army, as everyone else now did.

It was a road which few enough of us who lived around Loughrea found occasion to travel along, but the map will show you that our three towns formed a kind of triangle—Loughrea, Gort, Portumna, with rich pasturelands at each of its points, but the triangle itself sprawled across the Slieve Aughties; mountains barren and savage, nothing at all of the romantic and picturesque about them, and we used on occasion, in earlier years, to drive across the mountains to friends in Mountshannon, on the Clare side of Lough Derg. In those days, before the war, indeed before my marriage, and certainly before the motorcar, we would drive over, the four of us, Father and Mother and Betty and myself, with Father driving of course, why we kept a coachman was always a mystery, but the O'Gormans had always had a coachman, and if the weather was good, as it was likely to be, because it was likely to be mid-August and we would be on our way to Mountshannon, to the Fitzhughs, at Lakeview, for a shooting party, but even then, even in mid-August, those hills would feel bare and inhospitable, and we would be eager for Lakeview and tea.

But ever after that winter's day in 1919 when the news first came to us of the ambush, the "slaughter" was the word I heard first used, I would remember not summer drives to Lough Derg but rather a false memory. In my mind's eye, I would see the lorry hurrying along the road, and in the distance leafless trees, a lorry full of men, and on the road's either side, behind rocks, men waiting for them with rifles. I would not imagine the fighting, nor the unimaginable scene which followed it, bodies stretched along the road, rather it, my memory, would be frozen in time and yet swift-moving, the lorry quick-moving toward a bend of road which imagination forbade it from reaching. But now, a year later almost, one heard less often a word like "slaughter" and far more often "ambush," a neutral word, and, on occasion, the word "battle," "The Battle of Dawson's Cross," and "the Fourth Battalion of the Galway Brigade," whose officers now were on the run, in an "active service unit," and people knowledgeable in such matters would say, nodding wisely, that the Battle of Dawson's Cross had in fact been directed not by the local men, but by Francis Lacy, whose name had become an overnight legend, as things were likely in those days to do, heard less often than the names of farm-boy guerrilla captains, less often surely than that of Collins, whom the English generals and journalists and politicians had helped to make famous as the elusive generalissimo of what they insisted on calling "the murder gang," although Christopher Blake and the other Republican publicists had done their part. Francis Lacy, like Earnan O'Malley, was a legend of a different kind, shadowy and yet sharply defined, resourceful and deadly. "The Battle of Dawson's Cross," it was being said now, a year later, had been the "war's" first major "engagement," or so the Irish newspapers, some of them, were beginning to say, but other papers, like all of the English papers, spoke of attacks by "armed civilians" upon forces of the Crown.

But for me the change between the two winters was far different, for midway between them, in the spring, to be exact, Christopher Blake and I fell in love, and I became his mistress. And after that, what was happening in Ireland could no longer be held off at arm's length as the "Troubles," nor something to talk about with Father and his friends, nor even only the terrible scene, real yet utterly imagined, of the men at Dawson's Cross driving toward the other men with their guns. Not after that, for Christopher and Francis Lacy and Collins the legend were members of the same organization. Like someone in a shopgirl's romance, I had fallen in love with an "Irish rebel," except that it wasn't like that, not at all, because shopgirls' novels have the great blessing of simplicity, and from the first everything about Christopher and me was complicated in ways that lay beyond such reckoning.

We met, for example, Christopher and I, because we were both friends of Patrick Prentiss's, who had taken me to have lunch at Jammet's, and then on to one of Catherine Lawlor's Thursdays "at home." And I was in Dublin for the day, staying with friends in Merrion Square. Patrick was very distinguished-looking, now that he was in his middle thirties, and the empty sleeve was like a badge of sorts; after a bit, one didn't notice it.

Dublin in those days was very curious. There was a war of sorts going on right in the middle of it, but it was for the most part an invisible war, save for the soldiers one passed in the streets, and once in a great while armored cars going from one place to another. And on my first night in the city, lying in bed, but not asleep, I heard gunfire from somewhere, from Baggot Street, I thought, and was right because the papers that afternoon described "armed civilians" there opening fire on policemen, and one of the civilians was wounded but the fellows with him had spirited him away.

And the next day, as I was walking to Patrick at the Dolphin, a lorry passed me, filled with policemen, and most likely, so Patrick explained to me, the "auxiliaries" to the force, recruited in England, veterans of the war, most of them, and already famous as "Black and Tans," from the hastily assembled uniforms that the first lot of them had worn.

"The sweepings of the English jails," Patrick said, "if you believe Christopher Blake's newspapers, and so some of them may be. They are certainly a nasty lot."

"We have Black and Tans in Galway," I said. "People say that it was the Black and Tans who burned down a creamery in Oranmore last month in revenge for a policeman who had been killed."

"Reprisal is the polite term," Patrick said. "Not revenge. Of course, it depends on who is doing it."

Two officers, a major and a captain, were having a meal at the table next to ours, and the major sat facing me. He was deep in conversation with his friend, but his eye kept wandering back to me, not rudely, of course, and it was as though he could not help himself, which was flattering.

"You could discourage him, you know," Patrick said, breaking off his story, but he was smiling at me. Once, long ago and briefly, there had been something between Patrick and myself.

"Poor dear," I said, "he means no harm. He must be very lonely here in Dublin."

"Not in the least," he said. "Life goes on. There are dinner parties, dances, all the rest of it. More exciting than lonely, I expect."

"Once you wore that uniform," I said, "yourself and Charlie. Are you sorry now that you did?"

"My dear Janice," he said, "what a direct question. I don't think it has ever been put to me that directly, not even by Christopher Blake. There he goes again, you have made another conquest, dear."

"You have always been wonderful at avoiding direct questions," I said. "Your legal training, no doubt. Who is Christopher Blake?"

"Who is he?" he said. "I thought you might have known him. From London."

"You see?" I said. "You are incorrigible. Why should I have known him from London?"

"Because he worked for that publisher, the one who publishes those friends of yours."

"Carter and Hazlon? Bobby Hazlon? I don't remember a Christopher Blake. Should I? Is he memorable?"

"And he writes himself," Patrick said. "Carter and Hazlon did a book of his on the Irish brigades who served in France in the eighteenth century."

"We were in one of those brigades, I think. The O'Gormans were. And Charlie's people certainly were. The Nugents had an entire brigade, I think."

"That must have been very grand," Patrick said, in a dry way.

"Was he in the war?" I asked, "your Christopher Blake?"

"Not as you mean it," Patrick said. On the table between us there was a bud vase with a single pink rose in it. When the major next looked over toward me, a sidelong glance, I touched the flower, running my finger slowly along its length. It was warm to the touch.

"Poor major," Patrick said.

"Poor major," I agreed. "I am doing my bit for Ireland."

With an effort, the major tore his glance away from me. In these peacetime days, he was young to be a major, about Patrick's age. It had been different during the war. This major had close-cropped hair, sandy and wiry-looking, and a small blond mustache.

"Christopher is in *this* war," Patrick said, "the one that is going on around us. He was in the GPO during the Easter Rising and in prison after that. Now he is in the Dáil, the Parliament, whenever it meets and wherever, and he is something or other in the cabinet, and he is one of their directors of publicity. And he is close to Collins, everyone says."

He touched his wineglass and signaled to the waiter, who poured more of the lovely Graves that Patrick had ordered. It seemed so strange to be hearing of such matters in the Dolphin, and with two serving officers sitting almost in earshot.

"Would you like to meet him?" Patrick asked. "Come to Catherine Lawlor's with me."

"Just like that? A desperately wanted gunman, and we can meet him at one of Kitty Lawlor's 'at homes'?"

"In theory he is on the run," Patrick said. "But he isn't wanted all that badly, the police and the military have to pick and choose. He is not a gunman, after all. But he is close to them, he knows them, perhaps once in a while he gives them an order. It is a strange war."

It seemed to be more awful than strange, and so it had from the day that I had seen that poor man shot down on the station platform at Moate and had knelt beside him.

"Are you for them, Patrick? On their side? Your Christopher Blake and all those people? Tell me, don't give me another question."

"I don't know, Janice. I honestly do not. Christopher is a different matter, Christopher and I were friends long before this started and we are so still. I am of service to them from time to time. They may not recognize the courts, but barristers are helpful to them all the same. What I do know is that I'm not on *their* side, not on the side of the English, the major and his friend."

"At home in Galway," I said, "the Jelliffes were raided for arms and the Peterses and the Ruthvens, but we were not, and Sally Ruthven says it is because we are Catholics, do you believe that?"

"It's possible," Patrick said, "but not certain, not if the boys get desperate for arms. Your father might be well advised to hide his regimental swords, and those assegais in the hall."

"Regimental sword," I said, and it was as though the words held much of my bewilderment. He didn't have it hanging in the study, there is that to be said for him, but it was on his bedroom wall, and beside it three photographs, yellowing nicely now, one taken in India and the other two in Africa. In one of the African ones, he sits with three other young officers around a table, outside a tent, their tent perhaps, all of them absurdly young, and three of them, Father is one, with fierce mustaches. A servant stands near them in jacket and skirt. They had put on their swords for the photograph, and Father's hand rests with assumed negligence upon the hilt of his, the same sword which now hung in his bedroom, and which once, when we were children, Betty and I had carried to the lake to pretend that it was Excalibur.

"How is your father?" Patrick asked. "How does he feel about all this?"

"We have a motorcar now," I said, "and Father adores it. We motor each Sunday to Mass, of course, and he has taught me to motor, after a fashion. And we motor to visit neighbors. I must meet Christopher Blake, a man wanted by the police, that must be exciting."

As I spoke, suddenly I caught sight of myself in a tall, slender mirror which hung on the wall at a right angle to us, soft and at the edges faintly mottled. I saw myself leaning a bit toward Patrick across the table, the rose between us, and our glasses. And I saw myself talking, saw that I was talking for effect, and was angry with myself.

"And how does your father feel about all this?" Patrick said a second time, smiling not at me, but at my reflection in the mirror, as though he knew that the reflection was scolding me.

"He doesn't know how he feels about it," I said. "Mostly, he thinks that it is dreadful. And so does Father Cusack. But neither of the curates think that it is dreadful, so we hear."

The captain must have said something witty or else had come to the end of a story, because suddenly his friend the major gave a short, loud bark of laughter, and brought his hand down smartly upon their table. Patrick turned his head to stare at them, almost rudely, and his eyes carried a hostility I had never seen in them before.

I reached my hand out toward his and stroked it, until, aware of my touch, he turned to me. I remembered, an instant, a flicker, the cinematograph, distant and forever, Patrick and myself and the lake at Coolater, willow-fringed, deep summer.

"I am sorry," he said, "I am sorry, my dear. History."

Which was always one of the very nice things about Patrick. That he could say something oblique or fragmentary and leave it at that, as though confident that you would flesh it out, as swiftly as he had spoken it.

"It must be wonderful, Patrick," I said, mockingly and yet still letting my hand rest upon his, "to see history everywhere."

At that very moment, as if upon cue, one of the dreadful klaxon horns sounded, by which both the tenders and the armored cars plowed their ways through the streets of the city.

Whenever we met, Patrick and myself, we found ourselves not talking about Charlie or about Patrick's empty sleeve or about the Somme or Gallipoli. I cannot say why. But the war was history, surely, and history more monumental by far than a lorryload of English soldiers pelting down a Dublin street or the disagreeable barking laugh of an English officer in a Dublin restaurant.

"You used always to be talking about history, Patrick," I said, as I drew my hand away. "Enough to drive a girl mad."

"Not quite always," he said.

Patrick called round for me that evening and we walked the short distance from Merrion Square to Mespil Road. It was lovely, the days lengthening, and at this hour the eighteenth-century houses, old gold, some of them, but others their bricks the color of dusty roses, and at the ends of the streets, the hills of Dublin rising up in the near distance, brown and green, against a reluctantly darkening sky, the air soft, washed clean by recent rain. It was difficult to hold in a single thought that reality and that other reality of tanks and Crossley tenders and gunmen on the run. From the square, we walked along Mount Street to the canal, whose waters, dark now, came to us from the distant midlands of pasturelands and boglands, soft hills and harsh hills. It was a comfortable small city, large town, settling down into a comfortable dowdiness amidst the echoes of vanished elegance in fanlight, brick, smooth water beneath dressed eighteenth-century stone. Once, when Betty and I were small, and for some reason that I cannot now recall, we had spent Christmas week, the four of us and a maid for Mother, in rooms at the Shelbourne, and Betty and I had been taken to all of the pantomimes, clowns, fairy godmothers, dancers and a chorus. I remember blue transparent gauzes spangled with stars silver and golden, through which, magically, a sudden burst of light, we could see cavorting camels and elephants, dancing on their hind legs. Much later, when I was fifteen or so, Mama and I spent a few days at the Shelbourne, on our own, and attended a reception at the Viceregal Lodge, in Phoenix Park, and all the time that our cab was rattling through the city and then through the park, Mother was complaining about how awful the Dublin shops were, not at all like London, and then, the next year we were in Dublin again, when Betty and I were presented at the Viceroy's Court in Dublin Castle, when we stayed at Buswell's. Atmospheres, small worlds of remembered colors, odors, are stored up somewhere and return to us unbidden.

Charlie and I had been once or twice to a Kitty Lawlor "at home" and had not found them exciting. She lived on Mespil Road, not a stone's throw from Evie Cunningham, and ran a sort of rival salon—nationalists of the milder sort, Castle officials of the more agreeable sort, journalists, people like that, and once in a while people like Charlie and myself, birds of passage between London and Galway or London and Cork or London and Meath. It was a lovely house, built early in the nineteenth century, but in Ireland styles of architecture have always been delayed, so that Kitty's, like all the houses along the canal there, was charming in an older way, the eighteenth century still lingered in warm brick, and Kitty, being an artist, had done the rooms with an elegance you did not often find in Dublin. Dublin, in my experience, ran to heavy oaks and walnut, vast oil paintings done in brown gravy of hunting scenes or shepherds or a landscape before rain.

But Kitty's paintings—one or two of her own and others by her London or her Dublin friends—were a different matter. Bright splashes of color, vivid and challenging, so that one was bidden to reimagine the world. Her own paintings were as often as not of Galway, of my own county but not inland, not Loughrea or Coolater, but rather the long stretch which ran from Oughterard to Connemara and the Atlantic. It has been painted hundreds of times, the browns and greens, the magical skyscapes, but Kitty had turned her back upon all that way of doing it, and one saw colors only, masses of color, shape, design, but you could stand before one of her paintings and your heart would nearly break with your longing for Connemara. I was to know that, a few years later.

It was as crowded as ever at Kitty's, when Patrick and I arrived, and presently I found myself in the rear drawing room, standing before the fireplace, and drinking claret cup as I listened to a bearded man in Connemara cloth talk to me about astral bodies or Irish folk belief or something of that sort. Crowded as the room was, he had no difficulty in making himself heard, by me at least but also I should judge by anyone at all close to him. He must have been longing for his pipe, so I thought; a pipe nearly always goes with a beard and Connemara cloth. Above the chimneypiece hung one of Kitty's possessions, a painting of a young woman with one hand just touching her throat, a woman in a gown of yellow silk. Far beyond us I could see Patrick, looking very distinguished, talking to a man in dark blue flannel.

"Who is that with Patrick Prentiss," I said to Connemara Cloth; his name, Patrick told me later, was Russell, but he was also known by some initials which I heard as A.E.; "is that someone from the Castle? he looks like someone from the Castle."

"At Kitty's?" he said, politely but I think a bit annoyed at being interrupted, "not likely, not at all likely these days, Mrs. Nugent, not likely." How kind of him, I thought, to remember my name. "Our English cousins aren't welcome at Kitty's any longer, not for a while, at any rate."

"Not everyone at the Castle is English, surely?" I said. "We have friends—my husband and I had friends—"

"Of course, Mrs. Nugent," he said, "of course." He was quite a kind person really, and I remembered then that when we had begun talking he had told me that he had met Charlie once, and that he was very sorry. Perhaps that is how we began talking about astral bodies.

"Now over there," he said, "that is an interesting young man named Blake."

"Blake?" I said. "Christopher Blake?"

And that is how I first saw Christopher, before ever he saw me, standing, half-turned toward me, with a face too thin to be handsome, but clear, regular features, and eyes, even in that light, of bright, blazing blue. That is as close as I can come, now, to remembering how he looked then, as I looked across the room toward him. It is strange how difficult it is to remember how those we have loved looked to us before we came to love them, when they were strangers. I wish that I could remember Christopher as he looked to me then, at Kitty Lawlor's.

I cannot even remember how he seemed to me a half-hour later, when Patrick brought him over to me, all that I remember is that the face was too thin and the eyes so extraordinarily blue. Much later, he told me that he had been attracted to me at once, but there was no need for him to tell me because it was clear to me at once that he was, but it meant little really, because for some reason I looked wonderful that evening and I knew that I did.

But I remember what we talked about, talking as strangers, first beside the fireplace, and then we drifted apart, and then later, when we had moved, as others had, into the rear garden among the roses and with the small trees and the wall of soft, old rose color.

Once I said to him, "How do you know? What of Ireland do you know that you are entitled to lecture me about it?" but I was smiling as I asked him. "You Dublin people," I said, "what do any of you know about Ireland? I am Galway, you know. Galway is Ireland."

"Yes," he said, "Coolater. The O'Gormans of Coolater."

"My God," I said, "however did you know that? Did Patrick tell you?"

Which is why, the next afternoon, a messenger brought round to Merrion Square a copy of *Irish Brigades in the Service of France,* by Christopher Blake, with a card at page 122, where Christopher said in a footnote that "among those killed that July 2 of 1747, near Maestricht, was Major the Chevalier O'Gorman, of Coolater in County Galway, who acquitted himself well upon the field, but who is known also as the Matthew O'Gorman, who fitted words—words of Irish of course, not English or French—to one of the loveliest of Jacobite airs, known even now, 'The Royal Blackbird.' "

But at Kitty's, he said, "I am delighted that I know anything at all about you, Mrs. Nugent."

"I know about you, Mr. Blake," I said. "Is it true that you are wanted by the police or by the army or the Black and Tans or whoever? How exciting, I have never known anyone who was wanted by the police, it must be very exciting but I can scarcely believe it true. Why don't they come in and arrest you, that would be exciting, and Patrick could defend you."

"I don't think that I am very badly wanted," he said. "There are hundreds of people whom they want more badly than they do me. I am a member of what they call an illegal organization and an illegal assembly. It will be ages and ages before they get round to me."

Which may have been true enough in its way, but that wasn't all that he was. And it was later, weeks later, that he explained to me that he was well looked after, a bodyguard named Sonny Conlon across the road from Kitty's, whom I was later to know, a fellow not much older than twenty and thinner even than Christopher, and always, rain or shine or cold or whenever, save in the blazing heat of August, always in a brown mackintosh, and an unlit cigarette in the corner of his mouth.

"No," I said, "people are forever writing about Ireland and then people—other people—are forever going out and getting killed because of what has been written and they don't know Ireland at all. I don't mean to be offensive."

"Of course not," he said, smiling at me.

When I said that to him, I did not know or else had forgotten, if Patrick had told me, that Christopher had been in the Post Office through all of Easter Week, and had served his term in one of the English prisons. And I expect I should have been angry had I remembered, what many of my friends called the stab in the back, when our men, Charlie for one, and Patrick as well, had been off in France fighting. Or in the Dardanelles. But I wasn't thinking that as I stood talking to Christopher. Instead, I had told him the truth. I was remembering Galway, a thick, deep world of fields and low hills, lake water.

He was not tall for a man, an inch at most above my own height, but there was a sureness about him that gave him an air of height, although later I knew that the sureness was manner only, that he was tentative in many ways.

"You think of yourself as Irish, then, Mrs. Nugent. I am delighted to hear that."

"*Think* of myself," I said. "I like that!"

"We Blakes were once Galway," he said. "Long ago. It is a Galway name, of course. But we have been Dublin for a very long time, as long as anyone can remember. My father and my grandfather were doctors here in Dublin. But I know Galway a bit."

"Holidays in Connemara," I said, nastily.

"Yes," he said, and he was still smiling. "That sort of thing. And then I was a planning a book about— But then I was busy doing other things."

"Dodging the police," I said, "and sending young lads out to shoot at them."

"Yes," he said, "that sort of thing. You are out of sympathy with us, then, Mrs. Nugent. Yes, of course you must be. I quite understand."

"You understand nothing about me," I said. "How could you? We have only just met. How angry it makes me when people say they understand me. I don't understand myself."

"I seem to be saying the wrong thing to you," he said. "That isn't my intention, I assure you." The smile was still there, but the eyes, those splendid blue eyes, seemed worried. It is curious the way things like marvelous eyes are simply there, givens, unearned. And I knew very well that that was not his intention. I knew that he was drawn to me, but I was not to him, not then, not just yet, not that evening.

The book, when it came the next day, carried a short, charming note and I set to work at once reading it. I'm not sure how I felt about it, the style was bright and vivid but the subject seemed to me so distant, a dead world in which the writer was interested but the interest did not sweep from writer to reader, not to this reader, but you were aware of a genuine presence upon the page as always you are with a true writer, writing with quiet ironies and amusement which complicated what he said. The subject was the career upon French battlefields and in French history of those Irish regiments raised by the Catholic gentry of Ireland after the calamitous defeat at the hands of William of Orange, when the island lay entirely at the mercy of its Protestant masters. It was the sort of thing Father knew a bit about, of course, and well he might, not only because he had been a soldier himself but also because, as Christopher's book told us, there had always been a few O'Gormans in the brigades, first in Lord Clare's, and then later in Lally's and Dillon's. In a few months' time, when Christopher had become a visitor to us at Coolater, this was fortunate, because it gave Father and himself something to talk about, that and the book he had begun but set aside on what he called "the hidden Ireland," of families like our own. He wrote of us—of families like ours, I mean—with irony, as of families which once had been splendid, but then had fallen away, had shrunk, had lost a promise. None of it mattered a damn to me, but I was angry on Father's behalf, because it was the sort of thing which did matter to him.

And so I wrote and suggested to Christopher that we might have tea about it at the Shelbourne and he wrote back to say that that was wonderful but suggested instead a hotel down on the quays across from the Four Courts.

He was there waiting for me, wearing the same dark blue suit that he had worn at Kitty's, but a necktie with a curious and lovely design on it and in the dark-paneled room he had found us a table beside a tall window which looked out upon the river and across it to the Four Courts.

"This hotel must be convenient for you," I said. "Whenever they arrest you, you have only to walk across the bridge with the policeman."

"Almost that easy," he said. "The two times I have been arrested, I was taken the first time to Dublin Castle and the second time by the Black and Tans to their barracks. But then they took me to Mountjoy Gaol, across the river." He smiled at the waiter who had come to us, and ordered our tea.

In those early days I knew nothing about the "Cat and Mouse" act, by which suspects could be released and then arrested again, but I had heard about the Black and Tans. It was extraordinary how that nickname of theirs, applied first in derision, had now an entirely somber ring to it. It was startling to hear him say what he had said, in so casual a tone. He must have read my expression.

"Nothing happened," he said. "It was a busy evening for them. They held me for an hour or two and asked me rude questions and then put me with some other fellows and took us by lorry to Mountjoy. I was there for two weeks for 'spreading disaffection,' but the case was not pressed and I was released."

I had never before heard people speaking about jails and charges and releases and arrests, and certainly never by someone with Christopher's pleasant accent.

"You must not draw any conclusions from that," he said. "They mistreat prisoners, brutalize people, in the country they are savage indeed, they have burned down towns."

"That is what you do, is it not?" I said. "Tell the world how awful they are and how noble the rebels are?"

"Yes," he said, in a surprised tone, and suddenly he smiled at me. "Yes, I expect that is what I do. I have never put it to myself so crisply."

I cannot say that I fell in love with Christopher then, that afternoon, in the lounge of the Clarence Hotel, with the sunlight of late afternoon pouring in upon us, but I did know then, that afternoon, that I was drawn to him, as he was drawn to me. I knew it when he smiled a smile equally delighted by what I had said and how he had answered me. And it was true enough, what I had said, about Christopher and one or two others who managed the press for the Dáil, Sinn Féin, the rebels, however you chose to call them, the Irish Republican Army. But I did not know then of what else he did, that he was one of their intelligence people, which meant that he worked with Collins. That might have mattered, a bit, because I am certain that then, when first I felt myself attracted to him, an edge of danger was a bit of his attractiveness, that he had been arrested and might soon be again, and yet here we were having tea and cakes with the river and the Four Courts beyond the window, glinting in the sun.

We found ourselves looking at each other without speaking, and so I said, "He wrote poems, did he, this great-great-whatever grandfather of mine?"

"Who?"

"The Chevalier O'Gorman," I said, "who was killed at a place called Maestricht, and put words to a song about a blackbird."

"It is still sung in parts of Galway," he said. "Have you never heard it? 'The Blackbird.' The blackbird was the Stuart claimant."

"Jacobite," I said. "There is a small lake at Coolater, and when my sister Betty and I were children, we would go there, where Father kept a boat drawn up on the grasses, and play that we were Bonnie Prince Charlie and Flora MacDonald."

"Which were you?" he asked, and I said we took turns.

"You should always have been Charlie," he said. "Flora MacDonald was a brave young woman, but plain-featured, by all accounts."

Suddenly, frighteningly, from somewhere close at hand, there was a series of shots, a half-dozen of them at least and then, after a pause, two others. There were people at two of the other tables, a middle-aged couple and a party of four men with the look of solicitors or accountants, and we all looked at each other and then away from each other and when I looked back toward Christopher I realized that my hand was at my throat.

I don't know what I expected, men rushing past our window and then soldiers, a lorry of them, and more shooting and noise. But there was nothing, nothing at all. No one said a word, and then the waiter, who had drawn back against the wall, came forward, unsmiling and unhurried, to see if one of his tables was in need of tea. Then the footpath directly outside the window was filled with small children, a crowd of them, making the sounds of rifles going off and a few of them carrying sticks.

At last, Christopher said, "That is all it will be, most likely. Soldiers firing at our lads or else the other way round. There will be something about it in the morning papers, most likely, depending upon what paper you read."

I said nothing but sat looking at him, trying to read his eyes.

"It is not much of a war," he said, in mock apology. "Not like Flanders." Then, hearing what he had said, he reddened. "I am very sorry," he said, "that was thoughtless."

"It doesn't matter," I said, and shook my head. "Charlie wasn't killed in Flanders nor anywhere near it. A long time ago, four years."

"Yes," he said.

"Thank you for the book," I said, "I am glad for our tea that your book made possible for us. Will we see each other again?"

It was his turn to stare, and then he said, "You are a very direct young woman."

"How old are you?" I asked.

"Direct and more direct," he said, but he was over his shock and was smiling. "Twenty-eight."

"I am twenty-nine," I said, cutting a year from my age. "At my age I must favor directness. An older woman, a widow."

And that is how it began. Now it seems to me that the mark, the inscription of that day was not the sunlight falling upon our table nor beyond the window the river glittering in that light, people passing by, but that rattle of gunfire, distant from us and yet close at hand, closer than I could then have known.

John and Helen Ryan, with whom I had been staying in Merrion Square, were disapproving, not simply of the love affair after it had begun but of my seeing Christopher at all, although the two times when he called in for drinks we were all civil to each other. Helen spoke to me about it directly one evening, after Christopher had brought me back from the theater.

"John has asked around about Christopher, here and there," she said, "and it is known about him, he has been in prison and he is a gunman himself or at least he apologizes for them."

"Really?" I said. "That could be. I have never seen his gun." But this was not quite true. Once, in the flat in Fitzwilliam Square, I had passed his desk and there, in a drawer only half-closed, lay a revolver, dark and somber, but it did not startle me at all, at Coolater Betty and I had grown up close to guns. How odd that Christopher's flat in Fitzwilliam Square and John and Helen's in Merrion Square should be a ten-minute walk apart and yet they were in different worlds. John was something in Dublin Castle, in the under-secretary's office.

"They are called Castle Catholics," Christopher said, when I told him about Helen's warning. "People like John Ryan."

"I always thought that Castle Catholics were Catholics who had castles," I said. "Like us, like the O'Gormans." Not that Coolater was much of a castle, but rather a wretched modern version of one. "And I was presented at the Castle, you know. To the Viceroy."

"Yes," Christopher said, "I expect you were. James MacMahon, the under-secretary, is a Catholic. John Ryan is a member of his staff."

"I cannot imagine what they want, people like Christopher Blake," Helen had said to me that evening. "Things were rattling along quite nicely, all the old prejudices breaking down. Look at the country now—gunmen in the streets terrifying the people, soldiers in lorries, and the Black and Tans swaggering about, terrifying everyone."

"They want a republic," I said, and she echoed the word with derisive anger, as though I had said that what "people like Christopher Blake" wanted was a cageful of giraffes or whatever giraffes are kept in.

Two worlds were living side by side in Dublin in 1920, our world, the world of John and Helen and myself, and of Sir James MacMahon in Dublin Castle and Christmas pantomimes and tea at the Shelbourne and the Russell and the *Irish Times* at breakfast before John set off for the Castle, with "the Troubles," as everyone was now calling them, no more vivid and actual at times than the sentries at the Castle, the rolls of barbed wire, the armored cars in the Lower Castle Yard. And that other world in which Christopher lived and which, illogically, I associated with the midnight-to-five curfew, a world of gunmen moving upon deadly errands, waiting outside the house of a policeman in Phibsborough or Clontarf to shoot him as he came home, without warning, and of men in offices with the blinds pulled closed or in the back rooms of public houses. But some of that world lived in sunlight—great crowds of men and women on their knees, praying, at Mountjoy, during the hunger strikes, and the funerals through the city streets, from the church to Glasnevin, of Volunteers "killed in action," the coffins draped in the tricolored flag of green, white, and orange, and pallbearers, not in uniform of course but everyone knew who they were, Volunteers, Republican soldiers, black-suited, bareheaded, the next day there would be photographs in the newspapers, even the *Irish Times*. It was the side-by-sideness of the two worlds that seemed to be strangest of all, a member of the Dáil or perhaps a gunman known by reputation sitting in one row at the Olympia or the Royale, and two rows away perhaps a British officer or perhaps John and Helen and myself. Or Christopher accepting a drink from John in the room looking out upon Merrion Square, Irish whiskey, Jameson's as I recall, and a splash of soda.

But now my world was becoming more and more the world of

the flat whose windows looked out upon Fitzwilliam Square, although I knew that soon I would have to leave it, leave Dublin, to return to Coolater and Father and Betty and the small lake of Coolater. It was midsummer now, July, and I would walk there at night, after dinner, not bothering by then even to make excuses or explanation, although I knew that John and Helen were moving beyond disapproval to anger and it was not fair to them, a most respectable pair the two of them, and good friends. Sometimes Christopher would be waiting for me, but more often the flat would be empty and I would move from room to room, turning on lights and making tea, and then would settle down to read a book taken from the long, sagging shelves of them, books from Christopher's other life, in London, before 1916, when we might easily have met, but it would have meant nothing because there was Charlie then, but our tastes were very alike, and I would take down a book from the shelf and remember holding it in my hand in London, that very edition, color the same and the look of the page and its type and perhaps I could remember reading it in our flat, Charlie's and mine, or in Regent's Park.

If he was not there by nine, I would begin to worry, and, turning off the lights again, would stand by one of the two windows that fronted on the square, looking down upon gardens and small walkways behind the iron railings and the lovely houses of an earlier century darkening. Presently, he would walk toward me, along Fitzwilliam Street, walking swiftly past the few others abroad, in his gray suit most likely, mackintosh slung across his arm. We would have only a few hours because I was careful always to be back in Merrion Square before curfew, although once I spent the night and once we drove down for three days to a cottage in Wicklow which he had borrowed from a friend.

"It could be awkward for you," he said once in early days, "if you should be here and the police decided to come calling, or the Black and Tans."

"Awkward," I said, sleepily. I was in bed, and he was standing by the window, looking down into the rear garden. From where I lay, I could not see the garden, but I could see a full, vivid moon, and imagined its light touching the small, perfect pear tree and the flowers crowded beneath the wall. I was very happy. I could see Christopher faintly, half-turned from me.

"What do you do all those hours when I don't see you?" I said. "Or should I not ask?"

"It is very dull, most of it," he said. "I write accounts of our military actions, once in a great while I go out into the field to talk with our commanders, I talk with foreign journalists. Once in a very great while there will be something more exciting to do. Twice in the last month, we have had to move offices. Once we had ten minutes' notice, but the earlier time we had a bit more leisure. Our intelligence is very good, better than theirs. You should tell that to John Ryan. Tell him that he is on the wrong side."

"Poor John," I said, "a decent, respectable fellow. He was in school at Clongowes Wood, with Patrick Prentiss, did you know that?"

"I do mean it," he said, sharply. "He is on the wrong side. He is an Irishman, he should be with us."

"It isn't that simple, I expect," I said.

"Of course it is," Christopher said. "Whenever people want to avoid a decision, they say, 'It isn't that simple.' "

"John didn't say that," I said. "I did."

But then he turned away from the window, and I saw that he was smiling. "It doesn't matter," he said, "we can get along without John Ryan." And he came over from the window, sat on the edge of the bed, and took me up in his arms.

Much later, that time in Wicklow, in the cottage near Laragh, I said, "Did you really mean that, what you said to me once, that you—your crowd—could get along without people like John Ryan?"

He had been putting turf into the fireplace, but he paused and looked around at me. "Of course I meant it. And it is your crowd as well, you know. It is even John Ryan's, although he cannot realize it. We are fighting in this country for our existence as a people."

I was sitting curled up in a chair as I watched him, one of those scruffy kinds of chairs that make their way to weekend cottages.

Then, in a lighter tone, turning it to a pleasantry, he said, "Perhaps you should approach him for me. It would be quite a feather in my cap."

"I daresay it would," I said, "an official in Dublin Castle."

"We have them," he said, and stood up and dusted his hands. "We have our people in the Castle."

"Spies?" I said. "Spies in Dublin Castle? Sometimes it all seems like John Buchan."

"It's real enough," he said. "It's no shilling shocker."

"You don't really mean that, do you?" I said. "That I should approach John? Because I never could you know, not ever."

"No, of course I did not. John Ryan would never help us. It wouldn't be cricket. Did you know that they play cricket at Clongowes Wood?"

"Dreadful," I said. "Dreadful."

"But not everyone who works in the Castle went to Clongowes. The Special Branch operates out of the Castle, and those lads were bred in a tougher school. A few of them are looking ahead, preparing their futures."

"How patriotic of them," I said; "after independence they will be able to move from the old secret police to the new secret police."

"Exactly," Christopher said. "And wearing medals in recognition of their contributions to the national cause. As I say, our intelligence is good, better than theirs. But people like John Ryan are too proud to move with the times, they have been recruited to serve the Empire, and they cannot believe that the Empire will ever fail. It will, though. It will fail here, right here, in this country."

"People like John Ryan and my father," I said. "And Charlie," I wanted to add but did not. He did not reply, but instead knelt again to light the fire.

"It is always chill enough for a fire at night in these hills," I said.

But those three nights we had for ourselves and the chill did not matter any more than politics and history and gunmen and Dublin Castle, and upon two of those nights, after we had both fallen asleep, I would wake up and not be able to return to sleep, and would sit bolt upright in bed, to think about Christopher and about Christopher and myself and about love and about men and about what was to become of us, and when.

Now, when I looked at Christopher I could not remember how it had been, weeks before only, when we had talked together as strangers or when we had tea at the hotel on the quays, but of course it wasn't as if we had known each other always, as the popular songs would have it. His body was still strange to me, and exciting in its strangeness, as I expect mine was to him. And thinking that at night, when I was awake in the darkness, I would move my hand across his body, feeling the skin which was always a bit less strange after each of our couplings, touching his hair, moving my hand across his cheeks and his throat and then down the length of his body. Once he woke up.

I had not known many men other than Charlie. There had been Patrick before the war, before Charlie, and then after Charlie died, there had been two brief times in London, of which I had decided that one of them had been foolish indeed, a way of working something out, of saying goodbye to Charlie, that he was truly gone, but the other one had been very great fun indeed and the most fun of all was knowing that it was for only a time. I had not begun it with that knowledge but I had come to know it quickly enough, and of course where we come to know such things, in bed, one night as I had turned toward him, and I knew from the way he was looking at me that for him this was not serious at all, I just knew fully and accurately, and for a moment I felt both angry and full of shame and guilty about Charlie, and then I thought, what the hell, and for another month we had a marvelous time of it, better than ever it had been with Charlie although I could not bring myself then to admit that. But it was different now, because Christopher and I loved each other. Charlie and I had come slowly into love, over the better part of a year, deepening week by week, night by night, by everything we saw and heard and did together, music and paintings and trees and lovemaking. But Christopher and I had burst upon each other like freshets. Woke up, and took me into his arms as easily and fiercely and as softly as if we had been always in bed waiting for each other.

He never liked to watch me dress when I would get up to make certain that I was back in Merrion Square long before the curfew. The very idea of curfew frightened me a bit, not of anything that might happen, but the idea of the forbidden, and I would imagine the empty wide streets with nothing abroad in them save foot patrols and armored cars and gunmen. But once, when I was beginning to dress, as I sat on the side of the bed drawing on a stocking, he reached out and pulled me down toward him and kissed me with our bodies stretched together. There was a small lamp on the table that we kept burning and we saw each other clearly. We had a way of falling in love with each other over and over again, and I would look into his eyes and feel dizzy, drunk, and I would reach out toward his eyes, which had become soft and unfocused with passion, and I knew that we had never been in love before, either of us, with anyone. That is what all lovers believe, that is what love is. We would talk about marriage.

It was different, those three nights that we had in Wicklow, in the cottage outside Laragh, when we could sleep the night through and wake up to morning light. Beyond the bright-painted sill of the window, we could see hills, the dark green hills of summer with the wide far stretch of bogland upon them and blue sky. "Listen," I said, "a curlew." "A curlew," he said, with his hand resting lightly upon my breast, with the ease that comes quickly to lovers, "the poets of this country would be lost without it," and he said a poem in Gaelic and then said it again in English, and it was not Wicklow at all that I heard but my own Galway, its wide skies and far mountains with wind upon them. "Whose poem is that," I asked him, "is that your poem?" "No," he said, "not at all, I haven't written poems since I was a boy and they were all of them awful. This was by a friend of mine, of mine and of Patrick Prentiss's in fact." "It is lovely," I said, "it sounds like Galway, he grew up in Connaught, this friend of yours, I am certain of that." But he did not. He came from the midlands, Christopher said, and he was a lecturer in the university in Dublin. *Was?* I asked. "Was," Christopher said. "He was executed in 1916." And for a moment it seemed that the war had followed us from Dublin, striding along after us in long boots. But Christopher kissed me just then, and poetry and guns alike were held far away from us. It was lovely making love in the morning, in lazy morning light.

Only last year, ten years or more after our "Troubles," a young man came to me from the university who is writing a book on "the revolution" as he calls it, Patrick had sent him to me, who said that he had heard from Patrick that I could talk to him about Christopher Blake. He was nervous, of course, because many, many people know about Christopher and myself. It is not the sort of thing that gets itself into books, but people talk, people in Ireland talk. *Our Struggle for Freedom,* he said he plans to call the book, and I said, "What a dreadful title." I am acquiring a reputation as someone who says dreadful things, and he smiled politely. "What was he like?" he asked. "What was Christopher Blake like?" I smiled at him, and said, "I don't know. Ask someone else. Ask Patrick. Many people knew Christopher."

"There is a photograph of him," the young man said, this young man named Eamonn Hennessy said, "a photograph taken during the Truce, on Dawson Street outside the Mansion House, himself and Collins and old Count Plunkett and one or two others. Cathal Brugha, Harry Boland." He said that he had brought it with him, in case I wanted to see it, but I shook my head. I may not have seen that one, but I had seen others like it. They are in the books that are beginning to appear now.

"I did not know the man in those photographs," I said. There is one that I do remember, taken also at the time of the Truce, which shows Christopher and Collins and Mulcahy, a newspaper photograph, striding along a city street, Christopher bareheaded, his hair wind-ruffled, and Collins's face shadowed by a wide-brimmed hat. It was not a clever thing I had said, but the simple truth, I did not know the public man who did whatever things it was that Christopher did in the revolution, nor during the Treaty negotiations, nor in the Troubles that followed, when he was a cabinet minister. I never knew the people whom he worked with, not Collins nor De Valera nor Mulcahy nor Lacy nor O'Malley nor any of them. I only knew Christopher. I knew him in Dublin and then for days in Wicklow and then in London and then in Galway at Coolater and then, finally, I knew him in Connemara, in the cottage on the strand.

"They are all still there for you to talk to," I said, but of course that was not true, because Collins was dead and Boland and Lacy. And Christopher. "Yes, of course they are," he said. "It is difficult talking with them. So much has happened between them. Bad blood." Christopher's blood, some of it, Christopher's and Collins's and Boland's and Lacy's and Cathal Brugha's. So much bad blood. "Christopher Blake seems to have been different from them, from most of the others. A bit more—more reflective. That book he wrote, and the one that he had put aside. He stood apart from them, it seems to me," Eamonn Hennessy said.

"I don't know about that," I said, although I knew what he meant. "I don't know. I know that he admired Collins immensely.

And that he and Rory O'Connor were friends, until they all had their falling-out."

"Falling-out," he said; "most people call it the Civil War."

"Civil War, revolution," I said, "grand names given to things, to blood." I could see that Eamonn Hennessy was one of those who gave things their grand names. "My relationship with Christopher was entirely personal," I said, "surely Patrick Prentiss told you that. I cannot imagine why he sent you to me." "But of course," he said awkwardly, "at the end, at the very end of the—" "Of the affair," I said, "yes, there was history mixed up with that."

I remember the day, about two weeks before I had planned to return to Coolater, when Christopher went on the run. I was walking toward Fitzwilliam on a clear, lovely evening in early August. It had been warm all day, too warm almost, and Grafton Street had earlier been filled with shoppers in their summer frocks and the men in hats of cream-colored straw. At the corner of Grafton and Chatham streets, there had been two soldiers standing, on duty of some kind, because they carried rifles. But now it was evening and the air had cooled; there was a breeze coming down from the mountains. Suddenly Christopher's young man was walking beside me, too warm now for his trench coat, but wearing a dark suit and a gray felt hat shoved up away from his clear-eyed face with its dusting of freckles.

"You'll have to meet in a different place, Mrs. Nugent. Captain Blake's place is being watched."

We had reached Baggot Street now, and there was noise coming from the big public house at the corner.

"Where?" I said. "Will you take me to it?"

"I will," he said, "myself or someone else. But not tonight. We have to be cautious. You may be followed yourself, you see."

And so the next day at five, as we had arranged, I was in Bewley's teashop on Grafton Street, and took a table by myself upstairs, near one of the windows that looked out upon the street, ordered tea, and began to read the book I had brought with me. And it was fortunate that I had, because it was a good half-hour before I was joined by a young lady, in a blue, light linen frock and straw hat. I thought at first that she was simply a customer but before I could speak, she said, "I am the one you've been waiting for. I will have some tea." I set aside my book to look at her. She was pretty, with fair, close-curling hair beneath the straw and wide-open blue eyes, her mouth full and unsmiling. I motioned to the waitress. "You have not been followed," she said, "I made certain of that." Her tone kept a distance between us. "My name is Janice Nugent," I said, and would have extended my hand to her, but she shook her head. "We are old friends," she said, "chums. Meeting for tea, as we often do." She put her purse on the table, and said, "My name is Elizabeth Keating," and then looked around the room, at the tables of shoppers and office workers and accountants. She looked down into the street, while the elderly waitress put the tea before her. "It is very warm," she said to the waitress. "Tropical," she answered, "tropical. We could be in Africa."

"Can you tell me anything?" I asked her, when the waitress was out of hearing, but she shook her head and then relented a little. "We got word yesterday morning that they would be taking Christopher in. It might have been for questioning only, but we could not take the chance." "No," I said, "of course not," and with a lover's pride, I said, "He's important, is he not?" She had been without expression, but now she darted me a look of sharp, fierce dislike. "Everyone working with us is important," she said.

"Yes," I said, and would have let it rest there. I have never liked expressions of political virtue, of any sort, and I was anxious to get to Christopher. "You may not accept the fact, Mrs. Nugent, but we are at war." "Yes," I said again, "of course." "If my own opinion had been asked," she said, "I would have said that the safety of our fighting men should not be put in danger for the sake of a social visit." "How fortunate," I said, "that your opinion was not asked for."

"And especially," she said, "the widow of a British officer, who is staying with an official at Dublin Castle." "And I know so little about you," I said.

She seemed to enjoy her tea, and when she was done with it, we walked to Suffolk Street and took a Number 10 bus to Nelson's Pillar, and then a short walk brought us to Parnell Square, as now it is called, and down a side street to a building whose ground floor was occupied by a tailor's shop. At the door beside the shop, she said, "The fellow you are looking for is on the top floor. He will be expecting you." She turned round then and left me, without saying goodbye. The stairs were clean, they had recently been swept down, but the paint had worn off them, and the walls, of a dirty creamy white, were peeling in long flakes. On the third floor a young fellow sat keeping watch, about the age of Christopher's watcher or bodyguard or whatever, but short and overweight. He glanced up at me, heavy-lidded, and then returned to a book.

But I was to know a bit more about Elizabeth Keating, none of it of a sort to make her more appealing to me, although I came to marvel at her energy and her resourcefulness. We met a half-dozen more times, and each time I would discover something about her that I had not seen before. That she had a lovely figure for example and was well aware of it. I remarked upon that when I saw her in the safe house in Delgany where she had a half-dozen young women working under her direction, folding copies of the *Republican Bulletin* and making them up into bundles and tying them. She walked over to the window, and stood, in profile to me, looking out across fields toward the distant hills. Seen thus, her face had a cameo's clarity and grace of outline; she was wearing a shirtwaist of peach-colored silk, beneath which her small breasts were firm against the afternoon sun. When she became aware that I had been looking toward her, she turned away, back into the room, but not before a moment's pause within which she was aware of what I had been thinking.

But that was later. That afternoon, Christopher must have heard my step upon the stairs because he was holding open for me the door into what looked a quite ordinary office sort of room, with two desks, papers scattered across both of them, and against one wall a long table upon which papers were not scattered but rather had been piled neatly, row upon row. Above the table hung one of the 1916 posters you now saw everywhere, which the police and the soldiers, unless drunk, did not bother to tear down.

There were two chairs, but I walked past both of them, and stood looking out the window. The garden below was untended and overgrown.

"It isn't very comfortable, I'm afraid," Christopher said. "I can offer you tea."

"I have had tea," I said, "at Bewley's with your Miss Keating."

"Elizabeth," he said. "Elizabeth Keating."

"She must be great fun," I said, "when you get to know her."

"No," he said, "I doubt if she is. What I know of her is that she has courage and brains, and that she can be depended upon to take orders."

"Even foolish ones," I said, "even an order to bring a British widow here to your headquarters."

"Our headquarters!" Christopher said. "We're not that badly off. This is where I've been editing the *Bulletin,* where I've been spending some of my hours, waiting until I could see you."

I turned away from the window then. He was half-smiling, as I knew he would be, because he was using that mock-serious tone which sometimes I liked but not always. I did not like it now.

"What does that mean, really?" I said. "To be on the run? What does it mean for you?"

"They have been keeping me on a long string," Christopher said, "and they've decided to pull me in. Because of the *Bulletin,* most likely, but in the past it has shielded me. I am friendly with the foreign journalists, the French ones and the Americans."

But that was not the reason. As he knew, of course, it was because they had at last connected him with the intelligence work that he had been doing for Collins. He was to tell me that, but only later.

"What will happen to you if you are arrested?" I asked.

"What will happen! I'll be put in jail, of course. It's not bad, really. I have friends in Mountjoy, it wouldn't be lonely. But I will take good care not to be arrested."

"Elizabeth Keating will be watching over you, no doubt."

"Among others. You need not be jealous of Elizabeth. Her affections, as they say, lie elsewhere."

"With Ireland," I said, relieved and trying to keep irony from my tone.

"Elizabeth was in the Post Office in 1916," Christopher said. "She was one of Pearse's couriers. Later, at the end, she carried the final order out to O'Riordan at the South Union."

There would come times, in the year ahead, when I would hate those photographs—Pearse with the dreamy abstracted look of a crank, Tom Clarke a befuddled old conspirator, and the others. It was as though they had found ways of reaching out from the grave.

"And us," I said, "what will happen to us?"

"Why, nothing, Janice. Nothing at all will happen to us." Until that moment we had been standing apart, but now he walked quickly toward me, and put his hand on my arm. "We shall be able to see very little of each other for a while, I am afraid, but only for a while."

"I am going back to Coolater," I said, "to Father and Betty."

"Yes," he said. "You see? We would be separated in any event, but only for a while. Someday I will be visiting you in Coolater. Exchanging war stories with your father."

It was only then that I realized that Christopher and I had loved each other, were loving each other without context for our love of any kind. Now we were saying goodbye in this vile room with its view of a scrubby back garden.

"What will become of you?" I asked. "Where will you live?"

"Oh," he said, shrugging, "here and there. No shortage of beds. There are hundreds of us on the run, you know, but none of us lack for beds."

"Yes," I said, "the country is at war. Elizabeth Keating is a mine of information."

He laughed outright at that and took me in his arms and we kissed. I felt his hardening body pressing against me. And as we kissed, before we drew away from each other, I thought, with a shock, half an angry shock, He is enjoying this. He has been forced onto the run, like Irish rebels in the days of Robert Emmet and those people, and he will be sleeping one night in this house and one night in that, and on the table by the bed will be the revolver which I had seen in his flat. He will have a bed one night somewhere in a suburb and another night somewhere in the Liberties and the third night he will be in the country somewhere, and he will like that best of all.

He will like that best of all, I thought again, as I sat in the cab that I had found at the rank in Sackville Street—O'Connell Street, we are now to call it. He will like that best of all, a farmhouse in the countryside, with a view toward mountains, and a chance perhaps to use the revolver. Halfway down the street, we passed the Post Office, which was by now half-rebuilt, people going in and coming out, as though nothing had happened there, but much of the street was still in ruins.

I left on the morning train for Coolater, and my goodbyes with the Ryans were stiff and awkward. John offered to drive me to the station, but I said no, that a cab would do perfectly well, and he said, "Well," and the three of us stood awkwardly in the front hall until it came round for me.

"The police have orders to bring Blake in," John said, "but of course you know that."

"First they must find him," I said.

"And that could be difficult," he said, and gave me a smile. Helen put a hand on my arm. They are quite sweet, really, I thought. "He seems a decent fellow," John said, and Helen echoed him, "We liked him, Janice."

"But he's in with a bad lot," John broke out. "I'm sorry. A bad lot. Last night another policeman was shot dead as he walked home to his family."

"I know nothing about that," I said, "about any of that sort of thing."

"Of course not," Helen said, and as she spoke we could hear the cab outside, mercifully.

"He knows about it," John said, "that is his job, to apologize for them, apologize for murder."

"John," Helen said.

John opened the door to the cabman's knock, and then saw me to the cab and opened its door for me.

Early on in my visit, the Ryans had showed me in their album a photograph taken by a street photographer that April just before the war when they had visited us in London. The four of us are standing, arms linked, and laughing, outside Saint Paul's, only six years before, and yet it seemed to me a picture preserved out of some earlier world, the four of us looking not happy merely, but absurdly young. Charlie has just grown his mustache and is touching it absently, and smiling at Helen. Everything else, everything other than the four of us, looks absolutely forever, like the great dome of the cathedral.

"Kingsbridge," John said to the driver, and then leaned into the window. I thought he was going to kiss me, but he said, "Our love to Betty and to your father. We are very fond of you, Janice." "Yes," I said, "yes, I know." And because I knew that he would not, I kissed him, lightly, on the lips. That is the last time I saw John. I saw Helen again, but only once. We never visit, of course, even after this long a time.

"Kingsbridge," the driver said when we were in Clanbrassil

Street. "Have you heard what happened last night, outside Harcourt Street station? A policeman was shot there and killed. On his way home."

"Yes," I said, and wondered, for a moment, how John had heard. At the corner of Kevin Street, he put on his brakes in haste, to let a lorry of soldiers rush past us. We said nothing about it, either of us.

"It is grand weather to be going down the country," he said, when we were close to Kingsbridge. "This is the very best of the summer." And so it was. Along Thomas Street, children were playing, girls at skip-rope, and boys playing cowboys and Indians, or more likely Shinners and Tommies. A boy ran from a hallway into a fusillade of bangs shouted by his chums, and he flung up his hands in a theatrical manner and shouted, "Up de rebels," before slumping to the pavement. "Begod," the driver said, "they are at it early enough." "Early enough," I said. It was on an April day in 1916 (the twenty-fourth) that Charlie and the other Dublin and Munster Fusiliers attacked the beach at Gallipoli, near a village called Sedd el Bahr, and it was on that same day, so Patrick Prentiss once told me, that other Dublin Fusiliers near a French mining village named Hulluch, parts of the Sixteenth Irish Division, were attacked by poison gas. And on the twenty-fourth, on that very day, the rebels and Christopher among them occupied the GPO and declared their Republic. Bang bang, men playing at death in Flanders and Gallipoli and Dublin, where the GPO was being rebuilt while gunmen and soldiers were shooting at each other, shooting at policemen. "It's better to die 'neath an Irish sky," the ballad says, "than at Suvla or Sedd el Bahr." Perhaps it is. Now Charlie was dead and Patrick went about with an empty sleeve stuck into his pocket and Christopher was in a shabby room off Rutland Square—now we call it Parnell Square—guarded by an armed boy.

Sometimes, I thought, as the train moved out from Kingsbridge to cross the landscape of heartbreaking beauty to Galway, sometimes in London in those first lonely months, I would wake up and go into the drawing room to pour myself a whiskey and would sit drinking it neat, listening to the night noises of the city. He did not die on the beach, I had been told, but drowned in the waters of the bay, and I would imagine him washed forwards and back forwards and back, a bay ended by sands of a white, blazing purity and the waters so clear that on the floor of the bay could be seen pebbles washed smooth. He would be lying facedown. There would be a little blood, a curl of red blood in the water.

There were no soldiers in the train. They had their own trains now, and the lorries to carry them across the countryside.

VII

DUBLIN, LONDON, 1920

At ten-thirty at night, on June 9, 1920, as he was walking on Northumberland Road, about one hundred feet from his house, Sergeant Michael Casey, of the G Division of the Dublin Metropolitan Police, was shot dead. He had spent the evening at work in the Brunswick Street headquarters of the division, where he served as a liaison between itself and the political branch in Dublin Castle, and he was entitled to be driven to his home. But it was a pleasant night of early summer, and so he walked, on his own—a tall, well-built man, as were all members of the DMP, well liked and respected by his colleagues, silver-haired by now, a broad, confident face.

His assassins had been waiting for him at the Pembroke Street turning, three of them. They waited until he had passed them, and then one of the three called out, "Casey, turn round, 'tis all over for you." He had half-turned round and was fumbling for his shoulder-holstered gun when the first bullet caught him, at the shoulder, smashing his hand, and was then deflected by the weapon to his clavicle. The second bullet grazed his back, but the third caught him in the side, smashed through both lungs, and buried itself in muscle and bone. He sank to his knees, and his screams were blood-drenched. The gunman in command of the detachment ran over to him, bent, and fired a shot into his skull. Then, while the other two stood guard, he quickly patted the dead man's pockets, taking out a wallet, a notebook, and a sheaf of papers. Then, having looked up and nodded, he reached inside Casey's coat and pulled out the revolver. It was blood-smeared, and the grip had been smashed by the bullet, but he put it in his pocket. The three gunmen looked round. Nothing was moving, there were no sounds along the road nor down Pembroke Road. They separated then.

But from the time that the three men had moved toward Casey, people had been watching from behind lace-curtained windows in the quiet, middle-class street, and two telephone calls had been placed to the police. After the gunmen had left, a half-dozen people ran out toward the body, stretched in its gore upon the pavement, and one of these was Theresa Casey. She knelt beside the body and began to scream, and continued screaming after a neighbor had put his arms round her heaving shoulders.

The leader of the Squad, Dermot Hatchey, was twenty-three, and this was the fourth such task that he had carried out since he had been recruited a year before from the ranks of the Volunteers. He was wearing a cloth cap and a fawn-colored mackintosh. He walked along Northumberland Road, and then Mount Street to Westland Row, and as he walked, his hand, buried in the pocket of the mackintosh, fingered the beads of his rosary. Like Sergeant Casey, he was deeply religious, a weekly and at times a daily communicant, and as he walked, in the clear Dublin June night, with a faint light still upon the streets, he prayed for the two of them, for himself and Sergeant Casey, whom he knew by reputation and by a few glimpses upon streets of the city, glimpses so full that he had recognized him at once.

In Westland Row, with the dark forms of the railway station and the church before him, he turned sharply, rapped on a door beside a shop, climbed a flight of steep stairs, and was admitted to a shabbily furnished flat, where a man youthful but balding sat behind a table. Two young fellows sitting together by a window that faced the street talked and joked.

Standing before the table, Hatchey made a brief, sketchy salute and then nodded. " 'Tis done," he said.

"You are certain of that, are you?" asked the young, balding man, Commandant Tom Fleming.

"Oh yes," Hatchey said, and hoped that he would not be pressed for details. He remembered firing into Casey's skull, the shattering sound in the quiet street, the explosion of bone, blood and matter, lurid in the light of the streetlamp. He did not like to think about blood growing sticky on the damaged revolver in his pocket, which he would hand in to the armorer in Talbot Street, a wizard in the repair of weapons. Now he took out the wallet, the notebook, the papers, and placed them on the table. Fleming glanced at them without reading them. "There is tea in the kitchen," he said, "and the most of a naggin of whiskey as well. Help yourself to a drink if you'd like."

"If it is all the same, Commandant, I will not. I have a hard day's work before me." He was a clerk in a large company of carters and haulers.

When Hatchey's hand was on the door handle, Fleming called out to him, "It will be all right, Dermot. Take care of yourself now. Get yourself some sleep. How are the other lads?" But Hatchey, as though he had not heard him, nodded and left.

Once, a half-year earlier, before Collins had placed him in command of the Squad, when they had begun the business of shooting G-men, Fleming had had such an assignment. With another Volunteer, Peader Mulvey, he had waited outside the cinema at the top of Grafton Street for a G-man named Sam Anderson, who had been on his day off, watching the afternoon showing of D. W. Griffith's *Broken Blossoms*. As Anderson, with the other patrons, came out into a street filled with gritty sunlight, Fleming and the other gunman cut loose. Anderson was hit twice, one bullet shattered his arm, the other nicked his lung. All the other bullets went astray, and one of them shattered the thigh of a thirteen-year-old girl named Nora Hanly. Collins was furious. He found a sum of money for the Hanly family, who lived in a slum off Cuffe Street, the father a casual laborer who had served in the British Army. He waited five weeks, and then had Fleming finish off what he had begun, shooting Anderson dead as he left the Jervis Street Hospital, leaning on a stick and accompanied by his wife.

Now it was Fleming's task to send out fellows like Hatchey, upon Collins's orders, fellows whom he thought of as very young, although in fact he was himself only twenty-six. The week before, he had scouted Northumberland Road and Casey's house, and tonight, as he waited for Hatchey to report, he had seen in vivid reverie what would happen, what was happening, a tall, confident man, swinging along with the unmistakable stride of the DMP, and then seeing Hatchey and the other lads dashing forward out of darkness, and then Casey lying dead in his blood, and Hatchey hurrying here through the darkened streets, a wary eye out for patrols, his soul darkened and sickened by what he had done.

At last, Fleming began to read the papers and the notebook, which in the morning he would hand over to Intelligence. What he read made little sense to him, but was not, strictly speaking, his concern. The papers seemed to be roster sheets, but he could not recognize any of the names, although he had by heart the names of members of the G Division. The notebook was a different matter—scribbles in fountain pen or blunt pencil, difficult to decipher because of awkward penmanship and abbreviations beyond the stilted language of reports by policemen—"subject held under scrutiny," "desperate Shinner," "subject's place of employment." Tomorrow all of that would be interpreted without difficulty: to Fleming's knowledge, five members of the DMP were Collins's agents, two of them members of the G squad itself, and Fleming had no doubt that there were others. Toward the back of the notebook, as the entries became more recent, names started to appear which he did recognize.

By the next afternoon, papers and notebook had come to Christopher Blake, not in the rooms off Parnell Square from which he edited the *Bulletin,* but rather in a room off Dame Street, almost within shouting distance of Dublin Castle, in which he conducted far more dangerous work as an intelligence officer. He set aside the notebook, without bothering to interpret it: that evening, when Dave Shelley had finished his duties at the Castle, he could attend to that. The sheets of paper with names and symbols upon them interested him more, but no more than Fleming did he recognize the names. They seemed more English than Irish—Huntley, Taylor, Carver, Salmon. But then, you never knew about names. What could be more English-sounding than "Shelley," but it was an old Skibbereen family, and no one more Irish than Sergeant Dave Shelley of the G Division of the Dublin Metropolitan Police.

"I will tell you what that damned fool Casey did," Shelley said that evening, fingering the notebook. "He brought papers home with him from the Castle. Strictly against regulations, need I say. This book isn't important. Rough notes, which later he would write up neatly. We all do that. There isn't much in them, but we should tell Rory O'Connor and Bill Lynch to keep a sharp lookout, Casey's lads have them under round-the-clock watch. But this thing, the other thing, is a real puzzler."

He shook the typed sheets indignantly, as though their unintelligibility was a reproof. "I declare to God, Chris, I can't put a name to it, not that every detective in the G Division knows everything that's going on, but I would have sworn that I had access to anything that Mick Casey had access to."

As Blake had reason to know, for it was a warning from Dave Shelley that had put him on the run himself, and it had been a warning, a week before, that Casey knew more than was good for him that had sent out Fleming and the Squad to kill him.

"Look there at those markings against the names," Shelley said. "What the hell are they supposed to be, secret signs of the Masons or some such rubbish?"

"Not that bad," Blake said, "not quite. They are letters in the Greek alphabet—sigma and delta and theta and the rest of it." As he spoke, he saw himself in a university lecture hall, half-asleep, but the other half of his mind saw the coast of Greece, bright sun, gnarled olive trees.

"Whatever it is," Shelley said, "it should not have been on his person, he should not have been taking it home with him. Things are getting very lax at the Castle."

In Shelley, as in the two other G-men who reported to Blake, there was a fascinating division of loyalties, of which the men seemed unaware. Once, so Blake had gathered from scattered conversations over the past year and from the intense interrogation which he and Collins had conducted at the outset, once there had been a young Dave Shelley up from Kerry, tall and rawboned in the Kerry manner, confident and yet shy in the manner of tall strong young fellows from Kerry, the very stuff from which members of the Dublin Metropolitan Police were made. Nothing in the service of those early years had disturbed a patriotism rooted not in newspapers and meetings but deep within Kerry fields, salt winds from the Atlantic, networks of family, alliances, friendships flung across fields and hills. Weighed and measured in Dublin Castle, drilled and marched on the barrack square, hours spent studying the Police Manual, swimming lessons at the Iveagh Baths, point duty splendid in the DMP uniform, waterproofs, capes of black wool, padded tunics, night duty, ten at night to six in the morning, heavy boots sounding upon deserted streets. Monthly kit inspections, annual examinations for promotion.

A single man, Shelley had lived in barracks, but with marriage had moved to a small house in Clontarf. His wife had been a maidservant in a house in Leeson Street, from the country like himself, but from County Longford in the midlands. The G Division, when he was recruited for it, gave him a bit more pay, got him out of uniform, got him out of night duty. He was issued a .38 automatic, and housed at first in Brunswick Street, and then, when things got hot, in the Castle itself. Inside the Lower Yard of the Castle, by late 1919, were crammed the headquarters of both the DMP and the RIC, the army's Dublin Command, the telephone exchange, the house of the chief superintendent. Later, the Auxiliaries kept a company inside the Lower Gate. By mid-1920, many of the officials were living there. G Division had a messroom of its own, bedrooms. An inspector was in charge of them.

"By God," Shelley said one night to Blake, " 'tis like some fort in Timbuktu or Peshawar. The deputy commissioner has taken to wearing a steel vest under his shirt."

"He is a sensible man," Blake said. The deputy commissioner's predecessor, a Belfast man named Redmond, had been shot dead outside the Standard Hotel in Harcourt Street on the twenty-first of January, by Daly, a member of Collins's personal Squad.

"It is a disgrace, the demoralization of the G Division," Shelley said, without, so far as Blake could tell, a hint of irony.

At first, in 1910 and '11 and '12, it had seemed little different from the kinds of work done by detectives in the ordinary criminal division, more pleasant, indeed, for it was mostly a matter of keeping files in order and updated—the handful of old Irish Republican Brotherhood veterans reliving the ancient glories of *Erin's Hope* and the attack on the police barracks at Kilpeder and the running gun battle up into Clonbrony Wood. Even the sporadic violence of the Land War had by the turn of the century died away into the occasional assault upon the cattle of a rich grazier in some remote county, which was plainly the work not of a conspiracy, but of a few disgruntled small farmers or drunken, boastful agricultural laborers, lads of the sort that Shelley knew well. To keep the files supplied with notes set down in fresh ink, the speculation was kept alive that membership of the Irish Republican Brotherhood included such men as John Dillon, whom age had shaped into a conservative, law-abiding member of Parliament. From time to time, a member of the American wing of the Brotherhood, the Clan na Gael, would arrive from Manhattan or Yonkers or Pittsburgh to confer with the veterans, and one of the G-men, Shelley perhaps, would have the task of following him from his hotel to his various meetings and then to the hotel lounge, where the Yank would regale his chums with tales of derring-do in the old days, and reports of the growing impatience of the Clan na Gael for some action to help the "dear old country."

Beyond Dublin, such matters were handled by Crimes Special of the Royal Irish Constabulary. When, for example, Peter Falvey or another of Devoy's people went down to Limerick to visit Daly, the old Fenian, before sailing back to New York from Queenstown, the tracking would pass to them. Occasionally, after hours, Shelley would relax with one of his opposites in Kidd's Tavern off Nassau Street, or the bar of the North Star.

"I declare to God," he would say, "you should hear the Yank accent on Peter Falvey, 'tis his first trip here since he was a lad, a builder's helper in a place called Passaic in New Jersey. And Devoy sends him over to tell the Irish people what they should do for 'dear old Ireland,' as the Yanks always call it."

And if his opposite was Hanratty, a Limerick man himself, a tenant farmer's son from Bruree, "Old John Daly, sure he's not the worst, but he lives in the past, they all do. That day is past, not but what there hadn't been great lads in it."

When Tom Clarke arrived in Ireland from America with his wife and settled down as a newsagent and tobacconist at 75A Great Britain Street, he was placed on both lists—RIC Crimes Special and DMP G Division—because he was married to Daly's niece, and because he had contrived a commission as agent for Everard's odious-tasting and -smelling Irish tobacco, which gave him an excuse for traveling, but his name was telegraphed from place to place. He was on the B list of suspects, but Daugherty, the under-secretary, was not greatly concerned—"A pair of old jailbirds, terrorists, toothless tigers," Daugherty said, and both Hanratty and Shelley were impressed by this cool professionalism.

"There you are, you see," Hanratty said, "Mr. Daugherty was

in the police, out there in India. The lads who run the Empire know what they are about."

And as it was with Daly and Clarke, so would it be when, a few years later, a different sort of young fellow began using Clarke's shop as a kind of club, not the usual clerks and laborers with the look of obscurity on them, capped or bowlered, but handsome Gaelic League fellows like Sean MacDermott, still holding himself like the athlete he had been before the polio of a few years before, Bulmer Hobson, a round-faced, yellow-haired Protestant of all things from Belfast of all places, Frank Lacy, the son of an editor in Kilkenny, Home Rule stock.

Shelley had made a point of calling in himself for an evening paper from time to time or a tin of tobacco. He and Clarke would exchange brief, mild pleasantries, customer and shopkeeper, and Shelley, eyes mild as he tamped down new-purchased tobacco into his pipe, would eye Clarke with deceptive casualness, so he hoped, a gaunt, balding man, plates of false teeth, a thick long mustache of smoke-tinged gray, polite and distant, but this had been the man who was second-in-command at the time of the London bombings in the eighties, second-in-command to the hardest case of them all, Ned Nolan of Clonbrony Wood, and after the dynamiting long years in Chatsworth Prison, never breaking, never giving up his real name to the warders, arrested, tried and convicted as "H. H. Wilson," years in solitary confinement, chained. And twice, in the shop, for a moment, behind mild shopkeeper's manner, heavy-hedged defending mustache, Shelley had glimpsed not old Tom Clarke, but H. H. Wilson, gunman, terrorist, dynamiter, as, at the zoo, you will catch the tiger's eye, and think that *he* is stalking you, and then remember that thick bars hold him encaged.

"A vivid moment that must have been," Daugherty said, when Shelley, standing stiffly before his desk in the Castle, had ventured to report it to him. "Yes, vivid." Daugherty had never imagined Shelley to be capable of such a poetic if lurid flight of fancy. "A tiger behind bars, stalking us, as it were. Well, of course, it should remind us to keep on our toes. Fellows like Clarke are a rum lot, toothless or not. They have some bad marks against their names, as we both know, Sergeant. They bear watching," Daugherty said, "the old fellows, and some in this newer lot, the Sinn Féiners and the Gaelic Leaguers, and the boyos in the Gaelic Athletic Association. Tigers, eh? Tame tigers. But we'll have them in our drawing rooms, if some of this lot have their way." He nodded across the distances of Dublin Castle, through brick and stone, across cobbled courtyards, to the apartments of the chief secretary. "Our present lords and masters believe that Irish disaffection can be killed by kindness. That is their phrase, Shelley. 'Killed by kindness.' I saw my share of tigers killed in my India years, but never by kindness, eh Shelley?"

" 'The tiger never changes his stripes,' isn't that what they say out there in India?" Shelley had never encountered Daugherty in this unbuttoned mood, and he relished it.

"Or words to that effect," Daugherty said. "Sit down a moment, Sergeant, you're not on point duty now, padded tunic and thick boots and all the rest of it. We are in the same service the two of us, good decent Irishmen doing our best to keep the old Empire going for a few more years." "Yes, sir," Shelley said, as he placed himself gingerly, on an edge of the straight-backed chair that faced the desk. "Have the tigers in our drawing rooms," Daugherty had said, and Shelley had thought of the small, seldom-used front room in the house in Clontarf, the table of black walnut with the statue of Our Savior on it, a long forefinger resting against an exposed, bleeding Heart, the plaster painted a bright scarlet. And on the wall facing it, a large photograph, tinted, framed, behind glass, of the Gap of Dunloe in Killarney.

The reports which Shelley had filed in those years, his observations of men in public houses and on obscure platforms with banners and buntings of emerald-green with gilt lettering, "Ireland a Nation," had been harmless stuff. Somewhere, somehow, dimly perceived and massive, old Ireland lumbered along toward something called Home Rule, and was lumbering there without help from the Fenians and the Separatists and the Socialists and Gaelic Revivalists and the rest of the crackpots. At Mass on Sunday, in the Clontarf church, and in all the other churches in Dublin and across Ireland, there were prayers, and a comfortable feeling that Ireland was in safe hands, the old constitutional party under the leadership of Mr. Redmond, silk-hatted, paunched, the very spit and image of respectability.

Things began to change a bit, perhaps, when the guns were

unloaded in Howth harbor, and the soldiers, turning on a jeering crowd at Bachelors Walk, had opened fire. But after that came the Great War, and Ireland standing side by side with England for the defense of little, heroic, Catholic Belgium. "Our place is here," Daugherty had said, calling G Division together. "I know where we all want to be, off there in France, we are a fighting race, we Irish, and among those of us who are Catholic the blood is boiling hot to avenge poor slaughtered little Belgium, the ravished city of Louvain, the murdered nuns. But our place is here. There are people in this Ireland—I refuse to call them Irishmen—who would make use of this grave and awful hour to stab us in the back, to stab old Ireland in the back."

It had never occurred to Shelley that his place was in France, a man in his mid-forties, with a wife and five children, only two of them grown and on their own, but it was good to know that G Division was doing its bit. And a vital bit it came to seem; the Volunteers, as they called themselves, were a handful, ten thousand as against the hundred thousand or more decent young Irishmen who were off serving in France and later in the Dardanelles, at Gallipoli. But there was no doubt of busy, malicious minds controlling them, nor any doubt that money was coming in, from Germany and from New York. Through 1915 and on into 1916, Shelley kept at his task, keeping his subordinates on the job trailing Arthur Griffith and Tom Clarke, and himself reading and annotating the copies of *Sinn Féin* and the *Irish Volunteer* and the *Irish Worker*.

Once or twice, when he was certain that he would not be recognized, he would call in at one of the public houses which his men had marked down as a center of disaffection—the Brazen Head or perhaps Hartigan's in Camden Street. It was as though he had fallen into Irish history itself—festering, cloacal, familiar, heartwarming, harmless. They were younger than himself, most of these pint drinkers, but there were a few men his age and some far older, men in their late sixties who sat together at a long table, taking a sip now and then at porter dark as night, amber whiskey, ginger beer. Unobtrusively, he listened to their talk, exchanged guarded remarks with the two fellows who stood beside him at the time-darkened, smoke-darkened bar. Toward closing time, there was a bit of singing from the lads: songs, a few of them, that Shelley had been hearing all his life and a few new ones, but set in the same key, both musical and political. Some of the older ones he had sung himself, in his day. Before going to bed that night, he wrote out his report, dismissive and indulgent. In Irish tavern warmth, treason was a theme, like love and whiskey and place names.

Shelley's loyalty to the division, to the force, to the Castle, survived Easter Week, battered but intact. The people "over there," as Daugherty had called them with an indulgent jerk of his head toward his and Shelley's lords and masters, the chief secretary and the under-secretary, together with their "kill Sinn Féin with kindness" policy, were in disgrace, but not G Division and not Crimes Special. They had been urging arrests of the Volunteer and Citizens' Army officers, the known IRB men, the whole lot. Now they were vindicated. In early April, when Henry Edward Duke replaced Nathan as chief secretary, Duke made a point of visiting G Division and praising them upon their diligence and perspicacity. Things were going to be different, he said pointedly.

And so they were, but not in the manner that Duke had had in mind. In Dublin and across Ireland, memorial photographs began to appear upon walls of the men whom the G had treated as items upon files, cards, reports—Clarke, Pearse, MacDermott, Connolly. Pearse's pale face glimpsed by Shelley at an ill-attended meeting of Gaelic-language enthusiasts; Connolly's heavy-jowled mustached face—Shelley had known them all, knew their files. The files were still in place; no one, not even Daugherty, had suggested that they be placed in the "Dead Box" with O'Donovan Rossa and Ned Nolan and Lomasney, the Little Captain, a dynamiter of the eighties. The tangled ends of their conspiracy existed in their hundreds, the Volunteers and IRB men sentenced to death after the Rising but then pardoned and now alive and well in English prisons and detention camps—De Valera and MacNeill and the rest of that lot. MacDermott and Clarke might be dead, but not their files. So Daugherty reasoned, and he was right, of course, but for Shelley and some of the others, there was a bit more to it.

In the churches, nearly all of them, the war was still supported but not conscription, and the Rising was condemned but not roundly, and if the leaders were called, almost invariably, "brave but misguided," increasingly the emphasis fell upon the "brave" rather than the "misguided." And as 1918 dragged itself toward its close, through the carnage of the final German offensive, as the call for conscription went up from London, increasingly the sentiment in Ireland held that Irish lads were to be conscripted because Irishmen could not be trusted unless they were off in foreign fields, and that, in some obscure way, conscription was to be Ireland's punishment for having dared to rebel.

"Would someone be so kind as to tell me when people began calling it 'the Rising,' " Hanratty said to Shelley one night in the lounge of the North Star. " 'Rebellion' was a good enough word at the time, good enough for the lads themselves and for the military and for the Castle. 'Rebellion' is a good old Irish word." But "Rising" was a word heavy with significance—one of Pearse's poems spoke of "the Risen People," and the rebellion had been timed to coincide with an earlier, a sacred rising, a resurrection.

More and more, policemen like Shelley and Hanratty grew conscious of themselves upon one side of a divide, and their own people on the other. It was different for the ordinary fellows in the DMP, on night duty, uniformed and helmeted, as Shelley himself had once been, keeping the peace in quarrelsome neighborhoods, trying hall doors to make certain that they were locked, the doors of jewelers' shops. Those fellows might expect a few jeers in Finglas and the Coombe, but they always had, more or less. It was different for Irishmen working in Crimes Special and the G Division.

Not different, to be sure, for their superiors, for men like Daugherty, Catholics like themselves but Catholics subtly yet vastly separated by class, caste, speech, accent, years in India, cricket at school—Downside or Ampleforth or Clongowes Wood. In Dublin and across Ireland in 1918, the Volunteers were being reorganized by the survivors of the GPO, and men who had served prison terms were standing on anticonscription platforms with John Dillon and the other parliamentarians. At the general election after the war, the old parliamentary party sank forever, to be replaced by something calling itself Sinn Féin, but a far cry from that small gang of cranks who had borne that title before the war. Sinn Féin now was, one way or another, the party of Catholic Ireland, prepared, at the very least, to wink at a new campaign of treachery and rebellion. Daugherty stood by the old order of things in the Castle, an order that included an occasional tea party at the Viceregal Lodge, shooting weekends in Wicklow and Westmeath, yachting in Dublin Bay.

So too did most of the men in G Division, but not all of them, not Broy nor Nelligan nor Dave Shelley. For Shelley, it was a holiday visit home to Kerry that had settled matters. The Shelleys were a Rathmore family, the mountainy Slieve Lucra region between Kerry and Cork. Shelley was the son of a small farmer, now old, blind and a bit simple, the farm now in the hands of Donal, Shelley's older brother; another brother, Ignatius, had a small shop and licensed premises in the village. From the slopes of the steep hill near the Shelley farm, one could look beyond bare mountains scattered with black rocks, tough-rooted gorse and heather, toward Cork. More often than not, there was a wind in those lonely hills, the Derrynasaggarts, a wind, faintly salt, from the Atlantic. In winter, when darkness fell swiftly upon stiff fields, rime-edged roads, the loneliness was intense, and the families would visit each other to talk or play fives, or the men would gather together in the public houses, small crowded rooms heavy with a fug of tobacco smoke, the smell of porter, clinging together until long past the legal closing hour and then straggling home in twos or threes, or in their carts. Above them, in the clear, wind-scoured skies, stars distant, bright as ice. But in summer, the evenings were endless, bathed in light, the air heavy with odor, fruit, dung, the heavy-scented hedges, the knowledge of ripening crops certain upon the senses, and at evening, the two public houses, not blinded against chill, against chilly rain, would be open to yellow sunlight.

Once, on that visit home in the heavy summer of 1919, Shelley and his brother Donal walked beyond the farm, beyond townland, to where the shallow, narrow stream was crossed by a hump-backed bridge.

"Great times ye must all be having above in Dublin," Donal Shelley said in Kerry's guarded, noncommittal tones.

"Great times entirely," Shelley said. G Division had trained him in its own kind of guardedness, probing, bland, a hint of affable menace in the words, but this was the indirect converse of Kerry, oblique, circumspect, a habit.

"They have their own thing set up there, as it is understood here," Donal said, and leaning over the bridge's low parapet, he spat reflectively. "A parliament of their own set up there in the Mansion House or wherever."

"They do," Shelley said, and waited.

"Here they swept all before them, Kerry North South East West—Jamesey Crowley and Austin Stack and Finian Lynch and Pierce Beaslai. The old lot did not even trouble to put up men of their own, for they would have been swept away. Sinn Féin held sway."

"It did," Shelley said. "It did, begod."

There were files upon all of them in the Castle, and had been since 1916 or before. Before certainly in the case of Stack, who had been a commandant in the Volunteers, and was so still. But for all that, they were an old Kerry family, the Stacks, older than the Shelleys. It was Stack who had led the prisoners' strike in Mountjoy Gaol two years before, when poor Thomas Ashe had died. During those weeks of the strike, people in their thousands had gathered outside Mountjoy, a week or more of sodden September skies, crowds somber beneath dripping umbrellas. It was detectives under Shelley's supervision who had made note of those who filed past the emaciated body, an athlete's once, lying in the City Hall dressed in Volunteers' uniform. "I left poor Ashe," O'Neill the lord mayor had said at the inquest, describing his visit to Mountjoy. "He died. It is for his country to say whether it is in a good cause or not." "A choice Larry O'Neill gambit," it was said in the Castle, "slippery as a greased pig." But Shelley had known better even then, in bleak September.

"Ye must be far removed from all that yourself," Donal said, "in your pursuit of burglars and the like."

"Not as far as I might wish," Shelley said, and they left it at that. In his brother's shop, behind the bar, hung the photographs of the Easter Martyrs, and beside it was a colored print of Ireland portrayed as a radiant young woman, sword upraised, and standing on her either side, young Volunteers, green-tunicked, slouch-hatted, with rifles and bandoliers. In Ignatius Shelley's shop, or in the other licensed premises across the road, Shelley was welcome of a summer evening, as he had always been, was he not Dominick Shelley's second son, but he could sense the talk turning a corner as he walked in, a barely discernible hollowness in the greetings of fellows he had known all his life, some of them lads who had been at school with him.

When he was back in Dublin, he set to work making contact with the Volunteers HQ, a delicate and torturous operation. He had a brief conversation with Cathal Brugha, a member, as he knew, of the Sinn Féin cabinet, but nothing came of it.

Brugha, a small, sharp-featured man, his body twisted by the metal it had taken during the fighting at the South Dublin Union in Easter Week—rifle bullets and bomb fragments—met him in the rear room of a candlemaker's factory on Ormond Quay. He let Shelley talk, in a hesitant, oblique manner, for four or five minutes, before cutting in: "You are a detective in their G Division, keeping tabs for them upon the fighting men of Ireland, and now you want to turn upon them. Is that it?"

There was no give to Brugha. He was the manager of the factory, and sat at his high-topped desk, his back to it, facing Shelley. "Well, Mr. Shelley, is that not the long and the short of it?"

"There is a bit more to it than that, if I may say so," Shelley said stiffly.

"There always is," Brugha said, "but I lack time to listen to it. Trust one of Dublin Castle's detectives, is it? I'll see you all in hell first, and you can go back to the Castle and tell them that."

Shelley stared into Brugha's dark eyes, and saw there cold, unreasoning detestation. For a terrifying moment, Shelley thought that Brugha had passed a sentence upon him. Brugha swiveled his chair back toward his desk, and, in a theatrical way, picked up some invoices and began to read through them.

"Mr. Brugha," Shelley said, in throat-constricted tones, "I have in mind a suggestion which you should give some thought to."

"I doubt that, Mr. Shelley," Brugha said, running a pencil down the items on the top invoice. "I think we have had our say."

Outside, standing on Ormond Quay in summer warmth, looking across the green, opaque river toward Dublin Castle, Shelley felt, for the first time in his life, entirely alone, as though a country, a world, had denied him. Over in the Castle, in the files room, Brugha was a name and a fuzzy prison photograph, with the unimpressiveness of all such photographs, holding a numbered board against his chest, hair uncombed, badly shaven. He had been sentenced to death, but the sentence was not carried out: he had been too badly wounded. On sheets of blue-lined ledger paper, reports about Brugha had gathered through 1918 and on into the following year, in different handwritings, initialed, some of the initials "D.M.S.," David Michael Shelley. In the Castle, Brugha was name, photograph, entries, but in the scruffy rear offices on the quay he spoke in Ireland's new voice, bleak and contemptuous. Shelley walked back to the Castle, barbed wire, sheets of metal at the gate, over the bridge and up Parliament Street, billycock hat shoved high on his head, shoulders back, arms swinging.

Six weeks were to pass before the message came to Shelley that he should visit a certain room in Vaughan's Hotel, on Rutland Square, at half-past nine that evening, if he was prepared to continue a discussion begun in a rear office in Ormond Quay. When he went there that night, he had his .38 nestling in an elaborate chest harness which had been issued to G Division some weeks before, and for a dreadful minute or so thought that he might have to use it. The lad lounging next to the closed door off the landing was Batty Quinlan, whom he knew by sight and file, a slope-shouldered, quiet lad from Finglas, marked down because of his cold, quiet violence. Quinlan made a quick, darting move toward his hip pocket, like a Wild West cowboy in the films, and then grinned and opened the door for Shelley.

Christopher Blake was sitting at a table spread out with papers in neat stacks, and a teapot, with a china sugar bowl, and milk in a battered creamer from the hotel dining room below them.

"Now then, Sergeant," Blake said, "as you can well imagine, we have been most interested in the visit you made to us."

"Have you, indeed," Shelley said, spooning sugar into his cup. "You have a strange way of showing it."

Blake smiled and shrugged. "You know what government offices are like, Sergeant. Better than I do myself, I'm certain. Things float from this department to that, one person to another."

"I was given the impression that there was scant interest taken in what I had come to propose."

"Ah well," Blake said. "We must be very careful, Sergeant. You know that yourself."

Shelley knew Blake, from the files, writing the *Bulletin* and spreading disaffection; he had been arrested and taken in once or twice under the "Cat and Mouse" act. But he had not known, was certain that no one at the Castle or in Brunswick Street knew, of the responsibilities which carried Blake to meet with him in this room. What the devil was Blake doing with these fellows, gunmen, killers? Blake had been to university, a doctor's son, selling books and writing them, off there in London, before the war. But then Shelley remembered: Blake had been in the GPO, had served his time in prison, but you would not know it to look at him, a neat, gentlemanly fellow. He resembled Mr. Daugherty a bit.

"Relying upon you, Sergeant. It is a great temptation, but it is also a great risk."

"Your friend below on Ormond Quay," Shelley said, "had scant interest in the risk or the temptation or in myself or any of the rest of it."

Blake nodded and looked at Shelley steadily for a moment or so, then looked back at one of the papers on the table, a letter, Shelley could make that much out.

"Cathal Brugha was quite right to be cautious," Blake said. "Quite right. Are you still of a mind to be of help to us?" Suddenly, he lifted his head and looked at Shelley again, smiling. "Or have we put you off entirely?"

Shelley took a sip at the tea. It had lost its first heat. "We tend to be very cautious ourselves," he said, "in—"

"Across the road," Blake said, and Shelley looked at him with pleased surprise.

"Once or twice," Blake said, "fellows have come to us with stories to tell, and they were not trusted. You will remember the poor lad who called himself Mavor, and the fellow who called himself Taylor. To be sure, they were not inspectors nor sergeants nor detectives in the division."

"They were not," Shelley said. "Those fellows beyond there in London sent them over—"

"We know that," Blake said. "And of course it would be a great help to us if we knew who was being sent over from London, and when."

"Yes," Shelley said, expelling the word as a sigh. He had committed himself fully, in advance, to what he proposed, but had known that there would be a bad moment, when he handed over, for the first time, information from the files.

"Well then," Blake said, and held out his packet of Churchman's to Shelley. He took up a half-sheet of paper. "There is a fellow named Herlihy that I keep worrying about. He sounds solid, right enough, and he came to us well recommended, but there is something there that doesn't ring true."

"Herlihy," Shelley said, and the word was a double sigh. "Let me tell you about Bob Herlihy." It took him a good ten minutes, because of interruptions from Blake, who was making notes, to tell the little that needed telling, a man who had fought with the rebels in 1916, but had been recruited by G Division for all that, because of an unfortunate incident that involved a young lad, and as he talked, he could see Herlihy the one time he had seen him in the interrogation room, a day's growth of beard, holding for dear life to a mug of tea, while two detectives leaned over him. That was Herlihy past, so to speak, but there was also Herlihy future, that Shelley could also see, like the Christmas in Dickens, with two of the fellows in the organization, some rainy night, coming out of a public house with him, and then leading him down a back alley to shoot him. In the particulars, Shelley was wrong: somehow, a month after the talk between Blake and Shelley, somehow Herlihy, nervous as a cat, got the wind up, and in the lavatory of the flat which he shared with his mother hanged himself with his necktie. But the particulars would not be important: at that first conversation with Blake, Shelley had signed the execution warrant of an informant to G Division, and after that, there would be no looking back.

Blake kept him talking that night for close to three hours, and he knew that other talks would follow. For a time, the naming of names forced him to fight against the feelings and loyalties of all his career, and, deeper than that, forced him to fight against the deepest of tribal taboos, the taboo against the informer. As he talked, he would find himself envying the fellows you read about in the newspapers or the files, fellows in the flying columns in Cork and Tipperary and Clare and Longford, living like Ned of the Hill and the Bold Rapparee and Galloping Hogan in *Ireland's Own,* waiting in ambush for a British column or moving across the hills by night in silent companionship and trust. Here, in the rain-slashed streets of Dublin, banks, shops, theaters, great electric signs—"Bovril," "Churchman's"—here nothing was simple, files passed from one office to another and the files leading to men shot dead in alleyways, a metaphysical conundrum. But toward the end of the three hours almost, the names came more easily. It was almost like having a chat with Under-Secretary Daugherty,

Blake, like Daugherty, soft-spoken, educated, with a dry, tolerant, understanding wit.

In the course of those hours, Blake had had Quinlan bring in a fresh and then yet another pot of tea, and the second time, Quinlan had grinned again, street Arab's impudence. Shelley admired Blake's method, taking notes but not many of them, a few words, a few names more likely, scribbled down on half-sheets of lined paper. Toward the end, it seemed to Shelley that Blake, although he continued to ask questions, was filling time, drawing matters out. Once, he asked Shelley if he would take something to drink, and, when Shelley declined, nodded with approval.

When the door was flung open, it was not by Quinlan, but, as Shelley had half-expected, by Collins. "Well now, Chris," he said to Blake, who nodded again, decisively, and he drew up the third chair to the table, and sat astride it, resting heavy arms upon its back. "And Shelley," he said, "Sergeant Shelley of Dublin Castle. This is a pleasure certainly for us, and for yourself as well, I trust. Has Chris here been a good host?" He put a hand on the teapot. "God, that must be as cold as the water in a ditch. Should we shout out for some fresh tea? I am here myself just for a sec. I have some fellows meeting me below."

There was a legend in the newspapers believed by half Dublin, half everywhere, that Collins could not be caught because there were no photographs of him nor any accurate descriptions, but that was nonsense. Any man who served time after the Rising was well photographed and he had been photographed too when he spent a month in 1917 for spreading disaffection. Well into 1918, he had been speaking on platforms and going in and out of the Mansion House. There were a dozen photographs of him; and Shelley, like every inspector in G Division, had spent hours studying them. Once there had been a full meeting on the subject of Collins. When Reynolds came down from Belfast to take command, that had been his first question, "Why have you bastards not been able to take Collins?" In another of the legends, Collins was called a man of disguises, a priest one day, a Tommy in uniform the next, then a laborer. But he was the same man in the photographs, save for a time when he wore a mustache. To Shelley, looking him in the face now, he looked like the kind of fellow who would have been a splendid sergeant in the DMP.

"The sergeant here has been helpful indeed, Mick," Blake said. "He confirmed our misgivings about Herlihy."

"It was the right thing to do, Sergeant. The only right thing. We've got the goods on Herlihy, we've known for weeks that he has been reporting to the Castle."

Shelley should have expected that; it was what he would have done himself.

"A bit of a test," he said, in what he hoped was an easy tone.

"A bit of a test," Collins said, grinning. "And you passed it with flying colors."

Shelley looked at the two of them, at Collins and then at Blake and then back at Collins, who was still grinning. Shelley might as easily have been back in the Castle, reporting to Daugherty and Reynolds. Everything in Shelley's world he had deliberately turned upside down and yet he had a feeling of familiarity. He never knew whether or not the IRA intelligence staff had had the goods on Herlihy: it would have been like them to make a play of omniscience: at the Castle, they were the same.

"You have done the right thing, Dave," Collins said. It was Dave now, not Sergeant, and Shelley felt absurdly flattered, like a schoolboy, by this fellow ten years at least younger than himself, powerful and clever-looking. "You have moved over to where you belong, among your own people. Fighting for Ireland, not our bloody English masters in the Castle."

It was what Shelley wanted to hear, was desperate to hear, although he was troubled by what seemed a smile behind Collins's smile. From then, though, straight through to the end and afterwards, he was Collins's man. Later, he would be working with men who felt the same. But others felt differently, he had had a policeman's instinct for that, from the day on Ormond Quay, where Collins's name was not mentioned.

"I hope so, Mr. Collins," he said, testing the waters, "I hope so. I was made less sure of a welcome a few weeks ago, as no doubt you know."

He marked a swift exchange of glances between Collins and Blake, swifter than a gull's wing skimming upon the Liffey.

"Cathal Brugha is minister of war," Collins said. "He is a fine soldier, he carries English lead in him from Easter Week. He was a bloody Cuchulain there in the South Dublin Union, smashed by English lead, English steel, standing up against the wall to lead his men." Collins was resting his arms still upon the back of his chair. Now he lowered his head, and looked, not directly at Shelley, but at the wall beyond. "We are fighting a different kind of war now, you are and I am and Chris here, and that bloody little desperado outside the door. Not war at all, as Cathal measures such matters—he sees men led out in battle against other men, and perhaps a warpipe in the distance, or a drum at least. Gunmen plugging coppers and the other way round, that's how he sees our kind of war. And does he not have the right of it, Dave."

Shelley had nothing to say. The coppers who were being shot down were his chums, or at least had been until tonight or until he had walked into the office in Ormond Quay or perhaps until he had gone back to Kerry, stood with Donal upon the bridge in Rathmore on a quiet evening.

Collins said, "We are neighbors in a way, Dave, yourself and myself, yourself from Rathmore, and me from Clonakilty, and nothing between the two of us but the Derrynasaggarts. Dublin fellows like Cathal Brugha or like Chris here, they see matters differently." He suddenly swung his hands together in a loud clap and stood up. "But we're after the same thing, all of us. A Republic for Ireland. You have the look of a footballer, Dave," he said, "am I right?"

"I was in my day," Shelley said, "but my football days are well behind me now."

Collins nodded, then turned toward Blake. "Dave here and yourself will not lose sight of each other, will you? And Dave, I will want to know whatever comes your way." At the door he paused, turned as though about to say something, and then left.

"As simple as that," Shelley said dryly, and Blake, as dryly, said, "You have no idea."

It was to Blake that Shelley made his reports, one a week at least, and there were drops where he could be reached in an emergency. They were never seen together, of course, although they risked a pint and a plate of sandwiches once in the room off the front lounge of a small hotel in Howth. It was a warm day in early autumn, and beyond the window the bay was glistening, far off they could see the mailboat, and there were fishing craft tied to moorings across the road almost from the hotel.

A half-dozen years before, Blake had been one of the men unloading the Mausers here and distributing them to the Volunteers.

That was how it had all begun. Between then and now, there had been a world war and a rebellion.

When they had finished the business, Blake said, "That list of names that Sergeant Casey was carrying, Dave."

They were on Christian name terms by now, Dave and Chris, although Shelley was not entirely comfortable with this. Collins was someone you thought of as Mick with his jokes and his roughhousing, but Blake was a different matter, different accent, different manner.

Shelley shook his head. "Those are names that I have off by heart," he said. "Huntley and Salmon and Carver and the rest of them. There is a fellow came over from London named Salmon who took up a position in the Sun Life Assurance. And there is a fellow named Ferguson—that is another of the names—who has been hired on as a clerk at Grubb and Co., the solicitors. But Ferguson is as common a name as you would want to find."

"At the top of the sheet, off to one side, you saw the word 'Cairo,' Blake said. "Do you ever hear it around the Castle?"

"I do not," Shelley said, "and you may depend upon it that I have kept my ears clean. I have heard two of the typists decide to have tea and buns at the Cairo Café in Grafton Street, and Major Price was stationed in Cairo during the war, and he is inclined to wax eloquent on how preferable it is to Dublin, the warm sunlight and the women of Egypt and all that. But there you have it."

Sunlight sparkled upon the distant mailboat, and, nearer at hand, the sails on the pleasure craft took the wind. Blake remembered Erskine Childers, a brilliant sailor, bringing in the *Asgard,* the boxes of oiled Mausers.

"How did Major Price spend those war years off there in Cairo?"

"Reading invoices, lists of boots and leggings most likely," Shelley said.

"Is that what he does here? In the Castle?"

"More or less," Shelley said. "The War Office sent him over to carry messages between ourselves and the Army. It has a pretty title, what he does, but that's it, more or less. He's a decent old skin, Major Price. His Christian name is William, but all of his chums call him Reg."

"Find out whatever you can about him, Dave. Nose around a bit."

"About the major?" Shelley asked, surprised. "I will if you want me to, Chris, but there will not be much. The army and the DMP are in different compartments entirely."

"If nothing else," Blake said, as he watched a ketch veer sharply to starboard, "you can find out why he is called Reg."

Shelley laughed and picked up his pint.

It was two weeks before Shelley had anything to report, and in that time, without telling Shelley what he was doing, Blake had had Ferguson, the solicitor's clerk, shadowed, and Salmon, who had taken up a position with the Sun Assurance in Dame Street. Ferguson had brought his wife over with him, but Salmon had made a friendship with an Irish girl, a redhead named Slattery. She had moved into his flat in Upper Leeson Street. Liam Finnerty, one of the fellows who was shadowing Salmon, was of a religious turn of mind, and was shocked by this. "Dear God," he said, "what kind of people are the English? Right there in a furnished flat in Leeson Street, with the landlord and his wife living in the ground-floor flat and knowing all about it. What kind of people are those two, if it comes to that?" But he was good at his work, and was able to tell Blake that four times in those two weeks, in the early evening, Salmon had had tea in Bewley's with a man of middle years, with sandy, thinning hair, and a down-turning yellow mustache. Once Finnerty had contrived to sit close beside them, in the room of crowded shoppers, students, office workers, but heard nothing more than Salmon's complaints about the dullness of life at Sun Assurance, his companion's consolatory grunts and wheezes.

"There is little enough to tell," Shelley said to Blake. "There is talk of some kind of reorganization, but I don't hear the major's name mentioned in connection with it. It's hard to believe, Chris. He's a bit ponderous and heavy-footed in the English way, if you take my meaning."

"When I look for the major in my crystal ball," Blake said, "I see a middle-aged man, going a bit thin on top, yellow mustache, wheezes a bit. Overweight, I'll wager."

"And average height," Shelley said, after a long pause, and smiled. "Well, I'll be damned. How did you do it?"

"I had two of them shadowed, the two you mentioned, Ferguson and Salmon."

They agreed that the other names on the list were worth attention, and for this, Blake would use men in HQ's Intelligence Squad, who would keep the major under surveillance. Shelley, and Collins's other men in the Castle, were to stay well away from it.

"What do you make of it, Chris?" Shelley asked.

"I'm not certain," Blake said, "and I am not certain what is to be done about it."

But he told Collins, who nodded. "If you need more men," he said, "I can lend you one or two."

Three nights later, Shelley and Major Price chanced to be leaving the Castle together, walking across cobblestones toward the gate in the Lower Yard, heavy guarded these days, barbed wire, a corporal and a squad of Tommies. Price was dapper in a city suit, well tailored, a soft gray hat canted over one eye.

"Another day's work done, another pound earned, eh, Sergeant?"

There had been a comfortable ease between Shelley and Price, the times that they had met. Their social classes were not the same, but Price had a hail-fellow-well-met attitude, a bluff recognition that they were working together. Major or not, the squad at the gate had been trained not to salute when he walked past them onto Dame Street. As the two of them were walking out, Mr. Charteris, one of the clerks in John Ryan's office, was coming in. "Evening, Price," he said, "evening, Sergeant. Off to tell more yarns about Cairo with your chums, are you, Price?" Price smiled, and shrugged. When they were standing in the open courtyard beyond the gates, Price, his face very slightly reddened, said, "The chaps rag me about Cairo, but it was a bloody fine town in some ways. Couldn't hold a candle to Alexandria, of course."

After that, Shelley and Blake and Collins and a few others with whom they were working spoke of the men who reported to Price as "the Cairo gang." And they might not have been far wrong, Blake told Collins a week later. "During the war," he said, "Price was a lieutenant colonel in Egypt. King's Own Regiment, but he had been seconded to staff headquarters."

"Intelligence," Collins said flatly, but a question nevertheless. Suddenly he laughed. "Can you blame them," he said, "setting up an intelligence unit of their own in the Castle? Is he any good, this Major Price or Colonel Price or whatever?"

"Colonel must have been a temporary, wartime rank. I don't know if he was any good. I was lucky to find out as much as I did."

Collins was quiet for a full minute, and then nodded. "Right," he said. "We'll have to wait and see."

They did not have long to wait. Three weeks later, a party of military and police raided the Royal Hotel in Parliament Street, in the shadow of the Castle, and shot dead a guest named Lynch. The shooting took place at 1:35 in the morning, and a report was phoned to College Street Station at 2:15. No other details were given, and when Blake was phoned from College Street by a G Division detective named Broy, his immediate fear was that Liam Lynch, commandant of Cork No. 2 Brigade, had been killed. But by the time Blake reached Vaughan's at five, Dublin still black, traveling through patrolled streets, it had been learned through Broy that the man killed was a John Lynch from Kilmallock in Limerick.

Collins had somehow found time to shave, but he wore neither necktie nor collar. Like the other men at the table, he was drinking tea in full, noisy gulps. Blake drew up a chair to join them.

"They might have thought it was Liam," one of Collins's intelligence officers said, a quick-witted deadly man named Thornton. "Sure, who the hell was poor John Lynch, was he an officer at all?"

"I will tell you what he was," Collins said. "He was one of the Loan organizers in Limerick and that was well known about him. He came up yesterday on the afternoon train, and handed over to me a black Gladstone bag with almost twenty-five thousand pounds in it. I told him to watch his step. He was tailed here from Limerick, or else the news was phoned ahead and he was tailed after he reached Dublin. He met me at the North Star, and we had best stop using it. I stuffed the bag with newspapers and told him to book into a hotel on the South Side. And he did, by God, under his own name."

"Poor bastard," Thornton said again.

"Try to look at the bright side of it," Collins said, "the money is safe." He laughed at Thornton's shocked expression, and reached over to thump him on the arm.

"But I meant that, you know," Collins said later to Blake, when they were alone. "Sinn Féin Loan organizers are thick on the ground, and until now, if they were arrested, they suffered little enough. But without money we'd be done for. It's all well and good talking about money from the States, but in the heel of the hunt, we have to depend on ourselves."

"It's something else that worries me," Blake said. "It took fairly good intelligence work to hunt poor Lynch down, and it took a new way of operating to kill him like that, in cold blood."

Collins nodded, but he said, "We have killed that way ourselves. To protect the Loan. We took Bowers off the Galway train and shot him, and we shot Bell from off a tram here in Dublin. We should have expected this, sooner or later."

"A friend—my friend—was on that train that day."

"Yes," Collins said. "I know. You told me."

"She knelt beside him, there on the railway platform in Moate. She says that she dreams about it. Her husband was killed in the war, but it was off in Gallipoli. The postman brought a clean telegram round to her, unsoiled, without blood on it."

"I know," Collins said again. "You told me. I don't know any other way to fight this kind of war. Now they have begun to fight it that way themselves. And you can expect worse."

The Dáil was less certain. As far back as the summer of 1919, Brugha had insisted, against Collins's opposition, that the Volunteers should be preparing for an open fight against the enemy. Collins, so it seemed to Brugha, had maneuvered himself into an extraordinary position. In the Dáil, he was minister of finance, responsible for the Loan. In the IRA, he was director of organization and director of intelligence. Behind all of this, he was president of the legendary, secret, oath-bound Irish Republican Brotherhood. What pleased Brugha was news of victories in "the field," as he called it—Treacy and Breen in Tipperary, Barry in Cork, MacEoin in Longford, O'Malley and Lacy wherever they were sent by headquarters.

"I don't know any other way to fight this war," Collins said. "We can never defeat them in the open, they will wear us down. The people have been splendid, but you cannot expect them to be splendid forever. It will be an ugly war. Sooner or later, the English will get tired of it." He raised his head to stare at Blake, almost with belligerence, a heavy lock of hair falling forward. "What do you say to that, Chris?"

"Doing what I've been asked to do, by the Dáil, by yourself, keeps me busy enough, Mick."

"And you have never heard voices raised in anger at cabinet meetings or Headquarters meetings. You're a lucky man, Chris. Or else you're going deaf."

"Going deaf, Mick. We have an enemy to fight, not each other."

"God send it stays that way," Collins said, but his voice had an angry rasp to it.

For the hour, they had enough to do, the two of them. There was a British intelligence network in operation, and so far as could be told, for the hour, it was not strictly speaking army nor police nor administrative, but a bit of each perhaps. It had a man in the Castle, an army officer named Price, who had agents in the field—probably the dozen on Casey's list, whom Collins and Blake called "the Cairo gang," and perhaps more. Price's network might not be the only one, but it was something to be going on with.

It was morning by the time they separated, late morning.

By late morning, Reg Price had been up and breakfasted, and was ready to take the tram into Dublin. The house which he and Lucy had rented in Kingstown faced the bay, and they had fallen into the habit of taking their breakfast at a small table set beside one of the tall windows which looked across the road toward the sparkling bay, looked across the bay toward Howth, with its marvelous gorse-covered hill and the Bailey lighthouse stretching away, pointing across the Irish Sea toward Wales. Because he breakfasted so early, Lucy would still be in her dressing gown, but Price would be shaved and dressed and brushed, his cheeks glowing from a close shave with the straight razor that he had used from his days at Sandhurst and from a brisk, rough toweling. Lucy would be seated at the table when he came downstairs, and the *Irish Times*, unfolded, would be resting on his plate. Their housemaid, a cheerful willing girl named Hennessy, not more than seventeen, would be in the kitchen, having her own tea with Cook but with one ear listening for the bell.

Lucy, Price knew, was not entirely happy here in Ireland, coming as it did after two full years of the war had separated them, the Egyptian years. That was why he had chosen a house here in Kingstown. It had an English feel to it, the houses which fronted the sea especially, the look of towns along the coast in Devon and Dorset, and the neighbors, many of them, were English, or at least Irish Protestants, who were English in a way, decent loyalists at any rate, king-and-country people.

Price kept a motorcar, although he used the tram to go to work. Occasionally, he would need it and so he put down its expenses in his supplemental, but in good weather, he and Lucy would use it to motor, on a Saturday or Sunday, down into Wicklow, or sometimes as far afield as Kildare, where he had a chum, Charlie Kellett, ex-King's Own like himself, living there in retirement, with his wife, a marvelous old girl. The Kelletts gave them Sunday lunch once or twice and once or twice they had taken the Kelletts to lunch at the hotel in Blessington. Through Charlie, they had come to make a few other friends, ex-army for the most part, but not entirely.

Price was forty-eight, far too young for a serving officer to think of retiring, although they could if they wanted to, Lucy had money and Price had a bit himself, they had the house in Cheltenham where they intended eventually to settle, and where they spent their leaves. He could have returned to his regiment, of course, but after Cairo, intelligence work was in his blood. In Cairo, just as here in Ireland, he had had his own team, although there resemblances ended. Cairo had its extremists, of course, its extreme nationalists, but by and large, the task had been one of keeping an eye on pro-German activity. He had loved the long evenings, when the earth began to cool, the color of the marketplaces, the evening visit to Shepheard's, which everyone swore was the best hotel in the world, best bar certainly. The sun at evening turned the very air crimson, the air cooling as it bloomed, and then the light fading, at first slowly and then swiftly, and before you knew where you were, you were in the dark night of Egypt, black beyond the lighted gardens of Shepheard's, on Saturday fairy lights strung between the palm trees. The Ezbekieh gardens were heavy with odors.

In all his time in Cairo, there had been only two incidents in which it had been necessary to go behind the backs of the Egyptian police, take action on his own, as it were. In one of these, two of his Egyptian agents had taken care of matters for him. The other was an Armenian named Aram Tartanian, a crooked diamond merchant, which was no concern of Price's, but a clever fellow who was starting to fabricate a net of German agents, fellows clever as Tartanian himself. Price had had Abdul Nazar arrange to meet with him in Kafihey's shop, but instead of Nazar, young Steve Reynolds and Price himself had turned up, and without discussion of any sort had shot Tartanian with their service revolvers. He might, of course, have been tried, *in camera*, that sort of thing could be done in wartime Egypt, but there were reasons which made it highly inconvenient. "Poor old Tartanian," Brigadier Hatchett, Price's superior, had said to him next morning, "he bought it, there's a report here on my desk. Chaps who did it got clean away." "One of his diamond transactions gone sour, I expect," Price said; "no need for us to go near it." "Good heavens, no," Brigadier Hatchett said, "no concern of ours." Good man, Hatchett, best sort of OC for that sort of work, no questions asked, a wink as good as a nod, as Sergeant Mullaney would have said.

Dublin by contrast was a labyrinth of complexities, conflicting authorities, confusions, uncertainties. He had known Dublin a bit before the war, a city somehow hung up pleasantly somewhere in the Victorian past, tatty in bits and elegant in patches, the people courteous, friendly, a bit mad and irresponsible, marvelous parties, balls, good hunting in Wicklow and Kildare. There was all of this still, but beneath the crust, it had turned murderous, Ireland had turned murderous, and that made the charm and the courtesy sinister. Parts of the city center were still burned-out ruins from a rebellion launched when Britain was fighting for her very life, in France and off in the Dardanelles.

Before leaving England to report for duty at the Castle, Price had been taken to lunch at White's by Winston. An amazing survivor, Winston. His enemies thought they had him on the run after the Dardanelles, dumped the whole blame upon his shoulders, but he was back the next year with Lloyd George as minister of munitions, and here he was in this present cabinet, secretary of state for war.

He was in fine mood that day, he could be a wretched companion or the finest one going, bubbling with ideas, enthusiasm, wit, what have you. They had had a few whiskies in the bar downstairs, and there had been a lovely Moselle with the oysters. "We had to win the war, Reg," he said, "get our hands on some decent German wine." Price laughed, and looked with demure greediness round the handsome, dark-paneled room, dark-suited men, crisp-collared, the occasional country member in tweeds. He had been given meals at White's any number of times, but he was not a member. Out in Egypt, it had been one of a score or more places which would pop into his mind like picture postcards from home, what they were fighting for, as the posters said. And he was a bit flattered that Winston had asked him. They had met, four or five times, a half-dozen perhaps, they knew each other, Winston knew who he was, and Lord knows he knew who Winston was, who did not? But they were acquaintances, at best.

Winston had had little enough to say until they had finished their oysters. Winston would go at his with a peculiar stabbing, jabbing motion. They were excellent oysters, Dunstables, full and plump, and the liquor in the shells tasted of the sea, of submarine grottoes. When Winston had finished his dozen, he sipped his wine, finished it, nodded to the wine steward.

"Not half bad, these oysters," he said, patting lips with unfolded damask. "A surprise, really. The food here is indifferent." It was a habit they all had, all members of serious clubs, the clubs that counted. They always disparaged the food, but what they were saying was something different; they were saying, Don't you wish you could disparage it, don't you wish you were a member. Lucy's father had been a member, but the Army and Navy was quite good enough for Price.

Winston had ordered mutton chops for the two of them, and as they were waiting, he called over the waiter and said that they would have the red straight away, not wait for the meat.

"Different from Shepheard's, eh Price? God, how I love Shepheard's. And who wouldn't, tell me that?"

The room seemed to Price dense, solid, unattainable.

"I remember Ireland from when I was a boy," Winston said, "when my father was over there with the lord lieutenant. I can remember riding with him in his carriage on a brisk autumn day near winter, out through the park and down into town. We had a heavy plaid lap robe flung across our knees, and beneath the robe, my father was holding my hand and in his other hand he held a great heavy revolver. This was in the days of the Invincibles or not long before them, an under-secretary butchered in that very park, by the Polo Grounds. When I think of Ireland, I think of my father's hand in mine and his other hand on the revolver."

Quietly, the elderly waiter refilled their glasses.

" 'Ulster will fight and Ulster will be right.' My father coined that, Price, in later years. And was he not right! I learned that to my cost in 1912, at the time of the Home Rule crisis. A difficult people, Price, difficult. Do you know what Walter Scott said of them, he only visited them once, once was enough. He said that they were like blind men, fighting with daggers in a hogshead. Neat, that, is it not? With daggers in a hogshead. The daggers are out again, Price, our task to do something about it. Can't solve the Irish problem, never be solved, my father couldn't solve it, I cannot, no one can. But we can keep it controlled at least. Good people over there, Protestant and Catholic alike, during the war they fought bravely and well, hundreds of thousands of them, stained the fields of Flanders, the sands of Gallipoli. We must not judge the brave men and women of Ireland by the murder gang in Dublin, and the gangs of peasant murderers in the hills of Cork and Tipperary. They may have the people frightened into silence, but that is a different matter. That will be part of your task, Price, to make Ireland safe for the people of Ireland to stand up and speak out their minds, shake off the murder gang. Eh, Price?"

"We'll certainly give it a try," Price said, in his best bluff soldier manner.

"Down through the park into town," Winston said, his eyes slightly unfocused, as though he were seeing not Price nor the plate of plump mutton chops, their fat still faintly heavy-odored, nor the other diners, but that day in Dublin a half-century before, the carriage moving through the chill of late autumn, and Price, who knew Phoenix Park well, imagined it, brown leaves raked into the hedges, the trees bare-branched the wide meadows, imagined a plaid robe, black, dark green, flung across the joined hands of father and son, the heavy, long-barreled revolver. Price had gifts of imagination. They had both helped and hindered him.

"Shake off the murder gang," Winston said again, and his eyes were focused now, upon his sharp knife cutting into one of his chops. "But how do we go about that, eh? We are very fortunate, are we not, to have as astute and as resourceful a prime minister as we do, eh Price?" And when Price did not reply at once, he said again, "Eh?"

"I am a soldier," Price said, "I leave that sort of thing alone."

Winston was holding a bit of mutton speared upon his fork; above bow tie and stiff collar, his smooth, full face broke suddenly into a vulgar grin. "You do, do you, you soldiers, leave politics to the politicians? Tell that to Wilson, tell it to Gough and Seeley. Leave politics alone, do you? I am an old soldier myself, Price, don't forget that."

Winston himself certainly never forgot it, those years in India with the Hussars, and then riding down upon the Sudanese at Omdurman, blazing away with his revolver at spear-carrying wogs, like Buffalo Bill polishing off Comanches. Forgot it, why he was forever writing about it. After the calamity of the Dardanelles, he had seen active service in France, it was true, commanded a regiment in the trenches, but within the year he was back in Westminster as minister of munitions and here he was, secretary for war. Omdurman or not, Sixth Royal Scots Fusiliers or not, Winston wasn't a soldier, he was one of the frock coats, as General Wilson called them.

"An able man, the prime minister," Price said. "Able."

"Able," Winston said. "Yes, you could say that. Able. He managed the war well, and the peace well enough. An able man. And he should be able to manage the Irish, he's a Celt, after all. He's something new, this fellow, a radical out of Wales, shoved up into power by that gang of miners and hymn singers and chapel people. I like that, shows energy, cleverness, we haven't always had that at the top and we know the result. He is going to need all that cleverness, in that patched-up Coalition we have, Liberals and Tories hanging together because we want to stay in power. Ireland could ruin this government, Price. Sooner or later, the Liberals will want to give in to the murder gang, give the Shinners what they want. And the Tories will want to bring fire and sword into Ireland, do a Cromwell. I know them, was a Tory once myself, may be one again. Anyone can rat once, but to rat and then re-rat, there's boldness for you, the Prince Rupert touch."

Why is he telling me all this, Price thought. Why are we having a meal together and why here, we don't know each other that well. For all he knows, I'll leave here and walk up to the Army and Navy, read the papers for an hour or two, and then make a yarn out of this in late afternoon, when fellows begin drifting in for a whiskey or two.

"Matters will have to be settled in short order, Price, a year, eighteen months at the outside, or this government will go smash."

"Settled?" Price asked. "I thought the Irish problem can never be solved. Isn't that what you said?"

Winston's prediction was wrong: the chops were excellent, but Price was not really attending to them. The waiter was scrupulous in his attention to their wineglasses, but neither was the wine taking hold upon Price. He found that he was listening to Winston cautiously, as though shoals and rocks lay hidden behind that seductive voice with its orator's lisp, a defect put to use.

"It can always be settled for a time," Winston said, "for a generation. Gladstone settled it, made his pact with Parnell and the murder gangs of those days, Fenians and Land Leaguers. My father could have solved it if he been let, they hate people with imagination. Lloyd George would like to do a Gladstone, make a deal with the murder gang over there, murderers and arsonists, hiding behind hedges to gun down soldiers on church parade. He's ready for war one day, ready to deal the next. Beefing up the Royal Irish Constabulary is the way to do it, the Auxiliaries and the Cadets, and they must be allowed to fight with the weapons of the country. Michael Collins and his chums don't fight by Marquis of Queensberry rules."

The church parade had been early on, in September of 1919, eighteen men of the West Kent's Infantry on their way to the Methodist church in Fermoy, and a soldier killed. The following day, some two hundred soldiers fell upon Fermoy, sacking and looting.

"The weapons of the country," Price said. "What are those?"

But Winston said, instead, "Your friends call you Reg, I'm told, but that isn't your Christian name. Nickname, is it?"

"Yes," Price said, and felt an ancient embarrassment, now a faint scratch.

"Reg then, if I may," Winston said, and lifted his eyes to the waiter. "I think we can safely broach a second bottle, eh Reg? No harm done, the weekend almost upon us."

His face, the face of a dissipated cherub, pink and polished, seemed to glow upon Price. "Murder gang," Price seemed to recall, had been a phrase of Winston's coinage, either his or Lloyd George's, but the newspapers had taken it up, the leader writers at all events, just as "Michael Collins" had become almost a generic term for the murderous leaders of the Sinn Féin conspiracy.

"Hopeless," Winston said, "hopeless but perhaps not fatal. Look at us, look at Europe, the world, old empires smashed, ancient kingdoms gone down in ruin, and across the steppes of Poland from us a new kind of barbarism triumphant in Moscow and St. Petersburg, gunmen and assassins skulking in the alleys of Munich and Trieste and Vienna and Berlin. Half-naked fakirs in loincloths working their magic upon the millions of our Empire in India, beyond India, in the Sudan, along the Nile."

It was like a passage that Price had read as a schoolboy but had not forgotten, the world, in which the reader, the ideal reader, a schoolboy perhaps like Price himself at Birkhamstead, not the best public school in England but by no means the worst, had been placed upon the strong pinioned shoulders of some powerful bird, the roc out of the *Arabian Nights* perhaps, and carried high enough to look down upon the world, with Europe of course at the center and stretching away from it, from the turquoise Mediterranean, the desolate marshes which reached toward Siberia, the sands and the magical names of Asia. England lay to the north of the world's center, sea-begirt, meadowed, flower-strewn, fog-defended, and yet guarantor of the world's stability as it hurtled through time.

"To lose Ireland," Winston said, holding his glass and peering into its red depths, "would be a challenge to Fate, and Fate always wins. Couldn't put it that way on the floor of the House, of course, couldn't put it that way in the bar of this club, for that matter. How can we hope to maintain the Empire when we cannot keep the King's peace in the nearest and oldest of our possessions, the guardian of our sea upon which the Empire depends. The *Lusitania* was sunk by the Hun just off the coast of Cork, and the people of Cork, of Queenstown, of Kinsale, were splendid. But today, when one of the gunmen of Sinn Féin is shot down by our chaps, with his German gun in his hand, the juries of Cork, the coroners' juries, bring in judgments of murder against Lloyd George, against the army or the police, against the cabinet. Against anyone they please, against the sovereign." The pink, balding head nodded. "Lose Ireland, and the rot begins." Suddenly he smiled. "We are laying a heavy task upon you, my dear."

"Upon the army," Price said, "yes, I can see that."

"Upon the army, to be sure. So far as it is able. And it may come to that, martial law, fire and sword, the mailed fist of old Oliver Cromwell. But I trust not. That would be a kind of defeat for us in itself, a kind of triumph for Sinn Féin. The maintenance of law and order is a police function, and Ireland has for a century had one of the finest police establishments in the world, earned the respect of the Irish people themselves, put down the Fenians, the terrorists, the dynamiters, the Invincibles, the boycotters. And did it, mind you, because the RIC has the respect of the Irish people. No fairer prospect for a young Irish lad, a young Protestant lad in Antrim, a young Catholic lad in Kerry, no fairer prospect than a life of service in the Royal Irish Constabulary. All swept away by the murder gang." He nodded again, and as the waiter stood beside him, he said, "Some of that excellent Stilton must still be here, Murphy. And a taste of brandy, eh, Reg, a taste of Hennessy. No harm done, the weekend is almost upon us."

As the waiter moved away, the creak of ancient, polished shoe leather, Price said, "Where would we be without the Irish, a glass of Hennessy, a waiter named Murphy?" Then he ventured, a bit tentatively, "Eh Winston?"

Winston looked at him blankly, and then said, "Never thought of that. He's been here for years, been here as long as I can recall. There you are now. But they're leaving the RIC now, frightened to stay, frightened for their families, that's why we've begun recruiting in England. Auxiliary policemen, eh? Ex-servicemen, and a tough lot they are, you can't expect choirboys to sign up for work of that sort. You'll be seeing a bit of them, I expect, Reg. Our hope, Reg, is that the Army and the RIC will be working together, pooling what they know, pooling ways of doing things. That's why we—why I—am counting on chaps like yourself. That's what you were so good at in Cairo. A bit of the soldier, a bit of the bobby."

"I was in intelligence," Price said, a bit stiffly. He would not himself have described it as "a bit of the bobby."

Murphy held the salver firmly, so that Price could scoop out Stilton for himself.

"Most English of all the great cheeses," Winston said. "An old soldier, are you not, Murphy, like Colonel Price here and myself?"

Murphy smiled, a glimpse of ill-fitting dentures in a pale, lined face. "Indeed I am not, sir. You must have me confused with someone else. I took service here when I was fifteen and have not budged. I was too old for the war."

"No doubt," Winston said, a bit nettled. "I asked for you myself, you know, Price. Your posting to Irish Command is my doing. And do you know why? I asked Hatchett to recommend to me someone with a particular kind of experience, and he recommended you. He had a story or two to tell me. There was a diamond merchant in Cairo, for example, he told me the name, a Copt or a Jew, I think he was."

Winston sat patiently, waiting for Price to respond. As he waited, he piled crumbling Stilton upon a biscuit.

"An Armenian," Price said at last. "His name was Tartanian."

In the cramped office, a single dusty window looking out upon a bare courtyard, Brigadier Hatchett had nodded, looked not quite directly at Price but beyond his shoulder to the closed door. The sound of a typewriter came to them, and a sergeant's throaty shout. "Poor old Tartanian," the brigadier had said. "No concern of ours. Good heavens no."

"That's the name," Winston said. "That chap and a few others. People here think that intelligence is all mapmaking, dreary little dons breaking codes or making them up or whatever. Or else, Colonel Lawrence dynamiting railways and leading wild bedouins into battle. We know better, eh? It's codes and dynamite and bedouins, but it's also nasty things that have to be done to nasty people. Like that Armenian."

"Tartanian," Price said. It seemed absurdly important, now that the name was out, to say it.

Tartanian had had an assistant, but they had waited until near sunset, after the assistant had left for the day. Tartanian was wearing a black alpaca jacket, and a necktie of green silk, with a diamond pin in it, an advertisement perhaps or a signal of his trade, like a shop sign. Price and Reynolds opened fire at the same moment, and the room seemed filled with murderous thunder.

Price had imagined that he had left that sort of intelligence behind him.

"The glue that holds empires together," Winston said. "If we think the Empire is worth anything, it must be worth a few pairs of hands with glue on them, dirty hands, bloody hands, whatever."

"Tartanian was setting up an enemy spy network," Price said. "We were at war."

Winston grunted, and held his brandy in his cupped hands, to warm it.

"There is an illegal parliament in hiding in Dublin," Winston said, "professing itself at war with us, terrifying a decent people into acquiescence. Magistrates have been murdered, soldiers, inspectors of police. Police barracks have been attacked. Our lorries have been ambushed. We must not call that war, must not even call it rebellion, but it is, we know that, everyone knows it. The Special Branch is useless. Gunmen in city streets slipping back into their slums. Gunmen in the hills, farm boys by day, casual laborers, murderers at sundown. How do we fight that, eh Price, eh Major?"

Price said nothing.

Winston sipped his brandy and grunted again, this time with satisfaction.

"There are matters best not discussed in Whitehall or an HQ somewhere or in Dublin Castle. Even over lunch in a chap's club, it is best not to discuss matters too bluntly. No need to, really. They are not all farm boys and city gunmen, that's the problem, be a simple matter if that were the case. But they have some damned clever people over there, on their side. Michael Collins is half journalists' poppycock, but not the other half. We trained him ourselves. First in the Post Office over here in London, then in a stockbroker's office, then in a bank. Read the newspapers and you'd think he was some kind of Garibaldi or Hereward the Wake or Rob Roy. Not a bit of it. He's a broker's assistant gone bad, a clerk with a Parabellum. He's clever, but he's ruthless and his hands have touched the springs of murder. His operation must be smashed and he must be destroyed. One way or another."

Winston's voice, or so it seemed to Price, had taken on a tone which curiously mingled loathing, fierceness and admiration. It was as though, Price thought suddenly, as though a part of him had never grown up. Politician, minister of state, architect of an immense campaign, an immense armada, but a part of him was still flourishing a pistol, patrolling the Northwest Frontier, escaping from the Boers.

"My duties," Price said, "are simple enough. Coordinating the intelligences, army and RIC and DMP."

"I daresay some of your old Cairo crowd are spoiling for another fight," Winston said, as though Price had not spoken. "Bring them over. Have you stayed in touch?"

"A few of us have," Price said, "two or three of us. Reynolds and I have a drink now and then." Reynolds was Gamma: Price had given each member of the squad a Greek initial.

"You'll need more," Winston said. "You can have as many as you need. See if you cannot find some sound Irish chaps."

Everything was happening too quickly for Price's liking.

They were in the billiards room, in deep chairs of brown leather, fresh brandies in their hands. Close at hand, there was a game in progress, and Price thought he recognized one of the players, the attorney general, his jacket off, his stiff cuffs a dazzling white as they moved above the green felt of the table. With a long, lantern jaw, eyes glittery blue. In a swift, fluid motion, graceful, masculine, he shot forward his cue. Then he straightened himself, and picked up his glass and his cigar. He nodded toward Winston and smiled. He looked reckless, clever and not entirely sober.

Price was beginning to feel his own brandies. Victorians stared down at them from smoke-darkened oils, gilt-framed.

"Must say I envy you," Winston was saying. "In the field, one has a sense of accomplishment. All confused here, tangled."

He seemed confused himself, but only slightly, gesturing with his own cigar, a magician's wand, so it seemed to Price. His cherub's face was rubicund, glowing.

"Do you know, Major," he said. It was Major again, as though Reg had had a mayfly's flickering life, "there is an old prediction, Nostradamus sort of thing, that our empire began with Ireland, will go if Ireland goes, first crack in the wall. Barbary apes on Gibraltar, that kind of prediction." He exhaled smoke, held the cigar between short, stubby fingers, and studied, as at an augury, its glistening end. "We were debating Ireland as the war began, and here we are, still at it. A great war has come and gone, great empires overturned, the waves of history engulfing lands, nations, continents. But as the deluge subsides and the waters fall short we see the dreary steeples of Tyrone and Fermanagh emerging once again. The integrity of their quarrel is one of the few institutions that has been unaltered by the cataclysm."

Tyrone, Fermanagh? Counties in Ulster, surely. Price would have a lot to learn, and in short order. He remembered newspaper photographs of the northern loyalists marching on their Orangeman's Day, sashes, banners, bowler hats, hard faces.

"My father gave them their marching orders," Winston said. " 'Ulster will fight and Ulster will be right.' A stiff-necked people, Major, I tried to thwart them once, and was badly chewed. Should have listened to my father's ghost. 'The Orange card is the one to play,' he said, 'and pray it comes up trumps.' We may have to play it again. I trust not. But first, order must be restored, eh Price?"

"All that is a bit beyond me, I am happy to say," Price said. He had declined a cigar, but was smoking one of his own Virginia cigarettes. "All that is well beyond me. I'm a simple soldier."

The blue eyes, deep-set, studied him. "Yes," Winston said. "So you told me. But I cannot afford to be, was once. We're a patchwork cabinet, but we're the chaps who won the war. They're after us. The Tories and General Wilson yapping on our right, screaming 'Save the Empire,' and the Liberals sniveling on our left, getting up a committee every time some wog out in India contrives to get himself skewered on a bayonet. We have to settle things and settle them quickly. In the Levant, in Ireland. Good people over there, you know, bullied by a few hundred gunmen, and a handful of counterjumpers like Collins. Let's root them out, eh?"

From the four billiards tables, all of them in use, came the pock, pock, of ball striking upon ball.

Twice, two summers when he was a boy, when his own father was off in India, Price had gone with his mother and his two sisters and his brother on a holiday in Ireland, on the Cork coast near Glengarriff. It was a fishing lodge belonging to friends of theirs, the Ellises, a low, ramshackle building, sparely furnished, fronting on the water. Earlier in the morning, Price and his brother, Hugh, who would be blown apart at Passchendaele taking his men across mud to a machine-gun nest, would go off on their fishing, mist, fine rain, the tall grass as they walked to the strand wet against their leggings. At evening, the woman who came from the village to do for them would prepare a simple meal, gammon and potatoes. And later, Price and Hugh would mend their gear while the girls played draughts and his mother, by the fire, would write letters, to India perhaps, or look through the *Tatler* or the *Sketch* and say, about something going on in London the week before, "All that seems a million miles away, all that could be happening on the moon."

"I would never presume, of course, to interfere in military matters," Winston said. "Secretary of state for war is an armchair title, after all, budgets and funds and that. But a quiet talk over a meal and a few brandies, different matter entirely, eh? My view of the matter is that if these gunmen were quietly to depart from this vale of suffering not too many questions would be asked. Not too many." He motioned in the air with the broad-bottomed glass and caught the barman's eye.

Later, they stood in Pall Mall. Winston leaned upon his ebony stick, solid and cheerful-looking, the jaw thrust out, as Price had seen it in dozens of newspaper photographs, but the eye mischievous, young, a young Hussar riding down upon the robed followers of the Mahdi.

"Back to the office for me, I'm afraid," he said, and placed his hand, briefly, upon Price's elbow. "No sport for poor Winston, down by the Liffey-side, worse luck. Did you know that the Shinners have banned hunting, raided a few hunts, one in Galway and another the South Union. I have ridden with the South Union myself a few times. My God, what a country they have over there, eh?" He lifted his stick. "Walk me to Admiralty Arch. Splendid day, eh? Splendid day."

Price stood for a few minutes at Admiralty Arch, watching Winston walk to the War Office, a stumpy, jaunty figure. His friends in the service, most of them, cursed the very sound of Winston's name. Still, you couldn't help liking him.

The John Lynch who was shot in the Royal Exchange Hotel in Parliament Street by a mixed squad of policemen and soldiers had been a courier carrying Republican Loan funds to Dublin. Ten days later, a clerk in the Four Courts named Henry Dennehy was shot at six in the evening, after work, as he walked along the quays to the tram which would take him home. For almost a year, Dennehy had been passing to IRA headquarters information as to forthcoming arrests and charges; a prudent, rather timorous man, he had done so carefully, with meticulous attention to security. If Dennehy could be ferreted out, Blake knew, then Dublin Castle must have been able to build up a far better network than G Division could boast. Blake's men—Shelley, Nelligan, Broy, the others—could tell him almost nothing. It took him the better part of two months, working with the team lent to him by Collins, to put together a file, dropping from Casey's list two men who had returned to England and adding two others. There were twenty names, in all, by the time he had finished. Some of them held rank in the Auxiliaries, the others worked at this job or that in the city, a few were commercial travelers.

On the morning of November third, two men, Johnny Harte and Tim Brennan, were found shot to death in a field in Rathfarnham, a Dublin suburb. Before being shot, both had been severely beaten. A statement issued by Dublin Castle suggested that they might have been murdered by "Sinn Féin extremists." In fact, they had been tortured in the guardroom of the Castle by Auxiliaries, then killed, and their bodies carried by lorry to Rathfarnham. Collins had from Nelligan the names of the Auxiliaries.

"But how did they get the names of Harte and Brennan?" Collins said. "That was the work of Price's fellows, and they will have the lot of us, if we aren't quick about what we must do. You are sure of these fellows, are you, Chris?"

"Most of them," Blake said. "Morally certain."

"Morally certain," Collins said. "There is a phrase I have always admired. Morally certain. It means not quite certain, does it not?"

"There is a man named Fitzmaurice," Blake said. "He was an officer in the Munsters during the war. He's a chum of Eames, who is one of Price's Cairo lot. They have dinner once or twice a week, and they have called in on Price a few times, at his house in Kingstown. But there is nothing more against him; he is agent here for a company in Manchester."

"He keeps bad company," Collins said, and kept Fitzmaurice's name on the list.

VIII

FRANK LACY

By the autumn of 1920, Lacy had been in the field for well over a year, moving from one brigade to another, reporting back to HQ in Dublin for assignment every six weeks or so, and it had come to seem to him his second life, one with obscure beginnings and an unimaginable end. He still held the rank of a headquarters captain, although the men with whom he worked in the field were brigade commandants or battalion commandants, but by now a legend attached to him which was weightier than rank. Brigade actions, battalion actions, were legends blown across hills, valleys, from one town to the next, magnified, embellished, and Lacy was a veteran of many of these, had instigated some, arrived to take part in some, and for a few arrived in time to take down reports of action. He had led the attack upon the first police barracks to be captured, at Ballytrain in Monaghan, on February 14, and had fought beside the local commanders when Kilruddy barracks was attacked on May 27. He had helped to organize the ambush at Rathmore by joining Kerry and Cork battalions. He had trained recruits and shown Volunteer officers how to train them. He had been in a score or more of small shooting incidents on the road, or when a patrol was encountered crossing fields. In July, at a road crossing outside Bandon, he was forced into a running gun battle with a squad of Auxiliaries; he brought one down and was himself struck in the shoulder; then his Parabellum jammed, but the three Volunteers with him were locals and they found their way, the four of them, to the house of a farmer named Hennessy. In August, when the first flying columns were organized, he and Ernie O'Malley were sent out to work with them, O'Malley to Liam Lynch's command at Mourne Abbey, and Lacy across the border, to Tadgh Cummings's brigade headquarters in Lisfarran.

The land was beginning to seem to him at once immense and intimate. In Lisfarran, he would learn that an attack by O'Malley's column at Kanturk had failed, with three Volunteers captured by soldiers, and would know from his map that Kanturk was a bare twelve miles away, but those miles were crowded with blue hills, boulder-strewn, mauve heather and yellow gorse, a different world, the speech of the locals subtly different. A battalion headquarters might be a blacksmith's shop on one visit and, on the next, an outlying farm, an abandoned schoolhouse. He visited O'Malley in Coolea once, after Lynch had moved his headquarters there, an Irish-speaking district. At night, billeted with two others at a farmer's in Gougane Barra, he listened to verse and song in Irish, understanding half the words, but the music clear as larksong. There was singing, too, late one night at Lisfarran, a long summer's night, the singers shy or boastful, and in the safety of the farmhouse they drank porter. As always, they were ill equipped, thirty men who would be put to drilling for all of the next day, but with nine rifles, two shotguns, two revolvers. A boy of fifteen or so kept sentry outside, with a heavy bandolier strapped around him, and carrying a Lee-Enfield. The song, the vivid clarity of night, the murderous weapons, formed a whole for Lacy.

Three days later, traveling, he was outside Rosscarbery, near the coast, with a farmer named Neafsey, whose son was a battalion adjutant. The son was a cheerful, voluble fellow, Brendan Neafsey, heavy-shouldered but light on his feet, upon whom five pints of porter in the course of a long night had no effect. Neighbors called in, a dozen or more of them, and the night was spent with porter, songs, a bit of music and dancing, followed, a few hours before dawn, by sandwiches and mugs of heavy, sweetened tea. They had three days to wait before the attack on the Rosscarbery barracks. Those two nights, there was no porter beyond a glass for each of them after a heavy tea of sodden cabbage and fatty bacon. Later, the men of the battalion who would work with the column were drilled in a field by Neafsey and Lacy together. There would be eight of them, and Lacy expected Brigade to bring in a column strength of thirty. Amongst the eight of them, they had four Lee-Enfields and a shotgun.

Later, Neafsey and he walked across a field and through bracken to the strand. The night was moonless, but by starlight, Lacy could see water and hear the rattling of tide against rocks.

"'Tis a wonderful life you must have for yourself," Neafsey said, "here one day and above in Galway the week later and in Dublin for all the plays and music and the rest of it." His tone was bantering, challenging, but if Lacy were to speak the truth, it all *was* wonderful. He remembered the days alone in the shed in the hills of Claregalway after 1916. Now there were battalions and brigades stretched across Munster, parts of Connaught, columns in the hills. Every rise of road brought him to action.

"How will it all end, Captain?" Neafsey said. "Do we have a clear sight of that?"

"It will end with the Republic," Lacy said, "it will end with a free Ireland."

"It will indeed, of course," Neafsey said. "It will end with a Republic."

"Republic" had been a way of saying that it would end in triumph, though few enough of the men fighting could say exactly what they meant by the word. "Republic" had been the word on the Proclamation outside the GPO in 1916, the Fenians had called themselves the Republican Brotherhood. A teleology, the people had been moving through centuries toward a republic, not knowing it most of the time. The first business of the Dáil, when it met in 1919, had been to declare its loyalty to the republic which did not yet exist. Republic, Lacy said, half-aloud, and tried to match the word to the night's immensity, starless, the rasp and suck of the water at their feet.

Beyond them, to their left, three hundred yards away, glimmering through thick entangled autumn branches, was what Lacy knew to be the late lingering lights of Moorings House, where a family of loyalists named Sparrow lived. Loyalist families were scattered across this part of West Cork, from Clonakilty to Castletownshend—Moorings House and Burgatia House beyond it and beyond Burgatia House, Cooldrinnen. A different world, upon which the word "republic" made no claim.

"They are fierce loyalists," Danny Neafsey, Brendan's father, had said that night of singing and porter. "Fierce loyalists." The phrase was an awkward fit in his mouth. The word he had in mind was "Protestant."

"Fierce," one of the older men said, a man older than Danny Neafsey. "They have a flagpole there at Moorings House, and on the day that the Great War ended, the eleventh hour of the eleventh day of the eleventh month, there was a Union Jack run up, by God, I saw it with my own eyes."

"Well you did," a man as old as himself said. "Because there was lashings of ale and porter and grub laid out, beneath the Union Jack, and there were you with your two hands upon a pint of porter, and I can swear to that because I was there myself."

"The eleventh hour of the eleventh day of the eleventh month," his neighbor said again, as though the words were an incantation to shield him from embarrassment.

Brendan Neafsey and the intelligence officer of the battalion, Peader Murphy, laughed along with everyone else.

"They're not the worst," old Neafsey said, "as Cromwellians go. They are not exterminators, as the Coswells were of Cooldrinnen, driving the poor and the starving out upon the road in the old days."

Now, deep night as they stood together by the edge of the water, Lacy said to Brendan Neafsey, "they have a large staff there in Moorings House, do they?"

"Large enough," Neafsey said, "maids and a cook and gardeners and a coachman and that sort of thing. 'Tis well for such people."

In the end, they could not take the barracks, their explosives were faulty, and the police kept up a heavy fire upon them, until Barry, the column commandant, blew the whistle to signal retreat. As they moved away from the barracks, toward the woods of Burgatia House, a young fellow named Timsy Brennan was hit by two bullets, one of them passing through his lungs. Neafsey and Lacy carried him with them into the woods, and were kneeling on either side as he coughed up blood in great gouts and then died.

But four months later, when Lacy was west in Galway, Barry attacked again, this time using Burgatia House as a billet for the column. When they moved away the next hour, they piled up bedding and furniture in the rooms, doused them with paraffin, and set Burgatia House ablaze, then waited in the woods for the Tans to send their lorries. Lacy heard about it from Lynch, months later, when battalion officers were meeting with Brigade at Kippagh in North Cork. "It meant naught to me, that house," Barry said, "an outpost of the enemy. The fellow whose house it was, Burgatia House, was bloody lucky we did not court-martial him and shoot him out of hand. 'Tis well known that he was carrying letters for the Tans between Clonakilty and Rosscarbery, he as good as admitted it. We told him he had twenty-four hours to get to hell out of the country and he took our advice. 'Twas not advice, 'twas an order."

Barry was twenty-two, a veteran of the Great War, and the best field officer Lacy had met, cool and resourceful. He was pleasant-featured, smiled often, and had a wild shock of hair that stood upright. In the field, he wore two Webleys in British Army holsters which a cobbler had modified for him, and he carried Mills bombs. By then, he was known by name throughout Ireland. As the English newspapers put it, he headed a murder gang in West Cork, the most vicious in Ireland, save for one in Tipperary. "Dan Breen and Sean Treacy they mean," Barry said, "but sure I'm just as vicious as those two." Had said that earlier, but now Treacy was dead, shot down in Dublin.

Lacy remembered the houses, Burgatia, Cooldrinnen, Moorings House. Burgatia House was cool gray stone, a carriageway, Virginia creeper. He thought that he remembered tall windows looking out across smooth lawn to the sea, but that could have been Moorings House. He imagined a wall of books, faded binding of calf, faded gilt, tall Chinese urns, paintings of Cork landscapes, seascapes, a watercolor on a piano, resting upon vivid silk from India, vermilion, emerald, photographs in frames of heavy scrolled silver, a young man in uniform, a tennis party lounging upon the steps. Flames splashed across them, sickly-sweet smell of paraffin. Beyond, down a hall, a dining table of heavy walnut, a sideboard.

"I have no tears to shed for the master of Burgatia House," O'Malley said when he and Lacy talked of it, briefly, one night in East Limerick, "nor for Burgatia House itself." O'Malley, like himself, operated directly out of Dublin HQ, organizing first at the division and battalion level, but working now with the flying columns. But he was like Lacy in other ways as well—middle-class, bookish, vague leanings toward literature. Whenever they met, it was as though they shared a secret. Villon and Rabelais were the meat upon which O'Malley thrived, and he was delighted, satirical, the time he found the Loeb Virgil in Lacy's pack, with two boxes of ammunition resting beside it. He read his Rabelais in the Uruhart translation, but he could pick his way through Villon's medieval French. "Virgil," he said. "Dear God. Building up an empire for the Romans, and we are tearing one down here." Had said that once in Dublin to Lacy, when they were spending the night in the Dawson Street flat of an Abbey playwright, but now, in East Limerick, he said, "Nor for Burgatia house itself. The bloody Auxies are burning down the houses of the people, and it is the master of Burgatia House and that lot whose interests they serve. If the landlords would throw in their lot with the Republic, their sideboards and their silver and their dragon-fierce vases from Peking would be safe."

It was true enough, Lacy knew. If the Black and Tans and the Auxiliaries had not been deliberately turned loose upon the people, as a matter of unstated policy, then discipline was being deliberately kept lax. Now an ambush or a shooting would be followed by a raid upon the nearest town, houses and shops burned, creameries destroyed, and as likely as not, a man shot, two men. Drunken Auxies, dark jackets and light trousers like the Tans but with their identifying glengarry caps, would fall without warning upon a town, smash open a public house. Sober, they moved their lorries warily along country roads, rifles at the ready. Their prisoners were invariably beaten up and most of them tortured. On occasion, a prisoner would vanish and his body would later be found by a roadside. Once in a while, a casual effort might be made to make the death seem the work of rebels. "Spies Beware," a placard might read on the chest of a body found among the furze.

But the IRA was in fact executing prisoners, at first suspected spies and informers, and then soldiers and policemen held as hostages. In September of 1920, Lacy and the officers of an East Kilkenny column had tried and then killed a Volunteer named Conor Goff, who had been a private in the Leinsters during the war, but had joined the IRA early in 1919 and since then had taken part in raids for arms and twice in ambushes of policemen. It was in the aftermath of the second of the ambushes that Goff and another Volunteer, Pax Cooney, were seized by the Tans and taken to their headquarters in Inistiogue. Cooney was not seen again, but Goff was released after a week and went back to his work in a shop in Urlingford, on the Tipperary border, and reported back to his section commandant, Charley Parkinson, also of Urlingford. Almost before he had returned, the raids by Tans upon the houses of battalion members were begun.

Parkinson was away when the Tans fell upon his house, and took his father and young brother out into the yard, where they were stripped and beaten. A cocked revolver was rammed into the boy's mouth and he was forced to kneel. "Give it a squeeze," a Tan said to his chum who was holding the revolver, and another said, "I have something better for him to suck on." That remark was remembered and told in Urlingford. "It tasted cold and bitter," young Parkinson said of the gun barrel. The commander of the raiding party stood a bit apart from his men, a man named Seeley who was said to have been a major in the war. Terrified though he was, young Parkinson remembered hearing Seeley twice mention Goff by name, and this, with other evidence, was used at the court-martial in a farmhouse outside Callan, to which four witnesses had been brought by motorcar. "How in God's name can yez say that, after the way those devils tortured me in the cellars there at Inistiogue that they keep for torturing our fellows. Would you give a look, some of yez have seen these." He rolled up his trouser legs to show the cigarette burns, still recent enough to be scabs. "Give me a second to take off my shirt and coat and yez can have a look at my back."

"There is no need for that," Cline, the commandant, said to Goff, "they had a go at you, right enough."

"And before it was over," Lacy said, "you had handed over to them the names of your entire company and any others you could think of. Two nights ago they took our explosives dump. It would have been better for you if you had cleared out of the country entirely."

"You lads know me," Goff said, "ye have known me all our lives the most of you. Sure we're all Kilkenny men, even yourself, Captain Lacy."

They were in the kitchen of the farmhouse. Lacy sighed and walked over to a window. It was dark night, a few stars.

"That was a terrible thing to have done, Conor," the commandant said. "'There is nothing that I have done, will yez in God's name believe me. We've known each other all our lives, some of us."

"There are lads in that cellar in Inistiogue this night because of you," the commandant said.

Lacy, with his back to them, said, "This serves nothing, there is no more evidence, send the witnesses away and we will vote upon this."

The commandant was acting as president and he turned first to Lacy. "Guilty," Lacy said.

Shiel, the adjutant said, "Conor Goff and I were schoolfellows, and he was at my side in the Thomastown ambush."

"This serves nothing," Lacy said again; "anyone can break under torture, spill what he knows. Goff came back among you as an informer. There is only one judgment upon an informer, and the country must learn that."

They were behind the table, and Goff was some distance from them, on a straight chair, facing them. He had not rolled down his cuffs; his trousers were fawn-colored and his short jacket black. His shirt was collarless. He looked like what he was, a farm boy; you could see scores like him any day, on carts, shouting and laughing to friends, or driving cattle homewards, cap pulled low against rain. When sentence was passed and before anyone could move, his face worked and he began to cry; then, a widening stain upon which he looked in shame, he wet his trousers.

Three volunteers formed the squad, but from the look of them, Lacy was afraid that they would bungle the matter, and, as they stood with rifles awkwardly sloped, he executed the sentence. He told Goff to stand against a tree in the pasture at a distance from the house; his hands had been tied behind his back and a rosary twined between the fingers. Lacy asked him whether or not he wanted a bandage, but Goff did not hear him. He squeezed his eyes shut and he began to recite the Hail Mary over and over and over again. "Holy Mary, Mother of God, pray for us sinners." The one shot to his head was ferociously loud, but had died from the air as Lacy turned toward the house, leaving the Volunteers to attend to Goff's body.

"The master of Burgatia House was sent packing off to England to his chums," O'Malley said to Lacy that night, months later in East Limerick. "But I've been in the hills with a column when hostages were shot, three of them. You shot an informer yourself, you told me that."

"I did," Lacy said, "in Kilkenny."

"And he was an informer, right enough, you made certain of that."

"Certain enough," Lacy said. "How can you be all the way certain ever? How can anyone. He admitted nothing, not even to save himself."

"Would that have saved him?" O'Malley said, and Lacy did not answer.

In December, O'Malley himself was captured in Kilkenny by the Tans and taken to Inistiogue, where he was beaten in the vaults by the same intelligence team that had worked on Goff. Later, after he had escaped from Kilmainham in Dublin, he told Lacy about it. "I was not the only one. When prisoners came in, they would be beaten in the guardroom and then thrown down into the vaults. I thought my feet had been crushed forever, and there was blood from their bayonets streaked down my back. They never found out who I was. I said I was Bernard Smith, a farmer in Inistiogue, and I stayed with that. On the way up to Dublin, they showed me the house where I had been taken, the O'Hanrahans'. They had burned it to the ground, and the family was under arrest for harboring rebels. I was taken first to the Auxiliaries' HQ at Beggars Bush and then to the guardroom at Dublin Castle, where they had killed McKee and Clancy a week or two before. For a time they thought I was Jack Ryan, who had been with me when we attacked Hollyford, they checked me against their description of him in the *Hue and Cry*. In the intelligence room I was paraded with others, then held there on my own, two men from the Castle intelligence team went to work on me, a major and a captain. 'Put your coat in front of you,' the major said, 'we don't want blood on the floor. Nice small hands for a farmer,' he said, 'you're a nice bloody farmer.' He began then to hit me, himself and the captain taking turns. I tried at last to get up, but my leg buckled under me. Back in the guardroom, one of the Auxies said to me that it was a rotten job but what was he to do, he had been an officer in the war but now he was out of work. He had a Scottish accent. I told him I was sorry for his trouble. After a while, I was moved from the Castle to Kilmainham. Things were better there."

But at times, Lacy wondered if he could hold out as O'Malley had, and he would think of Conor Goff, a farm boy of nineteen, bewildered. By the time the Tans released Goff, they had burned down his father's farm, and they held the father under arrest for a time. When he remembered Goff, he saw rope loosely binding the wrists, the heavy rosary of dark metal and a kind of silver, weeds at their feet, the harsh horrified sound of Goff's voice, "pray for us sinners now and at the hour . . ."

"I've been called back to Dublin," Lacy said. "To HQ."

"Things are hotting up," O'Malley said, "we have made this a real war. The Black and Tans don't have police barracks, but they may call them that. They have fortresses. They are here as an army and so are we."

It was true. They had been pulled back from the small barracks and the outlying ones. In April, on the one night, and across the country, 258 of the abandoned police buildings had been burned down by the IRA. You could not travel fifteen miles without encountering one of them, a blackened hulk, and with that wide stretches of country lay open for the rebels to move in, but the Black and Tan barracks and the Auxiliary barracks were heavily manned and fortified. The face of the country was changing. On June 19, Lieutenant Colonel Gerald Smyth spoke to the RIC in Listowel, and set down the new policy. "The more you shoot the better," he said, "and I assure you no policeman will get into trouble for any man shot." But on July 17, it was Smyth himself who was shot and killed by Volunteers who walked in to him in the country club in Cork City.

Before Lacy went up to Dublin, he spent a night with the battalion commander at Coolpartry, who complained about supplies, as all commandants did. "When you are there," he told Lacy, "you tell those lousers that this battalion has rifles, more than twenty of them, but we have damned few rounds of the three-oh-three, and what good are the rifles on their own?" He was a man named Quinlan, with great heavy shoulders, and long, full cheeks the color of young beef. "Will you tell them that, now?" There were framed prints on the wall of Robert Emmet and Theresa, the Little Flower of Lisieux. By the door leading to the byre there was an elaborate holy-water font. Quinlan was an unmarried farmer in his thirties. His mother and her sister lived with him, women heavy themselves, but in a soft, shapeless way. The mother served out bread and tea to Lacy and Quinlan and Quinlan's adjutant, and then went back to rejoin her sister by the fire.

"Winter is setting in," Quinlan said suddenly, changing the subject, "and a cold winter it will be, with those poor fellows on hunger strike in Cork and MacSwiney on the hunger strike beyond the sea over there in London." It was MacSwiney, as commandant of Cork No. 1 Brigade, who had ordered the shooting of Colonel Smyth.

"I will tell them in Dublin," Lacy said.

"Tell Brugha and Mulcahy, to be sure," the commandant said, "but make it your business to let Mick know. Tell Mick we used up damned near all our three-oh-threes when we shot up that lorry outside Urlingford last month."

Early in the morning, Keohane, the adjutant, gave Lacy a ride into Urlingford on his cart, and in the town a lorry driver was waiting for him, with tea in a closed pail. The driver, a local also named Keohane—it was a local name—was a thin, tall, edgy man, and not an active Volunteer. "It is not for lack of goodwill, you understand," he said, "when I am needed I am there, as I am this day, but there are the three children and a fourth on the way." "I understand," Lacy said. "There have been patrols," Keohane said, "between here and Abbeyleix. What will we do if a patrol stops us?" "It depends," Lacy said, "if it is a foot patrol, only the two of them, it might be best to give the wink and the high sign. They say Tommies have a weakness for Irish boys." Keohane took his eyes off the road to look at Lacy.

"But if there is a squad of them," Lacy said, "we'll take them on, the lot of them. I have a Parabellum and a Webley and you are welcome to the Webley. By God, we'll take a couple of them down with us. They'll pay dear. *Sinn féin amanh.*" "But there may be no patrols at all," Keohane said, "that would be best." "Yes," Lacy said, "that would be best."

In the early evening, they reached Dublin, and Keohane left him at Dolphin's Barn, and he walked through the city in darkening light, through the Coombe and down Winetavern Street to the river, and crossed over to Ormond Quay and along Swift's Row to Abbey Street. On Ormond Quay, he stood with others, pressing themselves against the window of a closed shop, as a lorry of Auxiliaries sped past them. Behind the metal mesh which protected the Auxies from grenades and Mills bombs, he could see them dimly, sitting on benches. Outside the mesh, one on either side, hostages had been spread-eagled and fastened. The one near Lacy was ashen-faced beneath the streetlight, a round, soft face with wide terrified eyes. "That's a new one," the man standing next to Lacy said; "I wonder will they keep things quiet in the Dardanelles."

He spent the night in the house off Denmark Street which he had been told to use. An old woman gave him tea and a plate of bacon and then showed him to a bare room with an uncomfortable bed, a plain dresser, a print of the Sacred Heart. He took razor and toothbrush from his case, the two weapons with which he had terrified Keohane the lorry driver, and his copy of Virgil. But he was too tired to read.

The old woman was awake and dressed by the time he came into the kitchen in the morning, and she had hot tea waiting for him. There was another print of the Sacred Heart on the wall, and, facing it, the photograph of a young fellow in Volunteer uniform. As he drank his tea, she stood by the stove, facing him.

"It is very good of you to put me up," Lacy said. "I will only be here for the two days or three at the most. So far as I know."

"Stay as long as you like," she said. "I am on my own here, and I don't mind the company." Her eyes moved to the photograph and then back to Lacy.

"That is my grandson," she said, "Francis Joseph Carmody. He is in Mountjoy. Do you know of him?"

Lacy did not, but said, politely, "I have heard his name."

"He was taken prisoner not five minutes' walk from here," she said. "In Capel Street. Himself and another Volunteer named Meagher. They had been in a scrap, but they contrived to get free from their weapons before the Tans seized hold of them, thanks be to God."

"Thank God," Lacy said. "What is the Dardanelles?"

"It is where Camden Street narrows down. There have been a half-dozen or more attacks upon lorries there, with shots or else with Mills bombs. Everyone now calls it the Dardanelles, the Tans themselves call it that." She refilled his cup and then her own, but did not join him at the table. The bread was several days old, and should have been toasted. Lacy put bits of butter upon the slice and then folded it over upon itself. "Mountjoy is full of prisoners, Francis Joseph and his chum Tansy Meagher. There is talk that they will go on a hunger strike in sympathy with the lads in Cork and poor MacSwiney off there in London. Would it come to that, do you think?"

"I don't know," Lacy said. "I have been down the country for the last two months."

"Down the country," she said, as though naming some remote and exotic land. "How is it down the country?"

"Fine," Lacy said. He took a swallow of tea to wash down the bread.

The old woman's name was Carmody, like her grandson's, and she seemed well into her seventies, thin gray hair caught loosely in the back, a long, thin nose, long lip. Gray, shapeless skirt. She looked a bit like the Witch in Lacy's childhood copy of Grimm, and for a moment he remembered the books of his childhood, a long row of them in the house in Kilkenny, in his room overlooking the back garden, which ran down to the river. He remembered his mother reading the tale to him when he was very young, seven or eight, by the window in the front parlor, his mother dramatically impersonating the Witch, the two lost children.

"Fine is it you say?" Mrs. Carmody asked. The accent of the Dublin streets was heavy in her speech.

"There are stretches of Munster that are in rebel hands," Lacy said, "and hundreds of RIC barracks have been burned down across the length and breadth of the country. You must have heard of that, Mrs. Carmody."

"You cannot believe everything you read," she said. "Poor Thomas Ashe died upon his hunger strike, and Terence MacSwiney may die as well."

But in the daylight, in the crisp sunlight of late autumn, you could not believe that this was a city at war, the shops open and people strolling about, housewives doing their messages. As he passed a national school, he could hear the children within, chanting a rhyme to memorize the alphabet. At a public house, lorrymen rolled barrels of Guinness down the areaway. A policeman stood nearby, DMP, unarmed and unconcerned. Across a wall, someone had chalked "Up the Rebels," but the letters looked skinny and inconsequential. Placards in a butcher's shop window advertised performances at the Royal and the Empire, at the Grafton Street Cinema. In Moore Street, the traders were setting up their stalls, cabbages, apples, bags of onions.

In a back parlor on the second floor of Vaughan's, Collins and Christopher Blake were waiting for him. Brophy, the bodyguard, recognized him, nodded and knocked on the door.

"You're quick off the mark, Frank," Collins said. "It is just now eleven."

He has been up for hours, Lacy thought. He was wearing a dark blue suit, dark tie. At the small, paper-strewn table, Blake sat at right angles to him, a younger man, Lacy's own age, slender, triangular face.

"You have been keeping yourself busy, Frank," Collins said.

"There is a deal to be kept busy with," Lacy said. "The night before I came back here I stayed with Paddy Quinlan at Coolpartry. He sent up a message that they are in bad need of three-oh-threes. He asked me to tell Cathal Brugha and Dick Mulcahy but in particular he asked me to tell you."

"Why me, for Christ's sake?" Collins said. "Mulcahy is your man."

"I am carrying his message," Lacy said. "Now you have it."

"They all want more weapons," Collins said, "and when they have the weapons, they want ammo for them. There are lousers down in Leitrim who haven't fired a shot in anger, and they want ammo. For pheasant shooting, perhaps."

"Quinlan has been hammering at more than pheasants," Lacy said, "and well you know it."

"Still and all," Collins said, "I have nothing to do with armament." But he scribbled a brief, quick message to himself. Quinlan will be getting his ammo, Lacy thought.

"Are you being well looked after, Frank?" Blake said. But before Lacy could answer, Collins said, "Of course he is. By Joe Carmody's grandmother, a decent old lady."

"When I was on my way," Lacy said, "a lorryful of Auxiliaries came down the quays, with a couple of fellows spread-eagled on the wire."

"We heard about that," Blake said. "They have been taking

hostages along with them for some time now, but that's a new one."

"The Auxies may have been drunk and out for a bit of devilment," Collins said. "They have a hard life, poor fellows. Miles away from home, and every man's hand against them so to speak. Even the loyalists are getting fed up with them."

"I have scant sympathy for them," Lacy said, "and neither would you, if you saw some of the work they have done, in Cork and in Galway."

"They are like loose cannon rolling about on the deck of a warship," Collins said. "Crozier, their commanding officer, cannot keep a proper leash on them. No one could. There are fellows in the Auxies were majors and colonels in the war, a couple of them were brigadiers, like Crozier himself. Now they are policemen with rifles and Lewis guns and armored cars in a country they cannot understand. They serve their purpose."

"They serve England's purpose right enough," Lacy said.

"And ours," Collins said, "and ours. For a hundred years or better, England has controlled this island with policemen and a few regiments of soldiers. In the villages and towns across the length and breadth of this island, there were few fellows liked or respected better than the Royal Irish Constabulary. Damned few of us do not have a brother or a cousin or an uncle in the RIC. What else was there for the younger sons of the small farmers but the constabulary if they were lucky, or if not, the ship to New York or to Boston. There were towns after towns where the man most respected after the priest was the RIC sergeant. But not now. Not now, by God."

He said it like a schoolmaster working out an equation on the blackboard. Lacy remembered the first time he had led an attack on a police barracks, the night before carefully warming the frozen gelignite in an iron pot, chancy work; it was some sticks of the gelignite that had been taken by Treacy and Breen at the commencement of operations in the field, in January of 1919. But in the end, it could not be used, the inside of the barracks was eight feet above the outside level. They attacked with everything they could use, paraffin, petrol, grenades made from tin cans packed with iron. But the constables were a tough lot and the barracks was held. Treacy and Robinson had climbed to the hot, sliding slates of the roof to hurl down grenades. Later Treacy, as commandant, had made a report to Brigade, and it was a sentence or two somewhere on paper, somewhere in Dublin.

"I need not tell you," Collins said, "you have been out there, on the move. By God, I envy you, the two of us envy you."

Perhaps they do, Lacy thought, looking first at Collins, then at Blake, then back to Collins again, who was grinning at him, a grin of approbation. They had been there in the GPO right enough, Lacy thought, and Collins had seconded O'Rahilly in the final charge up Moore Street, toward the barricades and the machine guns. And they had been in the prison camp in England. But their lives since then had been in Dublin, moving from one place to the next, files in shallow boxes which could be lifted in case of a raid, or else burned, moving from one bed to another, hurried cups of early tea in kitchens like Mrs. Carmody's, on the run, prices on their heads, but moving through the city in which restaurants still served dinners, in whose cinemas beams of flickering light flung huge, familiar shadows upon the screen—Lillian Gish, Charlie Chaplin, Mary Pickford, America's sweetheart—in whose music halls and theaters, plays were brought over from England after runs in Bristol and Hull, English casts, leading men in dinner jackets, leading ladies with ropes of false pearls. Outside, beyond the theaters, there would on occasion be a burst of gunfire which traveled faintly in. It was a different world, a different war, and Lacy, for all that he was back in Dublin every month or so, was not easy with it.

"You know the drill," Collins said, "a full report, everything you can think of to Dick. And a polite visit to Cathal. Cathal likes to feel the reins between his fingers."

Dick Mulcahy was chief of staff of the invisible army, and Cathal Brugha was minister of defense of the Dáil, the outlawed parliament. Now and then, the Dáil would meet, those of its members that is who were not in prison or interned, in the front parlor of some well-to-do sympathizer, or else the cabinet would meet. In theory, Paddy Quinlan below in Coolpartry was answerable to the chief of staff and the chief of staff answerable to the minister of defense and the minister answerable to the cabinet and the cabinet to the Dáil and the Dáil to the people. It was a neat, tidy theory, but Paddy Quinlan knew that he was answerable only to Ireland, to the Republic. So did Lacy. Lacy felt tensions in the air, between Collins and Brugha; Mulcahy and Brugha, lines of command.

"I am borrowing you for a few weeks, Frank," Collins said. "It has all been arranged with Dick. He will tell you that when you report to him."

"I know precious little about finance," Lacy said, "or intelligence either. Is that the sort of thing you had in mind, Mick?"

Blake had said nothing thus far. He sat smoothing out the papers before him on the table, a handsome tweed jacket, white shirt, tie of pale blue. Beside the powerful Collins, Blake looked almost a dandy. Blake's paper, the *Republican Bulletin,* had once or twice published stories about operations that Lacy had been part of, colorful and high-pitched.

"You could call it intelligence," Collins said, "but there are uglier words that people could find for it. Tell him about it, Chris."

Collins leaned back, and folded his arms. He was smiling slightly. Blake was looking at him with what seemed a faint annoyance, as though he had not expected to be called upon. At last, he shrugged, and gave a final tap to the papers, then pushed them away from him, and looked Lacy in the eye. There was something else that Lacy should have remembered about Blake, but he could not think what it was.

"The enemy intelligence organization," Blake said, "is headed up by what Mick here and myself and a few others call the Cairo gang. It is controlled by a regular soldier named Price. He was a colonel during the war, but now he has reverted back to rank as a major. He operates out of the Castle, and in theory, he is there to coordinate the police and the military effort, but that is a lot of nonsense. He has about thirty, thirty-five subordinates, all of them with British Army commissions, most of them English but a few are Irish. And each of them has been busy setting up a private little network. They operate out of Dublin, most of them, but there are five who have set up shop in Cork. Those are the ones we want you to help us with."

It took Blake a full twenty minutes to set forth the case, and Lacy admired the crisp, well-ordered account, even as he felt himself distanced from the world it disclosed, of informers and counterinformers, agents, files, killers, Collins's men in the Castle and in the G Division, Volunteers who had been pressured or bribed or blackmailed or in some way or other corrupted. Blake's voice had a clean, surgical edge to it, a surgeon probing a growth, a tumor, laying back sickly flesh.

"There you are," Collins said, "what do you make of it, Frank?"

"It is something that I would as soon have no part of," Lacy said, "what I've been doing is more badly needed."

"There we are, nevertheless," Blake said, soft insistence. Lacy stood up and walked away from them, to the window. He was looking into an untended garden, a few meager bushes and a growth of weeds, coarse grass.

"We may need it done," Lacy said, "but not by me." The wall at the end of the garden was topped by a layer of cement into which bits of broken bottles, jagged, had been set, white, green, colorless. A flat sun fell upon them.

"We need you to set up the operation in Cork," Collins said. "I could find someone else, but it is a task you could do. I could—we could—rely on you."

Lacy did not answer him.

"The main operation will be here in Dublin," Collins said. "And I will stand over it. Clancy and McKee and Christopher here will stand over it as well. There is no operation in the field more important than this. They are beginning to get very close to us. We were depending on a shipment from Italy that Michael Bellew was organizing. Last week, they were about to arrest Michael in a newsagent's shop in Blackrock. He tried to shoot his way out, and he was shot dead."

"For Christ's sake," Lacy said, and he turned away from the window to face the two of them. "Get rid of the bastards, do whatever needs to be done. I said only that I have experience by now doing other kinds of things."

"You do, do you?" Collins said so quietly that Lacy felt a warning tug at his temper, but he went on.

"The lads are keeping themselves busy in Tipperary and Cork and Kilkenny," he said, "but you should send me to Galway, or to get to work on those lousers in Mayo, that think themselves heroes that they have frightened a landlord or driven off cattle or burned down an abandoned barracks. Mind you, I will do what I am asked to do. I will do what I am ordered."

"You will, will you?" Collins said mildly. "You will obey orders? You will do what you are asked to do, will you? By God,

Horatius at the bridge is not in it, nor the Spartans at Thermopylae." He shoved the heavy head forward and stared at Lacy, then stood up, pushing back his chair with such force that it clattered over onto the stretch of uncarpeted flooring. "Dear suffering Jesus! A soldier, do you call yourself, boy? Don't you ever tell me again what you are willing to do, like some girl at a crossroads dance, picking and choosing among improper suggestions." The words, with the quick, heavy singsong of West Cork, tumbled out, and his shoulders were heaving. His face was twisted with anger. He began to speak again, but instead, he turned and walked to the door. He stood there a moment, with his hand on the knob, and then, without turning around, said, "Other kinds of things!"

When he had slammed the door behind him, Blake said, "We have a lot to do, Frank. Perhaps you should take a couple of notes, but as few of them as possible."

"That temper will get him in trouble one day," Lacy said.

"It already has," Blake said.

"Barry would not hold still for that," Lacy said. "Barry is West Cork himself." It was a gallery of deeply held superstitions, the temper of West Cork, the boastfulness of Kerry, the meanness of Carlow.

"He is on edge about this," Blake said. "Bellew and he were chums, but there is more to it than that. Mick and I had to go before the cabinet and justify what we intend to do, name by name, the fellows in Dublin and your lads below in Cork. You would not like it here in Dublin, Frank. They are close to quarreling at times, himself and Brugha, and as often as not Brugha is in the right. Collins tramples over people. Do you know what he said to Stack? 'Austin,' he said, 'your department is a bloody joke.' Austin has not forgotten that."

Lacy laughed, a quick, amused bark. "I would not think so. Is his department a joke?"

"Worse than that," Blake said. "Austin is a fine man to go on hunger strike with you, but he has no head for organization. But he is a Kerry man, and they stick together. You know what they are like."

"I do indeed," Lacy said.

"And he has friends beyond Kerry, he is a well-liked man."

"Well liked he may be," Lacy said, "but there is the fellow who keeps things moving, that bastard who left us just now."

But that night, in Vaughan's again, when Lacy had a short one with Collins in the bar, in the hour before curfew, it was as though Collins had forgotten the matter entirely. He was sitting against the wall, his coat unbuttoned now, and tie and collar removed. Two of the fellows in his squad, whom Lacy knew by sight but not name, were sitting beside him, but he was giving his attention to Feeney Harris, a commandant from Limerick. Lacy knew him well. Harris was sitting across the table from Collins, and Lacy joined him there.

"You are just here in time," Collins said. "Harris was giving us an account of the raid by himself and the lads on Kilmallock. Do you know about that one, Frank?"

Harris shot a wry glance at Lacy. "Well he might. Frank was there two days before, and showed us how to handle the gelignite. 'Tis wretched stuff, with the temper of a cross-grained woman."

As Harris talked, staccato outbursts of speech, awkward, a man unused to narrative, Collins leaned forward, his hands on his knees, and his lips parted. When Harris described climbing up on the roof of the barracks, himself and Tim Mooney, Collins slapped his thigh. "Jesus," he said, "are you not the lads. Up onto the roof, is it?" And he seemed, at that moment, himself a fellow up from the country for the day, a farmer or a dealer. Sackville Street was distant by a ten minutes' walk, hotels and restaurants, the theaters crowded. But Collins, in imagination, was in the streets of a country town in Munster.

The next day, Lacy and Blake held a second and final discussion of the Cork operation.

"Once," Blake said, "Mick was describing for the *Bulletin* what his position was. " 'I stand for an Irish civilization,' that sort of thing. It was not very impressive. Then he said that once a crowd of them—Irish fellows working in London—were going along Shepherd's Bush Road and out of a lane came a chap with a donkey. 'It was just the sort of donkey,' Mick said, 'and just the sort of cart that we have at home. We all cheered the donkey.' 'Well?' I asked Mick. 'Are you planning to move back from the donkey to Irish civilization?' 'I haven't left it,' Mick said; ' 'tis all there, young Irish fellows on their own in London, wishing they were home, and then the cart and donkey come out of the lane.' Then he laughed and gave me a shove, as though he had been joking."

Once, at a meeting of brigade commandants, Lacy had been trying to set forth Headquarters' notions of how the campaign in the field should proceed, and had drawn an ordnance survey map of Munster toward himself across the table in the paraffin-lit kitchen, and uncapped his pen. "Christ," Paddy Tunney said, "we've been fighting this war with hurley sticks, but we will be ending it with fountain pens." In disgust, Tunney spat into the ashes of the dead fire.

"Did you use the bit about the donkey?"

"I dressed it up a bit," Blake said. "Something about humble scenes, a drover on the road, a donkey and cart in a laneway, fishing nets drying beneath a Connaught sky, can remind us of the abiding verities of our ancient Gaelic civilization."

By now, thanks to English journalists and Irish publicists both, Collins's name had become a legend, swollen beyond proportion. It did not go down well with some people, with Brugha for one, as Lacy discovered when he reported to him. He was a fierce, humorless man, lips pressed tight even in repose.

"That is not warfare as I understand it, Captain Lacy," he said. "Rival gangs of spies shooting each other down like criminals in the streets of New York and Chicago. It may be necessary. I joined with Collins to persuade the cabinet that it was necessary. But it is not my idea of honorable warfare."

"It may not be Collins's either," Lacy said, and there was an eloquent hesitation before Brugha said, "No, perhaps not." And then, much as Collins would, he asked for Lacy's account of operations in the field.

Late that night, after Lacy had walked home, a shadow in streets of shadows hurrying home before the midnight curfew, sitting dressed and propped against the bedstead in Mrs. Carmody's flat, he thought that they all wanted reports of actions in the field, as though the actions possessed a purity impossible in a city's soiled air, the oppressive weight of buildings, the sluggish dirty river, the pressures of bodies, jealousies, sweat-heavy air. Brugha's hands had not always been so clean. At the time of the conscription crisis, he had gone over to England to organize the assassination of cabinet ministers.

That afternoon, out of the blue, suddenly, Brugha had said,

"Bear in mind, Captain, that we are lending you to Mr. Collins. You are still under orders of the Irish Republican Army."

"Of course," Lacy said. "Mick—Mr. Collins made that clear to me."

"We all serve Ireland," Brugha said. "We all serve the Republic, for which we fought and men died in Easter Week, for which they are dying now. Men on hunger strike in Cork, Terence MacSwiney across in Brixton Prison."

"They are dying as well in the streets of Dublin and Cork," Lacy said, "thanks to the problem that Collins has asked me to lend a hand with."

And in the next instant regretted his sharpness. Brugha was a cripple because of Easter Week, his leg dragged, he carried English metal fragments. They were sitting in the small office in the rear of the candle factory, Lalor's, on Ormond Quay, which Brugha managed. The air was heavy with the odor of wax. "There is no finer man in the movement than Terence MacSwiney," Brugha said, "a poet and a visionary, but a man of great practical ability, the commander of Cork Number One Brigade. But he will die, over there in that miserable prison in London. And in his dying he will make his contribution to the Republic. Only the Republic is important, Mr. Lacy."

"Yes," Lacy said. It was a matter so self-evident to him that it did not require statement, much less argument.

"Heroes are needed to keep up the spirit of the people," Brugha said. "The Irish people have never lacked for heroes even in the most somber of times, and it is proper that the names of commanders should be carried from one glen to the next. But no one man must ever be allowed to use reputation as an excuse for seizing power, for tyrannizing over his own comrades and colleagues. We are not getting rid of a king in order to give ourselves a Cromwell." He winced at his own words, and shifted his weight in his chair, to give relief to his wounded side. "Not that we have one of those on our horizon, you understand. I was speaking of tendencies, that is all."

By the weak light in his room, Lacy, composing himself for sleep, turned the pages of his Loeb. All the world was the theater of Virgil's poem, or at least as much of the world as had been opened to the swords of Rome. Not Ireland. When Rome was at her greatest stretch of empire, after Virgil, after Augustus, Ireland had been a fog-shrouded island, unknown, unregarded.

"Perhaps you should exchange your Virgil for a copy of Plutarch," Christopher Blake said on the evening before Lacy set out for Cork. "They are ideal types in their way, Brugha and Collins—the Republican and whatever it is that Collins is."

"Whatever it is," Lacy said. "But then, who would know about that better than yourself?" No one had done more than Blake to create the Collins legend, in the *Bulletin,* in interviews with visiting journalists from abroad.

"I am getting away myself for a few days," Blake said, "before we put this operation in train. Out to the West, to Galway."

"It is lovely in Galway, on the coast, the air like wine."

"I am going to the coast," Blake said. "A friend has lent me his cottage there. Near Renvyle."

"I have passed through Renvyle," Lacy said. "Lovely right enough, but bloody lonely. You are on the run, are you not? You'd best keep a wary eye."

And as he spoke, he remembered what he had heard, that Blake was involved with a woman—loyalist or Castle Catholic, something like that. The widow of a British soldier. Beyond the small village of Renvyle, white strand stretched toward the Atlantic. There was an immense quietness, Lacy remembered.

"I don't expect to be lonely," Blake said. "I would like to live there someday. After this scrap has been settled."

Faintly, Lacy resented his use of the word "scrap." That was what fellows in the field sometimes called it, "There was a nasty scrap last month at Kanturk," or "We had a good scrap last week." It was not a word that Dublin had earned a right to use. There were not yet enough flying columns, and they were concentrated in a few counties. For the most part, the brigades and battalions were still part-time soldiers, farmers and drapers' assistants taking time out for an operation. But the columns moved across the hills, bivouacked in friendly houses and barns, attacked suddenly and then moved away, carrying their wounded when they could. After the scrap was settled, Blake said, he would like to settle in Galway, with the woman perhaps, whom Lacy imagined as blond, white as snow, cool, her hands cool, a voice like tarnished silver. And write his books, perhaps a book about the scrap.

"You will visit me there, will you not?" Blake said.

Lacy realized, just then, that he had never imagined a life after the scrap was over, after the Republic had been established.

IX

PATRICK PRENTISS

On the ninth of November 1920 at the lord mayor's dinner in London's Guild Hall, Lloyd George assured the banqueters that in Ireland, the government had murder by the throat. It may have seemed so. Both the Auxiliaries and the soldiers were now conducting reprisals, and, more to the point, as the public would shortly and shockingly learn, a formidable intelligence operation was being brought into play, in both Dublin and Cork. On the twelfth of August, as a Brigade Council meeting was being held in Cork, some 300 British troops in lorries and armored cars had surrounded the venue and captured them all, including Terence MacSwiney, the officer commanding. In October, Sean Treacy and Dan Breen, up to Dublin from their Tipperary flying column, had been hunted down by intelligence agents, and Breen was wounded in a running gun battle. A few days later, Treacy was run to earth by a squad of Auxiliaries guided by intelligence agents, and killed in a second battle. Treacy managed to kill one of his assailants, and two civilians were killed in the crossfire. It looked very much as though a skillful and experienced intelligence team had moved into action with permission to shoot on sight.

Whether by accident or design, a cinema cameraman was in Talbot Street when Treacy was killed, and within days his film could be seen in the Classic Theatre in Grafton Street. "Armed Gunman Battles the Law," white letters told the spectators, against a background dark as night, the letters appearing suddenly, a message from history, "Death in Dublin Street." Gray, black, dim figures came into view, soldiers leaping down from lorries, a flurry, mouths shouting in full silence, and then the soldiers drawing back, bodies fallen upon the pavements, shapeless. Outstretched arms, sprawling legs. Helmeted soldiers picked up one of the bodies, flung it to the floor of a lorry. Two tall men in slouch hats could be seen hurrying past.

There it was, it happened just so, it is all on film, a record, history in moving pictures. Black night fell and then Mustafa Kemal was in the saloon of his special train somewhere in Asia Minor, a stiff, uniformed figure sitting uncomfortably among patterned cushions. He laughed briefly, and touched fingers to the grip of a holstered revolver. Night again, and French and English women footballers were seen lined up against each other in a stadium outside Paris. Jerseyed, bare-kneed, they did not look cold in the air of late October. Out of darkness, out of night, out of film, out of nothing, the white lettering of history which had recorded Treacy's death asked, "What Will the Ladies Try Next?"

Treacy had been shot in Talbot Street, to which the spectators in the theater could walk in ten minutes, after they had walked out into the grainy sunlight of late afternoon. This was the hour of the shooting affray; the cameraman was fortunate to have caught the last light. Much of what was happening is there on film, but the film stock no doubt tossed into a warehouse, crumbling, eroding. Terence MacSwiney's coffin bobs through an ocean of mourners in Cork City and lies in state, the open coffin flower-bedecked, beside it a guard of honor, uniformed Volunteers. Outside Mountjoy Gaol, bareheaded men, black-gowned women kneel waiting for the news that Kevin Barry has been hanged. Glimpses of De Valera, tall, bespectacled, long-lipped as a woodkerne, shy awkward smile, of Collins at a 1919 meeting, the heavy body leaning forward toward an audience, in the background what may be College Green, indistinct, fuzzy, a fist pounds into an open palm, over and over, the face is full of energy. Lorries of Auxiliaries, of Black and Tans, move through city streets, along twisting country roads, in the distance the wall of a shattered keep, the stone walls of the West. Two small girls, sisters perhaps, smile toward the camera, they are holding hands; behind them, a parked lorry, the Auxiliaries in tunics and glengarry caps grin and give the thumbs-up.

It is all there and we have created a counterreality which is brought back to us for as often as we like, if we know where the reels of film are stored. In Sarajevo, the archduke and his consort leave the Town Hall and climb into their open car, excited local functionaries bow and gesticulate; the archduke looks bored, heavy. Over and over again, on hundreds of thousands of feet of film, Tommies march through French villages, poilus, Germans, past shell-smashed churches, village halls, out of darkness, star shells burst into light and below them the lunar landscape of the western front, across the plains of Russia, Poland, cavalry sweeps, long-coated horsemen with lances or down-swinging sabers, in dugouts soldiers smoke, laugh, wave toward what, whom, us, the camera, the cameraman? A squad, gas-masked beneath helmets, moves across broken ground, in poor light, the film light-blotched. Outside a building in Versailles, before an ornate door, stand frock-coated statesmen, mustached, wrinkled, their eyes bright with mischief and the loot of reparations, one of them, the statesman from London, long gray hair wind-stirred, is smiling. Impulsively, he gives a friendly jab to the ancient Frenchman. The American president, tall, smiling toward them but looking puzzled, pince-nez flashing above elaborate dental work.

"We have murder by the throat," Lloyd George told the lord mayor and his guests in the immense banquet hall in the center of the City of London, and perhaps there is somewhere a film of it, the vast wood-paneled hall and the top-heavy grotesque figures of Gog and Magog, lights brilliant upon shirtfronts, white waistcoats, the lord mayor's elaborate robes and chains and seals of office, and Lloyd George, hypnotic orator, roller-out of cadences powerful as hymns in chapel. "We have murder by the throat."

On the day of Barry's hanging, in the Galway village of Kiltartan, a young woman named Ellen Quinn was shot dead by Black and Tans from their speeding lorry, as she sat on her garden wall; a military investigation concluded that it was "a precautionary measure." And there were killings, similar in kind, on the fourth and the fifth and the sixth and the eighth and the tenth and the twelfth. On the thirteenth, a lorry-load of Tans, firing into a Dublin laneway, killed a girl of eight. And killings in Galway, Cork, Kerry, Tipperary. "We have murder by the throat," Lloyd George said in the City. But for none of this is there any celluloid history, nor for the other record of "spies" and "informers" shot by the rebels, soldiers taken prisoner, held as hostage, then shot in retaliation for military executions. In imagination, a scene or two can almost be seen, in the theater of the mind, the young mother, the garden wall, the speeding lorry, with Tans perhaps frightened themselves, perhaps sullen and vengeful. The poet who had a tower in neighboring Kiltartan would mark the death of Ellen Quinn: "Now days are dragon-ridden, the nightmare/Rides upon sleep; a drunken soldiery/Can leave the mother, murdered at her door/To crawl in her own blood, and go scot-free."

That autumn and winter of 1920 and on toward the spring of 1921 murder was not held by the throat, far from it. Lloyd George was something new in English politics, mountebank, charlatan, trickster, scattering decorations, knighthoods, baronetcies, an earldom or two, in exchange for political support, financial support, by rumor a table of prices laid out, a jaunty, fiery little figure, presaging a new Europe, a hieroglyph, which none could yet read. That he had unleashed upon Ireland two irregular armed forces, and what was at first an unofficial, then a declared policy of reprisals by arson and murder, that he accepted the program of dealing with Sinn Féin by quiet murder, all this was at first unknown in England, and then, when once known, accepted as part of that changed world which ten years before would have seemed unimaginable and awful.

The "unofficial" reprisal exacted upon the town of Balbriggan was the first to make an impact in England. There had been others before Balbriggan, but they had been given at most a paragraph in English papers. Balbriggan, though, was an hour's motor drive from Dublin, and Blake and the other directors of Sinn Féin publicity made certain that foreign journalists were taken there. Thus, on the night of September 20, the night of the attack on Balbriggan, houses in Tuam and Carrick on Shannon were wrecked by the Black and Tans, and on the night afterwards in Drumshanbo, and a night later in County Clare, in Lahinch and Ennistymon and Miltown Malbry. But journalists and cameramen were taken to Balbriggan.

At Balbriggan, on that night, a police constable and his brother were shot dead in a public house, and when word of this reached the Black and Tan depot at Gormanston, about a hundred and fifty of them fell upon the town. The people of the town fled and spent the night in ditches. A month later, Sir Hamar Greenwood, the chief secretary, speaking in the House of Commons, came very close to condoning what the Tans had done, at Balbriggan and elsewhere.

After Balbriggan, newspapers routinely carried photographs of burned-out homes, city halls, creameries. At Caernarvon, on the ninth of October, Lloyd George announced that there was "complete anarchy" in Ireland now, "where a small body of assassins, a real murder gang, are dominating the country and terrorizing it. . . . It is essential, in the interests of Ireland, that that gang should be broken up, and, unless I am mistaken, we shall do it." In the photograph, his hands are just joined, fingertips touching; he looks earnest, resolute.

"The Camera as Recorder: News in Photography," the *Illustrated London News* proclaims, and Alderman John Roll is elected lord mayor of the City of London on September 29 by the Liverymen of the City; he had worked his way up from office boy to insurance agent. A farmer in Mallow stands among the ruins of his house, and two men stand beside one of Mallow's burned-out shops. Chief Secretary the Right Hon. Col. Sir Hamar Greenwood strides through the garden at Phoenix Park, stick in hand, rough tweeds. The Prince of Wales, returning from his tour, declares himself to be "most deeply touched and impressed by the unity and strength of sentiment which make the future of the British Empire secure." Lenin addresses a crowd in Petrograd, in the Place Ouritzsky; he leans foward, fierce, intense; below the platform are soldiers, sailors wearing bandoliers and carrying rifles; the lettering on banners is indistinct.

Accompanied by an armored car and lorries of troops, the body of Michael Fitzgerald, who had died on hunger strike in Cork Gaol on October 19, is carried back to Fermoy.

In that way, in the public perception of England, of the world, it became a fact that order, as conventionally understood, no longer existed in Ireland, a fact competing for interest with the death of the King of Greece, who had been fatally infected by the bite of a monkey. But for the cabinet in London, of course, it was a matter of greater consequence than king and monkey. Something would have to be done. There were now, in Ireland, two kinds of funerals, "Crown" and "Republican." In "Crown" funerals, a member of the armed forces, a Union Jack across the coffin, guard of honor, is carried through the streets of Dublin to the North Wall; in England, another guard of honor beside an open grave outside a country church, or a cemetery in London or Cardiff, wind ruffles the clergyman's surplice; there will be a photograph inset, perhaps, an oval, a young man in uniform, a subaltern, fair-haired, mustached, and an account of service, service in Mesopotamia in the War, wounded in action, held the D.S.O., aged twenty-six. In "Republican" funerals a coffin bobbing through crowded city streets, then carried along a country road, before it a priest in cassock, surplice, biretta, and on either side, men in dark suits, ties awkwardly knotted, on the coffin, a tricolor and a crucifix. In the background, a village street, straggling, mean buildings unraveling toward distant hills. "Michael Hanratty," it might say beneath the photograph, "aged twenty-four, a farmer, reputedly a brigade adjutant in the Irish Republican Army, killed by forces of the Crown who were defending the police barracks in Kilmallock." Or Kanturk, or Dungarvan, or Newcastle West.

Toward the end of November, the defense of a Volunteer on trial for his life at the Old Bailey took me to London. I spent the night in my old room in Pump Court, and the next day walked across Gray's Inn to meet with Barnabas Boland, with whom I was to be associated in the case.

I found him in chambers, looking, as always, hangdog and, as always, not quite properly shaved, bits of nascent brown beard on either side of his lips, and the foam from shaving lather dry, white upon a cheek. On a stand by the door hung his silk gown, for he had taken silk sometime in the past, and his wig lay before him on the table. He was drinking tea, and when I walked in he shouted to the clerk, "Tea, more tea." "Good morning, Barney," I said. Barney was one of the Bantry band, the Healys and the O'Higginses, he had married the sister of Conor Tully-Delaney, of Cork City and Kilpeder, and the future lay all before him.

"A fine bloody day for a couple of our lot to turn up at the Old Bailey," he said, "they are likely to batter us to death, am I right, Pat? Turning up there to defend a Sinn Féin gunman, today of all days."

"You seem a bit upset, Barney," I said, "to call me by the humble Pat. Things are never going well when you don't call me

Padraic." I had never discovered the Gaelic for Barnabas, but he was happy enough with Barney.

"And I have a bloody well right, have I not?" he said. We had our tea by now, given over to us by the clerk, a nervous Cockney, and after the clerk had left, "Would you like a bit of stiffener in it?" Barnabas asked, and from his desk he hauled out a half-bottle of whiskey, and not, I realized at once, for the first time that morning. "I do not," I said, "nor do I prefer to appear in this court or any court with a man who has taken drink."

"For the love of God, Pat," he said, "fairness is fairness but it can be carried too far. I was thinking, do you know, that there are grounds upon which we could ask for a day's adjournment, to compose ourselves, like. Old Avory isn't the worst in the world, good old Judge Avory."

"I'm not so certain of that," I said, "he hanged poor little Crippen, and Big Tim MacDermott did worse than Crippen."

"Is charged with having done," Barnabas said, the law rising within him as instinct, Healy blood will always tell. "Dear God, Pat, do you never read the newspapers?"

"I read Saturday's *Irish Times,* I seem a bit more exclusive in my patriotism."

"Fuckin' *Irish Times,*" Barnabas said, "what does the fuckin' *Irish Times* have to do with patriotism." On his own, prepared to drink alone, he splashed a sturdy dollop into the Cockney's execrable tea.

And then, gathering the pages together slipshod, he handed me the *Morning Post.*

"APPALLING TRAGEDY IN IRELAND," I read, "Wholesale Murder by Sinn Féin, Brutal Gunfire on Sunday Morning in Dublin Cuts Down Fourteen Serving Officers in Their Homes or Hotel Rooms. Some Butchered before Their Wives. Five Other Murders in Cork. Sir Hamar Greenwood Promises 'Full and Total Response by Crown Forces' to Outrage in London."

I sat down on the chair by the side of Barney's desk, with its customary litter of briefs, scrawled messages and notes to himself and to others, framed photographs, indistinct family groups, men in frock coats and silk hats, a snapshot of himself hurrying into court, gown trailing and wig askew, followed by his clerk, and, as well this morning, the newspapers.

" 'Tis in all of them," Barnabas said, the tony English accent brushed away from his voice like the wisps of seafoam that it was, and it was Cork City's quick singsong, nervous, challenging and cajoling all at once. " 'Tis being talked about as a brutal massacre, and what else can you call it, my God, 'tis the slaughter in Dublin they dwell upon, and fair do. Dublin fourteen, Cork five." He made it sound like the score in a hurling match. "But I can tell you," he said, "it was bloody enough in Cork, I was on the phone to Conor. Two of them in houses in Sunday's Well and one in Montenotte, and one in the Metropole itself. They shoved the night porter into a closet, and went up to the third floor, no hesitation, they knew exactly the room, kicked open the door, and blasted away at the poor bastard. There you are."

I was trying to listen to him and read at the same time, and he was quite right, it was Dublin that dominated the *Morning Post* at least. In a concerted move, it told its readers, Sinn Féin's murder gang struck throughout the city, at the same hour, in bands of two or three, shooting down officers, who were roused from their sleep and stood against bedroom walls, or murdered in their beds. A few of them survived but only long enough to be taken to hospital. The actions, all of them, took place at nine or a few minutes later, after the bells summoning worshipers to Mass had fallen silent. In four instances, at least, wives had witnessed the killing of their husbands.

"What purpose can be served by mass slaughter?" Barnabas said. "My own sympathies are with the national movement, to be sure, as are your own." As he spoke I laid aside the *Post* and picked up the *Times:* it told much the same story. "Dear God," he said, "my wife's nephew is in the Dáil, and I am certain that he had no hand or act in such a catastrophe. There are wild men on the edges of the movement, we all know that."

Once, in an earlier decade, the clutter of fetishes on his desk had included, placed in prominence, a photograph of himself, very young, flanked by Dillon and Redmond, but after Easter Week it had disappeared. And so too in time, in a few years' time, there would, I was certain, be a photograph of his wife's nephew.

"Nor is that the worst of it," he said, "did they think that they could wreak such havoc without retribution, not with those murderous Black and Tans roaming the countryside." He looked a bit thirstily toward his whiskey. "Did you read that stop press in the *Post?*" I had, without paying it much heed, a shooting affray at the semifinal in Croke Park, Tipperary and Dublin, Auxiliaries and gunmen in an exchange of shots. "Is that what you mean?" I asked Barnabas.

"Exchange of shots!" he said. "There is a good one for you. I have heard from Conor what happened. When the Tans and the soldiers heard about the killings they went mad, prisoners in the Castle were tortured and then killed. And that afternoon, at the match, the Tans went berserk with rage. Lorryloads of them swept up to Croke Park from their barracks at Beggars Bush, and cut open with machine guns, Lewis guns, rifles, the lot, for ten minutes they poured lead upon players and spectators alike."

I rested the *Times* on the desk, atop the *Post,* and it was as though my mind refused fully to accept what he was saying. Later, government would profess, and rightly perhaps for all anyone knows, that IRA gunmen had begun the fire, but nothing could erase, for it was beyond a denial, the ugliness of that imagined scene, the Tans in their lorries and armored cars, from the safety of which they played automatic weapon fire upon a crowd at a hurling match. Before they had finished, fourteen had died, and the wounded, of course, were many.

"There you have it," Barnabas said, "we should consult with Givney when we go to court, and recommend an adjournment." Givney was MacDermott's solicitor, and MacDermott was charged with having laid explosives aboard three ships moored in the Thames. "There will be no justice given out to Irishmen in London today, or for days after."

"You're right about that, Barnabas," I said, although our task would have been in any case a brief one, because MacDermott, so he had let us know, intended to deny the authority of a British court. "By all means let us talk with Givney." Which in fact we did, but it all mattered little. The request for adjournment was denied, and MacDermott, a large man with flaming red hair, denied the authority of the court, and was tried and sentenced and shouted "Up the Republic" before he was led downstairs by the warders. Testimony, speech by the prosecutor, summing up by Judge Avory, and sentencing took a bit less than two hours.

Later we stood outside the Old Bailey, Barnabas, Finbar Givney and myself. Givney's was the fierce Republicanism you sometimes encountered among the London Irish. "Bloody bastards," he said, "with their scales of justice and their sword of justice, much justice has an Irishman ever taken from their hands."

"We must try to console ourselves," I said, "with the knowledge that our client is as guilty as sin."

"Guilty of what?" Givney said, "guilty of bringing the war into the enemy's camp? Is it that they can set fire to our towns and the homes of our people, but their bloody London is not to be touched?"

"Dear, dear," Barnabas said, and he looked left and right toward the indifferent streams of barristers and solicitors and law clerks.

"I will tell you this as well," Givney said, "those fourteen men or is it twenty who were shot in Dublin and in Cork were not anglers over for a bit of trout fishing, they were bloody serving officers, scourges of our people."

"He's right there, Patrick," Barnabas said concessively, "and the horror of Croke Park to cap it all."

After we parted, I walked to Blackfriars Bridge and then along the Embankment to the Temple. It was a chill, raw day, sunless, a sky of lead. Christopher Blake was later to tell me, that night in Wicklow, what I already had suspected, that the men shot down that Sunday morning, Bloody Sunday, as it was to enter historical memory, were the directors of the British intelligence operation in Ireland, save for two of them, who were shot in error, and the one most senior in rank, a colonel, one of the ones shot in the presence of his wife, was the director of the operation, a man named Price. "They were going to put us on the spot," Collins said, using a gangster phrase picked up from Edgar Wallace, "so we put *them* on the spot." And later still, years later, I talked with one of the gunmen, by then an auctioneer, portly, balding, a Pioneer pin. Tim Brennan and another volunteer had shot a captain named Tarleton in his room in the Gresham. " 'Say your prayers,' I said to him," Brennan told me, and stuck out two fingers in imitation of a revolver, " 'say your prayers' I told him and then bang bang." He nodded at his recollection. "Myself and George Coughlin both. Tarleton was one of those in bed with a woman, but you will find no mention of that anywhere because it was not his wife. He had a wife safe home in England. I hope to God he did take that second or two to say his prayers. A bitter November morning but she had less on her than a Hottentot would have. The one in bed with him I mean, not the poor missus beyond in England." He had recently taken up golf, and spent his Saturdays at the club in Portmarnock no doubt, holding the mashie with fingers that once had gone bang bang.

At the Embankment, in that bitter November chill which Brennan was later to recall for me, I looked out upon gray, chill waters. The history of our present hour comes to us in images, words, broken, a child's puzzle thrown toward us. MacDermott, in Criminal Court No. 1, shouts "Up the Republic," and Tim Brennan and his chum shout "Say your prayers," whom I would not meet for another ten years but I could imagine steps along a hotel corridor, a door kicked open and screams, lorries and armored cars moving into Croke Park, I could see the Lewis guns stammering but could not see the faces of the gunners. From waistcoat pocket I took out what I never thought of as my watch but rather always my father's watch, and snapped open the cover with its elaborate engravings of deerhounds couchant beneath thick-branched trees. Ample time to pack and make the night boat at Holyhead.

X

FRANK LACY

On the last Sunday in November 1920, a week to the day after action was taken against the British intelligence officers in Dublin and Cork City, Black and Tans on lorry patrol to Dunmanway from their headquarters in Macroom Castle were ambushed and destroyed at Kilmichael by the flying column of the Third Cork Brigade, commanded by Tom Barry. Two weeks later, farther westwards in Cork, near the edge of the Kerry border, on a stretch of road which leads across the Derrynasaggarts from the market town of Kilpeder in Cork to Killarney in Kerry, two lorries of Tans were attacked by Sixth Brigade's column, under the command of Patrick MacCarthy, with Frank Lacy from Dublin HQ serving as adjutant and second-in-command.

Kilmichael became a ballad within weeks, and in the best traditions of balladry, no one would ever be certain of its authorship, but many attributed it to the principal teacher of Castletown National School, Jeremiah O'Mahony, "a well-known local genius of history and literature," who lived by chance a hundred yards or so from the graves of the three Volunteers who were killed by the Tans at Kilmichael—Pat Deasy and Jim O'Sullivan and Michael MacCarthy. "And the flames of their lorries gave tidings," it sang, to the tune of an earlier song, "that the Boys of Kilmichael had won." The song floated backwards into legend, gathered itself about a twist of road at Kilmichael, moved outwards in Galway, Mayo, Dublin, wherever, forwards into a disputed present.

In point of fact, Kilmichael had been carefully planned and

prepared. Later, during the Civil War, when Barry and Lacy, on the run the two of them, had a quiet night together in Clondalkin outside Dublin, Barry talked a bit about Kilmichael. "On the twenty-first," Barry said, "on that Sunday when you fellows in Dublin and Cork City were busying yourselves with your assassinations, there was a brigade meeting at Curraghdrinnagh, and one after another of the battalion OC's came forward to describe the depredations of the Tans operating out of Macroom, but not a word was said at that meeting about the Kilmichael ambush which then was well in train."

The road at Kilmichael would never have been Barry's first choice, nor O'Malley's nor MacEoin's nor Lacy's. Bogland, heather, rocks, poor cover or none at all.

Kilmichael had been imposed upon Barry by his needs. The Tans had arrived in Macroom in August and had taken over the castle, a sensible and obvious choice, because Macroom was one of the two gateways upon which entry into West Cork swung. Their lorries moved out each day from Macroom, southwards toward Dunmanway. Attack them too close to Macroom, and you risked their being reinforced from the castle. Attack them south of Gleann Close, and they would have fanned out, or so at least they had done so the four Sundays earlier. That left Kilmichael. "And the problem, do you see," Barry said to Lacy, "the problem was how to make the bastards slow down long enough for us to kill them." Barry was twenty-two.

"You know yourself what they are like, those lousers," Barry said. "They would throw those lorries into a village and commence shooting. Go smashing into the public houses, and they may not have been drunk when they arrived but they would by Christ be drunk when they left, and if they saw a fellow fleeing down an alley they would take a shot at him. Burn down a man's roof over his head, that is their idea of a pleasant Sunday evening. A poor lad fifteen years old, the near side of Dunmanway, they caught him out on his own and fired so much lead into his two legs that there was little enough left afterwards for the surgeons to cut away. They have done worse, Frank, you know that yourself."

In the Dublin suburb of Clonskeagh, a long late-summer evening in 1922, in the long narrow garden of the safe house, green wherever they looked, a green so rich and luxuriant that it seemed to Lacy almost to be staining the air. Lacy said, "Yes, I know that."

"We fell in at O'Sullivan's of Ahilina," Barry said, "at two that Sunday morning, the twenty-eighth, and God but it was lashing rain, there were thirty-six of us in the column that morning, but if you are to credit what the British were to put out there were hundreds of us, but there were thirty-six. We had to borrow rounds from one of the other columns, a few of the officers had revolvers, I did myself of course, and I had the two Mills bombs that I captured at Tourneen. You've heard about Tourneen. The two Mills bombs were essential to my strategy." He ran a hand through the shock of tall unruly hair. It had all been less than two years before, Lacy thought, but it was all different now, a different kind of war, a different kind of enemy.

"You know how it is yourself, Frank," Barry said, softly, as though disclaiming any particular distinction, "when you struck beyond Kilpeder, in the Derrynasaggarts, you brought your fellows to the spot by forced march, did you not?"

"We did," Lacy said, "but it was a fine clear winter's day. A cold, bracing day, with a rime of frost on the rocks."

He was thinking that the two of them could be veterans of the Grande Armée, discussing Austerlitz in the inglenook of some *auberge* in Normandy, and not two Irish fellows still in their twenties, a war against empire behind them and in the midst of a civil war which they did not entirely understand, but understood a bit better than many, understood at least to the knowledge that it had to be fought. "Mind you," Lacy said, one Grande Armée veteran to another, "we had Kilmichael to look back to as precedent. You showed us the way to set about it, Tom."

A week before Kilmichael, Barry had said, there had been a brigade meeting at Curraghdrinnagh, "when you fellows were busying yourself with your assassinations."

When Lacy thought about the operation he had directed in Cork that Sunday, the kind of thought which would come to him late at night, in bed, without light by which to read, unable to sleep, he thought of it as ugly but necessary. He had schooled himself to think as surgeons, so he supposed, must think, or the commanders of uniformed armies. It was far different in tone and texture from his memories of the Kilpeder ambush, the air glistening, touched with a faint odor of the Atlantic, carried across Kerry by swift cold winds.

The Cork City operation had been different, delicate negotiations with No. 1 Brigade, for all that Collins and Mulcahy had sent instructions before him, and the meetings with the fellows who were to make up the squad, city lads all but one of them, drilling them in a task which was new for most of them, new enough for himself, although two of them had done the shooting of Inspector Massie in late August, walking up to him as he strolled in the flower garden of the hotel in Montenotte and cutting loose on him, then vaulting over the wall. Those two, Lacy made his seconds-in-command, and he himself, with a gangling, Adam's-appled young fellow named Finbar Tuohy, attended to a lieutenant colonel of the Argylls on detached service and passing himself off as a medical officer, living not in barracks but in a room at the Metropole.

When Tuohy joined Lacy at half-eight that morning, across the road from the Opera House, he was fifteen minutes late. There was a fine mist, and Tuohy had his coat collar turned up, his mackintosh, and his two hands buried deep in his pockets. "I am not late, am I, Captain?" he said. "I went to the early Mass, but left for here directly after communion." "Fifteen minutes late," Lacy said. For all his weedy height, Tuohy had the look of an altar boy. "But we have time and to spare," Lacy added. It was not the time for a reprimand.

At the Metropole they gave holy hell to the night porter, and then herded himself and the boots and two skivvies into a small side lounge, where Tuohy kept watch over them while Lacy took the lift to the fourth floor, walked down a frayed, pretentious runner of red Turkey carpet, passed closed doors and prints of fox hunts, a waterfall, sparkling waterfront at Glengarriff, to room 411. "A message marked urgent, Doctor," Lacy said, "it was brought by a corporal on one of those motorcycles." He was a paunchy man in his nightshirt, sandy hair thin, receding, red cheeks, puzzled and half-awake. Lacy shoved, prodded him backwards into the room with the muzzle of his automatic pistol. "Now see here," the fellow said. Lacy kept prodding him backwards until he was standing by the far wall, beside the bed. Above the wall was a colored photograph of some sort. Lacy picked up one of the pillows and wrapped it about the pistol, holding it, with the one hand, awkwardly in place. "Mistake," the man said, not hearing any part of Lacy's sentence but the final words, "authorized by the Irish Republican Army." The pillow muffled the shot, although not as completely as Lacy had hoped, and he walked back quickly to the lift.

The officer had been passing himself off as a medical doctor named Leith, but his name in fact was Campbell, no better name for the Argylls, and he was buried a week later, with full military honors, outside his parish church in Perthshire. As for Lacy, who had killed him, he and Tuohy and the other members of the squad, they met with Bassett, the vice-adjutant of Cork No. 1 Brigade in the house where Lacy had been staying, the house near the top of Blarney Lane owned by a prosperous contractor named Donovan. There was a full breakfast waiting for them in the kitchen, but none of them had stomach for more than cups of sweet scalding tea and some toast.

Afterwards, Lacy remembered it all, the red Turkey carpet, the colonel's paunch taut against his nightshirt, the mist outside the Opera House as he waited for Tuohy. Remembered it as something seen through the wrong end of field glasses, focused, but so distant as to be denied precision. Far different to remember the battle beyond Kilpeder, in the Derrynasaggarts.

It was in August of '22, in the Civil War, that Lacy and Barry sat talking together in the garden of the safe house in Clonskeagh. A year before, to the day almost, during the Truce, Barry had been married in Dublin, and there was a reception afterwards in Vaughan's Hotel, with a photograph afterwards in the rear garden of the hotel—the lot of them, Lacy thought, all of them, Harry Boland and Liam Deasy, Pat's brother, a brigadier, and Emmet Dalton and O'Duffy and Dick Mulcahy and Christopher Blake and Madam Markievicz and Liam Mellowes and Sean MacEoin. At the center of the photograph is Dev, president of the Republic or however it was that he styled himself that month, earnest and somber. Lacy himself is standing beside Mick Collins, the two of them with their heads tucked down because at the last minute Collins muttered to him that the photographer was a police informer. A moment later, the photographer's flare exploded like a harmless grenade, and the man himself crawling out from beneath the hood, Lacy said, "Jesus, Mick, an informer, are you serious?" Collins gave a whoop of laughter, and punched Lacy's arm. And here we are now, a time's time, stalking each other and killing each other.

Barry said, "I remember a time in October, a month before Kilmichael, some lads from the column were chatting in the kitchen of a farmhouse in Ballimphellic, and I walked in, Charley Hurley was there and Paddy Crowley, and over by the wall Sean Hales and Dick Barrett were talking with cups of tea in their hands, the four of them there, and all four were to die by the gun, Charley and Paddy killed by the British, and Dick to be executed by the Free Staters and Sean to be killed by our own crowd. Would you ever have believed that, would you have thought that possible?"

August, but a chill wind touched the garden, rustled leaves, fell across Lacy's face, died away and it was autumn heat again. He shivered.

"Kilmichael, Kilpeder," Barry said, Aeneas remembering windy Troy, "were we not the great lads then, and we're not so bad now."

Lacy had had to argue hard at Headquarters with the lot of them, Brugha and Collins and Mulcahy, before they would authorize the attack on the Auxiliaries operating out of Ardmor Castle in Kilpeder, westwards of Macroom, beyond Ballyvourney, almost on the Kerry border, and then argue with them, a less difficult task, to appoint him to a temporary joint command with Pat MacCarthy, who commanded Sixth Brigade's flying column, and then, after he had reached Kilpeder, to argue his case to MacCarthy, a shrewd, hard-headed commander. It was too soon after Kilmichael, Mulcahy said, and Collins and Brugha were for once in agreement. Kilmichael had stirred up a hornet's nest, Mulcahy pointed out, and the Tans and the Auxiliaries were fierce with rage and watchfulness, and so too was the army on the spot, the Second Essex, with Percival, their bastard of an intelligence officer, turning prisoners into informers with his pincers and hot wires. But Lacy argued a different case.

Kilmichael, he argued, had put heart into the people in West

Cork, had frightened the landlords, and had persuaded the British that they were dealing with something more serious than scattered bands of cowboys with stolen shotguns. The strategy of the Tans and the Auxiliaries had been to take over a large, well-fortified RIC barracks or a big house like Macroom Castle or the one in Kilpeder, bases which could never be attacked with any hope of success, and then rove out to terrorize the countryside. Barry had taught them manners in the only way possible, by using the strength of the flying column, its mobility, and ambushing their lorries on the road. It was going to take them a bit of time to sort this out and devise a strategy to meet it, and they should be hit again, and hit hard. "They will go on calling us the murder gangs," Lacy said, "but they will know that they are dealing with an army." It was an argument designed to appeal to Mulcahy and Brugha, who were keen on legitimacy and respectability.

Ben Cogley, the IO of the column that moved to the west and to the north out of Kilpeder, saw no need for help from Lacy nor from anyone else. He was shop assistant to the chemist in town and married to the chemist's daughter. A brisk, sardonic young fellow with ginger hair and mustache, he was behind the counter when Lacy walked into the shop, but he shouted out up the stairs that he would be away for a bit.

"I am astonished that you are not on the run," Lacy said.

"I am safe enough for the moment," Cogley said, "some of the lads are on the run, and Pat himself is of course, but the Tans think I am a harmless crank in a chemist's shop, if they think of me at all. 'Twas a different matter when the RIC was here in their barracks, a fellow named Gerry MacDonagh was the sergeant and he knew bloody well who I was and what I was about. He's handed in his retirement papers, but he was a helpful fellow while he was here. The barracks closed up shop when the Tans took over Ardmor Castle in August, and we burned the place a few weeks later. The Tans came streaming down into town here in their Crossley tenders but there was little they could do."

They stood together in the quiet street of the market town, a road stretching eastwards toward Macroom, westwards toward the Derrynasaggarts and distant Kerry. There was no mistaking the barracks, a shell of smoke-blackened brick.

"It took a long while to get that barracks burned," Lacy said, and when Cogley looked at him, puzzled, he said, "a half-century or more." A smile of pleased surprise. "You know about our barracks," Cogley said. A famous barracks. In the Fenian uprising in 1867, the locals under the command of a gunman named Nolan had tried without success to take the barracks, and had then moved out to make a stand somewhere beyond the town. There was a ballad about it, there was a ballad about everything, a place that Lacy could not recall by name, somewhere beyond the town, but he remembered Nolan's name.

"Ned Nolan," Lacy said.

"Ned Nolan," Cogley said in agreement. "You know your Irish history, as the schoolmasters like to say. Ned Nolan, he was a blow-in, a stranger sent down from Headquarters to take command of the lads here. But as the story has come down to us here, the real man in command was the man on the spot, a fellow named Delaney, it was from Delaney that the boys of Kilpeder took their orders."

"Delaney," Lacy said, "I don't remember that."

"Why should you," Cogley said, "Nolan was a hero-commander from headquarters, and Delaney was but a shop assistant."

The point had been made with an impressive swiftness and neatness, and Cogley, looking a bit pleased with himself, drew a forefinger along the mustache. "I thought we might have a glass in the pub, and then walk out a bit into the country. After dark, we will go out to Shanahan's of Aherbowey, where Pat and some of the lads are staying." As they talked, standing outside the shop, two Auxiliaries walked toward them along the far footpath, dark tunics, glengarry caps pulled over one eye. One of them carried a swagger stick. They were striding along but without haste, and unlike the Tans, they carried themselves like soldiers. One of them looked thirty or more, but the other was young, fresh-faced.

"Do they drink here in town?" Lacy said.

"Not officially," Cogley said, "they have their own canteen here in the castle, but out of uniform, they will call in at one pub or another, and they are never denied their order, you may depend upon that. Their officers drink in the Kilpeder Arms."

Once, they had all been officers, it was a condition for service in Ireland as a cadet, and when one of them was killed, you would read of the murder of Cadet Arthur Sinclair, late captain in the Second Lancashires. Disbanded temporary officers, drifting about after the 1918 armistice, no jobs to go back to, a taste for action unslaked by the slaughters along the Somme. As the ballad about Kilmichael had it, their wages were twice that of Tommies or policemen, and they killed twice as many.

The two Auxiliaries walked into the large shop across the road, handsome ornate scrollwork, great gilt letters upon a red background, "Tully and Son." "The local fellow who shared command of the Fenians in 'sixty-seven was an assistant in the shop there," Cogley said. "He married the owner's daughter."

"A well-known road to prosperity in such towns," Lacy said with a mildness that deliberately called attention to itself. He looked down the road toward the gutted barracks which once, a half-century before, had been attacked by laborers and potboys, most likely, led by a shop assistant and a gunman from headquarters.

Cogley looked at him with sudden, brief irritation and then smiled. He took Lacy's arm and turned him around. He extended his arm as though stretching but in fact he was pointing. "Do you see down there, the gate opposite the Protestant church, that is whence the two Auxies came, it's the rear entrance to the castle, the main entrance, the grand one with gatehouse and dressed stone and all the rest of it, is almost a mile outside the town, the Sullane flows beside it. When they move out on patrol, that is the gate they use, they cross the bridge and then a wide arc of a side road brings them to where they can move westwards toward Kerry or northwards towards Millstreet."

"Or southwards towards Dunmanway," Lacy said.

"Yes, of course, but in fact they have never patrolled towards Dunmanway. Dunmanway is covered by the garrison at Macroom."

"Macroom Castle," Lacy said, "Ardmor Castle, Daintree Manor in Kilmallock, they are housed in comfort."

Cogley grunted. "They are supposed to be in company strength of one hundred, but they lack the full complement. There are eighty-seven of them, four Crossley tenders, four armored cars with Lewis guns, two staff cars."

"Right," Lacy said, although he knew that already. He had read Cogley's intelligence reports, no nonsense, no boasts, clear, legible chemist's script.

"Our column, you understand," Cogley said in the same mild, low voice, a voice full of irritability, "is half-armed at best."

"We can do something about that," Lacy said.

"Something should have been done about it months ago," Cogley said.

In the snug of Conefry's public house, glasses of amber whiskey before them, Lacy said, again, "We can do something about that. There is great respect at headquarters for Sixth Brigade flying column, respect for Pat MacCarthy and for yourself as intelligence officer. It is shocking, the intelligence reports some brigades send in, half-literate scrawls." It was three in the afternoon, the time of day when Lacy liked a public house best, they had it to themselves, save for a toothless old pensioner at the far end of the bar from the snug's open door, and the barman, who kept himself at a studious distance out of earshot, dipping glasses first into a sink of sudsy water, then a sink of clear water, and then setting them into place, upside down, in the racks above his head.

"You are asking a great deal of us, is my judgment," Cogley said, "there are columns pampered by headquarters beyond belief, and the country knows it, Breen and Robinson in Tipperary and Sean Treacy while he was with us, God rest his soul, Sean MacKeon above in Longford, Galvin in West Galway. In and out of Dublin all the time, and they have Mulcahy's ear, or Mick's ear."

Through frosted glass, colored glass, winter's watery light fell upon sawdust, a bar whose edge had been worn by decades of fingers, behind the bar, sunlight fell upon bottles—Midleton's, Powers, Jameson's. Along the bar, halfway toward pensioner and barman, elaborate beer pulls of polished ebony, brass, ivory. A self-respecting house.

"All that is neither here nor there," Lacy said.

"You are right," Cogley said, and sighed as he moved away from the subject. "In any case, it is a matter for Pat and yourself to discuss."

On the front wall, beside a door closed against the cold of winter, a large, lurid poster of Hibernia, a maiden of towering proportions, demure and triumphant.

"The Auxies who come here to drink must be a tolerant lot," Lacy said, looking toward the poster.

"Most likely they don't know what the hell it is," Cogley said, "a Papist saint or whatever. Before the Tans arrived in August, there was a framed and glassed tribute to the martyrs of 1916, but Conefry got that out of sight quickly enough, and an engraving of the heroes, the GPO blazing, and Pearse standing defiant, with poor wounded Connolly propped up against a wall, but still directing the battle."

The iconography of public houses, Lacy thought, and Cogley, as though he had read the thought, said, "I have not the slightest doubt in the world that the tribute and the engraving are stowed safely away, and will be gracing the walls again one of these days."

"God willing," Lacy said.

"God willing," Cogley said. "There was also an original oil painting of the lad himself, our hero-commander, Ned Nolan, done not from the life of course, but ten years or so ago by a talented artist from Cork City. Fenian wideawake hat of deep-brimmed black, and two American six-guns strapped to his waist like Buffalo Bill. And in a semicircle above his head, the words from the ballad, 'Death lay waiting in the snows of dark Clonbrony Wood.'" Cogley lifted his glass in salute to Nolan or to the artist from Cork City or to the publican's prudence or to all three.

"Kilpeder's flying column has a tradition to live up to," he said courteously to Cogley, and Cogley, nodding, said, "We will take the other half, and then take a short walk to fill out the early evening."

"The other half is mine," Lacy said, and was about to hail the barman, when Cogley rested a hand on his arm.

"Not at all," he said, "not at all, you are a guest here," and he smiled at Lacy. Cogley never missed a trick, Lacy thought, and felt a mild, amused sympathy for the chemist father-in-law, with this swift, assured successor to the shop.

"Do you have children, Ben?" Lacy asked, moving strategically to Christian names, but asking out of genuine interest.

"I do," Ben said, "three girls and a boy. Clare and I have been married seven years."

They walked out of town by a side road, beside the Protestant church, and at right angles to the castle gates, handsome dressed stone, each of the pillars topped by a stone globe and atop each globe a stone falcon with fierce outstretched wings. Between the two pillars had been placed a makeshift gate of heavy metal bars around which barbed wire had been strung. Behind it, a loose-jointed Auxiliary walked sentry-go, forwards and back, his Lee-Enfield sloped; he was wearing a holstered automatic pistol. "Are they all that well armed?" Lacy asked, looking up toward the gilded hands on the Protestant clock. "They are indeed," Cogley said. It was past four, hurrying toward Munster's early winter evening.

The walk upon which Cogley led Lacy took them for three miles, the side road swerving to meet a larger one which ran beside farmlands, the winter soil hard, dry, leafless hedges, scattered houses, cabins, barns, past a creamery, past the ruins of a chapel, the one remaining crumbling wall of a Norman keep, up a rise of land, to a disused house, its garden untended, a garden wall, once trim perhaps but now neglected.

"Now then," Cogley said, with an intelligence officer's vanity, knowing the right spot to inspect terrain. "Over there are your Derrynasaggarts and there, northwards from here, are the Boggeraghs." Distant hills, browns, blacks, a chilly winter green; late sunlight fell upon rock.

"And eastwards from here," Lacy said, "passing through Ballyvourney, the Macroom road?"

"Indeed," Cogley said. He took Lacy by the elbow. "Look there, there is their base, there is Ardmor Castle."

From this distance, they had a clear view of the two chief roads which led to the castle, behind its demesne walls, the straight road from the falcon-gates in the village, a service road, moving past barns, outbuildings, and, far off from it as it seemed, a road which led by twists and turns past unheeded garden, a scattering of decorative summerhouses, past pasturelands and plantations, to an avenue running between tall elms, the bare branches on either side arching toward each other, to a great circular carriageway beyond which lay the steps leading up to the castle. At the farthest end from the spot upon which Lacy and Cogley stood, just this side of the demesne wall, slanting sunlight fell upon the river, the Sullane; a river walk ran beside it, bleak and uninviting. From the castle itself, broad, stepped terraces moved down toward the river, circular flower beds. Far off the one side, and as though in challenge to the formality of the terraced lawns and gardens, a wide pond, ice-covered now, glinting;

willow trees, bare-branched, touched its frozen edges. A small summerhouse, the deliberate parody of a pavilion, lay beside it. Pond, willows, pavilion, the stream which moved away from it to the Sullane, made a moment of their own. Obscurely, despite ice, neglect, bare branches, the dead stalks of reeds, Lacy felt himself stirred. It reminded him of something far different seen elsewhere, of Japanese prints.

The castle itself offered an immense Palladian front, tall windows looking past terraces, past gardens, past a little obscure Japanese-y cameo, past the Sullane, past the demesne walls, built so solidly as to survive frost and rebellion, past the town, toward the Derrynasaggarts, toward where, invisible, beyond Kerry, lay the Atlantic, from which came winter winds, faint now, which fluttered, faintly, the Union Jack, hung from a flagpole planted upon the highest of the terraced lawns. Eastwards from the castle proper lay stables and outbuildings, and in the stableyard two of the Crossley tenders, ugly vehicles, stood parked, without the overguarding of steel mesh with which Lacy had become familiar in Longford and Kilkenny.

"One of the Crossleys has been seized up," Cogley said. "It is in the far stable being attended to. A pity the Auxies could not get assistance from Pat MacCarthy. He is an automobile mechanic by trade, and has a shop just outside town on the Macroom road. Had, I should have said. His brother Dennis is tending shop for him."

The commandant's shop. "A wonder that the cadets have not burned down the kip and Dennis within it."

"They have been commendably circumspect in their dealings with Kilpeder," Cogley said, "the cute hoors." Lacy savored the mixture of dictions. "There is an old adage cautioning against shitting on one's own doorstep."

"Four Crossleys," Lacy said.

"Four," Cogley said. "There is for some reason but the one on patrol today. It moved out this morning, at ten, patrolling northwards to Millstreet, and it should be returning"—he broke off to take a gold watch from his waistcoat pocket—"oh, within the next hour, certainly within the next two, unless they have been up to some deviltry. The armored car and a Lancia. The Lancia has a driver and a gunner. The tender has a complement of fourteen, including the driver, and a lad sitting beside him with a Lee-Enfield."

Lacy turned away from the castle, to study Cogley. He was running his forefinger along his mustache again, a witty, vain, reliable man.

"The lad with the Lee-Enfield," Lacy said, "sitting beside the driver. Could you put a name to him?"

"Cadet Officer Thomas Neville," Cogley said, "late a captain in the Welsh Fusiliers. His father is a clergyman in Cardiff. A congregationalist clergyman."

Lacy's derisive smile detonated a laugh which had been building. "Get out from that, you low cunt," he said.

Cogley accepted the compliment with a show of demure pleasure. "You put me to the challenge," he said, "but you can accept the rest. We have been keeping tabs on them. And don't draw wrong conclusions. They are a bad lot, good soldiers but right bastards, they are worse than the crowd in Macroom Castle."

"They need manners put upon them, do they?" Lacy said.

"They do indeed," Cogley said, "but not here. They are secure and safe within the falcon-guarded gates of Ardmor Castle."

The immense demesne behind its walls, beside its river, lay spead before them beneath a dying sun.

"Whose castle is it?" Lacy said, and Cogley shrugged.

"No one's in particular," he said, "it belongs to a syndicate in London, it was sold off to them ten years ago as a speculation. It belonged once to a family named Forrester, Cromwellians, but the last of them died off somewhere in Italy. He was still alive when I was a young lad growing up, not here but in Millstreet, but I knew Kilpeder. The Big Lord, he was called by old-fashioned people. Is that sort of carry-on over and done with, do you think?"

It was Lacy's turn to shrug. "A tender and an armored car," he said.

"Some days," Cogley said, "and on some patrols. But on other patrols there will be two tenders and I have counted as many as twenty cadets."

Lacy turned away, and found a place to sit on the low wall which edged the disused cottage. Cogley joined him there. Lacy took a packet of Senior Service from his pocket and they sat smoking.

"Do the lads use this place?" he asked.

"We did, for a while," Cogley said. "Pat was here for a month almost when he was first on the run, but then we got the wind up. It is too close to town."

" 'Tis pleasant enough," Lacy said. "It must be grand in summer."

"There was once a rose garden," Cogley said, "but when the cottage fell into disuse, everything ran wild. It was the house of a retired schoolmaster, and it is still the property of his son, who is a lawyer off in America, in Philadelphia."

"God help him," Lacy said, "I have been to Philadelphia. A desperate quiet place."

Cogley looked over at him, startled, and then nodded. "You have of course, I had forgotten. You were in the Rising in 'sixteen, above in Galway with Mellowes, and from Galway you escaped to the States."

"The Rising in Galway was more of a farce even than the Fenians of 'sixty-seven. We have learned a bit since then."

Seated on the wall, Lacy could still see the castle, center of its miniature world. Mountains sprawled westwards and northwards from it.

"The Tans are not likely to invite us in," he said, "we must find a way of inviting them out to us."

"That will be a matter for you to put to Pat," Cogley said. "By God, you are a single-minded sort of fellow, Frank. Such was the reputation that traveled out ahead of you, and you are living up to it."

Lacy began to say something, but then changed his mind, and said instead, "I know that, Ben. 'Tis a fault. I know that."

" 'Tis well known, Frank, that you organized that ambush at Tourmakeady last summer and blew a lorryload of policemen to kingdom come. But it is also known that that night, after you had gone back to Dublin or off to God knows where, the RIC came out of their barracks and savaged Tourmakeady in reprisal, burned houses, took men out of houses and stripped them naked and whipped them with their women forced to watch and then shot them in the road. Life doesn't end with an ambush, Frank. Things happen."

"I know what happened that night at Tourmakeady," Lacy said. It had come back to him three or four times at night, whiskey would not deaden it, nor Virgil, nor music hummed aloud, tunelessly, beneath the music he would hear about the sack of Tourmakeady, as it was called, as it had been told to him not in Christopher Blake's comely paragraphs, but by Paddy Bawn Coogan, who had been one of those whipped, although he had escaped death by a wound in the thigh. It was not men only who had been stripped naked in Tourmakeady, but this was never mentioned, save for the occasional drunken Paddy Coogan in a Finglas public house.

The Derrynasaggarts, austere, desolate, tumbled, recalled to Lacy the weeks which he had spent on his keeping in the Slieve Aughties, after the Rising. He had never felt the land, the country, more intensely than then, alone, hunted, earth, rock, sky, water possessing an urgent purity.

"I know about Tourmakeady," he said again.

Abruptly, as though sensing the bitterness in Lacy's words, Cogley changed the subject.

"It was its own lovely world below there once," he said, "before your day and mine, terrace upon terrace and great beds of flaming flowers, lovely. My brother above in Millstreet is married to a young woman whose father was for a few years one of the gardeners at Ardmor. To hear him talk you would know that it was its own world, and a lovely one."

"Days gone by," Lacy said, "days over and done with."

"Perhaps . . ." Cogley said, who was less certain. The days of Ardmor Castle might be over, if by this was meant flowers, a young nobleman bringing home his bride, the carriage rolling across the miles from Macroom, those days might be over, but the Ardmor lands still paid over heavy dividends of rent to the syndicate in London, and would do so no doubt whatever the outcome of battles between Volunteers and policemen with Lewis guns. And on other estates stretched across the length and breadth of Munster, there were still flowers, still house parties, guests arriving now by motorcar, chattering about some incident in their neighborhood, a creamery burned down perhaps in army reprisal for an ambush, or an army motorcyclist fired upon and killed, left dead upon the roadside, sprawled beside his machine.

"Over and done with," Lacy said again, and Cogley said again, "Perhaps."

He happened then to look into Lacy's eyes, and was startled by what he saw there, eyes cold and pale as the Atlantic.

"Men have died for the Republic, and men have killed for the Republic," Lacy said. "We will put all that behind us, by God, English lords and their brides, glasses of porter for the servants. Do you think it is by accident that Ardmor Castle lay ready to be taken up by the Black and Tans and used as their base of operations? That is what the Ardmor Castles and the Macroom Castles and the Fitzherbert Houses have always been, when the waltz music and the beds of flowers have been scraped away. They have been the fortresses by which England has held us down. Take a look at Ardmor below there, and you will see what it has always been, with its guns and its British soldiers and its armored cars, as though we were holding upon it one of those yokes that the hospitals use which let the surgeons look past flesh and fat to see the bony skeleton."

In the few days that he was to spend with them in Kilpeder, Lacy never in Cogley's hearing made so long a speech again, not even when he and Pat MacCarthy were explaining the operation to the column, and it was not the words which Cogley was to remember, but rather the tone of voice and those murderous eyes.

Some twelve years later, Joseph Haggerty, a journalist at work upon a book, was to ask Cogley about Frank Lacy and the civil war in which he and Cogley had fought upon different sides. The journalist had put the question with appropriate circumspection. Cogley was by now a cabinet minister in the native government, and they were speaking over brandy-and-sodas, in the bar of Buswell's, a hotel across narrow Kildare Street from the Dáil. Cogley's father-in-law was long dead, and the chemist's shop was Cogley's; he employed two assistants, one of them herself a qualified chemist. Cogley had a paunch by now, and his thin, sparse hair was combed carefully across his freckled skull. At home in Kilpeder, he fought the paunch by beagling, but in Dublin, when the Dáil was in session, he golfed, with crisp winds from the Irish Sea weathering his broad, strong-jawed face.

"What was he like, Mr. Haggerty? A determined man, yes, you could say that." Cogley smiled down into his glass of watered brandy, pleased with his sardonic understatement. It all seemed so much longer ago than twelve years, like a different age almost, when the now cabinet minister had been intelligence officer to

West Cork No. 6, Pat MacCarthy's flying column. "He was a bookish man, everyone knows that, carrying the Roman classics in his case with his Parabellum, but he was a bookish soldier, as you might say, talking of tactics and strategy and sieges and Julius Caesar. He drove Pat MacCarthy up the wall with his pedantry at first, but then they got along well enough."

At Shanahan's, the safe house in Aherbowey, Cogley and Lacy sat waiting for MacCarthy that night, together with three lads who were on the run, simple country lads no older than eighteen by the look of them. Shanahan's wife kept tea fresh for them, and slices of soda bread, buttered and raisin-flecked, lay heaped in a plate on the deal table. Earlier, Jimmie Raleigh, the most recent of the three to be forced onto the run, had taken a half-bottle of whiskey from his pocket, but Cogley said, "There will be none of that. By God, if the commandant were to see that, he would rip it from your hand and send it smashing into the fire." Raleigh sighed and addressed himself to his tea.

It was close to half-ten before they heard, in the distance, the sound of a motorcar, and Cogley said, "There he is, I would know that motor anywhere." "I would myself," Shanahan said, "I remember when he bought it, below in Bantry, five years ago, and brought it limping and coughing into Kilpeder. He kept it three months in the shop, tinkering with it, and when he had finished with it, by God, he could have raced it in France." "A bit of a risk is it not," Lacy said to Cogley, "driving about in it like that?" But Cogley shook his head. "Not these roads," he said, "there are no patrols along these roads."

And of course there were not. Lacy realized that as soon as he had spoken. With Cogley, he left the kitchen, and stood in the cold winter night, starry and clear. Far below them, the headlights of MacCarthy's motorcar cut the darkness as he moved cautiously along the narrow, twisting boreen.

Shanahan's farm lay in the foothills of the Boggeraghs, the mountains which stretched northwards, from Kilpeder, across the Kerry border, toward Killarney and Kenmare. Even here, as he stood upon land sloping gently upwards, Lacy had a sense of hills, of roads moving upwards toward tumbling stone. Shanahan's byre was close to the farmhouse, and Lacy could smell beasts, dung, straw. Almost, not quite, he could hear the heavy-breathing beasts, but there were no sounds save, faintly from behind the closed door, the laughter of the three lads, and, below, the chug of MacCarthy's motorcar, heavy and insistent as it traveled through darkness, the two lights stretching forward like antennae.

"Shanahan has the right of it," Cogley said, "Pat made a beauty of that motorcar, it can do fifty if he pushes it."

They walked back into the kitchen, and it was another twenty minutes before they heard the motor switch off at the head of the boreen, and another five before MacCarthy swung open the door.

There was a captured three-page Dublin Castle file upon MacCarthy which Lacy had studied, but no photograph, and yet he was strikingly close to what Lacy had imagined, heavy-shouldered but quick-moving, in the flickering lights from the fire and the paraffin lamp, a ruddy-featured man, heavy-jowled. He wore frieze trousers and a black jacket, which once perhaps might have done for Sunday Mass, but now was worn, a gray streak along one arm; a clean white shirt, fastened at the collar below a prominent Adam's apple. He was carrying a heavy outer coat, which he hung on one of the pegs beside the door. He was not armed, so far as Lacy could tell, although a police description, one of the three documents in the HQ file, described him as going heavily armed; it also described him as having "the build of a blacksmith, and with a sullen bulldog cast of countenance."

He nodded toward Lacy and held out his hand, but before they settled down to talk, he took the newly arrived lad aside and questioned him sharply, nodding once or twice, and reaching almost absently for one of the thick-buttered slices of soda bread. Then he turned toward the table and sat down facing Lacy and Cogley, who sat side by side on the seat of the high-backed settle bed. They talked at random for a bit, sipping sweet, scalding tea, about a police inspector who had been shot dead in Millstreet the week before, about a hurling match in September between Cork and Kilkenny, about a gunman who had died of his wounds in the infirmary of Kilmainham Prison.

"There is many a good man who has died in Kilmainham," MacCarthy said. Before Lacy could respond to that, MacCarthy pushed aside his cup. "You have come down here to ginger us up, is that it, Frank? Do you mind if I call you Frank, the titles that have been handed out to us stick in my craw, my own included. Commandant, how are you!"

"Frank will serve fine," Lacy said. "By no means to ginger up your lot, Pat, not the West Cork flying columns, neither your own nor Barry's. Mind you, I have been sent out by HQ to do that to this battalion and that. But not here, not in Kilpeder."

"There is sweet fuck-all that can be done now, now that the Tans are installed in Ardmor Castle, and not with the arms that we have to hand. But you are here to change all that is it, and get us killed in the bargain and the town of Kilpeder burned down around our ears."

"I don't think so," Lacy said with deceptive ease, "I think that we can make West Cork so hot for the Tans that they will be well content to stay within barracks. Macroom last month and Kilpeder this."

"That is what you think, is it, Frank?" MacCarthy said, a flat statement, and he looked briefly toward the window, opaque, beyond it sleeping cattle, a rise of hills, the blackness of a December night. Lacy said nothing, he sat facing MacCarthy, and there was what seemed to Cogley an uncomfortable silence. Then MacCarthy reached into the pocket of the worn, shapeless jacket for a packet of cigarettes, and, when he had held a match for the three of them, he tossed the packet to the lads who sat near the fire, studiously not listening, talking to themselves in low voices.

"The Tans are neither British Army nor proper RIC," Lacy said. "They are turfed-out soldiers from the war, heroes one day and shiftless vagabonds the next, an embarrassment on Armistice Day. It is one thing for them to get drunk and shoot up a town, but it will be another if a stretch of countryside is made so hot that they cannot patrol it without being mauled. Barry left no survivors at Macroom, took no prisoners."

MacCarthy took a long drag on his cigarette, and held the smoke in his lungs, then released it explosively.

"That is their notion in Headquarters, is it, above in Dublin?" He rubbed the smooth table top in a circle of his large, heavy hand. "Mulcahy and Collins and Brugha?"

"Headquarters has approved the attack on the Kilpeder garrison," Lacy said.

"That is not what I asked, Frank, and you know it. They approved the plan, but I doubt if they proposed it. And I know that Liam Lynch did not. This was your own idea, was it not?"

"Yes," Lacy said. "It was, but that is neither here nor there. They did more than approve it, once it had been approved, it was sent down the line to Lynch, and Lynch approved it, and now here we are, with a plan to attack sent down from Headquarters to Brigade and from Brigade to Column."

"From Headquarters to Brigade," MacCarthy said with heavy sarcasm, and lifted his hand to run it through his thick, chestnut hair. "Those messages and demands for information and directives as you call them that come down from Headquarters and from Brigade are a wonder to me, I declare to God. I don't marvel at Headquarters, there they are up in Dublin dreaming their dreams, but Lynch is himself below there in Cork with us, himself a man fighting in the field."

"That is how it is with armies," Lacy said.

"Armies!" MacCarthy said, and raised his voice upon the word, but when he spoke again, it was so softly that his words did not travel beyond the table. "Armies is it? Take a look over there at them, armies is it? The freshest of them, the one I spoke to a few minutes ago, is a seventeen-year-old named Tommy Noonan. A few weeks ago, he walked up to a Tan in the main street of Kilpeder, and put a bullet into the fellow's chest, and he is now a hero on the run."

"Sixth West Cork is not Tommy Noonan," Lacy said. "Sixth West Cork has a reputation and a well-deserved one."

It was time for him to say something, Cogley knew, and he sighed. "Those requests and directives do not come to Pat, Frank, they come to me, I am the IO, as you people like to say, and I am the one who answers them, and I make out the monthly reports, for Brigade and for Headquarters. Pat here has other things on his mind. And I can tell you if you did not know that most of them are damned bloody nonsense, the tables of organization and all the rest of it. In this part of the world and in other parts as well, I daresay, commanders are not appointed from a distant city, they are chosen by the men. And in Pat's case, it was not a difficult choice, there was no competition."

No competition surely, Cogley thought, for a chemist's assistant who lived about the shop with his wife, the boss's daughter. Cogley knew that he was well enough liked in the town, and by the outlying farmers and their wives who would come in for their liniments and poultices and Father John's Mixture and syrups for colds and croup and something known as "a binding feeling like in my guts," and, once in a great while, a prescription. In Kilpeder, MacCarthy was the natural leader, once it had been at the hurling, and then in the livery stable which had slowly changed itself into a shop for the repair of motor cars and then in the Volunteers.

"Oh, I know that well enough," Lacy said, "it is because Sixth West Cork is commanded by Pat MacCarthy that I know that we can pull this off."

"Get on out of that," MacCarthy said, not pleased by the praise but not contemptuous of it. "If the lads look up to me, it is because they know that I would never throw away their lives." He flicked his cigarette, a long arc, into the fireplace. "And I don't give a damn for approval for orders or any of the rest of it, because so far as I am concerned, I have been asked by headquarters and brigade to take a look at an operation, and to use my own good judgment. That is my reading of things, and although I am no great scholar like Ben Cogley here or yourself, I will stand over it, and I will stand answerable to Mulcahy or to Mick."

Lacy exchanged a quick glance with Cogley, gave a brief grin, solicitous of complicity, but Cogley said, flatly, "There you have it, Frank."

"Did you bring a plan out with you, Frank?" MacCarthy said.

"Of course I did not," Lacy said, "this is your country and not mine. I have been thinking that one day soon we can take a look together at the road across into Kerry and the main road up into the Boggeraghs, and see where we stand. If you think the entire thing is impossible, then so be it."

"And you would abide by that?" MacCarthy asked.

"Who am I to abide or not abide," Lacy said, "if I am here at all, it is on your sufferance."

MacCarthy grunted, and let the grunt stand for speech. Lacy's reputation had gone before him, a cold, reckless fighter, careless of his own life and that of others.

"One thing is certain," Lacy said, "Ben here and myself stood today upon a rise of ground looking down toward Ardmor Castle. If you have five times the strength of the column, and them fully equipped and with proper transportation, they could never make a dent there."

MacCarthy smiled suddenly, and the smile transformed his face, a broad cheerful grin; Lacy could imagine him upon smooth turf, a hurley stick in his hand, broad grin.

"My grandfather," he said, "was one of the stableboys in Ardmor in the days of the last lord. God, you should have heard him talk about it, you remember him, Ben. Red face wizened like an apple, and two long yellow scraggling teeth. He could neither read nor write, but he had had the Gaelic in his boyhood, a young lad down from the Boggeraghs, but by our day, he had forgotten part of it and was ashamed of the rest. He lived to see me come into possession of the shop, and that was a great pride to him. You remember him, Ben."

"I do, of course. And I can remember us teasing him to give us a bit of the Gaelic, and he could not understand what we were on about. He was ashamed of it, the language of helots and starvelings down from the hills. It was at the end of his days that I knew him. I recall that he drank in Spellacy's, with a crowd of old gaffers who had worked for the Ardmors—gardeners and gamekeepers and the like."

"The very thing," MacCarthy said, "and there was a row of laborers' cottages that they had, just off the road, beyond the RIC barracks. God, the Castle and the Ardmors were the beginning and end of their lives, there was for them no other world needed."

"There was an old gamekeeper," Cogley said, "mind now, all this goes back to my first years here in Kilpeder, an old gamekeeper named Foxy Gaffney—"

"His Christian name was Aloysius," MacCarthy said, "small wonder that he was glad to settle for Foxy."

"And Foxy Gaffney claimed to remember the Fenian Rising of 'sixty-seven, and claimed to have seen Ned Nolan as plain as day on the streets of Kilpeder, a hero-commander carrying a sword, and with a black wideawake hat with a long green plume."

"Interesting lives you must have here in Kilpeder," Lacy said, "long winter evenings in Spellacy's listening to Foxy Gaffney." He smiled, half-challenge, half-banter, and the smile conveyed his point with precision. They had been telling him, in the oblique manner of County Cork, that he was a blow-in, a wandering busybody sent down from Dublin, but this was their countryside, a known terrain and not marks upon a map, pencil scratches and smears of crayon.

"Interesting is no word for it," MacCarthy said, and he returned the smile, as though somehow the air had been cleared. "You should see Kilpeder on a fair day or a market day. 'Twould put Macroom or Clonakilty to shame, if not Skibbereen itself."

Two weeks were to pass between Lacy's meeting with MacCarthy and the Derrynasaggart ambush, and for Lacy they were weeks of the strange, exhilarating heightening of perception which was his before action. But it was action beneath the open skies of Munster and Connaught, not the bloody shambles of Cork City, the musty hotel corridor, and the sleepy-eyed man in his nightshirt opening the door, "What, what, what is it?"

That first night, Cogley had gone back to Kilpeder, but Lacy, like MacCarthy, spent the night at Shanahan's, sharing the settle bed, with the three lads who were on the run dossing out in the barn, upon straw.

He was up before any of them, watching first light creep westwards along the Boggeraghs, the dark hills a soft, ambiguous purple at first and then blue, row upon tumbled row, reaching northwards toward Kanturk. It would be at such times, in such silent spaces, that Lacy felt most certain of what he was about, why he was at war, had the deepest sense of Ireland.

The next night, MacCarthy moved the two of them, MacCarthy and himself, to the house of a farmer named Cahill, Jamesey Cahill, beyond Ballyvourney and closer to the Derrynasaggarts. It was a large, sprawling house, and the two of them slept on camp beds in a room half-filled with farm equipment. In the barn of trim, discolored stone, MacCarthy kept most of the column's armament, and on their second day, he hauled it out for Lacy's inspection—eleven rifles, Lee-Enfields most of them, four shotguns, four revolvers, three Parabellums, a flare pistol.

"There it is, Frank," he said, "there is the arsenal with which yourself and your chums at HQ expect me to attack fully armed Tans escorted by an armored car."

"We can do better than that, Pat," Lacy said, "a bit better. Wait a bit."

"This is not quite all, I confess," MacCarthy said, in tones of sarcasm. "There are three or four lads who keep their shotguns at home, and bring them along when we go into action."

"Two months ago," Lacy said, "you engaged the enemy just here, did you not, outside Ballyvourney."

MacCarthy smiled and drew in on his cigarette. He had been working on his motorcar, and finger and cigarette were smeared with axle grease. "Engaged the enemy indeed. We bushwhacked two Tans on their way by bicycle to Killarney. We did it for the sake of the rifles. We dropped one of them, but the other got clean away. That is how we laid hold of the Lee-Enfields for the most part, by bushwhacking, once in Kilpeder itself. Another came to us with a deserter from the Essex regiment. And two of them we bought from Tommies. There is the way we have been engaging the enemy. Oh, and of course we burned down the barracks in town once it was empty."

"Where is the deserter?" Lacy asked and MacCarthy shrugged.

"He drifted away. Neither Ben Cogley nor myself liked the look of him, and he was not encouraged to make one with us, for all that he had an Irish mother, or so he claimed."

Four times in those two weeks MacCarthy and Lacy crossed the Derrynasaggarts into Killarney, taking not the motorcar but Cahill's horse and cart. Once, wind-driven rain came to them from across Kerry, carrying the salt savor of the Atlantic.

"Far Kerry," MacCarthy said, "Iveragh and Dingle, have you been in those places ever, Frank?" Lacy said that he had not.

"I was once in Dingle," MacCarthy said. "My mother's sister married a Ballyferriter man, and we were all down with them once on a visit. If you think that is rain and wind, you should try Dunquin. Great gusts that would frighten a giant, and black waves rolling up towards lonely strands. Do you live near water yourself, Frank?"

"A river," Lacy said, "a great, quiet river. The Nore. I am from Kilkenny."

"God, I would have taken you for a Dublin man. Farming people, are they, your people?"

"No," Lacy said, a bit awkwardly, "we have a newspaper

there, in the city of Kilkenny. Or rather, my father does. It was his father's before him."

"Ah," MacCarthy said, and the polite exhalation measured the distance between them, not the width of the island alone, that least of all.

Lacy knew the sound. For the most part, the men in the columns and the battalions were small farmers, sons of small farmers, farm laborers. MacCarthy was an exception, a skilled mechanic, grandson of an under-gardener, and Cogley, a chemist's assistant, was another. Lacy, on his assignments from Headquarters, could sense their resistance to him at first, and in a few instances from first to last, distrusting his accent, the words he used, the books in his case. The war—Lacy thought of it as a war—was being fought, for the most part, by lads who had never traveled thirty miles beyond their barony, breathing their own speech as the air itself is breathed. At first, sitting late at night with them, Lacy had tried his clumsy Irish upon them, but few of the columns knew Irish, for all that they held it in political respect. Lacy's classroom Irish was another form of distancing.

The road rose stiffly now before them, and MacCarthy gave an idle flick of his whip to the horse's gray rump.

"All this is on its way out," he said. "Your motorcar is your only man. It holds the future."

But Lacy made no answer. His mind was held by empty air, December's chill, by bare distant blue hills, across the county border in Kerry.

"Your only man," MacCarthy said. "When all this fuss is over and behind us, there will be no holding me back, Kilpeder will not hold me, what I see is shops for the repair of quality motor vehicles in Kilpeder and Macroom and Skibbereen, and why not in Killarney itself, why not Killarney? I will tell you, Frank, without modesty that there are damned few in Killarney who know the ways of motorcars as I do. And not quality vehicles alone, of course. For the average fellow as well, the average farmer."

Whenever talk turned to what life would be after all the fuss was over and behind them, Lacy listened with puzzlement, acceptance, a faint irritability. The war was his present but his future as well, and, in a sense, his past, their past, the past of the Irish people.

"It will require capital, of course," MacCarthy said, "but sure that will be little enough of a problem, when the country is in our hands after the long centuries, the government and the banks and all."

"To be sure," Lacy said.

"The capital is there," MacCarthy said, "waiting to be put to wise and proper use. Conor Tully-Delaney has buckets of it, and he spends most of his days in Cork City, but he is a Kilpeder man, right enough, the son of one of the heroes of Clonbrony Wood, Robert Delaney, and the nephew of another."

The wind was stronger now, cutting toward them against silent space, across mountains. The horse gave a sudden snort of dismay. Across the Kerry border, in Kilcarra, they called in by arrangement on Dinny Brick, who commanded the flying column out of Killarney, although he was a Rathmore man himself. The mountains were at their back now, and they had been traveling the road beside the Flesk, farmlands held in winter quiet. But Kilcarra was a lonely village off the road, and Brick's safe house for that month was a shop and public house in one, with flour and sacks of sugar and spades and pitchforks sold in its front, and beyond, without demarcation, a tall counter in the fashion of an earlier day, and bottles of whiskey and porter ranged behind it.

The shopkeeper, in a shapeless gown of drugget, with a bit of soiled flannel petticoat hanging beneath it, stayed near the door, with the sacks of flour and flitches of cured bacon, and Brick, as though the publican, had taken over the bar, standing behind it to pour out measures of Mitchell's for the three of them.

"My aunt," he said by way of explanation. "She is Rathmore as I am myself, but she married the shop here in Kilcarra," and then, dropping his voice, said, "God help her. Have you ever seen such a kip?"

"It must have been a terrible shock to her, after the excitements of Rathmore. You must visit Rathmore one day, Frank."

"You must indeed," Brick said, "a quiet place, but at least it is not a landlord's town like Kilpeder."

When, after pleasantries, after a second round of Mitchell's, they addressed themselves to business, MacCarthy said, "We have a proposal to make to you, Dinny. A request would be more like it." And, as he explained it, Brick pushed himself away from the counter and stood listening with folded arms, his head cocked to one side. He was a small man, not much more than five foot three or four, compact, with the face of an intelligent young monkey.

"Engage them for how long, Pat?" he asked. "That could be bloody brutal, the barracks there is heavily manned, thirty or forty of the bastards, and the barracks itself is solid. Solid and sandbagged. They are dug in there."

"Engage them with all that you have, Dinny," MacCarthy said, "and with as many boys as you can muster, not your column alone, but lads from Brigade. It must be bad enough for them to telephone to Kilpeder for help."

"If it is as bad as all that," Brick said, "the Tans in Ardmor may put more on the road than your lads can handle."

"We don't think so," Lacy said, "we will have the element of surprise."

."Of surprise," Brick said, "to be sure." He was a farmer's younger son who had been marked down by HQ, so Lacy remembered, as able but hot-tempered. "Our own column had surprise on our side, as you call it, two months ago, but three of our lads were cut down by Lewis-gun fire from one of their bloody armored cars. Two of them died, and one is in hospital."

"I know that," MacCarthy said. "I remember that."

"Sure, I know that road as well as you know it yourself," Brick said. "Where is it that you plan your element of surprise?"

"We have been traveling the road between Kilpeder and the county line," Lacy said. "We have not yet settled upon our site of ambush, but there are two or three likely prospects. As you must know yourself."

"Site of ambush," Brick said. "To be sure." He was still standing, arms folded, his back braced. "Your fame has preceded you, Frank. Pat Sheridan was down here some months ago, on the run after Tourmakeady, and he sang your praises. A great fellow for the strategy, he said you were." The words were cordial, but not the tone.

"Tourmakeady was an ugly business," Lacy said. "There were two Crossleys expected, but instead we had three lorries, and a Lancia with a Lewis gun."

"I know about Lewis guns," Brick said.

"An ugly business," Lacy said, "but I make no apologies for Tourmakeady. Either we fight the English or we pack it in, and if we fight them, there will be mistakes and reprisals and all the rest of it. That is the way of it, Dinny."

"That is the way of it," Brick said. Repetition seemed the only weapon in his arsenal of sarcasm.

"I will tell you the way it is," MacCarthy said, with sudden blunt irritation. "I will tell the way of it to the two of you. Frank here has the right of it, Dinny. We cannot let the Tans sit safe and secure in Ardmor Castle, sending out their patrols in whatever direction they like, and they have swung deep into Kerry more than once. But if we fight them, we must ourselves choose the ground, and Frank has proposed a way. Now there is the beginning and the end of it, Dinny. Frank Lacy does not command Number Six Battalion, I do, and the plan is one that I stand over."

There was a pause so long that Lacy could hear Brick's aunt wheezing and then Brick, with a quick nod, said, "Right," and uncorked the bottle of whiskey. "Right," he said again, as he put double measures in the glasses and then held a jug of water above them. "It will take care and time," he said, "if the column is needed and lads from Brigade as well. It might well need to be cleared by Brigade Headquarters in Tralee." MacCarthy gave him an encouraging smile and raised his glass.

All that about care and time and the Brigade HQ was a bit of face-saving, Lacy knew. It was clear that there were days and days of preparation yet before them, but today's business had been accomplished. Brick had committed the column to an attack on the Tan barracks in East Kerry, and would hold the barracks engaged at least until a relief force had been sent out from Ardmor Castle along the country road.

"You pour a generous glass," MacCarthy said, " 'tis well for the aunt that you are neither barman nor potboy here. You would drive her into the ground."

"Not that one," Brick said.

On the road home, MacCarthy was pleased with himself, as Lacy could tell. He was humming, of all things, "It's a Long, Long Way to Tipperary," a British music hall song, British Army song. He broke off to say, "Dinny is a fine, swift hurler, despite his height or lack of it, a fierce little runt. This scrap has been the makings of him. He was bullied at home by the da and the older brother, but by Jesus they walk in fear of him now. A fellow from his column tells me that Dinny and himself called in on the old man a few months ago, and it was a treat to see little Dinny swaggering about with pistol and bandolier, like Pancho Villa in the cinema shows."

And someday, Lacy thought, as winter's quick-coming night closed in upon them, someday the scrap would be over, he knew that, and what would become then of Commandant Brick? MacCarthy looked toward a garage in Kilpeder, in Macroom, in Skibbereen, someday when the "scrap," as they all called it, was over. In the shop-cum-pub in Kilcarra, Lacy had admired MacCarthy's air of easy authority, the manner in which he had sorted matters out with a few brusque words. But now, as MacCarthy joked about Brick and Brick's bullying father, about Pancho Villa seen in the flickering light of a village hall, Lacy felt alone again, the air darkening. As they approached the crest of the Derrynasaggarts, the road was treacherous, narrow and rutted, and the pony faltered, halting once but then driven forward by the whip in MacCarthy's casual, skillful hand. "A thing of the past," MacCarthy said, as he had said on the journey eastwards. "The future belongs to the motorcar."

On the journey home to Kilpeder, they passed, although they did not yet know it, the site of the ambush which would take place in eight days' time. Twelve years later, when Ben Cogley gave his interview to Joe Haggerty in Dublin, that site was marked by a memorial, a Celtic cross standing on its broad, heavy limestone base, with its inscription on one side in Irish, on the other in English. The inscription in English read: "Sacred to the memory of Lt. Michael Brennan, No. 6 West Cork Battalion, Volunteer Peter Fleming, Three Millstreet Battalion, Volunteer David Harty, 6 West Cork Battalion. On this lonely spot they gave their lives for Ireland, December 18, 1920. In triumphant battle against the enemy."

Lonely it was indeed, Cogley thought twelve years later, a faint image of it flickering before imagination's eye, flat boggy land, low, roadside hedges concealing the trench which they had dug, and where they had waited with their shotguns, primed to engage the Tans from the rear, when the main battle was joined five hundred yards along the county road. There, at the dogleg bend, at the wide outcropping of rock behind which MacCarthy and himself had taken up position, or else by the exploded bridge, a year later restored, where Lacy and Bill Sugrue commanded the second unit, might have been a more dramatic siting for the cross, but as it was, when the cross was placed there in 1929, the air still quivering with Civil War recriminations, it was best as it had been done, a memorial to the three slain Volunteers. And now, Cogley thought, I will drive across that road, as we all do, in my own case on political business, Cumann na nGaedheal business, or merely, perhaps, to play a round at the Killarney links, and the memorial will be but that, limestone, a clumsy Celtic cross, an outcropping, as indifferent to the eye as a holy well or some remaining screen wall of a Norman tower house, an abandoned cabin. But once, once or twice, with the color of the air exactly right, color of thick grass, color of rock, reddish-brown bogland, once or twice I have remembered that day, the hours of waiting, and then, far off, the sound of the klaxons that heralded the Tans moving down upon us from Kilpeder, lorries and the tender, the armored car, heard before seen. But twelve years is a very long time as such matters go.

Haggerty, the journalist and would-be writer, had been for a time with the *Irish Times,* still Unionist in sentiment but peace made with the Free State, with Cogley's party, that is to say, and was now on the staff of the *News-Chronicle,* in London, too young to have been himself involved in the scrap nor in the Civil War that followed, but he was Irish right enough, with a glib line in "Ireland's tragedy," and all the rest of it, but it was difficult to feel tragic in the lounge bar of Buswell's, over whiskies, air heavy with tobacco.

In his previous conversation with Cogley, he had said, "I have no ax to grind, you understand, it is the drama that one finds so gripping, and they know nothing about it in England, let alone the States. Fellows with a few thousand rifles bringing an empire to its knees, an imperial army no less, and then to fall fighting among each other, killing each other."

"Why Lacy?" Cogley asked, and Haggerty shrugged. "Why not Cathal Brugha if you wanted one from that lot, but the Big Lad was the lad who led our crowd, my crowd. Collins was the Big Fellow."

"Too big for what I want," Haggerty had said. Now they were

in Buswell's, where "our lot," the Free State lot, drank, the other crowd preferred Cummiskey's in Duke Street.

"There is already a little book about him, a wretched book put out by the Sinn Féin Publishing Company," Haggerty said, "have you seen it? *Frank Lacy and the Bright Sword of Freedom.*"

Cogley, by way of answer, shuddered slightly and picked up his glass. "There are fellows who could tell you more about Frank Lacy than I can myself," he said. "I knew him for a while, and then we ended up on different sides, you know. In the Civil War."

"You were by his side at the Derrynasaggarts," Haggerty said, "one of the great battles, like Kilmichael and Crossbarry."

"Great battles," Cogley said, "mother of God"—he was beginning to feel the whiskey—"they were but ambushes, Derrynasaggarts and Kilmichael, that is all the fighting ever was, ambushes, or potting a Tommy on his bicycle, the only times we ever took a decent-sized barracks, it was after it had been vacated. Great battles!"

But Haggerty was not put off, and at last Cogley said. "I remember the night hours, the hours before that dawn, we had made our way from the two farms that Lacy called the staging areas across scrappy farmland at first, and then moorland, a bright clear winter night with a peppering of stars and a pale half-moon, but light enough for us to see our way. There were forty-two of us by then, forty-seven it was, our own lot and the lads who had been sent forward to us from the Dunmanway and the Millstreet columns, and we armed with whatever we had and what had been lent to us by Brick and by Jerry Conlon, who commanded the Millstreet column, rifles and shotguns, but pride of place was given to the two dozen rifles with which Lacy had persuaded HQ to part, the real articles, British Army issue, that came to us in cosmolene. It was the only operation during the entire scrap when we had enough weapons to go around, I can speak only for our own lot, but the same was true of all the columns, but I can tell you that there were brigades throughout Ireland which did little at all to justify their existence but they held on to their weapons which might better have gone to the columns and battalions who were in the head of the battle—Cork and Tipperary and Longford and Clare. Be that as it may, the officers that night were carrying rifles as well as sidearms, and we had long loops of ammo bandoliers slung across our shoulders, and Frank

Lacy was wearing as well the field glasses that he had recovered from one of the Tans killed in the scrap at Tourmakeady. I remember at one point he had taken the lead, walking ahead of Pat and myself and the others, standing on a small rise of land, and looking backwards toward us, he was wearing a belted trench coat, with all the armament buckled or slung around him, and a dark, soft hat. He turned around to us and smiled, and I swear to God it was not to buck up the lads' spirits, as Pat might have done. It was sheer pleasure. Lacy was having the time of his life."

"But you were not," Haggerty said, and although he nodded with easy, affable sympathy, Cogley knew that he was seeing the picture which he had himself sketched upon air, Lacy turning around to smile, and wondered whether his memory was actual, or was he not inventing as memory what he suspected of Lacy. "Indeed I was not," Cogley said, "I was frightened out of my wits, Pat MacCarthy was as well, we all were. It was no light matter to lie in wait for fellows better armed than yourself and perhaps more numerous. Frightened out of my wits. Those Tans were right bastards. I can still see them in the mind's eye, swaggering about the streets of Kilpeder in their glengarries and their great bloody revolvers." "Some of them put paid to their swaggering that day in the Derrynasaggarts," Haggerty said. "Yes," Cogley said, "some of them paid."

He had no great gift for narrative, Haggerty discovered, and his account of the battle, as Haggerty insisted on calling it, had little to add to what was given in the newspaper accounts, of which the calmest by far was that in the *Freeman's Journal:*

> On the afternoon of December 12, civilians attacked and destroyed a police convoy in the Derrynasaggart Mountains, a few miles on the Cork side of the Cork-Kerry border. Twenty-three members of the Auxiliary force and the three officers in command were slain. There were no survivors. The attackers may have suffered casualties as well, but if so, they were carried off when the civilians left the scene.
>
> Less than a month has passed since the attack at Kilmichael, outside Macroom, in which seventeen Auxiliaries were killed, and this present one surpassed that in its savage thoroughness.
>
> Major-General H. H. Tudor left no doubt that such attacks will serve only to strengthen the determination of government that order and stability will be restored to the country by measures more drastic

than those already employed. "The morale of both the Royal Irish Constabulary and its Auxiliary Division remains high," General Tudor said, "and their discipline remains excellent." He took occasion to note that the town of Kilpeder has enjoyed tranquility in the two days following the incident, despite all rumors that the Auxiliaries pursue either an official or an unofficial policy of reprisals.

The bodies were removed to Cork, where a funeral procession took place. At Custom House Quay the coffins were placed in the gunboat *Hazard*, which took them to Queenstown. There they were transferred to the destroyer *Neptune* and conveyed by her to Pembroke Dock.

According to Colonel Richard Stoddard, officer commanding in Ardmor Castle, the two lorries of Auxiliaries, accompanied by armored cars, were proceeding to Rathmore barracks in Kerry, which telephoned for help in consequence of an attack there. That attack was unsuccessful, and after several hours of sporadic rifle fire, the attackers withdrew. It is possible, indeed likely, Colonel Stoddard speculated, that the Rathmore attack was a feint, designed to draw the Ardmor Auxiliaries into the ambush which awaited them. He denies, however, the suggestion that the armed civilians are gaining skill in their deployment of men. "It takes little skill to skulk behind rocks and ditches," he said, "and no skill at all to commit butchery after a fight has ended."

"To be sure, the scrap had ended," Cogley said. "What were we to do? We called out twice to them to throw their weapons away, out toward the hedges, but they did not, they held on to them. Perhaps they were petrified, perhaps they did not know what was happening to them or what would happen. But after Kilmichael, they should have known. They had leaped out from the lorries, you understand, and were lying flat in the road. Pat gave the order for rapid fire, and told them to keep firing until he passed the word. Afterwards, he and Frank Lacy walked among them, with drawn revolvers, firing. It seemed to go on forever. I looked away from the road, up towards the hills, and they kept firing. We lost three men there, as you know, the three men whose names are on the memorial, and three others were wounded, two of them badly. We withdrew with our dead and our wounded. There it is, there is your battle."

One of Cogley's colleagues, a TD from Westmeath, paused beside their table to chat with Cogley for a minute or two, and then walked out of the lounge, a heavyset man, going a bit bald, the beginning of a paunch. He was carrying a half-smoked cigar. "Gerry MacGarret of Athlone," Cogley explained to Haggerty. "The Imperial Hotel in Athlone, you must have heard of it. Gerry is a great one at golf. Golf and Rotary. Gerry is a devout Rotarian."

"I have heard it said," Haggerty said, "that Kilmichael and Kilpeder, coming on top of each other, seventeen killed in one and twenty-three in the other, helped prompt the British to turn their thoughts toward a truce."

"Yes," Cogley said, "I have heard that as well, and it was heard at the time. So many kinds of things were happening at the same time or almost the same time. The ambushes and Terence MacSwiney dead on his hunger strike and the others dead in the jail in Cork City, and young Kevin Barry hanged in Dublin, our crowd killing hostages and the other side hanging our lads, shooting them, and then the government in London standing over reprisals, houses and cottages burned down in retaliation for the ambushes and then our lads commencing to burn the houses of landlords of known imperialist sympathies, as well Bloody Sunday, put the wind up the British, the cream of their intelligence operation wiped out, in Dublin and in Cork. History can thank the Big Fellow for that one, history can thank Collins, Ireland can thank him."

"To be sure," Haggerty said, "to be sure, a great man." But he knew that if he were to walk down Duke Street, to Cummiskey's, to the Fianna Fáil crowd, he would be given a different version of Collins, and if he were to talk to the true Republicans, the legion of the rear guard, he would hear still another version, even more venomous.

"During all of this time, as I am certain you know, Mr. Haggerty, Mr. De Valera was off in America, for most of the scrap he was away, on matters of urgent national concern, so he would have us believe, but he returned to us on the Christmas Eve of 1920. He returned as a Christmas gift to us from St. Nicholas. Mr. De Valera had set sail from New York on the eleventh, on the very day that the Tans sacked Cork City as a reprisal for Kilmichael and Kilpeder. Mr. De Valera has always had an exquisite sense of timing, has he not?"

But Haggerty knew that no reply was expected from him, and he smiled. A bit of post–Civil War savagery. He came himself from a family divided by the Civil War, his father a Free Stater, with a framed photograph of Collins in the office of the creamery, the famous photograph of Collins in uniform, striding forward, but with the head turned to look backward, beginning to turn, and a holstered Webley at his hip. "And was he not right to look behind him, by God," Haggerty's father used often to say, "as things turned out."

Haggerty's mother would limit herself to saying that General Collins was a fine-looking man and had been a fine soldier, but she would be speaking with care because her own people were Republican, and stood by Dev. The two families did not speak, by and large, but Haggerty's mother was a link, she would visit her people, and bring along Haggerty and his sisters. In the parlor of the Kilfenora farm there was a photograph of Dev, long scholarly face, mathematician's eyeglasses, wide, firm, thin-lipped mouth. "To Patrick Culhane," Dev had written, followed by some words in Irish to Haggerty's grandfather, and then the signature. County Clare was one of Dev's strongholds. But Haggerty had seen another photograph, of Dev after his reluctant surrender to the English soldiers after Easter Week, on the final day, a fierce mustache and eyes wild after sleepless nights directing the battle at Boland's Mill on the South Side, reluctant at first to accept Pearse's order to surrender when it was carried to him by Nurse O'Farrell, like some of his officers he had been ready to cut his way up into the hills. When he surrendered to the soldiers, at Lower Mount Street, he had said to the gawking civilians, "If only you had come out with knives and forks." The knives and forks had passed into the folklore about Dev, Haggerty, a child, had heard it first from his grandfather, who had been Sinn Féin in 1919 but now was a member of Fianna Fáil, the party that Dev had founded to win in the Dáil what had been lost on the battlefield during the Civil War. It was from his grandfather that he first heard of Frank Lacy, although his grandfather had never met Lacy.

"And I don't mind telling you," Ben Cogley said to Haggerty, he had prudently splashed water into his brandy, but it was nevertheless his third, "I don't mind telling you that if you were not your father's son, I would not be sitting here talking to you about Frank Lacy. He was by our side in the Derrynasaggarts, by Pat MacCarthy's side and mine, but within a year was he not roving the hills with wild men like Lynch, bent upon destroying all that we had worked and fought to achieve. And for what?"

But Haggerty could not say for what, any more than he could say why he had elected to write a book about Frank Lacy, because Lacy's name was not one of the towering ones of their recent past, not the name of a Collins or a De Valera or a Brugha or a Griffith, not even a great guerrilla commander, like Barry, who had gone with the Republicans in the Civil War, nor MacKeon, who had stayed with Collins and the Free State, not one of the men of ideas, like Christopher Blake on one side and Erskine Childers on the other. Perhaps it was because of that odd detail which everyone seemed to remember, that there was always a book in his case, the *Aeneid* or Ovid or Homer in an English translation or the poetry of Browning. That and the snapshot which one of Lacy's friends had given to Haggerty, of Lacy and Ernie O'Malley walking together into the Four Courts in 1922, after they and the other Republicans had seized it, holding it until Collins directed the Free State Army to shell it with artillery, with field guns borrowed from the departing British. The two of them bareheaded, fair-haired, young men looking confident despite the puzzlements of civil war, part of Dublin in their hands, theirs and their friends. They seemed to be smiling, but the quality of the photograph was too poor for certainty.

"That night," Cogley said, "back in the safe house, Pat relaxed enough to let us have two heavy tots of whiskey but no more, because we knew that the Tans would be out scouring the hills for us, both the Tans from Ardmor Castle and those from Kerry and from Macroom as well, beyond doubt. And I cannot speak for the others, but never had hard drink been more welcome. I would be lying were I to say to you that I heard in my mind the revolver shots of Pat and the shots from Frank Lacy as they moved among the dead and the dying and the terrified as they lay sprawled upon the road, or flung against the hedges by the impact of our rifle fire. If it was slaughter, it was as much my doing as it was Pat's or Frank Lacy's. We knew that we would take no prisoners, any more than Barry took prisoners after Kilmichael." He took a long sip of the watered brandy. "It was nothing you could talk about with Pat, we were close friends and had no secrets from each other, but there was a wall there I knew. Pat had schooled himself to do whatever things it was that war might require, and he was not what you would call a reflective man, bright and clever in his way but not reflective.

"Frank Lacy was reading, sitting hunched beside a candle, whose light fell upon the page and his face, white despite the rough life we had been leading. 'What are you on to there, Frank?' I asked, and it took him a moment to answer, as though hauling himself up from whatever world it was that the page offered him. By God, if it was not a novel by Balzac, Balzac in West Cork. I had read a few bits of Balzac before, years before, the Christian Brother who taught us said that he was on the Index, like Rousseau and Rabelais, and so I took it from the library in hopes of racy passages or at least some exciting blasphemy, but there had been neither. 'I am shaken by that business today, Frank,' I said, 'not the battle itself, but what had to be done afterwards.'

"He closed the volume, and sat looking into the candle's flame, and at last said, 'We cannot take prisoners, Ben, you know that. And we have a need to show what losses we can make them suffer. Each coffin that we send home to England will be a message to some town or other, and at last the people over there will ask is it worth it, are we worth it.' He did not speak the words in a rush, but they came too pat, as though he had used them before, if only to himself, to assure himself perhaps.

" 'Yes,' I said, disappointed, because Pat MacCarthy would have said the same, for all that he was no reader of Balzac or the *Aeneid*. He went back to his book, and the two of us sat together in silence. At length he said, 'It can never be undone.' "

Cogley shook his head, as though to clear the memory from it, as a man will rise up from water.

"They were bloodier than we were, you know," he said. "Oh, they had jails and prisons and detention camps to shove us in, they could afford to take prisoners, but the Tans were sent over here and turned loose upon the countryside. I had no tears to shed then for the Tans and I have none now." He shook his head again. "They burned houses and they stripped prisoners and whipped them in the public road, unashamed of what they were about, and they did far worse than that in their interrogation rooms. There is a Macroom man, Jamesey Maher, who sits witless today in his sister's house because of what was done to him by the Tans in Macroom Castle. That is all over and done with, thanks be to God."

But Haggerty heard, as though by ventriloquist's magic, a young man's voice in a mountain farmhouse, "It can never be undone."

XI

JANICE NUGENT

When I remember the times we had together, Christopher and myself, three days here, a week there, two days here again, wherever here might be, I can remember each of them with what seems a full and entire recollection, all the colors and shapes preserved intact, without blurring, without fading. This surprises me, because I do not fully understand why it should be the case, I keep wanting it to fade, not my recollection of our love, of course, nor how Christopher looked, nor what he said, but the bowl of flowers on the table between windows in the London flat, the feel of the wet, salt-laden air outside the cottage in Connemara, dog roses there with a drenching of dew as though spray from the sea itself. Or driving out to Renvyle, out along the road from Clifden, the dark greens and grays of rock-strewn moorlands, the small islands of Lough Corrib, a sudden shower, I can remember all these and all the others, and at times I want them to fade a bit, but they do not.

It may be perhaps because all we had were those times together, scattered, not enough of them to make a whole, times scattered over two years, and there was never enough time for us to settle down simply to loving each other, for the time we had we were not loving but being in love, which is different, as everyone knows. When we are in love, as everyone knows, the world is vivid, the colors hectic as autumn leaves, as the blooms of deepest summer, and perhaps, if the world is ripped away from us, if love is, the colors remain, vivid as wounds. All of the rooms, all of the roads, have, each of them, their own atmospheres, unchanging. Perhaps.

I remember the times that he visited at Coolater, remember Father and himself sparring, wary, and then moving to something that might have become friendship, if there had been time. And I remember the "safe house," as such places were called, the "safe house" in Wicklow. I remember the flat in Chelsea, and I remember the week when for some reason using the flat seemed a bad idea and we used Patrick Prentiss's rooms in Pump Court. I remember all of those times and the other ones. But of those times the ones that I like best to remember are the times in my old flat, the flat that had been Charlie's and mine, I remember the first day and night that we stayed there, Christopher moving from the sitting room to the bedroom and then back to the sitting room again, touching a picture frame, a paperweight, a bottle of scent, touching a window latch, and I knew what he was doing, that he was discovering the mysteries of the life of someone with whom we have fallen in love, the life that existed earlier, and we think, "Here, he touched this," or "There, she looked at this." In the hallway, there was a poster, framed, of one of the ballets from Russia that everyone was so excited about before the war, oranges and browns and blacks, and the date was on it, a week in the early spring of 1914, on the ninth of June, to be exact, and I said, "*Scheherazade*. It was gorgeous. Do you go, did you go to the ballet?" "Once in a while," Christopher said, "but not then, not that June. I was in Dublin then. It was in that month that Redmond forced the crisis in the Volunteers." "Whatever that means," I said, and I touched his hair and turned away, and thought, as I turned away, that before that month had been out, everything would have fallen apart, all our lives, but we did not know it at first, an archduke shot dead in a dusty Balkan town, the newspaper photographs showed him in his pompous Franz Lehár uniform. "The Volunteer crisis," Christopher said, as I walked back toward the sitting room, "and Childers landing the first shipload of Mausers at Howth a month later, but it was in the planning then." He was speaking idly almost, it seemed to me, and I turned round to look at him, but he seemed absorbed in the poster, those wild designs of leaping, near-naked black men and veiled houris.

That would have been an evening in the spring of 1921, and Christopher was in London on one of those errands which he would not talk about. An evening in April, when we had the whole of one week and a half of the one that followed. He had been on the run now for a year almost, and more and more, this at least he told me, he had left to others, and especially to Elizabeth Keating, the task of editing the *"Republican Bulletin,"* and was at work on—well, on other matters, is how he would put it. But his visits to London were strange, this one and the ones which followed it, straight up to the Truce. He was on the run, which meant that there was a warrant out against him, and he could be picked up any time on the street, or by a rap on my door, our door. "Not now," he said to me once, as though in explanation, "not this time, not yet at any rate. I think that this time they know quite well where I am," but he would say nothing beyond that. Later, of course, he told me that these were the early, tentative days when "certain people" in government were putting out feelers to Sinn Féin, and Christopher was talking, once or twice, regularly for a bit, two times a week, with these "certain people." "I am a messenger," he was to tell me, "an errand boy, and so are the people I am talking with, a third secretary, a few civil servants. Collins says that the way I can talk with the English goes down a treat with them. Nothing important happens because of it, I talk a bit and the third secretary talks a bit and then he goes back to tell his cabinet and I go to tell mine." They were incommensurable, those two cabinets, the one in Ten Downing Street which I imagined as having a boardroom of some sort where they all sat before green baize, with pads of legal paper before them and on the walls time-darkened portraits, a tall window looking out upon Downing Street or else upon a neatly currycombed garden.

Beyond the closed door, along hallways and the walls of stairways, so I once read in *Country Life,* there were portraits of the prime ministers—Pitt and Salisbury and Russell and Gladstone and all the others. Someday there would be one of Lloyd George, but for the present one made do with the newspaper photographs of Lloyd George chatting with a few of the ministers outside Number Ten, Chamberlain and Birkenhead hovering above him, and Churchill, a man of his own stature, schoolboy's round face smiling or scowling. But I would imagine them in council, if that is what it is called, at the long table, perhaps, but this would be too much, no doubt, vulgar really, on the wall a map of the globe with the parts of the Empire tinted pink or red—India and much of Africa and Ireland and Australia. I would see their hands resting upon the table, beside yellow paper and pink sealing wax, hands pink and soft, beyond starched white cuffs, stiff, gold cuff links.

And the other cabinet, Christopher's cabinet, outlawed, in English eyes at once ludicrous and sinister, aping the titles of Westminster ministries, issuing pronouncements, prayers, pieties, threats, from undisclosed venues, grieving and wailing over deaths by hunger, deaths upon the gallows, by rifle fire in prison yard, but themselves sending out their squads of gunmen. But the starched cuffs and white, soft hands had their gunmen as well. Oh, yes; indeed they did. When I was not in London, I was home in Galway, at Coolater, and all of Galway knew by now about the government's gunmen, the Auxiliaries, Black and Tans, the Army itself, whose uniform Charlie had worn, been killed in.

After a bit, Christopher would tell me about those meetings, when he was being an errand boy, as he would put it, meetings in the most unlikely places, a house in the suburbs, a public house in Hammersmith, once in a great while in a government building. After a time, Christopher made a kind of composite third secretary or go-between, or whatever, and called him Soames Godolphin, who had been to Charterhouse and then Balliol, a year or two years in France in a good regiment, mentioned in dispatches, and then Whitehall. (Soames Godolphin, I learned, was mostly a fellow named Robert Soames.) "Soames affects a languid manner," Christopher said, "but deep inside, he thinks of himself as keen. Often, the first thing he says is, 'This meeting has never taken place, you do understand that, Blake, do you not?' He sees himself as one of the hard young chaps out of Kipling, staunch there on the edges of empire, Matabeleland, the Khyber Pass, Tipperary, wherever. If we are in a public house, he will have two tots of whiskey, as he will call them, as he sits in the saloon bar, but never a third. Sometimes I will have a third, to put him at his ease. They expect it of the Irish. 'What are they like, your chaps,' he will ask me, after we have transacted our nearly useless, formal business, 'Griffith and De Valera and the others. What is Collins like?' That is really what Soames wants to know, what all of the Soameses want to know. 'What is Collins like?' And well they might. The English will always choose some enemy and develop a crush on him, Collins is like the Scarlet Pimpernel to them. Then another detective will be shot down in Grafton Street or outside his house in Sunday's Well, and Collins will be a butchering gunman all over again."

I used sometimes to think that Christopher was taking delight in it, a kind of Irish Soames Godolphin. He seemed more at ease, there in London, and with each night, each evening, each morning that we had together, we seemed closer than ever we had been, and our lovemaking was as much bond as passion, as if our bodies spoke to each other of matters deeper than lust or even pleasure. We were easy with each other, as though husband and wife, loving and yet easy. In Ireland, whether in Dublin or in Wicklow or in Galway, and I could never forget it entirely, there would be a gun close at hand, a revolver on the floor beside the bed or on a bedside table. Here in London, there was no gun and I liked that better. Once, in London, with the gun distant by the wide Irish sea, I asked him if ever he had used it, but he had not. He was expected to carry one, as a deputy junior cabinet minister or whatever he was then, but he had never used it. "Good," I said, "it is good that you have never used it." "Yes," he said, "it is."

"I would use it, Janice, you do understand that," he said to me the next morning, as I made the tea, and I knew at once what he meant. "Of course, dear," I said. "To defend yourself." "Or if I was ordered to," he said.

After a bit, it was clear that no attempt would be made to pick him up on the warrant, although he was expected to be discreet, and three or four times he visited with English people and groups who were sympathetic or at least curious—he even went once to visit Shaw, who was later to describe him as "one of my clever young fellow Irishmen," and I think had a bit of a crush on him, as he did on clever young fellows, everyone knows how he felt about T. E. Lawrence. And once Christopher spoke at the William Morris Club in Hammersmith, arriving late and talking for twenty minutes, which was not reported in the newspapers. And once he went to Garsington to talk with the Morrells, and that time I went along with him, because I knew them a bit. There was a Liberal politician there, Teddy Bonneville, and he and Christopher spent a few hours talking together, in the Orchid Room, as Ottoline called it—an affected woman—but Christopher said later that it might have done some good. "The English are a wonderful people," he said to me as we drove back to London in our hired car,

"Bonneville said that they—he spoke for the entire people, of course—they felt that the Irish have not been dealt with generously. He said that history is to blame. A wonderful people."
"That is how politicians talk," I said. "All politicians, everywhere, the Irish ones will be as bad. Worse, probably."

One of the surprising things about Christopher was that he was a splendid driver, far better than Charlie. It was an open car, and the day was crisp and clear, the crisp, cold air of March, and as we drove past fields, sped past them is more like it, I could sense winter's final grasp before it relaxed, before the freshets of spring.

The battles being fought in Ireland seemed distant and unreal when I would read about them or when, as would happen, Christopher would speak about them to me. It was the other kinds of things. Betty wrote to me from Coolater, to say that in Kiltartan, on Lady Gregory's lands, a woman named Ellen Quinn, who had been sitting on her garden wall with her infant daughter, was shot dead by soldiers or police or Auxiliaries or whatever they called themselves from a lorry as they went speeding down the road. And then, the body of Father Griffin, a Loughrea man, was found in a bog: he had been murdered by the soldiers of the Crown. But then she followed that up with a letter written the very next day, with news that one of our own laborers, Gerry Foley, whom we knew well, Betty and myself, knew Gerry and his family, with children the oldest of them our own ages almost, had been found beside our own small lake, his hands and feet bound together and his head blown apart, with a sign on him, "Informers beware: Irish Republic Army."

"And none of us knows what that means," Betty wrote, "for what in God's name was there for a man like poor Gerry to inform upon even if he wanted to. All this is very hard on poor Father, as you must have seen when last you were here, but on myself as well, and on all of us. Major Leamington's house, you will recall it, Walnut Grove, was burned down last week to its foundation stones, the family and servants given twenty minutes to clear out before it was doused with paraffin, and then set fire to. Do you remember when we were young, and Major Leamington was master of the hunt? A jolly man we thought him then, jolly but elderly, but he could not have been past fifty, a few years home from India. He was shattered by the burning, everything gone. Those paintings that the Leamingtons thought so fine, you remember them, country bumpkins with white stocks, eyes like unshelled pecans, standing beside horses, and in the distance a folly thrown in gratis by the artist, the Leamingtons never ran to follies any more than we did ourselves. That awful umbrella stand burned down, made of an elephant's foot, those bound volumes of the *Illustrated London News*, and the piano that Sally Leamington played until the last months of her life, songs from London revues and bits of Liszt and Chopin. Don't I sound superior, but I don't feel superior at all. Bits of stick and canvas are nothing beside poor Gerry Foley tied up like a goose and shot dead beside our lake, and yet I feel the loss of the Leamingtons' umbrella stand, is that not wicked of me?"

Christopher read that letter from Betty, I passed it to him after I had received it, and when he had read it, he said, "I don't know, Janice. What is it that you want me to say? I have no idea why that fellow was killed, nor why Leamington's house was burned. Why Leamington's in particular, that is. The British now have an official policy of reprisals, setting fire to houses near the scene of an ambush, or burning down one of the creameries on which our farmers depend. And now there are—" He hesitated for a word. "Reprisals for the reprisals, is that it?" "Yes," he said, "that is exactly it. Houses of loyalists who have been cooperating with the Crown forces. Would that suit Leamington's case?" "I don't know," I answered truthfully, and yet as I spoke, I thought to myself, My God yes, no doubt it does, Toby Leamington was a ferocious fire-eater, and, I seemed to recall, a magistrate, fierce against the "Shinners" as he called them. "And Gerry Foley?" I said, "poor Gerry Foley?" But Christopher shook his head. I never learned what Gerry had done nor why he had been killed, but it was not held against his family.

Our "arrangements," which was the word I always used to myself and on occasion with Christopher, inverted commas and all, were absurd. Absurd for me to be a part of the time in Coolater and a part in the Chelsea flat, and certain to receive a letter from Betty if I were away from Coolater for so long as a fortnight. Letters like the one I passed to Christopher over teacups, with winter flowers, white, pale yellow, on the table between us, full of accounts of things close at hand but out of sight, "noises off," as theater people say. Betty's letters had always their faint, unwritten reproach, that I was not there to be horrified by the news of poor Gerry Foley, or shocked a bit, thrilled perhaps by the news about the Leamingtons, or about the creamery outside Ardrahan being burned down by the army as one of their "official reprisals."

But of course there was always another reproach, buried at the heart of things, beneath even unspoken words. "Father and Mrs. Donovan and I," she would write—Mrs. Donovan, Frances Donovan, was our cook-housekeeper for as long as ever Betty and I could remember, cook-housekeeper in Mama's day—"Father and Mrs. Donovan and I had tea together last evening, a Sunday, in her parlor off the kitchen, and the two of them were remembering when you and I were small girls and would play beside the lake or on it, Launcelot and Guinevere, or Sarsfield's men riding down upon the enemy at Ballyneety, or we would be the last of our breed to stand beside Gordon at Khartoum, with our revolvers and drawn sabers, just as it was shown in the frontispiece to Steevens's book, standing beside Gordon at the stairhead and swarming up the stairs from the courtyard, the Mahdi's wild followers crazed upon drugs or whatever. Do you remember, Janice? What tomboys we were! At least I was Guenevere!!"

Do you remember, Janice, she was asking me, do you remember how simple it all once was? Because she knew about Christopher and me, because of course I had had to tell someone, and she was one of the two whom foolishly I had chosen, Hazel Lockhart was the other one, two Irishwomen, dear God, two Galway women, when there were a dozen, two dozen friends in London whom I could have confided in and would not have cared thruppence that Christopher and I were sleeping together. Not that Hazel cared about that part of it—stones and glass houses—but she was quite simply horrified by Christopher's politics, "that gunman," as she called him, after that one time when we called in on her at Colleycourt House, and I told her that he was a Sinn Féin journalist, which she translated into "gunman." Which I thought was hilarious, of course, because in those days, even though Christopher had fought in Easter Week and even though he did carry a revolver in Ireland, I could never have thought of him as a gunman. I know better now, of course.

Once, I even got a letter from Colleycourt, it came in the same post as one from Betty, and I knew at once what it was, in Hazel's fierce, flamboyant script, the l's and the t's stabs upwards and the p's stabs downwards.

> All bleak, bleak awful Galway winter here, stay away until Spring if you can. Does your lover get across to see you ever, these days. I expect not, he has been busy here in Galway, last week he and some of his local pals burned out poor Toby Leamington.

It was a part of what Hazel thought great fun to pretend that Christopher was no ordinary gunman, but some kind of Whiteboy-in-chief, organizing all kinds of misdeeds and atrocities.

> You assure me that he has good taste in art, and now he has gone and proved it, getting rid of all that awful stuff at the Leamingtons'. Do you remember in particular that great-grandmother or whatever she was that the Leamingtons always said was a Romney but none of us believed she had been done by Romney, with those great pop eyes. Your gunman I am certain spotted her as a fake. "Away with her to the flames. Her and that elephant's-foot umbrella stand! In the name of the Irish Republic." But in truth it is quite awful, dear Janice, and I honestly do not know what will happen to us all. And the awfulest part is that all this goes on, shootings from hedges and burnings and all the rest of it, not everywhere but in this place or that, and there are wide parts of the county where you would think that nothing has been happening at all, the people do not have their dances, because of the curfew, but there are football matches as always there have been, and the churches are full and there are market days. What does your gunman say? I will tell you straight away what Derek says. No, I will not. You know what Derek says. "Shoot them all," Derek says. Derek has taken to carrying his service revolver, and has since last month when the Carstairs were stopped on the road and their motorcar taken away from them. But I don't find Derek's Browning exciting in the least. They order these things better in the Navy, or so they used do. So I have heard. Stay in London until Spring, dearest Janice, but you will not, you will be hurrying back to help Betty care for your dote of a father, and we can have long chats.

Once, long before, in 1915, in the first spring of the war, when Charlie was gone, sailed away off there to Alexandria with the Munsters, and Hazel's Derek was in France, Hazel came over to

London to visit me, or so the story went, but in fact because she was seeing a chap, a friend of theirs, who was serving with the fleet in the channel. Having a bit of a flutter is how she put it. She would tell me the most shocking things, knowing that they would shock me. I thought it was perfectly awful of her, two young married women, two service wives as the newspapers had begun to call us, and Galway women at that. Once I suggested as much to her, but she burst out laughing so loud that it startled everyone who was having tea at Fortnum and Mason's that afternoon.

"Tell me about your friends," Christopher said to me once. "Not your London friends. Tell me about your friends in Ireland."

And so I began, plucking friends from the air, without pattern, Charlie's friends and mine in Westmeath, and Dublin friends: Caroline Huggard, who made things out of glass, had made a lovely stained window for the church in Ardrahan and was a friend of Sarah Purser's and Evie Hone's; and Sarah Mulherne who had been in convent school with me was married now to a merchant-prince in Cork, as he was always called, Conor Tully-Delaney, the merchant-prince of Cork; and the Cavanaghs, who had the stud farm outside Cashel; and then, when I came to Hazel Lockhart, I began laughing, because Hazel was my secret special friend. And of course Christopher caught that, and asked me to tell him more about Hazel.

"To begin with," I told him, "they are Protestants, Hazel and Derek." Which is something one would never think to say about English friends, but was always in Ireland the very first thing. Although it was an unnecessary thing to say. I may not be much of a Catholic, but at least I know that children should be named for saints, not trees. "They have property," I said, "and an oldish house, Colleycourt, built ages ago, and beside it an old tower house that I am certain you would approve of, very Gaelic. Derek was in the war, all through the worst of it, there in the trenches. Does that put you off?"

"No," Christopher said. "Not at all. My brother was a doctor in the Medical Corps, you forget that."

But I had not forgotten it. Like everyone in love, I had set my mind to work upon his life, peopling it and furnishing it from the scraps that he had given me—his father the surgeon who had died when he was small, and his mother who had been to convent in Louvain, and his brother who had become a doctor, like the father. I would imagine the house in Sandycove, a five-minute walk from Dublin Bay, would see it on a winter's evening, the early darkness of Dublin winters, and would contrive to imagine a younger Christopher, beside a gray, roiled water, looking across the bay toward Howth. I could imagine that Christopher, and the Christopher who had lived in London, the Christopher who had written that book of his on the Ireland of an earlier century. It was my own Christopher, the Christopher whom I loved and who made love to me, that I could not imagine, the Christopher who had been in the General Post Office, firing off his revolver, and then fighting in some muddy awful lane and then in prison, and who now was at work supporting the gunmen. That was the Christopher whom I could not imagine, the Christopher whom I imagined becoming a different person whenever the door closed behind him.

"He's very sweet," Hazel said to me, that time I had brought him to call at Colleycourt, on an afternoon when I knew that Derek was away in Ballinasloe. "And quite civil and well-mannered. Quite the gent." Hazel was an incorrigible snob, and endlessly malicious.

"Don't be awful, Hazel," I said.

"I like him, dear Janice," she said. "I cannot believe that he is a wanted man. Is that really so?"

"I think so," I said. "He was brought in and questioned and then he was in a prison in Dublin for a bit, with hundreds of others, and then he was released and since then he has been lying low, but not too low. It is very puzzling."

"And he is staying with you at Coolater. What does your father think of all this?"

"We are very decorous and well-behaved, as you can well imagine. And Father can have a blind eye when he wants to. He is an old soldier after all. Betty, now! Betty is a different matter."

"Not about that," Hazel said. "What I meant was, how does the old soldier feel about having one of the King's enemies beneath his roof?" But before I could answer, she said, "I'm becoming a bit of a King's enemy myself, these days. These bloody Black and Tans are awful, like a pack of Greek bandits, and the Auxiliaries are worse, and the soldiers are only a shade better, if truth be told. Not that your lover is much of an improvement with his gunmen and arsonists. Those fools over in London don't know what to do, those fools over in London have never known, not for hundreds and hundreds of years. Derek is furious with everyone." She was pouring the tea when Christopher came back into the drawing room through the tall windows.

"It is lovely here, Hazel," he said, "as lovely as Coolater."

"Calm at any rate," Hazel said. "Those plantations were the work of my grandfather, and damned clever. They keep us sheltered from the worst of the winds. Colleycourt was an Eyre house, Janice must have told you that. Derek is only a blow-in from County Sligo."

"A pity that Major Lockhart and I missed each other today," Christopher said, in dry, social tones.

"Yes," Hazel said. "That would have been interesting." And she handed Christopher his cup.

"Interesting?" Christopher said. "In what way?"

"Blow-in he may be," Hazel said, "but it is Derek who has read up on the history of Colleycourt and the old castle down by the keep and a battle that was fought here once. Janice tells me that you are keen on history."

"It is an Irish failing," Christopher said.

"But scarcely a universal infection," Hazel said. "I am Irish myself of course, and I do not care thruppence about history."

Christopher smiled, delighted as men often were by Hazel's heady cocktail of impudence and seductiveness.

Later, as we drove back to Coolater, Christopher said, "I like your Hazel."

"So I noticed," I said.

"At the door," Christopher said, "she took me aside, and whispered very fiercely that I must be certain to take good care of you."

"That was sweet of her," I said carelessly, "and mind that you do." But I could almost hear her saying it, and was touched. "I expect you know all about the great battle that was fought at Colleycourt."

"More a skirmish than a battle," Christopher said. "Not even that, perhaps. A dozen or so of Lally's men, sloping away home after Aughrim, were caught by chance here, by a Williamite company, and they were finished off. It is a wonder that it got recorded at all. That sort of thing was happening all the time."

Was happening still, I thought, and thought of Volunteers behind hedges, waiting with Mills bombs and rifles for the Lancia and the tender, and the Black and Tans, half-drunk in their Crossley, firing away outside Gort at the young woman sitting with her infant. And I remembered the railway train outside Moate, and the frightened, bewildered man being shot down as he walked forward.

" 'It was a famous victory,' " I said, quoting the comic poem which Betty and I had once thought so funny.

And Christopher, not quite understanding, smiled over at me. I can see him as clear as clear. He had taken off his cap, and the wind ruffled his hair.

It was on the second day of May in 1915 that the wire from the War Office came to tell me that Charlie had been killed off there in the Dardanelles, as we called it then, the word "Gallipoli" came later, and all those other awful words, the Somme, Ypres, Verdun, Passchendaele. But the wire about Charlie came so quickly that it seemed to me an immense mistake, as though some telegraphist had punched the wrong key. It was in March that the Munsters, and one of our other regiments, the Dublin Fusiliers, the Dubs, everyone called them, had sailed out for Egypt, and I had had letters from Charlie from Alexandria, with talk about a "big push," but that was something which I thought would come later, much later, and I had been delighted that Charlie had been shipped off to Egypt, and kept out of harm's way, out of France and Belgium.

After the wire, there were letters, one of them from Charlie's CO, which I read through weeping with grief and anger, more anger than grief, and then threw away, not into the fire or into the river or whatever, but dropped, uncrumpled, into the wastebasket, with all its stupid, murderous adjectives, "gallant," and "splendid," and one or two others. It was not until a year later, almost, that a chum of Charlie's, a lieutenant who had gone out to Alexandria with him, but was a captain now, and on a sick leave from Flanders, came to visit me and took me out to tea and told me about April 25, at V Beach, at what everybody now called Gallipoli.

It was one of those bright ideas, he told me, a bright young man himself, named Donald Culhane. There was an old collier, the *River Clyde,* and the Dubs and the Munsters were to be put aboard her or else, others of them, aboard cutters, and then the

River Clyde would be run aground, and the troops would come swarming off and onto the beach. The Turks were heavily fortified in a castle above the beach, and they held their fire until the Dubs had come ashore from the cutters—wooden boats propelled by oars—and then they opened fire. "The fellows with me were all shot down within minutes, save for a handful of us, three or four, and we made our way over to another company, just as that company was taking its fire, and we did not know which way to move, it would have been senseless to charge the guns, and we could scarcely think. It was just then that the *Clyde* dropped her sally ports, and when the Munsters came down the gangplank, they were shot down, and that is when Charlie was killed. Later a chum in the Flying Corps told me that he was overhead, and the Aegean there had turned red." He would have told me more, but I stopped him then, but it was good that I learned that much from him, it is important to know where a loved one dies, and how, but not in all its miserable detail. I think that part of what he told me was in that letter, and in the other one, no doubt, from the War Office, but I had read neither with care, not wanting Charlie's death to be stained with "splendid" and "gallant" and all that. "And that was the very beginning of it, the very beginning of Gallipoli," Donald Culhane said, "the first half-hour. A place called Sedd el Bahr."

A few years later, when I told Christopher about it, he said, "It is a line now in an Irish song, 'It is better to die 'neath an Irish sky than at Suvla or Sedd el Bahr.' "

"It isn't better to die anywhere," I said. "The sky doesn't matter, skies don't care."

Far above, in a sky which I imagine as pale, white-streaked, Donald Culhane's aviator chum leans over the cockpit side, to anyone looking at him, his plane is a speck, a dragonfly, but it is life-sized to him, and below him he sees the Aegean, loveliest of the world's seas, a deep blue, Homer's sea, and he sees the red stain streaking outwards from the wreckage of men, but he cannot see the wreckage, only the red. Very lovely.

"It would not have seemed lovely to him," Christopher said, "it would have been sickening."

"Lovely," I said, like Lady Macbeth's bloody hand, 'The multitudinous seas incarnadine, Making the green one red.' "

"Poor Janice," Christopher said, "first Charlie and now me. You're not lucky with your men."

And it was true, Christopher with his revolvers and his rebellion, and before that poor Charlie, his blood staining the Aegean. And before Charlie, Patrick, come to think of it, and now Patrick has his empty sleeve tucked neatly into his jacket, but if you looked at it, and thought just a little, you could imagine the explosive ripping the arm, mangling it, and then later a surgeon in bloodstained apron and smock neatly cutting away what was left jagged, flesh and vein and bone. Not lucky at all.

A bit later that evening, after two, no three glasses of wine darker than the wine-dark Aegean, I said, "Donald Culhane was a chum, off there. Before Gallipoli, they were all on Lemnos for a bit, one of the isles of Greece."

"Like the Argonauts," Christopher said. "And once there was no one on Lemnos but women who had murdered their husbands."

"My God," I said. "The things you know. After we had had our tea, Donald Culhane took me back to Chelsea. In the cab, he began kissing my neck, and then he ran his hand up and down my leg, under my skirt. I had given over wearing mourning, thank goodness, and he was very nice about it. I took his hand away, and he sat up straight for the rest of the trip, looking very sheepish."

There was a great tremendous row about Gallipoli afterwards, it was reckoned a horrible disaster, and there was an inquiry, with everyone putting the blame on everyone else, but most of the blame went to Winston Churchill. I did not follow it closely, they all looked awful to me, Kitchener with that hideous enormous mustached face, and Fisher looking less like an admiral than like a Chinese laundryman dressed up for a panto, and Churchill, with that fierce baby face always scrunched up into a scowl. And that awful Lloyd George.

"At the end of the day," Christopher said, "those are the ones we will have to deal with, Lloyd George and Churchill."

And it seemed so odd to me, that Christopher and his chums, hiding out in Dublin flats and waiting behind hedges with a few rifles and explosives, should imagine a time when they would sit down in Downing Street across the table from the men who had thrown thousands upon thousands to their deaths in the Aegean and in the trenches of France.

"At the end of the day," I told him, "you will have to deal with me." When we kissed, I opened my eyes wide, and could see the winter flowers in their tall brass vase between the windows, and the curtains with their small Chinese-y black dragons against vermilion. Third time lucky, I thought, and I will bring good luck to Christopher.

XII

ELIZABETH KEATING

Elizabeth Keating's alarm clock rang at four on the morning of Wednesday, the eighteenth of May, 1921, and she dressed and went downstairs to the kitchen of her Leeson Street boardinghouse, where she turned on a single small light and boiled water for her tea. It was too early for even the skivvy to be abroad, and Elizabeth had the roomy kitchen to herself, chill even in spring, with its broad flags. She held the cup in her hands, and looked out into the kitchen garden as it slowly lightened. She had brought her bulky purse down with her, and now, between her first cup and her second, she sat down at the table and drew from the purse a broad stenographer's notebook.

"May 18th," she wrote, "to Mountjoy Prison, at five A.M., when the curfew has been raised, to attend the executions by hanging of four Volunteers—Terrence O'Brien, Joseph Gaffney, Edward Hennessy, Robert Malone." The fountain pen, a present to her on her twenty-fourth birthday from Christopher Blake, had an enameled casing of mottled black and maroon. It reminded her of those days, two years earlier, when she and Blake had worked together on each week's issue of the *Republican Bulletin*, when Elizabeth, a national schoolteacher with no training in such matters, had learned from Blake the art of sorting out facts and arranging them, writing a proper lead paragraph, learning the mysterious symbols by which editors and printers spoke silently to each other, a language beside the language of the story. But now, Elizabeth was the sole editor, with two assistants of her own to instruct, one a young teacher like herself, and the other a university student.

She hated Mountjoy. Kilmainham was awful enough, but at least it was close to the Phoenix Park, and its ugliness had been touched by history. But Mountjoy, ugly, beside the stale waters of the Royal Canal, was the repository of present disasters, hopes, deaths. It was from a cell in Mountjoy, in September of 1917, that Thomas Ashe began his hunger strike, bare months after the executions of the 1916 leaders in Kilmainham. And yet, with Ashe's death, something which moved beyond 1916 began to take place. The prisoners in Mountjoy, led by Ashe and Austin Stack, used hunger as a weapon when no others were available. Ashe's body, in the uniform of an officer of the Volunteers, lay in state, and then on the thirtieth, there was a procession of at least thirty thousand, through the streets of the thronged city, to Glasnevin, with the Volunteers in uniform, and the British authorities not so foolish as to make a move against them.

Two years before, on August the first of 1915, the old Fenian, Jeremiah O'Donovan Rossa, had been buried there in Glasnevin, with a procession almost as large, and Patrick Pearse had spoken at his graveside. Elizabeth, then a student, had been standing on the pavement on Dame Street. But when Thomas Ashe was buried, in 1917, she had marched with the Cumann na mBan, and had stood with them, so far in the rear that she had seen little, but had heard the three volleys fired by the honor guard of Volunteers, and then there was a silence, and she could make out a voice but not the words. When Pearse spoke at Rossa's grave, the words became famous, "They have left us our Fenian dead," at the end of a great oration, but it was only later that Elizabeth learned what the young officer, Michael Collins, had said over Ashe's grave, a few words in Irish, and then in English, "Nothing remains to be said. That volley which we have just heard is the only speech which it is proper to make over the grave of a dead Fenian." Speaking that day in Ennis, in County Clare, another of the men of 1916, Eamon De Valera, told his listeners, as he stood at the foot of the O'Connell monument, that the Irish people would accept nothing less then freedom, and would die, one by one, rather than submit. "The circumstances of Ashe's death," an English newspaper, the *Daily Express*, noted, "have made one hundred thousand Sinn Féiners." On the Friday of Easter Week, Ashe had fought a five-hour battle and earned himself a death sentence, but it was in death that he was enshrined. Parnell's grave, and

Rossa's grave, and the grave of Thomas Ashe. For Elizabeth Keating, Ashe's grave was touched by a special seriousness and solemnity. Rossa had dragged out long, humiliating years in America, before, almost forgotten, white-bearded, he had been in death shipped back. But Ireland had watched Thomas Ashe die, the tall, broad-shouldered body wasting away, without boots or bedding. The Lord Mayor had visited him, and found him shivering upon the floor of his cell. "He died," the lord mayor said at the inquest, "it is for his country to say whether it is in a good cause or not."

It was six months after Ashe's death that Elizabeth reported for work to Christopher Blake, but the *Republican Bulletin* now bore her impress rather than his. He had moved over to whatever intelligence duties he performed for Headquarters, and she seldom saw him, but when they met, he always made it a point to praise what she had been writing.

"No suggestions?" she had asked him once, and he had said, "No, no suggestions." Their final weeks together had been in the last weeks of October, of 1920, when Terence MacSwiney was on hunger strike in Brixton and eighteen-year-old Kevin Barry was awaiting execution in Mountjoy. Elizabeth had been outside Mountjoy on the early morning of November 1, with thousands of others, a damp, cheerless morning, but those thousands were kneeling, and were kneeling when the prison's death bell began to toll, and, when it had ceased, they said the sorrowful mysteries of the rosary. When Elizabeth rose to her feet, she went to the prison wall and copied down the typewritten notice: "The sentence of the law passed on Kevin Barry, found guilty of murder, was carried into execution at 8 A.M. this morning." Flecks of light rain had already fallen upon it. She talked to Jack Cunningham, a Volunteer who had visited him two days before, and got from Cunningham a description of the corridor leading to Barry's cell, and of the cell itself. When she began to write, she was weeping, and so set it aside, walked the four sides of the Green, and then, back in the Harcourt Street office, sat down dry-eyed, lit a cigarette, and began.

> November 1. This morning, a gray, cheerless morning, while thousands knelt to pray in the roadway, a roadway guarded by Auxiliaries and armored cars, Kevin Barry, an eighteen-year-old soldier of

the Irish Republican Army, was put to death by John Ellis, the common hangman, who had come from England for the purpose. The rope too, a new rope, had been brought over from Pentonville Prison.

At noon, when Christopher Blake came in to look at her copy, he read that first paragraph, and then placed the pages beside them on the table.

"I thought I would begin it that way," she said. "We cannot be printed and distributed before Thursday, and this afternoon every paper in Dublin will have the details, and photographs of Kevin and of Mountjoy. I thought that by doing it this way—"

"Yes," Blake said. "This is fine, Elizabeth." He picked up the story. "How do you know about the rope?"

"I talked last evening with one of the assistant warders, a decent fellow named Mahon. The rope is always new. Mahon says that Ellis looked in on Kevin through the spyhole, and calculated the drop, as they call it, and let the rope hang all night from the roof of the hanghouse, weighted down. Then he went to bed and had himself a good night's sleep. It is all there in what I have written."

And much else. On Saturday, the body of Terence MacSwiney was sent back to Ireland, and was to have been borne in procession through the streets of Dublin, then carried to Cork. But at Holyhead, the government insisted that the body be carried by boat directly to Cork. The requiem Mass, preceded and followed by an immense Dublin procession, took place without the body, which was buried in Cork, at a ceremony even larger, and after the body, in Volunteer's uniform, had lain in state. Elizabeth's article wove together the two deaths. The plaque upon the coffin spoke of him as "Murdered by the foreigner in Brixton Prison, London, England, on October 25, 1920, the fourth year of the Republic." The essay describing MacSwiney's death and his burial had been written for Blake by Maurice Harte, a young playwright at the Abbey. But Elizabeth merged the two deaths, and with them the death of a man who had died on hunger strike the week before, and one who at the moment lay near death. Harte gave attention to MacSwiney's burial in Irish Republic Army uniform, and his role as commandant of the Cork No. 1 Brigade, but Elizabeth laid stress upon words spoken by MacSwiney months earlier, and prophetically, before his arrest. "It is not those who inflict the most suffering but who suffer the most who will conquer."

They had been the first, MacSwiney the first to die upon hunger strike and Barry the first to be hanged, because Ashe's death had been caused by a clumsy doctor shoving a tube down his throat, which had put an end to forcible feeding.

"It is as though," Elizabeth Keating said to Blake that day in Harcourt Street, the day of Barry's execution, "it is as though—" She hesitated, not because she was looking for words, but because she had the words. She commenced again. "It is as though the meaning of our history has at last become clear."

Blake looked at her quickly: someone familiar had become subtly but suddenly different.

"As though," she said, "as though we are what we have endured." She looked beyond Blake to the quiet roadway. When Sarsfield sailed away in 1691, after the surrender at Limerick, the women of the soldiers whom Sarsfield carried off to fight beside him in the wars of France waded through the water, waist-deep, clung on to the anchor chains and the ropes, begged, but were left behind, and many of them drowned. Some were dragged by the ropes, and the seawater choked them to death, and other women went beneath the waves and were drowned as the ships moved outwards, a terrible wail rising up from the shore. In Elizabeth Keating's girlhood, they all knew the songs about Sarsfield, "O, Patrick Sarsfield is Ireland's darling," with his sword from Ferrara and his white cockade, and the men who had sailed off with him, " 'tis but by chance, he's gone to France, his fame and fortune to advance, to follow the fleur de lys." But Elizabeth thought these days, more vehemently, of those wails from the shore, which were the wails of women. Behind them Sarsfield and his bright swordsmen had left a wasted island, a people suffering through an indifferent and cruel century and moving forward to the disaster of the famine. But an enduring people were becoming risen people, able to conquer, as Terence MacSwiney had said, because they could suffer the most.

"It will take more than suffering," Christopher Blake said to her. "MacSwiney commanded a brigade."

"A brigade with a handful of weapons, as you well know," she said, "a brigade of country fellows and Cork City fellows who leave their shops or their farms for a day or two to attack a barracks or a lorry and then go back to work, or else, with bad luck, are put on the run. Terence MacSwiney did as much work for Ireland stretched out upon a cot in Brixton Prison as ever he did commanding First Cork Brigade."

"I know that," Blake said, "but—"

"Kevin Barry, who was hanged this morning, who was murdered by the hangman this morning, you will read in the English newspapers that he was hanged because he shot dead a soldier in a gun battle, and the soldier was himself but eighteen years old. But the soldier was well armed, and old or young, he was here as the agent of a powerful empire."

When she had finished her second cup, she carried it to the sink and washed it out, and washed out the teapot. The boarding-house was owned and managed by a Mrs. Theresa Leahy, who knew of course that Elizabeth was in Cumann na mBan and suspected that she had other responsibilities, but was careful not to inquire into them too closely. Once, six months earlier, when one of the rooms was empty, Elizabeth had organized it for a fellow on the run, a grim, gawky, frightened young fellow with a large Adam's apple. He drifted away two weeks later, leaving nothing behind him but a scent in the room of cheap cigarettes, and a celluloid collar, grimed and somehow pathetic. Mrs. Leahy hinted to Elizabeth, with the elephantine delicacy of her calling, that she did not welcome such lodgers. "Not that I am not for the boys heart and soul," she assured Elizabeth, "and not that I am not proud of yourself. I would be in the Cumann na mBan myself, if I were a younger woman." She was the safest sort of landlady, Elizabeth decided, sanctimonious and adroit.

By the mirror over the dresser Elizabeth adjusted her overcoat, and fixed her hat by pins to her full dark hair. Then she climbed upstairs, and, drawing back the lace curtains of the front room, waited for Joe Timins, Christopher Blake's helper, to arrive with the motorcar which was to take her across the river to Mountjoy. Timins was in fact her helper now, with most of the editorial work and decisions in her hands, but of course he thought of Christopher Blake as his "chief," although he followed Elizabeth's instructions cheerfully and accurately.

Curfew was ended, but there were few motorcars on the roads.

A few buses had been laid on to take demonstrators to the prison; most of them would be on foot, and the Dublin cumann was marching there.

"It will be a beautiful morning that those poor young fellows will be dying in," Timins said. He was young himself, but going bald early, the high, bare forehead shielded now by a soft gray hat.

"They will see nothing of it," Elizabeth said. Months before, the friendly warder had given her a description of the hanging shed. She took out her rosary beads, and as they drove through the quiet spring city, she moved through her fingers the smooth beads of polished bog oak. She prayed swiftly, silently, and was saying the last decade as they crossed the river by the Capel Street bridge. She kissed the crucifix, and put back the beads in their leatherette case. The beads had been given to her by the family of Florry Brosnan, who had been hanged with Tom Trainor the month before. There were glints of early-morning sunlight on the river's muddy green.

When Timins saw that she had finished praying, he said, "There was a raid last night upon the Ministry of Labor, but they got naught for their troubles. Most of the files were away safe in Sheriff Street, and the two girls on duty climbed down the planks to the rear garden and away with them."

"Who were the women on duty?" Elizabeth said.

"Nell Purdom was one of them, and I am not certain about the other one."

"Tell Nell Purdom to write a little account of it," Elizabeth said. "About four inches' worth. Auxiliaries hammering on the door with rifle butts and all the rest of it."

"By God, Elizabeth," Timins said, "you let nothing go to waste. You are a better man on the task than Christopher Blake was. Blake is too literary altogether."

"That is not the report of him that you would get from Mick Collins," she said. "When there is need to be hard, Chris Blake is as hard as anyone." But privately, she agreed with Timins.

The roadway outside the prison was already crowded, but the air was quiet. Out of respect, the crowd was well dressed, the men bareheaded, holding hats or caps in hand, and the women in somber hats, dark coats. A few held placards denominating groups. One placard, the largest, read, "Another Martyr for Ireland, Another Murder for the Crown," but four rebels were to be hanged today, the placard was quoting the street ballad which had been sung since Kevin Barry's execution in the winter. Along the narrow footpath, between wall and crowd, Auxiliaries made their way, their rifles slung. Elizabeth studied their faces, faces kept deliberately blank. She glanced at her watch, a half-hour to go. They were always punctual. Somewhere in the crowd would be the families of the lads who were to be hanged, but it would be best to leave them alone with their grief. Or with something worse than grief, more shattering. She could not imagine the feelings of parents, brothers. All four of the fellows had been captured in a house in north County Dublin, in the course of a gun battle in which two policemen were killed. Around her, discordant, she could hear muttered and whispered prayers, "Holy Mary, Mother of God," "May the perpetual light shine upon them, O Lord." Shortly before six o'clock, she knew, the hour appointed for the first two hangings, the crowd would fall to their knees, and commence the rosary, saying the words aloud this time. The Auxiliaries would stand motionless. Then the death bell would sound.

At a half-hour after noon, Elizabeth went into Switzer's, the large shop at the foot of Grafton Street, upstairs to the teashop, where she ordered tea and scones and waited. She tried making notes for the articles she was to write, but found that she could not bring herself to write. By order of Dáil Eireann, enforced throughout the city, no business had been transacted before eleven, but the offices and shops were open now, and the teashop was beginning to fill with shoppers, some of them carrying paper bundles or bags, and chattering. At the near table a woman said something which made her friend laugh, and the friend put a hand upon her forearm, the two of them laughing. For a year, now, it had amazed Elizabeth that there should be shopping, gossip, the routines of offices, on the morning and in the city of such deaths. But it was an amazement without accusation; she herself, although she could not make notes, was enjoying her tea. It would be different, so she thought, to be shot down in battle as the two policemen had been, and a Volunteer, wounded but dying later in hospital. There would be four ropes, her friend the warder had told her, all of them new, and the day before, the families had been allowed a visit. An altar had been constructed in one of the cells, and all four of them received communion from the prison chaplain, as did the warders who had guarded them. Kevin Barry had been hanged in winter darkness, with yellow gaslights burning in the alleys, and arc lamps on the main road, but it had been bright morning almost when the first pair of today's four were hanged.

It was a quarter to one, almost, when Sarah Byrnes joined Elizabeth, a country woman from Killenaule in Tipperary, with fierce dark eyes. "I am sorry to be late, Elizabeth," she said, and rested a parcel on the empty chair. "I am staying in Rathgar with my aunt, and we went to the Three Patrons to pray for the lads above in Mountjoy, and then the trams were off until eleven and then they were all of them crowded."

After tea had been brought, she said, "I took just a minute to look at the shirtwaists and the skirts below. They are Irish-made the most of them, I would never have expected that in Switzer's. Is that not wonderful?"

"It is wonderful if you don't mind ill-made skirts," Elizabeth said.

"Wonderful, I mean," Sarah said, "to find all of that on sale in Switzer's. They do not have a good national record."

"They do now," Elizabeth said. "Their windows were broken in by demonstrators throwing stones."

Before hanging, a white cotton cap is placed over the head, so the warder told Elizabeth, so that the fellow being hanged is spared knowledge of the exact moment. But it is also merciful to the witnesses.

"There is everything that you asked for there in the string bag," Sarah said, "and other material as well, that Commandant Tansey wants handed in directly to headquarters. I don't know is it safe to carry such material around with myself or with you in the center of Dublin, but I did as you bid me do."

"Nothing more safe than this," Elizabeth said, "two young women meeting for a late-morning tea in Switzer's. There has never been a raid upon Switzer's, nor any of the shoppers hauled off for interrogation."

"You are very right, I am certain," Sarah said, and looked about her with what might have seemed timidity but was in fact a country person's awkwardness in the city. In Tipperary, in the hills outside Killenaule, Sarah, who had been trained as a hospital nurse, ran a combination of safe house and hospital for men on the run or else serving in a flying column. One of its rooms served for a time as a bomb shop, and she was knowledgeable about explosives.

"It is heartbreaking, those young fellows in Mountjoy this morning," she said. "Did you know them, any of them?" But Elizabeth shook her head. "Paddy Tansey," Sarah said, "says that Headquarters knows damned well that the fellows in his column have less than twenty rounds apiece, and he says what more can they do but take a shot at a soldier on motorbicycle or a lone motorcar. He will not waste rounds by firing them off uselessly against armored cars and he will not put his men where they can be pinned down and short taken. If headquarters expects more from him, let them give him what he needs." Her voice had risen, and Elizabeth put a warning hand upon her elbow.

"Dear goodness," Elizabeth said, "did Paddy Tansey have you learn that off by heart, or is it written down?"

"It is written down," Sarah said, "and for me to give to you and you to pass on to Headquarters in writing. But he does wonder," and here she lowered her voice once again, "if you could find some way to say a word about it to Mick."

"To Mick, is it?" Elizabeth said, and smiled. " 'Tis little enough that I see Mick, and especially in these days. I am editing the *Bulletin* and am grateful for what material you bring me, but beyond that, as regards other matters, I am only a courier like yourself." But then, seeing the look that had passed over Sarah's face, she said, "I will see what I can do. When a person chances upon Mick, high or low, he will have time for that person, or else, if he has not time, he will chew that person's ear off and tell them to go to hell."

Sarah was looking about the room. "In the middle of a war," she said, "and people shopping and all the rest of it, the men in the pubs, no doubt, and all that."

"You are very concerned for Paddy Tansey," Elizabeth said, "do you see much of him?"

"I do," Sarah said, and carefully, warily, she continued to look at the other tables. "He brought a young fellow to me three nights ago who had been shot in the thigh outside Tipperary town. Dr. Lyons in Tipperary took out the bullet, and Paddy brought him up to me. It was when he heard that I was going up to Dublin that he entrusted the report to me, and then sat down and wrote out his letter to HQ. It is a mercy the boy lived. He had lost buckets of blood before he could be seen by Dr. Lyons."

A countryside which Elizabeth had written of but had never seen, an imagined countryside, fellows in action, on the run, a dozen of them, twenty perhaps, breaking up into smaller groups, and a wounded boy brought to the doctor or the doctor to him, the rough wool of his trousers sodden with blood, dank and with blood's metallic, terrifying smell, acrid. As now she imagined a hill-edged horizon, the smell of earth, dark, loamy, an imperiled body.

"He is well spoken of here in Dublin," Elizabeth said in the tearoom of Switzer's in Grafton Street, speaking of Paddy Tansey, whose name had become known, like the names of Tom Barry, Sean MacEoin, Frank Lacy, Ernie O'Malley.

"As well it should be," Sarah said, still guarded but smiling a bit. "They can carve up Munster into divisions, if that is what they have a mind to do, but for West Tipperary to be as active as it is, that is the doing of Paddy Tansey's column."

"You are a bit sweet on Paddy Tansey," Elizabeth said suddenly, "a bit gone on Paddy Tansey, are you not?"

Swiftly, Sarah brought down her eyes to study her cup of tea. "Indeed I am not," she said. "How could I be sweet on Paddy Tansey, he is as good as spoken for. Everyone knows about himself and Mary Noonan."

In Sarah's string bag, Elizabeth knew, would be accounts, meticulously written in Sarah's classroom hand, of attacks upon RIC barracks in Tipperary and across the border, a fight battering itself through an army roadblock, an evening, danger-edged, of music in a country farmhouse, and threading though all of the accounts, the surname concealed, the account of the column's commandant, chosen two years before by acclamation.

"Mary Noonan," Elizabeth said, her tone flat and derisive.

"It is true enough what Paddy Tansey says about supplies by way of complaint," Sarah said, swerving away from the subject. "The poor lad that I am tending says the same. Twenty rounds a fellow is the height of it, and there are all makes and kinds of weapons—Lee-Enfields, Mausers, some Browning automatic pistols, and beneath the floorboards of my safe house we have three useless Remingtons from the States. Things are as bad almost for First Tipp and Second Tipp and I have heard as much about West Cork and West Kilkenny."

"I know," Elizabeth said quietly, and she put her hand upon Sarah's. "But they work wonders for all that. They are the talk of the country, those fellows in the columns in Cork and Tipp and Kerry. They put the rest of us to shame. They will never be forgotten."

"Not forgotten is not good enough, Elizabeth," she said fiercely but she did not draw her hand away. "That is not good enough. They need a bit of help, more help than is going out to them."

"I know," Elizabeth said.

But in a way she did not know. She knew only what came in reports and stories told to her in front rooms in Rathgar and Clontarf by young commanders up for the day to make their meetings with the war council who would then be sent along to "have a word with Elizabeth for the *Republican Bulletin*, Elizabeth is a grand girl and she is doing great work for us on the information front, keeping up spirits like." She had talked once or twice with Paddy Tansey, Sarah's Paddy as now Elizabeth thought of him, and Liam Deasy, and once with Tom Barry. Ernie O'Malley talked with her for hours after his escape from Kilmainham, the *Braggart's Journal*, O'Malley called her newssheet, but O'Malley and Frank Lacy were different from the other fellows in the field, resourceful fellows like the others, and having ballads made up about them in the countryside, but they were very much fellows from Headquarters. O'Malley she did not entirely like, a fierce, capable fellow, able for anything, but a bit of the posturer, theatrical. Once, before he moved south to take command of the division, he had insisted on taking her to dinner at Jammet's, and there, as soft lights subdued by shades of pink silk fell upon the tables, he described for her the raid on Kilcorum Barracks, where he had shared command with Charley Neafsey, and it was as though he remembered everything almost too well, colors and atmospheres which there was no need to remember, how the rank raw grass, rain-sodden, smelled, as they mustered, to move across country upon the barracks, a snipe wheeling in the sky, the taste of tea as they shared it out. He knew that he moved within history. Frank Lacy was like him in many ways, but never a trace of the posturer, a hard, determined young fellow, his wit a bit bookish, like Ernie's, but dry, sardonic. But the two of them were far removed by temper, background, from the real commanders—the Barrys and Deasys and Haleses and MacEoins, fellows who had been mechanics, workers on the railways, small farmers. Or fellows like Sarah's Paddy Tansey. Their stories, as they would tell them to her, would ramble, gather slow strength, and there would be pauses within which, she would imagine, a shouted order would be remembered, the sound of gunfire. Often they were shy, country men's quick, sly smiles, the awkwardness of talking of such matters with a woman.

When they were ready to leave, Elizabeth picked up the string bag as easily as though she had brought it there herself, and they walked out into a midday Grafton Street which was as busy and as cheerful as though the city, the country, were entirely at peace. At the foot of Grafton, the eighteenth century confronted itself, the Bank of Ireland looking across College Green toward Trinity College. As the two young women stood together, an armored car came upon the Green from Dame Street, from the Castle, no doubt, and moved easily, cutting between two trams, into Nassau Street. And then the scene was as pacific as it had been.

"Will you be here in town long?" Elizabeth asked. "We might take in a film together, or have an early meal one evening, before curfew." And realized that she sounded as pacific as the street itself.

"Ach, no," Sarah said, "I will be staying tonight with the aunt, and we will have all sorts of family matters to catch up on, and then the train tomorrow morning." And Elizabeth imagined for herself, no doubt wrongly, a house tucked away behind high hills, a wounded Volunteer, and Sarah straining her ears in the Munster night for the sound of a motorcar.

"Time enough for all that later," Sarah said, and once again, Elizabeth imagined, tried to imagine, what later would be like, but, as always before, she could not.

She walked northwards, and crossed the river at O'Connell Bridge. On the north side, she turned left, and walked along the quays. At her back, over her right shoulder, hidden by buildings, lay the half-repaired wreckage of the Easter Week fighting, but the great, bullying, graceful buildings along the river were solid, domed and massive, the Custom House behind her, and the Four

Courts toward which she walked. In the five years since the Rising, so she told herself often, so she told her readers, the country had been transformed, the city had been transformed, freedom rising from the ashes of shelled buildings, buildings gutted by the fires of battle. But the unburned seemed not to know it. On the Custom House pediment, carved in flamboyant curves, lion and unicorn faced each other, emblems of the British Crown. Someday, she had said once to Christopher Blake, someday we will haul those fellows down, drop them into the Liffey. "That would be a pity," he answered absently, his mind elsewhere. "A pity," she echoed, faintly outraged, and the tone drew him to her words. "Yes," he said, "of course. We may not like what they did, are doing. But they have been rather splendid in their way. They made this into a great city, lions and all, unicorns and all." And there was no need to specify who "they" were. Remembering now, Elizabeth thought, we will see about that, we will see what happens to you later, Mr. Lion, Mr. Unicorn, Lord Unicorn. The river sparkled as she walked along the quays, arched by the graceful bridges which "they" had flung across it, the lords and masters of the Irish people, and she looked across the river toward where, beyond Wellington Quay, lay Dublin Castle. What would happen to Dublin Castle, she wondered, when "later" happened, with its statue over the gateway of a blindfolded Justice. There had been blindfolds for the four soldiers hanged that morning, white caps, hoods, to fall over their faces, and the hoods had a command upon Elizabeth's feelings stronger than domes, blocks of stone, a blindfolded Justice.

Once, another time, when she and Christopher Blake had been working together, she had said, "It must be spelled out very clearly, that a Republic was proclaimed by Pearse from the steps of the GPO and it was ratified by his blood and the blood of the other men who were shot with him at Kilmainham. It was ratified by the Dáil when first it met, three years later, that we stood by the battle fought in 1916, that we are fighting for a Republic."

Christopher Blake seemed to study her before he answered. "Is that needed, Elizabeth, do you think. After all, what do we call ourselves, if not the *Republican Bulletin?*" "It is needed," Elizabeth said, "because you hear the talk I hear, and you hear more of it no doubt because you are closer to the center of things than I am."

"And what talk might that be?"

That was in one of the weeks when they had edited the *Republican Bulletin* in the two small rooms in Mary Street, above the tailor's shop. Christopher was standing by one of the two front windows, which they deliberately left dusty and streaked. "Well you know," she said, "that sooner or later some form of bargain will be put on offer by the English, and the people must be put on guard against that."

"There is no bargain that is not worth at least a look," Christopher said, "need I tell that to a woman?"

"We are not talking about hats or frocks or furnishings for the home," she said, "we are talking about Ireland, about the Republic which was declared just down the road from here."

Copies of the Proclamation were everywhere now, and its language lay along the nerves. *We hereby proclaim the Irish Republic as a Sovereign Independent State. . . . In the name of God and of the dead generations. . . . The Irish Republic is entitled to, and hereby claims, the allegiance of every Irishman and Irishwoman. . . .*

She surprised herself that she was talking to Christopher Blake, who was after all her superior, with angry vehemence. She had never heard such talk from Blake, nor ever had expected to. And yet she found that her arms were shaking and she rested them against the table on which she had been correcting proofs. In her room, as in many rooms, there hung one of the reproductions by camera of the Proclamation, with its variety of typefaces, its broken R, and at the bottom the names of the men who signed it and signed knowing that they would have days only to live, a few weeks at best.

"We should tell that to the people," she said. "That we will take nothing other than a Republic, and that we will fight until we have one and die if need be." If she remembered rightly, they had been talking before even young Barry had been hanged, the first of them to have the white hood over his face, and the rope of new hemp.

"Perhaps," Blake said, "you may be right, Elizabeth. But that is a political matter."

She could not believe that she had heard him properly. The Republic lay well beyond politics, it was what history had been moving toward and sanctified by the blood of martyrs. By the grave of the old Fenian, O'Donovan Rossa, Pearse had said that life springs from death, and that living nations rose up from the graves of martyrs, and had not meant that as stirring language only, as the parliamentary blatherers would have meant it.

"We have done with politics," she told Christopher Blake in the chill, dusty room in Mary Street, "Sinn Féin has swept politics away and the blather about Home Rule and all the rest of it."

Now, as she hurried along the quays, she could not remember how Christopher Blake had replied to her, nor even, exactly, her own words, could remember only, but that vividly, her anger, her hands pressed down upon the table top to curb her trembling arms. It was not on behalf of politics that those four young fellows had given up their lives that morning, a sacred trust for those who lived after them.

Before she came to the Four Courts, sprawling and imperious, with its wide bullying wings, as she thought them, and its great green-tinged dome, she turned and went down Capel, but before turning she paused, a moment only, to look upon river, bridges, the shops which lined the far quays, bookshops and printshops, the offices of corn factors and solicitors, a cabinetmaker's shop. Here, for that moment, there was not even an armored car in view, and it was as though, for that moment only, she and Christopher Blake and the hanged Volunteers and Frank Lacy in the hills were invisible, phantasmal, fighting an invisible war.

But once she had walked into the rooms which that month were being used by the Ministry of Defense, she knew that the struggle, although invisible, was real. In the hallway, as always, a guard slouched against the wall of grimy green, straightened when he heard footsteps, and then relaxed. The guard was always a Dubliner, recruited from the city brigade, always young, and seemed always, spring or winter, clear weather or rain, to be wearing a tan mackintosh. Nearly always they were polite, in a distant way, and this one, who recognized her, smiled and jerked his head toward a closed door at the end of the corridor. He could not have been more than nineteen, with a round, open face, a scattering of freckles across his nose.

William Considine, whom she had come to see, the deputy minister below Cathal Brugha, was sitting behind a time-scarred oak desk, its top scattered with papers. He was working in his shirtsleeves, and there was a tray of snubbed-out cigarettes beside him, a man gaunt as Brugha himself, but much taller, with a long, Red Indian face, and close-cropped hair. His necktie was black, and Elizabeth knew that like herself he had been outside Mountjoy that morning, kneeling in the roadway, and waiting for the mourning bell.

"Well then, Elizabeth," he said, "what brings you to us?"

"My friend Sarah is in town to me," Elizabeth said. "She has written out a sheaf of stories about Tipperary—battles by the columns and what the Tans and the Auxies have been about. I have not had a chance to read through it, but what she writes is always good—good, sound, strong stuff."

"For the *Braggart's Journal,* is it?" Considine asked. "Not our department, girl. If you think it should be cleared, take it to Christopher Blake or Erskine Childers. If you can ever find Blake, that is."

"I am in charge of the *Republican Bulletin,*" Elizabeth said, "and I no longer need bring my material for clearance to Blake or to Childers or to Fitzgerald. Much less, as you say, to yourself."

"My God," Considine said, "I was chaffing you, girl, could you not see that? You are doing great work, and with scant resources." His voice held the flat, faintly northern tones of Louth. He reached over for his packet of cigarettes, and Elizabeth said, "May I have one of those, Bill?"

His hand resting upon the packet, Considine shot a quick glance at her. "You may, of course. I should have offered you one at once. Great ones for the cigarettes, you young ones."

Elizabeth held his eye as he lit it for her. "No," she said. "Once in a great while. It is of little consequence." But she relished the sweet, acrid taste of the tobacco, the sudden, mild jolt of well-being.

"The day or two before Sarah Byrnes came up," she said, "Paddy Tansey called in on her, and gave her the battalion report to bring up to you, and I have it here."

He took it from her, some sheets of white, unlined paper, folded twice. " 'Tis well for Paddy Tansey below in Tipperary," he said, "that he has two fine young women to carry his dispatches for him."

"Sarah Byrnes controls a safe house in Tipperary," Elizabeth said sharply, "she tends the wounded of Paddy Tansey's column and the other two Tipperary columns as well, and the house is used also as an arms dump. For a time last year it served as a bomb factory. They make their own bombs in Tipperary, they have given up on your ministry."

Wary now beneath his easy manner, Considine said, "There is nothing I can say this day that you will not take amiss, is there?"

Although she did not know Considine well, he had her confidence, a bitter man with an ease of manner entirely foreign to Brugha. She could not herself explain the edginess which he always set up in her.

"By rights this should have come to Headquarters," he said, "and not to the ministry, but there is no need to stand upon ceremony. I will see that it is passed along." He tapped it by its edge upon the desk, and then dropped it upon one of the piles of paper.

"He sent along a message as well," Elizabeth said, "for Sarah to tell me, and for me to tell the people in Dublin."

"Ah," Considine said, "we have it now. Well, Elizabeth girl, out with it."

Elizabeth drew in on her cigarette, and thought how best Paddy Tansey would want it phrased. It gave Considine a moment, casual, half-smiling, to study her, a handsome young woman, serious and capable. Too serious, perhaps.

"It is all there in the report, at any rate," she said, "but he was anxious indeed that HQ should know how things stand in his column. They are bad off for ammunition."

"I know that," Considine said. "There is no one knows that better than myself and Brugha, 'tis true for all the columns, every last one of them, and we wake up thinking that. 'Tis a marvel what they are doing with the little they have. And will keep on doing, God willing."

"God willing," she said.

"And that was the message so?" Considine said. "That was the whole of it?"

Sarah paused, for a moment only, but Considine caught it. "Yes," she said, "that was the whole of it."

"Are you certain that Paddy Tansey and Nurse Byrnes did not bid you slip round to Mick Collins, and have a word with him on the subject?"

She thought of sliding around the question, and then changed her mind. "Something like that," she said, and smiled to take the edge off the admission. "You know what they are like, those fellows down the country, in the columns and battalions. And most especially in Cork and Tipp, like Paddy Tansey. They swear by Mick. But sure, that is no concern of mine, I am carrying along the word."

"You may be doing yourself an injustice, Elizabeth," Considine said. "There are times when I think that the *Republican Bulletin* is in competition with the English newspapers to build up the reputation of Michael Collins. Not that he is not an able man, one of our very ablest. I have not a word to say against him. But he is neither the minister of defense nor the chief of staff of the Volunteers. And far less is he president of the Republic."

"I will try to remember that," Elizabeth said.

"You will of course," he said. "I had not meant to be critical, even if I sounded so. You have your tasks to perform, and every army has need of its shadowy legends, and especially an army like ours, fighting in the shadows, darting out upon raids, and then back into darkness. The Big Fellow, isn't that what the lads down the country call him? Do you know, I have never heard the words used here in Dublin."

But even Elizabeth, who as a publicist was on the edges of HQ only, knew that there was a bit more to it than that. Once she had been talking to Jamesey Loftus, who commanded one of the flying columns in East Limerick. "I declare to God, Miss Keating," he said, "I sent my lists to Brigade and to the HQ here in Dublin, and there was naught done, and I came up here and gained naught, and all this time operations in my command were slowed almost to nil, and then word came to me to have a chat in the back room of Vaughan's in Parnell Square on a certain night. And before I left, I had put four balls of malt and a pint of stout inside me and I had a promise of ammo from the Big Fellow himself. He took out his fountain pen and made a note in a book, and the thing was done. 'But I don't know why I am giving it to you,' he said, 'you lousers in East Limerick will only use it up. The fellows in Queen's County and other counties I could name, if you give them rifles, they will store them carefully away in straw and cosmolene.' By God, he is a rare one, Miss Keating."

"I have heard the words used here," Elizabeth said, and she reached for her bag, which she had rested beside the chair.

"I misspoke myself," Considine said, "I am sorry. I am out of sorts today."

"We all are," Elizabeth said. "It was an ugly morning."

"An ugly morning," Considine said. "I knew one of those lads, as decent a fellow as you would want to meet. He had just turned nineteen. Sure, you must know that."

She did. He had been in command of lads younger than himself who had made an attack with pistols on a lorry in the Dardanelles, as they called it, where Camden Street narrowed. A bullet had caught his ankle, and the others had had no time to drag him away.

"They shame us all," Considine said, "lads like young Martin Brophy. They—" He paused, and in the pause Elizabeth knew how much there was for her to respect in him, despite her nagging sense of some quality held in reserve. Give or take ten years or so, and he could have been Martin Brophy's twin, rigid, unhesitating patriotism; he carried in his body bits of shrapnel from the defense of Jacob's Factory in 1916, and walked with a limp. Although not wounded so badly as Cathal Brugha, who had held to his command, bleeding, bone-shattered. They were like figures in Plutarch, Considine and Brugha.

"It is not the kind of battle he would have chosen," Considine said suddenly, "fellows hiding in doorways and jumping out with pistols, blazing away and hoping for the best. He would have chosen open warfare, on the field of battle. And death if it came from the guns of the enemy, and not a shameful rope, the knot of the common hangman."

"The rope is not shameful," Elizabeth said with sudden fierceness, "not for our young fellows, that is. It is shameful for those who make use of it, who have not the chivalry to see in lads like Barry and Brophy soldiers fighting for their country. Our men have given honor to the rope and the white cap."

"It would be grand, though, would it not?" Considine said, "to see our fellows take the field again?" The words sounded boyish almost, but Considine looked anything but a boy, the lines beside his nose deep-drawn, traceries of lines beginning to form themselves about the eyes. He had been on the run for more than a year, but by profession was a civil engineer.

"We are fighting as best we can," Elizabeth said, uncomfortable to be discussing such a matter, however casually, with the deputy minister of defense. With a greater discomfort, she thought of Paddy Tansey and Jamesey Loftus, who thought themselves lucky to have enough ammunition to attack a pair of soldiers on motorcycles.

"As best we can," Considine said, but his words were a hollow echo, as though his thoughts had suddenly moved somewhere else. It is a terrible responsibility, Elizabeth thought, that Considine and Collins and the others must shoulder, send men like Martin Brophy out into the streets. "And we will fight," he said into his own silence, but turned toward her now, and his voice not hollow, "until we have won the Republic."

"We will of course," she said, in faint puzzlement at his intensity. "Who would say otherwise?"

"Yes, to be sure," Considine said, as though he had somehow been indicted. And she remembered, for the second time that day, her conversation with Christopher Blake. "That is a political matter," Christopher Blake had said, speaking of the Republic itself. "That is a political matter."

"Nothing less than a Republic is worth thruppence," she said. "Much less the blood of Kevin Barry and Tom Trainor and Martin Brophy. It was for the Republic that they died."

Considine nodded, and when he looked at her again, Elizabeth had the feeling that he was seeing her for the first time, seeing the whole of her, seeing who she was.

"Yes," he said, and, almost absently, he laid both hands upon his bad leg, with its dose of shrapnel, and shifted its weight. "For the Republic. And there are other lads fighting for it today and will be tonight on lonely hillsides, lads like Paddy Tansey." This time, when he picked up the packet of Senior Service, he held it toward her, but she shook her head.

"Mind you," he said, "we are wearing them down, we are wearing down the Crown and its Auxies and its Tans and its Lloyd Georges and Churchills beyond in London. We are holding firm and fast and we are wearing them down. The people know that, there is no need to tell them that, but reminders never hurt. You are doing great work with the *Bulletin*, and you will be needed in the days to come. I have heard the Chief himself speak in praise of it."

Once, a few months after his return from America at Christmas, she had spoken with De Valera in the house which had been found for him in Strand Road. They had had almost an hour together, with Elizabeth taking notes steadily, and De Valera talking quietly, with assurance, the accents of Limerick falling strongly upon his sentences. Midway through, his secretary brought them tea and small sandwiches. He had spent the hour describing his mission to America, threading his way carefully through a complicated story. A tall, dark man, dark-suited, with a slow, quiet courtesy, and unexpected flashes of dry wit beneath his gravity of manner. When they had finished, she closed her notebook, and De Valera rose up and walked with her to the hall door. "You will send round to me what you write before you publish it, will you not, Miss Keating? You are a very accurate young woman I am certain, but it is best to make doubly certain." But what she had written came back to her unchanged, save for some improvements which he had made upon her punctuation, and with a little note of thanks.

And now Considine, with a courtesy of his own, stepped with Elizabeth to the door of his office and opened it for her. The limp was a slight one, but one noticed it. Impulsively, as he reached for the knob, she placed her free hand on his forearm. "You men," she said, "the men of 1916. The Republic is safe in your hands. The people know that."

"Ach," he said, and smiled in pleased embarrassment.

Elizabeth left Considine's office and walked out into Dublin's summer sunlight as it glistened on the river, on domes, on streets crowded with shoppers, on two armored cars, one behind the other, moving along the quays on the far side of the Liffey, on the remaining wall of a building shattered by artillery in 1916, on two shopgirls or office girls hurrying along together in bright shirtwaists, quick legs flashing beneath skirts, one green, one black. And beyond, less than a mile away, the prison where that morning young fellows had died for the Republic, blinded by white hoods.

"We have declared for a Republic," Cathal Brugha had said, "and we will have no other law."

It was a week, though, before she had a chance to put in a word for Paddy Tansey with Collins, and it was by chance. An hour or two before curfew, she had gone to Vaughan's Hotel to have a chat by arrangement with one of the solicitors who was guiding the Republican courts, and almost collided with Collins, as he was striding down the corridor with Christopher Blake and, a step or two behind them, Harris, one of the gunmen in Collins's Squad. Collins was in one of his black moods and Elizabeth should have seen that, because she had heard of them, the heavy face set into a scowl, heavy brows pulled down over eyes which seemed to have sunk, dark hair falling forward. His unbuttoned jacket was pushed back and his hands shoved into trousers pockets.

When she spoke to him, he pulled his head toward her, and said, eyes focusing upon her, "Ach, Eliz'beth. Good evening, Eliz'beth," without breaking stride, so that she called after him, "Mr. Collins," and when that did not stop him, she said, in a loud voice, "Mr. Collins." And then he stopped and turned. "Just one word," she said. "Jesus, girl," he said, "if you were to shout out my name after me that way in Grafton Street, you could alter the affairs of state." But the face remained unsmiling, the sullen, hostile face of a Munster farmer. She had seen Collins a dozen times at least, and had talked with him here in Vaughan's and in Harcourt Street, but she had not seen this face before, the fellow on platforms, a bank clerk once in London, clever with files and balance sheets, a mask fallen away.

"A word Paddy Tansey sent to you," she said with determination. As he looked at her, his eyes flickered, and he nodded to the fellow from the Squad, tapped Blake on the upper arm, and took Elizabeth into a small, dust-filled room halfway down the corridor.

"Paddy Tansey has sent a report up here to HQ," she said. "He is desperate for supplies and has asked for them. But he sent word to me through my chum Sarah that I should say a word to you." He rested heavy shoulders against the pale green wall, and he might have been any fellow after Sunday Mass in Clonakilty, waiting with his chums for the pub to open up, his mind on a pint. "I will take a look at his report, Elizabeth, there is not much I can do this time round. I took care of him four months ago and damned near had my head chewed off me. Is that it, Elizabeth?"

"Yes," she said, "I was given that message and I carried it."

"Fair all round," he said, and walked to the door and opened it; he had almost walked through it when he remembered her and stepped aside. " 'Tis your own fault," he said as she slipped past him, "taking country lads like Dan Breen and Paddy Tansey and making them into Wild West heroes like Buffalo Bill." She turned toward him with such quick annoyance that their heads almost met, and she saw that the sullenness was gone. He was grinning at her.

"Jesus," he said, "now don't you take my head off." They were very close, and for that moment she saw him as one of those country lads at a dance, the room crowded, and a lad like this one, the pint half-drunk in one hand, and the other slyly, briefly, groping thigh or haunch. For that moment, but then he said again, "Don't take my head off, Liz. And make certain that you are home before curfew." When she was a bit down the hallway, he called out to her, "Mind now, take care. There is a good girl." But when she turned round, she saw that his mind was on something else, and the sullen look was settling itself back into place. Beyond him, just at the corridor's turn, the fellow from the Squad lounged, wearing his unbuttoned mackintosh despite the heat, a hand plunged deep into a heavy pocket.

It was not until long weeks afterwards, and from Frank Lacy, that she learned that what was being argued out that day and night—at Headquarters and in Vaughan's Hotel, in the back parlor of a house in Mountjoy Square, in a house in Ringsend—was the decision to launch an attack in strength against the Custom House. She was talking with Lacy in that strange, fatal period of the Truce, between War and Civil War. In London, the Irish and the English delegations were meeting in Downing Street, facing each other across the table of long, polished walnut at Number Ten Downing Street, and in Dublin there was in the air a still, strange, poised expectancy. The Dáil was once again meeting openly in the Mansion House in Dawson Street, across from the Hibernian Hotel, where Elizabeth and Frank Lacy were having their tea. Some of the fellows in from the field—Paddy Tansey for one—were as nervous as cats to be out in the open, who had for so long been hunted and hunting men, looking, those fellows, like what they were, country fellows up for the day, and if, in their own areas, they were brigade commanders and battalion commanders, men who had led flying columns into action, now they were fellows ill at ease in the city. But others of them—Tom Barry, for one, the most famous of the commanders, save perhaps for

Sean MacKeon and perhaps Frank Lacy himself—were quiet and watchful, with a sureness about them as they walked city streets, in Volunteer uniform some of them, or in bits and pieces of uniform, leggings, a green tunic, a slouch hat. There was good reason to think that the London talks would break down, and the two sides, British and Irish, were poised to resume the fighting.

Frank Lacy was quiet and polite, watching Elizbeth with the care of someone whose life had depended upon attention to detail, watched her as her hands moved above teatime china and silver. He was dressed in a well-cut suit of light gray tweed which, as he had told her, he had picked up the week before in a visit home to his parents in Kilkenny. His eyes moved swiftly, with deceptive casualness, across everyone who came into the large, cheerful room. Many of them were members of the Dáil. "Who is that one?" he would ask her, and Elizabeth would say, "Cornelius Cahill, he is a TD from Kerry," and Lacy would nod. "And that one?" "That one is not a TD at all," she would say, "he is a journalist. Like myself." There were TD's whom Lacy knew, of course, but they were either themselves in the army, or had close links with it. Peader Burke and Charlie Coffey came in, had a fast cup of tea and left, heavyset men, the one of them a battalion commander in East Munster and the other his adjutant. They held teacups of thin china in huge, thick-fingered hands and wolfed down small, pale sandwiches. They grinned over at Lacy, and Burke held a teacup at eye level in salutation. Lacy smiled at them with affection. "They are a right pair of bastards, the two of them." With the politeness of country men, they did not look at Elizabeth at all.

It was after they had left that Elizabeth learned, from Frank Lacy, what else had happened on the day that the Volunteers had been hanged in Mountjoy.

"Peader Burke's column," Lacy said, "was holding a pair of RIC inspectors, a man named Jameson and a man named O'Shannon. They had picked them up a week or two before, and were holding them in a hut a few miles north of Ballycotton. What the hell were they to do with them was the question. It would not have been a problem for MacKeon, MacKeon is all for standing his prisoners on their feet and dusting them and sending them on their way. And it would have been no problem for Tom Barry. Barry does not take prisoners. They only get in the way and cause trouble and are extra mouths to feed. Barry has a stern, Spartan view of such matters. But there you are, Jameson and O'Shannon, Jameson a Black and Tan, but O'Shannon RIC of the old school, devout Catholic, large family and the rest of it, well liked in the locality in the old days. And Cork Intelligence had heard that he was disgusted with the Tans, and was thinking of sending in his papers, or even throwing in his lot with us. But he had let matters slide a bit too long."

Elizabeth listened with a chill foreboding. A waitress whom she had known for years, Ellen something, Ellen Quigley, a matronly woman with a soft, agreeable face, leaned forward between them and replaced the teapot. At some moments, at this moment for example, it seemed to Elizabeth incredible that she should be hearing a story such as the one that Lacy was telling her, in the Hibernian, where often she had tea with her mother, and had since schooldays, and in all those years had known Ellen Quigley the waitress and the heavily patterned Hibernian wallpaper of white and green. But incredible too that she had knelt in the roadway and prayed for the Volunteers as they died, and then, two hours later, had walked through the crowded sunlight of Grafton Street.

"It occurred to Headquarters," Lacy said, "that an exchange of prisoners could be proposed, our lads who were waiting for the hangman in Mountjoy for the lads who were being held by Peader Burke's column outside Ballycotton. We sent word to Dublin Castle, and Cathal Brugha sent me down to East Cork to put Burke on the ready. We had tried exchanges before and they had never worked, but we thought we would try again. And back the word came from the Castle, there was no way in which sentence of death would not be carried out, but if O'Shannon and Jameson were turned loose, four of our fellows in one of the internment camps would be allowed to escape. Accidentally, of course. I learned about that afterwards, after I was back in Dublin."

"Afterwards?" Elizabeth said, in a small, questioning voice.

"By nightfall," Lacy said, "we knew that the lads had been hanged. The whole country knew. And Peader Burke carried out his orders."

Where? Elizabeth thought. Frank Lacy had said a few miles outside Ballycotton, and Elizabeth, although she knew that area only from maps, imagined not a farmhouse but a cottage, high upon a hill, tall grasses, looking southwards toward water, and the two men, toward nightfall or else early the next morning with the grasses wet against ankles, being taken to a field by the two men whom she had seen holding teacups in thick fingers and by Frank Lacy, who sat beside her in his suit of well-cut tweeds. She heard rifle shots and the screams of wheeling, frightened seagulls.

Lacy sat quietly, his two hands resting upon the table top, across one hand, close to the knuckles, a wound not recent, a trench cut across the hand, the skin reddened, a dry, rusty red. It seemed to Elizabeth that he was studying her.

Everyone knew that the IRA had been taking action in reprisal, and increasingly so in the final months before the Truce—informers shot, hostages shot, the houses of loyalists burned down. She had written of this in the *Republican Bulletin*, but discreetly and in general language, without imagined screaming seagulls, rifle shots, bodies stretched along wet grasses. Deaths for Elizabeth were Volunteers shot down in running gunfights, martyrs on hunger strike, young fellows set swinging by a hangman from England. Deaths endured, not inflicted.

If the talks broke down, or if proper terms were not placed upon offer in London, the war would go on. Everyone knew that. And it would be a different kind of war, the attack upon the Custom House had been a sample of what kind of war it would be, not ambushes now but open warfare, pitched battles. More than a hundred men of the Dublin Brigade had fought the action by which the Custom House was destroyed.

"I was here that day," Lacy said, "I was here on the twenty-fourth, when the final word was given that the Custom House would be attacked next day, it was all put on an exact schedule, the Dublin Brigade to assemble in places near the Custom House, and then to attack at one in the afternoon. One precisely. But at one the next day, I was on my way back to Munster. I remember looking at my watch, and thinking, 'God help them.' "

" 'God help them'?" Elizabeth said.

She had not known anything about plans for the attack, of course, until, like hundreds of others, she had heard the gunfire and had run out from the office that she was using that week, and almost collided with two fellows coming out of the turf accountant's. "Jesus," one of them said to her, a gangly young fellow with a pale blond mustache, "stay out of that, girl. What the hell is it? It sounds like Easter Week all over again." It was at one exactly that Tom Ennis led his second Battalion into the enormous, lovely building, and set them to work destroying it with paraffin and torches. And at about ten minutes after the hour, six Lancias moved across O'Connell Bridge and into action. A party of Tans stationed along the quays came following after the armored cars. The active service unit and Collins's own Squad had been given the task of helping to keep the army at bay, and Elizabeth was later to talk with one of them, Brendan Lucy, who had taken six men into position on the railway bridge. When the Lancias commenced machine-gun fire, Lucy's men responded with grenades and with rifle fire. It was these exchanges which had drawn Elizabeth into the street, but by the time she had reached the river, the Volunteers on the bridge had expended their ammunition and were in retreat, with two of the Lancias keeping up a steady fire upon them, while the others covered the Auxiliaries moving into position. When she looked down along the quays toward the Custom House, she could see windows red with the flames behind them. She was standing with spectators, drawn as they might have been to a pantomime, but with the smell of fear in the air. "God almighty," a woman standing beside her said to no one in particular, and, as the woman spoke, one of the machine guns commenced firing again, and Elizabeth could see the tall windows shattering. Above the gunfire, above the shouts, she could hear klaxons. She was close enough now to see that the machine-gun fire from three armored cars was being returned by fire from inside the Custom House and from Liberty Hall. This is a battle, she thought, an open battle in the streets of Dublin, and it seemed a fact so strange to her that she repeated it aloud. " 'Tis a bloody war," the man standing beside her said, a man shorter than herself, with a soft hat; he had a cigarette which had gone out in the corner of his mouth.

It was a full two hours before the Auxiliaries and the soldiers were able to secure the area, and by this time more than a dozen Volunteers and a half-dozen Auxiliaries had been shot down. When the Volunteers inside the Custom House had exhausted their ammunition, they surrendered, leaving the blazing building with their hands above their heads. Some of them came from the building, so she was to learn later, with their clothes soaked with paraffin they had been using to set the fire. The fire burned for days, it was still burning when she wrote her story for the *Republican Bulletin,* and by that time she had been able to talk with several of the Volunteers who had contrived to escape.

"You wrote a wonderful story," Lacy said to her in the Hibernian. "I remember your account of the Volunteers being marched along the road, and beside the road, the body of a dead volunteer, a young one by the look of him. Could you see that?"

"I saw well in the distance from where I was able to reach the fellows with their hands in the air, and beside them the Tommies with bayonets and the armored car, but I could not see the dead Volunteer. Francey Coughlin told me about him. He looked like a boy of sixteen, he said." Francey could not have been much older himself, one of the quick lads from the north city who were being sent out in squads these days to hurl grenades at the mesh-protected lorries.

Lacy nodded. "It was quite a battle," he said. "More than a hundred prisoners taken."

"I was writing it the next afternoon," she said, "when the copper dome melted. There was a great crowd watching it, in perfect safety, and they gave a great cheer. It must have been quite a spectacle."

Lacy was smiling at the excitement in her words, and she returned the smile. "Well," she said, "it was. Quite a spectacle. And the building was still burning, the fire could not be put out, even a day after that it was burning. It was a thorough job that was done."

With the great building went the records of nine government departments, the files of the taxing departments, all the records of the local government boards. With the destruction of the Custom House, what remained of England's bureaucratic control of Ireland had been wiped out.

"It was a great victory," Elizabeth said, and tried not to think of the boy that Francey Coughlin had seen, but she could not drive from her mind what his words had created for her, a boy lying facedown, his dark-jacketed back ripped across by machine-gun bullets, blood-sodden.

But that, so she was to think about it a year later, that was why the summer of the Truce seemed to everyone so filled with yellow-honeyed sunlight.

"And what now?" she asked Frank Lacy a bit later, as they lingered over teacups, reluctant to leave.

"I am going back to Munster this evening," he said, "back to my command."

That was what the commandants had been doing, she knew, ever since the Truce, coming up to Dublin for orders, for discussion, even for a bit of idle socializing, seeing how the winds were blowing, and then moving back to their commands, waiting and watching to see what might happen in London, at the great burnished table in Downing Street.

"After all of it, I mean," she said. "If our delegates come back from London with the treaty we want, if it is all well and truly over, what will you do then with yourself, Frank, have you thought of that?"

He had been shoving papers back into the jacket of his suit, but he stopped now, suddenly, and looked over at her. How old is he now, she thought to herself, twenty-eight, twenty-nine, a bit older than many of them, but young, a young man. He looked at her as though he did not quite see her, and the silence was awkward.

At last he said, "We had best attend to what we have in front of us. We are an army in the field, and we cannot let our men slack off."

"It would be a different kind of war," she said, thinking of the battle of the Custom House.

"It would like hell," he said. "Another victory like that and we are done for. Eight men of the Dublin Brigade killed, and a hundred of them put into prison. A hundred men of the brigade! Mick Collins would not give the word to put his own Squad into the Custom House, they were with the defending force along the bridge. And he had the right of it. The poor bastards inside fought until their ammunition gave out, and then they surrendered. That is no way to fight battles."

Elizabeth had been holding her purse, ready to rise from their table, but now she sat quiet and confused.

"We are not that kind of army," Lacy said. "We have had two years to learn how to fight and where to fight and where not to fight."

Now, in imagination, Elizabeth was back on Eden Quay, with gunfire and frightened crowds, back with explosions, the sounds of klaxons, the awful chattering machine guns, the spreading red glare behind the windows of the Custom House.

"It was a battle," she said stubbornly. "As Easter Week was a battle, and where would we be now without Easter Week and the men who gave their lives for us there?"

"Easter Week taught us a lesson," Lacy said, "should have taught us a lesson would be a better way to put it. At Easter Week, the lads were bottled up in Sackville Street, until the British Army had its chance to move in upon them, or else they were pinned down at Jacob's or at Boland's Mill or the South Union or the College of Surgeons. They fought with their backs to the wall, and no lines of retreat."

"Where would we be now if they had not put their backs to the wall?" And as she spoke, she remembered that Frank Lacy had himself been one of them, not in Dublin but far to the west, he and Liam Mellowes had raised up Galway and in the heel of the hunt, Lacy had been on the run for weeks as Mellowes had been.

And as though he had heard not her words but her thoughts, Lacy said, "I had a chance to think it all out, in a dreary shed in the Slieve Aughtie's, between Scarriff and Portumna. There are fellows in the cabinet and in Headquarters if it comes to that who have never heard an angry shot, who have not a notion of what it takes to move across a stretch of bad country nor to keep open your lines, nor bandage up a lad's foot that has been laid open. Open warfare!"

And the wonder of it was that Lacy was keeping his voice if not his temper entirely in check, so that it did not move beyond the two of them, beyond their table. And on his last words, promptly, two members of the Dáil came in, and looked round as though for company before taking one of the empty tables.

She put her hand on his forearm, and said, "My God, Frank, there is no need for you to take my head off," and the words had an echo in her ears that she could not place until, an hour or two later, after she and Lacy had parted, she recalled Collins, his hands shoved deep into his pockets, courtesy eating at the edges of his scowl. "Jesus," he said, and she remembered it now, the swift mocking singsong of West Cork, "now don't you take my head off." And remembered Considine at HQ, Cathal Brugha's deputy, "Would it not be grand to see our fellows in the field again, open warfare, as we fought in 1916."

Later, much later, Elizabeth was able to make a pattern of the echoing words: open warfare and a gunman's unbandaged foot, Considine leaning forward in his chair, and Collins, angry, rocking backwards and forwards on his heels, and Lacy angry across teacups. By then, much later, six months later, with the country balancing upon the brink of its Civil War, and charges and countercharges hurled across the floor of the Dáil, lines of disagreement which had been concealed came uncovered. But that was later, and now, in the tearoom of the Hibernian, Lacy's anger ebbed away at his words, and he placed his own hand upon hers. "A fine conversation over teacups," he said, and smiled, and the smile almost reached his eyes.

In May, a week after the burning of the Custom House, Elizabeth walked along Eden Quay to the smoke-streaked shell. The great copper dome was gone, and the four statues which once had crowned the south portico, allegorical embodiments of who knew what abstractions, Industry, no doubt, and Perseverance and Prosperity and something else. All gone, and gone with them much decoration in elaborate stone. But at the two end pavilions, there still stood, smoke-darkened but secure, the arms of the kingdom of Ireland, Britannia's arms, surmounted by the crown, and, on either side of the regal arms, rampant or whatever the term of allegory or heraldry was, regal or rampant or regnant, the lion and the unicorn, the unicorn with its long, fierce triumphant horn, like a jousting lance or something less delicate. Someday, Elizabeth thought, someday when peace has come, we will take crowbars to those things and topple them into the river below them.

XIII

CHRISTOPHER BLAKE/JANICE NUGENT

When Christopher Blake returned to Ireland that week, on the Thursday, the Custom House was still burning, and it was on that day that its great metal dome, the copper of the eighteenth century, melted, but south of the river, at Kingstown, where the mailboat put in, the sky was the clear, pale gray and white of a Leinster morning, in the distance mountains of blue, streaked by brown boglands. Blake stood at the rail beside two Auxiliaries, fierce-mustached the two of them, their glengarries at a jaunty angle. Pale clouds stretched across a windless sky.

Peter Devlin had been waiting for him, and they drove to the house in Blackrock, on Merrion Avenue, where De Valera had set up headquarters for himself.

"There is something in the wind," Devlin said, "and if you can smell it here in Dublin, you must have been able to smell it in London."

"What you smell here is the Custom House," Blake said. "That is getting great play in the London newspapers. Sinn Féin barbarism and all that. Wanton destruction of national treasure."

"Much concern they have ever shown before for the national treasures of Ireland, save to carry off those that were portable," Devlin said.

Devlin and Blake had been friends from the days together in Dartmoor Prison, after Easter Week.

"On the night after the action," Devlin said, "the Liffey was red from the flames bathing down upon it, and the next night as well. It was worth it, from all I can tell, with the destruction of the records, and it was great publicity, not in England alone, but in the States and in Europe. If you were still editing the *Republican Bulletin*, you could make great play with it."

"Trust Elizabeth Keating," Blake said, "she has a nice touch." The bay was sparkling, and on its far shore, the hill of Howth stretched out like a comfortable old bear, brown and heavy-muscled.

"But the English papers have the right of it, it was a fine old building, the finest in Dublin I have heard it said." Devlin was a Dublin man, with fierce local pride. So was Blake, if it came to that, but Devlin was North Dublin, and the distinction was a crucial one.

"You will hear the battle argued about one way or the other," Devlin said. "There are those who argue that we have no business making that kind of pitched battle, and that burning up a batch of records was not worth the men killed and the men of the Dublin Brigade taken prisoner. Eighty men is what we are giving out, but the loyalist papers have the right of it, it was a hundred or more. Mick was against it, I can tell you. The final meeting to decide was held at The O'Rahillys' house in Herbert Park, and Mick was cursing a blue streak. You know how he gets, with the scowl, and the fists shoved in the trousers and that heavy bull head of his flung back." Devlin leaned over as though to impart a confidence. "The entire HQ was there at Madam O'Rahilly's," he said, "and Cathal Brugha of course, with Dev in the chair. Dev was in favor of the action, but between you and me, Chris, Dev is a great man, but he is no military genius. That is between ourselves. One week he is presiding over a cabinet meeting, and arguing that we should slack off on the military campaign, and a month later, he is arguing, do you know what he is arguing, that we should attack the Black and Tans at Beggars Bush barracks with five hundred men. Mother of God, what a mess that would have been!"

There was almost no traffic on the early-morning road. The breeze was pleasant against Blake's face. He lit two cigarettes and handed one over to Devlin.

"Mind you, that is between ourselves," Devlin said.

But matters of that sort never stayed in confidence. Back in January, a few weeks after De Valera had returned from America, Collins and Mulcahy had summoned Ernie O'Malley and Frank Lacy, and Lacy gave Blake a comprehensive description. This was in the earlier of De Valera's headquarters, on the Strand Road, with tall windows looking beyond a garden to the bay. Across a broad library table, Mulcahy, the chief of staff, had spread out a map of Munster, and guided by questions the report which they were giving to Dev. "Things have changed a bit since I was last in the field, President," O'Malley said. "I have been otherwise occupied." De Valera looked up from the map, studied O'Malley for a moment, and then, slowly, a smile broke across the long, solemn face. "So you have, Mr. O'Malley, so you have. I am delighted that you are here with us today." In December, O'Malley had been captured by the Auxiliaries in Inistiogue and brought up to Dublin Castle and then to Kilmainham. A month later, with help from Collins, he had made a spectacular escape, together with Frank Teeling, one of the gunmen from Bloody Sunday. First Lacy, then O'Malley, would point to roads in Clare or in Tipperary, lines across mountains, toward safe houses, toward barracks, would name a commandant. "I see," De Valera would say. "Yes, yes, I see. It all seems very admirably organized, very admirable. The sinews of a national resistance. You are all to be commended. Very fine work indeed." But when Lacy spoke, or O'Malley spoke, they would see lonely moorland, men straggling to a muster in early-morning light, the dawn light watery, nibbling at edges of chilly darkness, a few of them on bicycle, but more on foot, carrying shotguns, a few rifles. "It is clear that you have established a perimeter," De Valera said approvingly, schoolmaster's voice, soft, polite Limerick tones, but his long finger, by ill chance, was resting upon the town of Kilpeder, the most secure of the Auxiliary strongholds east of Macroom. Lacy kept his eyes fixed upon the map, but O'Malley looked up to see Collins and Mulcahy exchanging amused glances, as De Valera prepared to leave with his papers.

Later, O'Malley and Lacy met alone with Collins and Mulcahy. The army was being divided into divisional areas, of which Lacy would take one and another, the second, would go to O'Malley, the Second Southern, two brigades in Limerick, two in Tipperary, one in Kilkenny.

"We will go over it in detail later," Mulcahy said. "But I want you two lads at your work down the country by early next week."

"The local commanders will not take kindly to this, some of them," Lacy said. "They are the men on the scene. It has been easy enough this far for Ernie and myself, coming down from Headquarters, and giving a bit of assistance and then moving off again. The command of a division will be a different matter."

"A golden opportunity for growing lads like yourselves," Collins said. He was in fine fettle, balancing the straight chair in which he was sitting by its two hind legs, and holding out his arms to steady himself.

"That was a most instructive hour with the president," Mulcahy said, his tone dry, opaque. "I am certain that he left us with a clear, firm sense of operations in the field."

"When will Commandant Lynch be able to move upon Fermoy in full brigade strength?" Collins said, the singsong of West Cork gently mocking the tones of Limerick.

The mockery was friendly enough, a kind of easy, high-spirited affection, but the meeting had not gone well as far as Lacy was concerned, as he told Blake a few days later. "They are big men, the two of them," he said, "we are lucky to have the two of them, Dev and Mick Collins, but big men tend to crowd each other. If it comes to that, what does Mick know about combat in the field? I would like to see how Mick would fight his way out of an ambush."

As O'Malley and Lacy were leaving, Collins crashed his chair down firmly on its four legs. "You heard the president," he said. "Take care of yourselves, lads. By God, you are a rare lot, the two of you. Do you still carry your Virgil in your knapsack, Frank? 'Tis Virgil is it not, or is it Plutarch?"

"It was Virgil, of course," Lacy told Blake. "Imagine a mind that can remember a bit of detail like that. He is a wonder, the Big Fellow is."

But later, much later, two years later, when Blake had cause to remember the account which Lacy had given him, he thought that Plutarch might have been a better object of study, for Lacy or for any of them. By then, the personalities of the leaders, Collins and De Valera, Griffith and Brugha, had taken on some of the meanings of allegory. It had begun early. When De Valera, traveling secretly from America aboard the *Celtic,* had arrived in Dublin, Collins had Tom Cullen waiting for him at Custom House dock. "Things are going great," Cullen told him on board the ferry, "the

Big Fellow is leading us, and everything is going marvelous." "Big Fellow!" De Valera said, and he slapped the guardrail. "We'll see who's the Big Fellow." Within three weeks, De Valera was suggesting to Collins that he should take De Valera's place in America. The suggestion was made formally, a long letter to which Collins made a formal response, polite and evasive, but to his cronies he was pithier. "The long hoor won't get rid of me that easily." Or so the words passed into folklore, though Blake never accepted them as factually true. But the exchange of letters was real enough: Collins had shown them to him. " 'Tis not Dev who wants to get rid of me," he said to Blake, " 'tis Brugha and his sidekick Stack. They hate my guts, the two of them."

Now, driving from Kingstown to Blackrock for a meeting with De Valera and Collins, Blake said to Peter Devlin, "Whose plan was the attack on the Custom House?"

Devlin took longer than needed to answer. "Dev approved it, an action fought out in the open, with the eyes of the world upon us, not some hole-in-the-corner ambush or a detective shot down. But it was not his plan."

"It was Brugha's plan," Blake said suddenly, flatly.

"And why would it not be?" Devlin asked, his tone deliberately light, as though the question was one which a skillful motorist could deal with. "He is the minister of defense, after all."

"He is, to be sure," Blake said, "and Dick Mulcahy is chief of staff, and the orders would be sent down from him. What did Dick think of the plan?"

"Dick Mulcahy is chief of staff, and he was carrying out an order given to him by the minister of defense after cabinet approval. Most of the cabinet, that is," Devlin amended.

Devlin remained with Blake throughout his interview with Collins and De Valera. It lasted for the better part of two hours, and halfway through, they were joined by Brugha and Charles Quinlan, the deputy minister for foreign affairs, now that Griffith was back in Mountjoy. De Valera sat awkwardly at the spindly desk with his back to windows looking out upon a spring garden. From time to time, he wanted to compare something that Blake was reporting upon with a document, and his secretary would bring it in to them, a calm, dark-haired young woman who had been with him upon the American mission. Brugha and Quinlan sat at angles to Blake, Brugha shifting his weight from time to time, as though the lead within his legs spoke to him. Collins sat facing them, in theory at least, but he was out of his chair as often as in it, jumping up and walking to the garden window to look out at heavily banked fuschia in flower.

"And there you are," Blake said at last. "You hear gossip here and there, of course, but not a crumb of it worth giving thought to, and the newspapers will one day be saying that the government should take murder by the throat, send in ten thousand more troops, should that be what is required. And the next week they will be saying that force solves nothing, that at the end of the day, we will have some kind of self-rule here, but what kind is the nub of it. But I doubt if the gossip is worth anything, and you have yourselves been reading the newspapers."

"This fellow that you have been meeting with, this Robert Soames," De Valera said, "would you call him a reliable sort of person?"

Blake shrugged. "He is doing what he has been told to do, as I have been doing. It suits their cabinet to have a fellow like Bobby Soames to send a bit of gossip over here, and I carry it over because it suits our cabinet to listen to it."

"But how much does your chum Soames know and how much of the things he tells you is the truth?"

"Very little," Blake said, "very little on both scores. He is an errand boy, like myself."

"Is he an honest man, do you think?" Brugha asked.

"He is honest enough to his masters, I daresay," Blake said. "I doubt if he is often honest with me. Why should he be?"

A morning quiet fell upon the room. Blake knew that he and Soames, this third assistant secretary, temporary, to the English cabinet, made up one thread only. For months now, peace feelers of one sort or another had been stretching themselves out from Dublin to London and from London to Dublin. And of them all, the important one by far was not from London at all, but from Dublin Castle, from an assistant under-secretary named Cope. Blake's meetings with Soames did little more than test out gossip.

"What sort of fellow is he?" Collins said. "A likable sort of fellow, is he?"

"Likable enough," Blake said. "We went together to the theater one night, and had dinner first off at a fish restaurant, a good one. It is not at all hardship duty that you have put me to."

"Jesus, they have great fish restaurants there, as good as the Red Bank," Collins said. "What was the play you saw?"

"What matter is it, what the play was?" Brugha said. "God almighty."

"It may not matter at all," Collins said.

"*Shall We Join the Ladies?* it is called," Blake said to Collins.

"Ach," Collins said in mock disgust. "James Barrie. Well, at least you were in no danger to your immortal soul." He smiled over at Brugha, the smile challenging and cold. "A terrible worry," he said, "sending simple Irish lads over to the great metropolis, with their painted women. And worse. But James Barrie is safe enough. Peter Pan in tights is the depth of it."

But Brugha, a man of legendary propriety, and the son of an English father, did not rise to the bait.

"If you have been reading the London papers," Blake said, "you will know that there is a great deal of sympathy developing for us over there, and not among Liberals only. Churchmen, editors, a few fellows in the House on both sides."

"A bit more than that will be needed," Brugha said.

"Perhaps," Blake said. "And even that is likely to fade away if you send your squads of dynamiters and arsonists over to set fire to their cities. It may not be my position to point that out, but you asked me about the state of the country."

"The war must be carried to the enemy," Brugha said. "Pay them back blow for blow. If an army cannot take the offensive, if it cannot carry fire in the camp of the enemy, it is not an army at all." His voice had the hard, flat accents of Dublin.

"They burned Cork City," Collins said. "Never forget that. They set the center of Cork City afire, on both sides of the river. The bastards. They are still swaggering around, the bastards who did it, with burned corks stuck into their glengarries. They earned Liverpool a few explosions and a few warehouses down on the waterfront, from which the supplies of war are shipped over here."

"War is dreadful," De Valera said, "truly dreadful, and those who wage it must be brought to a knowledge of that."

"The army of our people," Brugha said, "is fighting to sustain in arms the Irish Republic. It will take what measures are deemed necessary."

"Deemed necessary by itself," Collins asked, "or by whom?"

"By the cabinet, of course," Brugha said, "acting through its appropriate ministry, the Ministry of Defense."

"In short, Cathal," Collins said, "by yourself."

"I cannot believe," De Valera said, "that Mr. Blake is interested in these delicate matters. You are doing an excellent task for us, Mr. Blake, most commendable. And I agree with Michael here, you are entitled surely to the occasional fish meal, and a harmless play by Mr. Barrie. I would be most grateful to you if you would write up as fully as you can what you remember of your conversations with Mr. Soames."

"Yes," Blake said, "I have done that. And I stand ready to go back to London, if that seems useful to you."

"I would remind you, Mr. President," Brugha said, "that Christopher Blake here is not acting under orders, not anyone's."

"He went over because I asked him to," Collins said. "My God, Cathal, I am director of intelligence, after all, and talking to a deputy sub-assistant temporary secretary or whatever the hell Soames is comes under the heading of intelligence. Christopher holds the rank of a captain in the Volunteers, as surely you must know."

"And he reports to you."

"At the moment," Collins said, "he is reporting to the president."

"Yes," Brugha said. "At the moment."

"I dislike being talked about in my presence," Blake said. "Either talk to me, or else dismiss me, and then you can talk about me to your hearts' content."

Brugha began to speak, but De Valera held up a long, bony-knuckled hand. "You are quite right, Mr. Blake," he said. "Quite right."

An hour later, the three of them walked along Sandymount strand, Collins, Devlin and Blake.

"Jesus, he sets me the wrong way," Collins said. He picked up a stone, and sent it skipping along the gray waters of the bay. "Talk about oil and water."

"Have you thought about letting up on him a bit, Mick?" Devlin said. "You are forever trying to get a rise out of him, and he is not that sort of fellow. I have a lot of time for Cathal, I can say that to you."

"So do I," Collins said, with a terrier's bark of laughter. "That is the odd part of it. He is as straight as they come, and he was a bloody hero in 1916. No doubt about it, the rest of us did our bit, but Cathal was a bloody hero. Oil and water."

"It is a bit more than oil and water, Mick," Devlin said, "and you know it. You have been cutting into Cathal's ministry, sending out orders over his head, making certain that the fellows in the field take their orders from yourself or from Dick. There are fellows out there in the field who are loyal not to the Dáil nor to Cathal or even to Dev. They are loyal to Mick Collins."

"You are damned right they are," Collins said. He stopped short, and swung to face Devlin. It was one of his civil servant days, black serge suit, dark tie primly knotted, soft gray hat, soft-brimmed. But the hat was shoved to the back of his head, and the heavy face was scowling. "If a fellow out in the field, Paddy Tansey say or Tom Barry, with thirty or forty weapons of all breeds, if such a fellow has need to take out his men with more than three or four cartridges against lorries and tenders with their Lewis guns, do you know what Cathal and Austin and those chaps would have Paddy do? Of course you do. Write out a form in triplicate and send it to Brigade for transmission to HQ, and thence to the responsible ministry, as Cathal is forever calling it."

"But you can always find a few rounds, can you not, Mick?" Devlin said. "Especially if they are for one of your favorites."

"I pay for results," Collins said. "Is it a battle in the field that Dev wants? Let him think about Crossbarry. Tom Barry and a hundred men fighting their way through five times that many British troops. They fought because they had the arms to fight and because Barry knows how to use them. The responsible ministry would have sent them to lousers in Sligo and Roscommon who have yet to set fire to an abandoned barracks."

But Devlin said nothing in answer to this; neither did Blake.

"How about it, Chris?" Collins asked him. "What are our English cousins up to above there in London?"

Blake shrugged. "It is as I told the president. There is something in the wind. Soames is being very delicate and cagey about it. I have a suspicion that Dev and yourself know more about it than I do."

"They are a right lot of bastards there in the Castle," Collins said. "The only one I have any time for is Andy Cope, and he is as twisted as a ram's horn. At least he does not pretend to have principles."

"Soames did drop me a small hint about Cope," Blake said. "But I do not know why he did. He hinted to me that Lloyd George sent Cope over as his own man in the field, with instructions to sound out Sinn Féin."

"I have heard that," Collins said. "If that is the plan, he has not made his move yet."

In Blackhall's, Robert Soames delicately filleted a Dover sole, extracting white, fragile bones. He kept his eyes on his task. "I must say, Blake, that there are men in Sinn Féin that anyone of proper feeling must admire, but some of that crowd are a right lot of bastards. Blowing up warehouses in Liverpool of all places, and letting unarmed watchmen take their chances. The Yard, you know, has passed along rumors that they will try their hand at assassination next. Right here in London. Of course I know that you yourself have nothing to do with that sort of thing. Wouldn't be breaking bread with you if I thought otherwise. Would I now?"

Blake smiled and lifted up his glass. The Sauternes was cool; his tongue touched the vineyards of France.

"Most of what I hear comes at third or fourth hand," Soames said. "At best. There are those in the cabinet, those in Commons, who know that some sort of self-government for Ireland is on the way, but what sort will it be? But there are those who say that we must take murder by the throat, send over enough troops and armament to smash Sinn Féin into surrender, and that can be done. Make no mistake about that, my lad. I am betraying no confidences, you can hear this argued out on the floor of the house, read it in the morning with your tea. Smash them up, Winston says, make a proper job of it, or else toss in our hand. One or the other. And of course Henry Wilson has the ear of the diehards, eager to become another Cromwell."

The restaurant smelled pleasantly of flowers, perfume.

"I expect Sinn Féin has the same sort of division, same divergences, the men of reason and the crazy chaps, the fire and sword and burn down Liverpool chaps."

"I wouldn't know," Blake said.

"I have a tip for you, a small hint, no more," Soames said, "and someday you may have some small hint for me. Fair exchange. Lloyd George has his man in the Castle. Andy Cope. Andy reports back directly to the PM. If Sinn Féin is ever on the lookout for a line of that sort, Cope is your man. Unusual chap, not the sort of stuffed shirt that you behold in me. Andy Cope began his days as a detective in Customs, a man on the make, resourceful sort of chap, no great respecter of red tape."

"A man after Lloyd George's heart, in short," Blake said.

"And Mick Collins's, I should imagine. Started out over here as a bank clerk, as I understand it."

"Actually, a clerk in the post office," Blake said. "After a few years, he moved over to a bank, and then to a firm of stockbrokers. The Guaranty Trust. I expect the Yard has all of that in a file by now."

"The Yard!" Soames, amused, echoed. "The Yard and at least two of our intelligence services. Bank clerks, schoolmasters, tailors, Welsh solicitors. We are moving into strange new times. The old order changeth, Master Blake."

"Not entirely," Blake said. "There will always be room for a duke's grandson. Churchill. Winston, as you call him."

"Ah, now, Winston!" Soames said. "Winston is somewhere betwixt and between. Let me give you another little tip. Don't be fooled by that Lord Macaulay rhetoric and all that. Winston had to climb his way up, hand over hand. Winston is a toughie. As tough as they come."

"You are very generous with your tips this evening. Are you telling me that Winston is a bitter-ender, like Wilson, bring fire and sword to Ireland, smash the Paddies?"

"Not at all, quite to the contrary, indeed. He's all for martial law and backing up the Black and Tans. But at the end of the day, Winston may well be for compromise. That is a real toughie for you, Wilson would not know how to be tough, he is all swagger. I must say, Blake, that I toss out these tips in the hopes of getting a crumb or two in exchange, justify our soles on the bone to my lords and masters."

"Fair enough," Blake said. "At the end of the day, you may discover that our man Collins and your man Winston are two of a kind. Two toughies."

"No need to tell me that," Soames said, as he dabbed at sauce with a bit of bread. "Your Mick Collins fascinates them all. A veritable Pimpernel, we seek him here, we seek him there, is he in heaven or is he in Dublin?" If we must, Churchill had said in the House, we will make Ireland a hell to live in; was there an echo there in Soames's bantering? "But for all that, he's a gunman, a murderous gunman, shooting down policemen, murdering loyalists. Cannot expect us to deal with a brute like that. Fascinating brute, though."

"Collins is one of our leaders," Blake said, "one of the ablest of them, but your lords and masters will be much mistaken if they assume that he is the only one."

"Ah," Soames said, "of course, there is De Valera, the schoolmaster. And that fellow who sells ecclesiastic candles and religious medals. But surely . . ."

But Blake would not be drawn out beyond that point. If it pleased them to imagine that Sinn Féin was an army led by an implacable gunman, then let them. Blake himself had helped to create Collins's legend, a legend being burnished now by other publicists—Elizabeth Keating, Erskine Childers. And the legend was powerful because it was half-true at least.

"No matter," Soames said, "one leader or a dozen, what your chaps are doing, have done, is quite astonishing really. You are likely to be getting your damned Home Rule, which is something that Redmond and that crowd were never able to pull off."

"It is no longer a matter of Home Rule," Blake said, as Soames stole a glance at his wristwatch and then nodded to the wine waiter. "A Republic was proclaimed in 1916 and was defended in blood. That Republic was reasserted when Dáil Éireann met for the first time in 1919. It is for a Republic that men are dying now in the mountains of West Cork and in the streets of Dublin."

"Just exactly time for small coffees," Soames said, "and that good port that they keep here. Yes, but of course you know as well as I do that that simply is not on. No one would hold still for that, those tiresome Orangemen in Ulster, the poor afflicted loyalists in the south, the Tories, the Liberals, no one in short. The real question is how much are we prepared to give, how much are you chaps prepared to settle for. But not a Republic. Good heavens no."

Blake did not reply. As they waited for their coffees, he looked around the large room, its feeling of well-being, of ordered comforts, at shaded light falling upon stiff white linen, at rich-textured curtains, tall, brocaded, drawn across the garish lights and noises of the Strand.

After a time, Soames said again, "You do know that, old chap. If peace comes, it will be a negotiated peace. Not that chaps like yourself and myself will have much to say about it. Your, what is it Edgar Wallace would say, your big shots and my big shots will have to sort things out."

On Sandymount strand in Dublin, Collins and Devlin and Blake, Collins said, "Sort things out, is that the way he put it? By Jesus, I would like to see him trying to sort things out with Cathal, or with Liam Lynch below in Cork. But we have them on the run, lads. We have them on the run. Once they have begun to talk about people sitting round a table, they see the end in sight."

Sunlight sparkled upon the bay, and, far off, approaching Howth harbor a collier moved in slow, cloudless clarity.

"When all is said and done," Collins said, "the attack on the Custom House may have done some good, and warehouses burned down in Liverpool may have done even more. We mean business, and by God, they know it." He swung his fist into the palm of his opened hand. "Am I right? Am I right?"

"Back to London for you, eh Chris?" Collins said, before the three of them separated. "You are a lucky man. I love London, do you know that, lads? I should not admit that, but 'tis true—the theaters and the art galleries and the bookshops. And the grub. Twenty decent restaurants for every one of them in Dublin."

"If we have been reading the signs aright," Blake said, "you may be back there before you know it, yourself and Griffith and Dev and the others, walking through the door of Number Ten with your velvet-collared coats and your dispatch boxes."

"Ha!" Collins said. "Not me. Dev tried to get me to America, and without luck. Far less could he get me to London. When those negotiations are sorting themselves out, I will be far away from London. I'm a bit too clever for that, lads. Someday, we'll all be there, eating sole on the bone. But that is someday, a long way off from now."

* * *

In those final days before the Truce, as the country moved through bloodshed, arson, hangings, executions in jails and in open fields, moved through rumors of peace and polite words between intermediaries, as they moved toward the lovely summer of 1921, a summer gripped by exaltation and expectation, Blake was to remember Collins as he stood upon the pebbly strand, grinning and self-confident, at ease with himself and confident that there was nothing that he could not master.

Collins waited until Blake had walked a short distance away, and then called out after him, "When you are in London, Chris, be certain to give my very best wishes to Mrs. Nugent."

Blake turned toward him, caught between irritation and amusement. "Where do you keep that filed away, Mick, under what heading?"

" 'My Friends and Their Romances,' " Collins said, putting the words into loud capital letters. "A special file of its own."

But two nights before, late that night, after love, as they had sat in dressing gowns in the sitting room, and he had sat watching her measure cognac into glasses, she had said, "I do not think I would like your Mr. Collins. He seems an awful man. There is quite the Michael Collins cult sprouting up here. I have never understood bohemians. They all say that they are in favor of peace, and eating lettuce, and dressing sensibly, and then they let their heads be turned by some brigand. Not me." She always measured out very small cognacs with scrupulous care, cocking her head to one side and pursing her lips.

"You need not like him, Janice. You need only like the cause for which he is working. As I am."

"Cause," she said. "I should have thought the world had seen quite enough of causes, for a few years. Bloody Europe in shambles."

"Don't say 'bloody,' dear. It is not ladylike."

"Don't say 'ladylike.' It is an awful word." She carried the two glasses over to the sofa, and handed him his. "There," she said, and sat down beside him. "That was a bloody awful thing to say," she said. "And in any event, I'm not much of a lady, am I? Ladies don't make love to unmarried gentlemen and pour them drinks and sit around in bare feet. Do they?"

"I have been having a series of meetings," Blake said, "with a young fellow named Soames who is a junior assistant something or other at the Foreign Office. Ever hear of him?"

"No," she said. "Probably a pervert. Sally Sertaine tells me that all the young men at the Foreign Office are pederasts. How does she know? Trial and error, I expect."

"He tells me that Winston, they all call him Winston, is only barely a gentleman. Isn't that peculiar—a grandson of a duke? What a complicated country."

"Perhaps his mother sets him a bad example. Still, they say she has been a great help to him. They say she's not very ladylike."

"He says that Winston is what he calls a toughie, just as much a toughie as Michael Collins."

"I would not doubt it. They all are. They are all talking now about the hard-faced men who are taking charge of things, the new men. But the old ones were just as bad, a bit smoother perhaps."

"And what about me?"

But she did not answer him directly. She turned her glass round, and looked down into the cognac.

"I loved Charlie very much, you know. Just as now I love you. And I lost Charlie and I could not bear it if I lost you. Truly could not bear it."

"Not very likely," Blake said. "Things are winding down, you know. There is more going on than Robert Soames and myself talking. Someday before long there will be a treaty, can you imagine that? A country the size of a postage stamp, and we will be forcing an empire to a treaty table. Doesn't that cheer you up at all? Your own country, Ireland."

Suddenly she laughed. "It was Winston who did for Charlie, Winston and his awful Gallipoli. Everyone says that it was Winston who did for all those poor fellows, Charlie and all of them, thrown out upon the beaches to be shot down. My God, he did for Charlie, and if he moves fast enough he still has time to do for you."

"He may not be quite that bad," Blake said, "history may be kinder to him than you are."

"History is a lying bitch," she said, "and I am not. That is the great difference between history and me."

"One of them," Blake said, and bent down to kiss her, but for a moment she held him off, her free hand against his mouth. She had a way of laughing at the oddest times. "Churchill is always scowling or smiling. I want this, I want that, I want Gallipoli."

When Blake put her glass on the table and took her hand away from his mouth they kissed, and reaching through the low collar of her gown, he took her breast.

"Now Christopher," she said when she could, and pretended to push him away, "we were discussing matters of state, and not whatever it is that you have in mind."

But he kissed her again, and this time more deeply, and for a longer time, and felt her stiffen beneath his fingertips.

That awful young man from the university was here again today, and this time he had with him a sheaf of photographic reproductions of things that Christopher wrote during the Truce and then afterwards, in the terrible months that followed. By then, of course, he could sign his own name to what he wrote, and with two of the stories, there were photographs of him, one a quite good one really, showing his thin, serious face. You could never guess from those pages how much fun he could be. "Mr. Christopher Blake," it said beside one of them. "One of the young men who is shaping Ireland as a Free State. He is an associate of Mr. Michael Collins. Mr. Blake took part in the 1916 rebellion in Dublin, but before that worked as an editor in London, and is the author of a work of history."

"No," I said to the young man, "I do not remember them at all, and perhaps I never read them." He offered to leave them with me to read, but I said, "No, politics has always bored me," and he looked at me curiously. "Always," I said, "always bored me." He showed me a photograph he had also brought with him, a large one, eight by ten, and there are Christopher and Michael Collins striding along together, the two of them with light coats flung open, smiling toward the cameraman, and with sunlight behind them. It is a London street, because there is a *Daily Express* hoarding close by, on which the word "Irish" can be made out. A policeman and two passersby are looking, one of them smiling, at the two Irishmen. "They look exactly like themselves," I said to young Eamonn Hennessy, "is that what you want me to say?" "No, no, of course not," he said, "but I thought you might like it." He wasn't awful at all, really, quite a nice young man, it was what he was doing that was so awful, rummaging over those dead days with dried blood upon them. "Thank you," I said, "that is very kind of you." But I remember Christopher, I need no photographs. "It was taken during the Treaty negotiations," Mr. Hennessy said, "when Collins was in London as one of the plenipotentiaries, and Christopher Blake was one of the advisers on the Irish side."

"Yes," I said, "I know." Poor Mr. Hennessy. Because I have no use for politics, he thinks that I have no memory. But of course in his heart of hearts, he believes that I am very political, that all people are. "It is an excellent photograph," I said, unbending a bit, as it were.

"That is when you first met Michael Collins, is it not?" Hennessy asked, "during the Treaty negotiations."

"Yes," I said.

"And you must have come to know him well, of course, because of your friendship with Christopher Blake."

"Christopher and I were lovers," I said, and he began fussing with his notepads and lead pencils.

That was a very long session for Mr. Hennessy and myself. He came at one and stayed well into teatime, writing away in his notebooks, and from time to time not writing because he decided that I was deliberately saying something outrageous or frivolous or provoking. The provoking Mrs. Nugent, Christopher used to call me. Provocative, surely, I corrected him. A nice distinction he said, as of course it is, and I wonder if I was not being provocative with Mr. Hennessy. Old habits die hard.

"It is very difficult," Mr. Hennessy said, "trying to piece together those days," as though he were talking of the Punic Wars. But in fact "those days" were, what, twelve, fifteen years in the past only, and he was not all that young, he must have been a schoolboy at the time. I remember it as a wonderful time, those first months of the Truce, before everything began to be difficult, and I went home to Coolater for a week, and Christopher was able to visit me there, quite properly, and then afterwards, back in London, there were parties, and Mr. Hennessy, as though he had read my thoughts, said, "Our own household was divided, my father all for the Free State, and my mother a diehard. But that was later, of course, what I best remember is those first months, with the tricolor flags everywhere and the end of the curfew. That sort of thing."

I remembered going back to Coolater, and how strange Loughrea seemed, with the British soldiers back in barracks, great loops of tricolor buntings, green and gold bunting.

Mr. Hennessy had forgotten me for a moment, was looking beyond me toward the vase of bronze-colored roses, their leaves dark green against the cloisonné vase, egg-white, and upon it Chinese birds, pink, lime-green, faint yellow.

"But it does not matter anymore, does it, Mr. Hennessy? All over and done with." Which carried him back into the present, his present that is, not mine, because the present for me will always be a summer evening in Connemara, the long stretch of road toward Oughterard, behind me that slowly declining sun, thick-spreading mosses upon mist-darkened outcroppings of rock, lake water almost still, a faint wind stirring tall green rushes.

XIV

FRANK LACY

Notification of the Truce came to Lacy at Lughnavalla House, a shooting lodge between Kilpeder in Cork and Rathmore in Kerry, at the Cork edge of the Derrynasaggarts. It was owned by an Englishman named Townshend, who had not visited it in two years, and in early July Lacy had commandeered it to serve as divisional HQ. The tall front windows looked beyond empty pasturelands, a swift stream, a dense woodland, beeches and alders, past dry walls of rough stone, past two abandoned cottages, the thatch caved in, the walls long ago scrubbed clean of whitewash by rains, past these toward the fierce mountains, brown and desolate. A twisting boreen, hedged by thorn bushes, led down to the county road, and at the junction, two small farm-houses faced each other. Lacy had posted sentries in both of them. Three other riflemen, on loan to him from Pat MacCarthy's active service unit, lived with him in Lughnavalla.

Lacy worked in a small front room which he had decided to call "the library," because bookshelves stretched across one of the walls. On a long, low table he had spread out his battalion and brigade reports, and copies of the summarizing reports which he sent up to Dublin every two weeks. The reports varied in nature and appearance, one or two of them actually typed, but for the most part they were written by hand, ill-formed scrawls some of them and others neat, products of laborious lessons in penman-ship. Against one wall, facing the bookshelves, stood Lacy's own typewriter on a small table, a battered but usable wreck liberated from the house of a loyalist in Millstreet. Above the table, he had nailed an ordnance survey map of western and southern Ireland, with the borders of his division, the Fifth Southern, marked off with heavy black lines. Within the lines, he had inked in battalion areas, areas of General Strickland's enemy forces, the Irish locations in blue triangles, and the enemy in brown.

A week before the Truce, when Lacy had held a divisional meeting in Lughnavalla, Charlie MacNamara, who commanded an active service unit, said with a contempt part joking and part genuine, "By God, we began this scrap with hurling sticks, and we are ending it with fountain pens."

"You should visit O'Malley, beyond in Cahir," Pat MacCarthy said, "he had six fountain pens, two of them with black ink and the other four with various colors—green and red and the dear knows what else." "Why does he need two black fountain pens?" MacNamara asked. "One of them is the one he doesn't use. A gift from a young admirer."

Lacy, leaning against a wall with a glass of ale in his hand, was amused and friendly. They were fine field commanders, the two of them, and MacCarthy had all of his reports written up for him by his IO, Ben Cogley, the chemist from Kilpeder, on the run now, like MacCarthy himself. "Make bloody certain to write legibly," MacCarthy had told Cogley, "not that bloody gibberish that yourselves and doctors use, like a kind of code, to tell each other how much it is safe to overcharge the poor patient."

Twenty riflemen made up MacCarthy's column that summer, most of them casual laborers, but there was also a house painter from Millstreet, a railway signalman, an auctioneer's helper from Kilpeder, a farmer who had had his farmhouse burned down by the Tans as a reprisal after the raid on Cooltoomey barracks. Not even an officer as determined as Cogley could keep close tabs on them. A Volunteer might slip off without permission to spend two nights with his family, and then come back with a side of bacon, or else soda bread or cakes, as though in explanation. But they always knew, as though upon instinct, when an operation needed to be put in train, and they were always on hand for it.

"Do you send up a chit to HQ, Frank," MacNamara asked, "when you are in need of fresh fountain pens?" He was a heavy young man, a great paunch flowing over his wide, heavy belt. "If that is the way of it, you might write on the bottom, 'Active Service Unit Number Three could use a bit of explosive.' Whatever they have on hand, gelignite or dynamite or whatever comes handiest."

The British were extending their patrols, wide sweeps across selected areas, Limerick, Cork, Tipperary, Clare, across the mountains into Kerry, and both columns and brigades had been keeping themselves busy felling trees across roads, digging up the roads with pickaxes and shovels, smashing at small bridges with sledgehammers.

"You are becoming very forward and rude for the foreman of a road gang," Cogley said, and Lacy watched MacNamara flare into brief anger before he smiled, the smile spreading against the great expanse of jowl and full cheeks in which, in a few years' time, small red veins would show themselves, like the lines on a map.

When Lacy had first begun to operate in the field, the men with whom he was working had all seemed to him simply "the people," some of them able, some worthless, some clever and others dull, but that was the end of the matter. On rare, splendid nights, sitting at ease on a straight chair balanced against a kitchen wall, or sharing a bench with others, holding a glass of stout or porter in his hand, listening to unaccompanied song, or to music played upon squeezebox or fiddle, air thick with tobacco smoke, with days' odors of bacon, cabbage, fresh-baked bread, it would seem to him, perhaps the stout, perhaps the rare glass of whiskey, that he had been carried into the very heart of the Irish people, a warm organ, beating with lifeblood, encompassing, nourishing. Middle-class, university-educated, he had felt the walls dissolving, and all were together in the kitchen, tightly bound, the young singer, the men leaning forward to catch his words, the women carrying round the platters heaped with thick-cut bread, slabs of the boiled bacon. He was wiser now, could catch the edginess in voices, the bantering which concealed divisions that separated Pat MacCarthy, skilled motor mechanic, livery owner's son, from Charlie MacNamara, officer now of Volunteers, who once, a few years before, had been a railway ganger, as Dan Breen of Tipperary had been, who now was liaison officer in Ernie O'Malley's Second Southern Division.

"One way or another," Lacy said, keeping his tone light, "we will find some, our work is cut out for us for the next week or so."

With British operations that heavy, and with their ammunition as low as it always was, they had been limiting themselves to small engagements that luck brought to them. Tom Russell's column had attacked and killed a bicycle patrol of three Tans on the Millstreet road, and MacCarthy had engaged a lorry bringing in supplies to Kilpeder Castle. But there was a British net of at least a thousand men, soldiers and Tans in grudging cooperation, spread out across that part of Munster—Lacy's division and O'Malley's and Liam Lynch's. Once, in early June, as Lacy was cycling to Aghabullogue, he had seen a spotter plane circling the hills beyond the village, a lovely craft with double wings and concentric circles painted on its fusilage, red, blue, white. He had imagined the pilot, young, goggled, friendly, pleased by the company of tumbling clouds, studying the landscape spread out beneath him, strange words upon a map, pasturelands, roads, abrupt hills. The enemy were getting themselves ready for a drive, organizing a grid. Lacy kept his division busy smashing telegraph apparatus and telephone equipment in Millstreet, Ballingeary, but spared the telegraph in the Kilpeder post office. The Tans in Ardmor Castle had their own, and Lacy had plans for the post office key. But if the British intended to pin down the area, they would need more bases than were offered by the castles in Macroom and Kilpeder. The likeliest venues would be the old workhouses, bigger than barracks some of them, and these Lacy proposed now to destroy. He had been set an example by Barry, in Liam Lynch's division, and by Liam Deasy. Between them they had destroyed the workhouses in Skibbereen and Bandon and Schull.

"And how are we to destroy a solid workhouse?" Tom Russell asked. "Without explosives, is it?" He was MacNamara's opposite, a scrappy little terrier with bright, darting brown eyes. "With pickax, is it?"

"Those bloody workhouses," Cogley said. "When the British put them up, they put them up knowing that they could be used as barracks when need arose."

"Need has arisen," Lacy said. "I'm ashamed of the lot of you. Tom Barry and Liam Deasy needed no instruction when it came to putting an end to the workhouses in Skibbereen and Schull. All they needed was paraffin and matches and a bit of ingenuity and determination."

"I have a box of matches," Cogley said. "We are halfway home."

Russell reached into his pocket for a packet of Woodbines and handed them round. With a flourish, as though demonstrating his point, Cogley lit a match and touched it to Russell's cigarette and his own.

On the night of the twenty-third, Russell's column struck the workhouse at Rathcreevey, and MacCarthy's the one in Kilpeder, on the outskirts of the town standing on the road to Macroom. Russell's task was an easy one, the workhouse at Rathcreevey stood on its own, a dreary pile of somber Victorian stone, like some Gustave Doré nightmare; there was neither farmhouse nor police post within two miles. Russell and his adjutant herded out the inmates and staff into the chill nighttime, beneath a starry, cloudless sky, sloshed paraffin on walls and ceilings, and tossed in a grenade.

"When we had withdrawn," Russell said later, after we had made a forced march of two miles or three, we came to a rise of ground and looked back. The sky was lighted up for miles it almost seemed, like a false dawn."

The Kilpeder workhouse was a trickier affair. It was two miles beyond the town, but the Tans were still quartered in the castle, which had an estate gate opening into the town itself, and MacCarthy expected them to come swarming out, as did Lacy, who accompanied him. It was not long since the column had made its ambush upon those Tans, and there was every reason to expect that they were within the castle walls aching for action. The column moved this time from the north, using the Aghabullogue road, the full force of them, twenty-three men, all of them armed in one fashion or another, the most of them with the Lee-Enfields captured the year before, but a few with carbines borrowed from Liam Deasy in Lynch's adjoining division.

By one o'clock they had reached the mound known as Hurley's Hill, and stood looking down upon road and workhouse. They had been on the hike from Aghabullogue for four hours, and their eyes had become accustomed to the faint starlight. Beyond, to their right, at the edges of the town of Kilpeder, the castle was a dark hulk, within which, faintly visible, lights were burning at three windows despite the hour.

" 'Tis well for them, the hoors," MacCarthy said, "taking their ease in a castle, and the decent poor soldiers of the Republic trudging the midnight roads like a band of beggars." But his anger was half banter, as Lacy could tell from the shape of his words. They had worked out their plan in advance. Once they had made certain that the workhouse had not been placed under military guard, five of them would rouse the inmates and lead them out into the fields across the road and set fire to the building, but the body of the column would take up positions behind the stone fences on either side of the road leading from the castle. Back at Lacy's headquarters, back at Lughnavalla House, he and MacCarthy and Cogley and Russell, who had been visiting, discussed strategy. Very briefly, and at Cogley's suggestion, they considered opening fire on the Tans, and then holding them down to a pitched battle. But the others looked at Cogley as though he had gone mad. "Please God, we can be well away before the Tans arrive," MacCarthy said. "We will be holding our positions just long enough to give a bit of cover to the lads with their paraffin."

"We lured the bastards out once before," Lacy said, "and from that very castle. Once bitten, twice shy. They will remember that and they will remember how Barry dealt at Kilmichael with the Tans from Macroom Castle. When they come out, they will come with the lot, armored cars, Lewis guns, the lot."

But in the event, no one came, neither Tans nor soldiers. It took twenty minutes at most for the wood and plaster of the floorboards to catch fire, and there was a bright blaze by the time the boys who had set it reached the near edge of the road, where Lacy and Cogley had taken up their position. Cogley stood up and waved to MacCarthy, on the far side, and faintly they could see him wave in acknowledgment.

He waited for five minutes, and then stepped across the road, carrying his rifle in the crook of his arm like a shotgun. His left arm, as he walked, grazed the butt of his revolver and the deep leather holster that he had taken from the Tan lieutenant's body after the ambush. He was without uniform, save for the holster and the leather gaiters, and might have been a farmer walking by first light to his pastures.

"Be damned if I know," he said. "They must be seeing the blaze in Kilpeder and in the castle, and they could be seeing it in Macroom itself."

"Those poor creatures are seeing it right enough," Cogley said, and nodded to where, across the road but below MacCarthy's position, the inmates stood looking toward the blaze, their faces invisible, but Lacy could imagine features torn by bewilderment and fear. There were no more than fifteen of them.

Later, Jimmy Dineen, the farm boy who had herded them out and across the road, said that it was dreadful, they were old people, almost all of them, six or seven of them from the men's wing, but the others old women, shivering despite the month that it was, and scarcely understanding what was happening. "One of them," he said, "old enough to be my own grandmother, was either drunk or a bit soft in the head, and kept screeching at me. Screeching in Irish, it was. The grandmother could have understood her, but I could not. She was damned displeased, I can tell you that."

"Mother Ireland," Cogley said, who was developing, so Lacy noticed, a fine touch for the sardonic. "Set them free, and what thanks do you get."

"They will be made welcome in the homes of Kilpeder," MacCarthy said, "one in this house and one in that. Until other provision can be made."

"Other provision," Cogley said. "If God's timetables are working, they will arrive at the workhouse in Cashel just as O'Malley sets it ablaze."

"God forgive you, Ben," MacCarthy said with genuine anger.

Lacy studied the two of them, as a field geologist would study a first, faint line of fissure, delicate and menacing, upon a sheet of rock.

But that was later; now, an hour after touching off the flames in the Kilpeder workhouse, they paused, as, fifteen miles distant, Russell had paused, upon a high, sloping hill, beyond boreens, because they had moved across country, across trackless moorland, and, as with Russell, the blazing building lit up the predawn sky. But to their right, beyond the town of Kilpeder, their own town, MacCarthy's and Cogley's, and half the column's town, there were no lights. The lights they had seen earlier studding the dark mass of the castle had been turned off. The lack of movement was eerie, inexplicable.

"By God, they are afraid of us," Bill English said, the Kilpeder farmer whose house had been burned down by the Tans as a reprisal. "With all their bullying great weapons and their armored cars and their Lewis guns, we have put the fear of God into them. MacCarthy's column has won the day, as the song has it."

But MacCarthy himself knew better, as did Lacy and Cogley.

"Tobias Sinclair has a cool head," Lacy said, "and the answer may be as simple as that." After the ambush of the Kilpeder Tans, months earlier, their commander had been relieved, and was replaced by a youngish Scotsman, Tobias Sinclair, who had risen to the brevet rank of brigadier in the war, a fierce, shrewd man, fond of reprisals and trusted by his men. Later, at the time of the Truce, he explained to an American journalist that in the final month the rebels had tried to lure him into a trap by setting fire to the local workhouse, "but we would not let ourselves be drawn out," he said. "As our intelligence learned later, there were close to two hundred of them lying in wait for us, on either side of the Macroom road, well armed, some of them with the new machine guns from America." The intelligence section did its most effective work upon prisoners in what once had been the wine cellar of the castle.

"We are safe enough now at all events," MacCarthy said. "If we move north, towards that other rise, that you can almost make out against the sky, we will touch the Aghabullogue road, and then Bob's your uncle. A strong cup of tea. Am I right? And an egg or two, am I right, lads?" There were commanders who had the touch, Lacy thought, and commanders who did not. MacCarthy had it, and Cogley, he suspected, did not. Barry had the touch, and Liam Deasy and Tom Hales and MacEoin above in Longford had it. It was a mystery compounded of spirit, race, instinct; dark, unreflective certainties.

First rims of true dawn now, competing against the blazing workhouse.

"All my life," MacCarthy said, "and your own as well, Ben, and the other lads, all our lives the workhouse has been there, a terrible reminder to us all."

They walked through brightening weather toward the Aghabullogue road, their backs turned against the burning workhouse, against the town of shops and public houses, against the castle, against the armed force which held castle and town, held the road from Macroom across mountains into Kerry. It had been a successful but curiously inconclusive operation, like the days spent felling trees and tearing up roads.

MacCarthy's column would be based for two more days at Aghabullogue, in O'Meara's, and Lacy left them there, after the tea and eggs that MacCarthy had promised, and set off, by bicycle, back to Lughnavalla House, the morning clear by then, a fine morning of early summer, the sky blue and white, and rich farmlands, deep green, lying to either side of him. There was an enormous silence, broken only by the whirring wheels, and once, close beside the road, a quick-rushing stream. Just as he was wheeling westwards toward Lughnavalla, he came upon another traveler, a drover without his beasts, a tall, skinny man, a long brown coat which was not needed in June flapping about his knees, carrying the ashplant of his craft.

On Wednesday, June 16, with rumors about a possible truce already appearing in the national press, the IRA attacked in force at Rathcoole, 150 strong, and with men drawn from five districts, a fulfillment of Brigadier Sinclair's fantasy, down to the particulars, because an Auxiliary supply convoy was lured into ambush. It was an operation of Liam Lynch's division, but Lacy had lent them Russell's column, and O'Malley had sent them a small active service unit from his own area. It was the magnitude of this Rathcoole operation which led to the meeting in London at which Field Marshal Sir Henry Wilson declared that England must either clear out of Ireland entirely, or else move in with total strength, admit that a war was being fought, bring back troops from Silesia if need be, declare full martial law throughout the island.

For all that some help was sent from beyond, from the west and the north, Rathcoole was in most respects an operation of Cork No. 2. with most of the units from the Newmarket and Millstreet, Kanturk, Charleville and the Mallow battalions, with Paddy O'Brien in command. Rathcoole is a village, a very small one, along the Blackwater, on the road from Millstreet. Along that road, on the sixteenth, moved four heavily protected Auxiliary lorries. O'Brien had been waiting for them, with seven land mines laid, and detonated one as the lead lorry passed over it, and another, almost simultaneously, beneath the rear lorry. The two were disabled, some of the Auxiliaries were wounded, and all four of the lorries were trapped on the narrow road. Some of the Auxiliaries attempted to outflank the Volunteer position, and O'Brien exploded the third of his mines.

"God," Russell said two nights later in the library of Lughnavalla, "Tom Barry had best look to his laurels. It was brilliant."

But it developed into a gunfight which stretched itself out for more than an hour.

"We moved back after that," Russell said. " 'Twill be written up by Elizabeth Keating and her chum Childers as a great victory, but what we did was, we moved back, Paddy gave the order for withdrawal, and properly so. What else could we do? The next morning, he sent out some fellows on reconnaissance to the site, and be damned if the Auxies hadn't left behind for us about a thousand pounds of ammunition, a bit more perhaps, when they pulled out under cover of night. We had them there, Frank, we had them there, in an operation as neat as Kilmichael, and we had to pull out, and you know why, damned well you know why."

"Yes," Lacy said, "I know why. Because you lacked ammunition to keep up the gunfire."

"That is it," Russell said. "At the end of an hour, we had enough to cover our withdrawal, but the Auxiliaries had their machine guns going at full strength, and no need for them to take thought. Did they not leave behind a thousand rounds. We are organized now, Frank, and we know what we are about. They can have their strong positions, their barracks and workhouses and the strong houses of the gentry, but what good will that do them, if they are pinned down inside. And they are. We know these roads and moorlands and hills, and we can drop down upon them. Or we could, if we were properly supplied."

"Yes," Lacy said, "I know that."

"The chat that we hear, about machine guns that are to come to us, what is that, Frank, only chat? There are no machine guns on our side, but only the Lewis gun from the armored car that Billy Larkin captured above in Limerick four months ago, or was it five."

"It is not chat," Lacy said, "but close to it. The battle will be decided this summer, and decided here in Munster—Lynch's division, and our own, and O'Malley's, and the heat of the day will be felt by Lynch's. There will be no distribution of machine guns, you can depend upon that. Will there be ammo for our rifles is the question."

Like the other commanders in Munster, Lacy was almost until the end dependent on the national newspapers for news of the impending Truce. It made no difference to operations in the field, neither to the British nor to the IRA. In late May and on into June, the British sweeps continued, and the brigades under Lynch's divisional command and O'Malley's, too low on ammunition to initiate attacks, made small raids upon the houses of loyalists. One of Lacy's columns came almost by chance upon a small search party in the Boggeraghs, commenced fire, and forced a British withdrawal with one of their men lying dead upon the desolate roadside. But there was no mistaking the hints and speculations in the newspapers, nationalist and loyalist alike.

It was on the twenty-third of June that De Valera received a letter from Lloyd George inviting him to a conference in London, made, Lloyd George wrote, "with a fervent desire to end the ruinous conflict which has for centuries divided Ireland." And, on the twenty-eighth, De Valera came out from hiding and set up his headquarters in the Mansion House, where Griffith and other Sinn Féin prisoners were released from Mountjoy to join him. And, on the ninth of July, General Macready, commanding general of British military forces in Ireland, and Irish delegates Barton and Duggan signed a truce.

On the night of July 8 and on into the morning of the ninth, Lacy was alone in Lughnavalla House, save for his two bodyguards and his dispatch rider. He took his evening meal at one of the two farmhouses at the juncture of the boreen and the county road, the house of an elderly farmer named Casey, a widower, a grown son living with him, and a younger one away with Cogley's column. Casey's maiden sister, older than himself, did the cooking, which never varied, boiled bacon, boiled cabbage, slabs of fresh-baked bread, tea. Casey, "young" Dan Casey, the squad of four riflemen and Lacy ate together at the deal table. Delia Casey would serve out the food, a platter of bacon and cabbage at either end of the table, and then move back to her stool beside the chimney. She had little to say, ever, and in any event her English was poor. Two of the riflemen had a folded-over copy of the *Examiner* resting between their places, one of them holding it flat with his elbow.

" 'Tis all over, Commandant," he said to Lacy. "It says here in the *Examiner* that it is over."

"We do not take our orders from the newspapers," Lacy said, "and from the *Examiner* least of all. Those lads had once or twice to be taught their manners. When there is a truce and if there is a truce, the word will be given out to me, and I will give it out to you straight away, you may depend upon it."

The rifleman, he could not have been more than seventeen, looked at Lacy with wide, serious eyes.

That night, in the long white light of Munster's summer, Lacy walked from room to room of Lughnavalla House. What marks history might have made upon it were vanished, although once, so Ben Cogley had told him, it had had its moment of fame as one of the boycotted houses of the Land War of the early eighties. Journalists had encamped themselves in the Kilpeder Arms and had ridden out to watch the boycott at work, and, at last, no one there but an emergency man brought in by the owner from Millstreet. But there were no echoes, only the sounds of Lacy's boots upon the floor. The lads who these days came and went, guards and riflemen, lads from the columns using the house for a night or two, had for the most part been careful, although the overmantel in the sitting room now was gouged with someone's knife marks, and carpets had been stained by spilled tea and porter, cigarette burns scattered like insects. It was otherwise unchanged from what it had been when the Townshends said goodbye to it, two Septembers before, at the start of the Troubles. The Townshends could be re-created from their casual use of Lughnavalla House as a holiday lodge. In the front hall, wicker creels hung from pegs, gunmetal weatherproofs, soft caps and hats of brown tweed the color of moorland, with lures caught upon hooks in their weaves, iridescent, china blues, speckled yellows. In a room off the rear sitting room, at right angles to the short passage which led to courtyard and stables, what had once been a gunroom, but the guns, of course, no longer there, carried back to London in their fitted cases, but an empty gun rack, and above it a heavy colored print of a plover in flight; below the imperiled bird chaps in tweeds and thigh-high waders. Through the dirt-streaked window, Lacy looked out upon light fading from the cobbled courtyard, the small stables, dressed stone from some earlier day, two stable double doors, one half off its hinges. On a cabinet in the drawing room, a half-dozen easeled photographs, a watercolor, a family group sitting on the steps outside Lughnavalla, a solemn father, bright-smiling mother, two boys, a slender girl, her face blurred. Another photograph showed one of the boys, looking not much older, but in uniform, on either shoulder the single pip of a subaltern. On shelves in what Lacy called the library were small piles of the *Tatler*, the *Sketch*, the *Illustrated London News*, the Sportsman's Library edition of a volume on stag hunting in the Scottish Highlands, a dozen or so mystery novels, a guide to gardening, a Thomas Hardy novel and one by Warwick Deeping. By now, Lacy had read all of them save the Deeping, sitting in late, lamplit nights. He was self-conscious now about his *Aeneid*, which had become a joke among the Munster commanders, even those who were uncertain what the word signified.

In the morning, he made himself tea, and carried it upstairs to the library, where, with drawing pins pressed into shelving, he had tacked into place the half-inch map of West Munster. He had turned away from it, a map which he had studied so well and for so long that he scarcely needed it, remembering shadings, faint browns, the veins and arteries of roads, rivers, the darker shades of hills, the blue of inlets, ragged bays, and had walked to the window where, sipping sweet tea, still hot, he saw the messenger sent to him by Cogley. A boy, pedaling quickly, wearing a peaked cap reversed as the young lads were beginning to do who thought themselves already Volunteers, running errands, carrying messages, helping to tear up roads. It was a single sentence, with a signature. For the seconds that it took Lacy to read it, the boy shifted weight from one foot to the other, tense with excitement.

> In view of the conversations now being entered into by our Government with the Government of Great Britain, and in pursuance of mutual conversations, active operations by our troops will be suspended as from noon, Monday, 11th July. Risteard Ua Maolchatha, Chief of Staff.

The boy's name, Lacy suddenly remembered, was Burke, Dinny Burke or Patsy Burke.

"Good work there, Burke," he said. "There is fresh tea in a pot below. Pour yourself a cup."

" 'Tis the dawning of the day, Commandant," Dinny Burke said, or Patsy Burke. "So Mr. Cogley said I was to say to you. The war is won. Up the Republic, Mr. Cogley says I am to tell you."

"Not yet, Burke," Lacy said. "Not quite yet. Not until noon tomorrow."

He stood by the window after young Burke had gone below for his tea. Bright July sunlight fell now upon the brown, bare hulks of the Derrynasaggarts. As he looked westwards, he heard, faintly, coming to him from Kilpeder, the sound of a church bell ringing, and thought, for a moment, that the bell was being rung in celebration, in anticipation, but then remembered that it was a Sunday morning.

XV

PATRICK PRENTISS

It is often said now that the summer and autumn of the Truce, before the disputed Treaty was brought back, before the quarrels and the splits, before the bloodshed and deaths of the Civil War, often said that those months were splendid, and the summer especially. It is how I remember it myself, Dublin in summer sunlight which did not fade until a late hour, the midlands, Cork which I visited twice, and two long weekends in Galway. First you would hear that it was over, that the fighting had ended, and then what a glorious summer it was, as though the fine weather had come to us as a prize. I am inclined to distrust such recollections of weather. All throughout the war, the Great War, the war in Flanders, we all looked back on the final summer of peace, the summer of 1914, and endowed it with sun-dappled magic, a honeyed sweetness in the air, as though felicity were making a last, full-bodied assertion. But I suspect that were some dryasdust to consult the records, the newspapers, he would find that it had not been a summer at all out of the ordinary, the leaves not vivid but dusty, the sunlight harsh on some days, nurturing and sweet upon others.

Once in early August, Myles Keough motored down to the midlands, to Dunadin, a market town eastwards of Birr, and the day, he told me, was marvelous, a day of the marvelous summer of the Truce. He was driving his new Hirondelle, a yellow deeper than jonquils or canaries, gleaming metalwork, leather seats, an elaborate windscreen. He had bought it six months before, but had kept it, for the most part, discreetly garaged, save for a

Christmas visit to friends in Wicklow. Myles had well-placed friends in the national movement, but it was best to be safe, and cars like the yellow Hirondelle were, in the final months of the war, being commandeered by flying columns or even by squads working on their own and out for some sport, or by Tans or Auxiliaries dressed in mufti and ready for a bit of outrage. But not today, not that day, as Myles drove eastward to visit his friends the Darcys, in their house outside Dunadin.

Myles was a master of survival, not that he had ever been in danger of losing anything, but he had been thick with the Castle crowd before the Troubles started, yet at the same time he and Griffith had been friends of long standing. And once or twice, during the struggle, he had sheltered in his house in Ely Place some member of the Dáil on the run, and once a gunman who had escaped from Kilmainham, and who had been given Myles's name by Christopher Blake. But now, Myles and Griffith were more than friends, they were inseparable, and of a summer afternoon they could be seen the two of them walking through Stephen's Green or along the strand at Sandymount, Griffith not strolling, to be sure, a brisk walker, with fierce, heavy mustache and pince-nez glittering as they caught the sun, beside him the taller Keough, dark sedate coat, elegantly cut, warred against by the primrose waistcoat, small flowers of silk scattered upon a field of white.

"God, Patrick," Myles said to me as he told me of his drive down to Dunadin, "this is the loveliest of God's many fair and lovely fields. And to drive through it in mellow summer, knowing that we had somehow moved through bloodshed, through centuries, through bunglings and heroisms, deceptions, fidelities, had moved through it toward the very edge of triumph, of independence. Here and there, along the Birr road, you could see a burned-out barracks, and there was one installation of Auxiliaries at least, it could be seen from the road just outside Mountmellick. They had taken over a big house, and beyond the walls you could see their tenders and armored cars, but by the terms of the Truce, they were lying low. In the town itself, there were bits of bunting, green and gold and orange, and in the square, a platform still standing from a political meeting of some sort, bunting still clinging to it. I called in at the hotel for sandwiches and a glass of porter. In the bar, there were still, as there had always been, photographs of the local hunt, grouped around the steps of what may well have been the manor house now occupied by the Auxies, great florid landowning faces. But facing them, now, the faces of the executed martyrs of the Easter Rising, and a spanking-new photograph as well, the members of the Dáil sitting or standing formally, row upon row, outside the Mansion House. I was sitting some distance away from it, but I knew that photograph well, it had been in all the newspapers—Count Plunkett cloaked and bearded, looking like Father Ireland; Collins bulky and full of energy even in the stiff photograph, De Valera, long, solemn, unsmiling face, and Countess Markievicz in an elaborate dark frock and dark hat, Mulcahy with his long triangular face, all of them.

"The landlord himself served me my drink, and sent a girl off to the kitchen for the sandwich. I nodded toward the photograph. 'A new day,' I said. He nodded and took a moment to measure me, studying my suit and style of haircut before answering. 'It is, thanks be to God,' he said. 'A new day.' Some glasses on the rack above his head did not satisfy him, and he took them down, one by one, to polish them with a soft, clean cloth. 'My wife's brother is there with them,' he said. 'He sent the picture down from Dublin. That is himself standing directly behind Arthur Griffith.' I stood up and walked to the wall. 'Francis Martin,' I said, 'a member of the Dáil for King's County. I have met Francis.' After that, introductions were in order.

" 'Have you had a lively time of it here?' I asked him, and again he paused before answering, but then smiled.

" 'Not too lively,' he said. 'The lads are up in the hills now drilling away, now that it is safe. But this was not one of the troubled areas, as the newspapers call them. Relations between the various factions have been quiet enough, and have been since the Land War. The barracks was burned down after it had been vacated, and passing lorries were shot at now and again. The worst savagery was the work of the Cadets. They took over Dunstan House, Lord Creswell's big house, and have left it in terrible shape. But sure, he will be indemnified by the Crown. Those fellows are never the losers. But you should see the lads at the drilling. I would put the strength of the battalion at twenty, give or take a few, but there is close to a hundred now that the war is over and it is safe to volunteer.'

"At the landlord's insistence, I joined him after my sandwiches in a small Jameson's, and he walked with me down the short corridor, and out the hall door, to where the town lay in summer's sunlight. 'We have lived to see great days, Mr. Keough,' he said. 'Great days indeed,' I said, antiphonally.

" 'We have come into our own at last,' Mr. Lawlor said. 'There we are, in the Mansion House itself, the free assembly of a free people in a free land. With nothing remaining to be done but the scribbling out of the Treaty, the dotting of the i's and the crossing of the t's.' He was either a simple man or a deep one—the latter, I decided—a man in his late forties, clean-shaven and soberly dressed, the hair thinned at the top but combed carefully across a burnished and freckled skull.

" 'Would you not think that the Treaty might have its rough patches before it is ironed out?' I asked him.

"He shrugged, and studying with admiration my motorcar, he said, 'All will go well with Francis Martin on duty in the Dáil. Nothing slips past the brother-in-law.'

" 'A well-kept house,' I said, 'has it been long in the family?'

" 'Since it was built,' he said with quick, almost affronted pride. 'We built this house in the first decades of the old century, when 'twas naught but a stage for the Bianconis, and the overflow from Dunstan House when they had their great balls.'

"In the center of the small marketplace, there was a statue of an idealized rebel of some gone past rebellion, a pikeman, and beneath it lettering which I could not quite read, but knew from the shape was saying 'For God and for Ireland.'

"From there, I motored eastwards through Birr to Dunadin, and almost without incident, one would never have suspected that this had been, a few weeks before, a country in rebellion, crisscrossed by rebels, by soldiers, by special troops. Sunlight turned corn to gold, and the stacks of mown hay were bright as in a Constable. Cattle grazed, soft and complacent creatures, and two girls walked past on the verge of the narrow road, long-skirted, the hems of their skirts carrying the dust of summer. But at a cross, a body of men, half-march and half-procession, was on the move, close I would say to two hundred of them, in jackets the most of them, jackets and collarless shirts, but quite a few had bits and pieces, odds and ends of Volunteer attire, and the two officers were in full fig, the two of them in their late twenties, eyes shadowed from the sun by the brims of their slouch hats. They were not armed, which by the terms of the Truce would have been judged provocative, although other counties were less scrupulous, in that regard. They could not, I thought, by any stretch be thought impressive. And then, but an instant later, I thought, impressive or not, they have won the day, they have brought the British Empire to the bargaining table. One of the two officers, the adjutant no doubt, gave a command in English, and then Irish, and they wheeled to the left, as though they had been learning drill and Gaelic in the same operation. I was touched.

"The full weekend with Emmet Darcy and dear Susan gave us the Irish summer at its best, and I will remember in particular the long Sunday evening, with light stretching itself out until long beyond ten, I swear, with a supper in the garden, wicker chairs and tables, and bowls of strawberries, a marvelous Moselle. Emmet was Crown solicitor for the county until he resigned in March, in protest against the manner in which the Tans had been carrying on. 'I resigned as a matter of conscience,' Emmet said, 'but conscience is rewarded now and then. It was a scant month later that the IRA declared open war against servants of the imperial state. Poor Christopher Fitzgibbon was shot down in the marketplace in Roscrae for doing his duty as God told him to do it.'

" 'A great mercy,' I said, 'that God gave you different instructions.'

" 'So it proved,' Emmet said. He was a slender man, but with the beginnings of a paunch, still in his early years, younger than forty, and a careful dresser in a provincial town, in his own garden, flannels and a blazer. 'So it proved, but it may have been a close-run thing, for all we will ever know. A resident magistrate in Parsonstown resigned his commission and within the week, he had been shot down by "masked men," as they are always called. The Crown of course said that he had been murdered by Sinn Féin, but it is certain that he was killed by the Black and Tans. They had their own little murder gang in operation, you know.'

" 'Yes,' I said, 'I know. But they are hunkered down in Lord Cresswell's, I take it.'

" 'They are,' Emmet said, 'and careless guests, from all we hear. Cresswell's collection of lewd paintings from Venice has been used by the Tans for target practice, putting holes where appropriate but often shooting wide of the mark.'

" 'Emmet!' Susan said, 'I cannot imagine what that means.' But their other guests, Brian and Sally Cusack, laughed in delight, less at Emmet's drollery than at Susan's affectation of shock.

"The bottles of wine had been cooling in the pond at the far end of Emmet's garden, dark waters sun-pointed, willow-shaded. Grattan Darcy, Emmet's younger brother, had been a captain in the Dublin Fusiliers, killed at the Somme. In Emmet's study, beneath glass, lay his Military Cross, awarded posthumously.

" 'A new world, Emmet?' I asked, and held my glass of wine against the slant, tiring sunlight. 'A new world, do you think?' "

Myles's account of his weekend in Dunadin, and as close as I can come to reproducing his tone of voice, the swiftness of his tone from one thought to the next, the way in which he could sketch in a scene, a person, a look. Rather a pointless story it might seem, but for Myles, narrative was allegory. "A new world, do you think?" Myles had asked Emmet Darcy, and as he talked with me now, a month later, I knew that he was putting the question, a question which we all had on our minds. "You are the historian, Patrick," he said, "what would you say?"

Two facts, so it seemed to me and to many others, were clear from the outset, and were set by implacably strong political considerations. On June 22, 1921, the King himself opened the newly created Parliament in Ulster, or rather, as it was now to be called, Northern Ireland, and, in the course of his address, hinted that some measure of agreement with the South was possible. Behind this lay the recognition by the cabinet in London that Sinn Féin could not be crushed in less than a year, and that a ferocious and full-scale military operation would be necessary. All this we know now, but even at the time it could easily be guessed at.

"A hundred thousand new special troops and police must be raised," Churchill said, who had just moved from the War to the Colonial Office, and was chairman of the cabinet's Committee on Irish Affairs. "Thousands of motorcars must be armored and equipped; the three southern provinces of Ireland must be closely laced with cordons of blockhouses and barbed wire; a systematic rummaging and questioning of every individual must be put into effect." This was not a course which Churchill himself was advocating, far from it. He was reminding his colleagues of what would be required if Sinn Féin was to be put down by military force, and he was in fact arguing on behalf of a truce, and the working out of a political solution.

On July 8, when General Macready arrived at the Mansion House to organize the terms of the Truce, he was meeting with Sinn Féin leaders who had been released from prison for the purpose, and he moved through cheering crowds. Later, he said that he went to the meeting armed, and newspaper photographs confirm this, the right-hand pocket of his tunic weighted down. The King, in his procession through the streets of Belfast on the twenty-second, had been escorted by the Tenth Hussars; when they were being brought back to the Curragh, their train was exploded by the IRA, killing four soldiers and about thirty horses. The explosion occurred near Dundalk, at a spot known in Irish history as "the gap of the North," and by the government's account it had been skillfully staged. A passenger train had been allowed to pass by unharmed, and then, precisely as the headquarters car of the military transport was moving along the track, the mines were set off. It is fierce country there, the country of the ancient sagas of Cuchulain and the other heroes.

Those two events, the opening of the Parliament in Belfast, with full regal pageantry, and then, a week or so later, General Macready meeting the Republicans in Dublin's Mansion House, the weight of his revolver pulling his tunic out of shape, those two events seemed to me to compress into images what was happening. It was clear from the first that the London cabinet was prepared to concede much, but not everything. Northern Ireland, with its Protestant majority, was to stand clear of the settlement, and the settlement itself would be for something less than a Republic. Given those two limiting conditions, London was prepared to negotiate. Everyone understood that—De Valera did and Collins, MacNeill and Griffith and Barton. Everyone understood except the men who for two years had been killing others and risking death themselves for the cause of the Irish Republic.

General Macready's apprehensions were reasonable. Three times at least, Collins had organized attacks upon him, for the most formidable of which he had brought Treacy and Breen up from Tipperary. For Macready this was not a meeting between contending officers and staffs, but rather a meeting with ruffians and murderers, who sent out shabby recruits to do their killings from dark laneways, or along country roads, men to whom it did not matter if their targets were unarmed. Only days before, on June 24, two young Black and Tans, Leonard Appleford and George Warnes, were shot down on Grafton Street in the afternoon, as they left the cinema. It was done with precision, gunmen holding the spectators at bay, while two others pumped bullets into the Tans. It was a commonplace occurrence.

By the terms of the Truce, though, Macready and the Crown authorities were compelled tacitly to admit that the Irish had put an army into the field. Both sides agreed that "there would be no provocative display of forces, armed or unarmed." By October, Macready was to be arguing that "advantage has been taken of the Truce to convert the IRA, which three months ago was little more than a disorganized rabble, into a well-disciplined, well-organized and well-armed force."

"We are out in the open now," Collins told Christopher Blake, "they can mark us out and then hunt us down if this thing fails. We were in shadows before, and that was our strength."

Across the country in that magical summer of the Truce, the lads who had fought in the flying columns came down into their towns to be fêted, standing half-shy, half-arrogant at dances, lads whose names had already traveled into folksong—Barry and Breen and O'Malley. Once in a while, and in violation of the Truce, of course, a motorcar would be "commandeered" for a day's outing, and few were the private streams and lakes that were not poached. When Tom Barry was married in August, there was a large reception in Vaughn's Hotel, which had been one of Collins's bases, and the guests moved out into the garden for the photograph, Collins and De Valera are there and O'Higgins and Christopher Blake, O'Duffy the commandant from Ulster, Harry Boland. Barry—General Barry as he now was by rank—looks absurdly young in his stiff, city suit, great crop of hair, open, candid face of a young fellow off the farm. Frank Lacy stands behind him, beside Ernie O'Malley. Barry had been made liaison officer for the Martial Law Area, with a two-room office in Cork City, but Lacy and O'Malley, like the other commanders of divisions, were having their hands full keeping their men drilled and prepared to take up the fight again. Save for the flying columns, it was an army of parttime soldiers, anxious now to take up their old trades and occupations. The new men, the "Trucers," were ready for excitement, but they were without experience.

* * *

"I had orders from Headquarters to arrange details of the Truce with General Strickland," Frank Lacy told Blake. " 'Now then, Lacy,' he began, and I said, 'Let's start matters out properly, it is General Lacy.' It was as though he had not heard me and he began again. 'Now then, Lacy.' 'Oh, well,' I said, 'if you are determined to be informal, bash ahead, Strickland.' He heard that one all right.' "

"He did indeed," Blake said. "Representations were made to HQ. The words 'insolent' and 'ill-bred' were used."

"I heard nothing of that," Lacy said. "How did Mick take it, do you know?" But Blake shook his head.

"The Truce won't hold, Chris," Lacy said. "You know that, don't you. The talks will break down, and we will be back in the field. The English will never give us a Republic unless it's at the point of a rifle. They have as good as said so."

"Let's wait," Blake said. "Let's see what is on offer."

"On offer," Lacy echoed with contempt. "The Republic is not 'on offer.' The Republic is not for sale."

But Blake began to question him about his command, and turned the subject.

It was months later when Christopher Blake, talking with me, recalled what Lacy had said to him, in tones which, for all the edging of contempt, were flat and unemphatic. Even then, even a month perhaps before the beginning of the negotiations over the Treaty, a division was almost visible, a tremor in the earth, and for Blake it was the flatness, the finality of the words, "The Republic is not for sale."

In those days, those later-on days, I was myself for the only time involved in events, one of dozens of so-called experts whom Sinn Féin was consulting, a Dublin newspaper describing me once as "a member of a distinguished legal family, and an historical scholar recognized both here and in London." But I had neither skill in diplomacy nor any knowledge of diplomatic history, and if the Irish cabinet was consulting me, it was, I suspected, because they wished to broaden the base of national support. Matters stood differently between Christopher and myself, of course, we were close friends, friends of long standing, and we talked frankly.

It is that frankness which has made it possible for me to give a narrative to the twisted events which carried Ireland from the Treaty negotiations to the quarrel over it to the Civil War from which the country, even now, more than ten years later, has not yet recovered. Much of the history was public knowledge, of course, and more has become known in the last few years.

It was on the eleventh of July that the Truce was officially in effect, and a day before, De Valera had received Lloyd George's telegram, offering a meeting. Griffith accompanied him to London, and Stack, with Erskine Childers as adviser, and Count Plunkett of Foreign Affairs for solemnity and appearance.

But not Collins. On that Monday, the eleventh, the day of the Truce, Collins drove out to Glenvar to remonstrate with De Valera, and returned after a talk which lasted for several hours. "He was furious," Blake was to tell me, "pacing back and forth in his office, and if a straight chair got in his way, kicking it to one side." "Making peace is more dangerous than making war," De Valera had reminded him. "But not the same kind of danger," and Collins shot a quick, angry glance at him.

Blake had been for several months in London, exploring very thin, elusive leads, meeting with liberal groups, writing an occasional article for the English newspapers. Every few weeks, he would report back to Dublin, two kinds of reports, a formal one to the cabinet, and another, a less formal one, to Collins. From all that he had been able to learn, the cabinet in London was of two minds throughout the spring, certain that if the IRA could not be crushed by the beginning of autumn, something more drastic would have to be swung into place—either a total military operation, or else a truce, to be followed by some kind of political solution. The Liberals in the cabinet, including Churchill, were all for a truce, all of them save Lloyd George himself. The military advisers, especially the ferocious Wilson, were for a massive campaign, the imposition of total martial law, drumhead courts-martial, and an immense augmentation of troops.

"That cabinet beyond there in London must be a sieve of leaked information, Mr. Blake," De Valera said once, "as bad almost as our own."

"They let us know what they want us to know," Blake said. "It is no great secret that they are divided on the matter."

"But beyond that," De Valera said, "the bits and pieces that you are able to gather together and stitch for us, how much reliance do you yourself place on them?"

"The fellow with whom I have most to do is a third assistant secretary something or other. He is close to Churchill, they have some sort of connection by marriage. He is doing his work, letting us know what they want us to know. Beyond that, one talks to journalists, one meets people." He shrugged.

Later, after that meeting was over, Collins said to him, "Watch your step, boy. The lads here in Dublin know about your relationship with a certain lady. The day may come when they will try to use it against you." "Use it against me," Blake echoed incredulously, "what the devil business is it of theirs?"

"None, none at all," Collins said, "but mind yourself for all that."

It was on the twenty-fifth of June that De Valera received the letter from Lloyd George, inviting him to London as "the chosen leader of the great majority in Southern Ireland, to end the ruinous conflict which has for centuries divided Ireland and embittered the relations of the peoples of these two islands." On the fourth of July, De Valera met with the Earl of Midleton and three other loyalist leaders in the Mansion House, while a great crowd gathered outside. And on the seventh, in London, Lloyd George indicated to Midleton that should the IRA suspend all operations, the British government would cease its own active operations. The Truce, it was assumed, would last for but a few weeks. And, on the next day, on the eighth, Macready, with his weighted-down tunic, came to the Mansion House, passing through crowds even larger.

I saw that crowd myself, it almost filled Dawson Street, and spilled into Molesworth. It is difficult to gauge the mood of a great crowd. There was jubilation, certainly, a sense, wrong perhaps, that the British government and the British Army had been brought to the bargaining table. But there was also, perhaps, and perhaps more strongly felt, a relief that it was over, the curfew, the soldiers with their bayonets and the Tans, the lorries and the sandbagged streets, the Custom House in flames, and the shadowy men in trench coats firing out from shadows. The city police, the DMP, tall and unarmed, were on duty, but there was no need for them, and as I turned away to walk toward the green, I collided with one whom I knew slightly, a sergeant who had testified a few years earlier in a civil case. "God, Mr. Prentiss," he said, "this is a grand day, is it not, the bloody British Army brought to its bloody knees." He stood swaying with well-being, a fine figure of a man as was always said about the DMP, a heavy red face above the stiff, constricting collar.

"It is, Sergeant," I said; I could not recall his name.

"I wish that the grandfather was alive to see it," he said, "he was a fierce old Fenian, and spent a year in one of Her Majesty's prisons picking oakum. A grand day," he said again, and with no sense of irony.

De Valera, as I have said, brought a team with him to London, but by his decision he met alone with Lloyd George in Downing Street, four times in all and stretched out over a week. They were alone in the Cabinet Room of Number Ten, the two of them, and Lloyd George sought to impress upon De Valera a sense of the occasion's solemnity. The chairs were laid out as they had been for the Imperial Conference, and he named for De Valera, one by one, the Dominion premiers who had occupied each of them—Australia, South Africa, Canada, and then rested his small, graceful hands upon the back of one. "This chair, Mr. De Valera, has been empty throughout the conference." De Valera made no reply. "Do you know whose chair it is?" Lloyd George asked at last, a bit vexed that his rhetoric had not budged De Valera's silence. "Ireland, Mr. De Valera," he said and with one hand he tapped the chairback. "This is Ireland's chair. This chair waits for Ireland." De Valera smiled, but still said nothing, and he glanced around the room at the portraits of his host's predecessors, Pitt and Salisbury and Disraeli and Gladstone. There had been others to look at, as he walked along the carpeted corridor—Perceval, Russell, Palmerston.

Lloyd George acted the eager host, intent upon at once overwhelming his guest and putting him at ease. "An historic room," he said, "an historic room, and we are met upon an historical occasion."

"Please God," De Valera said, politely.

Outside Downing Street, an immense crowd, singing, saying the rosary. Their voices carried through tall windows, closed despite the heat of July. "We are an emotional people, we Celts. The P-Celts and the Q-Celts, are we not called, the Irish and the Welsh. But which is which, which Q and which P, I can never recall, can you, Mr. De Valera?"

"Yes," De Valera said, and bleakly, dutifully, he explained a point in linguistics to the prime minister, short, a bit overweight, fierce mustaches, the eyes quick-darting, soliciting secrets, offering none.

Later, at a meeting where Blake was present, De Valera described the scene, reaching toward precision of evocation, his voice, low, Clare-colored, reached toward exactitude. There was a map of the world on the wall facing dead prime ministers, and Lloyd George called it to his attention, the world, in the Mercator projection, with the Empire and its possessions stained a deep pink shading toward scarlet. "We are a great empire," Lloyd George said to him, "the first to cover all of the globe, all of it. Times change, Mr. De Valera, times change, we look forward to an empire bonded not by the sword, but by confidence and trust and imagination. Imagination, that is where we Celts make our contribution, people of the imagination."

"I was grateful," De Valera said, in a different Cabinet Room, in Dublin's Dawson Street, "and I was properly collegial. As a mathematician I had my skepticism as to what may be learned from the Mercator projection, but I was a polite guest. I did not say, as others might have said, 'I thank you, Mr. Lloyd George, for calling the map to my attention. It will be a timely reminder of the British Empire's greed and covetousness over the centuries.' " He smiled, long schoolmaster's face, saturnine, relaxed for a moment.

It was on the twentieth that De Valera received from Lloyd George the proposals upon which the British cabinet had agreed, and it was clear, from the first, that there were two stumbling blocks—Ulster, and allegiance to the British Crown. And yet, what Lloyd George put on offer went beyond what would earlier have been thought possible, well beyond what the constitutional nationalist had thought possible. Tim Healy, the master realist, saw that. "The main fact stares you in the face, that the Sinn Féiners won in three years what we could not win in forty." And Field Marshal Wilson saw it: what we are offering to those Sinn Féiners, he said in fury, is "an abject surrender to murderers."

But the world had changed. To talk with Mr. De Valera, Lloyd

George said later, is like trying to pick up mercury with a fork. And De Valera, being told of this, said, "He should try a spoon."

"You realize, do you not, Mr. De Valera," Lloyd George told him, "that if you reject these proposals, it means war, I can put a soldier in Ireland for every man, woman, and child in it."

De Valera gathered his papers together. "You could, Mr. Lloyd George, no doubt of that. But you would have to keep them there."

The proposals were unacceptable. From the British point of view, there was much to be gained, either way. If Sinn Féin accepted, then the wretched Irish business could be sorted out quickly and shelved. If Sinn Féin did not, then the offer made would be visible to the public in England, to the world, an honorable solution rejected by intransigents. And there, with offer and counteroffer, the matter rested.

The proceedings dragged themselves on, interminably as it seemed to those of us on the outside, and with peace or a resumption of the fighting hanging in the balance. In May, general elections had been held in the two unequal halves of Ireland, and the South used the electoral machinery thus provided to return 124 candidates to the Sinn Féin Dáil, one of them being Christopher Blake.

I was myself brought in for what seemed to me the first of two inconclusive discussions. We met in an office in the rear of the Mansion House, Blake, who had persuaded the cabinet to talk with me, De Valera, Collins, Stack, Brugha and Griffith. Of them all, and apart from Christopher, I knew only Griffith, whom I had met twice through our friend Myles Keough, once for a lunch and once for a small dinner party. I liked him, an abrupt, edgy man, stocky, with mustache and pince-nez which seemed always to glitter, even in shadow. But he was a stickler for formality, and, when Christopher introduced us all round to each other, he nodded quickly. The small conference table was covered in green baize, and there were some pads of ruled legal paper. The night before, a messenger had brought to me, copied neatly out in a clerk's even script, a letter which De Valera had received from Lloyd George. I brought the copy with me, and handed it back to De Valera.

"I have no experience, you understand, Mr. De Valera, in either statecraft or diplomacy. I don't know how much use I can be to you."

"You are in the same position then as the rest of us," De Valera said. "We come from various walks of life, but none that includes statecraft, as you call it. We must do the best we can. Mr. Blake here has a high opinion indeed of your talents, and Mr. Griffith speaks well of you."

"Whatever help I can offer you," I said.

"Prentiss is an honorable name in this nation," Griffith said. "I remember your father well, although we never met. He stood by his fallen chief, he stood by Parnell in Parnell's dark days. That is remembered in this island, loyalty is remembered."

"It is remembered," De Valera agreed.

"Whatever help I can be," I said again, and looked toward the copy which I had handed across the table.

"The letter, of course, was shown to you in very strict confidence," Brugha said.

"So I gathered," I said. "It has 'most secret' written across the top of it."

" 'Most secret,' " Collins said, and laughed. "By tomorrow, whichever way we jump, that letter will be in the newpapers in London and Liverpool. 'Most secret!' "

"You would agree with that?" De Valera asked me.

"Yes," I said. "Oh yes, we can be certain of that." But I was looking across the table at Collins. I had heard much of him from Christopher, of course, but I would not have needed Christopher. The newspapers had been full of talk about Collins for three years, here and in England and in the States. He did look like a hurler who had gone on to make a success as auctioneer.

"Mr. Blake has told you something of the correspondence which has preceded this letter."

"He has," I said, "but I have been more or less aware of it, from the newspapers."

" 'Most secret,' " Collins said again.

"It is a cabinet document," Brugha said. "At the moment."

"You will notice," De Valera said, "that Mr. Lloyd George does not choose to address me as president of the Irish Republic, nor even as the president of Sinn Féin. He addresses me as 'Mr. De Valera.' "

"In the eyes of the law," I said, "the English law, the Republic of Ireland does not exist. And Dáil Éireann is an illegal assembly, or at least it was until a month ago."

"The Republic exists in the eyes of the Irish people," Brugha said. "It was proclaimed from the Post Office in 1916. It was affirmed by Dáil Éireann in January of 1919."

"The Republic is not mentioned in the letter which I have been asked to read," I said.

"Precisely," De Valera said.

"Mr. De Valera," I said, "gentlemen. If I may make a point, which I gather you have considered. Your cabinet has proposed to Mr. Lloyd George a meeting without presuppositions. A wise proposal. Lloyd George has accepted it."

"He has a strange way of showing it," Brugha said.

"He is a lawyer," I said. "Like myself. He is looking across the Irish Sea to you people. And he is looking across the table at his own cabinet, a coalition cabinet, and he is looking over his shoulder at Tories who would like to smash his government."

"He is looking three ways at once," Brugha said. "Typical of the English."

"At least three ways," I said. "He is looking over at Ulster and the Orangemen, and at the British people. And so on."

"He made quite a point," De Valera said, "of reminding me that he is not English, in fact. He is Welsh. I did not find that reassuring."

It was a lengthy letter, but required no great interpretive skills. "It might be argued," Lloyd George had written, that no purpose would be served by any meetings which implied in their language the possibility of an independent republic, but His Majesty's Government extends "a fresh invitation to a conference in London on October 11, where we can meet your delegates as spokesmen of the people whom you represent with a view to ascertaining how the association of Ireland with the community of nations known as the British Empire can best be reconciled with Irish national aspirations."

"It is proper to tell you," De Valera said, "that we have consulted with other legal scholars and with former members of the old Nationalist party and with others who have had dealings with political negotiations."

"I would be greatly surprised," I said, "if they do not all say what I shall say. Discussion would not be possible unless there were no preconditions, and this is what you have suggested, what the English cabinet has accepted."

"No preconditions!" Brugha said. "Their letter scorns our attempt to make clear what cannot be bargained away or sold away at a conference table in Downing Street or anywhere else."

"You are quite right, Mr. Prentiss," Griffith said. "That is by and large the advice that we have received. Not from all whom we have consulted but from most."

"To go beyond what I have said would not be my province," I said, and on that point at least there seemed general agreement.

They might have been given the same advice, it occurred to me, by any country solicitor, the affairs of state not being all that arcane. And I was struck, of a sudden, by the task which history had imposed upon these men—De Valera, a mathematics teacher, Brugha, the manager of a firm making ecclesiastical candles, Collins, a bank clerk. Only Blake, editor and would-be historian, and Griffith, journalist, publisher of politically sectarian tracts, had trafficked in ideas. Across the Irish Sea was waiting for them a cabinet old in the ways not of empire only but of politics, of maneuver. These men had indeed been consulting, how had De Valera put it, with other legal scholars. I had not any doubt that several or all of them had traveled up to Chapelizod to have a word with Tim Healy and to Great George's Street for a word with John Dillon.

"Without preconditions means exactly what it says," I repeated. "The prime minister's letter has been drafted with great care." I shrugged. "There is nothing that can be said beyond that, or that it would be proper for me to say."

"To hell with proper to say," Collins said suddenly. He had been drawing lines upon the green baize with a blunt lead pencil, which now he flung down. "Go on, Mr. Prentiss."

"The letter hints," I said, "that there will be no preconditions, but that at the end of the day, whatever else may be agreed upon, there will be no recognition on England's part of a Republic for Ireland. There may be concessions on their part, concessions on your part, but there will be no Republic. And the proof of that can be read in every London newspaper. The English will be willing to surrender much to Irish claims, more than might have seemed possible ten years ago. But not a Republic. They would not dare that, their enemies would tear them down."

It was De Valera who broke the silence that followed.

" 'Republic' is a word," he said, "it is the substance that is of concern to us."

"A word only doubtfully Irish," Collins said, "or so we have it on the highest authority."

When De Valera and Lloyd George had met, Lloyd George had made great play of the two of them being Celts. "Now," he said, "in the Welsh language there is no word for republic. This is not the case in Gaelic, I take it?" "There is some disagreement on the point," De Valera said, "there are some who lean to the word *poblacht*."

"But now," Lloyd George said, "in your correspondence with me, there is the heading *'saorstat,'* a different word would that be?" "Yes," De Valera said, "a different word. It means Free State."

"It is the word used in the Proclamation," Brugha said, "*Poblacht na h Éireann*, it says, stretched across the top line. The Provisional Government of the Irish Republic. It was for the Republic that I fought in 1916."

"You were not alone," Collins said, "Mr. De Valera here fought as well, and Mr. Blake, and quite a few others."

"Not enough," Brugha said. "Not nearly enough."

"I doubt," De Valera said, "if Mr. Prentiss need spend his valuable time upon such matters. We are most grateful to you, Mr. Prentiss, for your thoughtful words."

"Of little use to you, I am afraid," I said.

"You have been of use to us before this," Collins said, "we know that."

"Captain Prentiss, is it not?" Brugha asked. "Or do you use your British Army title any longer?"

"No," I said, "I do not, and I was never entirely clear as to army usages with respect to titles. Perhaps you should consult within your own cabinet. Mr. Barton was also a British officer in the war. Like your adviser, Mr. Childers."

A month earlier, two months, and the streets outside the Mansion House would have been crowded with spectators, but there were perhaps no more than thirty or forty of the curious and idle as Blake and I stood together on the steps in the mild weather of September.

"A trivial exercise, Christopher," I said. "If I had been advising professionally, my clerk would have sent in a bill for five guineas."

"Not trivial," Christopher said, "by no means trivial. We are sorting out the terms upon which to end a relationship that has lasted for centuries. We must be careful."

Across the road, at the Molesworth street corner, two boys, messengers by the look of them, studied us and nudged each other. Then one of them spoke and his pal laughed.

"What did you make of them?" Blake asked. "We must talk about it later. What did you make of Collins?"

"Very little," I said. "I was a bit disappointed." Collins had grown over the two years; in legend, in imagination, he was the dangerous man, the man whom the English most hated. "There is no love lost, I take it, between himself and Brugha."

"Very little," Blake said, "very little indeed."

A faint breeze stirred at bits of newspaper in the roadway, and a van passed us on its way to Nassau Street.

But it was some weeks before I saw Blake again, and before that I had had a chance to gossip with Myles Keough in our club facing the Green. Myles, as always, knew everything, or that at least was the impression he sought to create. He was close to Griffith, true enough, but Griffith struck me as a singularly reticent man.

"Oh yes," Myles said, "I have had my chat with the lads, very much like your own, same cast of characters, but Austin Stack was there, not Brugha. Flattering, in a way, but they have been consulting far and wide. You know the point of the operation, of course. There is a six-man cabinet, and only Arthur is whole-hearted about opening negotiations, Stack and Brugha are opposed to whatever might even seem to compromise the Republic, the great invisible Republic. And those two points of view have wide support, both of them in the Dáil. Dev is casting about for some way to persuade them that that we give nothing away simply by agreeing to negotiate. He will be able to swing them round for a time, God willing."

"And what about Collins?"

"Ah, yes," Myles said, "the mighty Mick. Where does he stand in all this? There is no one who has pushed the war forward as hard as Mick has. So far as the public is concerned, it is Mick who commands the IRA, not Brugha or Dick Mulcahy."

"Blunt fighting type of man he seemed to me," I said, "for the half-hour I had in his company. Energetic fellow, from all one hears. Christopher is close to him."

"Christopher is," Myles said. "Ah, yes, he would be. Christopher and Mick have this and that in common." He drew on his slender, pale cigar, and nodded as though he knew far more than he chose to tell. I could not even tell if he knew Collins well enough to call him Mick, because half of Ireland did. "Mick will win the day," they would say, and then, "By God, he has won the day, Macready coming to the Mansion House to make terms with the Volunteers."

"It is quite extraordinary," I said, "that we should be sitting in this club discussing the manner in which in the future we will be governed by gunmen."

Quickly, he put a cautioning hand on my forearm. "By no means," he said, "should the elected representatives of our nation be spoken of as gunmen." As he spoke the word, he pretended to shudder. "We Irish have exerted ourselves in arms, have established in arms our rights to self-government, but the day of the gun is ending, God willing."

About us in the lounge that late afternoon in early autumn were a few landlords up from the country, a few fellow barristers, a few solicitors, talking together over whiskies, in a far corner, as always, Charlie Fitzsimon and his friend Sinnott were bent over a chessboard, and, at a small table beyond them, a writing table, Philip Prendergast, a solicitor, was scribbling away at a letter.

"Do you think," Myles asked me, "that they should be put up for membership, Collins and his chums? They might ginger the place up a bit."

"Your friend Griffith is not a member, as I recall."

"No," he said, "not Arthur. Not a clubbable sort. And I doubt if he could have met the dues."

And indeed, Griffith lived on a very narrow income, editing his newspaper for devout nationalists in the days before the Rising. For some odd reason, of the men I met that day, I was most taken by Griffith, a straightforward man, serious and determined. But when Myles and I had had lunch with him, he had been brimming with good humor, jokes, snatches of verse. Of all things, he was a great fan of Kipling.

* * *

So the days passed, as September lengthened itself into October. And, whatever may have been the misgivings of a part of the cabinet, of a part of Sinn Féin, matters would seem to have sorted themselves out, for on the last day of September, De Valera sent to Lloyd George an acceptance of the invitation to a conference, to meet in London on October 11.

On August 26, the Dáil, meeting in public session, had elected De Valera as president of the Irish Republic, but this title, and indeed this word, was not used by him in his letter accepting the invitation to a conference.

When the cabinet met on September 9, to settle upon the delegates who were to negotiate with the English, the president of the Republic, Eamon De Valera, declined to serve on the mission. Griffith and Collins were named as the heads of the mission, and were joined by Robert Barton, Erskine Childers's cousin, and two members of the *Dáil* with legal training, George Gavan Duffy and Eamonn Duggan. The secretaries to the delegation were to include Erskine Childers and Christopher Blake.

As all the world now knows, much ink and much Irish blood flowed from De Valera's decision not to head the delegation. His decision can be justified upon several grounds, and they tend to support each other. When the Dáil met in the Mansion House in August, for its first day of session, 300 uniformed Volunteers kept order outside amongst an enormous crowd, and there, in the Round Room, De Valera was elected president of the Republic. It was as a head of state that he named his delegation. But it was certain to everyone that if a treaty emerged from the negotiations, it would not recognize Ireland as a Republic. Moreover, in the cabinet, at least two irreconcilables, Brugha and Stack, could only be won carefully and subtly to the acceptance of anything less than a Republic. In choosing Griffith as head of the delegation De Valera had made, granted that he himself would not be going, the obvious and the appropriate choice. He was a man whose passion for Irish independence was of long record and he was not a doctrinaire Republican.

But why Collins? A treaty would require the support of the army, and although Collins, in the cabinet, was "minister of finance," and, in the Irish Republican Army, "director of intelligence," it was to him that the army looked. In the eyes of the public, he *was* the army. He had argued strenuously, indeed desperately, against the appointment. And he accepted with bitterness.

The Irish delegation, all but Collins, left Dublin for London on October 8, a party of twenty-six, plenipotentiaries, secretaries, aides, stenographers. They traveled by special train from Holyhead to Euston Station, where they were met by an enormous crowd of the Irish in England. There was another crowd waiting for them at 10 Hans Place, which had been rented for them, and it was there, later in the day, that they posed for press photographers, in a handsome drawing room, scrolled mirror above white walls, paintings, a wide, marble table, a tall window looking out upon the Place. The secretaries were seated in the foreground, delighted and nervous, and the men in two rows behind them, Griffith, like a bulldog schoolmaster Churchill was to say of him, and beside him Erskine Childers, thin, ascetic even in a photograph, recessive, unsmiling. But Collins, the man whom the press and the press photographers had been waiting for, was not there. He had been delayed on urgent business, Childers explained.

When the cars drew up in front of Hans Place, they discovered that someone had scrawled upon the pavement, in large letters, "Collins the murderer." Barton scrubbed at the name with his boot, but the chalk-white letters remained clear.

Collins slipped into London on the morning of the tenth, and went not to Hans Place, but to a different house, at 15 Cadogan Gardens. The night before he had spent in a hotel in Greystones, "working almost asleep." It was at Hans Place that he spoke to journalists, on the morning of the tenth. "Mr. Collins has the Irish sense of humor," the *Daily Express* reported. "But this big, good-humored Irishman with the rich brogue and the soft yet decisive voice, has another side. His face grew stern as he said with something like emotion, 'The *Daily Express* was the newspaper that called me a murderer.' "

He had his own household in Cadogan Gardens, with a housekeeper and a waiter from the Gresham. But the building also housed the information bureau and Collins's picked intelligence agents, and members of his Squad. The group included Ned Broy, formerly a Dublin Castle detective, Liam Tobin and Tom Cullen, from his intelligence unit, Emmet Dalton of the Republican Army headquarters staff, and Diarmuid O'Hegarty and Christopher Blake, secretaries to the delegation. It was with Broy and Blake that Collins had slipped over, Broy with two heavy revolvers strapped to his chest beneath his coat.

The division between Hans Place and Cadogan Gardens had been dictated by prudence. Griffith was the leader of a delegation of statesmen, of whom, of course, Collins was to be considered one, but Collins was also directing an intelligence operation. On the morning of the twelfth, accompanied by Christopher Blake and a bodyguard, he traveled by taxi to Hans Place, to accompany the other delegates to Downing Street. The whitewashed legend had been scrubbed at, but his name, and the part of a word, "murd—", were legible. He stepped over them, and walked to the door.

XVI

JANICE NUGENT

On the last Friday in November, 1921, Christopher and I made a night of it—an early meal at Creveney's, and then Shaw's *Heartbreak House,* and then a party that Kitty Blackett was giving, and then to Patrick Prentiss's rooms in Pump Court, which Christopher had been using.

"Are you armed, Mr. Blake?" a girl at Kitty's asked Christopher. "Are you carrying your revolver with you?" And she patted Christopher's dinner jacket, and let her hand trail for a moment along the velvet shawl of the collar. Christopher did not seem to mind.

All that autumn and as winter approached, the Irish delegation to the Treaty talks were considered a rare social catch, and not by Liberal hostesses only; even the Conservatives, who thought of Sinn Féin and the Republican Army as murderers, bloody and cowardly, were eager for a look at one of them, but for the most part without much luck, most of the delegation kept to itself or else met with other Irishmen. But Christopher, of course, was different, he had lived in London before the Troubles, before Easter Week, and then, more recently, he had been all over London on behalf of his cause. The great catch of all, though, would have been Michael Collins, who was always described, in the newspapers and in conversation, as "the commander in chief of the Sinn Féin Army," and was credited with having ordered all the savage ambushes and assassinations. It was assumed by everyone that Collins was with the delegation to make certain that the demands of the extremists were heard. And that if negotiations broke down, he would resume the warfare. By rumor, at least, there was a chartered airplane kept ready and fueled for him at Croydon. When he would go out, to a discreet party or to the theater or to a walk through the streets or along the Embankment, there would always be, at a distance, two men in raincoats. It was that aura of danger, of course, which made him such an attraction, and it was undeniable. I was getting to know him a little, because he and Christopher were friends, and I was not the only one surprised by him, by the range of his reading and the quickness of his wit, but there is no denying that never, not once, did I forget what he had done, what he had ordered done, what even now he could order done by giving a shout to those two men. That damned girl at Kitty's would not have been likely to run her hands along Collins's coat nor ask him if he was armed.

"He is not a brute, you know," Christopher said to me that night. "He is quite civilized."

"No doubt," I said.

The newspapers were all full of chat about the Seven Tragic Centuries, the seven hundred years of misunderstanding and ill will and now a possibility of bringing it all to a peaceful resolution, and everything depending upon young men, young Irishmen, without experience of government and given, some of them, to violent ways. And if the talks should fail! Behind the delegates with their secretaries and their briefcases were men with guns and Mills bombs and grenades.

"What the hell do they think brought England to the conference table," Christopher asked me that evening in Creveney's, and he plunged a knife to cut open a grilled sole as though the poor creature were Field Marshal Wilson. "A century or so of talk did nothing. They were bombed and shot and burned to the conference table."

"Not these people," I said, and placed a warning hand on his forearm, looking toward the other tables. Not that he had raised his voice, but he was speaking with intensity.

"These people," Christopher said, and his glance chanced to fall on a harmless-looking baldhead of middle years and the beginning of a paunch, and his rather younger wife, who had been blessed or cursed with too much bosom, far too much now that bosoms had gone out of fashion. "These people," he said again.

"If they are decent sorts, they will tell you that the Black and Tans have gone too far, gone on a rampage, have to be curbed."

For months he had been dragging me to meetings in dreary parish halls, dusty seats and scraps of orange peel on unswept floors, while he described the atrocities inflicted on the Irish by the armed police and the Auxiliaries and the Cadets and even by regiments of regulars; but the Black and Tans were the worst. One regular officer, resigning his command, had said that they treated parts of Munster and Connaught as their private shooting preserve, with full hunting rights. Once, at one of these meetings, Christopher had quoted from a letter my father had written to me, describing him as an Irishman who had given long years of his life to the British Army, had retired from it full of honors and memories, and with the rank of colonel. Lieutenant Colonel, I reminded him later. You are a colonel's daughter when all is said and done, he said, the daughter of a British colonel. And the widow of a British captain, I said. In the letter, Father had said that things were being done in Galway that made him ashamed of the uniform he had worn, and he described what a friend had written to him of the Tans at work in West Cork, where matters were far worse. "You will not learn of this in its full horror in the newspapers in this country, you must look for it in letters written by old soldiers to their daughters," Christopher told his audience. On the platform, there were no tricks of oratory to which he would not descend. "You should tell them," I said to him later, "that the old soldier's daughter passed along the letter to an Irishman with whom she is having an affair." Sometimes he was preaching to the converted, to Irishmen living in London, but at other times to decent, dim, scant audiences of liberals with a small L.

"The Black and Tans are serving their purpose," he answered me, that evening in Creveney's. "The Black and Tans are what imperialism is about. Scrape away parliaments and regiments and rolls of honor and flags and Unknown Warriors and all the rest, and what you get, in the heel of the hunt, are men in ill-matched uniforms, black tunics and tan britches, armored cars, and torture rooms. There is a torture room in Dublin Castle itself, did you know that? Not the wing where your friend the civil servant spends his days. A far less pleasant room. There are friends of mine who were beaten and clubbed to death in that room. And that is what empire is about."

And all this in a wonderfully restrained voice, and in the midst of it a brief, social smile, so that anyone would think we were talking about Mr. Shaw and the play of his which we were to see that evening. You never know anyone, not really, not even when you are locked together breast to breast, sealed by the sweat of passion. Underneath all there was this passion in Christopher, a rage which condoned men shot from ambush, old houses set ablaze.

He had fallen into the way of describing people as "toughies" and "softies." Collins, of course, was a toughie, the supreme of them, and some of the gunmen who led the flying columns. Christopher had come to admire them, and to think himself one of them, but by virtue of what exploits he was reticent, save for a few things he had told me about.

Christopher could change mood and manner in the twinkling of an eye: it was part of being a toughie.

"How is your sole?" he asked. "Mine is very good."

"When you were taking out the bone," I said, "I thought that you were murdering Field Marshal Wilson."

"He could do with a bit of murdering," Christopher said. "He's the worst." Later I was to remember him saying that.

And Wilson was, even I could see that. The worst, and he looked it, had a shark's look, wide, thin, cruel mouth, an Irishman from County Longford, a ferocious hater of Sinn Féin, nationalists, Catholics, the whole lot of us.

There were so many other things we might have been talking of that evening: after all, the meetings of the Irish and the English in Downing Street were filling the newspapers, and Christopher's work brought him to the plenary sessions, in the Cabinet Room, and across the table, Lloyd George of course and Winston Churchill and Birkenhead. What are they like, I asked Christopher, and he was wonderful in his descriptions of them, being careful in his own mind to sort out his feelings, that he was talking about the other side, but he was fascinated by them and perhaps a bit frightened although he would never admit that to himself, all of our people were a bit frightened, except Griffith of course with his terrier courage, and the other secretary, Childers, who knew the English well, was English himself really if the truth be told, and who had served in the House of Commons before the war and in the Royal Navy during the war, a commander doing something in intelligence.

There was precious little socializing between the two sides of the table. They did not even shake hands with each other on that first morning in October, and they were all, Christopher thought, like the crowds in the streets and the journalists, they were all curious about one man, as though the others were clerks, or petty theorists or civil servants or what have you. They were curious about Collins, all of them, but Churchill and Birkenhead in particular. His hands, someone had quoted Churchill as saying of Collins, his hands have touched the springs of murder.

"A fine lot they are, those bastards," Collins said one night to Christopher, in a taxi driving back from Downing Street to Cadogan Gardens. "Lloyd George, with that bloody twinkle in his eyes, forever fluffing up his mustache like a foxy grandpa, and reminding us that we are all Celts together, himself and the Irish. Did you notice that when he and his chum Jones have something to tell each other, they tell it in Welsh, that none of us can understand, neither the Irish nor the English."

Beyond the windows of the taxi, London's autumnal darkness.

"The worst of the lot," Christopher said, "the one for you to keep your eye on."

"Worst of the lot, is he?" Collins asked impatiently. "Where would you put F. E. Smith, Galloper Smith, Lord Birkenhead we are now to call him, Carson's right-hand man when they raised up Ulster against us in the days before the war, the man who presented the Crown case against Roger Casement, and sent him on his way to the gallows. Mind you, I have a bit of a soft spot for Birkenhead, he's a tough one, you will see that for yourself at the end of the day. And his chum Churchill, I have the measure of that lad, a Tory and then a Liberal and trying to decide now which way to jump."

"What do you think of them yourself?" I had asked Christopher, and he answered me as though he had not heard me quite properly, as if I had asked him only about Churchill.

" 'Winston,' " Christopher said, "you can hear them calling down the table to him from one side or the other. 'Winston!' And he will turn his head to his left or his right, scowling one time and grinning the next. He has a stammer."

For months and months and months after Charlie had died, I hated that man as I would never have thought possible, because everyone said that Gallipoli was all his idea, and the generals had tried to argue against it, but Churchill had won the day, and all those poor fellows and Charlie among them had been thrown there on the beach, with the great Turkish guns pointing down at them, Australian boys and Irish boys and even a few English fellows. And all of them blown away or dead of dysentery. But they said later and still say that it had not been his fault at all, that the generals had not understood his plan and distrusted him anyway and they had let him down. But by then, I did not care whether it was his fault or not. I detested the look of him in uniform for a while and then in overcoats with fur collars and tall silk hat, grinning, and you would see him in some of the news photographs swinging a stick, swinging a stick and grinning.

How strange, I often thought, ordinary fellows, even Collins was an ordinary fellow when all was said and done, a post office clerk and then a bank clerk here in London, and now they are sitting across from the men who plotted wars and peace, who had sent great flotillas to Gallipoli and put them in the trenches of Flanders and the Somme, millions of them, to be shot down. What, besides that, were a few hundred soldiers and rebels shot down in the laneways of Cork and Galway?

But when I said that once to Christopher, he knew at once what I meant, and veered away from the point. "Do you know the one that they don't think is ordinary? Not ordinary in the least. They don't think Childers is ordinary, they hate him like poison, they don't even talk to him if they can help it, save in the way of business. Churchill doesn't look at him really, he studies him, as you would study something in a tank."

And he was a rare one, all right, from all that I could learn about him, an Englishman with Irish connections on his mother's side, the cousin of Robert Barton, who was one of the Irish envoys, but everyone, Irish and English, accepted Barton as Irish, Anglo-Irish and Protestant, a landowner, an English officer in the war, but Irish, like Parnell. Childers was a different matter, summers in Ireland with his cousin in Wicklow, service in South Africa in the Boer War, by occupation, for years, a committee clerk in the House of Commons, which now made him valuable to our side, a devoted Republican now, and for two years he had been living in Ireland, editing one of the underground papers, like Christopher and Desmond FitzGerald and Elizabeth Keating. I had never met him, but there he is, in the official photograph of the delegation, standing beside Christopher, and looking very pale and recessive, as though he wanted to fade out of the photograph entirely.

"He is invaluable to us," Christopher said, "he knows Parliament inside out, he knows the kinds of things we may be up against, the kinds of tricks. He has the training for that, none of us do."

"You must be great chums," I said.

There were plenary sessions and meetings of committee and all the rest of it, and Christopher would have told me all that I wanted to know, whether he should have told me or not, but it had little enough interest for me, even though, as he kept reminding me, the future of Ireland was at stake. For one thing, I did not really believe that. There were actually subcommittees meeting about fisheries and postal services, all of which seemed less than fascinating. "Mr. Collins must be of inestimable value in the subcommittee on posts and telegraphs," I said. "After all, he was a postal clerk, he has the necessary experience." Christopher had the courtesy to smile at that, but he did not like it, I could tell. "The colonel's daughter," he said, "you will always be the British colonel's daughter." "Perhaps they will make you a colonel, pet, an Irish colonel, and I can be the Irish colonel's wife." "Not me," he said, "once the Treaty is signed and things are sorted out, that will all be over for me." "For you," I said, "but what of Mr. Collins?"

During the Truce, Christopher told me, there were marriages all over Ireland, even some of the legendary commandants of the flying columns were married that magical summer as later we all spoke of it. Christopher was at Tom Barry's wedding in Dublin, which was a very proper and respectable one, although a few others were a bit, shall we say, hurried. It was a very romantic summer, and the heroes of the war were down from the hills and looking splendid, no doubt. It was a strange summer, because as Christopher told me, the soldiers on neither side were certain that the Truce would hold and they were making their preparations. Even in the final weeks of negotiations, there were photographs in the London newspapers of De Valera reviewing Republican Army soldiers at a small place in Limerick called Six Mile Bridge. He is standing on a platform, Cathal Brugha on one side of him, Richard Mulcahy on the other, he is a tall, gaunt man seen in full profile, dark overcoat, dark wide-brimmed hat, the president of the Republic, hand held, stiff-fingered, to hat brim. At the foot of the platform, soldiers in full Volunteer uniform are at attention, and the commandant of the troops marching past is in uniform, dark-eyed, a fierce mustache, but the soldiers behind him are in work clothes, cloth-capped, a bandolier or a blanket roll slung across their shoulders in token of military status. Because of the terms of the Truce, they are not carrying weapons.

"Damned fortunate," Christopher said, as we stood looking down at one of the newspapers. "If the Mid-Limerick Brigade were to muster fully armed, you would see Mausers and Lee-Enfields, a few shotguns, and there you are."

But despite the terms of the Truce, negotiations for arms purchases were under way on the Continent and in England itself. The rumor, heard everywhere in London, was that Collins was heading an armament and intelligence operation, which was why he needed separate headquarters.

Now, as we finished our meal in Creveney's, I asked Christopher the only question which mattered to me. "Could it all start over again, the guns and the ambushes, and the towns burned by soldiers?"

"Oh yes," he said, as he nodded to the waiter for the bill, "it could start again. If there are no terms on which the two sides can come to agreement, everything will break down, there will be nothing for it but to fight it out."

There were two real issues, and everyone knew what they were, and they had little to do with the fisheries and the posts and telegraphs on which the committees wasted their mornings. The Irish demanded a unified country, from the center to the sea, as the song had it, but the English, before entering into negotiations at all, had made certain that the Protestant North was provided for, with a statelet of its own, and no need to become a part of the Free State, unless it chose to do so, which seemed unlikely in the extreme, its Parliament having been opened by the King himself, with a grandeur and ceremony worthy of India or some other far-flung outpost of empire. And that was the other issue, the question of Ireland remaining inside the British Empire, and acknowledging King George as our sovereign. The true negotiations lay between these two poles, like iron filings caught between contending magnets. The Tories, on the one hand, were disinclined to sell out their Unionist henchmen in the North, and far less were they willing to let Ireland remove itself from the Empire, dissolve its supposed bond of loyalty and allegiance to the Crown. As for the Irish, they had won from the British an offer of far more than had ever been hoped for by O'Connell or Young Ireland or the Fenians or the Land League or Parnell himself. But it was *not* the Republic; and it was for the Republic that the gunmen had been fighting in the hills of Cork and Donegal, it was for the Republic that men had died on hunger strike and on the gallows and against rain-streaked brick walls.

Two irreconcilables were facing each other across the table in Downing Street, and the idea, as I gathered it from Christopher, was that there would be a bend here with regard to Ulster and a bulge there with regard to the oath of allegiance, and somehow things would work themselves out in a way that would satisfy the ferocious Tories and the fierce Republicans. But it was nasty work, and exhausting work. More than once, the Coalition government almost fell, and survived only because of what was always described in the newspapers as Lloyd George's "Welsh wizardry" but by Christopher in less genial terms.

It was astonishing to go from that meal in Creveney's, with its talk of cabinets and guns and loyalty to the Crown and oaths sworn to the Republic and all the rest of it, to go from that to the Haymarket, Mr. Shaw's *Heartbreak House*. Charlie had been very fond of Shaw and so too was Christopher, but I have always found him too clever by half, endlessly clever.

Michael Collins, so Christopher had told me, months before, was a great Shaw fan, during his years in London he was in the stalls every week and Shaw was one of his favorites. I tested that out, one of the first times I talked with him, at an evening party. Christopher, like most of the other men, was in evening coat, but Collins was wearing a very dark blue suit, so dark that there was almost a black to it, and a dark necktie with bits of red. He always made a great fuss when we met, because I was "Christopher's young woman, a fine young woman from Galway, from outside Loughrea," as he introduced me once to someone. He would always hold my hand a bit longer than need be, absentmindedly no doubt.

"Tell me this now, Mr. Collins," I said on that occasion, "Christopher tells me that you're a great fan of Mr. Shaw. What is your favorite Shaw play?"

He answered not my question, but my motive for asking it.

"Am I being examined?" he asked. "Put to the test?" He spoke in the quick, inflected accents of West Cork, the London years had done nothing to smooth them out, a country man's voice, Father would have called it. "Now then, Janice"—it must have been our third meeting, when first he called me Janice and not Mrs. Nugent—"now then, I will disappoint you, I do not think I have a favorite. But I will tell you my favorite line, and should anyone in London ask you, what is Mick Collins's favorite line in the dramatic works of George Bernard Shaw, you tell it to them. It is when Undershaft, the munitions maker, says, 'Nothing is ever done in this world unless men are prepared to kill each other, if it is not done.' "

He knew exactly what he was saying, and what its effect upon me would be. All of a sudden what I knew came to me with a fresh vividness, frightening, that the man to whom I was talking had done just that, and was ready to do it again, if need be.

He was still smiling at me, and holding a glass of red wine in his hand. "I have never seen *Major Barbara,* would you believe that? I read it in Frongoch, the prison camp in Mr. Lloyd George's Wales, in 1917."

He had a way of leaping from one subject to another when he was at ease or when he was bantering as he was now, but when he was serious, so Christopher told me, he was blunt and unyielding.

"Prison is wonderful," he said, "for serious reading, there is a kind of quiet in the center of a prison, for all its hubbub."

"Yes, I am sure of that," I said. "Christopher seldom talks about it. It must have been dreadful."

"Not at all," he said, "far from it. We had time for games, and singing and recitations, and there were parcels from home."

"No doubt," I said skeptically.

It was an evening party in Kedleston Place, and we were standing beside a tall curtained window which lodged along a crescent toward the small railed park, toward autumnal mists upon which the yellow light from streetlamps fell.

"They made a great mistake in the way they dealt with us after the Rising, after Easter Week." It was as though he was talking in Dublin or home in Cork, and not in a London drawing room.

"Yes," I said, "I know. Even here people say that those men should not have been executed, that they should not have killed your leaders."

"That was their small mistake," he said, "their great mistake was not to have killed all of us. It was a great training ground for us, Frognach and the other British prison camps. We came out of them knowing what kind of war would have to be fought and won."

In the theater that night, sitting with Christopher as we watched *Heartbreak House,* I took his hand and held it. It all seemed odd to me, that Irishmen were making a new nation in Ireland, and Poles in Warsaw, Czechs in what once had been a part of that old empire, and at the same time so many other things were falling apart, and Shaw making a design of it. We had taken seats far too close, so that I could see the makeup on the actors, the lip-rouge and the coloring on the cheeks and Captain Shotover's false beard.

That night, we were very happy, and lay close together. I was awake longer than Christopher, who lay beside me with his hand on my breast, and I put my hand on his hand, and then ran it down the length of his sleeping body. We would be married of course, but far more than that, I wanted everything to be over, settled, and a bit of peace for us and for other people. I was always a terrible disgrace to my sex, so Jennie Hunter would have said, who had been a VAD in France during the war, and so would have said Elizabeth Keating and Con Markievicz and all those. Good for them, but it was not what I wanted.

In the morning, I stood there by the window in Pump Court until it was full light, until I knew that in half an hour at most, Christopher would have to ring for a cab and set off for Cadogan Gardens. "All very respectable at Cadogan Gardens, I daresay," I said once to Christopher, "decent Irish chaps, and very respectable. Whatever would they think if they knew about us?"

"They know about us," he said. We were walking through the Green Park. "How could they not? You have met most of them, you have met Collins and Barton, and Griffith, I think, yes, you met Griffith once. Of course they know about us."

"Do they know that we make love?" I asked, "to give it no coarser name. They jolly well do not know that. They would be shocked to death. Mr. Griffith would be shocked."

Christopher laughed, and without turning toward me, said, "He would indeed. Very shocked." "But not Mick Collins," I said, and suddenly I wanted to know what he would say, "not Mick Collins." You can tell about some men, is a theory Hazel Lockhart and I used to have before we had had any experience at all with men, you can tell about some men. Men have the same notion about women. Well, I think there is some truth to it, and I could tell about Michael Collins.

"Mick Collins would not be shocked," Christopher said. "How could he be? He knows everything about us. I told him."

"Told him!" I said, and stopped stock-still. "Why in God's name?" I had always supposed that it was the sort of thing that men did not do, like cheating at cards.

"We were talking once," he said, "late one night. As friends will."

"As men will," I said, with a nasty edge to my voice, but even as I spoke, I thought that there was very little about me that Hazel did not know. But Hazel was different, Hazel was someone I had known forever, it seemed, and Collins was this almost opaque gunman, the head of the murder gang, as the newspapers in London were forever calling him. Collins, so all the newspapers said, was going to go home one day, if he wasn't killed, and marry a young woman from somewhere in our midlands, Longford, I think, whose people had a hotel.

Which shows, of course, how little I knew. The young woman from the hotel in County Longford was to have her photograph in the newspapers before many months had passed, a brisk, handsome, pleasant young woman with an engaging smile, but she was not the beginning and end of Collins's romantic life, if that is the word I want. Far from it. But Christopher, although he knew more than he was telling me, perhaps did not know everything, and I am not certain that even Collins's bodyguard knew everything, although I will wager that Scotland Yard did.

By the time Christopher had rung for the cab, I had his tea for him, and watched him with the wonder that I have always had when people slip out from love into the world, their voices taking on a different timbre, alien and strange, their smiles toward you a kind of negotiation. It is true of all of us, I saw myself in the tall looking glass above the fireplace, in Patrick's dressing gown trailing the floor and my hair disordered. I put my hand to my hair, and smiled at Christopher in the mirror, at myself in the mirror, and thought how lucky we were.

XVII

PATRICK PRENTISS

If I were to compose a "secret history" of the Treaty and the Civil War which issued from it, it is with Christopher that I would begin it, and at no place better than his visit to Dublin in November, when he spent the weekend with me. The delegation, all of them or some of them, made several visits back to Dublin, to report to the cabinet, and Collins was back more often than that, that much at least was common knowledge, because there were frequent photographs of him in the newspapers, heavy overcoat, pale hat. By Dublin rumor, Collins was over on matters that concerned the army, which was being kept in readiness lest the talks break down, to consult with Mulcahy and O'Sullivan and the rest of HQ, and to report, over the heads of the cabinet, as it were, to the Irish Republican Brotherhood, one of the several chains of power which he kept in his hands.

But on that occasion in November, it was the full delegation that had come over to Dublin, with both Christopher and Collins accompanying them, for meetings which went on all of the Thursday and the Friday until darkness had come to Dublin's autumnal streets, and the electric lights had been turned on in the Cabinet Room in the Mansion House. They adjourned then, and were to go back to London on Sunday's night boat. They had, most of them, houses or flats to go to, families, but Collins, as they all said goodbye to each other in Dawson Street, nodded and walked down Kildare Street, quickly, hands shoved in pockets. "There are a dozen places he could be going to," Christopher said, "safe houses that he used when he was on the run, but tonight he will be on the town with the lads, you may be certain of that." Christopher, though, did not go to the flat which he kept in Fitzwilliam Square, but instead came out to stay with me in Palmerston Park.

We had a long talk that night, and an even longer one the next day, when Christopher borrowed a car for us, one of those motorcars which were always being made mysteriously available to cabinets and headquarters staff in those days, and we drove across the Dublin mountains and down into Wicklow, and walked for hours, stopping for a meal at an old Wicklow coaching hotel, and then circling back, along the shores of Lough Dan.

"It seems likely," he said to me, "that on Sunday we will be traveling back separately, Collins and Griffith and Duggan and myself from Kingstown, and the other lads from the North Wall, things are that strained."

"Myles Keough tells me," I began, but Christopher stopped me with a burst of angry laughter.

"Keough knows gossip he has picked up at dinner parties or in the Four Courts."

"He is Arthur Griffith's great friend," I said.

"He is," Christopher said, "he is, and a more ill-matched pair you could not imagine. But there is not a more tight-lipped man in Ireland than Griffith is. Even though at this very moment, you may depend upon it, he is having a few quiet malts in the snug of the Bailey, and with Myles as likely as not."

Poor Arthur Griffith, with the small house in Clontarf, the modest house for which his friends had taken up a subscription, traveling into town each morning in the years before the Troubles on the tram to the shabby office of his newspaper, seated in the tram with neatly pressed suit, the trousers pulled up a bit to save the serge, short, compact man, compact of face, heavy mustache, polished pince-nez. When he heard of the 1916 rebellion, which he had opposed, he was stranded in Clontarf, minding the children; Mrs. Griffith had taken advantage of a cheap Easter excursion fare to Cork, but he had found his way to the post office. Never a Republican, but by accident he had given his name to what followed, *sinn féin,* ourselves alone. No, they would have seemed ill-matched, Griffith and Keough, but there was another Griffith who could relax over a few whiskies, sing ballads, warm himself before flashing wit, but never so warm, so relaxed, as to speak out of school. A small, stern patriot, bred in the school of John Mitchel and John O'Leary. "This is all a terrible strain for Arthur, poor fellow," Myles would tell me. "His doctor prescribed powders for him, and veronal, but he refuses to touch them. Decent Arthur Griffith, sitting there in Downing Street facing up to that gang of imperial ruffians, Lloyd George, Churchill, Birkenhead with his monocle and his drawl. And then, when he comes back for a few days to report to our crowd, what a crowd, De Valera the mathematics teacher and Brugha the fanatic and Austin Stack the fanatic held in reserve. And there are worse terrors beyond that Cabinet Room, the gunmen who will not be satisfied with any treaty, the lads in the hills and the back streets."

"Whether he heard that from Griffith or not," Christopher said, "that about sums matters up." And Christopher picked up the tale where he had left it off the night before in Palmerston Park, as we sat together in Father's study.

It is an extraordinary county, Wicklow, so small and so various. That morning, we had driven out from Rathfarnham, past the Yellow House, past Pearse's school in the Hermitage, through Stepaside and over the Scalp, with Wicklow lying before us, but first the barren boglands, red-brown that November day, an even stillness, not even a snipe, the distant mountains, a glimpse of sea, and then the long valley.

"We come close to a formula of words that we can accept," Christopher said, "the two lots of us, their lot and ours, and the centuries of battering away at each other could come to their close, a formula which the two crowds would accept, and then, there we are, up against two abstractions, the Republic for us, and the Crown for them. We could break down into a quarrel about two words."

"You forget that I am a lawyer," I said. "We live by abstractions. So do writers, priests."

"And other people die by them," Christopher said, "are killed by them."

It seemed a curious reflection on the part of a man who held officer's rank in the Irish Republican Army, and, as he would one day tell me, had helped in the planning of Bloody Sunday.

The men on the two sides of the table at Ten Downing Street, it seemed, were interested in some kind of accommodation, in some formula of words, but beyond the table, in London and Dublin, in England and Ireland, words like "Republic" and

"Crown" held magic, power, claimed loyalty, lives. Never, never conceivably, would the men on one side of that table surrender the Crown's right to claim Irish loyalty and allegiance. And as for the Irish . . .

On the day that De Valera appointed Christopher to his position as a secretary to the delegation, he reminded him that the negotiations would at best be torturous.

"I have my own long session with Mr. Lloyd George," De Valera said. "He is as wily as some creature out of Welsh mythology, some sort of sea serpent. And the others are adept, to be sure, in the arts of diplomacy. We are not. We are plainspoken country people, the most of us. And none the worse for that, mind you, but it is a different way of doing things, we have not their training, nor their wiliness."

In the Mansion House's small committee room, De Valera sat with his back to a window. Dark suit, dark necktie, a long face beginning to line, features almost mournful in repose, but his smile could be disarming, direct. "Michael Collins asked expressly that you should be added to the delegation, and I am delighted by the suggestion. My own suggestion is Erskine Childers, as you know. And I trust and am certain that the two of you will work well together. You have been working on similar tasks for the past several years, doing fine work with your two periodicals, and informing the journalists from France and America." They had been working well together, Christopher said, but De Valera caught a faint reservation, and the eyes behind the thick spectacles glinted a moment with curiosity, but he said nothing.

It was a conversation which lasted twenty minutes or longer, but it had not yet reached its point.

De Valera looked again into Christopher's eyes, and then toward the closed door, and then back again to Christopher.

"You are going to be present at some of the discussions in London, Christopher, and at others you will not. It is well that you should understand the problem as I understand it. We are pledged to the Republic, but no bargaining in the world will get us one. I am racking my brains for something that will get me out of this straitjacket of a Republic." As he was to tell the story later, it was while sitting on his bed, lacing his boots, that he came upon the idea of "external association," one of a dozen, two dozen, catchphrases which were to be invented in the weeks ahead, by the Irish, by the English. But for the British, it was unthinkable that some sequence of words would place Ireland outside the Empire, and for the Irish, it was intolerable that they should accept a formula that placed her within the Empire. "Association with the British Commonwealth" was countered by "association within the British Commonwealth."

"Each new version," Christopher told me, "is carried back to Hans Place to be argued over, and every week or two it is carried over here and amended and redrafted. Griffith is beginning to show his age. One night, it must have been after midnight, and Childers had been at him all night, with that precise, public-school voice, that House of Commons voice, analyzing for him every adverb, every semicolon, and poor Griffith fortifying himself with double whiskies, at last he pulled himself away, and walked up to bed none too steadily. 'Poor Griffith,' Childers said to me, 'a bit too fond of the native elixir, eh?' I did not answer him, and Childers sniffed. He has the most maddening sniff, the entire history of British imperialism is inscribed upon the air in that sniff. Someday, you will see, Ireland will be free, and Erskine Childers will be shot for his sniff."

I laughed, and Christopher turned his head away from the wheel to look at me, and the two of us were laughing. Brown bog stretched before us, and bare mountain.

The odd thing, Christopher said, is that of all the fellows on their side of the table and ours, the only two who have struck up a measure of friendship are, can you believe it, Birkenhead and Collins. Do you remember before the war, Carson and Galloper Birkenhead, Smith he was then, reviewing the Orangemen? "I like that fellow," Collins said to Christopher once, "he has a respect for the facts. Tough as a bludgeon, no Welsh charm, none of Churchill's blather, cuts straight to the point, a tough Tory and he lets you know it."

But Childers, for all that he was on the Irish team was a different kind of Englishman, Griffith couldn't stand him, "that damned Englishman," he called him, and whenever Childers walked in the room, you could see Griffith stiffen, more than once he changed the subject. Collins did not go quite that far but there was no love lost between them. Collins would bait Griffith about him. "Dev's little mouse, is that it?" Collins would say to Griffith, "pick up the stray remark and carry it over to Dev? You could be right." Until at last, one night, with two large whiskies inside him, Griffith took off his pince-nez and polished them and settled them back on the bridge of his nose, and said, "If it is only to Dev that he is making his report, then that is not the worst of the matter." Griffith had called in at Cadogan Gardens to talk over the subcommittee meeting that he and Collins would be going to in the morning, and they sat together in the drawing room. Collins saw at once, of course, the point which had been made, as Christopher did himself, but for a moment Collins said nothing, and in that moment, it seemed clear that Griffith would have drawn back the words if he could.

"That is as serious a charge as might be made against a man."

"I know it is," Griffith said, "I know that. And I would not for all the world . . ." But then he broke off, and said, the words falling out quickly, "Have you never thought it yourself, Mick, never at all?"

"I have been working with him for two years," Collins said, "since he came over here, and you have yourself, so has Chris here. Chris more than either of us, they ran Information as a team, the two of them. He has never been anything with me save forthright and candid. What about yourself, Chris?" But before Christopher could answer, Griffith said, "That is not what I asked you, Mick. I asked you had you never thought it yourself?"

Collins had been holding his own glass of whiskey, but he put it down, stood up, and walked to where the tall window looked out upon the darkened garden. He shrugged the heavy shoulders, and did not answer Griffith's question.

"They are getting round our chaps," Childers told Christopher once. "They are clever, the pack of them, Churchill and Lloyd George and that appalling Birkenhead and the rest of them. They are flattering our crowd one day and frightening them the next. There in that bloody Cabinet Room, with the map of the Empire on the wall. Breaking our chaps up into subcommittees, and working their charms upon them. What do our chaps know of such matters?"

There was something to what he said. The English had seen from the first that the two members of the Irish team who were worth reckoning with were Griffith and Collins, and they were discovering that Collins was far from being the bloodthirsty gunman they had thought him. The others were makeweights more or less, Barton, a decent Protestant landowner of nationalist sentiments, Childers's cousin as it happened, Gavan Duffy and Eamonn Duggan, solicitors—Duggan a member, as Christopher had himself been for a time, of Collins's intelligence team.

Once Childers and Christopher found themselves standing on the Embankment, and looking up toward the Houses of Parliament, crisp October weather, and a stream of traffic across Westminster Bridge. "For their chaps, you know," Childers said, "this is the center of the world, not the Empire only, mind, but the world. They are all grave and polite, courteous as they sit facing us, but they think us a pack of mutinous gunmen." His accent was Haileybury and Cambridge, its vowels and diphthongs pure and unadulterated by rebellion, and when he spoke about "our chaps" and "their chaps," as he did incessantly, you had to remember who was who.

Long after Christopher and I had had this talk, in the late 1920s, I found myself in conversation, in London, with Eddie Marsh, who had been Churchill's secretary, and who remembered the Treaty negotiations. "We had been at Trinity together, at Cambridge, Childers and myself," Eddie said. "A goodhearted, simple fellow, full of jokes. Once, he and Bertrand Russell and I took a reading holiday in Wales. He almost turned Bertie into a trout fisherman, can you imagine? Whatever happened to turn him the way he went? He took first class honors, you know, and placed third in the Civil Service examination, and he chose his clerkship in the Commons. And then, in 1921, there he was, at the council table, and when I looked at him, there was no recognition in his eyes. He had one of the sweetest natures in the world. What is it that that Ireland of yours does to people, Patrick? Look at poor Casement. Your Christopher Blake, now, he was a different sort entirely, would you not say? But of course, Blake was really Irish, not one of your hobbledehoys, like Casement and Childers."

And what of Collins, I asked Eddie Marsh. What did you think of Collins, as he sat there at the council table, what did Churchill think of him? "Ah, now Collins, there is a different matter entirely. 'I will not shake his hands,' Winston said to me at the outset, 'his hands are sticky with blood, his hands have touched the springs of murder.' And of course Winston never forgot that about Collins, if for no other reason than that Winston never forgets a vivid phrase, especially if it is a phrase of his own contriving. But he came to be very impressed with Collins, a formidable young thug, he called him once to me, and at the end, of course, he quite admired him, bloody hands and all."

"And yourself, Eddie?" I asked, and my curiosity was genuine, because Eddie Marsh could see people freshly and shrewdly when he chose. "Formidable," Eddie said, "Winston had the mot juste, a formidable young man. A bit rough about the edges, of course. Well, more than a bit, a boy from West Cork come to London to work in the post office, fond of the theater, reading books, becoming cultured as he would have called it, and now here he was, at Number Ten."

"He earned his road to that table," I said to Eddie.

"Shot his way to it, more likely," Eddie said. "London was dying to meet him, even when it looked as though negotiations would break off, even though it seemed as though the whole sordid mess would begin again, ambushes and those bullies in uniform that we had sent over. At the end, of course, Winston and Collins had come to know each other very well indeed, better, my dear, than history is likely to record." And at that moment, Eddie reminded me of no one so much as Myles Keough, dropping his half-hints, but Eddie Marsh's half-hints had genuine history in them, Churchill's secretary and Churchill had no secrets from him, so everyone said.

"The Irish delegation had a very cozy house that they had taken, in Hans Place, but Collins had his own establishment, not far away, now, where was it . . . ?"

"Cadogan Gardens," I said.

"Of course!" Eddie said. "Cadogan Gardens, and Christopher was staying there with him. I have read reports from Scotland Yard about Cadogan Gardens, that Collins was running his own intelligence operation, that he was buying up rifles and revolvers in total violation of the Truce, and that your friend Christopher was hand in glove with him. But Christopher did not spend every night there, as we both know. Christopher had that lovely young woman. I knew her a bit, you know, from before the war, Janice, that was it, a lovely name, and she was married to a nice young fellow, Charlie Nugent, and I met her in 1921, with Christopher. Poor Charlie was killed in the war, of course."

"Yes," I said, "at Gallipoli."

There was a moment's flickering, Churchillian hesitation at the sound of the word.

"He was killed that first morning," I said, without remorse. "They waded ashore onto the beach, and were wiped out by the Turkish guns firing down on them."

Later, Eddie said, "Winston was certain, almost from the first, that we could do business with Collins and with Griffith, that is why we proposed breaking up and meeting in subcommittees. Winston was certain of it, and so was Freddie Birkenhead, and so after a bit was Lloyd George."

For Eddie, it was an afternoon's gossip about a chapter in the thick volume that was the chronicled life of Winston, his great hero, but for us, it was our meager history, the war of independence, as the newspapers have come to call it, and the Truce and the Treaty, the fierce fighting about the Treaty, and then the Civil War, which still, as I talked with Eddie that day in the twenties, was an open sore. To him, it was moving into a past of committees and subcommittees, recollections perhaps of Winston sweeping into Downing Street in his fur-collared coat, of Collins and Griffith at the table; behind them, Childers and Christopher.

"Dear me, yes," Eddie said, "we would have every week our report from Scotland Yard, and I seem to recall that on occasion, when Christopher was not at Cadogan Gardens, he would be spending the night in rooms lent to him in Pump Court by a certain Irish barrister."

"Your memory is prodigious," I said.

"For gossip, my dear," he said. "A fair memory for business, an excellent memory for poetry, a prodigious memory for gossip." But for Eddie, as for Myles, gossip was a kind of poetry, poised between legend and brute fact, always with its lingering reticences.

"It was of far greater interest to the Yard, and to us, of course, that neither did Collins spend every night at Cadogan Gardens." Eddie was also a prodigious smoker of cigarettes, and now he extracted yet another one from his gunmetal case, and fitted it into its holder of onyx and amber. And, although I said nothing, he knew that he had my attention. "When we first met, Patrick," he said, "you were in the throes of your discovery that history can never really be written, the book you wanted yourself to write lying about you in shambles. It seemed to me then that you were suffering an Oxford plague, part of Oxford's lethal seriousness. Of course it cannot be written, not even if you read the minutes of every meeting, not even if you read every report by Scotland Yard. Is it true, by the way, that Collins had his spies inside Dublin Castle itself? Never mind, no need for me to know. But where Collins was when he was not in Cadogan Gardens, not sitting at the table of polished walnut, who he was seeing and why, that *might* be a part of history."

His eyes brimmed with mischief, but there was a faint tremor of caution about his lips, as though he were wondering how much might safely be hinted at. But he had my attention, and he knew it; it delighted him.

"Winston and Collins met more often than appears on paper," Eddie said, "and they met in unlikely places. An unlikely place, to be more exact. A certain painter and his lovely wife. Did you know that, Patrick?"

"I have heard the stories before this," I said, "there were many stories going the rounds in Dublin in 1922."

"To be sure," Eddie said, and he stroked a flame from his elaborate lighter. "Stories put about by his enemies. Absurd stories. What of his friends, though? What did you hear from Christopher?"

And I did in fact hear a bit of the story from Christopher that weekend in November, and a bit more in the few hours we had together on the last evening before they sailed back from Dublin a week or two later, and of course in the months that followed. But I best remember Christopher talking to me as we walked beside the November lake in Wicklow, the reeds dry, rattling in their faint breeze, and a rime of ice upon the lake shore.

"What a discreet fellow you are, Patrick," Eddie Marsh said. "You should have been a solicitor, not a barrister. Family solicitor, grave family secrets locked away."

I smiled without answering, because there was no need to. Eddie's love of gossip was genuine, but he could never have remained Winston's private secretary if he had been truly indiscreet. Eddie was a professional blurter, a font of carefully chosen indiscretions.

"In those weeks while the negotiations were going on in London," I said, "Christopher was a very busy man indeed, he was being a secretary, like yourself. He was not greatly concerned, I should think, about where Collins and your Winston were meeting, if they did."

"Oh, they did," Eddie said, "you may depend upon that. And it was I who arranged those meetings, at a certain house in Cromwell Place. Most appropriate name, Cromwell!"

"It is very difficult entirely to blame Childers," Christopher said to me that afternoon, as we walked along the dry woodland path which skirted the Wicklow lake. Childers once took Christopher to a Lyons Corner House, and bought tea and buns for them. That would have been before they went back to Dublin for that final consultation with the cabinet. Childers was stretched almost to the breaking point, his skin tight across his cheekbones, and he was quick, too quick, with his reproaches.

"I have spent a good part of my life with these people," he said to Christopher, "and I think I understand them. It is their world, it is the lake in which they swim." Westminster, he meant, Whitehall, government offices and, beyond the offices, beyond Whitehall and Westminster, a web, a network of schools, Oxford or Cambridge or Sandhurst, nicknames, house parties, shooting parties, grouse and trout streams. "We are a burden to them at the moment," Childers said, "a serious burden, they want to deal with us, make us happy, send us away. We are a problem to them. But it is quite different for us, it is our freedom, not something which we are at liberty to bargain away."

Christopher said it was always curious to hear Childers talk about "them" while using their very accents. A friend of Roger Casement's had told Christopher once that most people had the wrong idea of him, years in the consular service, the knighthood, that romantic appearance, bearded and handsome. In fact, the friend said, he had never been to university, you know, not especially well read, and a strong north of Ireland accent. Perhaps so, but Childers, unlike Casement, was the real thing, a member of the English governing class who had drifted over to our side. And what he had to say was, Christopher knew, worth hearing.

"Mind you," Childers said, "I have the greatest respect for

them, for Griffith and for Mick Collins. I mean, where would we be today without Mick Collins, but his field of action is over there, back home in Dublin. You know why Dev insisted on sending Mick over here, because they were bloody well horrified by him, Collins the gunman, Collins the murderer, the man they would have to mollify, but it is not working out that way, Collins is being far too accommodating, he is awed to think that he is sitting in Number Ten, bargaining with a prime minister, with Winston and Birkenhead and Austen Chamberlain."

"Perhaps Dev should not have sent him over here," Christopher said, keeping his tone as mild as he could. "Perhaps Dev should have come over himself."

"You know perfectly well why he did not," Childers said. "Dev is more than president of the Republic. He is our conscience. Whatever we can work out here, hammer out here, must be referred back to Dev."

"The Republic," Christopher said in a questioning tone.

The Corner House was crowded, shoppers, clerks, people in town for the day. The women, many of them, had string bags resting on the floor beside their chairs. It was not yet December, but there was already a Christmas feel in the air. What would the word "Republic" mean to them, Christopher thought, what would it mean to most of the shoppers in Grafton Street or Sackville Street, the ladies from Rathmines and Rathgar having tea in Switzer's. For Childers more than for Christopher, the word was sanctified.

"Lloyd George is delighted that he does not have Dev to deal with, you may be certain of that," Christopher said.

"It was a bad move," Childers said, "to agree to meet in subcommittees. It is an old trick of theirs, divide and conquer." His words flung out a historical tapestry stretching back to the Tudors, Cecil and Walsingham dazzling visiting tribesmen. And as though he read Christopher's smile, he said, "I know them. I have seen them at work. I have worked for them."

Once, in Downing Street, Christopher looked up to see Churchill studying Childers with undisguised loathing, and I was myself to hear that he spoke of him as "an unnatural creature, a vile and loathsome renegade," much as Griffith spoke of him as "that treacherous Englishman," but Childers, who must surely have been aware of all this, soldiered on, working twice as hard as anyone, obsessed by his certainty that Winston and Birkenhead and their gang would swindle them out of their Republic.

"I have been preparing a report for Mick and Mr. Griffith to read at their leisure," Childers said, "it bears upon what the English are prepared to concede with regard to fisheries and coastal defenses." As he spoke, he carefully smoothed strawberry preserve across half a scone, alert that it did not spread beyond the edge. He did everything with careful precision, his handwriting, trained by his writing of minutes, small and shapely. But he had managed to bring the *Asgard,* with its cargo of rifles, through stormy seas, in 1914.

Childers could not get it through his head that he and Christopher were not deputies but secretaries. And of course he was more than merely a secretary, he was De Valera's eyes and ears, everyone accepted that. De Valera would have made him a delegate, but Griffith would never have agreed.

"He's all right," Collins said once about Childers, "perhaps Arthur does not trust him, but I do. He's an odd sort, but sure he's not the only odd fellow we have working with us." Throughout all of the Troubles, the only weapon that Childers carried, so far as anyone knew, was a small automatic which Collins had given him, so small that he would carry it pinned to his braces by the trigger guard, and he wore it less from a wish for protection than out of affection and admiration for Collins.

"They are not Mick's sort," Childers said to Christopher. "They know how to get round him." He shook his head.

The last day of all, there in London, Christopher would later tell me, began in the Cabinet Room at three in the afternoon—Lloyd George, Chamberlain, Birkenhead, Churchill; Collins, Griffith, and Barton for the Irish. It was a closed meeting, and lasted until after seven. At its conclusion, Lloyd George held up two envelopes. "There are two letters here," he said, and he held one in each hand, "and they go tonight, one of them, to Sir James Craig in Belfast. One letter will tell him that articles of agreement have been signed between Sinn Féin and the British government. The other letter will tell him that Sinn Féin refuses allegiance to the British Crown, refuses to come within the British Empire. It is the final breaking of the ways. If I send this letter it is war, and war within three days. Which letter do you want me to send? It is for you to decide."

"And how long have we to decide?" Griffith asked.

Lloyd George looked down at the watch which lay on the table before him, bedded on the coiled gold links of its chain. "You have less now than three hours. Mr. Shakespeare is waiting outside in the Special Lobby. At ten o'clock, there will be a special train to take him to Holyhead, and there is a destroyer at Holyhead to take him to Belfast. It is the end of the road, gentlemen, one way or the other."

Young Shakespeare was waiting there with Christopher and Erskine Childers. He made a decent effort at conversation. "This is quite as exciting as *The Riddle of the Sands,* Mr. Childers." Childers looked at him blankly. "You know, do you not," he asked Christopher and Childers, "you know, do you not, what is going on in there, you are going to know soon enough, I will be carrying a letter from the PM to Craig, special train, destroyer getting up steam at Holyhead." "What sort of letter?" Childers asked.

"Ah, they would not tell that to a humble junior like myself, you know that as well as I do, Mr. Childers." Childers looked across at Christopher. Geoffrey Shakespeare had a nicely polished face, and his hands, as he rested them on striped flannel, were pale and shapely. Christopher returned Childers's look, and went back to reading the *Tatler,* the account of a dinner dance, with photographs of a ballroom, dancers. When he looked up again, Childers was looking into space, one hand was squeezing the other tightly.

When the Irishmen came out of the Cabinet Room, Lloyd George walked with them, the courteous host; as he walked, slipping the links of his watch chain through a waistcoat buttonhole, he looked grave and preoccupied. Griffith's face was impassive; Barton, to Christopher, seemed agitated; Collins looked murderous. "A few hours yet," Lloyd George said to Shakespeare. "We are having a light meal here at Number Ten while we wait for our friends. You must join us." Shakespeare beamed; it was becoming a most exciting evening.

London's early winter night had fallen. Across the road, two bobbies walked quietly, in pace with each other; it might have been Kensington or Hampstead. The air was chill; moonlight shone through ragged clouds moved by a brisk wind.

"Well for them," Griffith said suddenly, "so securely set in their empire that two unarmed policemen is all they need for their safety."

"While the Truce lasts, at any rate," Christopher said.

"Two unarmed policemen," Collins said. "Do you really believe that, Arthur? Give a shout or better yet pull out a revolver, and see what will happen." He gave a smile over toward Childers. "Am I right?" But Childers seemed not to have heard him, and Collins's moment of levity flickered, faded.

Collins, Blake and Barton shared one of the taxis, Collins sitting behind the driver, his head turned toward darkened streets, the yellow lights, traffic. Presently, he said, "I am going to sign." For a minute or two, Barton said nothing, as though first astonished and then fumbling for a response. "Can you talk to me about that, Michael? This is the first I have heard of this."

"We have gone as far as we can go," Collins said. "We have got as much from them as we can get."

"It was bluff and theatricals," Barton said. "There may be war around the corner, but Lloyd George will not let it rest on a letter to James Craig."

"I know that," Collins said. "Special trains and destroyers with the steam up. Do they think we are children? Well, so far as I am concerned, little Shakespeare can carry word over that the Irish have signed."

"That some of them have signed," Barton said quietly.

"Some of them or none," Collins said. "They want the whole bloody roster. They want the lot of us. They have gone so far that they have put their own necks on the chopping block; their full delegation is prepared to sign, and they will require the same from us."

"Steamer?" Blake asked from the far side. "Special train?" And Barton described the final minutes in the Cabinet Room, and Lloyd George holding the two envelopes. Collins did not interrupt him. His heavy head was still turned toward the window, and his hat jammed down over his eyes. "He is a master of oratory," Barton said, speaking of Lloyd George, "whatever can be done by gesture and word, all of those resources by which the mind of one man oppresses the mind of another."

"Bloody Welsh dodger," Collins said at last, "but he is impressive right enough, Bob. You have the right of it there."

Blake remembered Geoffrey Shakespeare in the Special Lobby.

A special train waited to carry him to Holyhead, a destroyer, gray metal, guns, against a dark sky.

"What do you think, Chris?" Collins said, but without turning his head.

"Theater," Christopher said, "I think about that as Bob does and yourself. Scare the Paddies."

"We can get no more from them than this," Collins said. "Do you agree, Chris?"

Christopher paused before answering, paused a moment too long.

"Well?" Collins said. "You know damned well what you think. Let's have it."

The unheated taxi was cold in the December night.

"Thank God that I am not a delegate," Christopher said.

"You are a member of the Dáil," Collins said. "If we sign you will have to vote upon what we have done. And you are not here as a secretary merely, neither Childers nor yourself. You have a voice. Let's hear it."

Christopher could almost feel the tenseness of the two men sitting beside him.

"If the delegates sign," he said, "I will support them."

"But should we sign, Chris?" Barton said. "That is the question Mick put to you. A fair question."

"You have been thrashing this out with them since three this afternoon," Christopher said, "and you have all the ins and outs of it."

"We know where Erskine will stand," Barton said. Pure Rugby and Christchurch in his voice, no Irish at all. In easier moments, it had amused Christopher that the two cousins, Barton and Childers, Rugby and Christchurch, the one Haileybury and the other Trinity, British officers the two of them during the war, should have been, in the delegation, the voices of the Republican conscience.

"Oh, to be sure," Collins said. "We know where Erskine will stand. Erskine will stand wherever Dev wants him to stand. That is why Dev sent him over, Dev's man with the delegation. And Dev believes that we are empowered to sign nothing until it has been referred back to him."

"Until it has been referred back to the cabinet," Barton said.

"To be sure," Collins said, "Dev and Austin Stack and Cathal

Brugha, the Republican red-hots. Austin and Cathal would accept nothing short of some sort of total and abject surrender." As he talked, he turned his head, but his face was obscured by the winter darkness.

"Arthur Griffith and yourself are members of the cabinet as well," Barton said. "You have tongues in your heads, God knows. The rights and wrongs should be argued out, before any names are set to that document."

"There is no bloody time," Collins said, "can you not bloody well see that? We are at the end of the day. We can have that bloody Treaty, or we can have war. Now which will it be?" Before Barton could answer, Collins put a hand on Christopher's arm. " 'Tis your answer we have been waiting for, Chris," he said.

"You got nowhere with the draft treaty we carried over with us from Dublin?"

"Nowhere at all," Barton said. "What we are left with is what we had last week, which the cabinet in Dublin would not accept."

"If you sign that thing," Cathal Brugha had shouted suddenly to Griffith, "you will split Ireland from top to bottom."

"No," Christopher said, in the darkness of the London night. "I would not sign it."

"We are not signing away Ireland," Collins said, "we are not signing away anything. The decision does not rest with the cabinet, it rests with the Irish people. It will be for them to decide if they want war. And that is by God what we will have."

"You asked for my answer, Mick," Christopher said. "You have it."

The light of a streetlamp fell suddenly upon them, and in its brief glare, Collins's face was dark and lowering, the jaw firm.

"Dear Jesus," he said, partway between a sigh and a snarl. He turned away from them again, looking out upon darkness, as they made their way from Whitehall to Knightsbridge. Neither Barton nor Christopher spoke again, until they had reached Hans Place. They were beneath its streetlamp as Christopher paid off the driver. Christopher looked at his watch: it was almost eight.

"This could be one for the history books, Mick," he said, "matters of state talked out in a taxicab."

But Collins had brushed past him, and was walking to the door. "This is very bad," Barton said, in his mild, even voice as they followed him. "Mick is very certain as to what must be done."

"But you are not?" Christopher asked. "You seemed certain enough a few minutes ago."

What happened that night, between eight and two the next morning, would bring Ireland, within months, into civil war, and in the years which have followed, its events have passed into documents, records, arguments and charges and insults on the floor of the Dáil, into the remembrances of men, into the histories of families. Once, in Annamoe, late at night, Barton talked with me, and once, most extraordinary of all, late on a night in the winter of 1922, I listened to a man who had not been there with them in London at all, a Republican with a price on his head, moving out of Dublin to join desperate men in the hills of Cork, but who imagined those hours with fierce, murderous anger. "They were the traitors," the Republican told me, "they were the ones who bargained and sold, they were the ones, the British were too clever for them, or perhaps they were willing to be hoodwinked." And of course, Christopher told me and at length as much as he could remember, not arguments alone, but gestures, tones of voice, memory, not once but several times, and would remember fragments of phrase, a look, everything enacted in those hours before and after midnight of the fifth and sixth of December. And yet, oddly, what stays most vividly with me is the account which Janice was to give to me of what Christopher had told her, how he had looked, when he came to her flat at almost three in the morning.

He had phoned her, and she was waiting for him by the window, saw the taxi pull up and Christopher get out, still black night, but by the lamplight from the taxi she could see that a light rain was falling. At that hour, the world seemed empty, save for the taxi and the silvery rain and herself at the window in her red dressing gown and Christopher coming to see her.

He brushed her lips lightly with his, and as she took his coat, he ran his fingers lightly along her throat, touched collarbone. His fingers had the cold of winter upon them.

"What is it?" she asked. "What has happened?"

"It is signed," he said. "Signed by every man on our delegation, and every man on theirs."

"And that is what you wanted," she said, "what we wanted. That is the treaty you were working for?"

She poured whiskies, and when he had taken his glass, she touched hers to it.

"Oh, yes," he said. "It cannot be called a treaty, 'Articles of Agreement' is what the document is headed. But it is a treaty, right enough."

He walked over to the thick chair which stood beside the fireplace and sat down heavily in it. He took a long sip of the unwatered whiskey.

"And that is what you wanted," she said, her voice making it a question.

"Part of it," he said, "the most of it, perhaps, as much of it as we could get."

"Shouldn't you be celebrating—isn't that what we Irish do?"

"We Irish," he said, and smiled. "Perhaps we should have celebrated. After the signing, and for the very first time in these months, the English came round to our side of the table, and there were handshakes."

"You shook hands with that awful Churchill, did you? Really and truly? The things you chaps will do for Ireland."

"We were all of us exhausted," he said, "their lot as well as ours."

As they were leaving the Cabinet Room, Birkenhead said to Collins, "This could be the end of my political life."

"Your *political* life," Collins said, with a savage weight upon the adjective. "It could very well be the end of my life."

"Most of us went back to Hans Place," Christopher said, "and Collins took a cab to Cadogan Gardens, I expect, God knows where Collins goes, and I came here."

By seven-thirty, the three taxis had reached Hans Place, and the arguments began in the conference room one floor above the drawing room. The typists brought in pots of scalding tea, and plates of sandwiches. At nine, copies of the Treaty, freshly typed to incorporate a few minor details, were brought over from Downing Street and spread out on the long table. Griffith, who was firm for signing, sat at the head of the table, and Collins, who was almost as firm, sat at his right, and beside him sat Duggan, who had come round early to signing, and across from those two, Duffy, who was against signing, and Barton. At the far end, facing each other, sat Childers and Christopher. In the hours that followed, Childers, so far as Christopher could recall, did not touch the food, although he had a cup of tea before him which he sipped from. He had taken one of the Treaty copies, and sat staring down at it, making notes from time to time on a pad. But he never lost track of the argument, and, from time to time, would break in upon the argument in his precise, dry voice, which held in control a fierceness of feeling that his pale blue eyes revealed.

"You cannot sign that thing," he cried out at last, "you cannot sign it. You have not the authority to sign it."

Griffith glared down the length of the table at him. "By God," he said, "I will bargain with the English at their table up there in Downing Street, but I will take no hectoring from the Englishman who sits here at our table."

Childers began to answer, but bit his lip, and Collins, although the Treaty was putting them on opposite sides, gave him a wink, as though to say that they were all of them nervous and overheated. Certainly Collins himself was, and at one point, he shoved back his chair, stood up, and paced the room back and forth.

"It is well for you," he said, wheeling suddenly, and speaking to Duffy and Barton, "it is well for you to say, let the war commence up again if it must. What the hell do you know about it, either of you?"

"I know a bit about it, Mick," Barton said, "and I'd know more without your help." In 1919, when Barton was in Mountjoy Gaol, Collins had organized his escape, smuggling in a file and a rope, and posting a squad outside the walls to carry him to safety.

"What the hell do you know about supplying it and fighting it?" Collins said, ignoring the pleasantry. "There are columns in the field in Cork and Limerick and Clare and Longford without proper weapons, without the ammo you would need to rob a bank. We are close to the end of the day when it comes to fighting, and you are asking us to begin afresh."

"It is the men in those columns," Childers said, "who are looking to us to bring back to Ireland the Republic that they have been fighting for, and not—" He paused to look for a noun, and then said, "and not this." He gestured toward the papers which lay before him.

Collins was still standing, and when he looked down the table at Childers he seemed for a moment blind with fury. "It will be for them to decide," Collins said, "the Dáil and the fellows in the columns and the Irish people. The Treaty will be wastepaper if the people do not want it."

"The people have given trust to their leaders," Childers said. "Yourself and Mr. Griffith here, but Dev as well and Cathal Brugha and there are others. It is monstrous that the English should hold a three-hour club over our heads. Peace or war by ten P.M., is that not what Lloyd George gave you? Decide war or peace for our country in three hours."

"It is already past ten," Collins said, "and we are here still arguing and it does not matter that it is past ten. Lloyd George is running a bluff, I know that as well as you do, Erskine. But I also know that this is a final offer. There is nothing more that we can get from them."

"Why?" Childers asked. "Why must it be now? Unless you know something, Mick, that some of the rest of us do not."

From his chair at the end of the table: "Are you suggesting, Mr. Childers," Griffith asked, "that Mr. Collins and myself have private knowledge, have had private dealings with the enemy that we have not disclosed to the delegation?"

There had been a time, in October, when Griffith had regarded Childers with a weary, puzzled exasperation. "Where is Erskine?" he said once to Christopher. "We are looking for fellows to take the typists to the Gilbert and Sullivan. They are doing *Iolanthe*." But Childers would be locked away in his room, or in the library of the House of Commons, where once, in another time, another world almost, he had worked, a promising civil servant, bright and eager, a veteran of the war in South Africa, decorated, mentioned in dispatches. But it was "Mr. Childers" now, and "that damned Englishman."

"Of course he is not suggesting that," Collins said impatiently. His coat was unbuttoned, and he hooked his thumbs into the band of his trousers. It was at Childers that he was looking, and not at Griffith. "Erskine knows damned well that he is not properly speaking a member of the delegation. He is a secretary to it, as Christopher here is."

"Erskine was made a secretary," Barton said mildly, "because he knows far more than all of us put together about the House of

Commons and English politicians, and their ways of thinking and doing. His advice I have always found helpful."

"It is not advice that he is giving us at the moment," Griffith said. "He is—"

"We have other matters before us," Collins said. "It is late in the bloody night, and how do we stand? Arthur stands ready to sign whether anyone else does or not, and so do I. And so does Eamonn Duggan. That leaves yourself, Bob," he said to Barton, "and Gavan here. Where do you stand, Gavan? Are you still holding back from us?"

In that time long afterwards, in that time a few years ago, Eddie Marsh passed to me a copy of the aide-mémoire, the dossier on the Irish delegates, which had been prepared by Whitehall. "*Gavan Duffy,* Catholic," it read. "Son of the late Sir Charles Gavan Duffy. Practiced for about ten years as a solicitor in London. Vain and self-sufficient. Likes to hear himself talk; will try to score points, even small ones; will attempt arguments in a legal manner." The stale odor of English condescension clung to the single typed page. "They are leaders in Dáil Éireann," it says by way of general comment, "which is a very nondescript assembly. They are absolutely without world experience, and considerable allowance will have to be made on this score. In overcoming their nervousness they may be a bit rude and extravagant in speech. . . . The two so-called secretaries," it notes, "although not delegates, are of consequence in the party and should not be underestimated. Christopher Blake spent several years in London as an editor and tried to make his way as a writer. Author of a book on early Irish history, over-lyrical, extravagant, not without charm. Took part in 1916 rebellion. Sinn Féin propagandist and intelligence officer. Friend of Michael Collins, and under his influence. The other 'secretary' is very different. Haileybury, Trinity Cambridge, civil servant, served with distinction in the Army in African War, Royal Navy in recent war. Holds reserve rank of Major. Skilled yachtsman. By now, a hardened fanatic and renegade. Close to De Valera. . . . Childers must not be underestimated, will operate in the background, demure civil servant. Watch him." Of Collins, it noted, " 'Minister of Finance' in Dáil Éireann, Chief of Intelligence in Irish Republican Army, so styled. Full of physical energy, quick thinker, impetuous, excitable. Strongest personality of party, capable of dominating all of them, save, perhaps, Childers and Griffith. A very dangerous man. He has murdered and has had murders done." In the margin of the copy which Eddie lent to me, his master had written, "His hands have touched the springs of murder. W.S.C."

Now, Christopher told Janice, there were two holdouts, Gavan Duffy and Bob Barton.

"Die for what?" Collins asked them. "Die for bloody what? By Jesus, if there is a new war in Ireland because the two of yez have refused to sign, there are lampposts in Dublin that the two of yez will be swinging from."

"That is a disgraceful argument to make, Mick," Childers said to him, "disgraceful."

"It is the truth of the matter," Collins said, "and we have no time to waste on Cambridge good manners. 'Twill not be our lads that will hang them, 'twill be the plain people of Dublin, the plain people of Ireland. We have hauled them along a long hard road, but we have come to its proper place."

"That," Childers said, his voice soft, held by iron control, "that agreement they have sent over to be signed. It was toward that that we have been leading the people?"

And in the end, Christopher told Janice, it was Duggan, not Collins, who turned the tide, Duggan whom the aide-mémoire dismissed with "Fought in 1916 rebellion; solicitor; completely under influence of Michael Collins. Neglible, and he knows it." First Duffy broke under the passion of Collins, under Griffith's arguments, and then, suddenly, as if a word by Collins had triggered it, Duggan cried to Barton, "You have served your time in Mountjoy, Bob, and so have I. I remember when Moran and Flood and the others were taken out and hanged. I saw the hangman. Will you send out more of our lads to be hanged because you don't like phrases on a piece of paper?"

"Phrases which time can change, boy," Collins said, "nothing is forever."

Dark night beyond the drawn curtains. During all this, Griffith had sat resolute and composed, certain in his feeling. "The signatures of the entire delegation are required, Bob."

"We are divided here," Childers said, "and so will the cabinet be and the Dáil and the nation."

But Barton shook his head. "I am sorry about this, I am not persuaded, but I will sign, let us sign the thing."

There may perhaps have been but the two policemen on point duty when they left Downing Street, but when they returned, close upon midnight, a half-dozen plain clothesmen came to the doors of the two taxis. Lloyd George and Birkenhead walked with them to the Cabinet Room.

"We are delighted to see you here," Lloyd George said to Griffith, "we were giving up hope. You are doing the proper thing, Mr. Griffith."

"There are some details of language which will require some redrafting," Griffith said. "An hour's work, perhaps."

"May we offer you something?" Birkenhead said. Griffith did not reply, but Collins shook his head.

It was after two before the redrafting was completed, a mechanical matter, and while they waited, there was polite talk, in bursts, across the table. "A wonderful night," Birkenhead said, speaking directly to Collins, "a wonderful night for our two nations."

"As much for this kingdom as for your own people," Sir Hamar Greenwood said, and he beamed across the table at all of the delegates who sat facing him. At two, they heard Big Ben strike, and ten minutes after that, the clear copies were brought in.

He could remember the words upon which the first paragraph closed, Christopher told Janice, "an executive responsible to that Parliament and shall be styled and known as the Irish Free State." They signed on the final page, the English delegates to the left of the page, and the Irish delegates to the right. After they had signed, the English delegates walked round the table and for the first time, officially at any rate, there were handshakes. Churchill shook Griffith's hand and then Collins's, the hand which had touched the springs of murder.

The air was cold, clear. Childers was standing by himself on the footpath, and Barton began to walk toward him and then paused. It was clear to all of them, to some of them at least, to Barton and to Christopher, that he was now standing alone, that he walked in silence with his grief and his anger.

"And that," Christopher said to Janice, "is how the Treaty was signed between Ireland and England." He looked down into his empty glass but when she reached for it, he shook his head.

* * *

The mailboat which carried Collins and Griffith back to Dublin docked at Kingstown on the morning of Thursday, December 8. There was a thin, chill wind in the air, stirring thin-branched winter trees. At Euston Station crowds, who had read of the Treaty in the papers, had followed the two men, and Christopher, who was accompanying them, jostling and shouting. Collins's hat, a trilby, was knocked off and left somewhere on the station platform, to be claimed as a souvenir. One of the press photographs shows him triumphant, an arm flung about Griffith, but in the others he appears preoccupied. One lingers over a photograph of Collins smiling at an elderly, heavyset man, broad smile of triumph, overcoat and jacket unbuttoned despite what must have been the cold, who is waving what might be a handkerchief, and perhaps shouting. There are other waving arms, grins, and toward the rear of the crowd a banner whose blurred letters are illegible.

In streaky dawn, Collins and Christopher had stood together at the railing looking toward a coast just visible. "PEACE IN IRELAND," one of the evening papers had said, in immense letters, "TREATY SIGNED." A newspaper hoarding, just visible at the edge of the crowd at Euston, carried a single word, illegible, which might have been "PEACE" or "IRELAND."

"An immense city," Collins said, "a labyrinth. But we hammered something out there, Chris. 'Tis done, signed and done."

Christopher waited for him to say more. They had spent the night like that, a few drinks in the bar, and another one, much later, in the cabin which they shared. For a few hours, they may have slept, or at least Christopher did, and when he woke to find Collins gone he went up on deck to join him.

"What is it that we are bringing back with us, they will ask. I can tell you this, we are bringing back with us something that Ireland needs and needs now."

"The Treaty is signed," Christopher said, "and you stand by it, Mick, and I stand by you."

"That is not much of a formula Chris, if you will excuse the bluntness. You are not a solicitor, Chris, but you are talking like one."

"We drove as hard a bargain as we could," Christopher said, "or rather, yourself and Mr. Griffith did. We brought the country back from the edge of war, and then moved off with the most that we could get."

"Not in Erskine's view," Collins said. "By God, I used to have a great fondness for that fellow, but he is like a field under water. Useless."

"You heard the crowd at Euston," Christopher said, "you saw them."

"London Irish," said Collins. "I know them through and through. I was London Irish myself for ten years or more. Whatever gives them a chance to wave the green banner."

"You are a hard man, Mick," Christopher said. "The Treaty went back to Dublin before us. We will know soon enough."

"Poor Duggan and poor FitzGerald," Collins said, and for once in the dawn light he smiled. "We shoved them into the line of fire." They had carried the Treaty with them to Dublin on the sixth, on the day of its signing, and delivered it that night to De Valera. In the morning, Duggan cabled Collins, "Document delivered, cabinet summoned by President." De Valera's wire reached Hans Place an hour later: "Urgent. Members of cabinet in London to report at once. Meeting fixed for December 8, noon."

"We know already," Collins said. "That was not a bouquet that Dev sent us."

"He is a frugal man when it comes to telegrams," Christopher said.

"The future has been put in our hand," Collins said. "We can stand now on our own two feet, develop our own civilization. After struggling for centuries." The words had a hollow echo, as though he were rehearsing them, but when Christopher said nothing, he burst out, in a more familiar manner, "We know damned well what they want, some of them, Brugha and O'Connor and Stack and those. They want a Republic, but a Republic is not on offer."

The coast was clear now, with mist drifting away, the town in view, a hotel, and along the seafront prim houses of the middle class, pastels, white, pale green.

"You live here, do you not?" Collins said.

"In Sandycove," Christopher said. "My mother lives there."

"Does she stand behind what you have been about, what we have been about?"

"More or less," Christopher said. "She is alone now, save for myself and a housekeeper. My father was a Redmond man, a friend of Redmond's, in fact. My brother was a medical man, he was killed in France a few weeks before the Armistice."

"By God," Collins said, "do you know, I cannot even be certain that my own family will stand behind me over this. West Cork people are fierce people, great tradition of patriotism there." Collins's family home, the farm at Sam's Cross, had been burned by the Black and Tans. Hatless, hat left behind on a train platform, he ran his hand through his hair.

Later, they had tea carried to them, and stood holding the warm cups against the morning chill.

"There is no great crowd there," Griffith said as he joined them. His face was expressionless, morning light glittered upon his eyeglasses. "This is not Euston Station, is it?"

People were gathered in knots, perhaps twenty of them or thirty, and the most of them were perhaps waiting for other passengers.

" 'Tumultuous ovation greets returning warriors,' " Collins said. " 'A grateful nation goes wild with gratitude.' "

"A bit early in the morning for tumult," Griffith said.

In the event, there were three old friends waiting for Griffith, and, for Collins and Christopher, three members of Collins's Squad, and Bill Sinnott, who had worked with Christopher in the intelligence bureau at the time of Bloody Sunday. Tom Cullen, of the Squad, was first up the gangway, and Collins seized him. "What is the country saying, Tom, what are our own lads saying?"

"The lads are with you, Mick," Cullen said. "If it is good enough for you, by God, it is good enough for them."

"But the country, Tom, have you a sense of the country?"

Cullen, it seemed to Christopher, was uncertain how he should answer: an urban fighter, a good man with a revolver. "Sure, why shouldn't they be for you everywhere, Mick. Haven't we won the war, the Treaty signed and all."

But on the pier, Christopher talked with Sinnott and Bob Bennett. "The fat's in the fire," Sinnott said. "That mean-spirited bastard, and his chums, Stack and Brugha. What the bloody hell did they want?" Christopher looked over at Collins, who was listening to Charlie Robinson; his hands were jammed into his overcoat pocket, and he had a sullen look.

"There is a cabinet meeting this noon," Christopher said.

"Nothing could be so bad, so soon." He remembered the crowd at Euston.

"They won't take what the Big Fellow signed," Sinnott said.

"Mick did not sign on his own, for God's sake," Christopher said, "the entire delegation signed."

Mrs. Griffith's hand rested on her husband's arm; she wore a heavy coat which she had bought in London, her one extravagance, dark wool, with a fur collar.

"The country will be quartered," Sinnott said. "Neither the Big Fellow nor Dick Mulcahy nor the two of them together will be able to hold the Army."

"It will not be that bad," Christopher said.

"Mind you," Sinnott said, "I stand by Collins."

But at noon, when the delegates and the members of the cabinet came to the Mansion House, it was a different matter. De Valera had given orders that there was to be no mention made in the press of Collins's and Griffith's arrival that morning, but by noon, Dublin knew of it in the papers, and knew that a cabinet meeting had been called. Not Dawson Street alone was jammed with people, but the streets leading off from it as well, and the delegates had to fight their way through cheers, and when Collins and Griffith arrived, together, someone in the crowd began singing, and other voices, hundreds of them, took up the words. "A nation once again, a nation once again."

Neither Griffith nor Collins gave any acknowledgment of either the song or the cheers. "Up Dev!" someone shouted. "Up Dev, up Mick, up the Republic."

XVIII

FRANK LACY

In early December, when negotiations in London were nearing their close, Lacy traveled northward to inspect the active service unit in Dunmaurice, at the edge of his division. He traveled in a Humber, a long saloon car of royal blue which his quartermaster had persuaded a landlord to lend to the army of the nation.

Lacy detested it. He had been using a secondhand Ford but three days before, on a training operation, it had broken down, and it was now in MacCarthy's garage in Kilpeder. Cogley, the Kilpeder chemist who had been MacCarthy's intelligence officer, was now Lacy's adjutant, and he was driving the Humber. They were in national uniform, the two of them, and Cogley wore his with flair, heavy greatcoat nipped in at the waist and the brim of his campaign hat pinned up. The insignia of a commandant rode on his shoulders. Lacy had not bothered with insignia, and he was hatless despite the chill of the winter day.

Ice lay in patches on the ground, and Cogley drove with great care. The road carried them through Millstreet and Kanturk, with the Derrynasaggarts to one side of them and the Boggeraghs to the other. The hills looked cold and bleak, and the hedges to either side of the road were leafless, brittle.

On the near side of Millstreet, still in the morning hours, they passed a farmer who had heard the noise of their approach, and stood to one side of the road, an elderly, tall, bent-shouldered man with a brown and white dog at his heels. He had time to peer into the car, and when he saw the uniforms he took off his cap and held it against his chest. "He may think that we are grandees," Cogley said, "or British colonels at the least." "He read us right enough," Lacy said, "the two of us got up like Hussars in an operetta and driving along in a blue circus wagon." The year before, when he and MacCarthy led the raid on the Millstreet barracks, they had worn bits and pieces of uniform, trench coats, bandoliers. In Millstreet, they passed the barracks, a blackened hulk in the wide street, facing a row of shops. Someone had strung green and orange bunting across its charred face, rain-bleached now and limp.

It had been strung up there, most likely, in the wild days of enthusiasm which followed upon the Truce in July. Six months before, on the July Sunday when the courier had brought Lacy at Lughnavalla House the dispatch from Mulcahy which made it official, church bells in Kilpeder ringing, trees stretching toward pasturelands were green, heavy-leafed, the boy said to him, " 'Tis won, Commandant. The war is won." Now the war was being fought at a table in Downing Street, and Lacy, like the other divisional commanders, was at work keeping his command on a war footing. His most recent dispatch told him that hostilities might resume in seventy-two hours.

In Kanturk, they stopped for tea in the hotel, and the girl brought it to them at a table drawn close to the fire. Vincent Carroll, the proprietor, was a friend of Cogley's, and he joined them.

"Did you hear that Dev was in Galway two days ago," he said, "and in Ennis yesterday? Dev and Cathal Brugha and General Mulcahy. In Galway, there was a review of the Galway army there, what is it called?"

"The Second Western Division," Cogley said. "Ennis is the First Western."

"Right," Carroll said, "the First Western Division of the Volunteers."

"The Irish Republican Army," Lacy corrected him. He preferred the more recent name. It said what they were about.

"My wife's nephew is with the Second, or however you call it," Carroll said, "he joined up in August and there is talk now that he will be made a lieutenant. My wife is a Galway woman. From Ballinasloe. Do you know Ballinasloe?"

"I know Haydon's Hotel," Lacy said, "and the RIC barracks across the road from it."

"My wife is related by marriage to that hotel," Carroll said, "or rather her first cousin is."

"The barracks is three stories," Lacy said, "a great solid hoor of a building. Dayroom to the left of the door, a small lockup to the rear."

"That's the one," Carroll said.

Since the Truce, young fellows had been joining the army in vast numbers. As soon as the rifle fire had died down, as soon as the terms of the Truce had put the Black and Tans on their best behavior. "Truceleers," Collins called them once in October, when Lacy reported to Headquarters in Dublin. "Truceleers," Collins said in the back bar of Vaughan's Hotel. "And if the Truce breaks down, they will vanish away like the wind that carried away your grandmother's last ha'penny. But what of the rest of us, with our snapshots in the newspapers, like rabbits forced up from their holes."

"Tell me, gentlemen," Carroll said, resting palms on fleshy thighs and signaling for fresh tea, "is there word of how matters are developing over in London?"

"If there is news, Vincent," Cogley said, "they have not bothered to send it down here to West Cork."

Their division, Lacy's and his, was the Third Southern, wedged between Lynch's to the east and O'Malley's to the west. And it was not quite candid of Cogley to pretend to such ignorance. The commanders in all three divisions knew that matters were being brought to a head. That was why they had been put upon seventy-two hours' notice.

"Ah well," Cogley said in the silence that followed, "we can only hope and pray."

"It would be a sorry blow," Carroll said, "if the fighting had to begin again, after these six blessed months of peace."

"Of truce," Lacy said, "not peace." He had unbuttoned his greatcoat, and its skirt fell upon his pistol in its low-slung holster.

Like the Wild West, Carroll thought, angrily. Cogley was a decent chap, first-rate, they had known each other for years, and in fact Carroll preferred him to the chemists in Kanturk and Millstreet. But Lacy was a sardonic, unsmiling fellow, quiet but with an edge of violence flickering like St. Elmo's fire. Carroll had met him only once before, but he had heard stories.

"A truce which may become a peace, please God," Carroll said.

"Please God," Lacy echoed politely.

"A decent fellow," Cogley said to Lacy as they drove out from Kanturk, past the great ruined MacCarthy castle, the walls stopping short at the corbels, "and he has always understood his obligations." When divisional funds ran out and HQ was late in sending a supplementary, Lacy would make a levy upon the countryside of his command, but everything noted down to the penny, receipts given, dated, pledges upon the future Republic. And Volunteers on their own were expected to pay for their own beer, whiskey, sandwiches, cups of tea. "Whether through patriotism or prudence does not matter," Cogley said.

"Within the present week," Cogley said, for at least the fifth time in the last two days, "mark my words, within a week those lads across will be coming back with a treaty signed."

"What kind of treaty?" Lacy said. Yesterday's *Examiner* had quoted Dev's words at Galway, when he reviewed the IRA. "This is a separate nation and never, till the end of time, will the English get from this nation allegiance to their rulers."

"Mick Collins is sitting over there at that table," Cogley said, "you can put your faith in the Big Fella. You have told me that often enough for the past year or more."

But Lacy veered away from the subject, almost. "Your man MacCarthy back there who built Kanturk's castle. He was a tough man in his time, until he went over to England."

Two rivers joined in Kanturk, the Dalua and the Allow: they flowed through Spenser's *Faerie Queene.* Half-remembered lines were a jumble in Lacy's mind.

"Have you read any Spenser?" he asked Cogley. "Edmund Spenser?"

"Jesus, Frank," Cogley said, his eyes fixed on the frozen road. "You ask the damnedest questions sometimes. We read the marriage one at school. 'Sweet Thames run softly till I end my song.' "

"Did they tell you at school that Spenser slaughtered us with sword and fire, starved us, here within these hills?"

"Did they not!" Cogley said. "I had my schooling from the Christian Brothers at the North Mon. They shoved the wrongdoings of the English down our throats like porridge." He spoke with teasing, faint irony of a history believed yet faintly doubted.

It was a well-traveled road, Lacy thought, as they bumped along the icy, rutted road northward to Dunmaurice, on their left a thin-iced pond edged by brittle sedge, a well-traveled road that carried Irishmen from home to London, sea road and road through Welsh mountains. Cogley had learned about it in his school, and Lacy in his. Con Bacach O'Neill had taken it in Tudor days, Con the Lame, Con the Cripple, wearing a fur-lined cape at the cost of twenty angels, ten pounds for a new escutcheon, kneeling before King Henry VIII and rising up as Earl of Tyrone. Twenty years later, another O'Neill, Sean an Diomas, Shane the Proud, had swaggered at Greenwich before Elizabeth with his band of gallowglass, too proud, the courtiers said, half-smiling, "to writhe his mouth in clattering English." Later, his murder was organized and carried out. Lacy and Cogley drove northwards through a landscape of shared history.

"Someday I may trust the English," Lacy said. "Some year. Not yet."

In modern times, in times which had ended barely five years before, Ireland had sent over her envoys to London, her Redmonds and Dillons and Healys. Once, young, Dillon had been fiery in the cause of the small farmers, courting arrest, prison, preaching sedition at torchlight rallies. Once, young, Redmond had stood beside the betrayed and abandoned Parnell. In the end, London had done for them as thoroughly as it had done for Con the Lame and Shane the Proud. Velvet-collared, silk-hatted, decorously bepaunched, they had become members of the Empire's finest club, the House of Commons.

Now, Ireland's fate rested with five Irishmen sitting at a table and facing a British prime minister and his cabinet.

By half after the noon hour, they had cleared a rise of hill, and saw the village of Dunmaurice spread before them, a Catholic church at one end of a short, straggling street of shops and public houses, and, at the other, a tidy, trim-spired Protestant church facing the gates of a demesne. Before they reached it, Cogley swerved the Humber to the left, and they drove down a narrow, deep-rutted road. Cogley, who like Lacy had paid earlier visits to the column, said, "Pray God we will make it, this road is barbaric in the freezing months."

Where a twisting boreen met it, a young fellow with a shotgun was lounging. He waved to the Humber. "You're welcome," he said, "go straight up to the house, but you had best go afoot. The boreen is not equal to the task." He looked to be seventeen, with an unformed face, a heavy brown down on his upper lip.

As Cogley climbed out, he said, "What is your name, boy?"

"Joe Rafferty," the boy said. He was holding the shotgun easily, in the crook of his arm, and looked like a lad out after rabbit or woodsnipe.

"And my name is Cogley. Not plain Cogley nor Ben Cogley, but when I am addressed by a Volunteer on active duty, my name is Commandant Cogley. Do you follow that? How long have you been in the army?"

"I follow that, Commandant," Rafferty said. He looked both impressed and annoyed. "For three months, Commandant. I was first in the Fianna, and then when I turned seventeen, I was allowed into the army."

Cogley smiled in spite of himself. "Allowed in. I like that. But you must mind your military manners. We are no longer fellows on the run, we are the national army."

"Yes, sir," Rafferty said, and shifted his shotgun awkwardly, as though uncertain whether or not to shoulder arms.

Lacy had walked straight up the boreen, and Cogley had to walk briskly to catch up with him.

"Bob Powers is running a damned sloppy operation," he said, "if that boy is an example of what we will find."

"Do you think so, Commandant Cogley?" Lacy said.

The road climbed steeply upward, and along one side ran a line of leafless birches. A bird, perched on a high branch, took fright at their movement, and rose quickly to circle above them.

"You know what I mean, Frank," Cogley said. "There is more need for discipline now than six months ago, when we were on the run."

He was right, Lacy knew. Six months of truce had left them in a kind of limbo, waiting for peace, waiting for war. Not easy, in this bleak, leafless winter, to remember the exhilarations of July, fellows who had been on the run for a year or more coming down from mountain huts and bothies, from safe houses with hidden rooms cunningly contrived. Against the terms of the truce, young officers of twenty would swagger into dances and public houses in full uniform, heavy revolvers snug in holsters. Discipline for men who had been on the run meant obedience to a signal from a curve of road, response to a warning shot. In those early weeks, early months, it was as though a war had been won, as though "truce" and "peace" were words with the same meaning.

Bob Powers, the commander of the column, had heard the footsteps on the hard-packed earth, and stood at the open door of the farmhouse, waiting for them. He was a good-looking fellow in his mid-twenties, black, tight curls crowding his campaign hat, his Volunteer's uniform unpressed but clean. He saluted smartly, and then stepped forward and shook their hands.

"Impressive, Bob," Cogley said. "A salute that would do credit to Sandhurst. You must teach it to Joe Rafferty below at the cross."

"Ach," Powers said, deprecating. "He's a young lad scarce out of the Fianna. He's clever, though; he learns quickly. You know who he is, do you not? He is the brother of Brendan Rafferty of Toor Hill."

"Jesus, no," Cogley said, remorseful. "I did not." Brendan Rafferty had been killed in May, in one of the last big ambushes, falling upon a grenade that a Tan hurled into his squad. "And I am after dressing him down." In moments of stress, Cogley's urbanity of speech, Kilpeder's leading chemist, would fall away from him.

"It did him no harm," Powers said.

"The new national uniforms," Lacy said, "should carry identifying insignia. 'Volunteer Joe Rafferty, brother of Brendan Rafferty.' "

Cogley and Powers exchanged annoyed looks. Lacy took pleasure from blasphemy, sucking at it like a hollow tooth.

"Come on in," Powers said, "you look to be in need of tea." They followed him into the empty kitchen.

"Are you holding the fort here, just the two of you," Lacy said, "yourself and Joe Rafferty?"

Two long deal tables ran down the length of the kitchen, side by side, with benches and an assortment of straight-backed chairs drawn up to them.

"Would you believe," Powers said, as he walked to the fire for the kettle, "that this morning thirty-one men had their breakfasts in here? We have a cook squad, and a cleanup squad. We are turning into a regular army."

"You seem to be missing twenty-nine men," Lacy said.

"Not missing," Powers said. "You are the cause of it all. They have all been sent off on a training exercise, and they wait only for yourselves to give the signal. I have them divided into two batches, Dinny Noonan in command of one, and Sparky Moynihan the other." Noonan and Moynihan were his lieutenants. "I have laid out an ambush plan. Dinny's lads are our lads, and Sparky's lads are the Tans."

"You should have asked the Tans up," Lacy said. "From Kilpeder or from Bandon. The Tans are getting as slack as our own people. They could use the exercise. A few months ago, some of our lads in Kilpeder began drinking in Conefry's with the Tans, having a singsong and exchanging war stories. I put a stop to that. We may go back to killing those lads, I told them, and it is always hard to kill friends."

Powers was pouring water into the teapot from the steaming kettle.

"Jesus," he said, "is it likely to come to that?"

"We have been put on seventy-two hours' notice," Cogley said, "as of yesterday. I have sent word out to the brigades, and we are carrying it up here ourselves."

"I cannot believe that," Powers said, "meaning no disrespect to your rank. Six months without action, and then seventy-two hours. There are many in this part of the country who would be reluctant to take up the fight again."

"Not yourself, though," Cogley said.

"No," Powers said, and he set down the kettle on the hob. "Not myself, but I would like to know what I am expected to do the fighting with. Only half of the lads have weapons."

"And you with a training exercise laid on," Cogley said.

When the tea had been poured, Lacy picked up his and said, "A few miles across the border, in Second Southern, there was a raid two weeks ago on the British Army hutments. Seventy rifles were taken and two machine guns and a quantity of ammunition. The British are raging about Treaty violations, and O'Malley has been hauled on the carpet in Dublin with the Big Fellow shouting at him on one of his trips home from Downing Street."

"I can imagine," Powers said.

"You would not know anything about that, would you?" Cogley said.

"Me?" Powers widened blue eyes above his cup. "Tell Ernie

O'Malley to put the question to his Tipperary ruffians, Breen and Robinson and that crowd."

"You would never be tempted, would you," Lacy said, "to slip over the county line into Second Division."

"Indeed I would not," Powers said. "I have some Huntley and Palmer tea biscuits for you."

"Packed in with the rifles were they?" Lacy said.

"By God," Powers said, blue-eyed mischief, "it must have been an event, O'Malley standing at attention while Collins shouts at him. And all for a few British rifles. We can all mind a time when a stunt like that would have earned O'Malley a commendation. He loves to be commended, have you noticed that about him?"

The training exercise was as boring as Lacy had expected it to be, although Cogley threw himself into it, examining the ambush position, and criticizing the way in which Sparky Moynihan deployed his men behind their imaginary tender. Joe Rafferty was an enthusiastic participant, leveling at the enemy a rake handle which was standing in as a rifle. If Powers's column had raided the British hutments, he was keeping their weapons well hidden. But it was more probably Breen's Tipperary column: Breen took a cavalier attitude toward the terms of the Treaty.

Lacy wandered off by himself, leaped a narrow, frozen stream and climbed a hill behind the house. From its slope, heather-covered, he could look down upon the mock battle, almost ending now with a surrender by the Tans, and beyond it toward, far off, the Ballyhouras in Tipperary. The sky was as blank and chill as ever, but there was a wonderful clarity in the air, and the mountains were clearly etched, browns and dark blues against the pale blue of the sky.

The early darkness of winter had almost closed in upon them by the time they all sat down to a meal, eggs and greasy rashers, thick-sliced bread smeared with butter, all washed down with cup after cup of sweetened tea. Lacy imagined his parents at that hour, in the heavy-wooded dining room in Kilkenny, tea in cups eggshell thin, thin-sliced cake studded with ruby-colored currants.

It was after their tea when, in the near distance, they heard the sound of an approaching motor. When the motor was cut off, they waited. Powers turned low the paraffin lamp, and Moynihan walked to the kitchen window.

"It will take them a good five minutes to walk here," Powers said, but the door burst open, and a young fellow who had replaced Joe Rafferty as sentry opened the door and said, " 'Tis safe enough, lads. 'Tis Ernie O'Malley."

"By God, lads," O'Malley said, "you have been dining well. I put on speed to get here."

Powers turned up the lamp.

He knows how to make an entrance, Lacy thought. He was dressed not in uniform but in high boots, a belted leather jacket, with a heavy automatic holstered to the belt, and he was hatless.

O'Malley talked as he ate, and the lads of the column pulled their chairs and benches closer to him, but unobtrusively. He had a flair for narrative, a sense of telling detail, and his stories were laced with wit.

He was on his way back to his division from County Clare, where he had been summoned to exhibit to De Valera and Brugha and Mulcahy the artillery piece which was the pride of the division. He and Bob de Courcy, his munitions officer, had loaded the gun onto a flatbed and shepherded gun and crew across the Shannon, where a guide met them and led them to a field. De Valera and Brugha and Mulcahy were waiting for him, Mulcahy in uniform as chief of staff, but De Valera and Brugha in civilian clothes as president of the Republic and minister of defense.

"But they had an escort finely turned out," O'Malley said, "you may be sure of that, looking like the Pope's Swiss Guard. I was a bit nervous. She had been testing well at home, and Rory O'Connor had passed on her, but you never know with these homemade creations. There was a bad time there in Kerry last year when the barrel of Kerry's pride and joy exploded and drove splinters of steel into its poor creator, and cut open the jaw of an innocent Volunteer. But things were far better today. We banged away at a pile of stones set up for a target, first with empties and then with live ammo. Cathal Brugha looked as close to happy as he ever gets. He went hopping after the shells to measure the distance. 'If we go back into action in a few days,' he said, 'we will have our artillery.' "

He made the final point in the same bantering, enthusiastic tones, but Lacy saw that the Volunteers exchanged looks.

"Dick Mulcahy," O'Malley said, "invited me to join him for

dinner this night with the Bishop of Killaloe, but I'm anxious to get back to Tipperary. There is much to do if we are getting back on a war footing. I'll stay here the night, with the permission of you lads, and be off by first light."

"Are you shifting your headquarters?" Lacy asked him.

"We are, where we are staying now is known to all, by the Tans and the British Army and any number of strollers. Before I left yesterday, I gave orders to burn our papers."

"Things are looking up for the good old cause," Moynihan said, "when bishops have places for them at table."

"Tell me, Ernie," Cogley said, "is that the new uniform for the Corps of Artillery?"

O'Malley's smile was not entirely affable, but Lacy was with him. The uniform made him feel stiff and awkward, and he wore it with reluctance.

"It was all well and good," O'Malley said, "a grand occasion. De Valera has a great sense of occasion, you have a sense of him as president of the Republic, a courteous, formal fellow, but he can unbend, he has a shy, sweet smile. Brugha and Mulcahy took me aside and began badgering me about that raid for rifles on the British hutments in Tipperary. I don't expect ever to hear the end of that."

"Dreadful," Powers said, and O'Malley looked at him sharply.

It was only later, when the three of them were sitting together in the small room with cots beyond the kitchen, Lacy and O'Malley and Cogley, that Cogley produced a half-bottle of whiskey and passed it round.

"What did you hear, Ernie?" Lacy said.

"Nothing," O'Malley said, "nothing that was said directly, you may be certain of that, mum was the word, amongst the grandees, and that word had been passed along to their staff. But they were tense as cats, Dev was in particular and Brugha. It's all coming to the boil, lads. Dev spoke at Sixmilecross, when he reviewed the First Western, and twice he said that we will never give allegiance to a foreign crown, and he said the same at Ennis. He laid stress on it."

"Well he might," Lacy said, "well he might. By God, we took an oath to uphold the Republic."

O'Malley nodded and their eyes met and locked.

Cogley stood up and walked to the window. A quarter-moon was pale, cloud-shrouded.

In the morning, the three of them made an early start, driving down the narrow, twisting road, and parting outside Dunmaurice. They paused there, and O'Malley left his long, pale-gray motorcar and walked over to the Humber.

"We should keep in touch with each other, Frank, yourself and myself and Liam Lynch in Cork. There is no telling which way the cat will jump." He reached into the car and shook hands with the two of them, and they waited until he had driven off eastwards, toward his command in Tipperary.

That was on the sixth. On the next day, on Wednesday, they learned which way the cat had jumped, and they learned about it as everyone in the country learned, as De Valera himself learned of it, from newspapers which carried the text of the treaty which had been signed in London.

Lughnavalla House learned of it from the *Cork Examiner,* the newspaper spread out on the reading table in the study. They read it to themselves, or half-aloud but speaking to themselves and not each other, and when Cogley would move to turn the page, MacCarthy, a slow reader, would put a restraining hand on his. After a time, Lacy moved back from the table and walked to the window. There was a fine mist of rain falling on the dead garden, and on the dead winter lawn which ran down to the small frozen lake.

"It says it here," MacCarthy said, "it gives the very words of the oath. 'And that I will be faithful to His Majesty King George the Fifth, his heirs and successors by law in virtue of the common citizenship of Ireland and Great Britain.' It gives the words of it here."

"For God's sake, Pat," Ben said. "Will you give over? We know what it says. We can all read." He called across the room for a second time. "Frank?" But Lacy neither spoke nor turned to him.

"It was signed by all of them, you know," Cogley said to the stiff back, unyielding or stunned Cogley could not tell. "By all of them, you know. By Mick Collins as much as by the others."

And when Lacy did not answer, Cogley turned back to the newspaper, and read through the text again.

"He did not sign for me," Lacy said. "Neither Mick Collins nor any of the others."

"Take another read of it, for God's sake," Cogley said. "Listen to the first article. " 'With a Parliament having powers to make laws for the peace, order and good government of Ireland and an executive responsible to that Parliament, and shall be styled and known as the Irish Free State.' That does not sound so fearsome."

But Lacy did not answer him. Above the frozen lake, two rooks wheeled, and Lacy studied the pattern of the flight. There was an old saw about magpies, one for joy and two for sorrow. What of rooks, black-plumed, no splash of white?

MacCarthy, aware of the tension in the room without fully understanding it, stepped away from the table, and took from a capacious pocket his weathered pipe and its pouch of tobacco.

"The good government of Ireland," Lacy said at last, but without turning away from the window. "Of a part of Ireland is what they mean. They accept that the country is split into two, and they leave part of our people trapped north of a border. They have bartered away a part of Ireland, so that they can call the other part a Free State faithful to the King of England."

"You can read it that way if you choose, Frank, but—"

MacCarthy's match made a faint crack as he lit it, and Cogley glanced for a moment toward the sound. MacCarthy had come to Lughnavalla from his garage, and the furrows on his broad, capable hands were lined with grease. There was a streak of grease along one cheek.

"I can read plain English," Lacy said.

"So can the cabinet," Cogley said, "and so can the members of Dáil Éireann. Most of them. The cabinet will have something to say, and then the Treaty must be put to the vote in the Dáil. Nothing is final."

With a final, wheeling arc, the rooks flew from view, and Lacy turned round.

"The *Cork Examiner*," he said, "has cast its vote already."

"The vast majority of Southern Irishmen," the newspaper declared in boldface, in words set off and boxed, "will accept this treaty with joy, the honorable resolution of an ancient quarrel."

"I am damned if I can see what you lads are quarreling

about," MacCarthy said, holding his pipe between clenched teeth, and striking a second match. "Kilpeder will be wild with excitement today, and we should be below there with the lads."

"We are not quarreling," Cogley said, but without taking his eyes from Lacy's set, strained face. "Are we, Frank?"

"No," Lacy said, "of course we are not, Pat. Of course not. It takes a while for great changes to sink in."

"That's right," Cogley said, "it takes a while." But his eyes and Lacy's met above the words, and Lacy's eyes, he saw, were furious.

After Cogley and MacCarthy had left, Lacy walked aimlessly from room to room of Lughnavalla House, pausing with unseeing eyes before framed sepia photographs of cricketeers, of a tennis match, of two young men and an elderly man (father? uncle?) kitted out for a day's shooting, pouches slung from one shoulder, shotguns cradled. He halted in the room which he had come to think of as his own, the room with books scattered along its shelves.

From a cabinet below one of the shelves, he took out whiskey and whiskey glass and filled the glass half-full, sipped from it, and carried it down the hall and out to the graveled entranceway. Beyond, the air was chill but not freezing, although there was a heavy wind coming down from the Derrynasaggarts. He began to sip again, but instead, before the glass reached his lips, he hurled it away on a long arc. It fell on the gravel.

He walked down the lawns, past the ruined garden, to the lake, and, crouching, tested its layer of thin ice. When he stood up again, he studied the empty, cloudless sky.

As he had walked down the hall, glass in hand, there came suddenly into mind Conor Goff, the Volunteer in Kilkenny whose execution he had ordered. He remembered Goff standing against a tree, at once terrified and bewildered, saying, over and over, "Blessed art thou amongst women," and he remembered the three appalled riflemen of the execution squad. He remembered the rank, wet grasses of the field through which they had walked across to the tree, Conor Goff stumbling and supported by one of the riflemen. He could remember everything save how he himself had felt in that hour, as though his feelings had been placed on a block of ice in a cool cellar.

After a while, he walked back into Lughnavalla House, and noticed, having formed the habit of observation, that the wind was dying down a bit.

XIX

ELIZABETH KEATING

On the noon of December 8, when the full cabinet was to meet for the first time since the signing of the Treaty, Elizabeth Keating fought her way through the crowd gathered about the Mansion House, carrying small tricolors, many of them, and many of them with tricolor rosettes pinned to their winter coats. It was a clear, cold day. She heard what she thought were the sounds of hundreds of voices, but in fact most in the crowd stood watching and waiting in good-humored silence.

"You just missed Cathal Brugha himself," a woman standing beside her said, and Elizabeth, abstracted, smiled her thanks and nodded. "He is terrible serious, that fellow," the woman said. "There was a cheer went up for him, but he gave no look to left nor right." The words confirmed the image shaped by Elizabeth's imagination. In six months, they had become faces familiar everywhere in Dublin. Before that, names moving in shadows.

"Is Mr. Collins here?" Elizabeth asked.

"Not yet," the woman said. "He's the lad we're waiting for. The boy who won the war, the boy who bet England."

But Collins's arrival, twenty minutes later, was a letdown. The crowd did its part, letting out a great shout, within which she could distinguish words, "Mick, Mick, Mick," a boy shouted in shrill soprano. And before Collins could reach the door of the Mansion House, they had him almost encircled, but there were no answering grins from him today, no hands joined above his head. Someone shouted a question to him, and he turned a head toward the questioner, whether curious or angry Elizabeth could not tell, and then one of the fellows from his Squad was ahead of him, opening the door.

"Terrible solemn they are today," the woman said, "and why not, on such an occasion."

There was no need for Elizabeth to reply. Someone else was arriving, and the crowd set up a fresh shout. The banners were waved again from side to side, and someone shouted, "Up the Republic," but whether in triumph or defiance she could not tell. She surrendered her place, and made her way down Dawson Street.

Earlier that morning, hurrying to her office, she had encountered Kathleen Riordan, a friend of hers from Prisoners' Aid. She was wearing one of the tricolor rosettes, and her cheeks were flushed. "I am just back from Kilmainham," she said. "Where were you? You were asked after. My God, what a day, Elizabeth, what a day!" She seized Elizabeth's arm.

Elizabeth looked at her a moment, puzzled, and then nodded. She knew that the prisoners were to be released that morning, some of them, that is, from Kilmainham and Mountjoy.

"Oh, dear God, Elizabeth," Kathleen Riordan said. "It was a lovely morning. There were a few motorcars laid on, and jaunting cars would you believe it, and a milk float, and whatever kinds of conveyance could be pressed into service. But that was far from sufficient for Kilmainham alone, let alone Mountjoy and Ballykinlar. They came out at Kilmainham through those great awful gates, carrying their parcels and looking fit the most of them. Oh, Elizabeth, had you only been there!"

"A splendid morning," Elizabeth said, "a splendid morning to be sure." And it was still early. As they stood talking, an island of two, men walking to work passed them to either side. Two young fellows who caught sight of Kathleen's rosette smiled and gave her the thumbs-up sign.

"Mind you," Kathleen said, "there are many of our lads still behind bars. It is the political internees only who have been released, and not any of our lads who have been convicted in their courts, nor those who are waiting their trials."

"Yes," Elizabeth said. "I know."

"But of course," Kathleen said, "they will be released straightaway once the Treaty has been ratified."

"Yes," Elizabeth said again, "I know. And there is one more

powerful reason to ratify the Treaty." Because she did not want to spoil Kathleen's morning, she kept bitterness and irony out of her words.

"Oh, Elizabeth," Kathleen Riordan said, "do you remember that terrible morning outside Mountjoy, the great crowd of us kneeling in that gray morning light outside Mountjoy, in that spitting dreary rain, kneeling to the rosary while the four of our lads were hanged within, poor Joe Gaffney and poor Terrence O'Brien and the other lads. A May morning, but as chill as winter. And the Tans in their armored cars. Oh, Elizabeth, what a difference!"

Elizabeth kissed her cheek, a cheek at once flushed and chill, and imagined the taste of dried tears. Then she turned and walked along the quays, past the Four Courts, and turned north to her office in Mary Street.

It was to that office, the morning before, that she carried the newspapers, all of them, the *Independent*, and the *Freeman's Journal*, and the *Irish Times*. Later in the day, one of the two young women who helped her in the editing of the *Republican Bulletin* would come in, bringing galleys from the printer's, but for the hour, at least, Elizabeth had the small, neat room to herself. All three of the newspapers carried portions of the Treaty's text, and by matching them up against each other, she had a fairly good sense of its provisions. All three made it a point that all of the delegates had signed, all of the English delegates, Lloyd George and Churchill and Birkenhead, and all of the Irish, Collins and Griffith and the others. The *Freeman's Journal* assured its readers that the Irishmen had signed in Irish. Art Ó Gríobhtha and Micheál Ó Coileáin and so forth.

Elizabeth reached into her pocket and took out her packet of cigarettes, and, as she read for perhaps the fifth time the fourth article of agreement and the language of the oath, she absently waved away smoke from her pale blue eyes. . . . *and that I will be faithful to H.M. King George V. . . .*

For all of that morning, or the better part of it, alone in the office, standing by the window and looking down into the street of shops, she had the odd and frightening conviction that she alone responded as she did to the news. From time to time, she would see acquaintances talking to each other, laughing, one clapping the other on the back, and would imagine that they were talking to each other in delight and triumph. Perhaps, she thought, the words held a meaning which escaped her, some subtlety of phrase, but she was certain that this was not the case. What the Treaty said could be distilled down to its essence: the Republic had been abandoned for half an island and something called a Free State. And it had been signed by Griffith, the creator of Sinn Féin, and by Collins, with the approval, for all she knew, of the entire cabinet.

Once, in April, in one of the final months before the Treaty, the office had been raided by the Tans, a half-dozen of them under the command of a rangy, sardonic captain, his glengarry cocked jauntily to one side, and accompanied by an elderly, phlegmatic inspector of police in civilian clothes. Elizabeth had asked to see his warrant, and the captain had smiled with delight, and set his men to work emptying papers and dead galleys from shelves and wardrobes, back issues, and carrying them to the inspector, who had seated himself at Elizabeth's desk. Patricia Gunning, Elizabeth's assistant, stood by the dusty, uncurtained window, a hand to her throat. All the correspondence, and the copies of Elizabeth's letters were in two folders in the desk, and the inspector devoted all of his attention to these, reading through them slowly, his ill-fitting dentures chewing steadily at an imaginary cud. While he was at work, the Tans lounged against a wall, and the captain read through one of the issues of the *Republican Bulletin*. "Are the articles yours, signed 'Granuaile,' Miss Keating?"

"No," she said truthfully.

"I am relieved to hear that," he said, " 'Granuaile' has a barbarous style, vivid but barbarous."

"I stand over what is written in the *Bulletin*," Elizabeth said. Privately, she quite agreed with the captain. "Granuaile" was a young woman named Henchey, with a fondness for lurid prose.

"There is nothing here," the inspector said at last. "There is no point in taking it away, even. Calculations of printing expenses, and a few letters. There is even a poem," he concluded with mild distaste.

"There you are," the captain said to Elizabeth and nodding toward the inspector, "the arts suffer in time of war."

As they were leaving, one of the Tans walked to the reproduction of the Proclamation tacked to one wall, and, lifting his rifle, ripped it in two with the front sight.

"That will do," the captain said. "Far better prose there," he said to Elizabeth. "'In the name of God and of the dead generations.' Stay out of trouble, now." He waited until his men were climbing down the stairs, and then saluted the two of them, Elizabeth and Patricia, and left.

When the clatter of boots on the stairs had died down, Patricia said, "Bastard!" "Not really," Elizabeth said. She retacked the Proclamation but left it in two pieces, a reminder.

Now, she rested her back against the wall, standing by the window, facing, without really seeing, the ripped Proclamation. "In the name of God and of the dead generations." "The Republic of Ireland."

By late morning, she could stand her feelings no longer, and, putting on her hat and her heavy coat of black, fur-trimmed wool, she left the office and walked back along the quays and up Sackville Street almost to the square, then turned left to the Ministry of Defense. The front room was crowded with men, some of whom she knew, and one woman, a young typist, sitting at a small desk close to a window. Elizabeth gave her name to the guard, and waited in the tobacco-heavy air, air heavy with the dark wool of overcoats. Half of the men, at least, were in national uniform, and she smiled at her chum Paddy Tansey from the midlands. He was moving over to speak with her, when the guard came back to bring her in to William Considine, Cathal Brugha's deputy.

He rose up when she came in, took her two hands in his and kissed her cheek. His own cheek was rough, as though he had shaved carelessly, and the iron-gray hair looked uncombed. "This is terrible," he said, and, closing the door, he led her to the straight chair beside the table at which he worked. "This is terrible," he said again, and with those three words she was reassured that she was not alone in Dublin, in Ireland.

"How did it happen?" she said, "how in God's name did it happen?"

"It should not have happened. It need not have happened. They were under strict orders that any articles or any treaty must be brought back here before signing. But this Treaty, as they call it, was not. Dev learned about it from the newspapers, as all of us did, after he came back to Dublin from the West. From an English newspaper, as it happens."

"Do you mind?" she said, looking toward the packet of cigarettes on the table, and he lit one for her but without pleasure. Considine was strict in his ways, and did not like to see women smoking.

"We'll not have long to talk," he said. "Everything is topsy-turvy at the moment. Collins is still in London, but he has been summoned back, they all have. Dev has called a cabinet meeting for noon tomorrow."

Not "Mick" this morning she noticed, nor "Michael Collins," nor even the formal "Mr. Collins" which Cathal Brugha favored.

"But they all signed it," she said.

"Oh, yes," he said. "They all signed it. And three of them are cabinet members themselves. We can expect a split in the cabinet. But it is not quite as bad as it looks, not quite as bad. The cabinet can only advise, it is the Dáil itself which must decide whether it wants this thing or not."

"Have you walked along the streets, Bill?" she said. "Have you heard people? It is as though we have won a famous victory, as though those people were coming back to us with the Republic."

"Yes," Considine said, "of course I have heard people. But I will tell you this, you will hear different talk from the fellows in the room beyond. There are angry men in that room. As there will be in the Dáil, and in the country when once it has been grasped that the Republic has been sworn away and signed away by men pledged to uphold it. I was with Dev and with Cathal in Galway and in Clare, you know. And each time that he spoke, Dev went out of his way to tell those who heard him that the people of Ireland will never swear allegiance to a foreign king."

"And while he was telling them that, those fellows over in London were putting their names onto paper with Lloyd George's name and Churchill's."

The quaver in Elizabeth's voice surprised and angered her, and her hand shook as she crushed the half-smoked cigarette in a tin ashtray.

Considine put his hand on hers, and held it close to the wrist, affectionate but impersonal.

"I cannot spare you much time," he said. "I am sorry. You can see the way things are."

"Yes," she said, "yes, of course." He drew back his hand, and she stood up.

It was only when she had reached the door that he called out to her: "Your paper is called the *Republican Bulletin,* Elizabeth. Don't forget that. It may be of great help to us in the days that are coming." He had half-risen, but it was plain to her that his thoughts were elsewhere.

When she went down the hall into the front room, she looked for Paddy Tansey, but he was gone.

She had half-turned to seek out a few close friends that evening, but instead she went back to her office and worked on her galleys, treated herself to an early meal alone in Bewley's, and then went home. In Bewley's she sat at a table close to three women who had been shopping in Switzer's. One of them, a large women named Florence, was the wife of a surgeon, who was going to take her to the South of France and perhaps Rome in February. "The Eternal City," one of the other women said, envious and awed: "I would give anything to see the Eternal City and Saint Peter's." "Now that all the Troubles are over," Florence said, "such wonderful news." "Do you know," the third woman said, slender with a close-fitting brown hat, "it was not as bad as people are forever making out. Except for the armored cars and the Crossleys and the Tans shouting out horrible things as they drove past." "Once," Florence said, "two gunmen brought a wounded man into Brendan's surgery to be stitched up."

At home, Elizabeth changed into a dressing gown, and sat in her armchair to read, sherry and a packet of cigarettes beside her. She had all week been reading *La Cousine Bette* in translation, Balzac carrying her within a paragraph to Paris and its dreadful household, the excitements of the boulevards. But tonight, as she had feared, he was unable to hold her attention, and after a half-hour she closed the book.

For a time she stood, cigarette between long, thin fingers, and looked out into the winter garden, light from a half-moon falling faintly upon two wide-mouthed, fluted urns. She tried to remember the urns as they had looked in summer heat and sunlight, blossoms violet and magenta on long, weak stalks falling over the mouths, almost touching tall, ornamental grasses.

Then she poured out a stiff sherry, carried it to the bed and lay down. Across the room, shadowed, a Renaissance madonna and child, eyes cloaked in darkness. When sunlight fell upon the reproduction, the madonna's robe was pale blue, the child's hair golden and curling.

Her memories were a jumble. The rainy morning when she knelt with the crowd outside Mountjoy Gaol, and the Custom House in flames, flames licking toward the imperial unicorn and lion, Terence MacSwiney on hunger strike in Brixton, and the funeral, in a Wicklow graveyard, of a Volunteer killed in action on a lonely road outside Blessington. In the snug of a public house off North Earl Street, Frank Lacy described a raid on a barracks in Clare, his words, careless but vivid, shaping from smoky Dublin air a countryside of tumbled hills, winding roads.

She lay for an hour or more, apprehensive and soiled, as though not merely the Republic had been betrayed, but some part of the self which for two years she had been shaping. Then, at last, she turned off the light.

Next morning, in her office but unable to work on galleys which needed her attention, she smoked cigarette after cigarette until, toward noon, she walked to the Mansion House, where she arrived not quite in time to see Cathal Brugha, lame skipping walk, but in time to see Michael Collins arrive, to hear the crowd cheering him. She remembered, as she walked down Dawson Street, Kathleen Riordan's joy as she described the prisoners released from Kilmainham, and tried, wanly, to persuade herself that their release was worth the sacrifice of the Republic. But she could not.

The cabinet meeting lasted until five that evening, and it ended with a split.

"What I signed I will stand by," Arthur Griffith said, "in the belief that the end of the conflict of centuries is at hand."

But De Valera said, "The terms of this disagreement are in violent conflict with the wishes of the majority of this nation. The greatest test of our people has come. Let us face it worthily, without bitterness and without recrimination."

When the country was at war with itself, Cathal Brugha talked with Elizabeth. "That cabinet meeting almost did not take place at all. There were commandants who wanted the delegates arrested for high treason as soon as they stepped off the gangplank onto Irish soil. But I forbade it. I now know that I was wrong." And privately, Elizabeth agreed with him that it should all have ended at the outset, with the arrest of the men who had signed away the Republic.

On that December night, Elizabeth lay sleepless, as she had the night before, but thinking now of Kathleen Riordan and the released prisoners, and of the crowd cheering the unsmiling Collins as he hurried into the Mansion House. It was not Collins who dismayed her, so much as the crowd and its cheers. They could not understand, could not yet understand, how much had been sold away or bargained away. Somehow, she did not know how, somehow the Republic would endure, despite crowds, despite Collins and the others who had signed that shameful Treaty.

XX

JANICE NUGENT

On December 22, I crossed over to Ireland, and Christopher and I motored to Coolater for Christmas.

I have always cherished secretly a child's fierce, warm, protected love of Christmas, and without ever knowing quite why. At first, of course, I thought that everyone loved it as I did, other children, parents, servants, shopkeepers, the red-and-green-and silver-spangled dancers in the pantomime. Only when I was a young woman did I discover, slowly and resentfully, that for most people, even for Father, even for Betty, Christmas was simply a very, very nice time of year, affectionate and sociable, a blazing Yule log to fight off the sniffles and bone chills of winter. Yule logs and holly and candles in the window for the Christ child and gifts of course and Dickens and a crèche.

Once, the Christmas that was midway between Charlie's death and Christopher's appearance in my life, I remember Betty telling me that she and Father hadn't been quite certain that I would be home that December. I had seemed from my letters to be so busy in London. Not come home, how could I not come home? Home was the center of all, and without Christmas the center would be sent wobbling off balance like a disturbed top. "To be sure," Betty said, "I had forgotten, you would miss the parties here and the dance at the Jelliffes'. You are an incorrigible flirt, Janice. But surely there are far grander parties in London." Betty, of course, was teasing me. I was out of mourning by then, but decorum was expected of young war widows. And now, from my jaded heights in the metropolis, I might be expected to smile down upon the

Havilland party as dowdy and provincial, as no doubt it was, but when Betty and I had first been old enough to attend, it had seemed part of Christmas's mystery, the men splendid in black and ivory and the women in ball gowns, flashes of red, lime, cherry, puce.

Part of Christmas's mystery, but not its secret center. Every year, in late November, the special Christmas number of the *Illustrated London News* would arrive, with its reproductions of Renaissance madonnas, and appallingly trite, as I later realized, novellas about the hearts of the jaded being melted by a cathedral choir, color illustrations of tales out of Grimm, and photographs of pantomimes, the principal boys who were really girls in their innocently seductive tights, their unbound and always golden hair. And even the advertisements, things that fathers would like for Christmas, walnut pipes and gold fountain pens and leather folders in which to carry motoring maps. After Betty had been given a fair chance to read it, I would take away the special Christmas number and hide it, in my bedroom after I had one of my own or in the tackroom with its Christmassy smell of leather and gun metal.

In the newspapers on Tuesday, the twentieth, Christopher's name appeared, Mr. Christopher Blake, a member of Dáil Éireann for South Wexford. For three days, the Dáil had been discussing the Treaty in closed session, but now, just before the Christmas recess, it was in public session, and there, quoted in the newspapers along with Collins and De Valera and obscure members from Kerry and Donegal and my own Galway, was Mr. Christopher Blake, speaking, as the *Times* put it, "with quiet intensity" in support of the Treaty against its enemies.

"Good for that chap of yours," Louise Greene said to me that night when we were both having dinner at the Robinsons'. "I expect you saw him in the newspapers. What in the world are those gunmen over there, what are they about? The whole thing sorted out, so everyone thought, and now they don't want their Home Rule or whatever it is."

"Whatever it is," I said agreeably.

But Alex Robinson, who had overheard us, explained it all to us, how the Treaty didn't give the Irish their Republic, but did give them the next best thing, after all, and now they were quibbling over words like "faithful" and "allegiance." Alex was very liberal and advanced in his views, youngish but with a paunch and receding hair which he set off against a neat, cropped beard.

"I must say, Janice," he said, "your chap comes off well, at least from what I saw quoted in the *Times*."

"Yes," I said, while my mind cast round for a way to change the subject.

"I mean to say," Alex Robinson said, "the gunman-in-chief signed, Michael Collins signed, a fellow who would as soon shoot you as look at you. Why cannot the minor gunmen take a lead from him? That is your Christopher's point, is it not, dear?"

"Not quite," I said, but we dropped the matter, they did not really care, either of them. Diaghilev had brought back *The Sleeping Beauty* with a new and sumptuous decor by Bakst, and had I seen it yet, at the Alhambra? This was closer to them, really, than peace or war in Ireland, and I did not blame them. Later that evening, a journalist just back from Vienna was telling me of the riots there, led by the "Communists," he said, thousands upon thousands of them, smashing restaurants and rampaging through hotels and attacking the parliament building, placards and torches, and finally, too long delayed, a massive attack by the police or was it the army? And it meant as much to me as the debate in Dublin meant to Louise Greene and Alex Robinson. I remembered newsreels of other riots in other cities, Berlin, Warsaw, grainy images of men in caps and mounted policemen. But when they spoke of Diaghilev and the Russian dancers, colors flooded my imagination.

I told all this to Christopher as we were motoring westwards on Thursday morning in the elaborate car which Myles Keough had lent him, fitted out with mirrors and windscreens that caught the winter sun.

"You should have gone," he said, "*The Sleeping Beauty* is as good as one of your Christmas pantos."

"Better," I said, "the piano does not have all of Bakst's colors and shapes, and that wonderful, wonderful music."

I linked my arm in his and rested my head on his shoulder.

"You should have gone," he said again.

We had lunch at the hotel in Athlone, soup and leg of lamb. The hotel stood out of sight of the Shannon, at its loveliest in Athlone, and the huge army barracks. As we walked to it, we passed soldiers sauntering in their twos and threes or on their own, and two middle-aged officers were having lunch in the hotel.

By the terms of the Treaty, they would all be leaving, and the barracks itself turned over to the new government.

"Will your Treaty pass?" I asked Christopher.

"I think so," Christopher said. "We will not know for a while. After New Year's, the debate will pick up again. No one will be happy, some very ugly things are being said there in the Mansion House. After New Year's, the debate will move to University College. Stay in Dublin. I will find a seat for you."

In Myles's touring car, he had given me his Christmas gift, an antique ring, three small rubies within intricately twisted gold. I had put it on my right hand, and now he reached across the table to touch it.

"I will stay where you want me to," I said. "In Dublin or London. Or I will wait for you at Coolater."

The British officers had begun their lunch before us, and now they were leaving. They both had close-cropped, graying mustaches. As they walked past us, they laughed together, the kind of easy, good-natured laugh which follows good food and a brandy.

"We wanted the British out of Ireland," Christopher said, "and they are going. Without our war, they would never have gone. They would have been here for another century. That is what matters."

Other times, in Dublin or in London, there would have been more about politics than I had time for, but now he seemed almost unwilling to talk about it.

"Do you know why the debate is moving its location? You will like the reason. The Mansion House was months and months ago booked for a Christmas fête, and that sort of thing takes precedence over the destiny of the Republic."

"Yes," I said, "I like that reason very much. My friends in London would call it a very Irish reason."

And it was then, as we moved across the Shannon into Galway, that I told him about Christmas, and its special, secret mysteriousness for me. He was a wonderful listener, asking the right questions now and then, but for the most part letting me talk, as we drove past bare-branched hedges, bare-branched trees, toward my Christmas at Coolater. I seemed to have his full attention, as though he was learning something secret and important about someone he loved. I had not put my gloves back on, and the hand which rested on his forearm held the ring which was more than a Christmas gift, but a bond between us, as we both knew.

"It is a lovely ring," I said, interrupting myself, "was it a ring in your family?"

"No," he said, "the Blakes don't go in for heirlooms." Which was not true, as I discovered when I met his mother. "It is from Weir's in Grafton Street." And, incorrigible, I thought of Grafton Street at Christmas, and Regent Street.

"Good for you!" I said. "It is a Christmas ring. Red for Christmas."

Or perhaps, I thought a bit later, as we drove across even countryside toward low, distant hills, perhaps he is giving me his full attention in these hours because he is keeping other thoughts away, placing a magic space about the two of us, in Myles's gaudy, expensive car.

Coolater does not have a very large demesne at all, and almost the first thing you see from the road, if it is leafless winter, beyond the walls, glinting for a few seconds and then gone again from sight, is a lake, nearly always frozen in winter, a surface of brittle ice catching the winter sun, and the ancient ruined keep by the shore.

"There, there we are," I said, feeling utterly happy, as the lake's gleam flashed past us, and then we drove through the gates, past the empty gate lodge. Once, in my grandfather's time, there had been a gatekeeper and a gatekeeper's family. I never knew them.

In the house, while our bags were being carried to our rooms, separated from each other by the entire length of the hall above, Father took Christopher to the library, as we always called it, for a whiskey, and Betty, taking my two hands in hers, drew me into the morning room, which had always been our special room, and we kissed each other, and she said, "Welcome home, Janice, oh, welcome home."

"Look," I said, when we sat together, side by side, and I held up my hand, so that she could admire the ring. "Now, don't misunderstand," I said, "it is a Christmas gift, don't make too much of it."

But Betty said, "Oh, Janice," and moved her finger across the laced strands of gold.

Long before, before ever I met Charlie, it had been decided, by

Betty and myself, that I would be the one to go off and meet men and marry, and she would be the one to stay home, with Father and Coolater House. Decided, but never, I am quite certain, talked about. It was odd, really, because Betty was every bit as good-looking, and good-looking in the same way, and her figure was almost as good as mine, although her frocks never showed it to advantage. But she was always eager to talk with me first about my young men and then about men, provided of course that I did so with discretion and delicacy. She knew quite well, I am certain, that Christopher and I made love, but not because I had told her so. It was one of the things I did, just as it was one of the things that she did not. I was free to hint, though, she welcomed my hintings. We had our hintings, secret languages, from when we were children and there were no men, except the gardener and the coachman.

"I like Christopher," she said, as we sat together, looking past glass, past early-winter blackness, toward faint, distant points of light. And I said, "I love him," and she put her arms around me again.

One thing that did trouble her a bit, so she told me later, was how I could "be with," as she put it, Charlie and then, later, "be with" someone else. I did not enlighten her, although it was a subject which I myself found of great interest. "Oh, Betty," I said to her impatiently, "the war has made millions of young widows, and what are we to do?" "Yes," she said, nodding, "I see."

But for the moment, as we sat in the morning room, we thought only, we sisters, that I was in love with Christopher.

"He will be very important," she said, "his name has been in the newspapers, he made a speech in their parliament."

"The Dáil," I said, giving it a pedantic pronunciation, as though I had been studying Gaelic with Christopher.

"Yes," she said. "Do you really grasp all of this? That we are to be a country of our own, with our own parliament?"

"And postage stamps," I said.

"Yes," she said, a bit doubtfully, as though she could not imagine postage stamps which did not carry the King's neat, bearded profile.

"Maud Gonne, perhaps," I said.

"Do you remember when we were girls," she said, "and we played 'Irish Army and English Army' by the lake and you would always insist on being 'Irish Army.' There is prophecy for you. Look now, you have Christopher, a commander in a real Irish army."

"Scarcely that," I said. "Christopher deals with the press, and he was a secretary with the Treaty delegations in London, very unwarlike duties."

We no longer dressed for dinner unless there were guests, and when Father decreed that this should be the case for Christopher's visit, I took this to be a favorable omen. And in fact, Father went out of his way to make dinner pleasant, beaming first at Christopher and then at me and then across the table at Betty. He was wearing his suit of heavy, orangey tweed from Scotland, a repellent color, and a waistcoat printed with tiny fox's heads, and, a bravura touch, a regimental tie, a bit frayed, that he must have rummaged up from some bottom drawer. I fancied, with a touch of fear, that he seemed small within the suit, as though he wore the jacket of some older brother.

"Now then," Christopher said. "You can neither of you guess how happy Janice is to be here."

"At Christmas!" Betty said. "We know about Janice and Christmas. Better than you do."

Father looked a bit puzzled.

The cuisine at Coolater was not elaborate, and Father invariably approved of it.

"Excellent," he said, as he nearly always did, a kind of second grace. "Splendid news, Christopher," he said, "splendid news. You chaps did wonders off there in London. Irish Free State. I like the ring of that. Mind you, I must be careful in making that point before some of my friends out here. In County Galway, in certain circles, the notion of an Irish Free State is not a popular one."

"Nor in Dublin, it seems," Christopher said, and smiled at Father and Father's words.

"Wouldn't have said that a few years ago," Father said. "But we have had a dose of English rule since then. Mind you, the army has been decent, the army always is. But the Black and Tans and the Auxiliaries and the Cadets, all of that lot—savages! About time we began managing our own affairs."

"The Treaty must be approved, Father," Betty said. "You realize that? By the Parliament in London and the one here in Dublin. Christopher is a member of the Dublin Parliament."

"I know that," Father said, putting down his soup spoon in mild indignation. "I know that. But who wouldn't approve it. The Irish will get their country and the other lot will be free of a sticky mess. Lucas doesn't approve of it, to be sure." He turned toward Christopher. "Lucas Fleming lives on the far side of the lake, fierce old bird, ex-Artillery. A chum of Henry Wilson's. Give the army its head, Lucas would say, send them over in proper numbers and don't ask too many questions of them. The army knows how to make short work of ruffians, gunmen. That's you, Christopher," he added with a glint of mischief.

I listened to Father, amused and puzzled. There had been a time when his views and Lucas Fleming's had not been that far apart, although surely as human beings there was no resemblance. Fleming was a dreadful man, foul-mouthed and hard-drinking.

"And do you know what the Black and Tans did?" Father asked, the mischief still in his voice. He picked up his wineglass. "The rebels laid an ambush on the Athenry road, and when they wounded a couple of the Tans, the Tans went berserk, and in their night of berserking they burned two of Lucas Fleming's barns, and drove his herd into Laney Bog. A few of them drowned, stupid creatures. 'Well,' I said to Lucas Fleming, 'there we are, swift reprisals and no questions asked.' And Lucas, to do him justice, did not reply." Father laughed, and drank off his glass of wine in a draft, looking significantly toward Mary Frances, who stood ready by the sideboard with a fresh bottle of the indifferent Médoc.

"Mr. Fleming and yourself—" Christopher began, but Father interrupted him.

"Colonel Fleming," he said. "Colonel Fleming, if you please. He insists upon the title. Pompous ass."

"Colonel Fleming and yourself have remained friends in spite of all," Christopher said. "That's to the good."

But Father's mood changed upon the instant, and he said, in a small voice, "No. We have not. Lucas and I are not on speaking terms." And, as Mary Frances refilled our glasses, he bent his head over his soup. When you faced Father directly, and when the light was helping him, you admired his shock of thinning white hair, but when his head was bent, you saw that he was almost bald. Almost bald and looking a bit small in his jacket of orangey tweed.

Father and Lucas Fleming had not been especially close friends, but friends of a sort nevertheless, with the army a bond between them. And friendship had always had special claims upon Father. It would be a blow to him, if he and awful Lucas Fleming were not speaking, and I wondered of how many of his other loyalist friends was this also true. His mild nationalist sentiments in the old days, shamrocks and whiskey on Saint Patrick's Day, they excused as a harmless consequence of his being a Papist, but support of the new Free State would be quite a different matter.

"You have heard about the Jelliffes?" he said to me suddenly, speaking of much nicer neighbors. "They are selling out, moving across to England, to Dorset. Stella has family there." The bald head shook, in puzzlement.

After dinner, after Father had insisted that we leave Christopher and himself alone for a cigar, he released poor Christopher, and the two of us, bundled against the cold, walked back and forth along the stone terrace. There was a chill, bracing wind.

"People fail," I said. "Father is failing."

"Your father is fine," Christopher said. "I wish more people had your father's sense. He is a bit abrupt, I admit."

On Christmas Eve, we had the O'Hallorans over for tea, and then went off for a drive in Myles Keough's motorcar, and, after darkness had fallen, one by one, the candles would be lit in the farmhouses beyond the lake, the houses of our tenants, some of them, not that we had many left. That was always an essential part of our Christmas, Betty's and mine, but in earlier days we would walk together to the rise above the plantation of birch trees, holding hands, and then for two Christmases, no, three, it had been Charlie and myself. And now Christopher. I loved Christopher and Father and Betty and the memory of Charlie.

The next morning was Christmas morning, and we went to Mass in two motorcars, the family in Myles Keough's, flashing the tidings of Christmas from mirrors and windscreens, and the staff in our own, and the church was already crowded when we arrived, the air warm and heavy with the special smells of Christmas at Mass, incense clinging to the air from the earlier Mass, and the boughs of pine and fir scattered about the side altars. Ours is the cathedral town of the diocese of Clonfert, and the cathedral itself is from the outside dull and undistinguished, modern and fake-Gothic like half of the new churches and cathedrals in Ireland, but the interior is magnificent, and often, although I would not call myself religious, I would remember it in London.

There was a Christmas sermon of the usual sort, comforting and familiar, with the story of the Nativity discoursed upon, as though the language of Scripture could be bettered, but at the end of the Mass, not the bishop, who was away, but the celebrant came forward to speak to the congregation.

"This is a season," he said, "of our greatest joy, a joy greater even than that of Easter itself. And this year, at this Christmastide, there is an occasion for joy greater than any which we in this country have known for many years. Peace and the restoration to us of our nation's liberty have been given to us in this season. For years past, we have all of us in this nation endured much, and we have witnessed the deaths of brothers and husbands and sons, stricken down cruelly. And, at last, in God's time, our struggle has been a victorious one. In Dublin, as you know, the representatives of our people have been meeting to debate whether or not to accept the peace which wise and patriotic Irishmen have brought back with them from London."

The priest was in his early middle years, but losing his reddish hair, and his cheeks had that particular brightness which I never see save in priests, as though they shaved themselves every hour. I was thinking more of that than of his words, when I sensed Christopher, sitting in the pew beside me, stiffen, and glancing toward him, I saw that he was looking forward intently. Gannon was his name, I remembered suddenly, Father Gannon.

"It is surely with heavy hearts," he went on, "that everywhere, throughout this island home of ours, we have learned of dissension and controversy within the Dáil itself, so grievous as to imperil peace. With what great joy did we learn of the release from prison of thousands of patriotic and manly young Irishmen, some few indeed, from this parish itself. And we know also that close to fifty young Irishmen remain still in the prisons of Dublin and Cork, condemned and awaiting their deaths by the hangman's rope, whose lives this Treaty would protect. Many of you, I am certain, saw, as I did, the headline in the most respected, dare I say, of our national newspapers. 'The Treaty or Chaos.' Let us have no mistake about it; the rejection of this Treaty must inevitably lead to war of such a destructive character as would lay Ireland out dead. I cannot begin to speculate as to the motives—"

I turned toward Christopher again, but as I was turning, a noise behind me drew me full round, and I saw that a man in the congregation had risen up. He was a youngish man, high-cheekboned, with a fierce shock of dark hair which the comb had not been able to subdue. He was staring dead ahead, at the priest, who had paused. And as he stood there another man rose up and then another, until presently there were, I would suppose, a score of them or more, some standing hesitant, but the most of them, following the first man's lead, stiff and angry-looking. All of the congregation, so it seemed to me, had turned to look at them. I put my hand on Christopher's arm.

Father Gannon had begun to speak again, but I have no memory of what he said, nor of the tone of voice in which he said it. But, as though his words were a signal, the youngish man, who had been standing at the end of a pew, stepped into the aisle, genuflected quickly, and then walked out. And the score of other men followed him. One young fellow at least had an awkward time of it, an older man beside him, his father no doubt, reached up to grab him by the sleeve, but he pulled himself free. Gannon had again stopped speaking, and in the silence we heard only the sounds of heavy boots on the flagstones of the aisle.

"Let us pray," Gannon said at last. "Let us pray for this unhappy island, which has good cause to be overjoyed in this season of the coming of the Christ Child . . ." He had little more to say, and when he had said it, he dismissed us all, and we all walked out into the sunlight of December.

For a short time, Father sat without stirring, until Betty nudged him, and then he shook his head and stood up.

It would have been the custom for the celebrant, his chasuble off, to join the congregation on the steps, but now he was nowhere to be seen. Across the road, standing in the roadway, with a field beyond them, were the fellows who had left the church. They stood ranged about the high-cheekboned young fellow. He had now a soft, wide-brimmed gray hat jammed onto his head, and his hands were buried in the pockets of his greatcoat. He was staring, I could have sworn, directly at Christopher.

"Dreadful," Father said to Betty and myself, "in church, and on Christmas morning of all the mornings in the year."

Now Father Gannon came hurrying along the path beside the church, an overweight man, with short legs on a heavy trunk, his vestments unseasonably bright and festive. No one seemed in any hurry to leave, and Gannon, as though intent upon some destination, threaded his way through small crowds. He was looking, as most of us were, across the roadway.

But then, to my entire surprise, Christopher said to Betty, "What is the priest's name? Quickly, Betty. And bring me to meet him. Right now, right away."

Christopher surprised me, but so too did Betty, who paused a brief moment, then nodded decisively, and the two of them walked away, toward Gannon.

"Do you understand this, Janice?" Father said, "any of it?" From within the open door of the church came a brief trill of music, as though the organist had set herself to practicing, and then thought better of it.

Presently, Betty and Father Gannon came over to us, and Christopher gave a skimpy sort of wave in our direction, and then walked across the road. He was suddenly full of surprises, a Christopher whom I did not entirely recognize.

"Dreadful," Gannon said to Father, without a word of greeting to me. "A fine gift for Christmas morning this is. The ruffian. It is his lead they are following, you may depend on that."

For a moment, I thought he meant Christopher, and then I said, "Whose lead, Father? What ruffian?"

"Ach, Mrs. Nugent," he said. "Forgive me. You are welcome home. A happy Christmas it must be at Coolater."

"What ruffian?" I said. Christopher had by now reached the roadway and had walked straight to the knot of men.

"His name is Brady," Betty said. "Sean Brady. He is the commandant of the Volunteers. He is a very well-known person." She was speaking, so far as I could judge, without irony, and she was looking toward Christopher and Brady, who were standing very close to each other, and seemed to be talking at each other, the two of them with hands in pockets.

"You would think," Gannon said angrily, "that I had taken it into my head to set forth upon my own to discourse upon politics. Not a bit of it. Every priest in this diocese has been instructed by the bishop to enlighten the people as to the Treaty. Not that they stood in need of enlightening. They are all for the Treaty, save for Brady and his crowd."

Once before, on that terrible day when I had seen the man shot down on the railway platform at Moate, I had the feeling which I had now, that whatever I looked at, heard, was informed, charged with an unreadable meaning, like electricity. The people on the steps of the cathedral were looking across the road, as I was, but they would now and then look over toward us.

Presently, Christopher gave a brief nod, and then walked back to us.

"I'm sorry," he said, in vague apology, and led the way back to Myles's motorcar.

We drove a part of the way back to Coolater with no one speaking, with Christopher seeming to concentrate upon his driving. Until at last, Father cleared his throat and said, "Disgraceful. In the church itself. At Mass."

"Do you know Sean Brady, then?" Betty said, but Christopher said, "I know who he is, and he knows who I am."

"A ruffian is what Father Gannon calls him," Father said, "and that seems precise enough."

"He is a fine column commandant," Christopher said, "and he is more than that at the moment. Ever since Paddy Hennessy died in hospital, he has commanded the Fourth Western Division."

"That fellow," Father said incredulously, "that Brady fellow with the hat pulled down around his ears. He looks more like a hostler."

"Close enough," Christopher, swinging his wheel sharply, avoiding a cur that loped suddenly onto the road. "He is a fierce, clever man, I can tell you that about it. He ambushed some Tans here a month or two before the Truce. I would not have envied the Tans. He is a bad man to cross."

"Father Gannon seems to have crossed him," Betty said, and we drove in another bit of silence.

"I am meeting with Brady and one of his officers tonight," Christopher said. "We have a great deal to talk about, as you can imagine."

"No," I said, shocked and angry. "I cannot imagine. It is Christmas night. A special night. A very special night." I could feel my words begin to quiver at the edge of tears, and was angry now with myself. From the moment that that man had stood up in his pew, I had felt something bad nibbling away at the edge of our special Christmas happiness.

"Don't be foolish," Betty said suddenly and sharply, "and don't talk like that. Of course Christopher and Sean Brady must talk. Do you pay no attention at all to what has been happening in your own country?"

A day before, Betty and I had been joking about what was happening, and would there be a postage stamp with a picture of Maud Gonne, and were we really to have our own country? But Betty, it would appear, had a few ideas. I turned round in my seat to look at her, and when she saw my glance, she smiled and was the old Betty again. "Well," she said, "I will say this for Sean Brady. He knows how to cut sermons short."

Father, sitting beside her, said nothing. He smiled a bit when she spoke, as though that was expected of him. He held his folded hands upon his lap, resting on his heavy coat.

But he was very much his old self when friends came in for afternoon drinks, the Frenches and the O'Hallorans, and my dear friend Hazel Lockhart but without her blood-and-thunder husband, Derek. There was a special punch, the O'Gorman punch, which requires several days' preparation, and then, at the very last minute, a thrust from a red-hot poker. The punch was laid out in the dining room, as ever from my childhood, and from the dining room one looked past double doors thrown open for the occasion, to the great Yule log blazing in the fireplace of the east drawing room, the smaller one, which we always used at Christmas. It was from there that Father carried in, a compound of the casual and the ceremonious, the red-hot poker, and thrust it into the punch bowl, with its carved elaborations.

The O'Hallorans had been at Mass with us, but the Frenches and the Lockharts had been at their church, trim and slim-steepled, at the other end of town. They knew, of course, what had happened at Mass.

It was a good half-hour before Hazel and I had a chance to speak alone. She looked splendid, as always, had put on a bit of weight, not much, and she was becoming quite shameless in her use of cosmetics. We were standing by the tall windows in the sitting room, warmed by the fire, and for a moment we had the room to ourselves.

"Tell me," she said—her cup had cooled a bit, and she was holding it in both hands—"where is your gunman? Derek will not enter the same room with him. Derek says that your gunman is like all the Sinn Féiners, his hands have touched the springs of murder. God knows where he found the phrase. He doesn't read, of course."

But I did not know where Christopher was, he had driven off an hour before, and so I told Hazel. It was turning into an awful Christmas, and I almost told her that as well.

She drank from her cup, and looked at me over the rim. Hazel had the gift of looking demure and wicked at once. I envied her.

"You have rooms at opposite ends of the hall, Betty tells me. Poor dears. What now for you both, now that it is all over?"

"It is not all over," I said, "you heard about what happened at Mass this morning."

And, as I spoke, Betty joined us, looking lovely in brown with a bit of fur at the high collar. I linked arms with her. Nothing that happened at Christmas could spoil the love I felt for Betty. And for Father.

"Gunmen falling out over the spoils is how Derek puts it," Hazel said. "And I must say there is something to it. Do you remember how awful it was here six months ago, Betty?"

"Something to it," Betty said. "If you think that, you are very foolish, Hazel. Our only hope of getting back to normal is that Treaty. Things could happen to all of us, to our country, far worse than what was happening six months ago. Worse than the Black and Tans. Worse than the British Army, even. Do people in this country never bother to think? Really think?"

As she spoke, I could feel her arm getting tense within the loop of mine, and she spoke with such an even, low intensity that Hazel and I looked at each other.

"To be sure, pet," Hazel said, gently, using her own familiar name for Betty.

It was late night when Christopher came back. I had been waiting up for him in the room that Father used as the estate office, sitting by a low fire and turning over the pages of Betty's magazines. After I had been there an hour, Betty came downstairs in her robe and joined me. When we were small, we used to sneak into that room, close the heavy door and tell each other stories. On one wall, there was a map of the estate as it had been in our grandfather's time, a much larger estate then, with the acres of each of the tenants marked off, and a small square drawn for each farm building and the name of the tenant—Cooney, Clohessy, Hogan.

"You have changed, Betty," I said, "you have changed and Father has changed." It had happened suddenly, since the summer.

But Betty shrugged and said, "Father is older, Janice."

When we heard the hall door, I went out to Christopher, and brought him back to the estate office.

"It is after midnight," he said. "No need for you to have waited up, either of you."

Betty rummaged in the deep pocket of her robe and brought out a packet of cigarettes. That too was something new.

For a space he sat smoking, almost forgetting us. "A very determined man, your neighbor Sean Brady."

"Once," Betty said, "a few months before the Truce, he sent four men here to demand arms. Father was in Athlone that day, thank God. I gave them the shotguns and both rifles, but told them we no longer had sidearms, and they did not bother to search. When Father came home, I thought he would be furious, but he nodded. As though he had expected it, or as though it did not matter."

"Did you report it?" I asked her.

"Good heavens, no," Betty said. "Report it to the Black and Tans!"

I imagined the fellows hammering at the hall door, or had habit sent them round to the kitchen? Sean Brady's men, but also, in a way, Christopher's men.

"A very determined man," Christopher said again, a thin trail of amusement in his voice.

"It could not have been easy for him," Betty said, "standing up at Mass and defying the priest."

"Not easy at all," Christopher said, "and relying upon his lads to follow his example. And on Christmas Day."

Betty stood up then, and went to one of the low cupboards which lined the room, below the shelves of estate papers, ledgers. She took out a decanter—whiskey, brandy?—and glasses, as though she had known exactly where they were.

"He had warned Gannon," Christopher said, holding out his glass as Betty measured spirits into it. "If Gannon spoke from the altar in support of the Treaty, Brady would pull out his men. But of course, Gannon had no choice."

When Betty gestured toward me with the decanter, I shook my head, and so she poured herself a generous dollop.

"It was a dry season," Christopher said, "two short ones to take off the cold and to show that there were no hard feelings on either side. Later on, a plate of sandwiches was produced. We met in rooms behind a shop in town, Brady and myself and a man named Henchey." He looked inquiringly toward Betty, but she shook her head. "Sandwiches," Christopher said, "and a few bottles of stout." He sipped at his glass. "Connaught is in a state of rebellion, as far as Brady is concerned. In rebellion against the Empire or the Treaty, he does not care which."

"That sounds very strong," Betty said. "Has he read the *Connaught Tribune,* let alone has he listened to his parish priest?"

"He does not give a damn for the *Connaught Tribune,*" Christopher said, "nor for any other newspaper. Nor for Michael Collins nor for Sean MacEoin, nor for myself if it comes to that, although politeness stopped him just short of that until the very end."

"People like Sean Brady," Betty said furiously, "why in God's name should anyone listen to the likes of Sean Brady? Because you can ambush a lorryload of policemen does not give you the right to pass judgment on something like the Treaty." I had never seen her in such a temper. And it was to Betty that Christopher was talking, as though I was not sitting across the small room from him.

"You had best take that up with him," Christopher said. "He will tell you about it with impressive fierceness.

"He wasted no time," Christopher told us, "we neither of us pretended that it was a social occasion. Despite the two small whiskies which he poured for the three of us. Henchey did not have much to say, a man with a small, contained face, thin-lipped, a high-arched nose like a parrot's. But Brady is impressive, with one of those high-cheekboned faces like a Red Indian's and a controlled voice, not slow but deliberate. Have you ever talked with him?"

"Once only," Betty said. "There have been dances at the parish hall during the Truce, and I went along to one of them. Brady was there in national uniform, with the insignia riding on his shoulders. He is engaged to the daughter of the Lakeside Arms."

I listened with mild incredulity. One of the daughters of Coolater House, one of Colonel O'Gorman's daughters, at a dance in the parish hall, herself and a commander of rebel gunmen. But then I thought, Like Christopher. Your gunman, Hazel would say to me when we talked about Christopher. That was different.

"You can see for yourself how matters stand," Brady told Christopher. "You were at Mass this morning. The Fifth Western wants no part of that bloody Treaty that you signed beyond there in London and brought back with you."

"I signed no Treaty," Christopher said. "I was there as a secretary, myself and Childers. But I will stand over it. It is not all we wanted, but it is all that we could get. I stand over it."

"Well, Childers does not," Brady said. "Not Childers nor Dev nor Cathal Brugha. They were here, you know, in this town. Dev and Brugha both, reviewing the division. 'You are soldiers of the Republic,' Dev told us, 'and you will never be asked to pledge your allegiance to a foreign king.' He said that here, and below in Ennis and below Ennis in Limerick. And by God that is good enough for the men of the West."

"What should be good enough for the men of the West," Christopher said, "and the men of the East and of wherever, should be the will of the Irish people. The Irish Republican Army are not gunmen setting up shop on their own, they are the army of the people of Ireland, and they are answerable to the people. The debate will be resuming at the new year, and there will be a vote. I will abide by that vote. Will you, Sean?" In the Irish way, they were Sean and Christopher, although they might never meet as friends.

"I cannot believe that Dev would ever ask me to swear away my oath to the Republic," Brady said. "Good God, Chris, do you think that I am on my own? The divisions and the brigades and the columns or however you want to slice us up are foursquare behind the Republic."

"Not all of them," Christopher said, "and perhaps not half of them."

"I can tell you where Liam Lynch stands and Liam Deasy and Ernie O'Malley and Frank Lacy and Seamus Robinson, and that is the beginning of the list and not the end of it."

"Across this island," Christopher said, "there are civic bodies making use of the Christmas week to vote their support of the

Treaty, civic bodies and newspapers and bishops and ordinary people."

"It was not the newspapers that fought the Black and Tans," Brady said, "nor civic bodies nor bishops. By God, it was not bishops. The Church was not behind us. Oh, a word or two whispered in private perhaps, 'Good on you, lads,' that kind of thing, but nothing more than that."

"Those lads of yours who followed you out from Mass this morning. Will you ask them to stand against the will of the country, should the people vote to accept the Treaty?"

"It will not come to that," Brady said. "Wait and you will see. You fellows above in Dublin have a queer notion of things, you should spend more time below here and get a sense of how things are here before you begin talking about the will of the country, whatever that means. The Tans thought that they could level us flat, but by God they could not. Do you think that the *Connaught Tribune* can accomplish what the Black and Tans could not nor the RIC nor the fucking British Army. The British army could not and neither can some schoolteachers and solicitors putting matters to a vote in the Mansion House in Dublin."

"And neither," Henchey said unexpectedly, leaning forward, hands pressed upon bony knees, "can those in this very country who call themselves Irishmen but behave like the enemies of Ireland and have behaved so for decades."

"All right, then, Mickey," Brady said, "that will do." And he shot an angry glance at his adjutant.

"Not at all," Christopher said. "What is your point, there, Mickey?"

"Few and far between," Henchey said, "are the big houses which gave help to the lads fighting for Ireland. They were more likely to go off to fight in the British Army. We know that and we remember that."

"That will do," Brady said again.

There were stacks of flour in the crowded room behind the shop, wooden and cardboard crates piled one above the other, a single, narrow window looked out into darkness.

The talk among the three of them moved back and forth, over the same matters, for hours, with neither Christopher nor Brady prepared to break it off, although Henchey gave signs of impatience. It was Henchey's shop. At one point, his son, a boy of ten or so, tight-faced like his father, brought in tea and sandwiches of ham and pork, thick-sliced bread.

"It will not come to that," Brady said, as he had said once before, this time with his mouth filled with pork and bread. He chewed and swallowed. "Sure, don't we know each other, by name at least, all of us do. We have been at this for three years, since Soloheadbeg and before, we have been tested."

"But we stand by the Republic," Henchey said, "you can take that back to your pals in Dublin, to Mick Collins and that crowd of his."

"This time last year," Christopher said, "I doubt greatly if I would have heard Collins spoken of here in that tone of voice."

"This time last year," Brady said, "he had not signed that Treaty."

"This time last year was the time when Collins wiped out the entire British intelligence operation in Dublin. This time last year, if I remember aright, is when Collins got a full crate of Lee-Enfields to you here, and ammunition to match it."

"I know that," Brady said, and sighed heavily.

"Good work that he did so," Henchey said, "and even so, we had to go hat in hand to the big houses of the gentry to beg the loan of a few shotguns."

Later, when Brady and Christopher stood alone in the dark street, outside the darkened shop, Brady said, "I will say this for you, Chris. You sought me out to argue the matter with me, you walked away from the church and across the road to me. I respect that."

"I doubt if your chum Henchey does," Christopher said, but he contrived to take some of the sting off his words.

"Mickey Henchey is a good man," Brady said, "make no mistake about that, a hard, bitter man, but a good one. He saved my life once, at the Carrowglass ambush, and at risk to his own. He will take nothing less than the Republic, Chris, and neither will I. Neither will other lads whose names you know as well as I do."

Christopher began to answer him, but stopped, lest the whole wheeling argument repeat itself again, in the street. In starlight, light of clouded crescent moon, he held out his hand, and Brady took it.

"When you go back to Coolater," Brady said, "give my best Christmas wishes to the Colonel and to Miss O'Gorman. She looked in at one of our dances, did you know that. Sure, Father Gannon was there as well. We were all one then, just a few months ago."

"Commandant Brady remembers you," Christopher said to Betty, "from the dance last summer. Have you made a conquest there?"

But Betty smiled and shook her head. "I am told that Commandant Brady's hand has been claimed by the Lakeside Hotel. And Ireland, of course," she added, with a flick of contempt at the tail of her words.

By the time that Christopher had finished his account, Betty had turned on another table light, and I was sipping at a glass of whiskey, to keep them company. Christmas had shriveled away, and all that I had hoped for it, present joined seamlessly to past, had shriveled with it. Instead, there now was Father, this strangely diminished Father, who nodded and smiled where once he would have roared and playacted rage, and Betty, who had always, to my best knowledge, cared as little for politics as she did for the history of Mesopotamia, becoming a fierce supporter of the Treaty being debated in Dublin, and, most astonishing of all, Betty at a dance in the parish hall.

When Betty, tactfully, had left us alone, I smiled at Christopher, but a bit wanly, I am afraid, because he put down his glass at once, and crossed over to me and kissed me. It was an affectionate kiss, upon my parted lips, not a passionate one, and he said, "Oh, Janice, poor Janice, what a poor sort of Christmas this has been for you," and he began to put his arms around me, but I held him away from me, with my hands on his chest, feeling the tweed of his jacket.

"I feel stupid," I said, "listening to what you were telling us, and watching Betty as she sat listening. All the world cares about such things and you do and Betty does, and perhaps I do, somewhere in my mind. But not the way I care about you and about Betty, not the way that I remember Charlie, and bits of music, and the lake in summer. When Betty and I were little, on Christmas Eve we would stand with Father by the window . . ." But I stopped there; twice at least I had told him about looking across lake and valley toward the candles, fallen stars.

He began to speak, but I still held him away.

"Do you know what that Treaty has meant to me, all those months that you were in London because of it, and telling me about it in cafés and in restaurants and even in bed? It meant that once it was signed, we would have our lives together."

"And so we shall," Christopher said. "Wait," he said, "you'll see."

"Wait," I said, "wait for what?"

But then, a minute or two later, I dropped away my protesting hands, or rather, felt them drop away, and he kissed me, this time with passion, and I kissed him back. And shortly, before we knew what was happening, we were conscious only of our kisses, and of our bodies, until all at once, and with difficulty, I broke away. His head was buried in my neck, his face covered by my hair. My lips were wet from his, and I said, "My God, Christopher, no!" And I began to laugh, but at first of course he thought I was crying, and he pulled away from me. "Oh, my God," I said, but I was still laughing, and I smoothed down my skirt over my legs.

"Oh, what an end to Christmas Day," I said, "making love in Father's office, with my skirt bunched up about my waist. What an end that would have been!"

Some men might have been furious, but Christopher, his eyes shaded, looked cross and puzzled, at least for the moment.

"It was beginning," he said, "to seem a very good idea," but I shook my head, and began laughing again, which wasn't fair to him of course because laughter can be very provoking, but I could not help myself, and, as well, I had a fear that the laughing might turn to tears.

"No," I said, "we will have New Year's in Dublin, New Year's is the time for passion and disarray."

I looked beyond him, beyond the paper-covered desk, to the estate map, and at this distance could not make out the little squares that had been penned in, decades before, to mark the farms of tenants.

"Christopher," I said, "I may need eyeglasses in a year or two. Will you still love me, even so?"

"It was beginning," he said, "to seem a very good idea."

"As good as arguing politics with Mr. Brophy?" I asked.

"Brady," he said, "and I have had enough of arguing for one night."

"Brady," I said, "to be sure." And kissed him good-night in a manner which I trusted was fond but undisturbing.

In my room, before I undressed, I stood in darkness and looked out upon the scene which in London I remembered so often, but a scene now in an almost entire darkness, starlight and faint moon. And I thought that I was finally saying goodbye not to Christmas but to childhood, long after marriage, after having been to bed with two other men I scarcely knew and certainly had not hungered for, and now after Christopher, after parties in London and being drunk too often, after the colors and sounds of the ballet, after whispers and flirtations and poetry in corners of Bloomsbury. After even that awful hour, the most awful hour that ever was, when I received that obscene wire from the War Office and I stood by the window in London, rain pouring down the panes, and outside traffic, taxicabs, people with umbrellas. Even then, there was always in some hidden center, Coolater and Betty and Father and the candles of Christmas, fallen stars.

But not anymore, and what happened, not simply but with entanglements had happened, struck not the mind but the bewildered heart, because what happens never happens entirely on its own, the telegram that tells of a lover's death is always mixed with rain and a window, umbrellas, the sounds of taxi horns faint, beyond glass. So now I knew that Coolater was changing, that Father would grow smaller, fainter, that there would be less of him. And that Betty had entered upon a kind of life different from the one that the two of us had known.

On my table, but hidden now by black night, a photograph of Mother very young in her wedding gown, fair skin, clear eyes, firm chin, the faint sketch of a smile. Mother remained the same, unknown, a photograph, changeless.

In the morning, Christopher set off for Dublin. I was to follow him by the New Year. He was making an early start, and so we had a quick breakfast, the four of us, Betty in her dressing gown, and Father, always clean-shaven however early the hour, tweed jacket and the regimental tie which he had taken to wearing, his hand, small and white, holding the teacup steadily. Christopher too was in tweeds, heavy tweeds; he had nicked himself shaving.

"Mind yourself, Christopher, until you have put Athlone behind you," Father said. "There are heavy Black and Tan patrols between Loughrea and Athlone. So I have been told."

No there are not, Father, I wanted to tell him, for six months they have been confined to barracks. Ever since the Truce. But Betty caught my eye.

"I will, sir," Christopher said. "Very careful."

"Good that you have been with us for Christmas," Father said. "You must be here every Christmas. Charlie was here every Christmas. Better here than that draughty Nugent house in Westmeath, am I right, Janice?"

We walked Christopher to the car, the three of us, and before he set off, mindless of Father, I kissed him on the mouth.

"Mind yourself, Christopher," Betty said. She had put a heavy, shapeless waterproof over her lemon-colored dressing gown. "Stand firm."

He looked splendid in his borrowed motorcar, hatless as always, despite the cold of the December morning.

It was not until the morning before I left myself that Betty and I talked.

We were back in the estate office, the two of us, and she had papers and ledgers spread out before her on the long table. From time to time, she would lick the stub of her pencil, as she had done from childhood, when we were doing our sums in the drafty school above our bedroom. In a week's time, George Fitzmaurice, our solicitor, would be up from Dublin to go over the accounts. Last year, he had gone over them, as always in the past, with Father, but this year Betty would be sitting by Father's side.

She saw me watching her. "He can be as shrewd and sensible as anyone can wish," she said, "but suddenly he will not remember something, something immensely important, perhaps. Or he will imagine something. Last week, for the better part of a day, he thought Charlie would be joining us here. It doesn't matter, really, but I have to be very careful. The staff is wonderful with him, they all love him, Mrs. Donovan in particular. She is a good ten years older than he is, but sound as a bell."

"Black and Tans in Loughrea," I said.

"Yes. And he will not get better, you know, he will get worse. You remember old Phillip Haskell, master of foxhounds one year, and the next thing you know—. . . At least Father has been leaving young boys alone." She giggled and looked away from me. "As far as we know."

"Betty!" I said, shocked.

"It isn't easy," she said. She put down the stub of pencil and looked at me straight, a young woman with handsome, delicate features. My Betty. "It isn't easy. He is a bit frail, but God willing, we will have years together here, Father and I." Her voice was even and matter-of-fact, but there was no mistaking the bitterness behind the words.

"Oh, Betty," I said. "How awful for you, for you both. What shall I do?"

"Nothing," she said briskly. "Write more often, he adores your letters, and perhaps, when things have settled down, Christopher and yourself will visit more often. You are more than welcome to settle down here, you know, the two of you, but I expect you would not find that great fun. City mice, the two of you."

And my first thought was, But that isn't true at all. All that I had been thinking of for weeks past had been Coolater and Betty, but that was not my second thought. With my second thought, I knew that she was right. And it was not Father alone who would be changing, bit by bit, year by year. It was as though a new Betty were taking shape, brisk and sensible, but I had never thought of Betty as sensible.

And it was the new Betty, the sensible Betty, who walked down with me to the lake late that afternoon, past the garden, and along the wintry, leafless path, the ground frozen.

"There is more to your Christopher than you realize," she said. "Being in love does not tell you everything you need to know. And neither does living in London and Dublin. Coolater is my charge now, just as Father is. And I know as well as I know anything that this country has contrived just barely to survive ambushes and houses burned and creameries burned and all the rest of it. I wrote to you, did I not, about the poor fellow who was murdered here, on Coolater land, one of our own tenants, and a sign pinned to his jacket, 'Informers beware!' That was our friend Sean Brady's work, I have no doubt, but you do hear it said that the Tans did it, the way they would black their faces and take Sinn Féin people from their houses and murder them. That happened in Loughrea and in Athenry."

She was speaking as she walked, decisively, and I had a time keeping up with her, our boots smashing down on dry leaves, on branches ripped off by autumn winds, winter winds.

"The Sean Brady who remembers you from a dance at the parish hall," I said, a bit spitefully.

"There will be scant peace in this country," she said, "if it is handed over to the Sean Bradys and the Derek Lockharts to quarrel over. We have been holding on to Coolater by our fingertips for the last ten years or more. George Fitzmaurice says that we should have sold out years ago, under the provisions of the Act."

"Oh, no, Betty," I said, horrified. "That would kill Father. This is his life."

"And my own as well," she said. "All of it. I know now that I shall never marry. I should have known that long ago as well."

"However can you say that, Betty," I said, but knowing that she was right, "you are a young woman yet, and not bad-looking, you know."

But she shook her head. "Oh, in five years' time," she said, "ten years' time, some widower . . ." She shrugged.

"Or Sean Brady," I said, "you could steal him away from the Lakeside Hotel." I said it to tease her, and she laughed a bit, but without real mirth. Because there it was, or a part of it at least. One of the daughters of Coolater House could not marry a Sean Brady, who for all one knew had a cousin in service with us.

"It would break my heart," she said, speaking of Coolater, and I knew that it would break my own, because Coolater was my heart's center.

Almost as though she had read my thought, she said, "Don't you worry, Janice. Coolater will struggle along. We have struggled along since, since when was it?"

We had reached the lake, with its covering of brittle ice reflecting the sun of late afternoon, winter sun. Always, from childhood, this had been our special, secret place, sheltered and inviolate. Once, one summer, there had been three swans floating on it, white, mysterious, full-bodied, elegant, their beaks savage jewels against white. Summer was its true season, hidden by thick, entangled branches.

"For ages," I said, and added, without thinking, "ask Father."

In a place of honor in Father's study had always hung the sword which an eighteenth-century O'Gorman had carried or was said to have carried when he served in one of France's Irish regiments. But for us, the history of Coolater began at the very end of that century, when Catholics were allowed to hold land on ninety-nine-year leases. And the house itself had been built by Father's grandfather, which of course did not make it old at all, but the shattered keep at the far side of the lake was, so we all piously assumed, a vestige of old O'Gorman grandeur.

"Oh, yes," I said, "we have always been able to struggle along." But that, I thought, was because of tough old birds like Father's grandfather, not dear, unworldly creatures like Father himself. The grandfather, I thought, had likely been a rack-renter or a grazier of some sort, tough and unscrupulous, which was how Catholics advanced in those days. There was a portrait of him in the dining room, the work of no wandering Romney or Reynolds, but an itinerant portraitist with a small stock of visages, to be given slight variations. The old boy was wearing a blue coat and yellow waistcoat, painted with care, and, above the wide stock, a full, florid face, broad nose, thin lips.

And suddenly I thought that no two faces could be less like each other than his face and Betty's, but that this new Betty, brisk and unbiddable, may have been proving his blood across the century and more.

She saw me looking at her quizzically, and smiled, uncertainly, and at that broken smile, my love for her broke upon me anew, and I flung my arms around her.

XXI

PATRICK PRENTISS

On January 7, 1922, in the Council Chamber of University College, Dublin, Dáil Éireann, by the perilously narrow vote of 64 to 57, approved the Treaty between Great Britain and Ireland. It was a night session, beginning at four in the afternoon, and continuing on until nine o'clock. The harsh illumination of electric lighting, massive chandeliers holding unglazed glass cups, fell flat upon members of the Dáil who faced each other in the front of the long, narrow room, and, beyond them, those who had managed to find seats in the rows reserved for spectators. I myself had managed, with little difficulty, to claim the seat which had been reserved for me by Christopher Blake, having first identified myself to one of the Volunteer guards who stood outside the hall, at the head of the stone stairs, young fellows with trench coats and cloth caps, pockets bulging heavily. It was a night of cold rain and blustery winds.

The debate had begun in mid-December, had suspended for Christmas, and had resumed on the fourth of January. I had sat through some of the early sessions, not all of them, but since the fourth, I had been a faithful, indeed a fascinated visitor. It is seldom that one can observe the nature and fate of one's country being debated and decided. For six months, since the Truce, the men who had been conducting the war against England had walked our streets, we had all seen them in public places, seen their photographs in newspapers, met them at the homes of friends. But they drew their authority from their years in shadow, directing operations which had created a government of shadow and gunfire, challenging that other government which existed by right of Westminster and Dublin Castle, by right of English rifles and, at the end of the day, by right of armed thugs in uniforms of black and tan.

Now, in the Council Chamber, they sat facing each other, in dark suits, hair combed and plastered into place, a few of them, a Count Plunkett or a Darrell Figgis in a beard patriarchal or bohemian, but for the most part clean-shaven. Some few had never been photographed, guerrilla captains from Munster and Connaught, victors of ambushes on twisting country roads, of jailbreaks and hunger strikes. Survivors of the 1916 Rising some of them, but some of them, more of them, men who had been swept up into Sinn Féin by the legend of Easter Week, by the exhilaration of the fight against conscription. The women members, most but not all of them, were the survivors of martyrdom—Pearse's mother, Tom Clarke's widow, MacCurtain's widow, whose husband had been murdered by the Tans, the sister of Terence MacSwiney, who had died on hunger strike in an English prison. They sat in the deep black of mourning, and they sat, all of them, with those members who opposed the Treaty, ranged behind De Valera and Austin Stack and Cathal Brugha.

For four years, the men who had conducted the government of shadows had offered to the public the image of a united movement, acting on behalf of, and with the authority of, a united people. The Treaty had ripped that image, like a photograph torn in two, jagged, angry, grieving. There was nothing in my experience, whether of men or of history, to match the bleakness of the occasion, of feelings carefully controlled and then lashing out into invective, words of scorn and rage from which the speaker would then retreat in phrases of muttered near-apology. Nothing, certainly, to match what could be witnessed for time to time in the House of Commons, from the Visitors' Gallery, furious oratory, the Empire in danger and so forth, from men who had had tea together a few hours before, on the terrace, and would be going off together, in an hour's time, to theater or dinner party. Here, in this harshly lit Dublin chamber, were friends separated not by rhetorical devices but by genuine anger.

De Valera, in a front rank, sat close to one end of the long council table, and would rest in front of him a stack of papers which from time to time he would sort through, restlessly, and twice at least that evening of the seventh, he would place his folded arms on the table and sink his head toward them, then raise his head again, an extraordinary head, long and equine, the face thin, long thin lips; he would remove his spectacles and rub his eyes. Cathal Brugha, fellow cabinet member, sat beside him, a small, contained figure, implacable, sitting for long periods almost without movement, arms folded across his chest. But Griffith, one of their two chief opponents, sat for some reason in the center of the house, facing the speaker, as stiff as Brugha, but sturdier, heavyset, trim, unyielding face guarded by mustache and pince-nez. Collins, with Christopher Blake beside him, sat directly opposite De Valera and Brugha, Collins restless, crossing and uncrossing his legs, hands in pockets or hanging at his side. Once, MacEoin, one of the flying column commanders who had become a legend, leaned forward to whisper to him, and Collins turned round to listen, then turned back and, in turning, flung back a forelock with an impatient, unthinking lift of heavy, strong-jawed face. It was a gesture which we would all become familiar with, from newsreels or from addresses, in the months ahead, to enormous crowds in Sackville Street and College Green. Collins, on that January night of the final Treaty debate, had eight months to live, as had Brugha and Childers and Griffith and Boland, eight months and a bit more, less than a year for all of them. And the germ from which their deaths sprouted and flowered was here, that night, beneath harsh, habitual light.

On the day before, one of the gunmen, Seamus Robinson, had risen up, "to fire a few shots," as he put it. It was Robinson, commandant of the South Tipperary Brigade, who had begun the armed fight by launching, with Treacy and Breen, the ambush at Soloheadbeg, and he hammered out now the names of commanders and commandants who stood by the Republic, and of divisions and brigades—the first, second, third, fourth, fifth Cork brigades, West Limerick Brigade, Waterford Brigade, Dublin Brigade, Tipperary No. 1 Brigade, Liam Lynch, OC First Southern Division, Earnan O'Malley, OC Second Southern Division, Frank Lacy, OC Third Southern Division. "The Republic," Robinson said, "is at stake, and I don't give a rap whose opinions are cut up for bandages." And when it was suggested to him that the gunmen were threatening to blast the country into chaos, replied, with a beautiful simplicity, "Chaos would be better by far than degradation."

This intervention by the gun, or at least, by the shadows of the gunmen, appalled even De Valera, who called out from his seat, "It is scarcely right for any officers to be using the name of the army at all." But Robinson swept on, undeterred, to use the word that had been hovering, all but spoken, itself a shadow, above the deliberations, the word "treason." Until then, hard words had been spoken and harder ones contemplated, but Robinson flung the matter on the table. "Delegates are in the dock, to some extent at least: they have done something that to some extent at least appears to be—well, treason. I maintain that they have been guilty of the act of high treason and betrayal." Other commandants spoke less flamboyantly, but to the same effect. Eamon Aylward, who commanded a Kilkenny brigade, spoke prophetically: "The Republican ideal has not died, nor will it die, even though there be but fifty men left in Ireland to carry it on. I was elected because I was a Republican soldier and I will remain a Republican and I will vote against that Treaty."

The great bulk of the objections to the Treaty, however, was not formulated or expressed by picturesque commandants, heroes of ambush, disguise, attacks upon police barracks. A formidable minority, as the vote was to demonstrate, believed, and with justification, that when Dáil Éireann had assembled in January of 1919, it had assembled on behalf of a republic, and that to bargain, negotiate, compromise, for anything less than this or other than this was in fact an act of betrayal. But a majority, slender but nevertheless a majority, held that in the three intervening years, something had happened, and that something was History. The word "Republic" had been a banner used to organize a people, to shape an underground army, to launch in that people's name a desperate, bloody, ingenious war against an empire, to kill and risk killing in that banner's name. It was a banner whose legend stretched backwards for a century, and a people's aspirations were gathered within its folds—Whiteboys, the rebels of 1798, the Fenians, Parnell, the Land League, martyrs, patriots, rebellious playboys, all, despite contradictions and sober realities, had been gathered up within that name, "Republic," and so too and in especial, was the most recent yet the most formidable myth of them all—the Rising of 1916, the heroic, weeklong defense of Dublin, the deaths in city streets, the firing squads at Kilmainham. But there was a time for banners and a time at the negotiating table. And in London, the delegates had won on behalf of Ireland, on behalf of the "Republic" as much as could be won. It was, or so it seemed to me, the Party of Reality and the Party of the Dream in conflict with each other, and with much to be said for both sides. Griffith, with plaintive accuracy, reminded the House that he had told the Cabinet: "If I go to London I can't get a Republic: I will try for a Republic, but I can't bring it back."

Today, when we read the debates on the Treaty as they run their way through four hundred double-column pages bound in the dull olive of the Stationery Office of the Free State, we can see, with very little exercise of the imagination, Griffith's stiff, sturdy figure, see the square head, thick mustache, a limited, sincere man, with an inflexible sense of honor, and now, at the close of his career, forced to defend—of all things—his honor. As he spoke, ungesturing, fists clenched behind his back, once, for a second, the pince-nez caught and held a reflection of the electric light, so that he seemed, for that second, blind. "I cannot accept the invitation of the minister of defense to dishonor my signature and become immortalized in Irish history. I have signed this Treaty; and the man or nation that dishonors its signature is dishonored forever; no man who signed that Treaty can dishonor his signature without dishonoring himself and the nation."

But Griffith, as everyone knew, had never claimed to be a Republican, not from his earliest days when he was shaping Sinn Féin. Collins was another matter, it was Collins who had sent out his squads in the name of the Republic, and Collins who had caught the public imagination. And it was at Collins, more than anyone else, that Republican anger was directed.

"What positions exactly did Michael Collins hold in the army? Did he ever take part in any armed conflict in which he fought by shooting, in fact is there any authoritative record of his having ever fired a shot for Ireland at an enemy of Ireland?" Seamus Robinson had put the questions in the speech which suggested that the signers of the Treaty should be in the dock for high treason, and he put the question with a fierceness that suggested an old bitterness. It was when he had put those questions that Collins turned around to talk with Sean MacEoin, who sat behind him. MacEoin was a column commandant as famous at least as Robinson, famous for the skill and efficiency of his operations, but famous too as one of the field commanders who held, as the saying had quickly gained currency, that "What is good enough for Mick Collins is good enough for me." It was not merely the Dáil which was splitting upon the rock of the Treaty, it was the army as well. Collins nodded, and turned away from MacEoin, but he made no response to Robinson, nor, the next day, to Cathal Brugha, who in the course of denouncing the Treaty turned viciously upon Collins himself.

It was in the night of the final debate, about an hour before the vote was taken, and Brugha was speaking, as he always did, with a bitter, humorless tenacity. "Members have asked," he said, "because it is known that many in this chamber, and many, many more in the country at large, are of the opinion that Michael Collins is a leader of the army and has fought many fights for the Republic, members have asked me, as the minister of defense, to say whether in fact Michael Collins has ever fought for Ireland, has he ever fired a bullet at any enemy of Ireland?"

"Is this in order?" MacEoin asked, but Collins shook his head and said, "Carry on, carry on, Cathal," and folded his arms across his chest.

What followed was, in the circumstances, grotesque.

"The minister of finance," Brugha said, referring to Collins's cabinet rank, "does not like what I have got to say."

"Anything that can be said about me, say it," Collins said, in a tone of rough-edged disgust.

And Brugha proceeded, with a meticulous pedantry, to define Collins's position in the army as a subordinate of subordinates, the head of a subsection of the headquarters staff subordinate to the chief of staff who in turn was subordinate to Brugha as minister of defense. And all of the heads of subsections performed their work conscientiously and patriotically for Ireland, with but one—and here he paused for effect—with but one exception. "Whether he was responsible or not for the notoriety, I am not going to say. What I do say is that one member was specially selected by the press and the people to put him into a position which he never held. He was made a romantic figure, a mystical character such as this person certainly is not. The gentleman I refer to is Michael Collins."

It was at this point, when Brugha in his excitement slipped

from the decorum of parliamentary usage and referred to Collins by name, that Collins's supporters erupted. "You can let the Irish people judge that," Eamon Duggan shouted, and Milroy said with a wise air, "Now we know things," a cryptic utterance which a fellow named Dan MacCarthy amplified, "Now we know the reason for the opposition to the Treaty." And Griffith, his anger under an iron control, said only, "Oh, bravo, Cathal! Bravo!" But the tumult, strangely, came entirely from Collins's allies. The opposition, although some of them shared Brugha's views, as we came shortly to know, sat fascinated and appalled, as though a dangerous secret had been hauled into the open. De Valera himself sat as though stricken. He had taken off his spectacles, and now, throughout the noisy interchange, he rubbed the bridge of his nose, looked toward the chandeliers, or toward windows beyond which lay black night. Once, at least, he looked over directly at Collins, as though trying for his eye, but Collins was looking straight ahead.

It was upon those of us who sat as visitors that the effect was strongest. All of Ireland knew that the divisions over the Treaty had brought to the surface divisions among personalities. It was hinted at in the newspapers, spoken aloud in parish halls and public houses, it was becoming the subject of satirical street ballads, but to watch it, thus naked, to hear it, was a different matter. And Brugha's anger against Collins was carrying him beyond the bounds of prudence. There were few within that chamber who would have agreed that Collins was the subordinate of a subordinate, with limited and clearly defined responsibilities. The subsection in question, after all, was Intelligence. Much that had been secrecy and whisper six months ago was talked about openly now. It was Collins who had smashed the British intelligence operation, Collins who had planted his spies in Dublin Castle and College Green, Collins who had managed to be everywhere at once, cutting red tape, standing pints of porter to flying column commandants, organizing prison breaks and the occasional assassination, settling quarrels between brigades.

And yet the damage, finally, was done by Brugha to himself, and not to Collins, as Brugha slipped deeper and deeper into abuse, at one point accusing Collins's claque of exaggerating the price which the British had put on his head, dead or alive. At this, Collins did lift up his head and grin, and I knew that he had gauged nicely the effect which Brughas's invective was producing. De Valera shook his head, and again sought to meet Collins's eyes.

Christopher rose only once to speak, and it was immediately after the tumult had exhausted itself. Although he was sitting close to Collins, he did not look at him while he was speaking, nor indeed did he look across the table at Brugha, his words seemed directed, if anywhere, at De Valera.

"I rise," he said, "to speak in support of the Treaty and because I intend to vote for it. And for that reason only. Every member of this house, every man and woman in it, has an obligation to the house and to the Irish people to explain his vote as clearly as possible, and to do so without the vilification of colleagues. I have served this movement since 1916 in one or another of several capacities, and most recently as a secretary, with Mr. Childers, of the delegation which negotiated the Treaty. I am persuaded that the delegates secured all that could be secured, and that the alternative to the Treaty was a resumption of the war. We did not secure a Republic, but—"

He was interrupted here. "You did worse than that. You surrendered the Republic which you had taken an oath to defend."

Christopher paused for a moment, and then began again. It was a lucid speech, well balanced and sinuous, I had expected nothing less from him, but for two days now I had been hearing speeches which went over the same points in one order or another, and my mind drifted away a bit to reflect upon what a curious assembly this was, of schoolmasters and gunmen and solicitors, even, in his case, a historian, even, in the case of Childers, a Republican diehard who had held during the war—during the Great War—a commission as major in the British Army. For two years, Christopher and Childers had been friends; now they sat on opposite sides, Childers looking intently forward, a frail man, the skin of his face pulled taut. At one point, so it seemed to me, he had been about to interrupt but had restrained himself. Old parliamentary courtesies die hard.

Childers, on this January night, had ten months to live. It is easy now, gratifying to one's sense of the tragic, of the grotesque even, to look backwards, past that bloody autumn and winter of 1922 to the afternoons and nights of the January debate. But it would be misleading. No one in that room was prepared to look down the perspective of short months to civil war. To the contrary, despite outbursts of anger and sophistry, there was a determination to maintain a membrane, at least, of unity. But the membrane frayed at points, tore loose, and in Christopher's case, it was an interjection by one of the Waterford members, who commanded a brigade.

He was a stocky young fellow named Patrick Burke, "Paudge" Burke was how he had become famous, the victor of a celebrated ambush outside the small town of Ring. His heavy, fleshy shoulders bulged against his dark serge jacket, and he had jumped up to speak, hands pressed flat against hips.

"Will the member yield," he asked, "upon a point of order? Will the member not declare his personal interest, that he is a crony and a confidant of the minister of finance, and that he did his best, as a pal of journalists in London and New York, to puff up the minister of finance as a romantic chieftain of the guerrillas and all the rest of it, as has been ably set forth for us by the minister of defense?"

"The chair will no doubt rule," Christopher said, torn between anger and amusement, "that there does not seem to be a point of order here."

"The chair does so rule," Professor MacNeill said. A smile slipped briefly across his grim, bearded face.

"Oh, to be sure," Paudge said, " 'tis easy to make up rulings. But I will tell you what is not easy. 'Tis not easy to be on your keeping, in winter rains, with no help save what people can contrive for you at risk of prison or of having their houses burned down by the Black and Tans. We have heard men stand up here to say that Michael Collins is the man that won the war, but the war was won upon the lonely roads of Munster and Connaught, by men who fought for a Republic and will still, please God, fight for a Republic. The war was not won in the back rooms of public houses in Dublin, much less was it won by Irishmen off in London hobnobbing with their society hostesses." Before he sat down, he paused to say, "And that is all I will say on that subject. A vote against the Treaty is a vote for the Republic."

"All right," Christopher said with a sigh. "I helped with our Republican publicity and so did Deputy Childers. We arranged interviews with the men whom foreign journalists wished to talk with, and at the top of their lists was always the name of Michael Collins."

"Not because he had led an ambush," Paudge said, "any more than you ever did yourself, and I do not say that with sarcasm, but I do say that the men who did the fighting should be heard here. You have heard me, and you have heard Seamus Robinson, of the Third Tipperary. There are two brigade commanders from Kerry sitting amongst the visitors and I can tell you what they think of oath-breakers who would betray the Republic."

"If we are going to count up brigade commanders and battalion commanders," Christopher said, "we are in a sad way indeed, if we are choosing up sides, this brigade on one side and that brigade on the other."

"Hear, hear," De Valera said, and now, for a brief moment, his eyes and Collins's met, and the two men nodded. It was a moment heavy with possibility, but brief. But Collins looked then, and a bit apprehensively, toward Christopher, who had grown angry during the exchange.

"We have no finer fighting man in Ireland than Sean MacEoin, the man who won and held the midlands, fighting battle after battle, the man who a few months ago lay in Kilmainham under sentence of death. And you have heard Sean MacEoin speak in support of the Treaty, as giving us not the form of freedom but the substance of it."

"Sean MacEoin can speak for himself," Collins suddenly interjected, "and he has done so. Leave that alone, now, Christopher." For all of the room's tensions, there were smiles on the faces of some of the deputies, on both sides. MacEoin was indeed a fine commander, and a chivalrous one, which was more than could be said of Paudge. When Paudge staged his ambush of the Tans at Ring, there were no survivors among the Tans, but MacEoin had been known to get medical help for the British wounded. British officers whom he had fought and beaten testified at his court-martial on his behalf. But he was not, to put it mildly, a master of oratory.

"You speak of the army," Christopher said. "The army's chief of staff is a member of this body, you have heard him speak. It would be a sorry day for Ireland were the people to think that their army was opposed to the Treaty. Some are and some are not. We all know that. That is why we are talking to each other or at each other. That is why very shortly we will be voting. We are a democratic people, please God, and that is how matters are settled by a free people."

Liam Mellowes had early made a powerful speech in opposition to the Treaty, but since the reconvening of the Dáil after Christmas, he had said almost nothing although in constant attendance, a nervous, fierce, high-strung man. In 1916, Mellowes and Frank Lacy had commanded in Galway the only Rising outside Dublin. Now Mellowes leaned forward, and hard upon Christopher's words, he said, "It is right for this house to know that my oath to the Republic, my oath at least, cannot be dissolved by a vote. The Republic exists, it is a living, tangible thing, something for which men gave their lives, for which men were hanged, for which men are in gaol, for which the people suffered, and for which men are still prepared to give their lives. There is no question of making a bargain over this thing, over the honor of Ireland, because I hold that the honor of Ireland is too sacred a thing to make a bargain over."

Cathal Brugha's words had had the hysterical intensity of a devout, and Paudge's words had the bravado of a moss trooper, but Mellowes, who was capable of both eloquence and close reasoning, spoke now, at the end of the day, with a sincerity that moved beyond eloquence, and Christopher, recognizing this, looked toward him with both distress and recognition. What was at issue in the chamber that night, as the minutes moved toward an irrevocable vote, was more than Republic or Free State or the sundering of old friendships and alliances, but two habits of mind and spirit. Christopher, like Collins and like all of those who had spoken on behalf of the Treaty, recognized what Collins, in a wonderful phrase, had spoken of as "the duress of the facts." You fought as hard as you could, ruthlessly if need be, unscrupulously if need be, and then, at the end of the day, you struck the best bargain you could get, and with perhaps a hidden resolution that someday, if conditions were right, you would fight to get back what you had bargained away. But Liam Mellowes reminded those who heard him that the fight had been waged by men who had sworn an oath to the Republic, and who were bound to that oath by the blood of fallen comrades. And more, were bound to it by history itself.

The final word before the vote was taken was spoken by

Griffith, bound as always by a code of old-fashioned honor. "I do not care," he said in his high-pitched, determined voice, "whether the King of England or the symbol of the Crown be in Ireland so long as the people of Ireland be free to shape their own destinies. We have the means to do that by this Treaty; we have not the means otherwise. I say now to the people of Ireland that it is their right to see that this Treaty is carried into operation, when they get, for the first time in seven centuries, a chance to live their own lives in their own country and take their place among the nations of Europe."

The vote, when finally it came, was so close that the chamber was silent, listening intently, and when it was at last announced, 64 in favor of the Treaty and 57 against it, there was an entire silence, which was broken at last by De Valera. His tone was personal and not public.

"It will, of course," he said, "be my duty to resign my office as chief executive. I do not know that I should do it just now."

"No," Collins said at once. "No. The president knows how I tried to do my best for him."

"Hear, hear," De Valera said, taking refuge behind the parliamentary formula, but Christopher, who of course was sitting close to him, only the table separating them, told me that De Valera's eyes, behind the thick spectacles, had begun to water.

"He has exactly the same position in my heart now that he always had," Collins said, and this brought applause from both sides. "We must reach some kind of understanding—" but there he paused, and shook his heavy head as though in bewilderment.

"I would like my last word here to be this," De Valera said. "We have had a glorious record here for four years. It has been four years of magnificent discipline in our nation. The world is looking at us now—"

At this point, in the printed record of the debate over the Treaty, the secretary found no other words than these, placed in apologetic quotation marks: "The President here breaks down."

And the poor secretary had no choice. De Valera had begun sobbing, and, out of grief or embarrassment, rested his forearms on the table, and buried his head in them. He was not the only man weeping. It was an unnerving moment, as though all the oratory had at last been scraped away, all the tributes to sacrifice and principle, and what was left was the ugliness of a division which few wanted, a division without victory for either side, and fraught with the possibility of something worse than mere division.

"Perhaps," Collins said, his tone faltering, tentative, probing for a stopgap, "perhaps we could form some kind of joint committee to carry on—for carrying through the arrangements one way or another—I think that is what we ought to do. Now I only want to say this to the people who are against us—and there are good people against us—so far as I am concerned this is not a question of politics, nor never has been. I make my promise to the Irish nation—"

"As far as I am concerned," Cathal Brugha said, "I will see at any rate, that discipline is kept in the army." He was speaking directly to Collins, and Collins, who understood what was meant, nodded his relief. Not all the army commandants were members of the Dáil, indeed most of them were not, but the most active of them had traveled up to Dublin—Liam Lynch was here, and Ernie O'Malley, and Frank Lacy.

But in that moment of transient reconciliation, of men moving slowly, warily across brittle ice toward each other, the voice of the future spoke through Mary MacSwiney.

"I rise now," she said, "to denounce the grossest act of betrayal that Ireland ever endured. Let there be no soft talk about reconciliation at the last moment of the betrayal. Make no doubt about it. This is a betrayal, a gross betrayal. There can be no union between the representatives of the legitimate Irish Republic and the so-called Free State."

She had more to say along those lines. Her attributes as an orator did not include a gift for the laconic. Statisticians with an interest in the matter were to calculate that during the debate she spoke for a total of five and a half hours, and, so far as I can myself judge, this lengthiness was not created by a love of sophistry or equivocation or out of a pedantic attention to detail. Rather, she swept forward, upon a torrent of words, to her irresistible conclusion that at the end of the day, at the end of the hunt, only civil war could preserve the Republic.

It became the fashion, among the Dublin wits, Gogarty and Myles Keough and Jimmy Montgomery and their pals, to make sport of the women who opposed the Treaty, Con Markievicz, who attended the sessions in her green Cumann na mBan uniform, and Mrs. Clarke and Mrs. Pearse and Mrs. O'Callaghan and Mary MacSwiney. There was a touch of unease even in their wit, because our bloody recent history was inscribed in this very presence. As they rose, at the first, at least, ghosts stood close to them—Pearse at the grave of O'Donovan Rossa, Clarke in the condemned cell in Kilmainham. In Limerick, on a March night in 1921, as his wife stood watching, armed men, Black and Tans disguised by goggles, murdered Michael O'Callaghan at the foot of his stairs. Now his widow stood up in the Dáil to denounce a Treaty which she, like others, regarded as betrayal. A month before, drunken police on a random raid had told her that soon she would "know more about murder."

We drifted out from University College into the chilly, rainy Dublin night, alone, or in small groups, struggling into greatcoats, voices subdued, on edge, angry, confused. The street which we faced, Earlsfort Terrace, a prim, respectable street, held a thin crowd who had braved the rain, and who cheered, but thinly, as we came out. A band of twenty, perhaps, were holding a long, stretched-out banner of white, upon which had been painted, in tall black letters, "Up the Republic." The letters were already smeared by the cold, drizzling rain.

Christopher came out with Collins and four or five others, not talking, any of them, staring straight ahead. Behind them walked one of the "boys" of Collins's Squad.

"By George," a familiar voice behind me said, "Mick Collins must be the safest man in Ireland. Before long, we will all be welcoming a bodyguard, but who will be able to afford him, and how do we know that we can trust him?"

Myles Keough was buttoning his overcoat of rich black wool as he spoke, and now he turned up the collar.

I touched his arm, and then walked away from him to Christopher, who smiled at me, but bleakly, without pleasure. He began to speak, but then shook his head, and stood looking at me, then shrugged and walked after his friends. I went back to Myles.

"Yes," Myles said, "yes indeed." Myles was a wit, with a reputation to maintain, and the occasion had challenged him. "You heard Dev, did you not? He will be meeting with his followers tomorrow. And why should he not, there are almost as many on his side as on the other. What shall we have now, Patrick, the True Republicans and the Not-So-True Republicans?"

Collins and his fellows were out of sight, somewhere toward Stephen's Green, and De Valera had not come out from the chamber, so far as I knew, nor Griffith, nor Brugha, nor any of the others who had been speaking with such passion. But, just then, the crowd gave a shout, and the banner of smeared black lettering on white moved jerkily from left to right, right to left. And, turning to my own left, mine and Myles's, I saw De Valera, tall, bent-shouldered, standing for a moment motionless, neither accepting the shouts nor rejecting them. The rain was heavier now.

Ten days later, though, when Dublin Castle was surrendered to Collins acting on behalf of the new Provisional Government, the skies were clear, but it had turned remarkably cold, even for January. It should have been a day of portents, of history and ceremony, the fulfillment of ballads and prophecies. And the departing, or at any rate retiring, British did their best for ceremony, a Castle guard drawn up for a final inspection by Fitzalan, the Lord Lieutenant, in the cobblestoned Castle Yard, and sentries in full battle dress standing behind the closed gates, watching through slits for the arrival of the Irish. And there were crowds outside on Dame Street, of course, waiting to cheer.

But when the Irish did arrive, it was almost matter-of-fact, three motorcars of them, with Collins in the first car and Christopher in the third—you can just make out Christopher in a smudged newspaper photograph. Collins waited impatiently, distracted, until his party was standing around him, and the heavy gates had swung open.

"Mr. Collins," a young English major, amused and impressed at the same time, said, after he had saluted, "you are nine minutes late."

Collins had walked past him, but now he turned around. "After seven hundred years," he said, "we don't begrudge you a final ten minutes."

"Yes," the major said, uncertain whether or not he was expected to smile. "Well. Lord Fitzalan is expecting you in the Privy Council Chamber. I have been detailed to escort you there."

"Yes," Collins said. "Very proper. Come along, boy. Mind you, I know where the Privy Council meets. I know Dublin Castle."

In the chamber, first Collins, as chairman of the new Provisional Government, and then the other cabinet ministers, and then Christopher and the other members of the cabinet staff, shook hands first with MacMahon, the under-secretary, and then with Fitzalan, a portly man, well-tended walrus mustache of snowy white. Christopher, recalling the scene to me, the transfer of power from English to Irish hands, best remembered of the room heavy wood paneling, dark wood, a heavy table, on a long wall, portraits, Victorian, most of them, or Edwardian, dark frock coats, white shirts, or court uniforms, stiff with gilt brocades, gilt sword hilts. On one of the narrow side walls, beside a door, hung a magnificent early map of Ireland, decorated in one corner by a florid, elaborate cartouche.

"Mr. Collins," MacMahon said, affable, himself a Catholic, one of the Castle "moderates," as the press called them, "I am delighted to see you here."

"You are like hell," Collins said.

MacMahon, Christopher told me, responded with a wintry smile. Fitzalan looked unsmilingly first at Collins and then back at MacMahon. Castle legend had made Collins out to be a jovial sort of gunman, full of Irish humor, but MacMahon did not seem amused, and Collins looked sullen. Fitzalan may perhaps have remembered that Collins, by repute, had organized the assassination of his predecessor, Lord French.

There were formalities to be attended to, Collins to say that he was prepared to take over the powers and machinery of government, in accordance with the seventeenth article of the Treaty, and Fitzalan to reply that he was prepared to communicate this intelligence to the cabinet in London, who would, in turn, inform His Majesty. The exchanges back and forth took ten minutes in all, and Collins walked through them like a man accepting a parcel at a sub–post office. Christopher turned away from the wall of portraits, and toward the wall of tall, leaded windows looking out onto the Castle Walk. Barbed wire and sandbags were scattered across the wide expanse, and soldiers in squads, weighted down with rifles, marched back and forth. The heavy doors opening out onto Dame Street were still open, and the crowd filled the street beyond them.

As the Irish walked across the cobblestones, back toward their waiting motorcars, MacEoin, who although in civilian clothes was acting as military attaché, grabbed Collins by the shoulder. "Mick lad, what a day! Dublin Castle in the hands of the Irish, by God. The bad centuries wiped away. *Sinn Féin abu!*" Collins snapped his head toward him, almost in anger, but caught himself in time. "A grand day, Sean," he said. "A grand day."

But on the short drive back to the Mansion House, Christopher sat in the car with Collins. Collins at one window and Cosgrave at the other, with Christopher between them. The crowd cheered them, but not all of the crowd. At the corner of Parliament Street, a sizable group, the women in black, most of them, and the men in dark overcoats, black or dark gray, stood silent, not cheering, not shouting. The banner which stretched behind them read "The Republic Cannot Be Destroyed."

"Would you not think," Cosgrave said, in his high, precise voice, "that they could leave us alone for a morning at least, give over that nonsense long enough for us to take over Dublin Castle on behalf of the Irish people, the lot of us, them as well as ourselves? Would you not think that?"

But Collins did not answer him. He had taken out a notebook and one of his stubs of pencil, and seemed to be making notes, but as the motorcar swerved into College Green, Christopher glanced over, and saw that he was drawing abstract patterns, uneven rectangles, jagged arrows, ladders that stopped in midair.

In the ten days that had elapsed between the vote on the Treaty and the "surrender" of Dublin Castle, Ireland had drifted into uncertainties, bitterness, confusions. De Valera had resigned as president, then offered himself for reelection, and had been defeated by only two votes, he himself not voting. Cathal Brugha had renewed his bitter attacks on Collins, and Collins's supporters had answered in language equally fierce. In a second vote, Griffith was elected president of Dáil Éireann, pledged to maintain the Republic until the Irish people had voted on the issue, and Mulcahy had pledged that "the army will remain the army of the Irish Republic." And, on the fourteenth, without vote or discussion, a Provisional Government was appointed, with Collins as its chairman. There was now, in existence, Dáil Éireann as an ongoing deliberative body, torn between supporters and opponents of the Treaty, and with a cabinet composed entirely of supporters, and a Provisional Government, shadowy in its own way, which existed for the accomplishment of such formalities as the transfer of Dublin Castle's authority from English to Irish hands.

As the cars swung down Nassau Street toward Dawson Street, Collins took off his hat and rested it on his knees. Despite the cold, his forehead was damp. He caught Christopher looking at him, frowned, and then, as though thinking better of it, smiled, and, so it seemed to Christopher, it was his first unaffected smile that morning.

"Bloody lousers," he said, still smiling. "Jesus, you'd have to be up early in the morning to be up before those lads. There must have been a few hours' work put into the construction of that banner. 'The Republic Cannot Be Destroyed.' Cathal Brugha has cut out a new task for himself, dictating placards." Brugha was no longer minister for defense. He was in the wilderness with De Valera, and Mulcahy had replaced him.

"Disgraceful," Cosgrave said.

"Do you think so, Willie?" Collins said. "By Jesus, this time a year ago, we were all of us shouting that the Republic could never be destroyed. Do you remember that, Willie?"

"I do," Cosgrave said, and in the crowded seat, he moved uncomfortably. "But things are said and sworn and promised in the heat of the day, said at meetings and in the newspapers and so forth."

"It was the lads lying behind the hedges, in rain and danger, waiting to cut loose upon soldiers in armored cars," Collins said, "those are the lads we told were fighting for a Republic." He nodded again, as though in argument with himself. "Ask Chris here. Am I right, Chris?" He pounded his knee, with some kind of self-lacerating anger.

Christopher and Elizabeth Keating had many months before produced a bulky pamphlet, "Soldiers of the Republic," with accounts of MacEoin's "battles" in Longford; Barry's ambush of the Tans at Kilmichael, and his "battle" at Crossbarry, where he hurled his column against a British force five times as large, with Billy Belton, his piper, droning full blast, and then fought his way out to safety, his column intact; Frank Lacy's attack on the Tans quartered in Ardmor Castle; Ernie O'Malley's hit-and-run assaults on police barracks scattered across the country—Tipperary, Mayo, Kilkenny, Limerick.

Half of the run of 500 copies had been lost when the Tans raided the house in Mespil Road, but Christopher remembered Collins leafing through a copy in the snug at Devlin's, off Rutland Square, sipping a heavily watered whiskey and with an uneaten ham sandwich in front of him. "This is great stuff, Chris," he said, and shoved the pamphlet into his pocket. He was in a hurry, late for a meeting with Mulcahy in Mountjoy Square; that would have been in the spring of 1921, when he was always in a hurry, always late.

There was another crowd, a smaller one, outside the Mansion House, but they seemed a crowd of the curious, and there were no banners or placards. When they saw that it was Collins, though, there were scattered jovial shouts. "Mick Collins, the hard man," a young voice shouted, and Collins, as though detecting irony, swung his head toward the voice. But then, unsmiling, he nodded, and touched his hand to the brim of his hat. The door of the Mansion House swung open for Collins and his party, and a newspaper photograph displays the black-clad arm of a civil servant, a small, decorous civil servant's head bent forward in greeting.

"A wonderful day, Michael," Arthur Griffith said. "Dublin Castle is ours. Dublin Castle is in the hands of the Irish."

Collins nodded and looked around the drawing room. He had taken off his hat but had made no move to unbutton his overcoat. There was a moment's delay, and then, as though seeing Griffith suddenly, hearing him a fraction after he had spoken, Collins nodded. "Yes," he said, "a wonderful day entirely," and, as though entering Griffith's mood with an effort, he said, "We have seized the Castle, by God. *Sinn Féin amhain!* Ourselves alone."

Griffith stood, a short sturdy pillar, dark-suited, wing-collared, necktie precisely knotted. Later, Christopher told me, he wondered whether Collins was seeing him as he himself was, as a man for whom a dream had come mysteriously true, Dublin Castle, the heart of British rule in Ireland, fallen to the Irish, a symbol toppled.

"It went off well?" Griffith asked.

"Indeed yes," Collins said. "They did everything but turn out a British regimental band to play 'Let Erin Remember.' They do that sort of thing well. Stiff upper lip."

A bit later, Collins and Christopher stood by the tall window, looking out upon Dawson Street. The crowd had drifted away, and there was no one to be seen save the occasional passerby. Dermot Breen stood beside them, a member of the Dáil for County Dublin, but related by marriage to two of the old, respectable nationalist dynasties, the Healys of Bantry and the Tully-Delaneys of Kilpeder, sturdy, prosperous Cork dynasties, solicitors and merchants and barristers. Dermot Breen was a solicitor himself; for the past year he had been serving as a judge in one of the Sinn Féin courts, and appearing in the Four Courts to defend Volunteers.

"A great day for Ireland," he said. "The guns of the Castle spiked after centuries."

The Provisional Government would be establishing itself in the City Hall, next to the Castle, and Breen was responsible for the arrangements, transferring records and settling the staff in their new quarters.

"A great day for Ireland," Collins said, mechanically. "The crowds have deserted us, Dermot, save for the odd surgeon hurrying along to a late lunch in the University Club."

"You should have been here earlier," Breen said. "Your blood would have boiled. Twenty or more of the other lot, you know the ones, the Childers crowd and the monstrous regiment of True Republicans, with banners and tricolors, clumped in front of the Royal Automobile Club." He coughed discreetly. "I think they were waiting for you. We made short work of them."

Collins shook his head, as though not understanding, and continued to look out upon the near-empty street. "What do you mean, you made short work of them? How?"

Breen laughed with delight. "Sure, aren't we the government now? I picked up the telephone and put in a call to the police."

"You did what?" Collins asked, and turned around to face him. "You phoned the bloody police? You used the RIC to scatter Republicans? Are you mad?"

"The DMP," Breen said, alarmed but keeping his tone jovial. "Dublin's own. A fine body of men, as the saying goes."

Collins began to speak, and then seemed to think better of it. He jammed his fists into the pockets of his coat, and stood rocking back and forth on the balls and heels of his feet.

"It was yourself they were waiting for," Breen said, "to barrack you when you came back from the Castle. You have heard the class of things that that crowd has been shouting out at you whenever you have been in view."

Traitor, Christopher had heard them shout, *renegade.*

"I will take my chances," Collins said, "if I am to be protected against Irishmen, it will not be by England's hirelings."

He nodded and turned back to the window, and Breen, rightly reading this as dismissal, stepped away from him, back to the long table stacked with papers. In all likelihood, Christopher thought, Breen had never set foot in Headquarters, had never seen Collins in a rage in the rooms above Devlin's public house or in the Heytesbury Street public house.

They were alone by the window then, Collins and Christopher, and after a silence, Collins said, "This has been a busy morning, Christopher. Jesus!" He smashed a fist into an open palm.

But before he left the Mansion House, he wrote out a statement for the press.

> *Rialtas Sealadach na Heireann* (Provisional Government of Ireland) received the surrender of Dublin Castle at 1:45 P.M. today. It is now in the hands of the Irish Nation. For the next few days the functions of the existing departments of that institution will be continued without in any way prejudicing future action. The various details of the handing over will be arranged forthwith. A statement will be issued tomorrow with respect to the immediate intentions and policy of the government of the nation of Ireland. For Rialtas Sealadach na Heireann. —Michael Collins, Chairman.

He read it over, blew on the ink, and screwed on the top of his fountain pen. He looked around, for Griffith perhaps, Christopher thought, but Griffith was not in the room. He nodded with cold, distant courtesy to Breen, and, impulsively, grabbed Christopher by the shoulders. "We showed them, boy. We showed them. The *surrender* of Dublin Castle. By God, I wonder how they will like that word when they read it in Downing Street. Surrender. We showed them."

Christopher watched him clatter, splayfooted, down the steps of the Mansion House, past the elaborate ornamental lanterns, past intricate ironwork, and turn left toward Stephen's Green. He was walking quickly, head sunk to heavy shoulders. Behind him, at a prudent distance, moved his shadow.

XXII

FRANK LACY

The Treaty had been signed and ratified in the depths of London and Dublin winters. In May, when Lacy drove north, the Munster countryside was in the fullness of late spring. The pasturelands were a deep, rich green, the trees were heavy with leaf, and Ireland was on the edge of civil war.

He was driving the open touring car of royal blue which he and Ben Cogley had used on tours of inspection. But Cogley, the closest that Lacy had come to having an intimate friend, was in Dublin now and on the other side in the impending war, an officer stationed in the Free State garrison at Beggars Bush. And on the empty seat beside him, because he did not know what final twists negotiations might have taken, Lacy had rested a loaded parabellum.

At Mallow, he stopped at what had once been a British Army barracks, but was now the headquarters of the Republican First Southern Division, commanded by Liam Lynch. The British, when they withdrew, had handed over barracks to whatever brigades of Volunteers were on the scene, whether pro-Treaty or anti-Treaty, which meant that most of Munster, save for parts of Clare and Limerick, had passed into Republican hands.

Lynch, who was now not only commandant of the First Southern but chief of staff of all armed forces in opposition to the Treaty, had been in Mallow for the weekend, but had taken the early train to Dublin.

"You would have to be an early riser to catch Liam," his deputy said, Charlie Mannion, a hefty, sandy-haired man in his late twenties. "With the road to Dublin before him, and a full day's work on his plate."

They were having tea in what had once been the wardroom. One wall still held a British Army map of Munster, a network of main and secondary roads in red and blue, arteries and veins. Someone, Lynch or Mannion or their intelligence officer, had peppered it with black and white pins.

Mannion nodded toward it. "We'll never have better maps than the British maps. Those lads are prodigies of mapmaking. By God, it was a marvelous day entirely, that day in February when we took over Mallow barracks. Sure, it must have been the same for you lads, when you took over from the Tans in Kilpeder."

There was an open window beside the map. It looked out upon the cobbled courtyard behind the barracks, and the sounds of a squad being drilled drifted into the wardroom. Presently, the squad came into view, farm lads in moleskins and dark jackets, bandoliers slung across shoulders. They were drilling with what looked to Lacy like Lee-Enfields. "Jesus," their corporal shouted at them, "can you not at least drill! Count cadence! On your left, on your left, on your left right left." He was wearing a Volunteer tunic, and a holstered revolver belted to his waist.

"I doubt," Lacy said, making a question of it, "if the British handed their weapons over to you when they vacated the barracks?"

"Indeed they did not," Mannion said. " 'The surrender of the Mallow barracks' is how the *Cork Examiner* described it, but it was more like one lot of tenants moving out and a new lot moving in. The Tommies moved out in good order, their weapons sloped. My fingers itched to get hold of those rifles, but Liam had his orders and he hewed to them. He is sorry by now that he did."

"I was as bad myself at Kilpeder," Lacy said. "I let the Tans—and Kilpeder was garrisoned by bloody Black and Tans, not Tommies—I followed orders, and off they went in their lorries, with their rifles and sidearms and Mills bombs and Lewis guns and Vickers guns and what have you. I had my mind set on keeping discipline. There are terrible things that the Tans were about in the cellars of Ardmor Castle, and my lads were ready for another go at them."

"They have not left the country, any of them, for all the fine words. They have been pulled back to Dublin, and they sit, waiting for Mick Collins to bring them cups of tea."

"You clumsy hoors," the corporal shouted, "lay down your left boots on the left beat. Do I have to call out hay-foot straw-foot for you?"

"A bit of a martinet beyond there," Lacy said.

"He signed up during the Truce," Mannion said. "One of the Truceleers. But he is a good Republican."

"He knows how to drill men," Lacy said.

" 'Tis in the blood," Mannion said. "His father was Connaught Rangers, killed beyond there in Mesopotamia." Suddenly, Lacy imagined sand, thirst, a strange language.

"The sun never sets on the British Empire," Lacy said. "Baghdad, Calcutta, Dublin."

"The sun has set for it in Munster," Mannion said. "We hold a perimeter from Waterford to Limerick. If the Free Staters move against us, we can pull back behind that line. Liam was busy all yesterday afternoon with that British map and a handful of drawing pins. We hold Munster for the Republic, Frank, yourself and Liam and Ernie O'Malley beyond in Tipperary. And not Munster only, the Republic holds parts of Connaught as well. Lads like Pilkington have not been idle. And we hold a part of Dublin itself."

"I know that," Lacy said, "but we should have been quicker off the mark. Ernie O'Malley made the right move, raiding the British police barracks in Clonmel while it was still loaded with British rifles."

"Rifles and land mines," Mannion said, grinning. "By God, Ernie is the hard man." He carried hot water from the stove, and filled their teapot. "Did you hear tell about Ernie at the Templemore barracks?"

Templemore, in O'Malley's divisional command, was held by Second Tipperary, and in theory, like all of his command, was loyal to the Republic, but O'Malley was less certain of it. It seemed to him that Leahy, the commandant, was courting first one side and then the other, first the Free Staters in Beggars Bush and then the Republicans in the Four Courts. The Free Staters courted them with promises of British rifles, and then, in May, had sent down an armored car with which to overawe them. It was in the courtyard, being overhauled by the battalion mechanics, when O'Malley made a surprise visit. O'Malley fell in love with it—plates of bulletproof steel, a long Rolls-Royce engine, loopholes with shutters, and a revolving steel turret with a Vickers gun.

"Take a look at that," Leahy said, "look away at your leisure. There is modern mechanized equipment for a modern mechanized state. It carries an armed crew and beside the Vickers they can maintain steady fire from the loopholes. How do you like her, Ernie?"

"I have fallen in love with her," O'Malley said, and as he walked along the carriage, he ran a hand affectionately along the side of tempered steel. "I have always wanted a Rolls-Royce," he said. "Gogarty above in Dublin has one, and he took myself and Christopher Blake out once for a spin across the Scalp into Wicklow. A different model to be sure, his is a lovely deep yellow, and fitted out with leather and windscreens and a trunk for picnic hampers, but the motor could be identified anywhere, a Rolls-Royce motor."

"You understand, Ernie, do you not," Leahy said nervously, "this armored car is the property of the Provisional Government, Mulcahy himself sent it down to us from Beggars Bush, a demonstration only, a driver went with it."

Lacy could imagine O'Malley, and he imagined him smiling. He was wearing, in Lacy's imagination, the tight-belted, long leather coat, with the automatic pistol belted to his waist, half-soldier, half-brigand.

"Have you forgotten, Tommy," he said to Leahy, "the Second Southern Division has repudiated the authority of the Provisional Government, we have declared ourselves for the Republic. And Dick Mulcahy has made us a present of an armored car. God alone knows why."

Now the armored car was in Dublin, at Republican Headquarters in the Four Courts.

"Do you know what the lads in Dublin call it?" Mannion asked Lacy. "They call it 'The Mutineer.' That is what the newspapers call us, after all."

"He is a wild lad, O'Malley," Mannion said, smiling and shaking his head in reminiscence. "I can remember the day in 1920 when Liam and Ernie attacked this very barracks, the one in which we are sitting, and overthrew the garrison, September of

1920, that was, the first major operation of the flying column, and by God if we did not teach the arts of war to the Seventeenth Lancers."

"I remember," Lacy said, "the lads in my own column were green with envy. What sort of load was it that you hauled away with you from the barracks?"

"Oh, by God," Mannion said, "rifles and revolvers and Very pistols, and four thousand rounds of ammunition. And two Hotchkiss light machine guns. Two machine guns," he repeated, rolling the words on his lips.

It had been a model operation, for all that it had been the first of its kind, and Lacy had lectured upon it in training operations, both later in the Tan war and then during the Truce. That is what the Republican soldiers were beginning to call the operations against the police and the British, the Tan war. As though to mark it off from whatever might now be at work.

Sketches had been made of the streets running off from the barracks, and a lad who worked there as a painter had drawn a map of the barracks itself, its courtyards and wardrooms. On the night of the twenty-seventh the column moved into town, across the bridge over the Blackwater, and took up headquarters in the Town Hall, which faced the barracks. The next morning, about nine-thirty, O'Malley knocked on the door with a message that could be given only to the barracksmaster, and, when the sentry hesitated, tore away his rifle, and shouted to the column. Three motorcars had been waiting, which drove into the outer courtyard, and into which the captured weapons were piled. "But it wasn't all that perfect," O'Malley protested later to Lacy, "we shot that poor hoor of a sergeant. I tried to bind up his wound as best I could, but he had been gut-shot. A brave man, that sergeant was, but he was screaming, you could not blame him." But it had been almost perfect, O'Malley admitted. "When our lads drove off in the motorcars," he told Lacy, "they carried lances shoved out the windows, with colored pennons flapping from them. The Seventeenth Lancers, there you are, a crack regiment, famed in song and story, as they say."

Now, in that barracks, Mannion smiled in reminiscence.

"I remember us standing in the courtyard below there, myself and Liam Lynch and Ernie O'Malley. We were watching some of our lads loading the motorcars, and another lot of us holding the garrison quiet at rifle point, a crisp autumn morning, the action had taken far less than an hour, but we had cause to work as quickly as we could. Here we are here in Mallow, take a look at us"—he jerked his head toward the ordnance map—"twelve miles from Fermoy, which in those days had a garrison of close to two thousand. And Buttevant, eight miles to the north and with a heavy garrison, a camp. They would soon be swarming upon us like the myrmidons of old." Myrmidons: Lacy savored the word, imagined Achilles, the chalk-clouded air of a classroom. "But for that moment," Mannion said, "time was lost, as a garrison of British soldiers, a garrison of Lancers, stood quiet under our weapons while we loaded the motorcar. The three of us stood together, myself and Liam Lynch and Ernie O'Malley. The air had its magic." A half-hour later, standing outside the barracks, facing the burned-out shell of the Town Hall, "What has happened to us, Frank, what in the hell has happened to us, can you tell me that?" But Lacy shook his head, he was looking down the side street toward the Fermoy road. It would be evening before he reached Dublin.

"Mind you," Mannion said, at once proud and edgy, "we have been fortunate here in the First Southern, the largest division in the island, and solid in our support of the Republic, every battalion, every column, every brigade."

"Rebel Cork," Lacy said. "You have good reason to be proud. But Third Southern is standing firm as well, you know that. Barring the occasional defector in this town or that, who has sloped off to join up with the other crowd."

The "other crowd" was the description of choice that spring. Neither side, neither the Free Staters nor the Republicans, could bring their tongues as yet about the word "enemy," when speaking of fellows who had been shoulder to shoulder with them weeks before.

"Oh, indeed," Mannion said in quick politeness, "indeed."

But the two of them were thinking in that moment of Lacy's adjutant. Ben Cogley.

"I will say only this on that subject, Frank," Mannion said, as though the two of them had been reading each other's minds, like witch doctors. "Kilpeder is a gombeen man's town, and a shoneen's town. It has been that way forever, with its great brute of a castle skulking over the town, glowering over it. Ben Cogley was a good fighter, I know that as well as you do yourself, but he is the sort of lad ready for what he would call a good bargain. When the smoke of battle clears away, Ben Cogley will once again be the premier chemist of West Cork, and hand in glove with Conor Tully-Delaney, the merchant prince of Kilpeder and Cork City. Mark my words."

"You are too harsh upon Ben," Lacy said, "and too harsh upon Kilpeder itself, if it comes to that. When good men were needed everywhere, in the snow-choked winter of 'sixty-seven, in the Fenian year, it was the chaps of Kilpeder who rose up, and the man who led on the van was Bob Delaney, Conor Tully-Delaney's father."

"That is as may be," Mannion said, "but as I have heard it told, it was in sober truth Ned Nolan from America who led on the van. And there is far more of Tully than there is of Delaney in the present lad."

"In any event," Lacy said, "the Fenian days are long gone, vanished with their snows. And if Ben has thrown in his lot with the other crowd, then so be it. We talked it out, the two of us, but there was no agreement between us. He is a good fighter, as you say yourself."

Mannion spat into the roadway, and ground the sole of his boot upon it.

"He may have a chance to prove it. Liam tells me that Ben is some class of a Free State colonel, there in their barracks at Beggars Bush. By God, Frank, if they make a colonel out of your adjutant, they would make you into a general at the very least."

"You are right about one thing," Lacy said. "He may have a chance to prove it."

"There is still hope that things can work themselves out," Mannion said. "Liam is still full of hope, and there are still meetings with the other side, Mulcahy and MacEoin and so on. Liam has even had talks with the Big Fellow."

"Mick Collins you mean," Lacy said.

"That's right," Mannion said. "Mick Collins." Collins was president now of the Provisional Government, and the jovial days of "the Big Fellow" were long gone, had perished when he put his name to the Treaty. But for a moment, Lacy, standing in Barracks Street in Mallow, remembered Collins in the upstairs room in Devlin's, sitting hunched in his dark heavy overcoat on a winter's night, and drawing out from pockets of overcoat and jacket memorandum pads and bits of paper, sorting them out and initialing some, scribbling notes on others.

"One thing I know," Lacy said, "if Ben crosses the Blackwater here at the head of Free State troops, he will have a chance to show how good a fighter he is. As MacEoin discovered back in February when he sought to wrest Limerick away from O'Malley."

"Ben Cogley, is it?" Mannion said. "Let Mick Collins himself chance it. For all that he may be a West Cork man himself, there are lads in these baronies would put paid to him if need be. We know that."

They did indeed. At Cork, on March 14, when Collins and Sean MacEoin tried to visit the Republican burial plot, they were driven back by armed men of Lynch's command, and the next night, as the two of them walked to the house of Collins's sister, a man jumped suddenly in front of them, waving a revolver. "I have you now, Collins," he shouted. In Cork City.

"Ach, sure God is good," Mannion said, and spat again, again ground it down with his heel, as though disaster were a gob of spittle. "If there is any man can guide us through this shambles, 'tis Liam Lynch. Meaning no disrespect to yourself, nor Ernie, nor Rory O'Connor. But Liam and Mick Collins are Cork men, the two of them, words have the same weight and shape for them."

"Not Dev?" Lacy asked, and gave Mannion one of his crooked smiles, rubbing the back of his hand along a long line of jaw.

"De Valera, is it?" Mannion asked, and matched Lacy grin for grin. "The mathematics teacher? Can anyone tell us what that lad is about, breathing fire one minute and spitting rosewater the next. He may know about binomial theorems but he does not know his own mind."

"Binomial theorems have more clarity," Lacy said.

What De Valera was about kept the entire country puzzled, still hinting that he was president, but president of what? Of the Republic? At Dungarvan, on the day that Collins was held back by gunpoint in Cork City, De Valera told a crowd that now they could only win their freedom by civil war. "If you don't fight today you will have to fight tomorrow I say, and when you are in a good fighting position, fight on." Either you fight on, he told the army in Carrick on Suir, or you will leave the task to your sons.

"Perhaps the fight will have to be made over the bodies of the young men with us here this day." At Thurles, with hundreds of armed men in the crowd, revolvers, rifles, shotguns, the men of the Tipperary battalions, he warned that they would "have to wade through Irish blood, through the blood of the soldiers of the Irish Government, and through, perhaps, the blood of some of the members of the government in order to get Irish freedom." It was a memorable phrase, and on many lips that spring.

" 'Wade through blood,' " Mannion said. "It sounds clear enough, but now he says that it was a warning only, as any statesman might make."

"Or whatever it is that lies beyond the binomial," Lacy said. "He is a great lad, Dev is, a great lad for the talking. But the fate of the Republic rests where it has always rested, with the rifles of the IRA. We all know that."

"Ah well," Mannion said, and he held open for Lacy the door of the royal-blue Humber. Bright sunlight fell upon the parabellum, clumsy, weighty and graceful at once.

"There is a formidable weapon, Frank," Mannion said, "do you look toward trouble on the road?"

"When I travel these days," Lacy said, "I travel armed. Do you not yourself, and Liam?"

Mannion shook his head. "We are not at war, Liam says, not yet. There have been blows struck and hard words spoken, but no blood."

But earlier, in Dublin, at one of the abortive meetings between their crowd and the Free State crowd, O'Malley had opened his jacket briefly, to show Lacy the two holstered revolvers strapped to his chest. "Young Wild West," Lacy had joked to him. "They'll never take you alive, is that the program, Ernie?" Now, in his own country, he never traveled unarmed.

"Safe journey, Frank," Mannion said.

From Mallow, Lacy took the Mitchelstown road, with the Ballyhouras on his left and, distant on the road before him, the Galtees. But on the day they raided Mallow barracks and the days following, Lynch's column had moved northwards, keeping the Ballyhouras to their right flank, moving past farmlands and big houses, low hills and plantations, until on the thirtieth they were able to move on the coming of darkness from Lombardstown to Ardglass in the Charleville battalion area. On that first night after the raid, a bit after first dark, so O'Malley had told Lacy, they saw a glare in the direction of Mallow town, that faded and then came again, and held itself now against the waning light. "Then," O'Malley said, "a bit later, with our ponies struggling against the hard road, another and brighter light took the sky, and some of our lads took the hill to have a look. 'Oh, Jay,' one of the lads, a Mallow lad said, 'I hope 'tis not the creamery.' " But it was, one fierce bright light was the creamery on fire and the other was the Town Hall. Before the night was over, creamery and hall were gutted, blazing shells, and ten houses in the town had been burned as well. There were the usual drunken British on the roam, hurling petrol-filled bottles, but Mallow was the beginning of something different and worse. These were not Tans, but British regulars, commanded by officers, and the destruction, beneath the familiar arc of drunkenness, was systematic.

The Ballyhoura Hills were cool and dark that later noontime as Lacy drove eastwards toward Dublin. He had not been in the raid on Mallow barracks, had not stood on the hill looking down toward the burning town, but he had seen Kyleabbey the day after he and MacCarthy had ambushed the convoy of Somersetshires. The smell of smoke and charring had hung heavy in the summer's windless air, and two families whose houses had been burned and gutted had gathered around MacCarthy and himself as the two of them stood beside a burned-out public house whose sign, although badly singed, survived: "Michael MacCluskey, Tea and Wine Merchant." The roadway was scattered with smashed bottles, whiskey, pint porter bottles dark in the sun of summer, shards of brown glass. Down the road, toward the burned and savaged creamery, two lean curs loped toward a neighboring field. Ben Cogley had been the only fellow to offer practical help that morning, taking names and ages, and organizing houses in which the homeless could be given shelter.

But the acrid memory of that morning faded for Lacy as he guided the handsome, "levied" motorcar, and he remembered, rather, the ambush of the evening which had preceded, caught in summer's late light, the column in three positions, freshly armed with the rifles that Lacy had wheedled from Collins and Brugha on his trip to Dublin two months earlier. There was, as they waited for the three lorriesful of Somersetshire Tommies, a feeling of summer's plenitude, laced by the brandy of expectancy, the smell of the saved hay heavy in the air, an air honeyed by harvest. Lacy and Cogley were lying prone, side by side, in grass- and dirt-stained trench coats the two of them. One of the Lee-Enfields lay on the ground between them. Cogley, Lacy saw, was studying him. "What the hell is this, Ben?" Lacy had asked.

"We could be taking our ease after a long day's fishing of the Sullane," Cogley said. "You enjoy this, Frank, do you not? Barring the danger to life and limb, you are having the time of your life."

"Get out of that," Lacy said, "do you take me for a maniac?" And Cogley, wisely, had not pressed the point.

Beyond the Ballyhouras, beyond Mitchelstown, he had moved from Cork into Tipperary, from First Southern to Second Southern, from Lynch's division into O'Malley's, but they were in Dublin now, the two of them, Lynch, who had gone up on the early train, had been there—Lacy looked at the heavy watch strapped to his wrist—for an hour or more, and was in all likelihood conferring with O'Malley in the Four Courts. Once the watch had been the possession of a young Somersetshire subaltern, who had been mortally wounded in the Kyleabbey ambush. A hollow-nosed bullet had ripped open his thigh and part of his upper leg, and blood was pouring out onto the roadway from the ruined femoral artery, unstanchable. "Be certain to take this bloody thing, Paddy," he had said, waving his wrist in Lacy's face, "carried the bloody thing from one trench to the next without a scratch on it, and now where are we, eh, where are we?" Lacy lit a cigarette and put it in the subaltern's mouth. "You're having the time of your life," Ben Cogley had said to Lacy an hour earlier, as they lay side by side.

It was the Galtees that lay now to his left, steeper than the Ballyhouras, heavy-sloped, held now in summer haze, lonely and harsh, but beyond the Galtees, hidden, lay Aherlow, loveliest of all the numberless glens of Munster, save perhaps for the valley of Slieve na Bhan, the mountain of the women. Unable to carry a tune, Lacy hummed what he believed, mistakenly, to be the tune of the old ballad. Once, a bit more than a year earlier, he had heard it sung in Aherlow. Those were the days when he was working with the Fourth Tipps, before the column had been formed, and he was on temporary assignment, taking over from O'Malley, who had left a name behind for himself, as he always did. They were crowded together in the kitchen of Shiel's farm, a good fifteen of them, from which, later, the core of the column would come, and people from neighboring farmhouses had come to visit them, carrying bottles, freshly made soda bread. There was a fiddler, an old, toothless fellow, dark jacket and waistcoat, clean work shirt buttoned across throat, slack and yellow as a chicken's skin, and a youngish chap, not one of the Volunteers, a farmer's only son most likely, with squeezebox pressed against swelling paunch. There was singing, the bottles of amber-colored whiskey passed around, and soda bread, raisin-studded, slathered with sweet butter.

The songs were the well-known ones, "Eileen Arroon" and "Clare's Dragoons," and "The Coolin" sung by a dark-haired girl eager to show off her Gaelic, wretched Gaelic it was but her voice had the clarity of silver-touched crystal. When, very late, one of the Volunteers commenced, without accompaniment, to sing one of the ballads in English which seemed these days to be rising up from the earth, thick with the savors and grief of earth or its exultations. "For the banshee cried," the Volunteer sang, "when young Dalton died, in the valley of Knockanure."

You heard these days whenever a column had a few hours to stretch out, or in a safe public house, mountain-sheltered, but most often in farmhouses like Shiel's, song rising out from the actual, glorifying, boasting, lamenting extravagantly, but always grounded upon the actual, upon some incident, a famous one that rose up after Barry had wiped out the convoy of Tans at Macroom, or this one, less happy, as it were, about the running gun battle in which young Charlie Dalton was killed. Lacy, tone-deaf, followed sounds of what was, had he known, an untrained but exquisite tenor. It was when someone picked up with the greatest song of them all, which was also the song risen from Aherlow itself, "Sean O'Dwyer of the Glen," that Lacy stood up and walked outside for a breath of smoke-clear air. At the open door, he paused and looked back, to where the young singer sat perched at chair's edge, motionless, calm, pale face. The boy was singing in English, Canon Sheehan's version of the old song, "For Sean O'Dwyer a gleanna, we've been worsted at the game."

He crossed the Suir at Cahir, putting Clonmel to his right, and heading north to Cashel. Cahir had once been a town important to any line of defense, the river passage guarded by the great Butler Castle, famous in Elizabeth's reign as "the bulwark for Munster, and a safe retreat for all the agents of Spain and Rome." Early in February, Denis Tuohy, who commanded Tipperary's Sixth Brigade, had raided Clonmel, had raided the barracks, taking out three hundred rifles, two hundred thousand rounds of ammunition, mines, a dozen Lancia motorcars, bombs, machine guns. Lacy imagined as a map the countryside through which he drove, saw the South of Ireland, saw all of Munster as a terrain to be defended, along a line stretching from Waterford to Limerick, with its positions of strength along roads and rivers, Cahir, Cashel, Clonmel, Kilmallock, Cork, Mallow, his own Kilpeder. It had not yet come to war, not yet, not quite, but it was coming close. When commanders met they matched up battle plans.

Ahead of him now loomed the great cathedral rock of Cashel, which once, in the early days of the war against the British, he had come upon suddenly, close to nightfall, and from the east, immense, ruined, unruinable, shattered cathedral, ruined chancels, stark against a westering sun, a great outcropping of history. Rooks had circled above it, unreadable emblems.

XXIII

JANICE NUGENT

The spring of 1922 was lovely, and the summer lovelier still, a season for festivals, parties, and weddings, and parties and weddings there were of course, all over Ireland, but Christopher and I had decided to put off ours until what he spoke of as "the mess" would have been sorted out, as he put it. And by "the mess" what he meant was civil war, which still remained unthinkable, but which every passing day brought closer to us.

It was an unreal time. I remember a Sunday, the first Sunday in April, when I went with Christopher to the wedding in the University Church on Stephen's Green of a young brigade commandant from Mayo named Michael Gaffney. The church was crowded, the women in all the lovely pastels of spring with the lovely names, violet, lilac, peach, and the marvelous, absurd hats, and the young men, a heavy sprinkling of them, were in the new national uniform which the Free State had adopted, looking a bit German, a bit English, a bit Graustarkian. But the other young men, officers on the "other side," the Irish Republican Army as it defiantly called itself, in dark, civilian clothes. Men who in a few months' time who be shooting each other were together that Sunday in the narrow, elaborate church, Cardinal Newman's church; who would be arranging ambushes, meeting each other in open, bloody battles, sentencing each other to death by firing squad or by a bullet fired into a lighted window. Collins and Rory O'Connor, Christopher's two particular friends, were seated not too far away from Mulcahy of the General Headquarters and Lynch, a divisional commander from the South, rival claimants to the army's loyalty, and, in civilian clothes, some of the column commandants whose names had become legend, hard Republicans now, Dan Breen and Tom Barry and Ernie O'Malley, but a commander whose name was as much legend as any of theirs, Sean MacEoin of Longford, fierce in his loyalty to Collins, was in Free State uniform. And I saw, in a dark jacket, a Republican jacket, you might say, Dinny Lawlor, the young farmer who, on that long-ago day, had taken the elderly man off the Galway train, and shot him down before my eyes. My introduction to Irish history. Christopher himself was in civilian clothes, because, although he held military rank, he was also a junior minister in the Free State cabinet, what they called a minister without portfolio. Those are a few of the men whom Christopher pointed out to me at the wedding, but most of them I forget, names and faces.

Michael Gaffney looked very handsome in his uniform, a serious young man with a full, red face and close-cropped hair, and his bride, whose family owned a hotel in Castlebar, looked lovely, but then they say that all brides look lovely. She was well formed, and the new fashion in wedding gowns suited her well; her hips were a shade too generous for the new fashion in such matters, but her full and no doubt virginal breasts were shapely. Someday, Christopher had told me, after "the mess" had been sorted out, Michael would be taking over management of the hotel.

Afterwards, as everyone stood outside the church, across the roadway the wide Green, with its combed and tended lawns, paths winding past a small lake, flower beds bursting with the colors of tulips, and all around Christopher and myself, the women in their spring finery, and spring everywhere in the air, lightness, the air itself fresh and light, with Dublin's special softness, a clarity warmer than haze. When I turned away from the Green, I saw that Christopher had moved away from me, and Myles Keough was beside me, looking especially vernal, with yet another of his carefully chosen waistcoats, not proper at all for a wedding really, vertical stripes of pale purple, dark purple, pink, but otherwise formal in attire. His stiff hat was cocked to one side to display his heavy, oak-colored hair, and his eyes a cornflower blue.

"What will it be like, our new Ireland?" he asked me. His years as a barrister had given him a voice that he could use however he chose, so that, as now, it could be full and a bit thrilling, and yet it would not carry beyond the two of us. "Christopher is looking splendid," he said.

"No, Myles," I said, "you tell me, what will our new Ireland be like?"

"Now over there," Myles said, "is a count, a genuine count, his poor son was one of the fellows executed in 1916. A Papal count, to be sure, not quite the top of the ladder, but there you are. And the fellow closest to him there, their shoulders almost touching, is one of our bandit chieftains, a brigade commandant or battalion commander or whatever. He began work as a shop assistant. Will we throw aside class distinctions in the new Ireland, do you think, Janice?"

"Not likely, Myles," I said. "Not bloody likely." There was always a mild, innocent flirtatiousness between Myles Keough and myself, in which I used naughty words like "bloody" and "bitch," and he, in turn, was scandalous and satirical about "the national cause," as he liked to call it, rolling the words on his tongue. And yet he was being satirical about himself as well, so it was turning out, because he had turned his house into a "safe house" during the worst months of the Troubles and had defended Volunteers when they were on trial for murder. "It is always wise to be with history rather than against it," as he told me once, but you could never tell when Myles was joking. He had been generous to Christopher and myself, giving us the key to his cottage in Connemara.

"Pray God," I said, "that there is a new Ireland," and he turned serious upon the instant, leaning down toward me, and touching my arm.

"It could be very awful," he said, "truly awful. We are very close to civil war." And I knew we were, but it seemed impossible.

That very day, that very afternoon, after the wedding, Sunday the second of April, by the order of the new Irish Republican Executive, as it called itself, those soldiers of the Dublin Brigade who rejected the Treaty assembled on parade at Smithfields, and took a new oath of allegiance. The photographs in the English papers and in our own, and a few days later a large photograph in the *Illustrated London News,* showed thousands of men in parade formation although in civilian clothes, and there were photographs beside the large one of their commanders, some of whom had been at the wedding a few hours earlier, and these officers had had time to change into uniform. The oath which they swore pledged them to the Republic and by implication threatened war against the new Provisional Government of the Free State.

I was "visiting" Christopher in his Fitzwilliam Street flat a week later when that copy of the *News* reached Ireland, and he saw me looking down at the photograph.

"Don't blame those lads," he said. "Decent fellows. There is no better crowd than the lads of the Dublin Brigade. Blame their bloody officers, and blame the bastards sitting in back rooms and plotting to preserve a Republic that does not exist. Never existed save as a form of words."

Christopher was drinking these days, not heavily, but he was drinking more than I had ever known, and as he talked he was pouring out a measure.

"Come along now, Janice," he said, "take a short one of these, it will do you no harm," and I said all right, that I would like a whiskey, because I remembered my father saying that people should never be let drink alone, it was not good for them.

"Once," I said, "a couple of my father's old chums from his army days came out to visit with us in Coolater, nice old boys, one of them clean-shaven with wattles like a rooster, and the other with a fierce mustache, whiter than white. And my father pulled up the cork from a new bottle of Jameson's, and then flung the cork into the fire. 'No need for the cork, lads,' he said, 'we will make a night of it.' And they did. That was a few years after Mother died, and at two in the morning, Betty and I were sitting up wide awake in our beds, listening to them singing and laughing and roaring down below." I saw us again, the two girls, looking at each other in wonderment, half-delighted and half-fearful. "Oh, but they were three sorry men the next day."

"Are you preaching me a sermon?" Christopher asked, and he threw rather than splashed water into his tumbler.

I shrugged and held out my own tumbler to him for water.

Both of our national newspapers had quoted the announcement by the Provisional Government. "The purpose of the mobilization announced for Sunday next is the seduction of soldiers away from the army of the Irish nation and its legitimate government. The real issue is not between a Free State and a Republic, but between a military dictatorship on the one hand and an Irish

Army functioning with the moral authority and sanction of the Irish people on the other. If you repudiate General Headquarters, you stand for a military dictatorship. There is no other issue."

The words were printed in the letterpress below the photograph. I turned the pages, and there was the Prince of Wales in India, riding atop an enormous elephant, a wan, melancholy-looking chap, and another photograph of him fly-fishing an Indian river. "Give her a pearl for Easter," a jeweler on Bond Street urged, "or better yet, give her a diamond."

Christopher was leaning over my shoulder as I turned the pages, but I knew that his mind was elsewhere, that he was seeing that photograph of a sea of dark-jacketed men at Smithfields, thousands of them, it had seemed. His breath smelled of the whiskey.

On a page all to themselves, three Japanese geisha girls, kimonoed and elaborately made up, holding quite lovely fans. Two of them were smiling, quite vacuously it seemed to me, but the third, her hand resting on a panel, looked without smiling, wide almond eyes unreadable, straight into the camera.

" 'The geisha,' " I read aloud, " 'has no prototype in Europe. She is unique—a purely Japanese creation. She is trained from childhood in the arts of music, dancing, singing, story-telling, conversation, and repartee. The geisha is in great request for boating and picnic parties.' I'll just bet she is. Do you fancy her, the one on the end? The other two look rather awful, is that rice powder, do you think, but the one on the end looks a true charmer."

But Christopher turned back to the photograph of the mobilization at Smithfields. By some fluke of the camera lens, the assembled men seemed to be stretching backwards towards infinity.

"We have fewer men than that under our command at Beggars Bush," Christopher said. "Dublin could be a battle, a bad one. But we hold the countryside, aside from Munster and North Connaught. They are not strong enough to win, but they are strong enough to turn this into a war. They are going to find that the people are not with them."

I drained off my glass of light whiskey and water, and put my hand on Christopher's. I remembered what I had been saying and felt cheap, as though I had myself been playing the geisha. But I did not know what to say. It seemed unreal to me, phantasmal, that men should attend a ceremony together, a wedding, nod to each other, and then—

"We are a sideshow, a carnival," Christopher said with sudden anger. "Look at the heading they have put on that. 'The Irish Army's Divided Allegiance.' "

After dark, I made us an omelet, one of my few culinary skills, a nice sweet omelet, and we had straw-colored wine with it, and then, after that, we listened to Schubert on the gramophone. We held hands as we listened, and several times, Christopher smiled at me, and once stretched out his hand to stroke my hair, as though the "defiant Dublin Brigade of the Irish Army Threatens Mutiny" was as far away as the poor little Prince of Wales looking handsome and foolish atop his enormous elephant. And then, before bed, we played a game of chess, sitting facing each other across the chessboard which once had been Christopher's father's, the pieces of ivory lovely and smooth to the touch. Christopher was not as good a player as I, not quite, but when playing he looked wonderful, and had I been a painter I would have painted him and called him "The Chess Player." He would study his move until he was quite certain of it, his forefinger pressing across his lips as though cautioning the world to be silent, and then he would dart out his long, graceful hand, and make his move swiftly and decisively. He was off in his game that evening, abstracted, and when I put him into checkmate, there was a second or perhaps it was a third brandy by his hand, but his hand was steady.

Later, in bed, I found myself giggling, and when he turned his head toward me, I said, "I should have let you win. *She* would have let you win."

"She? Who? Who are you talking about?" There was a slur, the faintest of slurs, in his voice.

"That geisha in the photograph, the one on the end, looking at us and with her hand upon the panel of the door. She would have let you win."

"If we are ever in Tokyo," Christopher said, "perhaps we should hire her for you. She interests you far more than she does me." And, tired but dutifully feigning the erotic, he ran his hand down from breast to belly and from belly to thighs.

"Only men," I said. "It says that they live to serve men. But of course, who knows what happens when the men are gone, and the geishas have the run of the house. Perhaps we will be in Tokyo, perhaps you will be the first Irish ambassador to Japan."

But he was almost asleep, or at least unlikely to be roused into erotic reverie, and I put my hand upon his, and lay there thinking. Life's important thoughts have a way of stealing upon you when you are least prepared for them, and what I was thinking was that in fact I *was* a geisha, that whatever my intentions might have been, I had drifted into being one. And I didn't much like the thought. What was it that geishas were adept at, dancing and singing, conversation, repartee, and the art of making men feel good. Well, that was me, and I didn't seem to be much else. In fact, I was deficient when it came to dancing. Oh, and singing! It had not been that way with Charlie, and perhaps it would not be that way with Christopher, after we were married, but everything in our future seemed indefinite, where we would be living and what Christopher would be doing. But whenever we talked about that, even when Christopher opened the subject himself, he would sooner or later break it off. There was no point in talking about any of that, save of course for the wedding, until after "the mess" had been sorted out. It is all well and good to say that living in sin is especially exciting, but it doesn't stick to your ribs, the way porridge does on a winter morning.

And the terrible thing is that I really did not care much about "the mess" one way or another, any more than a geisha would. I had really and truly become a geisha, give or take the slanted eyes and the rice powder. The Irish Republican Army to me was no more real than the photograph in the English weekly, flat, sepia, like the leaves of early autumn. Christopher's position as a junior minister in the Provisional Government meant that he was working in Dublin, at first in the City Hall next to Dublin Castle and then in Government Buildings on Merrion Street, but with frequent trips to London, on his own but more often accompanying Griffith or Collins. The Free State was caught between the Republicans on one flank, and the British on the other, pressing for a strict enforcement of the terms of the Treaty. It was far better for the two of us, for Christopher and myself, when his duty took him to London, because that was where my flat was, and I would follow him over as a good geisha should. And better also because my true life was in Galway at Coolater or else in London, where all my friends were. But not Dublin.

Did we know, in Dublin, that civil war was almost upon us? I did, of course, because of who Christopher was, but did most people? They did and they did not. They saw Free State troops moving through the streets in formation from Beggars Bush barracks, and they saw the Republican columns, they read in the newspapers of the rival Army Conventions, and they knew that semilegal headquarters had been set up throughout the city. But most people still went about their ordinary tasks, solicitors and shopkeepers and accountants and schoolboys and medical students and housewives and tram conductors and motormen. They brought home fish and chips after work and went to the races in Phoenix Park and Leopardstown and had long dinners in Jammet's and the Shelbourne and stood arguing politics in the Bailey and Davy Byrne's and went shopping in Arnott's and Switzer's and Clery's. Now that April had brought the good weather, they walked in the Phoenix Park and Herbert Park and Stephen's Green, whose buildings, on the west side, still bore the rifle and machine-gun scars of 1916.

And then, on the night of April 13, "while the city slept," as the newspapers of course declared, the Republican forces seized the Four Courts, the largest and the most imposing building in Dublin, and declared it their headquarters. Christopher did not have a telephone in the flat, junior minister or not, and an army messenger from Beggars Bush was sent round to summon him with the news, and waited below in a staff car while Christopher dressed. He was not back for two hours, and I had fallen back to sleep, but when I heard his key I woke fully and made him tea.

"It was the Dublin Brigade," Christopher told me, "at least two battalions of them. They have taken possession of the entire Four Courts, and have issued a public statement, addressed to Dáil Éireann, that they are pledged to maintain the existing Republic, and that they will maintain their army as the Irish Republican Army. To maintain the existing Republic. What existing Republic?" He left his tea untouched, and smoked cigarette after cigarette. "They have drifted beyond metaphysics into fantasy. They must be studying metaphysics with the mathematician."

De Valera had been a schoolteacher of arithmetics before 1916, and "mathematician" was now the kindest word that Christopher and his friends had for him.

"The Dublin Brigade," Christopher said. "You see how things

stand in the city. There is only one battalion that we can count on, aside from Collins's Squad."

As Christopher spoke, in my imagination I saw double columns of dark-jacketed men, their rifles sloped, marching along the quays to the Four Courts, in the chill of deep night, to their left, beyond a low parapet, the dirty, sluggish river. And, looming before them, the immense Palladian grandeur of Gandon's Four Courts.

"What statement?" I said. "Whose statement? Is Mr. De Valera in the Four Courts with them?"

"Not him," Christopher said, and looked at his cup of tea as though he had not seen it before. "Seizing the Four Courts moves us a step closer to civil war, and Mr. De Valera deplores the prospect of civil war. He says it would be a national calamity. Mr. De Valera, as you can see, is a natural phrasemaker. No, these are the Republican red-hots, Rory O'Connor for certain, and Liam Mellowes, and Ernie O'Malley. Liam Lynch is not in there with them at the moment, he is back home in Cork, but he will be there soon enough, he is their chief of staff, and Frank Lacy will be throwing in his lot with them." He sipped at the cool, sweetened tea. And then smiled at me. "Well, Janice," he said, "what should we do? Advise me. You are the daughter of a British colonel. What would Colonel O'Gorman do?"

And suddenly, in the midst of my concern for Christopher's distress, it occurred to me that over and above my being a geisha girl, if that is what they are called, he was treating me as one. It was a bad moment for him all right, a bad moment for the Free State, and his playful question made him feel a bit better.

I looked beyond him, beyond the window, into a rear garden filling with streaky light, washed out and pale.

I reached over for his packet of Players, and lit a cigarette. "Is that the fact?" I said, "that in the city of Dublin the Free State can count on only one battalion and a squad of gunmen and assassins? If that is the case, my advice to you is to change sides."

He looked at me as though he had been slapped, and then laughed. "That is the fact on paper," he said, "but we can call in massive forces at three hours' notice. We can drive them out at our leisure. Leave them where they are for the time being is Mulcahy's advice, and Collins's."

"I don't know," I said. "I expect Colonel O'Gorman would

have wheeled up cannon and artillery and given them an hour to clear out."

"And then open fire on his own countrymen," Christopher said, and shook his head. "Those are not sepoys in the Four Courts nor Boers nor fuzzy-wuzzies, those are our own fellows in there, O'Connor and I are friends." He drank off the rest of his tea, but I doubt if he tasted it.

The next day, out of curiosity, I walked across town to the Four Courts, down Patrick Street and past Christ Church and then down Winetavern Street to the quays, and stood there looking at the enormous building across the narrow river, James Gandon's great triumphant design, all the seriousness and swagger of the eighteenth century, lions and unicorns and a magnificent dome, pillars, statues of who-knows-what on the pediments, abstractions, no doubt, of Justice, Civil Order, Britannia, whatever. It seemed little changed from what it had been a few months earlier when Myles Keough had taken me on tour, meeting me in the front courtyard in flowing gown and white wig. Now, in that courtyard, two young Republican sentries slouched, rifles and bandoliers and cloth caps.

As I stood there, an old fellow came out of Winetavern Street and stood beside me. I looked over at him, cloth cap like the sentries, brown jacket, a respectable-looking old fellow despite a stubble of beard.

"Jesus, ma'am," he said, "the capture of the Four Courts, what next?"

"It seems quiet enough," I said. I was secretly a bit disappointed. Sandbags had been piled against the windows on the ground floor, but these and the sentries seemed the only sights out of the ordinary.

"I was by here an hour ago," he said, "and there was more then to be seen. There were two squads of soldiers, I guess you could call them soldiers, being drilled in the courtyard there." He looked down at the dirty, bilious river, and rested his forearms on the parapet. Sunlight struck the water, and gave it a transient charm. Without looking away from the water, he said, "I know nothing of your politics, ma'am, and I have none myself, but I can tell you that those two squads were badly in need of a soldier trained in the British Army. I say that as a simple matter of fact."

"I am a daughter of that army," I said, "my father served in it for twelve years."

He nodded. "Munster Fusiliers," he said. "I was wounded at Spion Kop and invalided out. They gave me a pension and two medals, neither of them for good conduct." He rubbed the back of his hand across the stubble. "Since then I have been doing this and that and not much at all latterly. I live with the married daughter beyond us there in Bull Road."

"Have you thought of walking over across the bridge and offering your services as a drillmaster?"

He laughed briefly. "To that crowd, is it? Or to the other crowd below us there in Beggars Bush? Begod, the way things are moving along, those two lots will be at each other's throats." He cleared his throat, and then added phlegm to the Liffey. "Your father was in the army, you say? An officer, I have no doubt." He paused as though weighing thought, and then turned to face me. Toothless, watery eyes of pale blue, red-veined. "And I will tell you something, ma'am, which your father would tell you if he were standing beside us. The two lots of them will discover with scalded hearts that there is more to warfare than hiding behind hedges to shoot policemen."

I looked round us apprehensively, but the people walking past us paid us no attention whatever, and even less to the Four Courts, across the river. Whatever my friend may have learned in the Munster Fusiliers and on the sands of South Africa, he was a Dubliner born and bred, with a Dubliner's ability to speak in normal tones which somehow could not be heard two yards away, an art acquired over years in public houses.

"I stood here, mind you, or if not precisely here, then not far distant, on this side of the river, a crowd of layabouts and old crocks like myself, and watched the shelling of Sackville Street in April of 1916. A band of military geniuses those lads were, bottling themselves up in the middle of a city, with no lines of retreat open to them." He made as if to spit again into the river, but his mouth was dry, or else he knew that he trembled upon heresy. And indeed, swift upon his own cue, he said, "But a brave lot, begod, they held out for a week against the might of the Empire."

I looked over again toward the Four Courts, spring sunlight still sparkled upon the Liffey, and, as I looked, three men, walking closely together, turned into the courtyard. The two sentries, slouching no longer, stood to stiff attention and saluted.

"The high command, no doubt," my old soldier said in mordant Dublin accent. "The Four Courts is not long for this world, ma'am, you mark my words. The city of Dublin is being sacrificed up, first the GPO in 1916 and then the Custom House last year, and it will next be the Four Courts." From where we stood, we could not see Sackville Street nor the ruined Post Office, but the fire-gutted hulk of the Custom House lay across the river to our right. Once it had matched and counterbalanced the Four Courts, twin triumphs of eighteenth-century swagger.

In the two months that remained before civil war in full fell upon us, I thought once or twice about the old soldier and myself, as we stood together on Merchants Quay, looking across the Liffey toward Inns Quay and the Four Courts. Almost, I could look down upon the scene and upon us within it, like the figures placed in paintings and engravings to suggest scale and perspective, the old soldier with a gesticulating arm outflung, and myself attentive upon him.

There was an unreality about the entire scene, as two parties moved beyond words toward warfare, reluctant, driven, and as a city and a countryside contrived to persuade themselves that nothing really untoward was happening, even as enormous crowds swelled first to hear one side and then another in College Green, banners flapping from platforms, Collins leaning forward into the crowd, banging fist against outspread hand, and De Valera, somber, a tall, bespectacled crane. Once or twice at such meetings, so newspapers gingerly informed us, revolvers would be fired off from within the crowd, but no one seemed ever to be hurt, not yet. Immediately after the taking of the Four Courts, other buildings were commandeered by the Republicans—Irregulars, one was supposed to call them, although they detested the word, Irregulars, or Mutineers—the Masonic Hall on Molesworth Street, and the Ballast Office, and, of all places, the Kildare Street Club, the citadel of Tory, loyalist staunchness. I would pass it, on my way to the library or else to meet someone for tea at the Shelbourne, and there would be not even a trench-coated sentry, but once, looking through windows from which the heavy curtains had been pulled back, I could see young men huddled together about a long table, a good dozen of them, heads bent.

Sometime around the beginning of May, and all of them on the same day, branches of the Bank of Ireland across the country, but especially in the South and the West, were raided by armed men, and something more than fifty thousand pounds taken. The next day, Rory O'Connor issued a statement to the press: Republican forces in the field were of course not being issued funds by the Provisional Government, and it was proper that they should pay off debts incurred to traders. The funds, he explained, had been "made subject to forcible possession." In all cases, he explained, receipts had been issued in the name of the Irish Republican Army. In the East, especially, in Wicklow and Wexford, railway lines were torn up to prevent Free State assemblies, and, almost everywhere, supplies and motorcars were being commandeered. In Killarney, where Collins was scheduled to speak, the platform was burned down as he was entering the town, and, on the same day, in Dublin, an unarmed Republican prisoner was shot down "while trying to escape." Both sides were developing a great skill at euphemism and bad prose. O'Connor, justifying to the press the destruction of rail lines while railway workers were held at gunpoint, put it that "those who move pro-Treaty troops from place to place in connection with political meetings are guilty of grave indiscretions which tend to create and promote bitterness which is liable to produce undesirable results." In Athlone, at the end of April, a Free State officer was shot dead.

Once, I walked past the Kildare Street Club, past the library, and up to the Shelbourne corner, where a political meeting was being held, about a hundred men and women gathered around a small platform, just large enough to hold the three speakers, a heavyset man, a tall, gaunt woman dressed in widow's black, and a remarkably pretty young woman. There were flags at either end of the platform, the tricolor of green, white and orange, and the older national flag, a harp against a green field. A banner, stretched between the flags, said simply, in elaborate letters, *"Poblacht na Éireann,"* "the Republic of Ireland." The pretty young woman was fair-haired and hatless, a firm, full mouth, and, so it seemed to me, she recognized me, because she stared at me intently, and I had myself a faint stir of recognition, but it was not until I was inside the Shelbourne and at tea with Margaret

Kilbride, the wife of one of Christopher's colleagues, that I said suddenly, "Of course," remembering the stern young woman who had taken me to Christopher's office that time when he was on the run. Elizabeth, I remembered, Elizabeth something.

"Oh, to be sure," Margaret said, "Elizabeth Keating. A very clever young woman, I am told. So many of the Republican women are very clever." Her tone was acid, as though cleverness were a moral blemish. Free Staters, Free State women that is, prided themselves upon other qualities, but I must say that not many of them were fun to be with; Margaret was an exception. "There was a time," she said, holding the teapot over my cup, "when I rather thought that something might be developing between Christopher and Elizabeth Keating, but then, of course, thank God, he met you. And I doubt if anything would have developed. Elizabeth Keating's great love is the Republic. The Republican women, Janice, honestly! They are a sex all of their own."

That was becoming another article of Free State gospel, that women were defending the Republic with a ferocity that unsexed them, and caricatures were in circulation of the Republican women as a band of maenads, black-garbed, gaunt, hysterical. And many of them, indeed, qualified for the black of mourning—the widows and sisters and mothers of men hanged by the British in 1916 or later, or done to death in cellars by Black and Tan interrogators. How, I once thought in secret sympathy with them, could they think of the Free State as anything but a shabby compromise for which lives had been sacrificed and taken? But my sympathy was not long-lasting. I knew a bit about grief. I knew that it was foolish to give it meaning or purpose.

"As if there was any need," Margaret said, "for them to preach from street corners like Protestant missioners, when they have their meetings in the Mansion House and in the Rotunda. Why, their army itself, as they call it, has met in the Mansion House to plot mutiny and worse, without let or hindrance. They were hard at work at it twenty minutes ago when I arrived, Mrs. MacBride, Madam MacBride she wants to be known as, with her clenched fist raised up to heaven and . . ."

But what else she said drifted away from me, and I was thinking that that was who the tall gaunt woman was, in her widow's weeds, and I was sorry that I had not paused for a moment or two, because she was once, everyone said, a great beauty, tall, skin like roseleaf, and beautiful eyes, as the poet had written of her, before she went into mourning for the drunken, wife-battering husband who had been shot by firing squad in 1916, when she was lovely and fierce, Miss Maud Gonne, for whom the poet had written those wonderful poems.

"Maud Gonne," I said suddenly, aloud, and no doubt cutting against Margaret's words, but she understood, and smiled at me.

"She is the most frightening one of them all," Margaret said, "and always has been, I suspect. I think she frightened poor Yeats into loving her, he did not dare refuse."

Was there another Troy for her to burn? the poet had asked. Not a Troy, perhaps, but she was making do with what lay to hand, the Post Office in ruins, and the Custom House a gutted shell, and now armed men, brother Irishmen, gathering in two armed camps, and almost ready to kill each other. Almost. In Kilkenny, on the very day in early May when we sat talking in the Shelbourne over our buttered toast, a large body of armed Republicans had swept into the city of Kilkenny, seizing two barracks and the Ormond Castle and the best barracks, and the next day the Free State troops moved into position against them and a trainload of reinforcements was sent down from Beggars Bush. Shots were exchanged for an hour or two, between the Free Staters on the roof of the Bank of Ireland and the Republicans in Kilkenny Castle. But a truce was patched up somehow, and the barracks and the bridges portioned out between the two armies, with Green's Bridge left to the Republicans and John's Bridge held by the Free State. It was all over by Wednesday, and by Thursday other ladies would be reading about it before tea, but perhaps not talking about it.

"It is a pity that she writes so well," Margaret said, and I knew at once that she was speaking about Elizabeth Keating. With part of my mind, I tried to remember everything we had said to each other, that day when she had brought me to Christopher's office. I had not remembered her as quite so pretty, but surely, as she had been standing just now, on the shabby platform outside the Shelbourne, she had looked poised and lovely, but then she had had other matters than poise on her mind, she had had the Republic.

"When you read that news sheet of hers," Margaret said, "you would never know, would you, that she and Christopher had once worked together, had been great pals. It was Christopher who gave her her start in journalism, helping him with the *Bulletin.*" And of course, I had not known that Elizabeth Keating now edited, with two other Republican women, something called *The Republic* which was for sale in all the Republican newsagents', and Republican schoolchildren sold it on the steps of the GPO.

"No," I said, a bit sharply, "I did not know that. When I need something to read, I do not go for it to the steps of the GPO."

Margaret noticed the faint sharpness, and looked at me with fresh interest.

"My dear," she said, "you should. There is scarcely an issue without some stern denunciation of Christopher. Far wilder denunciations, of course, of Collins and Griffith and Mulcahy."

She smiled. Margaret and I had become quite good friends. Unlike most of middle-class Dublin, she knew that Christopher and I were lovers, a word and a fact which would have shocked most of them. But she had Dublin's love of mischief, and now she said, again, "You really should read it. Are you ready for more tea?"

Then, a bit later, as we were gathering up our things, she said, "Brendan so admires Christopher, you know."

Brendan was a solicitor, and during "the Tan war," as people were beginning to call it, he had been a judge in one of the illegal "Republican courts," moving from one venue to the next. But now like Christopher he was a junior minister in the Provisional Government. He was drafting proposals for the new system of courts. It sounded dull, but Brendan himself was quite lively, like Margaret.

"I remember," Margaret said, "one evening Brendan came home, it was when we were still running the government from the City Hall, and as he made himself a Scotch and water, he said, 'There we are, fifteen or twenty young men standing amidst the ruins of one administration, with the foundations of another not yet laid, and wild men screaming through the keyhole.' Then he plopped down in his chair, facing me across the fire. 'Thank God,' he said, 'that I am only an administrator, only a civil servant, and not involved in—' " And Margaret dropped her voice here, and glanced about us. But the waiter had taken away the bill and her pound note, and the other tables were not close enough to overhear. " 'Thank God,' Brendan said, 'that I am not involved in the other matter, like Collins and Christopher and a few others.' "

"Yes, yes of course," I said, but I had no idea of what she meant. Christopher, so far as I knew, was kept busy drafting pronouncements of the Provisional Government which Collins headed, and serving as Collins's aide in the endless London conferences which followed after the Treaty.

She kept her voice as low as before, but spoke rapidly, because she saw that the waiter was crossing the room toward us. "Not that Brendan tells me much about it, I doubt if he knows that much to tell. But he loves to be mysterious, most men do, have you noticed? And to put on airs of knowledge. 'If the true history of this country is ever told,' he likes to say. But there!" Because the waiter was beside us now, with Margaret's change. "Can you wait?" she asked, and smiled up at the waiter, and picked up pieces of change but left a florin in the salver. "Can you wait until—until autumn, is it?"

"Oh, yes," I said. "My sister Betty is busy already with the planning, what flowers we will want in the church, and how many guests we will be able to put up at Coolater, and how many will my chum Hazel put up for us, and how many at the hotel."

"Can you wait?" she asked again, excitedly, and looking younger than her years, she must have been close to thirty.

"I certainly cannot," I said, and right there, in the lounge of the Shelbourne Hotel, I gave her a broad wink. After a moment, she understood, and actually blushed beneath her faint, discreet coloring. "Janice," she said, shocked and pleased, and put her hand again on my arm. Widows, I have noticed, can get away with saying the most shocking things.

Outside the Shelbourne, platform and flags and banners and black-clad orators had vanished entirely away, as though melted by the warm spring sun, and I kissed Margaret, and watched her hurry away to Buckley's, the butcher in Chatham Street. The fashion of the season suited her well, her silk-clad calfs suggesting supple, eloquent legs. Lucky Brendan Kilbride, I thought, but then I thought, what will they do, or rather, what will Brendan do, will he become part forever of the new government or the new civil service, or whatever, will they stay on forever in the house in Sandycove or else move to a larger one in Rathfarnham with a view of the mountains? And what of us, what of Christopher and myself? And even though I would be going back there in three days' time, I felt very lonely for London, for Regent's Park and the theater and Simpson's.

I bought a copy of *The Republic* and carried it back to my own hotel, in Nassau Street, and sat leafing through it as I sat by my window, which looked out upon Trinity College, snug and Protestant and Anglo-Irish beyond its railings, as though history had never happened. From Margaret's disparaging words, I had expected a shabby enterprise, the sort that might be expected from people who spoke on makeshift platforms. But it was quite professional, despite more than its share of misprints, and there did not seem to be anything in it about Christopher, much to my disappointment, but rather much nebulous rhetoric about "the Republic," and, as complement to this, much fierce and far from nebulous denunciation of "the traitors who bargained and sold" the Republic across the table at Downing Street, and there was speculation as to their motives—timidity, a covetousness of fame and power, and so forth.

But there was also a letter from "A Soldier in the Field," as he called himself, which was quite moving. "The Soldier" described nights on the run and times when he and his comrades had been under fire, times when they had been ill fed despite the generosity of locals, who would carry supplies, when able, to the column, which was for months bivouacked in two abandoned farmhouses in the Derrynasaggarts.

"We knew then," the "Soldier" wrote, "that we were doing our part in the struggle for freedom for which Pearse and Plunkett had fought and died, and for which Kevin Barry had suffered a felon's death in Mountjoy and for which Sean Treacy had been shot down on a rainy Dublin Street and for which Terence MacSwiney offered up his life in lonely Brixton Prison. They were not fighting and dying to make of our island some kind of Crown Dominion, or Free State, or whatever words are used. We are loyal to the memory of those brave men and we are loyal to the Republic."

Somewhere in the letter, the "Soldier" let fall that he was seventeen years of age. Something in the letter affected me more than I can say, and still less can I understand.

* * *

On the evening before my crossing over to London, Christopher and I had dinner in Jammet's, around the corner from my hotel, my favorite restaurant in Dublin, quite Londonish, really, in its dowdy Dublin way.

Christopher, as one of a party headed by Collins, would be crossing in a week's time, "on business," as Christopher always put it, and this gave me an opening.

"Christopher," I said, "what exactly is this business of yours that keeps you so busy?"

He looked at me, startled, and put down his fork. "I thought you had heard enough about my business," he said, "quite more than enough, has been my impression."

"On Wednesday," I said, "I had tea with Margaret Kilbride. Margaret tells me that Brendan is very mysterious with her about your business, whatever it is. She made it sound almost dangerous, or desperate."

"Brendan Kilbride must have a lively imagination," Christopher said. "Not a healthy trait in a solicitor."

But I sat looking at him, and took a sip of wine, and looked at him over the wineglass. Then I put down the glass. "So have I, Christopher. A lively imagination."

"Well, then," Christopher said, "here is how matters stand," and without lowering his voice, as Margaret surely would have done and Brendan most probably, he told me about the Free State's endless and tortuous negotiations, with the British cabinet and with De Valera and with the Republicans who were now in occupation of the Four Courts.

"Christopher," I said suddenly, "what is it that I do not know about? What was Brendan Kilbride hinting at to Margaret?" I had cut straight into his words, and my voice had been sharp.

"I told you, Janice," Christopher said, "a lively imagination. Brendan had a safe time of it, the past two years, settling disputes between farmers in the courts set up by Sinn Féin. He likes a bit of excitement to carry home to Margaret."

"No," I said, "I am not having that." And now I did lower my voice. "The country is on the edge of war, that is not Brendan's imagining. He coupled your name with Michael Collins's. Michael Collins and Christopher and a few others, Margaret said. Whatever Collins is doing, it is more than carrying over a briefcase to London to sort out papers. Do not treat me like a child."

My storm had come up suddenly, but Christopher recognized it. He was clever about things like that.

"You are not being treated like a child, Janice," he said. "You are a grown woman, and you are being treated like one. As I have always dealt with you."

Which certainly was true, but I was in no mood to agree with him. "You might in that case," I said, "tell me whatever it is that Brendan was hinting at."

He paused before answering, which was a maddening habit he had, and I did not know whether he paused to put down a flicker of irritability or to frame an answer. In the event it was a bit of both, and now he did lower his voice.

"Either what Brendan was hinting at is his lively imagination, or else it is none of your business. Or his, come to think of it."

And a silence fell between us upon the table, one of those messy silences.

"I am sorry," he said, and reaching across the table, put his hand on mine, and I let my hand rest there, mute and unresponsive.

"We should make an early evening of it," I said, "if you will see me back to the hotel. I have the boat to catch in the morning."

"Yes," he said. And then he said, "Some matters are not mine to talk about, Janice. It does not mean that they are important matters, or dangerous. I know, I think, what Brendan has got wind of, and it is not his concern. Or Margaret's, or yours."

"Yes," I said. "Of course." He did not answer that, and I said, "What shall we talk about?" It was as though a part of him was shut off from me, and I had now this nagging memory of Elizabeth Keating on the platform outside the Shelbourne, and I thought that once she and Christopher had been working so closely together that there had been no secrets between them.

Without waiting for coffee, we left Jammet's and walked back to the Nassau Hotel. Before he kissed me chastely good-night, outside the hotel, we spoke about what we would be doing in London, a play we had been planning to attend, and an exhibition of Augustus John's new work, as lovers will talk when they wish they had not quarreled. Or almost quarreled. That night I lay in bed being angry with myself, because I knew that I had provoked an argument on the wrong grounds, that there was something that I was angry about but I did not know what it was, it was not what Margaret Kilbride had said nor some faint jealousy of the Keating woman.

I knew no more the next day, as I stood at the rail of the boat for Holyhead, watching Ireland recede, its bays and the soft spring hills of Dublin and Wicklow, and the hill of Howth. The water beneath us was a cool, dark green. I was already missing Christopher and missing Ireland, but not Dublin. Ireland for me was Coolater, was Galway and the lands beyond the Shannon, but Dublin was entanglements, rain falling upon narrow streets that blocked off the hills from view, armed men in their rival camps. And I thought that save for Christopher and Coolater, I could do very nicely without Ireland, thank you. In my mind's ear, above the racket of the engines, I could hear Christopher telling me, about whatever it was, that it was none of my business.

XXIV

FRANK LACY

Beyond Cashel, that day in mid-May, Lacy drove hard toward Dublin, through Urlingford and Abbeyleix, through Maryborough and Monasterevan, across the Curragh of Kildare, stopping only for a glass of whiskey and a quick cup of tea in the hotel in Naas. It was as though he had left history behind him on the Rock of Cashel, and almost as though he had left Ireland, his Ireland, behind him. Always, traveling backwards and forwards across the country in the past three years, it had been the same. The River Shannon at Athlone on the western road, and Cashel on the southern—westward of them, layered in richness, of speech, sound, landscape, was the Ireland which held his deepest loyalties, the true Ireland. Driving westwards, or, as in the early days of warfare, traveling by cart or bicycle, the occasional "lift" aboard a goods van, there had been for him that rise of the heart as the great cathedral ruins of Cashel rose up, or the broad Shannon, sun-spangled or rain-drenched. Beyond, westwards, lay the deep-valleyed hills of Lacy's Ireland, rooks circling low above the stones of shattered friaries, nights in sheltered farmhouses, hillside bothies, song weaving outwards past turf smoke, tobacco smoke toward star-pierced blackness beyond which lay immensities of red bogland, black bog.

The bar of Lawlor's, the hotel in Naas, and the narrow hallway leading down to it, had walls of photographs of the Kildare Hunt and the Kilruddery Hunt, the sepia of autumn, huntsmen mounted in the street outside the hotel, and the hounds, sepia-mottled, gathered about the master. Photographs of officers stationed at the Curragh at one time or another, cavalry officers, necks choked behind high-collared jackets with elaborate froggings, hilts of swords. Garden parties outside the houses of the Kildare gentry, grouped three deep upon the steps of big houses, gentlemen leaning attentively toward the ladies, or else looking straight ahead, fierce-visaged, into the camera. Blurred photographs of horse races. In the bar, oil paintings of celebrated Kildare champions, jockeys astride them wearing shot silk slashed colors—scarlet, vermilion, emerald.

At the end of the bar, two men, one young and the other middle-aged, the two of them wearing jackets of hounds tooth tweed and trousers of cavalry twill, talked to each other in low voices, on the counter before them what looked like large gins. With his tea, Lacy ate a sandwich of thin-sliced pork, and, after his tea, drank a second small whiskey. The two horsemen looked at him with mild interest.

From Naas, he had a clear run through Tallaght into Dublin, threading narrow streets, and, at last, crossing the Liffey at Bridge Street. The room which had been booked for him at the Barristers Arms was waiting for him, and although he could hear convivial voices coming from the bar, he followed the boots upstairs, the boots a brisk, fresh young fellow with close-cropped red hair.

"You are only an ass's roar from the Four Courts," the boots said, resting thin shoulders against the open door. "But there is no legal business being transacted there. The Four Courts is now the headquarters of the Irish Republic."

"Yes," Lacy said. "So I have heard."

He had been given a front room. From its window he could look down directly at the night-shrouded Liffey, or look left toward the Four Courts, its high, massive dome faintly visible. There were no lights within it that he could see, but it was an elaborate structure, courts built in the complex ordering of the late eighteenth century, and for all he knew, lights could have been blazing in the eastern half, facing up the river to the ruined Custom House. Directly across the river from him, lights blazed in the public rooms of the Clarence Hotel. From his black Gladstone bag, he took out nightshirt, razor, and the two books which these days accompanied him, no longer *Virgil,* but Florio's *Montaigne* in the Everyman edition, and Balzac's *Père Goriot* in what was, he suspected, an indifferent translation, requisitioned from the library of a loyalist in the valley beyond Kilpeder. Then he removed his coat, and took from its holster, cross-strapped by leather across his chest, the weighty, loaded Parabellum. He placed books and weapon on the table beside his bed, and added, from his jacket pocket, the flask which he had had filled with tea in Naas.

Before undressing, he went back to the window. As he stood there, two of the lights in the bedrooms of the Clarence were turned out, but not the wide, bright lights in its public rooms.

In the morning, early, he had a quick breakfast, and then walked along Ellis Quay and Arran Quay to the Four Courts. There was a clear, clean feel to the early morning. He convinced the two young sentries as to his identity, and then walked down twisting corridors to where a uniformed Volunteer sat behind a desk with a ledger, a cup of tea, and copies of the *Independent* and the *Freeman's Journal*.

Sean Hulden, director of organization and a member of the five-man Army Council, had an office on the second floor of the massive, rectangular block which had been requisitioned as headquarters, but he was waiting for Lacy two doors beyond it, in what had once been a council room, long dark-wooded table and matching high-backed chairs. The air still had a chill in it, and Hulton's dark jacket was buttoned. Papers were spread out before him, and he was making rapid notes on a sheet of lined paper. When he saw Lacy standing in the doorway, he put aside the pencil, and shouted down the corridor for fresh air.

Waiting for the tea, they sat facing each other, with faint smiles. They had been together, during the Tan war, no more than a half-dozen times, but long enough for a trust and a liking to develop between the two of them. Hulden, like his friend Rory O'Connor, was a university graduate with a degree in engineering and a passion for classical music. It was a family passion: he had a brother who was a cellist in the orchestra in Boston and who had helped organize the first shipment of Thompson submachine guns from the States.

"They keep me busy here, Frank," he said. "On top of everything else, Rory and myself are trying to build a tunnel between this block and the Rotunda axis. Those sandbags that the lads have put in place are little better than useless."

"For all that, you are very cozy in here," Lacy said dryly.

" 'Tis a great barn of a place," Hulden said. "I grant you that.

But it can be defended, if worst comes to worst. It will take men and work, but it can be defended." He gestured toward the windows. "As you can see, we have the law on our side." The windows were blocked, two-thirds of the way up, with law books, calf-bound, thick. "Sure, they were useless on their shelves, dead old eighteenth-century statutes, George I and George II."

"If worst comes to worst," Lacy said, and the two of them were circumspect until the tea things had been brought in and laid out on the table. The wall facing the window was handsomely paneled, and carried portraits in oil, charcoal, crayon, of wigged and gowned barristers and judges.

"That first night," Hulden said, "Ernie O'Malley and myself climbed up onto the roof, and watched dawn come to the city. It was extraordinary."

"What lies behind us here?" Lacy said.

"The Public Records Office," Hulden said. "It has a fine, deep cellar. We are using it to make and store munitions."

All the records of Ireland would be in that building, so Lacy had always heard, charters and deeds and titles, paper, parchment, sheepskin, vellum, for all one knew. But he said nothing more, waiting for Hulden, who was loading his tea with sugar, pouring in sweet heavy milk.

At last, Hulden said, "The council has a matter to take up with you, before today's executive. But I told them there was no need for the full council. The two of us know each other well, and we can sort it out, the two of us."

"I hope so," Lacy said, in mild, neutral tones.

"Frank, back in the beginning of the month, when the army raided the Bank of Ireland branches, including your own raid on the branch in Kilpeder, that was done on the authority of Headquarters, and a statement was issued. We had been running up debts to traders across the country, and it was not right that they should suffer. The Bank of Ireland is the financial agent of the Provisional Government. Everything was in order and done properly. We gave receipts, you will recall."

"I do recall," Lacy said. "Mr. Caulfield seemed most grateful." Caulfield, a peppery, bald Protestant with a northern accent, had said, holding the receipt with theatrical distaste, "What the hell am I supposed to do with this?" "That is entirely your affair,"

Lacy said. There were no customers, and Lacy's men kept their carbines fixed on Caulfield and his terrified cashier.

"But that was not the case when you held up the Munster-Leinster last week. There is no way to put a good face on it. You did not trouble yourselves with masks. You had no authorization for that raid. It was simple robbery."

"I gave him a receipt," Lacy said, "just as I had Caulfield. He was more frightened than Caulfield had been: I liked Caulfield. A chap named Cassidy, a strong John Redmond man in the old days. 'What is the country coming to?' he asked me. A good question, I had no answer for him."

"It is nothing to make light of, Frank. Without authority it was a criminal act, in our eyes as much as the Provisionals'. O'Connor is furious, to say nothing of our friends beyond." He nodded across the river, toward the distant Mansion House.

"What's done is done," Lacy said. "The money is gone."

"Gone!" Hulden said. "You took away from poor Cassidy"—he paused to search out a paper—"more than twelve hundred, almost thirteen hundred pounds. How the hell could you get rid of thirteen hundred pounds in a week?"

"I am making an arms purchase," Lacy said, "carbines, revolvers, some Mills bombs. From a dealer in Southampton. We used him before, in the Tan war. Mellowes would know his name."

"I know his name myself," Hulden said, tight-lipped. " 'Tis that crazy Mexican or Portuguese, whatever he is. I know the gun merchant in Southampton. He is a bloody anarchist."

"He is as reliable as any of them."

Hulden was angrier than Lacy had expected. "You had no authority. Even such measures as we take under authority allow Griffith and his crowd to brand us as brigands. And you are prepared to behave like one. I understand that you have been driving about the country in an immense motorcar. The railway is good enough for Liam Lynch, and Liam is our chief of staff."

"The motorcar is a belated contribution to the Republic from a landlord in West Cork."

"Contribution!" Hulden said. "There are small farmers and landless men in Connaught driving cattle, and houghing cattle as in the bygone days of the Whiteboys. And there is talk of industrial strikes in Limerick and in the midlands. Fellows are holding up public houses not to buy arms, but because they are common criminals. In Mayo last week, two big houses were burned out and the people driven onto the roads not because they were loyalists but because they were Protestants. No better reason. We are the lawful government of this country, for God's sake, Frank. We are the army of the Republic."

"An army cannot fight without weapons," Lacy said.

"We are making arms purchases, damn it," Hulden said. "What it comes down to is this. The army is split in two, our lot and the Free State crowd in Beggars Bush. Our lot is open and aboveboard. We have an Executive which we asked you to join, and we have a council. And by God, we will not have a Republican division acting like a gang of cowboys in the Wild West."

Lacy did not answer him at once. He stood up, and walked to one of the half-barricaded windows. Beyond, a courtyard stretched to the Rotunda. Volunteers were filling sandbags.

"You cannot fight with sandbags, Sean."

Hulden spoke to Lacy's turned back. "With the help of God, we may not be fighting at all. The truce between the two wings has been extended for another two weeks. Fellows from the two crowds are meeting. When men are still talking there is still hope." O'Connor and Mellowes were talking for the Republicans, Hulden said, and Collins and Mulcahy for the Provisionals. "A few more for each side, but you can see that they are the top men. There is still goodwill on both sides. Our lot will continue to hold the Four Courts here, but we will pull out of the Kildare Street Club and the Ballast Office and all that. I am sorry to see us leave that club, the fellows holding it used to report here with fistfuls of excellent cigars."

"And what are Collins and Mulcahy doing as evidence of their goodwill?"

"Why, they have as good as agreed to let us stay here in the Four Courts, and to use it as Republican Army headquarters."

"Our lads have made a fool's bargain, Sean," Lacy said. The Volunteers working in the courtyard were all very young, and they were cheerful at their monotonous task. Two of them would hold open the bag, and the third fellow would shovel sand into it. "You have a building," Lacy said. "And you sit in it like custodians of some bloody palace or museum. It is not even defended properly. You have not occupied the outbuildings, or the hotels along the quays to either side of you."

Hulden gave a snort of laughter, and Lacy turned toward him in puzzlement.

"Outbuildings," he said, "that's a good one. At the very least they should be taken over, and the Four Courts Hotel in particular, it is sitting directly there under our wing, and do you know why we have not?" He laughed again. " 'Tis a good one. You know how ticklish matters are in Limerick, the two lots of us squared off against each other, in February it came almost to a battle, shots were exchanged. The goodwill of Limerick City is essential." He smiled, folded his hands across his beginning of a paunch, and waited for Lacy's question, but Lacy said nothing. "And why can we not send in the lads to occupy the Four Courts Hotel? Why, because it is owned by the mayor of Limerick, who has no wish to see his public rooms held by armed Dublin gurriers hurling out defiance past sandbagged windows. Wheels within wheels, as always."

Beyond Hulden's youthful, balding head, judges and barristers, bewigged and begowned, beamed down upon this worldly attitude.

"I have been well and truly reprimanded," Lacy said. "Is that the end of it, Sean, or must I answer to the full council?"

"Not at all," Hulden said, "not at all. Sure, where would we be, without your division and Lynch's and O'Malley's, and one or two others? At the end of the day, in the heel of the hunt, the Republic will sink or float upon the loyalty of the men in the field. 'Twas not even a reprimand, 'twas a word of caution."

"You summoned me all the way from West Cork to give me a word of caution. Now, Sean, that is not like you."

Hulden smiled and nodded. He leaned forward toward the council table, and his shoulders, Lacy noticed, moved more easily, as though a burden had been lifted from them. "Take a seat here, Frank," Hulden said, and gestured, with indifferent generosity, to the chairs on either side of him. Then he took a pink dossier from the untidy pile before him, undid its ribbon, and opened it. There were but two sheets of paper inside, and he placed them side by side. "Come along here, Frank. Take a look at this."

Months later, toward the close of what had indeed become a disastrous civil war, Lacy, alone save for two gunmen who acted as bodyguards, tried with but partial success to remember Hulden's look and sound that morning, as he sat at the council table in the Four Courts, behind the untidy piles of dossiers. He could remember Hulden's look, the early sunlight falling on the high forehead, an anxious smile, anxiety to please, strains of the unfamiliar. He remembered the smile, a desperate attempt at worldliness, as Hulden explained why the Four Courts Hotel had not been occupied.

One of the gunmen had gone down to the shop at the cross, and had come back with a copy of the *Cork Examiner.* Spread across the front page was the account of how four men, and Hulden one of them, had been executed by the Free State, shot by firing squad. The *Cork Examiner*'s account was cautious, the newspaper itself sympathetic to the attempts of the Free State to suppress "Republicanism and anarchism," but Cork City was held by the Irish Republican Army, and the newspaper was censored by gunmen. "Hulden went calmly to his death, with a quiet determination. He professed his continuing loyalty to the Irish Republic, and offered prayers for its safety in the field," the *Examiner* said.

It was not until late that Dublin night that Lacy entered into the planning that Hulden had opened up to him in the morning, from the two sheets in the pink dossier, and between morning and late night he had had a chance to talk with Ernie O'Malley.

"You are quite right," O'Malley said. "It is absolutely disgraceful. I spoke to Joe McKelvey, and told him we had need of an operations staff. If we are attacked, I told him, he should have plans for mobilization within the Four Courts itself, and we should be able to move out at once to establish a defensible perimeter."

O'Malley, commanding officer of the Second Southern, one of the divisions on Lacy's flank, had been detached for duty in the Four Courts, and he was garrisoned there, but he had also the use of a flat on Harcourt Terrace, which was occupied in winter months by a minor dramatist at the Abbey, a friend of Elizabeth Keating's. It was there that he and Lacy were meeting, in early evening.

In response to Lacy's questioning look, O'Malley said, "Joe sent me on to Liam Lynch, and I heard from Liam what you heard this morning from Sean Hulden. Matters will sort themselves out, there will be no war, no war between brothers was the way Liam kept phrasing it, there will be a joint Headquarters staff, pro-Treaty and anti-Treaty. It will take patience and restraint on the both sides, Liam assured me. Our lads have been meeting with Collins and Mulcahy. What need have we for an occupation staff in the Four Courts? Do you trust Mulcahy? I asked him, and he shrugged." O'Malley grinned savagely at Lacy. "He shrugged."

"What about yourself?" Lacy said. "Do you trust Mick, do you trust the Big Fellow?" He gave the words a sarcastic edge.

"I have no more notion than you have yourself what has happened to Mick Collins," O'Malley said. "Another of Ireland's bloody tragedies. But I do know this about Mick Collins, and you do yourself. When he gets the bit between his teeth, only a fool would stand in his path. It will be ourselves against Mick Collins at the end of the day."

"And there matters were left stand, were they, between yourself and Liam?"

"He relented a bit," O'Malley said. "Made a few concessions to reality. Paddy O'Brien and myself marked down snipers' positions, and organized the garrison into sections, set up more barbed-wire barricades at the gates, and strengthened the sandbagging."

"I know that," Lacy said. "I saw your lads at work with their shovels."

"Well," O'Malley said. "There you are. We need routes of escape, through the sewers if it comes to that. We are fairly well armed, and we have set lads to work making bombs and grenades."

Lacy stood up and stretched. He envied O'Malley the use of the flat, tall windows framed by flame-colored curtains; heavy, sagging easy chairs faced each other across the fireplace, deep-cushioned. On the walls, shadowy and indistinct beyond lamplight, hung framed photographs of performances' playbills, two unfurled Spanish fans at right angles to each other, framed posters, seascapes in watercolor. Along half of one wall, reaching to above eye level, books on bowed shelves were pressed tightly against each other.

"You may be well armed to defend yourselves, Ernie. When they move against you, you can put up a good fight for a few days, a week perhaps. Then what?"

"You answer that one," O'Malley said. "If you can." He ran nervous fingers through red hair. "When Paddy and I were making our inspection, I said to Paddy that I would be damned before I handed over the Four Courts. Before I handed it over, I would blow the bloody place up to kingdom come. And we could do that, you know, we have turned the Public Records Office into a bomb shop, a munition dump."

"The Republic will not be saved from Dublin," Lacy said, "but by the men in the field who have been fighting for it, the lads in the columns and the divisions, the men on the hillside."

"You are preaching to the converted," O'Malley said. "At the end of the day, matters will rest with the army in Munster. And look at us, would you, myself quartered in the Four Courts, and yourself summoned up here to atone for having lifted a few pounds from the Munster-Leinster like Jesse James."

"It was more than a few pounds," Lacy said, "to be honest about the matter." And he and O'Malley grinned at each other. "But I was given no more than a slap on the wrist from Sean Hulden. A good man, Sean."

"All good men," O'Malley said, "the lot of us. That's the problem."

At Lacy's arrival, O'Malley had brought out two glasses and a half-full bottle of the playwright's brown sherry, but they had left them untouched. Sunlight of early evening fell through glass upon warm brown. Lacy walked over to the low table and picked up one of the glasses.

"Once," he said, "during the Tan war, I came to this city to argue some arms for Paudge Brennan's column and got nowhere. That night in Vaughan's, Mick Collins scribbled out a note and told me to bring it round to Sean Hulden. Sean was deputy QM then. That note from Mick turned the trick."

"I have three stories that I could give you to match that one," O'Malley said, and he raised his glass. "But he is on the other side now, on the other side from Sean and ourselves. On the other side from Liam Lynch and Rory O'Connor and Tom Barry, all the fighting men that he should be with by rights."

Above the fireplace, splashes of vermilion, purple, a Jack Yeats impression of one of the Fay brothers as Cuchulain, his back against a wall of soft night, enormous arms, fingers white against colors, blues, magentas, an inexplicable swirl of yellow. Lacy took a step backwards to study it.

"Sean Hulden says that things can be somehow sorted out, even at this late hour. Do you believe that?"

"I do not," O'Malley said, "and neither does Rory. Liam Lynch may. There is cooperation between Beggars Bush and the Four Courts on the northern question, we are acting together to protect our lot against the Orangemen and their B-Specials. But it will not last, it cannot last. At the end of the day, the British will demand the surrender of the Four Courts, and then Collins and Griffith and that crowd will have to make up their minds, are they Irishmen or are they British hirelings in green uniforms? You do not make us a free country by wearing green trousers and painting the letterboxes green."

"It was not to slap my wrist because of the bank job that the council brought me up to Dublin. I am under orders from them to meet tonight with a few of the Beggars Bush crowd."

O'Malley clapped his hands together. "There you are. We are on the bloody brink of destroying each other, but when it comes to the North, we are still together. I have worked on one or two enterprises of that nature. My advice to you, Frank, if you are looking for it, is to go cautiously. The lads in the North need our help, God knows, but the Free Staters are looking to entangle us in flypaper."

Lacy took a sip of his sherry, thick and cloying on the tongue. "If war is as certain as all that, Ernie, you should not let yourselves be bottled up in the Four Courts. Beyond the Four Courts, you have the Dublin Brigade, or most of it, but the Free Staters have the better part of an army in Beggars Bush. They have been recruiting ex-British soldiers, and they are being supplied by the British with arms and vehicles. That is no military secret. I read it in the *Cork Examiner.*"

O'Malley sat forward on the edge of his chair. "I know that, Frank, I know that, God damn it. But I am not the Army Council. I will be in charge of defense when the worst comes, but there you are."

"What need is there to give you lessons in what you know?" Lacy said. "You should occupy buildings to form a perimeter, and you should have at least a line of retreat."

At first, O'Malley did not answer him. He stood up and

walked to the window, and when he spoke, it was to the window, his back to Lacy.

"Do you know what I think it is? I think it is 1916. In 1916 the lads sealed themselves up in the General Post Office, and fought until it began to come down in flames above their heads. And they set Ireland on fire. There are fellows on our side who would like to see the same for the Four Courts. Dig in there in the Four Courts, and hold fast until they smash the Four Courts and smash the lads holding it. The Four Courts aflame will teach Ireland what is still at stake."

It came to Lacy unbidden, the stabbing image of a building in flames.

"If they think that, they are entirely mad. If they have a war, it will be fought in Munster, along a line stretching from Waterford to Limerick, it will be fought by the Republican divisions and columns, your and Liam's and mine and the others. It will not be won by men holding the Four Courts until it is destroyed."

O'Malley shrugged. "Who knows? We have fought the war thus far on imagination and memories."

Neither of them had a mind to finish the glasses of brown sherry, but they sat together as the room quietly, imperceptibly darkened. At last, O'Malley said, "I mean that, you know. The bit about imagination. We have been at work improvising, ever since 1916, improvising parliaments and ambushes and rhetoric and history and laws and theories. But now we are in danger of running smash against something that does not give a damn about imagination."

From the street outside, the shouts of schoolboys floated to them. And then a girl's voice, high, musical, half-taunting.

The Free State officers whom Lacy met late that night proved to be Christopher Blake, Ben Cogley, who had been Lacy's adjutant in the days of the Tan war, and Collins himself. They met, for reasons of sentiment, in the abovestairs room in Vaughan's, three tables with a cluster of straight-backed chairs around each of them. On the walls, theater playbills beginning to fade, the poster for a race-meeting at Leopardstown, a full-sized copy of the Proclamation, framed in dark bog oak. The three of them were sitting at the table which Collins had always taken, nearest the door. He and Blake were in civilian clothes, but Cogley wore a handsome tunic, Sam Browne belt, his insignia of rank as a brigade commandant.

Lacy nodded to each of them and took a seat facing Collins. The barman—Lacy remembered his name from the old days. Tony Hassett—had followed him upstairs and stood waiting for orders.

When Lacy shook his head, Collins said, "For God's sake, take something to wet the dust. We have had more than one drink together in this room, Frank."

Lacy told the barman to bring him a glass of stout.

"Guinness," Collins said. "Do you know, Guinness is the one drink that I have never been able to abide."

"Yes," Lacy said. "I did know that." And let the words hang in the air.

"It has been a long time, Frank," Cogley said.

"A few months, Ben," Lacy said, but knew that the months were stretching like a crack on the surface of a desert.

Of all the men with whom he had worked over the last three years, he had felt closest to Cogley. Save for O'Malley, but O'Malley and himself had been on different operations in the South and the West, meeting infrequently. But he had known Cogley since first he came to Kilpeder to help in the organization of Patrick MacCarthy's battalion, when Cogley had been intelligence officer, and then, later, after the formation of divisions, Cogley had been Lacy's own adjutant.

Lacy remembered evenings in the rooms above Cogley's shop, before they had been forced on the run, Cogley and himself and Cogley's wife, Clare. Beyond the windows, darkness had settled upon the square, closing-time shouts floating upwards from Conefry's and the other public houses, but Cogley and Clare and himself deep in conversation, or Cogley trying out his rudimentary Gaelic. He was the same man now, Lacy knew, but seemed not the same in his brisk Free State uniform.

"How is life in the Four Courts, Frank?" Collins asked him. "Sean Hulden and yourself had a quiet chat, I have been told."

Lacy shook his head in mock admiration. "Your intelligence sources are as good as ever they were, Mick," he said.

"They are as badly needed as ever," Collins said. "But not this time. I talked with Sean on the telephone. Sean tells me what Liam Lynch has told me, that you are willing to talk to me." He sipped from a glass, almost empty, of deep amber whiskey. On the table stood an open bottle of Paddy, and a pitcher of water. During the years of the Tan war, it was more than stout that Collins had had an aversion to; never, while at work, had Lacy seen him with so much as a glass taken. Later on, business attended to, he might take a single glass, or, more rarely, a second, and then he would be gone, from this room, most often, but Lacy had met with him in safe houses in Mespil Road, Haddingon Road, Clonskeagh.

When, in these latter days, Lacy thought of that Collins, it would be a single image—here, in this room abovestairs in Vaughan's, deep winter, and Collins, struggling into a waterproof, translating himself into a respectable strayed reveler anxious to get home from his pub before curfew, but at the same time giving final instructions to one of his men, Blake here on occasion. And then gone, riding off through black, patrolled streets on the defective bicycle that he kept at Vaughan's, with the loose, clattering fender that scraped against the spokes, *creech,* pause, *creech.* "It would take less than a half-hour to repair that, Mick," Lacy told him once, but Collins said, "What! That *creech* is my safe-conduct past the Tommies. No wanted gunman is likely to ride through Dublin on a bicycle calling out *creech, creech.*"

Now, this night, Lacy said, "Liam was almost right, Mick. Not quite. I did not tell him that I was willing to talk to you, but that I was willing to listen."

For a moment Collins glared at him, heavy head shoved forward, and then he laughed. "Jesus, Frank, you have become quite the pedant. I should have known that." He drained the end of his glass, and picked up the bottle of Paddy, and held it toward Blake's glass, toward Cogley's, and they shook their heads. "You will so," he said, "a drop for old times' sake, with an old comrade," and he splashed whiskey in their glasses, and a larger measure into his own.

"How is that glass of Guinness holding out, Frank? We can ring for more. Quite the pedant and I should have known it. Back in the early days, when you were out organizing the columns, yourself and Ernie, the local lads on the spot, the company commanders and the battalion commanders, when they were up here in Dublin, they would say, 'What the hell have you sent down amongst us, Mick, 'twas a drill sergeant we had need of or a man skilled with explosive devices, and you sent down a university lecturer on the arts of war as practiced by Hannibal.' Sometimes they meant you and sometimes Ernie. And you are still pedants, the two of you, Ernie in the Four Courts and yourself below in West Cork. What the bloody hell do you know about West Cork, 'tis my own country."

As he was talking, he added water to the three glasses, a dollop for Blake, a dollop for Cogley, but he filled his own glass almost to the edge.

"I am listening, Mick," Lacy said.

" 'Tis Christopher here that we have asked you to come listen to," Collins said, and with the words, he put his hand on Blake's forearm. Lacy, following the gesture, saw with amusement that Blake was as well dressed as ever, a jacket of pale gray herringbone. They had much in common, Blake and himself, bookish fellows, middle-class the two of them, as O'Malley was also, in a world of hillside rebels, tough Dubliners. And yet Lacy had been drawn close to O'Malley, stayed aloof and wary in his dealings with Blake. It had not surprised him to learn that Blake had gone over to the Free State, why would he not, he was one of Collins's men, bound to him, like MacEoin the legendary fighting man and the members of "the Squad," by ties of personal loyalty. But there was more to it than that. Blake had been there when he was needed, fair enough, in 1916 and on Bloody Sunday, but there was something about him that Lacy distrusted, something that had nothing to do with the Collins connection.

Lacy shrugged, and looked into Blake's eyes, pale blue like his own. "I am listening, Christopher."

But before Blake could speak, Cogley cut in.

"Mick here and Christopher have talked with me about this, Frank. They asked me to come along tonight, because they know how things stand—how things used to stand—between the two of us. We have always trusted each other, Frank, and I pray God that we still do."

"I have never had occasion to mistrust you, Ben," Lacy said, but he did not shift his eyes from Blake's.

Blake moved slightly in his chair, as though sensing an oblique reproof, and Lacy would have let the matter rest there, unspoken upon the air, but Collins laughed.

"These days, a meeting of old friends is like walking across one of the minefields of Flanders. I declare to Jesus." He picked up his glass almost eagerly and there was a slight slur to his speech. You heard it said these days on all sides that Collins had begun to drink heavily, but the matter had been settled for Lacy moments before when he watched Collins adding water to his glass; Collins had had drink taken that night and was willing to let it appear so, but he was quite sober, the eyes alert and appraising.

"We are still talking, you know, Frank," Collins said, "the two crowds of us. We are still working together on certain matters that involve the North. Dev and myself are working on a formula to patch up matters until after the election. We are not quite at war with each other yet, Frank."

"Close enough to suit me," Lacy said, speaking beyond the watered whiskey to the clear, appraising eyes. "Shots have been fired. A man has been shot dead in Macroom. Barracks held by Republicans have been rousted by your people with their armored cars and with their weapons that have been handed to them by the British."

"This may not be a profitable discussion," Blake said suddenly; these were the first words, almost, that he had spoken. Collins had left his hand resting absently on Blake's forearm, and now he squeezed it.

"We need your help, Frank," Collins said, "for a particular matter."

"I will see you in hell first, Mick, before I will help your crowd, before I will help the men who bargained and sold away the Republic."

"Jesus, Frank," Ben Cogley said. "Draw it mild."

"Why, Ben?" Lacy said. "Why should I? I have been friends with the three of you, one way or another. I have never had a better man beside me in the field than yourself, and I am not one of those who begrudge all that Mick has done for us in four hard years. But it was not to friends that I took an oath. It was an oath to the Republic."

In the final days in Kilpeder, before Ben and himself split apart, the word had echoed back and forth in their arguments so often that at the end it was stale, drained of meaning. The Republic. The Republic. Cogley had made the point to him one night, almost the last night, in Ardmor Castle, which had been serving the two of them as divisional headquarters.

"Listen, Frank," he said, "to the sounds of our two voices, going over the same ground, over and over again, like a gramophone with a stale needle stuck in the middle. The Republic. The Republic. It is for Ireland that we have been fighting, for the living people in it, and not for a word."

And suddenly, when Cogley said that, Lacy knew that there were no longer bridges between the two of them, that bridges could not be built. The word "Republic" might go stale in the mouth, as any word will if you say it often enough and fast enough, children knew that. But the Republic was no mere word. It was the Republic which justified ambush and murder and translated willed starvation from suicide into sacrifice. That night in Ardmor Castle, Lacy looked down the long road and saw death and civil war at the end of it.

"Yes," Ben Cogley said this night in Vaughan's, and sighed. "I know, Frank. The Republic."

"You had best hear us out," Collins said. He spread his hand out on the porter-stained top of the table, a gambler's hand. "This is a matter that has been approved by your own Army Council. You are not setting up shop entirely on your own, are you? A one-man Republic with a one-man Irish Republican Army?"

"He would if he had to," Cogley said, and although the tone was no more than half-humorous, Lacy smiled for the first time.

"You are right, Mick. I take my orders from the Army Council. I told Sean Hulden that this morning."

"There is nothing in this that is in violation of any oath," Blake said. He was following Collins's lead dutifully enough, but there was an edge of irritation in his voice.

"Far from it indeed," Collins said. "Far from it."

"We need your cooperation," Blake began, and Lacy thought that it was perhaps Blake's preciseness of diction that he found offputting. He had found it so two years before, when Blake explained to him exactly how and when the Bloody Sunday operation was to be conducted in Cork City, timed to the hour to coincide with the shootings in Dublin. For Blake it had been words and orders, specifications, set forth neatly as they sat quietly at a table in Dublin, with a view beyond a narrow window of a winter garden, a leafless apple tree and beyond it a brick wall topped with broken glass. But for Lacy, Bloody Sunday had been the hotel corridor in Cork, a frightened half-dressed British officer, a blur of mustache, unfocused eyes, and revolver shots exploding in the musty hotel room.

Blake leaned forward across the table toward Lacy, and paused for a moment, as though his thoughts were cards which needed a final ordering. "On the twenty-fourth of June," he said, "within your division, four miles distant from Kilpeder—"

Collins's glass was half-empty. He set it down on the table, and peered first at Blake and then at Lacy, and his words cut across Blake's. His voice was a good-natured growl with a bit of mockery in it, self-mockery perhaps.

"We are going down to West Cork, boy," he said, "down into your stronghold."

"And it is your stronghold, right enough," Cogley said. His tone was wry, bitter. Lacy was a newcomer to West Cork, a blow-in, but Cogley had spent his life in the county, growing up in Millstreet and then marrying into the Kilpeder chemist's shop.

" 'Tis your parish," Collins said. "Fifth Division is solidly die-hard. Not like some that could be named, some to either side of you." It was open knowledge that O'Malley commanded a troubled, divided crowd to the left of Lacy's, and even Lynch's command to his right, the largest and most formidable, had its dissenters.

"I have had good fortune," Lacy said, agreeably, "I have Pat MacCarthy at my side." He knew that the words would hurt Cogley. In the years of the Tan war, MacCarthy, the garage owner in Kilpeder, had become one of the formidable guerrilla commanders, with men loyal to him out of instinct, love, as they would never be to either Lacy or Cogley. When the army units were choosing up sides, after the Treaty, MacCarthy's choice of the Republic had been an important event in Munster.

"MacCarthy," Collins said. "The hard man himself. How is Pat?"

"He is thriving, thank you," Lacy said. "He and I speak of you often, Mick. And of yourself, Ben." He made it sound as though Collins and Cogley, by putting on the uniform of the Free State, had drifted off to some foreign land, distant from Ireland.

Collins moved his heavy shoulders, and there was an instant's angry glint in his eyes. "You were saying, Christopher."

"Yes," Blake said dryly. "I was saying. Do you want me to outline this for Frank, Mick, or will you do it yourself? It does not matter to me, so long as he knows what is needed from him."

"You were mentioning a date in the next month, in June," Lacy said.

"Those bastards in the North," Collins said, "they have been mauling our people, butchering them. It is time that they were taught a lesson."

"The time for lesson teaching is long past," Lacy said with sardonic mildness. "The lesson should have been that the nation of Ireland would sign no treaty that split the country in two, and left our people in the North helpless and outnumbered, standing by while rifles and revolvers were placed in the hands of the Orange bullies."

"For the moment," Blake said, "that is neither here nor there. The question for the moment is what kind of protection can be given to our people up there. Not when we have a constitution down here, not after the election, but now. There are B-Specials roaming the streets of Belfast in armored cars, keeping order by spraying houses with machine-gun fire."

"I know that," Lacy said, his voice still mild. "I read the newspapers." But he was well informed, by Lynch and O'Malley, among others. Cooperation on the North even now, even on the edge of civil war, was extraordinary. Rifles had been exchanged between the Four Courts and the Beggars Bush barracks, lest any weapons supplied by the British to Collins's forces should turn up on retaliatory raids from the South.

"The Orangemen," Collins said, "are not alone in this, they are backed up by the British Tories, by Wilson and Chubb."

"Wilson isn't even British," Cogley said suddenly, "a Longford man, a turncoat Irishman. They are the worst, worst of all those turncoats."

But Wilson, Lacy knew, had not turned his coat, Anglo-Irish, Protestant, British Army, loyalty to the Crown had been bred into Wilson by generations of history, bred by the people who had given the British Army its commanders, Wellington, Wolseley, Gough. Wilson was almost a grotesque epitome of the breed, half-comic, half-terrifying. Field Marshal Sir Henry Hughes Wilson, Officer of the Bath and all the rest of it, former chief of the Imperial General Staff, and, more to the point, at the moment member of Parliament for North Down, and military adviser to the Northern government. It was at Wilson's advice that General Horace Chubb was placed in command of Northern troops, a bemedaled old soldier like Wilson himself, and, like Wilson, an Irishman by birth. Newspaper photographs showed them together, awkward in their well-tailored civilian clothes, Wilson immensely tall, a hawk, hawk's features, high, curving nose, staring eyes, and Chubb, a younger man, a man in his early fifties, solid, square bullish head. Dimly, Lacy remembered photographs of Chubb, in uniform, inspecting a company of B-Specials drawn to attention in a courtyard, the Specials looking, to Lacy's angry eyes, to be cast from a common mold.

"It is the Tories that must have a lesson taught them," Collins said. "If the Tories back away, we will be able to handle the Orangemen."

Lacy shrugged. Like many of the Republican commandants, he had developed an acute distaste for politicians, whether Irish or English.

"You can talk reason to men like Lloyd George and Churchill," Collins said, "you can talk reason to Birkenhead. By God, of all of them, it is Birkenhead that I prefer. But the Tories are deaf to reason."

Names in newspapers to Lacy—Churchill, Lloyd George. He had seen them in newsreels. At the conference at Versailles, they had stood together between the pillars of a building of state, the two of them, Lloyd George gesticulating, and Churchill, round-cheeked, his head bobbing: once he clapped his hands together, then put a hand on Lloyd George's forearm. Collins had sat across the table from them. Number Ten Downing Street, green baize table, writing tablets, on the wall, flanked by portraits, a map of the Empire. There, in that room, he had bargained away the Republic.

"I would not know," Lacy said. "I have never tried to reason with them."

Collins smiled, without humor, but with a wry, acknowledging wit. "Indeed you have not, Frank. There is that to be said. Yourself and Cathal Brugha and Harry Boland and Rory O'Connor and Liam Lynch and so forth and so on. You have never tried to reason."

"I can speak only for myself," Lacy said. "Reasoning takes

quiet and a time for contemplation. I have always been too busy, hurrying to this place and that place, carrying out orders. Orders from yourself, more often than not."

"You should make time for contemplation, Frank," Blake said. "Life cannot be all that bustling below in Kilpeder."

If I knew why I have come to dislike Blake, Lacy thought, I might know something about myself.

"You were talking, Chris," he said, "about a day in June, two weeks or so from this day. Before we drifted off into affairs of state, Winston Churchill and Downing Street and so forth."

Collins produced from the small serving table to their right a clear whiskey glass, and said, "Drink off the rest of that stout, Frank. Have a proper drink, for the love of Jesus." And Lacy, for the sake of sweet Jesus, let Collins measure out for him a decent glass, and for himself as well, and then the others. He watched Collins pouring out the water then, and he had been forewarned. Collins was a man with a few drinks taken, not drunk, but giving a calculated impersonation of it.

"Yes," Blake said. "On the twenty-fourth of June General Chubb will be in your division, a few miles beyond Kilpeder. His godchild is being married that day, a fatherless girl, the father killed on the Somme, commanding his regiment. General Chubb will be giving her away in marriage. The Armstrongs. You know the Armstrongs, Ben tells us."

"Not socially," Lacy said. "The Armstrongs of Glamorgan House, people of Welsh descent, as I recall. Glamorgan House is shoved over there against the borders of First Division. It has a fine view of the Derrynasaggarts."

"We raided it once for arms," Cogley said, "in the summer of 1920, before Frank joined us. Two rifles and four splendid shotguns." He smiled across the table at Lacy. "One of them was that over-and-under that you fancied for yourself, but Timmy Timmins had firm hold of it, by the time you joined us, do you recall?"

"Yes," Lacy said, "I recall, Ben, as well as you do yourself." He recalled the botched ambush at Derrynacoppel, and Timmy Timmins lying sprawled behind a hedge, the hedge cut into ribbons by fire from a Lewis gun.

"They are to be married in the Protestant church in Rathgorey, and there will after that be a reception in Glamorgan House,"

Blake said. "Friends and relations from far and wide, and General Chubb motoring down from Belfast."

"With an escort," Collins said. "An armed escort, no great flaunting display of troops, but an armored car before his own motorcar, and one to the rear of it."

"Driving down into my division, is it?" Lacy asked. "British soldiers in armored cars driving into Fifth Division, is that it, Ben?" He looked directly at Cogley, ignoring Collins and Blake.

"Hear us out now, Frank," Cogley said.

"There is no reason whatever," Collins said, "why General Chubb, or anyone else for that matter, should not attend a wedding in West Cork. The Provisional Government has assured him of this, but he would like a bit of insurance, two armored cars' worth of insurance."

"And you are asking me to make certain that he has it, is that it, Mick?"

"No," Collins said, "that is not it. Not at all." He had been leaning far back in his straight chair, and now he brought it crashing down and rested his folded arms on the table. "I want you to kill him for us, Frank. I do not care how you do it, you can do it by ambush, you can have him shot down outside the church, you can do it at Glamorgan House. And if you are too squeamish to do it at all, yourselves and your fellows, Christopher here and myself can send down a couple of the lads from my Squad. You can slip them in and you can slip them out, and no one the wiser."

He sat looking over his folded arms at Lacy, heavy shoulders hung forward. The room was entirely silent. Lacy said nothing. After a bit, after a few moments, Collins stretched out his arm and picked up his glass, and Lacy, as though the gesture had given him a cue, picked up his own. But no one spoke.

"Well now, lads," Lacy said at last, and he took a full, welcome sip of the whiskey. "So this is the Provisional Government at work, is it, on behalf of the Free State that is to be, and acting in full loyalty to his majesty, King George the Fifth?"

"It has been put to you fairly and squarely," Cogley said.

" 'Tis a handsome uniform you have there, Ben," Lacy said. "Will you be wearing it when you take your oath of allegiance to the Crown?"

"You can contrive it for us, Frank," Blake said, "but if you—"

"If you will pardon my curiosity," Lacy said, "Mick and yourself are members of the cabinet. Has this been authorized by the provisional cabinet?"

When his question hung unanswered, he prodded them with a second. "Has this operation been approved by Arthur Griffith and Cosgrave and FitzGerald, and has it been approved by Kevin O'Higgins, the nephew of Tim Healy?"

"That should be neither here nor there," Collins said at last, "not so far as it concerns you. What should concern you is that no objections will be raised by the lads on your side."

"These are deep waters, Ben," Lacy said to Cogley. "When you put on the uniform of the Provisionals, you moved into deep, murky waters." Cogley, he was pleased to notice, was growing uncomfortable.

"I was asked along here tonight, Frank, because we fought together, and because Glamorgan is close to Kilpeder, which is my own town, you will recall."

"Yes," Lacy said, "I do recall." He moved his whiskey glass in small, widening circles on the table top. "Is that all you have to say, Mick?"

"We are still working together so far as the North is concerned," Collins said. "By God, we could be killing each other tomorrow and still be of one mind about the North. You know what is happening there, we all do, it is what the newspapers call a pogrom, and they have the right word for once. The B-Specials and the other Orange bullies have been turned loose, with Field Marshal Wilson and General Chubb to give it a cloak of respectability. And the Tories are backing them to the hilt."

"Hilt is the right word," Lacy said. "Why settle for Chubb, a general of the second rank? Why not Wilson, field marshals are not machine-gunned every day?"

"Machine-gunned, you say?" Collins asked. "Then you are thinking of an ambush, are you? I could give you the lend of a Vickers gun, but you have two or three of your own, from what I have heard."

Lacy shook his head in rueful acknowledgment. "You haven't lost your nerve, Mick, I'll say that for you."

But as he spoke, he knew that at the end of the day, he would go along with the plan, no matter how mad it seemed, and provided it had the approval of his own Army Council. In March, when the MacMahon family were slaughtered in their Belfast home, five of them, with only a small child surviving by hiding himself, the killers were men wearing the uniforms of the B-Specials. But Lacy temporized. He wanted consultations in Dublin, he said. He would propose the notion to his staff when he was back in Kilpeder. He must be left to work out the details as he saw fit. But he would go along with the plan: he knew that, and they knew it.

"We will denounce it," Collins said. "You understand that, do you not? The mad act of a few diehards. We will promise to search out the miscreants."

"You should leave the denunciations to Griffith and to O'Higgins," Lacy said. "They will be able to put their backs into the task."

And Collins grinned. "By God, they will," he said. Griffith was developing into a fierce law-and-order man. And what else had O'Higgins ever been, Tim Healy's nephew, prudent and upright. What would they say, either of them, or Cosgrave or Professor MacNeill, if they knew of Collins, president of their precious Provisional Government, back at his old trade, arranging murders in the abovestairs room in Vaughan's.

"I will denounce the crime of course," Collins said. "An abominable deed."

Before the night ended, before he set off into streets no longer patrolled by Tommies and Black and Tans, Lacy allowed himself a decent whiskey as Collins would have called it, and arranged to meet with Blake the morning following. As they talked, Collins sat smiling at them both, as though, for the moment, time was suspended. Lacy was never to see Collins again, and within a few weeks' time, within a month or two's time, a bit longer, by the time of deep summer stretching itself toward autumn, he would have occasion to remember the room, and Collins, a bit more full-faced than he had been a year or two before, and whiskey, which he had been using earlier in the night as a trick, beginning, now that it was safe, now that the evening's task had been completed, to play its tricks upon him.

They left together, clattering down the uncarpeted stairs, and Collins directly behind Lacy, so close behind him that he could feel Collins's warm, whiskey-scented breath. Collins put his hand for a moment, a moment only, on Lacy's shoulder, and then pulled it back, as though he had committed an impropriety.

" 'Well, here's to good honest fighting blood,' " Collins said, in poetry-reciting tones, " 'Said Kelly and Burke and Shea. Oh, the fighting races don't die out. If they seldom die in bed.' " It was one of Collins's party pieces, a bit of doggerel ballad which went on forever and a day. Lacy had heard him twice recite it all out, once, at Christmastime in 1920, in a house in Mespil Road, past curfew time, the blinds drawn, and half the fellows gathered around the drawing room fire, wanted men, Collins standing by the fire, his necktie pulled loose, no bank clerk now, no accountant's apprentice, but a wild boy from West Cork. " 'Well, here's thank God, for the race and the sod, Said Kelly and Burke and Shea.' "

But they were standing now, the four of them, on Parnell Street, and for three of them, there was a staff car waiting with its uniformed driver.

XXV

JANICE NUGENT/CHRISTOPHER BLAKE

The "season" of 1922 in London, while Ireland was skidding and tumbling into civil war, was by general agreement the most brilliant in years, since 1914 in fact, the first truly postwar spring and early summer. "The clouds of war," as one newspaper put it, "have at last entirely rolled away and *le beau monde où l'on s'amuse* holds high carnival." The Duchess of Buccleuch brought out her daughter amidst flowery splendor, and the Royal Ascot was superb. There were polo matches at Hurlingham and Ranelagh and Roehampton, and without even going one could imagine horses, color, speed, the downsweep of mallets and the girls in their pastel frocks.

Best of all, Christopher was often in London in May and June, either alone on errands from his government or else accompanying Collins. We went together, the two of us, to see Sacha Guitry and Yvonne Printemps perform at the Prince's Theatre, and actually went together all three, Christopher, Collins, and myself, to watch Gladys George's daring bid to outshine Mrs. Pat Campbell in *The Second Mrs. Tanqueray.* At night, after the theater, before we went to bed, or else in bed, after love, sleepless, Christopher would pour out nervous accounts, splashed with anger and foreboding, of what was happening at home and in these fresh consultations with the British.

On a June day, in Saint George's Hall at Windsor Castle, there was an especially grand ceremony which should have held great meaning for Father, because on that day the King, as head of the army, accepted the colors of the now-disbanded Irish regiments, the

Royal Irish Regiment, the Prince of Wales's Leinster Regiment, the Royal Munster Fusiliers, and, of course, the grandest of them all, as we had been taught to believe, Betty and myself, Father's regiment, the Connaught Rangers. All the newspapers had elaborate accounts, and several of them, including the *Morning Post,* had photographs of the great hall, blazoned with coats of arms, and each of the color parties bearing two colors to present to the King, King's banner and battalion banner. "I pledge my word," said the King, "that within these ancient and historic walls your colors will be treasured, honored and protected as hallowed memorials of the glorious deeds of brave and loyal regiments."

But no, Betty wrote me, Father had cared nothing or almost nothing, after she had read him the two-days-late *Morning Post* at breakfast, and then passed it over to him so that he could see St. George's Hall, and the color-bearers of the Connaughts, on their one knee before the King. "Well, well," he said, "see there," and went back to tapping his spoon against his egg. I can remember seeing, a few months earlier, in an Irish newspaper, a photograph of the new government's troops taking over the barracks in Galway, the troops of Christopher's and Michael Collins's new government, which had until then been a barracks of the Connaught Rangers, many of the men still in civilian clothes, but the officers in the new national uniform, which the malicious said was British khaki died green. The soldiers, in caps and dark jackets, tieless many of them, bore rifles, bandoliers slung from their shoulders.

We would walk through summery Regent's Park, or in the evening, before the theater or after it, walk hand in hand along the Embankment. And once, walking toward Westminster Bridge, looking at the Houses of Parliament set against the evening sky, it seemed to me like an immense, intricate stage setting which might vanish upon some instant, like Father's old regiment, which had left not a rack behind but only a few banners. But when I told that to Christopher, he said, "It's real enough, all right." He was in no mood these days for fantasy.

These days, even the English newspapers were full of talk about the Irish almost at each other's throats, the Irish in the South, two rival bands of gunmen as one of the newspapers called them, but still more the awful things that had been happening in the North, houses set afire and entire families killed. We may still get through this, Christopher told me, if the pact will hold between Collins and De Valera, and if the diehards in the Four Courts can be kept in check, and if the election settles matters, and if the constitution survives. It was the new constitution which was bringing Irishmen over to London, Collins and Griffith and O'Higgins and Christopher, to argue with the British cabinet, Lloyd George and the others, but mostly with Churchill, who now was secretary for the colonies.

"We need, you see," Christopher told me once as we walked between flower beds in the park, "a constitution close enough to a republic to suit the diehards, and far enough away from one to suit the British."

"I see," I said, "and is that why you are so grave these days? Nothing else?" And he turned on me with chips of anger in his blue eyes. But I was sorry for my glibness, and put my hand on his forearm. My God, I thought, a constitution, what next, and cursed my frivolous nature. There had been a time, at the beginning of our love for each other, a time when Christopher was at work doing whatever it was that he did for the underground government and its army, a time when, so far as we know, toward the end, there was a warrant out for him and a reward posted; in that time, there had been a wonderful gaiety to Christopher, as though nation, nationality, was all improvisation and adventure and dash. On our weekends in Connemara, at Myles Keough's cottage perched above the Atlantic, we would sit in the long evening reading verse to each other, or reciting what we could remember, comic verse often, about the Jumblies and the Snark, and the Walrus and the Carpenter, and the unhappy Oysters. Things began to change, I think, with the Treaty. All the fun was being bled out of Christopher. Collins too, for that matter. I remember the night we went to the Piñero play, all through the first act, Collins was watching intently, lost in the drama, and lost perhaps in admiration for Gladys George, who was smashing, but it was different after the first interval, when he had knocked back two large whiskies, and for the rest of the evening he sat hunched forward, looking up at the stage for politeness' sake, but as often looking down at his large, joined hands.

One day, late in May or at the beginning of June, Christopher took me to the House of Commons, where we sat in the Visitors' Gallery, and looked down at them all, Lloyd George and Winston Churchill and all the others. They all looked exactly like themselves, so to speak—Lloyd George a vulgar mountebank, spry and resourceful in debate, the words rolling out with that hideous Welsh singsong, but the attention that night was upon Churchill, because the crisis in Ireland was the subject of debate and Churchill was the responsible minister. How he savored his combat with the Tories, hands jammed upon occasion in his trousers pockets, but often, more properly, holding fast to his lapels. His face was shining with excitement or perhaps wine, and he turned whatever he said into a page out of Macaulay. I told that to Christopher, who smiled absently. He would be reporting on the debate to Collins, and was being closely attentive.

"The troops in Dublin," Churchill assured the House, "will remain on the alert. In the event of the setting up of a Republic it would be the intention of the government to hold Dublin as an essential step to further military action."

He was being pressed hard by an extraordinary man, tall and gaunt, with a hawk nose, pop eyes, the kind of bristling mustache that cavalry officers wore in *Punch.* This man's voice was harsh and his language venomous, but what seemed to me most awful was that he seemed to enjoy the venom, to smack his lips over it.

"What an awful man," I whispered to Christopher, "what an ogre." The fellow was talking as I whispered, and Christopher replied without taking away his eyes. "Ogre is the proper word," he said. "The ogre's name is Wilson."

Yes, it is, it must be, I thought at once, because that grotesque face and body had been in the newspapers for six years at least, more like ten, and in recent years tricked out in the insignia of a field marshal. He was black-jacketed that evening, a raven. I seemed to recall that he was not British at all but Irish, and had grown up in Longford, close to Charlie's Westmeath. You would see him in photographs during the war, standing with Joffre or Foch or Haig, or inspecting troops, great storklike legs encased in handsome boots. But now, as Christopher told me later, as we walked home along the river, he was a member of Parliament from loyalist Ulster, back and forth to Ulster every few days, organizing their armies and their armed B-Specials, himself and another general named Chubb.

He could not bully Churchill; who could? "Unlike the secretary for the colonies," he said, "I have never shaken hands with gunmen." Collins, he meant. "I have never touched hands that have butchered." "Oh yes you have," Churchill growled, "many times."

"Is the Government prepared—" Wilson began again, and again Churchill cut him off. "We are quite prepared," he said, "to resume the long, bloody struggle to hold Ireland in her loyalty to the British Crown. The Irish leaders know that. The resources of civilization are not yet exhausted."

But it was not of the Crown that I thought as, later, we walked along the Embankment, but rather of that dreadful raven figure, the raven's rasping voice, and the specter that he summoned forth. A crown was a bauble, so far as I was concerned, a toy for grown men to quarrel about and kill for, and a republic was not much better. But a people were trapped to the north behind that new border, and that fierce-beaked raven had who knew how many thousands of armed men at his disposal.

"I almost prefer Wilson," Christopher said, suddenly and unexpectedly, "he is like a brutal old cavalry saber, slashing and cutting. But with Lloyd George and Churchill you never know where they are. That House is like a murky fish tank, and those fellows swim around in it." It did not seem a good metaphor, they were splashed with vivid color, the two of them.

At my door, Christopher kissed me good-night. His tasks were far from ended. He meant it as a brief kiss, but without troubling to look up and down the road, I held fast to him and opened my lips. His arms tightened about me, and when we pulled apart, my right hand still rested upon the back of his head. "My God, Janice," he said. "Be careful with me."

"Christopher," I said, "I am a skillful widow, I know all the tricks."

"Not all of them," he said, "not quite all."

"So you think," I said, "I am saving a few."

"So am I," he said, and we kissed again. It was like old times, it was like it had been two years before when we were much, much younger.

At one that morning, Collins was waiting for Blake in his room at the New Metropole Hotel. Collins was in shirtsleeves at the small desk, writing a letter.

"My own dearest," he wrote. "Am just scribbling a very, very hurried line—at the moment I don't know whether or not I shall be able to get back this weekend. Things are bad beyond words, and I am almost without hope of being able to do anything of permanent use. It's really awful—to think of what I have to endure here from the English crowd and then go back to endure as bad or worse from our own lot. Everything here is awful. I wish to God someone else was in my position. I wish to God someone else had gone over last year to negotiate the Treaty, and we both know who I mean—a certain tall, bespectacled mathematician. I am awaiting Christopher, who is more than two hours late. We have some matters of importance to attend to, and I am half-asleep. Lucky Christopher, his nights in London are never lonely. You will know what I mean." He scrawled his name, as he always did, in Irish, "Mícheál."

But he was all brisk, ribald energy when he greeted Blake. "By God, Christopher, the House was sitting very late tonight," he said with a broad wink.

But he listened soberly, sitting at the small, paper-strewn desk, as Blake gave him an account of the debate on Ireland. Blake was familiar with the manner in which Collins preferred oral reports, and in the cab from Janice Nugent's, he had gone over the headings in his mind, sorting them out, ordering them.

"And there is the gist of it," he said. "It will all be spelled out for you in the *Times*."

" 'Tis as we expected," Collins said. "Wilson waving his gauntlet and leading out his moss troopers, and Winston dancing about like a toreador, and waving in Wilson's face the bright scarf of his rhetoric."

"Gladstone's rhetoric," Blake said. "That bit about the resources of civilization not being exhausted. That's Gladstone's."

"Much Wilson would know," Collins said. "The ignorant hoor. And to think that he comes from Longford, of all places. Ah well, not for much longer. What was the mood in the House, could you put a name to it?"

"They were getting great entertainment from Winston, but the loyalists from Ulster were in an ugly mood, and they were grouped behind Wilson, no doubt of it. You need not be from Ulster to wish ill to Winston, there are fellows on both sides of the House would be happy to see him pulled down, and Ireland could do it."

"I know that," Collins said. "And so does he. We will be meeting tomorrow night for a chance to talk together. At—at a friend's."

There was no need for Collins's discretion. Blake was one of many who knew that Collins and Churchill met, from time to time, in the home of Sir John and Hazel Lavery. And he was one of almost as many who knew that there was talk of a serious flirtation, perhaps an affair, between Collins and Hazel Lavery, who was dark-haired and incurably romantic.

Collins was protean. Blake had long before decided that Collins's ability to become what was needed, hurler, bank clerk, accountant, bullying gunman, soldier, tavern chum, was no theatrical trick with costume and bits of props. It came from within a complex labyrinth of being. The Collins who attended Mass each morning in London was no less real but perhaps no more real than the Collins who flirted with the wife, dark-haired and romantic, of an elderly society painter.

"Things are bunching up toward a crisis one way or another," Collins said. "Winston is furious because of the pact that Dev and I have made. I'll be hearing about that tomorrow night, you can depend upon it."

And not Churchill alone. At the cabinet meeting in Dublin, when Collins announced that he and Dev would put up coalition candidates for the election in June, Griffith had sat in shocked silence for a full three minutes before at last stonily agreeing to recommend it to the Dáil. Since then, Collins was no longer Mick to Griffith, as he had become during the fight for the Treaty, but Mr. Collins.

Now, Collins shrugged to Blake. "How else can we have an election? We needed it, and I set it up. Did you hear what Liam Lynch said to Liam Manahan when he heard about it? 'Collins is back with his own crowd again.' "

"You may hear Liam Lynch saying that," Blake said, "but not Rory O'Connor or Liam Mellowes or the crowd in the Four Courts."

"No," Collins said, and rubbed his hand across his eyes, but he pulled it away, and the eyes looked bright and untired. "That is my crowd, you know, Christopher. O'Connor and Liam Lynch and Tom Barry, Frank Lacy, Ernie O'Malley. Boys, oh boys, the times we've seen. I would rather have Tom Barry at my side than

Cosgrave and Kevin O'Higgins and that crowd, warriors with fountain pens."

As Collins was himself, Blake thought, when all was said and done. He had been palpably hurt and furious that day in Treaty debate when Seamus Robinson asked what ambush Collins had ever led, what gun he had ever fired off in person against a Black and Tan? In the old days at Vaughan's he had always found time to listen to a column commandant up from the country, and by preference a commandant from his own county, from Cork, Barry or Lacy or Hales, and, as the fellow would describe the setting up of an ambush, an attack upon a barracks, Collins would nod, excited fingers drumming the table.

Remembering, Blake suddenly thought how seldom were the occasions when he had seen Collins alone, as though he moved always within roomsful of men or at public gatherings, or else hurrying down a corridor from one meeting to the next, or bursting into a room to shout out a joke or an order. But always the orders, the questions, the attentiveness came from some center of being inaccessible to others, inaccessible, perhaps, to the painter's dark-haired wife.

"Those lads think that they can sit in the Four Courts forever and a day," Collins said, "but the pot is on the boil. Those lads are spoiling for a fight. Dear Jesus, with them on one side of me and the English on the other side, and Griffith sitting next to me in the Cabinet Room polishing his bloody eyeglasses, I don't have enough sides to go around. And all this time, those blackguards in the North are making life hell for our people."

"They are leaning hard," Christopher Blake said. "Wilson had the bit between his teeth tonight, and the Tories were giving him all the 'Hear, hear' that he needed."

"They smell blood," Collins said. "They are getting ready to pull down the government, and they will use Ireland to do it. Our government over there lacks the will to govern, they will be saying. We are leaving armed enemies in possession of Dublin's central buildings, and we are letting our enemies arm themselves in the South, we are aiding and abetting raids into the North and reprisals."

"That is a fair summary of what Wilson was saying," Blake said, and again he saw Wilson leaning forward as he spoke, skin stretched taut over high cheekbones. "They smell blood." In Ulster, the blood was more than metaphor.

"Right," Collins said, and, walking to the window, he looked down into the depth of London's night. "We must put all this into train, you know, Chris. We have Frank Lacy in Kilpeder, precisely where he should be. By God, that is a bit of luck." He rapped his knuckle against the window frame. "There is a divinity that shapes our ends, as the man said."

"That night in Vaughan's last week," Blake said, "when we put the word to Frank Lacy, did you have any doubt?"

"About Frank Lacy?" Collins said, and laughed with what seemed to Blake to be genuine enjoyment. "Not that lad, he's one of the hard men, bred in a hard school." Collins was ready to take whatever weapon lay to hand, Frank Lacy and his Parabellum or a quiet chat with Winston, as he had taken to calling him.

"I wish that I liked Frank Lacy better," Blake said.

"You don't have to," Collins said. "You can depend upon him. That's better." As some of us, Blake thought, depend on Collins: right or wrong, we depend on Collins.

Once, in the run-up to the Truce, when Blake was talking with Soames, his opposite number in England's civil service, Soames had said, "Mind you, you have your irreconcilables, your romantic gunmen, and so forth. We can take that into account. Winston takes that into account. But Collins horrifies him. He calls Collins the mustang. A mustang is a wild horse on the American plains. You think you have him tamed, and then he breaks loose."

"Right," Collins said again, and turned away from the black London night to discuss with Blake the assassination of Field Marshal Sir Henry Hughes Wilson, former chief of the Imperial General Staff, Baronet, Knight Grand Cross of the Order of the Bath, DSO, Legion of Honor, member of Parliament for North Down.

As they had earlier agreed, it was to take place, if at all possible, on Saturday, the twenty-fourth of June, when General Chubb, Wilson's second-in-command, in fact if not in title, and military adviser to the B-Specials, was to be shot dead in West Cork.

"And after that," Blake said to Collins, an hour later.

"They have been smelling blood and tasting blood," Collins

said. " 'Tis about time they saw a bit of it. Their own, for preference."

After Bloody Sunday, in an interview with foreign journalists that Blake had arranged, Collins said, about the two teams of British agents who had been shot down in Dublin and in Cork, "They were going to put us on the spot, so we put them on the spot." He was quoted, word for word, in the American and French newspapers. Those were the days in which, as Cathal Brugha was later to charge, Blake was building up Collins's reputation as commander of the Irish revolutionary underground.

"Killing Wilson, you know, Mick," Blake said, "will be as though we had killed Kitchener."

Collins smiled, and scratched his hard, flat belly beneath the white shirt.

Blake, looking into the wide, clear eyes, translated the smile. The killing of Wilson and Chubb would be laid at the door of the Army Council in the Four Courts, O'Connor and Mellowes and the others, as would the killing of Chubb be blamed upon the Republican forces in Cork, the First Division, Liam Lynch's Division, Frank Lacy's of course, Ernie O'Malley's. But they had known this. Collins's decision to kill Wilson and Chubb had been discussed with their Army Council. It was his own government, the cabinet of the future Free State, who had been left in the dark, and who, as Blake knew, would have been appalled. No more did that cabinet know, save in partial and discreet detail, of Collins's cooperation with the Four Courts in the reprisal raids against the North.

"Nothing must be left to chance," Collins said. "I am depending on you for that, Chris. On Lacy in Kilpeder and on yourself here in London." He smiled again. "After all," he said, "at the end of the day, we must depend upon each other. We want what is best for Ireland, after all, the lot of us."

"But we never depend upon each other entirely, do we, Mick?" Blake said. "Back home, abovestairs in Vaughan's when we gave the task to Frank Lacy, there was nothing said to him about the killing of Wilson here in London."

"True enough, Chris," Collins said, mildly, absently, as though Blake had brought up a point of negligible importance. "True enough."

And only now, as though in signal that business had been concluded, did he put a bottle before them.

"He's the real thing," Collins said with unshadowed admiration. "Lacy the hard man. Is he fool enough to think that the Republic does not mean as much to me as it does to him, is Liam Lynch such a fool or Rory O'Connor?"

In Dublin, in Vaughan's, Collins had said to Lacy, half-joking, "Are you setting up shop on your own, Frank, a one-man Republic?" It was to himself, Blake thought, that Collins should be putting the question. Now, a nightcap, one for the road before Blake left, Collins looked at him across the glass of whiskey with clear, unreadable eyes.

"There are times," I told Christopher, "when I suspect that you are not so much in love with me as you are with Michael Collins." That was when Collins had returned on June the eleventh for a hasty visit, and would be leaving the next day, taking Christopher with him. He was visibly shocked, as any decent Irish Catholic would be, and I spoke with annoyance, half-anger and half-irritability, but no sooner had I spoken than a small but important part of my mind set perversely to work on what I said. You never know, I thought, because I found Collins quite attractive myself, and so, as half of London knew, so did Hazel Lavery, John Lavery's wife, who had made it her business to make certain that everyone knew that she and Michael Collins, a romantic gunman who had had his name on wanted posters, might perhaps, might just possibly, be having an affair.

We were sitting at breakfast as I spoke. "Why not," I said to Christopher, teasingly, lazily, "everyone seems to be in love with him, the young woman in Longford and Hazel Lavery and that woman with the double-barreled name, and John Lavery, I have always had a theory about himself and Hazel, and I have felt a twinge or two of passion myself."

"That's absurd," Christopher said angrily, but I could tell from his tone that he had heard stories himself. And why not? Something must explain the way people like Collins get chaps to follow them blindly, Collins and Nelson and Bonnie Dundee and so forth. "That's absurd," he said again, but a bit less angrily, and I saw that he was staring at me, as well he might, because my robe, above the waist, had parted slightly, and my hand, without my knowledge, or so I trust, had moved inside the parted collar, deep cut, and I was touching my unclothed body. I never have known what people mean when they say that they can feel themselves blush, but I knew that I should have been blushing. And yet at the same time I imagined my own unclad body and imagined Christopher imagining it.

"Well," I said briskly, "so much for that kind of talk, early in the morning," although it was not early in the morning, and sunlight fell upon us, upon the cheerful white and purple of the teapot.

But I thought, after Christopher had gone into the bedroom to dress, after he had stood behind me to kiss my unbound hair, I thought, surely bodies, our bodies, any bodies, are more important than arguments about the language in a constitution and a pact, an agreement, fragile as a salmon's bones, between Collins and De Valera. So I thought, and do not, even now, think myself in the least frivolous, not at all, because I hold that flesh and blood and bone are at least as real as clauses and articles and items.

And felt quite superior to Christopher when he walked back in, knotting his tie, blue-and-red-patterned, as he walked. Because I knew that there were great pressures upon him, and far greater pressures upon his chief, knew it of course because we talked endlessly about it, or rather he talked and I listened, caught upon all sides, the gunmen in the Four Courts and in the South, the pogrom in Ulster, the demands of the British, the demands of the conservatives in their own government, and yet, at that moment at least, I felt as though I knew something worth more than these.

"Polling Day on Friday," Christopher said. "Then things may sort themselves out a bit."

"Yes, dear," I said, "of course." And smiled, wise and secure in what I knew.

And of course what I knew then was nothing. Because I did not know then that Collins had given Christopher the task of organizing two murders, one of them in London and the other at a wedding in Ireland, in West Cork. Neither to be sure did Margaret Kilbride know, who had hinted to me in Dublin that Christopher had dangerous responsibilities which were not known to the cabinet itself. Christopher and Michael Collins and a few others,

Brendan Kilbride had hinted to his wife and his wife had hinted to me. But neither did I know then, on that June morning in London, of the part which Christopher had played in planning the murders of the English officers in Dublin and Cork on Bloody Sunday. I knew nothing of this until that final weekend in Connemara. And so, as Christopher straightened his jacket before the glass, I smiled, weighing bone and blood against papers and arguments and politicians, and I was myself the fool that morning, because Christopher too had bone and blood on his mind.

I crossed the room into his arms, and then, crossing to the table by the window, took a small yellow rose, and fixed it to his buttonhole. Christopher smiled down at me as I fastened the rose, holding a second straight pin between my teeth, and in my concentration my robe again fell dangerously loose. But already a part of him had left the flat.

I stood by the window and watched for him on the street, and before he walked off, toward Russell Street, he turned around and waved, knowing that I would be there. What does anyone know of love, what if there is a special kind of love, deep-tided, which will carry men off into warfare, or to do the bidding of a chief, be it good or bad, fair or foul?

XXVI

LONDON, 1922

It was a summer night so delightful that Winston chose to walk through Kensington to his late appointment at the Laverys' in Cromwell Place. For all its problems and difficulties and dangers, dangers to his own future of course, but dangers also to the Coalition, and, above all, dangers to the Empire, for all that, he knew that he was just now precisely where he should be, as secretary for the colonies. From here, from London, England cast out its great glittering web across the world, Mesopotamia, Palestine, Africa, Ireland. And now, more than ever, after a victory equally splendid and calamitous, with old kingdoms swept away, with ancient European cities being debated by armed gangs upon cobbled streets, with the terrible specter of Bolshevism risen across half of Europe like a gibbous moon, now, more than ever, Empire required a steady hand, a stout heart, and, above all else, a gift for imaginative understanding of history.

In the Middle East, he had posed with Colonel Lawrence, on camels, the two of them, in lounge suits, hatted, Lawrence looking uncomfortable in Western clothes, a splendid, shy little chap, with a genius for backing into the limelight, and there was history, Churchill and young Colonel Lawrence, what did it matter if crowds outside Shepheard's shouted, "Down with Churchill! Down with Empire!" In fact, matters were already settled, the conference in Cairo was theater. Back in London, over dinner in the Ship Hotel in Whitehall, he and Lawrence, Lawrence abstemious, picking at a plate of vegetables, sipping water, had settled matters, chosen a pair of kings, Faisal for Iraq, Abdullah for

Transjordania. That was how empires were ruled, not by splashy visits to their distant sands, tours of inspection guarded by circling aircraft, but by a quiet chat over dinner in Whitehall.

After he had settled matters in Cairo, he left the details to be sorted out by civil servants, and drove out to the desert in an armored car, guarded by police and soldiers, and set up easel and bench to paint the Sphinx, the pyramids, wearing his white linen smock and broad, floppy-brimmed hat.

It was Hazel Lavery, toward whose house he was now walking, who had shown him how to paint, during the bleak days of the Gallipoli campaign, when everything was going wrong in the Dardanelles, and hysterical politicians and generals were flinging accusations about. There he had sat in his garden, beads of color on the newly purchased palette, blue, white, rose, yellow, and he held the brush irresolute, hanging doubtful, portentous but impotent. He had just managed to put a dot of blue, pea-sized, on the appalling whiteness of the canvas when a car drove up, destiny-inspired, and Hazel Lavery jumped out, a flash of lilac skirt, white silk blouse, hatless, dark hair. "Here," she said, and took the brush from his hand, dipped into blue paint, white paint, and slashed colors boldly, without hesitation, upon a cowering canvas. "There," she said a bit later, handing him back the brush, "now deal with it, don't take any backchat from it." And she stood watching him, small fists resting upon hips. After that sun-drenched afternoon, he had never hesitated, whatever the subject, the Pyramids or Normandy, the Highlands, it was all a matter, after all, of imposing one's will upon paint, canvas, turpentine, landscapes. But only landscapes, buildings, seacoasts, strands. Portraits were a different matter, people's faces were mysterious, shifting, their contours hinting at unexplained life.

If he could do portraits, he thought as he swung into the Cromwell Road, he would paint Hazel, a great beauty who knew she was a beauty. Jack Lavery had done wonderful portraits of her, but then Jack was her husband, and she his favorite model. Jack seemed actually proud of her conquests, almost as though they were his own, and these were murky depths into which Winston had no wish to peer. Not that he was naive, not that he did not know the history of his own family, near at hand and remote. But surely this was the strangest conquest of all, the Sinn Féin gunman. Not that he was merely a gunman, of course, far from it, he had courage and intelligence, to be sure, but so did many, little Colonel Lawrence on his camel, for example, but there was something more, a quality to which Winston could not place a noun, dangerous and unknowable, like radium. And at the moment, Collins was the lynchpin that held together the entire shaky, top-heavy Irish scaffolding.

Winston was a jaunty, brisk-walking man, despite short, stubby legs flattered by an excellent tailor, and he had been coseted by an excellent brandy, three of them in fact, and the third, the final, had left faint, fragrant fumes within his head. A nightmare, you would hear a voice in the cabinet say about Ireland, a quagmire, a bog, a quicksand, in which politicians and their reputations were sucked up and smothered like Essex's troopers and their mounts. But the voice was never Winston's. He enjoyed battling toward a solution in Ireland, as he had in Egypt, in Palestine. And there was always the special pleasure of tidying house in some especially imaginative way. Those unemployed Black and Tans, for example, as desperate a gang of rogues as you would want to meet in a dark laneway, could be shipped off now to Jerusalem, to keep control upon Arab and Jew. He was not a cynical man, rather a sentimental one, in fact, but he enjoyed the mask of the cynical statesman, Metternich, Talleyrand. As he walked, he swung his stick, ebony, silver-handled.

God, but it had been a special pleasure to stand up in the House against that grotesque fire-eater Wilson, snorting defiance, calling for savage retribution against the Irish rebels, fire and sword against the rebels in the Four Courts, Collins forced to show his true colors once again, gunman and conspirator. For years now, Wilson had been contemptuous of the "frocks," as he called them, the frock coats, the politicians, and private encounters had led Winston to know that Wilson regarded him as the arch-frock, the very antithesis of a fighting soldier. Winston, who had ridden with Kitchener against the mad mullahs at Omdurman, firing his revolver, who had commanded his regiment in the mud of Flanders, after he had been given the blame for Gallipoli. Well, well, let us see.

The devil of the matter was that Wilson was half-right, more than half, Collins must be made to bite the bullet, as it were, drive the rival gunmen out of the Four Courts, disarm their seditious flying columns in Cork and Limerick and Galway. Or else, stand aside, and let the British Army do the job, ready and able under Macready, concentrated on the outskirts of Dublin, infantry, mobile units, artillery.

Jack and Hazel Lavery had given Winston and Collins Jack's studio as a place for their little chat, while below, their dinner guests were making their goodbyes. They had used it before, two or three times, and Winston liked its air of theater, improvisation, the raised platform upon which Jack liked to place his sitters, sketches nailed to the walls, a clutter of costumes in a doorless wardrobe, a few unmatched chairs. Winston and Collins sat facing each other in low chairs, almost too comfortable, Turkish in feeling somehow or mock-Turkish, soft heavy pillows a musky rose in the electric light, and between them a table inlaid with bits of ivory and colored stone, pale blue, lavender, and on the table a bottle of Rémy Martin. There was a smell of turpentine in the air.

"And there you are, Michael," Winston said, "won't do, won't do at all. We have been patient, God knows we have been patient, but we have a parliament to answer to, a country to answer to. And what does our parliament see when it looks across the water? Armed men defiant of any law, yours or ours, the Republicans arming themselves with the proceeds of bank robberies, robberies on the high roads, homes raided for arms by men with blackened faces. Are you a government or are you not? If you are not, say the word."

"It is your government," Collins said, "that has let the armed bullies in the North roam at will, fully armed, terrorizing Catholics. There is no need to remind me of what your government can do."

Winston rolled the brandy in his glass, and the fumes caressed his downturned face.

When he looked up, he saw that Collins was still sitting on the edge of his cushioned chair, bending toward the table, hands pressed down upon knees. A mustang, wild, unpredictable.

"At the end of the day, Michael, in the heel of the hunt, we must bow, the both of us, to the empire of fact, the legislature of reality. This government of ours is hanging on by the tips of its fingers, and you would not like our successors one little bit better, let me assure you. You would not be happy with the friends of Field Marshal Sir Henry Wilson. We gambled everything when we signed that Treaty, Michael, and by God you will live up to it, one way or another."

"You were not the only gambler at that table," Collins said, and picked up his own glass. No savoring of the bouquet for him, he drained what was left in the glass and then picked up the squat bottle. It was pleasant, Winston thought, to discuss matters over a bottle of brandy. Collins was drinking more heavily these days, but then, who could blame him? Those gunmen in the Four Courts and in the hills of Tipperary were a rum lot, but they had been Collins's comrades in arms, and now he might have to turn his guns against them. *Our* guns, to be more exact, Winston corrected himself with a small, unreadable smile. If he has to attack the Four Courts, he will need British guns.

Remembering politeness, Collins motioned toward Winston with the Rémy Martin bottle, and Winston extended his glass.

"A large one, Michael, if you please."

"There is a man in Dublin," Collins said, "a witty man, poet and surgeon both, and in a pub one evening a fellow asked the barman for a large whiskey, and the doctor said, 'There is no such thing as a large whiskey.' " He smiled. In the room's artificial light, his pale gray eyes glittered.

He has charm, Winston thought, and not for the first time. It was not difficult to see what Hazel saw in him. But Winston remembered Bloody Sunday, men shot down in Dublin and Cork on Collins's orders, poor Bell dragged off a city tram and shot dead in the roadway.

In shadow, along the wall to their left, was Jack's half-finished portrait in oils of a half-dressed beauty, dark-haired, her head turned, looking toward the viewer over bare shoulders, one bare breast, small and shapely, seen in profile. She was smiling faintly, and her expression held wit and excitement. Jack no doubt would call it *The Fair Unknown* or something of the sort, but everyone would know who it was.

"That pact you made with our friend De Valera put the fox in the henhouse," Winston said. "Cannot for the life of me think what you had in mind."

"An election for one thing," Collins said. "You have heard about those, have you not? We need an election, we need a constitution that we can live with, we need protection for our people in the North, and we need less bullying from London. 'Tis to the people of Ireland that I am answerable, not to you."

"But there is the rub, Michael. Can you not see that? You *are* answerable to us, a treaty is a solemn obligation. And you are allowing enemies, not only enemies of the Crown but your own enemies, to gather up strength on behalf of their cloud-cuckoo Republic."

"Have a care there with your language," Collins said, and looked away into the studio's shadowed right, where virginal canvases, stretched, were dimly visible ghosts. "Have a care."

Winston leaned forward across the table. He remembered Collins signing the Treaty, and throwing down the pen, looking like a man tormented, ready to shoot someone, by preference himself. "General Macready has his orders, Michael. No date has been set, but he has his orders. It is at my urging that no date has been set. I have assured my government that you will take action against your diehards. And for the moment, for the moment, Michael, they accept my assurances. They have a sort of half-knowledge that you and I meet from time to time."

Winston felt a twinge of sympathy for Collins, deep and painful. Collins's deepest loyalties lay not with the pince-nez and bone-white celluloid collars of his Free State cabinet, but with the reckless lads who were in mutiny against him. Rather like poor Colonel Lawrence and his broken promises to his wild bedouins. But we must all bow to the empire of fact, the legislature of reality; Winston rolled the phrases upon the palate of his imagination.

"You know, Michael," he said, "a dear friend of mine said to me once, in a bad moment, a very bad moment, 'It will all come right in the end.' And do you know what language he spoke it in? Afrikaans! Afrikaans! He was one of the Boer fellows who had been fighting us a year or two before, but now he is back by our side in the Empire. My Afrikaans is a bit rusty, he had to translate it into English for me."

" 'It will all come right in the end,' " Collins said. "You cannot translate that into Irish."

Winston added a prudent dollop to each of their glasses. Once, during the Treaty negotiations in Downing Street, Lloyd George had escorted Collins and Griffith to the map of the world that dominated one wall, facing the conference table. Splashes of red, deep pink rather, covered the world in the Mercator projection—

deserts, jungles, snow-covered prairies, the Great Trunk Road of India moving northwards beside sacred rivers, savannas, crowded cities, splashes of varicolored skins, brown, black, pink, through harsh lands of rock and thorn toward snow, and, in the center of all, England, and at England's center, London, an empire of fact girded by imagination.

"Come in there, the two of you," Lloyd George said, with the dreary music of his Welsh chapel voice, "come in, and help us to rule it." Griffith's pince-nez glittered, they were forever glittering, in sunlight or electric light, photographer's flashgun, a decent little fellow shoved into history. But Collins, towering beside him, stood grinning, polite but distant, as though the grin said, General Sir Michael Collins, is it, not bloody likely! But still, Winston thought, picking up his glass, you never know, circumstances alter cases.

"And there we are, Michael," he said. "There we are."

Later, Winston telephoned to have a car brought round to Cromwell Place, and offered to drop Collins off at his hotel. But Collins shook his head, and they made their goodbyes with Collins standing at the hall door with Jack Lavery. Hazel was not in view.

"You should do this fellow up in oils," Winston said to Jack Lavery, nodding toward Collins. And Lavery, a man of Winston's height, shot a glance over at Collins, half a head taller, and beamed. "Yes," he said, "yes indeed. So I tell him, but you can't get the fellow to sit still. Still on the run, eh, Michael?"

Collins, swaying slightly, nodded at the pleasantry, and answered in kind.

"Still on the run," he said.

"Indeed," Winston said, "but from whom?" He peered into the shadows of the house across the road, where once the painter Millais had lived with his Effie.

Jenkins, the driver, was holding the door of the motorcar for him, and Winston, before climbing aboard, turned around to wave. Jack Lavery gave a wide, grandiloquent response, and Collins, head thrust forward, nodded, amiably, Winston thought. Quite a personage, Winston thought, in his own rough-hewn way, and Jack Lavery should indeed do him in oils. Winston would have paid closer attention, of course, had he known that he would never see Collins again, that there were barely two months to go. He remembered the outthrust head against the hallway light, hands shoved in pockets, the heavy body swaying ever so slightly.

Curled safely in the car's warmth, Winston lit a cigar and looked out upon his city. Paris was a woman's city, some old jingle had it, but London was a city for men. London town. The joys of debate in the House, thrust and counterthrust, the play of wit, a bit heavy-handed at times, early evening in the smoking room of a club, rich leather, the smell of cigars, brandy or a mild whiskey from the Highlands.

XXVII

PATRICK PRENTISS

In the early-morning hours of June 27, Provisional Government troops moved through black, rain-spattered streets from the barracks at Beggars Bush to the streets which surrounded the Four Courts and to the streets and quays which faced it across the Liffey. Armored Lancias drove up to the gates of the enormous complex of buildings, sealing it and making withdrawal impossible. Two eighteen-pound artillery pieces, borrowed from the British Army, were placed in position at Bridgefoot Street and Winetavern Street. A dispatch rider carried an order to surrender to Rory O'Connor, Liam Mellowes and Ernie O'Malley. It was refused, and at four o'clock an attack by artillery, machine gun and rifle was begun. It was to last for three days.

Six days had passed since Sir Henry Wilson, dressed in the full uniform of a field marshal, had been shot dead outside his house in Eaton Square. Four days had passed since Brigadier Chubb, dressed in motoring clothes, his morning coat neatly packed in leather, was ambushed while on his way to attend a wedding in West Cork, near the Kerry border. Chubb's killing might well have been the work of some solitary, crazed Republican, the mountains were full of them, and he must surely have been a skilled marksman, two shots fired from a distance and landing, both of them, in the back of Chubb's skull. But Wilson's killing and the pursuit of his killers through London streets by a horrified mob were a different matter. They were captured with ease. Sullivan, a wounded veteran of the Somme, had a wooden leg; Dunne, who was in command, could have escaped, but refused to leave his comrade. Scotland Yard discovered on Dunne IRA correspondence, including a letter which referred to "an operation being laid on by the Big Fellow."

On the night before the Wilson killing, a night of heavy rain, Collins spoke to a large, cheering crowd outside Talbot's Hotel. Shots were fired from the edges, a dozen or more, but it was clear that these were young fellows firing into the air, reminding Collins that in Cork he would not have matters his own way. There was an uglier scene the next morning, when he went to St. Finbarr's Cemetery, to the Republican Plot, to pay his respects to Terence MacSwiney, who had died on hunger strike, and Thomas MacCurtain, who had been murdered in his house by British soldiers wearing disguise. Now, armed men, a dozen of them, barred his way, and the commander told Collins that he had no business at the graves of men who had died for Ireland.

"By Jesus," Collins shouted, his face working with anger, and he dug into his waterproof pocket for his own gun, but Christopher Blake grabbed his arm and one of the bodyguards threw an athlete's shoulder block against him.

"By Jesus," Collins said again, but he was sitting now, the next day, in the rear lounge of the hotel, his face angry once more, and flushed. "There were no two Corkmen closer than myself and Terence MacSwiney, and now a crew of gobshites think they can face me down. You did wrong to grab hold of me, Chris. They would have fled like mice."

It was there, in the hotel, that news of the Wilson killing came to them, in its first, garbled details, the identities of the killers not yet known, and as they drove eastwards, to Dublin, Collins sat in the staff car, arms folded across his chest, shaking his head from time to time, as though to clear it.

"A wooden leg," he said. "Jesus, Chris, could you not have found a lad with no legs at all, set him in a handcart and give him a push toward Eaton Square."

Christopher had in fact planned the operation with care, leaving everything save the choice of gunmen in the hands of Brigade Commandant London, but he knew better than to make excuses to Collins.

"They'll not talk," Collins said. "I know Reg Dunne. He's a good lad. We'll get them out. If we have to blow the prison apart, we'll get them out. We will set to work on that when we reach

Dublin, send over a few lads from the Squad to see how matters stand."

That night, a letter to Collins, signed by Lloyd George but drafted by Churchill, was prepared in London. "Mr. Rory O'Connor," it read in part, "cannot be permitted to remain with his followers and his arsenal in open rebellion in the heart of Dublin in possession of the Courts of Justice, organizing and sending out enterprises of murder. His Majesty's Government are prepared to put at your disposal the necessary pieces of artillery which may be required, or otherwise assist you as may be arranged."

In the House on Monday evening, and facing the possibility that the government might be overthrown by Bonar Law and the Tories, Churchill made clear the alternative. "The presence in Dublin of a band of men styling themselves the Headquarters of the Republican Executive is a gross breach and defiance of the Treaty. If, through cowardice, weakness, want of courage, or some even less creditable reason, it is not brought to a speedy end. . . ." The words that followed were drowned by cheers and applause from both sides of the House. Earlier that day, most members, like Churchill himself, like Lloyd George and Bonar Law, had attended the funeral services for Wilson in St. Paul's, where the pallbearers had included the great war leaders, Beatty and Haig and Robertson, walking in slow, measured, old men's steps beside the coffin draped by a Union Jack, on which rested a field marshal's white-plumed hat and baton. Among those marching in procession was a large detachment of the newly formed Royal Ulster Constabulary and the Royal Ulster Special Constabulary, the B-Specials, which Wilson had placed under his particular patronage and which Brigadier Chubb had been putting into aggressive military shape.

"Let Churchill come over here and attend to his own dirty work," Collins had snarled, the day after his return to Dublin, and he found time to send Cullen and Dolan to London to scout out rescue possibilities. But in Dublin itself, Collins faced an Irish cabinet horrified by the death of Wilson, and then, two days later, shots echoing northwards from a distant mountain road, the killing of Chubb.

It was a joint meeting, both Provisional Government and Dáil, and Christopher, who sat down the table from Collins and across, could study his expressions of outrage and shock, almost as though Collins had slipped into another role.

"It is an abomination," Collins said. "I cannot believe any Irishman capable of it, not even that crowd in the Four Courts."

"It is indeed an abomination," Griffith said, "and I know that you share our outrage, Mr. Collins. I have been saying for weeks now that that armed and mutinous garrison must be cleared out, and you know as well as I do that it can only be done with shot and shell."

"They have scant sympathy from me," Mulcahy said. "Even as we speak, they are holding Ginger O'Connell as their hostage, because the forces of this government have sought to exercise its legitimate authority, the authority to preserve order."

"Hostage," Collins said, with a flick of italic upon the word. "At the moment, he is doubtless there inside the Four Courts having a game of bridge with Rory O'Connor. Bridge fiends, the two of them."

That afternoon, a Republican active service unit, operating out of the Four Courts, had raided a large garage in Baggot Street, and commandeered motorcars for use in an operation in the North. Provisional soldiers from Beggars Bush had arrived on the scene, and the Republican commander had been captured in the scuffle. A few hours later, O'Connell, the deputy chief of staff, had been lifted by the Four Courts as a bargaining chip.

"It is not at issue," Kevin O'Higgins said, "whether or not General O'Connell is being made comfortable by his captors. What is at issue is that this is but their most recent outrage. They have authorized bank robberies, arms raids upon private houses, the bullying of civilians in towns scattered across the West and the South."

"The West and the South," Collins said. "You do not mention the North, I observe. There are matters which it would not be decorous to bring up in cabinet. It is no secret that there has been cooperation of an informal sort between ourselves and the other crowd on operations in the North. There is no need for detail. Dick Mulcahy here can bear me out. Those motorcars were intended for the North. And it might in passing be observed that the garage was owned by Ferguson, a right Orange bastard himself."

"Let us be clear about this, Mr. Collins," Griffith said. He took off his pince-nez, breathed upon them, polished them. "I cannot speak for our colleagues around this table, but for myself, I have been patient, week after week, while you have temporized. There are men in the Four Courts with whom you have served, they are your comrades-in-arms. We all of us understand that, but at this terrible crossroads—"

"I am not the only man sitting at this table who has called Rory O'Connor my friend," and Collins stared directly at O'Higgins, who sat beside Christopher. Christopher could sense his stiffening. In October, when O'Higgins had been married, Rory O'Connor had been his best man. O'Higgins would have responded, but Griffith held out his hand, palm down.

"We have reached a place, Mr. Collins, at which nothing matters save the expressed will of the Irish people. We can support them, or we can traffic with men who have done splendid work in the past, but who are determined now to work their will even if it drags us all down into anarchy."

Collins was rolling a pencil on the table, forwards and back, forwards and back. He would look toward one man or another, toward Griffith, toward O'Higgins, once toward Christopher, toward Mulcahy.

"The Four Courts," he said, "have walls like some medieval fortress. You will not bash them in with Lee-Enfields nor with Lewis guns."

"Of course not," Mulcahy said. "Cope has been on the telephone to Churchill. General Macready has been instructed to hand over two eighteen-pounders. More, should we need them."

Collins studied the pencil moving forwards and back. "We have lads who know the ways of such things, do we?"

Mulcahy smiled, thin-lipped, precise. "Not many, I grant you, but enough. Dalton knows their ways, he learned it beyond there on the Somme. If you are in agreement with us, Mick, we can send him up after nightfall to the British artillery lines. The guns can be hitched up to motor lorries."

"There is one final matter to be considered," O'Higgins said. "Churchill's speech in Commons was most unfortunate. It would be a disaster should we seem to be attacking in obedience to commands from the British. We have ample grounds ourselves, the protection of the people and their Free State."

"A dreadful business," Ernest Blythe said, "the kidnapping of a high official. There are wild men beyond there in the Four Courts. O'Malley and his sort."

The pencil rested now upon the table, Collins's hand pressed down upon it.

"The guns," he said, "must be manned by Irish soldiers, by our own crowd, from Beggars Bush or the Curragh, or wherever. If they are ex–British Army, so much the better. But they must be soldiers of Ireland, I will have no British experts coming along with the British guns."

"I agree," Griffith said, in a suddenly fierce voice. "I agree entirely."

In the event, it was not to matter. Street ballads were to shape popular memory:

England blew the bugle
And threw the gauntlet down,
And Michael sent the boys in green
To level Dublin town.

"We are agreed, so?" Collins asked, and he moved his eyes across faces. "Christopher?" he said suddenly.

Christopher had been dreading this moment, as he told me later, and when it came, it echoed that terrible half-hour in the taxicab, driving back to Hans Place from Downing Street, in the clear, chill December night.

But without a pause, he said, "Agreed," and his voice seemed to come from across a distance which could never be traversed again.

Collins was the first to leave, and Christopher accompanied him. At the door, Collins turned and said, "They must be given a full, fair warning. And if they do not heed it, they are to be given a final warning. Are we agreed on that, so?"

It was to Mulcahy that he had been speaking, but O'Higgins answered, long, firm, determined face, resolute and unflinching; level, even eyes. You would never have thought of him as Tim Healy's nephew.

"Of course," he said. "Full, fair warning. This is a dreadful business."

But when Collins and Christopher stood in warm June sunlight, Collins said, " 'A dreadful business,' by God, there is the lad for the mot juste." But he jerked his head toward the river, hidden by Georgian brick, Victorian granite, beyond which lay the Four Courts. "But that crowd must be taught their manners."

Christopher did not reply.

" 'Tis but a rump that has seized possession," Collins said. "You will not find Liam Lynch in there nor Tom Barry, nor many others of the real fighting men. If it comes to that, you will find few of the political crowd, not Stack nor Cathal Brugha nor Dev, if it comes to that."

"Not at the moment," Christopher said, and let the words rest upon the air. Collins responded to them.

"Nor Frank Lacy," he said. "We saved Frank from treason by sending him off to do killing. By Christ, is he not the cool lad? Two rifle shots fired from ambush, and a farewell to Brigadier Chubb."

"If he were not below in West Cork," Christopher said, "he would be in the Four Courts, if he had to get in disguised as a nun. You can depend upon that."

"Yes," Collins said, and sighed. "I know that."

The shelling of the Four Courts, ineffectual at first, continued all through Wednesday and Wednesday night, Thursday and Thursday night, and on into Friday. And as it went on, Republican forces outside the Courts, the First Dublin Brigade, took up positions north and south of the river, and established headquarters in the great hotels on the east side of Sackville Street, the Gresham and the Grenville and the Hammam. In the south, Liam Lynch, Frank Lacy and the other divisional commanders commenced operations to hold "for the Republic" a perimeter which was to extend across the island from Waterford to Limerick.

Of these events, which were to plunge the country into civil war, what I best remember, save for one vivid exception, is the extraordinary evidence they provided of the ability of the commonplace and violent, the tragic even, to exist side by side. During all of the Wednesday, if the fate of the Republic held by a thread, as the politicians averred, the shoppers on Grafton Street and the accountants and solicitors in their Dame Street of turreted mock-Gothic were unaware of the fact.

De Valera, to be sure, drove into town in his borrowed Ford, reported to his old battalion, the Third, and reenlisted as a Volunteer. When a brigade HQ was established, he reported there, on the Wednesday, and issued a ringing proclamation, urging support of the men "who have refused to forswear their allegiance to the Republic, who have refused to sacrifice honor for expedience and sell their country to a foreign King." In the Gresham, he was joined by Cathal Brugha and Austin Stack, by the fiery shades of what had once been an underground government. But the cinemas remained open that day and the theaters that night.

On the next night, on the Thursday night, I joined Christopher and Arthur Griffith on the roof of Government Buildings. In darkness touched by lingering, late light of summer, we could hear the shells exploding at irregular intervals, ten minutes or fifteen, machine-gun fire, rifle fire.

"Not very much like the western front, is it?" Griffith asked me. "Not very much like the Somme?"

"No," I said in agreement, but the Somme had been in a different, incalculable universe of sounds, bursting lights, mud, distant by six years that might as well have been sixty.

"We are fortunate," Griffith said, "to have General Dalton in command of the field guns. He was an officer on the western front, like yourself. Perhaps you knew him there."

"We had a friend in common," I said. Tom Kettle commanded B Company at Ginchy in September of 1916, and eighteen-year-old Emmet Dalton commanded A Company. Kettle died in his arms. I remembered Tom Kettle a month earlier, with his bottle of Jameson's in the ruined village, drunken and eloquent. "We will emerge with Irish freedom, Patrick, earned on the battlefields of France. Such is history's lesson for us."

"At first they issued shells loaded with shrapnel," Griffith said, "and that is why yesterday's shelling was so ineffectual, but now we have proper shells, would you not say, Mr. Prentiss?"

"I don't think you can tell by the sound, Mr. Griffith, if that is what you mean."

It was an extraordinary conversation, Irishmen shelling Irishmen. Griffith, in the fading light, looked tired, worn, but he stood erect, short and ramrod-straight.

* * *

By Friday, Free State troops had smashed in the outer buildings, and what the Republicans called the munitions block but the more legally or the more historically minded knew as Records was now aflame, the flames licking downwards from the roof, orange and scarlet. Within that block, stacked, docketed, piled in crates bafflingly organized, lay the history of Ireland, insofar as the law records history, from somewhere in the thirteenth century. Below, in the cellars, the Republicans had stored their explosives, their land mines, the shells for nonexistent fieldpieces, and what was later estimated as a half-ton of TNT.

At somewhere close to noon, the cellar exploded, destroying that block and a part of the block which was serving as HQ. It was an explosion heard almost to the outskirts of the city, and visible for miles, a column of black, dirty smoke rising some six hundred feet into the air. "Black as ink," the *Irish Times* was to report the next day,

> Black as ink, shot up a giant column of writhing smoke and dust, a mushroom glaring in the sun with lurid reds and browns, through which could be seen thousands of white snowflakes, dipping, sidling, curtsying, circling, circling, floating as snowflakes do. But the shower was not falling, it was rising. All around us as we stood, three hundred yards away, the bricks and mortar of the great explosion were dropping like hail, but the great white snowstorm eddied ever upwards.

Presently, one of the great snowflakes drifted to the feet of the *Irish Times* journalist, the last sheet of an order made by a probate judge. *And the Judge doth order that the cost of all the parties shall be costs in the cause.* The law, the records, the history of Ireland had been exploded by history, shot high into the air, and for days afterwards, carried by freakish winds, drifted upon suburbs, city squares, Georgian slums. Sheets of paper, parchment, tatters of vellum, fire-scorched, were preserved as keepsakes, but most drifted, defiled, into rear gardens, were drowned in gratings.

Ernie O'Malley signed the surrender, but not until he had made certain that all the machine guns had been smashed, the gunners stamping on the parts, and all the rifles and handguns had been stripped. Then paraffin was poured upon them, and, finally, incendiary grenades were tossed in. As they walked out to the gate, they could feel the heat behind them of the flames feeding on rifle butts. O'Malley, as he walked, ripped off the top mechanism from his Parabellum and tossed it over his shoulder. He walked over to the Free State officers in command, Daly and Lawlor, and told them that he was surrendering on behalf of the Republican garrison of the Four Courts.

"We will need your weapons," Daly said, gruff, angry, embarrassed. He and O'Malley had fought together in the Tan war.

"Go in there after them, so, Paddy," O'Malley said. "But mind yourself. We tossed belts of machine-gun ammo onto the flames."

Lawlor drew the back of his hand across his cheek. "You implacable bastard," he said, and smiled. In those days, in those first hours of the civil war, they were still smiling at each other.

O'Malley walked past him, stood by the stone parapet, and hurled into the Liffey what remained of his Parabellum, butt, barrel, trigger, trigger guard.

"And so much for that," Lawlor said. " 'Tis all over."

But minutes later, as Lawlor's sergeants were trying to make the prisoners form up in fours, the sounds of the fire, of random shots, of shouting quieted for an uncanny full minute, and they all heard gunfire, machine-gun fire and rifle fire, coming from their right. The battle for Sackville Street, for the center of Dublin, had begun.

"Not quite," O'Malley said to Lawlor. "Not quite over."

XXVIII

ELIZABETH KEATING

It was not until mid-July that Elizabeth Keating was able to make her way southwards to Republican headquarters in Fermoy, leaving well behind her the gutted hotels on Sackville Street which had been destroyed by field guns, armored cars, machine guns and incendiary grenades. Liam Lynch, the chief of staff, had established himself in the old barracks of the British Army, and when Elizabeth arrived she found him in the wardroom, bending over a map of the entire island. Frank Lacy stood bent beside him, and, on his other side, President De Valera, looking tall and a bit uncertain. She had last seen him in the besieged Hammam Hotel building in Sackville Street, standing beside a gaping sledgehammered hole in one interior wall. On the other side of the wall was the makeshift hospital where she had been helping nurses tend the wounded.

De Valera was in a dark suit, a white shirt soiled a bit at the collar; there were patches of dried mud on his trouser legs. Lynch and Lacy were both in uniform, though, tall boots, Sam Browne belts, holsters weighted down by heavy pistols. No one questioned Elizabeth's presence there; she might have stood there forever, listening, and if she had spoken, they would not have heard her. The room was unguarded, Volunteers moved into it and out, in uniform most of the officers, but the soldiers were most of them in farm clothes, jackets the color of rain. Many of the Volunteers were young, seventeen or eighteen, and they often laughed in joking excitement, which she took to be a good sign. She walked downstairs and out into the barracks square, where what looked to be the awkward squad of Volunteers was being drilled. At the far side, close to the barracks wall, two Lewis guns stood side by side, and a uniformed sergeant was giving instruction, a squat, capable-looking fellow.

Later, in the deserted commissary, Lacy took a small map of the country from his pocket, unfolded it, and, placing it before them, explained to her the map which was being studied in the wardroom. It was a much-used map, and repeated creasings had worn away a few towns, burrowed narrow trails of paper and buckram across hills and valleys.

" 'Tis no secret," Lacy said. "Everyone knows what we are about." Since they had had tea in Dublin, less than a year before, his voice, the rhythm of his words, had altered slightly, but she could not define the change.

With a red pencil, Lacy drew a circle around Limerick, on the west coast of Munster, and Waterford, on the east. Then he circled towns which lay almost on a straight line between the two—Tipperary, Golden, Cashel, Fethard, Clonmel, Carrick on Suir. "There you are," he said, "the front line, the Republic of Munster." He put down his pencil, and lifted his head to study her. "We hold those towns, and the most important of the towns to the south of that line—Charleville and Mallow and Fermoy here, as you can see; we hold Killarney and Kilpeder and Macroom."

But she did not raise her own head. She was lost within the map. The names were magic to her, potent and occult.

In the years of the war against the English, working first with Christopher Blake and then publishing the *Republican Bulletin* on her own, they had been the names of ambushes, attacks upon barracks, reprisals by the Black and Tans. Accounts had been carried to her by fellows up to Dublin on business at HQ or by women of the Cumann, or else she would talk with flying column commandants in teashops or on rare occasions in the discreet snugs of public houses. As they talked, terse and ungrammatical some of them, including some of the best, but some, like O'Malley, florid and protectively self-mocking, or like Lacy, intense yet ambiguous, as they talked she had spread out hillsides, twisting roads, village streets, upon the ordnance map of her imagination. During all of those Troubles, during the Tan war, as Republicans were now calling it, she had been out of Dublin only once, that time when she and Christopher Blake were on the run in Wicklow, and Wicklow scarcely counted, wild yet within the shadow of Dublin.

"Not to mention Kilmallock," Lacy said. "There are those who say that a battle for Kilmallock will be shaping up. We hold it now, at any rate. For the time being."

"For the time being," she said, echoing his words as a question.

Later that day, carrying with her a note from Liam Lynch, she walked down into the town, and rented a room from a Mrs. Kelleher, a high room with a fine view of the Blackwater and its bridge. Toward evening, bats would wheel within the arches of the bridge, familiar but frightening.

"I will be here for a week or two only, I am writing newspaper stories for the Republic."

"Man proposes and God disposes," Mrs. Kelleher said. Her son, who was in hospital in Cork City, had had parts of his body shot away by the Tans. She managed life through her storehouse of tags and sayings.

After Elizabeth had settled in, she cleared off the small table, set out tablets, pencils, notes, fountain pen, and recommenced her story of the siege of Sackville Street and the death of Cathal Brugha. But no words would come to her that pleased her, not even as a first draft.

The next day, De Valera, who had been appointed by Lynch to the operations staff, set off for Clonmel. Before he left, he gave Elizabeth an interview in the wardroom. The large map had been tacked to the wall, and drawing pins were scattered across it, pink, white, deep green. "Your words are a great comfort to us, Miss Keating," he said, "to all Republicans in these terrible times. You are a very brave and a very eloquent young woman."

"When we last met, Mr. President," she began, but he interrupted her. "President no longer, not for the time being I should have said. I am once more a soldier of the Republic. It is a title of even higher honor. I have borne it before, and without disgrace, I believe."

"You have indeed, sir," she said, and he peered out the window.

"I intend my story on the siege of Sackville Street to center upon Cathal Brugha," she said. "It is for him that the siege will be remembered."

A shadow seemed to play briefly across the long, patient, melancholy face. "The bravest of the brave," he said, brightening a bit. "A rock of courage in 1916 and a rock of courage last month. Bullets from the British in 1916 and from the hirelings of England in 1922. A sad, brave story."

"You have read what Michael Collins has said? 'I would forgive him anything. Because of his sincerity I would forgive him anything. When many of us are forgotten, Cathal Brugha will be remembered.' "

De Valera was still looking out the window. "I see that my driver is waiting for me in the motorcar," he said. "People here are very kind to me. People everywhere."

The long head turned full toward Elizabeth.

"It was Cathal Brugha's great fear," he said, "that next will come the setting up of a military dictatorship, with some popular hero in command, some figure of newspaper celebrity who has made his peace with the traditional enemy. We must hope not, Miss Keating. We must work to give meaning to his sacrifice."

Two days later, Limerick City fell to the Provisionals, and Lacy went south, to his headquarters in Kilpeder, to bring up men for the defense of Kilmallock. He was still driving his garish Humber, dirt-streaked now, but now, beside him and in the seats behind, sat Volunteers with loaded rifles, the butts resting on the floorboards.

Elizabeth walked with him across the cobbled parade ground.

"Mind yourself," she said in a tone more prim and distant than she had intended.

"I'm safe enough," Lacy said. "If the roads between here and Kilpeder are not controlled by Fifth Southern we are in desperate straits. I will be there by teatime, and Pat MacCarthy will have a hot cup for me."

Once, she thought, it would have been Pat MacCarthy and Ben Cogley, but Ben Cogley was now a general in the Free State army. Just before leaving for Fermoy, she had seen a newspaper photograph of four of them standing together, Mulcahy trim and whippet-thin, and MacEoin, genial and smiling, who now commanded at Athlone, and Cogley looking a bit ironical and uneasy, and Collins in a splendid new uniform, crisp and dramatic. Days earlier, he had resigned his civilian posts, and was now commander-in-chief of the Provisional army.

For the next week, she talked with officers and men, scribbling down names, villages, always making certain that the names were spelled correctly. Some of the men, the youngest, were lads who had joined after the Treaty. They talked about "patriots and martyrs" on the one side and "renegades and lousers" on the other, and made it seem like a hurling match. Few of them could handle a rifle or shotgun with familiarity, but they were willing, and they spent their days felling trees to use as roadblocks. After the great ten-spanned bridge across the Blackwater at Mallow was blown up by the Republicans, there was no access into the counties save by road. Elizabeth found ways of transforming every scuffle into a battle, and every battle into part of the undying defense of the Republic. She wrote her copy in duplicate, sending one of each story south to Cork City, where the Republicans controlled the *Examiner,* and the other eastwards, more uncertainly, to Dublin, where Eithne Mullane and Helen Maguire were printing *The Republic* on a handpress in Chapelizod.

Late at night, in her room above a Blackwater tinged by a full summer moon, she worked upon the elaborate essay which would describe the defense of Sackville Street and the death of Cathal Brugha. She would write a half-page in her forward-slanting script, then find herself balked, light a cigarette, and walk across the room to look down upon the river, night-shrouded shopfronts of the quiet town. But when she sat down again at her table and read over what she had written, as likely as not she would scratch out words and lines with angry jabs, or else tear the page in half.

By Tuesday, July the fourth, the Hammam Hotel was on fire, under a continuous bombardment: Provisional soldiers would run in close and hurl incendiaries and cans of petrol. Part of the garrison had surrendered under a white flag on Sunday, and on Monday De Valera, Stack and the other leaders had been guided through back lanes to safe houses. But now, on the Tuesday, the flaming building was held by seventeen men under Brugha, with three nurses to care for the wounded. They contrived to hold out through much of Wednesday, but then Brugha called them together and ordered them to vacate the building, whose walls were about to collapse. They left, under a flag, and surrendered to the soldiers who had sealed off the rear laneway. Beyond the barricades, watching with a small crowd in the blackened, acrid air, straining to hear despite continuous machine-gunning, Elizabeth stood with two other women who had managed to escape on Monday without surrendering. A press man with a heavy camera stood beside them, and one of Elizabeth's friends, in rage, kicked at it.

There seemed at last to be no one left in the building, and there was a shuddering, deep noise which may have been the buckling of a wall. Even beyond the barricades, the heat from the three burning buildings seemed to Elizabeth intolerable. And just then, Cathal Brugha came running from the building, soot-streaked, a wraith. He was holding a heavy revolver straight in front of him, firing at the soldiers. Or so she remembered it, but some remembered him holding two pistols, like a gunman in films about the Wild West, and some remembered that he had but the one gun and was holding it at his side. It was over in seconds, a minute perhaps. "Fire low," some heard one of the soldiers shout, but Elizabeth did not hear the shout. The figure, Cathal Brugha's figure, looked small and terrifying; she thought she saw him running toward the soldiers, silent, smoke-bedaubed.

In the event, a bullet that severed the femoral artery killed him. He was carried up Sackville Street to the Mater Hospital by ambulance, with Linda Kearns, one of the nurses, holding the artery's ends in her fingers. He took two days to die.

First, Elizabeth tried to describe what she had seen and heard, but only that, so that people unknown to her, with their backs turned against the laneway, carried him into the white-painted ambulance. And then, she tried to describe, through the eyes of her friend Linda Kearns, the ride beside the dying man through the ugly, flaming night, through the smell of gunfire, shellfire. But each time she knew, after she had written more than a few pages, that she was being literary in the bad sense of the word, and she would try, simply, to explain what was embodied by Brugha's death, who had been faithful to the Republic, to whom Ireland and the Republic were one, inseparable. But the words, after three years of using them, had become slippery counters, coins with the legends worn through. It was not the words which she blamed, but herself, as though she had lost, or more likely had never truly possessed, the powers by which language and passion are joined, language and history.

Every morning, however, she would be ready to talk once again: with commandants hurrying through upon their bewildered and bewildering tasks; a Volunteer who had exchanged gunfire with a Provisional tender; a lorry driver who had escaped from one of the Provisional prison camps. But the news which came into Fermoy in the first weeks of August put increasing strains upon her powers of invention.

The line was buckling, that bright girdle of colored drawing pins on the wall map. Golden fell at the end of July and then Kilmallock, Carrick on Suir fell in the first days of the new month, and then Clonmel and Macroom. The rail line had been destroyed, but the Free State landed troops and artillery at Fenit and Passage West, and began moving inland from the west and the south. Within weeks, within days, the Republicans had been driven from their fixed positions, all of them save Fermoy and, remote upon the Cork-Kerry border, Frank Lacy's headquarters at Ardmor Castle in the town of Kilpeder.

Fermoy barracks was evacuated on the eleventh. Lynch stood with his men in the barracks square, reluctant to walk through the gates into the streets of the town. He knew what needed to be said, that the war of fixed positions had ended, that they could turn now to the kind of fighting they knew best, flying columns on the run, attacks from ambush. It was a kind of warfare which he had helped to invent, himself and Barry and Lacy. He said what had to be said, with a flatness that held its own eloquence. Then, a strained awkwardness settled again upon the square, an awkwardness which was broken by what seemed to Elizabeth a kind of magic.

Dan Mulvihill, who had a fine, full tenor, began the aria from Verdi "Home to Our Mountains," and the square was filled with no sound save that of his voice, Italianate flourishes to a song of movement into Gaelic hills, dark, heather-shrouded. It was a moment crammed with meaning, Elizabeth knew, like the smoke-streaked ambulance driving up a shattered Sackville Street, and a nurse holding a slippery artery in bloody fingers. But she knew also that it was a moment which she could never translate into words upon paper.

After the barracks had been vacated, supplies and weapons and ammunitions moved out, carts of laundry and flour, cases of tinned beef, the walls were soaked with petrol and paraffin, and set on fire. The charred ruins had cooled three days later, when Colonel Ben Cogley reached Fermoy with his Free Staters.

The Republican garrison at Fermoy, like the one in Clonmel and the one in Kilmallock, broke into columns and moved into the hills, on their own keeping, but staying loosely in touch with each other. Elizabeth rode with one of them almost to the Knockmealdowns, and then traveled with a friendly carter to Waterford, where there was still train service to Dublin.

She was traveling not only to Dublin but to the years of her future—years in which the Republic, the true Republic, would exist in fugitive, ill-printed newspapers like those she would continue to publish, and in speeches delivered in drafty meeting halls or from rainswept platforms—a Republic protected by a handful of unforgiving gunmen.

XXIX

PATRICK PRENTISS

He wears full uniform as commander-in-chief in his most famous photograph, a uniform handsomely cut, gold on shoulder strap and cap; boots and belt so highly polished that they shine despite grainy newsprint; by his side, slung so low that his fingers almost graze it, a holstered revolver, the restraining strap of the holster unbuckled. He is walking, striding rather, across an open square and is by himself, space-surrounded, but behind him, at a distance, a crowd of the curious; a father, hat in hand, the other hand holding that of a daughter in holiday frock, and, a bit behind those two, a dark-skirted woman, dark hat. He is walking with what seems a brisk stride, the arms swinging, and he is looking off to one side, away from the camera.

What gives the photograph its haunting quality, though, is a boy of twelve or fourteen, in dress-up uniform, brass buttons and epaulets, large rosette, dark kilt and tall stockings. He is bareheaded. He walks in obvious imitation, not at all nervous but a bit shy. He is smiling.

Like almost everything in the final weeks, the final days, the photograph has grown in legend, and you will hear it said that it was taken on the morning of August twentieth, a Sunday, as he set off for West Cork from Portobello barracks. But he left Dublin at six that morning, long before small boys and press photographers were awake, and, despite the month, he wore his heavy greatcoat. There are many photographs of him in that Free State uniform, so many of them as to lead one to forget that he did not wear it before his appointment to military command, six weeks before his death.

A number of photographs were taken in Limerick on that final Sunday, and more in Cork on Monday, and there is one taken in Bandon, outside Lee's Hotel, on Tuesday, a few hours yet to go, sitting in the rear of his open Leland Thomas touring car, with Emmet Dalton beside him, still in his twenties but now a Free State general, the two of them with loaded rifles across their knees. In some of the photographs, the greatcoat is unbuttoned and thrown back upon his shoulders. Perhaps, somewhere, in some vault, some garage, some lumber room, there are newsreels of Collins in Cork City, in Skibbereen outside the Eldon Hotel, joking with admirers, grinning, his hand on one man's shoulder, leaning forward to attend to another man's words.

There certainly are newsreels of Collins at the funeral of Arthur Griffith in Dublin on the fifteenth, first as one of the pallbearers at the Pro-Cathedral, the right edge of the coffin resting on his shoulder, and then, spectacularly, thanks to Pathé News, which gives us history on celluloid, perishable but not for a while, scenes of the great funeral of state up Sackville Street, past enormous multitudes of mourners. On the one side, the General Post Office shattered in 1916, and, on the other side, facing it precisely, the buildings bombed, wrecked, burned, in the fighting a few weeks earlier, the fighting which, so all agreed, had hastened Griffith's death. Collins, in uniform, walks at the front of the military, the spruce and trim Mulcahy beside him. They look neither to left nor to right.

Legends cluster around what he did and said in those final days, about why he was determined to travel into a West Cork thick with Republican soldiers, blocked roads, exploded bridges, the sites of ambush. As always the legends include warnings and premonitions. On the night before he set out, returning from a dinner party with John and Hazel Lavery in Wicklow, the car was machine-gunned. At a meeting with his chief of intelligence earlier that day, he had been urged not to travel south, and the next morning he was warned again. "Sure, I am safe enough in West Cork," he said, "I am a West Cork man." And, as he was setting foot in the car, an old army friend dashed out of the barracks, and put a hand on his arm. "Mick," he began, or so, years afterwards, he remembered it, "would you in God's name—" But Collins shook off the hand. He was in poor health, some of the legends have it, troubled in body and spirit, and other legends have it that for weeks he had been drinking. Some legends hold that he thought the war was almost over, the Republicans defeated without a single position left, Fermoy abandoned, and then, on the Thursday, faced by Ben Cogley's advance along the Cork-Kerry border, Frank Lacy had moved out of Kilpeder, leaving Ardmor Castle a flaming ruin behind him. But other legends, the most persistent of them all, hold that Collins was arranging through old friends to meet with Republican leaders, with Liam Lynch perhaps, or Hales, or Lacy.

But Christopher Blake was not one of those who argued against the journey, although on the day before he met with Collins for two hours in Government Buildings. It was a business meeting, although not business of a sort which gets itself minuted and recorded. There were ten pages of instructions, written in the small pocket notebook, and as Collins read off each page, he tore it out, and handed it across the desk to Christopher.

He tugged at his belt to loosen it, and shoved two fingers into his collar to pull it away from his throat.

"Have you ever noticed, Chris, how much of the world's work can get itself accomplished by two fellows sitting quietly down to talk in a quiet room. We are being eaten alive by committees, interim reports and fact-finding missions and all the rest of it. By God, the country and the war alike were run more sensibly from the abovestairs room in Vaughan's, and on top of that, you could get a ball of malt liquor by ringing the bell."

But there was no better man at the committees, Christopher knew, using them and playing them off against each other. This was a role, now, that Collins had played before, the simple fellow up from the country, bluff and no-nonsense, manager of a creamery perhaps or agent for farm machinery. But it did not sit easily with the dramatic uniform, the gilt, the polished boots, the six-gun in its holster.

" 'Twill not be all business, Chris," he said. "I am damned if I will go downcountry that far without calling in at Clonakilty and Sam's Cross. You have never been there, Chris, you are a Dublin man, a jackeen. Come along with me now," he said suddenly, impetuous, as though the notion had just occurred to him. "Clonakilty, Sam's Cross, Skibbereen, a few balls of malt at the Five-Alls, we can make a holiday of it."

But Christopher shook his head. "Some other time, Mick."

"That whole land there is as thick with Collinses as berries on the bush. I will be welcomed by my own there, Chris, and as safe as houses."

"There are more to be found there these days than Collinses," Christopher said. "And well you know it. The woods and hills are thick with the fellows driven out of Cork City, and Kilmallock."

"For God's sake, Chris, keep a bit calm. You sound like our friends in the cabinet, with Ernie O'Malley hiding in every clothespress. There is not a town in Ireland that is not glad to see the last of those cowboys when they are driven out. When our lads took Clonmel and Macroom, the people were mad with enthusiasm. 'Tis all over, and the sooner lads like Lynch and Tom Hales know that, the better. I have not the least objection to talking with them. Sure if you will talk with Winston, you will talk with anyone."

He tugged at the tall collar, and pulled it open. "The weather cannot make up its mind is it to be the heat of the tropics or winter in August. Last night, I was so cold I was shivering with a blanket on me."

Christopher picked up the sheets of paper torn from the notebook, folded them, and put them in his coat pocket.

"Mind now," Collins said. "As soon as you have no need for those, do away with them."

"Have a pint of stout for me at the, what is it, the Four-Alls."

"The Five-Alls," Collins said. "But I will make it a pint of ale, if that is all the same to you. I am not partial to stout." He patted his tunic. "And neither is the gut."

On his way out, he paused by the open door. Christopher, from where he sat, could just make out a bodyguard's green-uniformed arm.

"I will bring you down there one of these days," Collins said. " 'Twill do you good."

Later, three days later, Christopher would turn the words over in his mind, as though reading runes, but there had been no portents in the words nor in Collins's manner. Once, a few weeks earlier, when he had met with Collins at the house in Kingstown, and Collins had had drink taken, it had been different. Collins had sat for an hour by the open window in the hot July night, with a sullen wind stirring the trees in the terrace garden. Beyond the garden lay Dublin Bay, and, beyond darkening waters, the lights of Howth. The day before, Harry Boland, who had been the closest of his friends, but who had taken the Republican side and had been shot down in Skerries by a Free State soldier, had died in St. Vincent's Hospital. "Boys, oh boys," Collins said, into darkness, to Christopher, "there were no two lads closer together than Harry Boland and myself. Sure, you know that yourself, Chris. There is no need for me to tell you. We go back to the beginnings of things, Harry and myself. 'Shot trying to escape,' did you read the report? Sure, if Harry had wanted to escape, he would have done it. He was a Houdini, that fellow was, a veritable Houdini. 'Twas Harry and myself organized Dev's escape out of Lincoln Gaol. You know that yourself, Chris."

He pushed his empty glass across the small side table to "Chum" Gaffney, one of his two bodyguards that day—the other one, Tim Hennefy, was sitting in the front garden, quietly smoking a Woodbine, beside the monkey-puzzle tree—and, when Gaffney had attended to it, "Have a jar yourself, Chum, and mind our friend's glass here," and he nodded toward Christopher.

Beyond the window, a ketch, seizing the sullen wind, moved toward Kingstown's harbor.

"The two of you always got along well, Harry and yourself," Collins said. "Dublin men, the two of you, Dublin jackeens. I had always a great mind to take Harry to Clonakilty, show him the real Ireland."

"It is all real," Christopher said, and held out his glass toward Gaffney's bottle of Powers. "Everything is real."

"Yesterday," Collins said, "when word was brought to me that Harry had died, I walked along the Green, past St. Vincent's. There was a crowd outside, but I passed by them unnoticed, and straight on towards Leeson Street and back at last to Portobello. I'd send a wreath, but I suppose they'd tear it up."

It was late on the afternoon of the twenty-second when he had his pint of ale, several of them to be exact, in the Five-Alls at Sam's Cross. The small room was crowded with kinfolk and neighbors, and he had asked in his drivers and escort, the machine-gunner and the crew of the armored car, the *Slievenamon*.

He was now in the heart, the dead center, of his own country, the publican was a Collins, and the public house was almost within sight of Woodfield, where he had been born, and which the Tans had destroyed in reprisal a year earlier.

The convoy had set off from Cork City for Macroom very early that morning—a young lieutenant on motorcycle who acted as scout, and then the Crossley tender carrying two officers and ten riflemen and two Lewis gunners, and then Collins and Emmet Dalton in the long, yellow touring car, and then, bringing up the rear, the Rolls armored car, with a crew of four and a Vickers gun mounted on a swivel. It was not, so it was later agreed, a particularly heavy convoy to be guarding two officers of general rank, and it was not an inconspicuous one to be traveling through what had become a forest of ambushes, felled trees, torn-up roads, twisting narrow alternative roads.

On the way to Bandon, they stopped at the crossroads of Beal na mBlath to ask directions from a man lounging against the wall of Long's public house, and there they made the first of several mistakes, for the lounger, although a local fellow, was an IRA sentry, protecting a meeting up the hill of two Cork brigades. He had heard the convoy approach, and had slipped his rifle behind the door. When the sentry made his report, Tom Hales, the local commandant, set up an ambush, and kept it in position from morning well into evening, on the off chance that the convoy would return through Beal na mBlath, and through all of that long, last day, it waited for him. Toward evening, Hales disconnected the land mine that had been set, and removed the barricade. Five or six men, however, were kept in position, on the off chance.

At Bandon, the Provisional commander, Sean Hales, Tom's brother, said, "Watch out for the brother, Mick. He's a hard man."

They had had a pint in Bandon, and now Collins and Dalton were back in the touring car. Hales had bent forward to speak to them, and he had lowered his voice.

"Don't I know that," Collins said. "By God, I had rather have Tom Hales on my side than any ten men. Tom Hales and Tom Barry, the two of them. And look now, would you, the one of them jailed in Kilmainham, and the other roaming the hills of West Cork bent upon mischief."

"Whatever he may be bent upon," Hales said, "Tom is a good fighter, a good column commander."

"Ach," Collins said, "take a look at the lads ahead in the tender. They are fit for anything, from the Dublin Brigade, the most of them, and with officers from the Squad."

"They may know how to give battle in the streets of Dublin," Hales said, "but what the hell do they know about fighting in the hills of West Cork?" And as he spoke, he thought, What the hell does Mick Collins know about it?

"We are fit for a fight or a frolic, Sean," Collins said, "depend upon it."

Hales dropped his voice still lower. "Can I put a word in your ear, Mick, not to the commander-in-chief, but one West Cork man talking to another. If you run into trouble in the hills, don't stop to fight. Drive like hell. Get this motorcar with yourself and Emmet here out of harm's way. 'Tis you would be the target, and not the jackeens ahead in the tender."

"Ach," Collins said again, "we can cross that bridge when we come to it."

Hales sighed and straightened up. "Most of the bridges have been blown up, Mick. Or hadn't you noticed?"

At Clonakilty they were halted by felled trees across the road, and took a narrow, twisting byroad into the town, but they had a clear passage from there into Rosscarbery, where Tom Barry, the year before, had burned down the British barracks. In Callinan's public house, Collins was warned that the Republicans in the towns and in the hills knew of the convoy and knew who commanded it. The publican, ceremoniously presenting a glass of the house's special whiskey and making a brief, flowery speech, said then to Collins, almost in a whisper, "It was said, General, in another public house not ten minutes' distance afoot, it was said, 'Collins is gone west, but he won't go east.' "

Now, in Sam's Cross, before returning to Rosscarbery and Bandon, to make for Cork by the road through Beal na mBlath, he had a final pint. " 'Twill be nightfall soon," he said to Dalton, "we have had a good, full day of it."

"Mind what Sean Hales told us," Dalton said. "He knows this countryside."

"*He* knows it!" Collins said. "I am standing in the crossroads of my birth, in a public house owned by my own cousin, and you tell me that Sean Hales knows the country or Tom Hales knows the country, or who will it be next knows the country?"

Light was darkening as they moved out of Bandon along the road. It was a landscape of rocks and low hills, hedges and thornbushes. Just before the first rifle shot, an eerie premonition came to Dalton, someone walking on a grave, and he shouted out, almost as he heard the shot, "Drive like hell. Don't stop for anything." And Collins punched the driver on the shoulder. "Pay no heed to that," he said. "We will fight them here."

Because the roads between Cork and Dublin were judged to be either impassable or dangerous, the body was brought back by ship, the S.S. *Classic,* the coffin draped in the tricolor, and, atop it, a bloody officer's cap. The boat's journey from the pierhead at Queenstown was a slow one, and the party of officers, colleagues and friends who stood waiting for it at the North Wall waited for hours in a cold, drizzling rain with the first hints of autumn in it. It did not arrive until close to three in the morning.

Christopher stood for a time with Myles Keough's friend Oliver Gogarty, who had also been Griffith's friend, a poet and surgeon. He would be doing the postmortem and the embalming in a few hours, readying the body for its brief lying-in-state at St. Vincent's, and then the public viewing in the City Hall.

Gogarty and Keough were two of a kind, learned, witty, licentious, but Gogarty was somber that morning, coat collar turned up to protect long, equine cheeks, a handsome, mercurial man. Later in the week, Emmet Dalton was to pass back to him the hall door key to his house in Ely Place, which Collins had used, on occasion, as a safe house. Grief had done nothing to quench Gogarty's legendary venom, though.

"What an unlucky handshake De Valera gives," Gogarty said. "He shakes hands to speed Collins and Griffith to London. They are dead within a year."

Weeks earlier, Gogarty had been summoned to the nursing home, but there was nothing to be done for Griffith. A long incision had been made along the pulse, the only desperate measure against cerebral hemorrhage, but there was no blood. His friend was lying on the stairhead. "Take up that corpse at once," Gogarty said to the nursing sister, letting his bitterness coarsen his words.

"What an unlucky handshake," he said again, to Christopher, as they stood on the North Wall, and Christopher, in the cold, spitting night rain, sensed the bitterness and chill fury which were about to become part of Irish life.

Presently, in the distance, they could see the running lights of the *Classic*. The guard of honor was formed up, and the gun carriage made ready to receive the coffin. "Time enough for all that," Gogarty said, "it will be the best part of an hour before they dock."

It was while the body of Collins was lying in St. Vincent's chapel that Sir John Lavery painted his portrait, just as, months before, his friend Winston had urged him. Hazel, Lavery's wife, visited the body, dressed in the black of mourning. But when the coffin, on its gun carriage, was drawn to Glasnevin up Sackville Street, past crowds larger than any seen since the funeral of Parnell, past the ruined General Post Office of 1916, past the more recent ruins which faced it, there rested on the tricolor a single rose from the young woman in County Longford whom he had been engaged to marry. The cortège passed close to Vaughan's, where Christopher Blake's memories of Collins were the brightest, the least shadowed by ambiguities.

XXX

FRANK LACY

By the early spring of 1923, Lacy was using as a brigade headquarters whatever seemed reasonably safe for a week or two—farmhouses for the most part, and once he risked taking over Lughnavalla House for a fortnight. He had a column strength of forty, all of them fellows on the run, like himself, and when a large operation was on hand, he could usually find a dozen or so more, but most of these were young lads indeed, who six months before would have been used to fell trees for roadblocks. Pat MacCarthy, his second-in-command, had been lost to him at the end of the last year, caught up by the enemy during the fight for Aghabullogue, and a prisoner now in Gormanstown. The two lads who had commanded his column near the Limerick border were both dead, one killed in a raid and the other dying in hospital a week later. It might be possible, in the public houses in Kilpeder and Millstreet and Macroom, late on a Saturday night, to hear fellows boast of their loyalty to the Republic, but this was never carried beyond the boasting, or the singing of a doggerel Republican ballad.

But all that was in fact; theory was entirely different. In theory his command stretched from the Kerry and Limerick borders across to that of Cork No. 1. The brigade areas were operating substantially on their own, with divisional meetings and meetings of the Executive difficult to organize, and more and more commandants were ending up, like MacCarthy, in the prison camps or in the large prisons like Kilmainham or the one in Maryborough. The operations themselves were being described, both in government announcements and in the national press, as acts of brigandage and murder, tumbling the country into anarchy. There was something to be said for such descriptions: Lacy's command, in the six months that moved it into spring, had twice held up post offices, and once the bank in Aghabullogue.

They were also, such operations, the only way in which the brigades could maintain themselves in the field. By now, by the spring, there were almost no sources of Republican news. For a time, Erskine Childers, on the run in West Cork after the fall of Cork City, had trundled a portable press around with him from place to place, following the Republican retreat northwards, a barracks at Ballymakeera, a cottage in Ballyvourney. But in October, Childers, traveling toward Dublin to meet with De Valera, had been arrested by Provisional soldiers, Free State soldiers they now called themselves, was carried to Dublin, tried by military tribunal and executed. His printing press died with him. There were then left a few sheets, printed by hand or by greeting-card companies, Elizabeth Keating's *The Republic* and one called *Ireland*. There were also posters and placards, run off on the same presses, and posted on walls at night. "The Republic Lives," a familiar one began, and there would follow, as brief bulletins, accounts of raids and ambushes by brigades—Barry's or Deasy's or Lacy's. They would be announced as major victories in the field. And some of them were. Tom Barry attacked and captured Carrick on Suir with about a hundred men from Cork and Tipperary, taking armored cars, Lewis guns, and a hundred Lee-Enfields. In midwinter, three towns in Kilkenny were taken. Then, in February, Lacy, moving across the Derrynasaggarts to the support of beleaguered Kerry, ambushed and destroyed a Free State convoy of three Crossleys and an armored car. As the Free State soldiers moved up the hillside in retreat, Lacy cut them down with their own swivel-mounted Vickers gun, the bullets stripping away dead branches from the trees behind which they sought shelter.

But these victories, as Lacy knew, as Barry and Deasy knew, were defensive. The war was being lost, and the only questions that remained open had to do with the terms on which fighting would end. In Dublin, De Valera and the ideologists of the Republic knew it as well, and from time to time, perilously, guided across broken roads and makeshift bridges, De Valera would journey south to confer with the military leaders. The people in the towns and villages knew it, waiting in disgusted horror and fear for the machine-gunning to end, whether by either side, Free State or Republican.

Lacy during these months did not touch drink, save for an occasional beer, but he smoked incessantly, his fingers stained yellow by the smoke from Woodbines and Players. At night, when his men would be asleep in the farmhouse or in its barn, and when the farmer and his family would be asleep, or lying in nervous wakefulness, Lacy would lean against a gable wall, lighting one cigarette from the butt of another. Whenever he could, he would take shelter with a sympathetic family, but it was not always possible, and there would be awkward hours when the wife would make up a tea in the kitchen, while the farmer and his sons looked with angry helplessness at rifles, at revolvers in waistbands.

Once or twice, young Joe Casey, who now was Lacy's seconder, had tried to argue things out with a reluctant host, but without much success. Casey was a decent fellow, his instincts were decent, but he was callow, and Lacy missed MacCarthy in his Gormanstown prison, and Ben Cogley, a general now in the Free State army, and commanding operations in mid-Munster. But it was Casey who had mastered the Lewis gun and the Vickers, Casey who fired the Vickers in the Kerry operation.

The war had become ugly in ways that would not have seemed possible to either side a year earlier, before the shooting of Collins, before the execution of Childers in Beggars Bush barracks. In Kerry, across the Derrynasaggarts from Lacy, the savagery was almost entire. At Carrigaphooca, Free State soldiers began to lift up a land mine, but the mine had been booby-trapped. In early March, at Knocknagoshel, Free State soldiers were lured into a trap and blown up. And a day later, at Ballyseedy, nine Republican prisoners, who had been taken from the jail at Tralee, were chained together and then blown up by a mine. The news of Ballyseedy came over the mountains to Lacy's command within hours, and he was hard put to prevent his men from exacting reprisals. Reprisals by both sides were common now, and for a long time Lacy was not certain how he felt about them. Rafferty, the Free Stater whom Ben Cogley had put in command in Kilpeder, was more decent than many of them, and he and Lacy kept a decent, respectful distance. Lacy would think about reprisals and executions, firing squads and mines exploding beneath prisoners, as he stood alone, leaning against a wall, fingers cupped about a cigarette.

The Free State executions had begun with Childers. Soon there were shootings every week, in Mountjoy, in the yards of provincial prisons, thirty-four of them in January alone. Lynch, commander of the Republican army, issued an order that anyone who had voted for the Free State's Emergency Powers Act would be shot on sight. In December, Sean Hales, who in August, in a West Cork town, had warned Michael Collins about hillside ambushes, was shot dead in a Dublin street by Republican gunmen. The next morning, at first light, the Republican commanders who had been captured at the Four Courts six months earlier—Rory O'Connor, Liam Mellowes, Joe McKelvey, Dick Barrett—were taken from their cells in Mountjoy and shot in the prison yard.

Lacy had known them all of course, but Mellowes and he had been together in the hills of Galway in 1916, when it all began, a thin-lipped, intense, bright-spirited man. There had been no trial, nor even charges, and the official report described the act as "a reprisal," a warning to those "engaged in the conspiracy of assassination." The report was carried two days later, in the *Examiner.* Lacy was drinking tea in the kitchen of a friendly farmer on the Millstreet road, a man named Charlie Cronin. "Fucking hoors," Joe Casey said. "Pay them back blow for blow." Lacy and the farmer, an elderly, intelligent, yellow-toothed man, looked at each other and said nothing. "There is no other way," Casey said, "blow for blow."

"We could go down into Kilpeder," Lacy said, "and kill Jerry Rafferty. Or would you rather wait until Ben Cogley comes home on a visit to his family." He did not put it as a question, and he could not keep the contempt from his voice.

Toward the end of February, a council of the First Southern Division was held at Coolea in West Cork, to which Liam Lynch had traveled, and where he heard from Barry and Lacy, from some eighteen officers. Indomitable, or else blinded by his ideal, Lynch argued against them all that the war could still be won. "We will keep on fighting," Barry said, "but we cannot keep on winning." Lacy, afterwards, rode southwards in a trap with Paddy Joe Murphy.

"Liam has the right of it," Paddy Joe said. "I had a long talk with him. The hills and the mountains are our allies, he says. Leave the towns and the road to the Free Staters."

"I see," Lacy said.

"Last week," Paddy Joe said, "when he was meeting with First Western, he revealed his plans to acquire mountain artillery. He has been in negotiations with big armament people in Germany and in the United States."

"I see," Lacy said again.

"One of those yokes, moved from one of our strong positions to the next, and the war could be won by the end of the summer."

"Did he reveal his plans for getting mountain artillery into the country?"

In the vast silence of the valley, Paddy Joe dropped his voice. "Submarines were mentioned," he said.

"A pleasant evening," Lacy said. "It could be an early spring."

In March, the Executive assembled in the Nire valley. The meetings began on the twenty-third, but there was heavy raiding by Free State forces in the neighborhood, and so, on the twenty-sixth, they moved from Bliantas to Glenanore, deeper in the valley. De Valera was present at that meeting, but for a time was made to wait in an adjoining room.

At this meeting, Tom Barry moved and Frank Lacy seconded, "That further armed resistance against the Free State government will not further the cause of independence in the country." The motion failed by one vote.

That night, in John Murphy's kitchen, before they climbed up to the loft they were sharing, Lacy did have a single glass of whiskey with Tom Barry, and then the two of them walked out in the yard.

"I never thought the day would come when I would move such a motion," Barry said, "nor that Frank Lacy would back it."

"Nothing is forever," Lacy said.

"Ah, well," Barry said, "we did our duty, we spoke as we thought best. Now we can keep on fighting with clear consciences."

There was to have been a final meeting on the tenth, at Araglin, northwards of Fermoy, between the Kilworth Hills and the Knockmealdowns, but it never took place. Liam Lynch, and with him what in effect was the headquarters of the Irish Republican Army, had been on the run, moving from place to place, a night in one farmhouse, a night in the next. On the night of the sixth, they crossed back over into the Nire, and Lynch slept at Knocknagree. By midnight of the eighth, they were at Goatenbridge, in the Sixth Battalion area of the Third Tipperary, and it was there that Lynch learned of the broad sweep by Free State soldiers which General Prout was sending through the valleys and along the foothills of the mountains, southwards from his base in Clonmel.

Early the next morning, Lynch and his party, in sight now of a Free State column, moved up along a hill of the Knockmealdowns, following a dry riverbed. There was firing upon them, but from a distance of three or four hundred yards, and it was when they had left the riverbed and moved into an exposed position that a soldier, a marksman or a lucky shooter, hit Lynch and brought him down, fatally wounded. He was carried by troops into a public house in Newcastle, and then taken by ambulance to Clonmel's hospital, where he died.

The men from Cork and West Cork and First Cork had been making their separate ways toward Araglin. It was too dangerous to travel in company; each day was bringing new arrests, or fellows shot down by Free State troops traveling in convoy, parts of Prout's sweep.

Lacy, having walked the last twenty miles on foot, reached Araglin at ten the next night, but there was no one in Carmody's save two, Bill Hassett from Kilkenny and Mick Dwyer from Fermoy. Dwyer had arrived but an hour earlier, and Martha Carmody was cooking up a fry for him, which Lacy shared. For a time, the men ate without talking about what had happened. Dwyer had possession of a Ford motorcar, but dared not put it on the road lest it attract attention, and his feet were worn out with walking. He had a full account to give of his journey on foot, and the others let him talk on; it filled the air and kept them away from other thoughts.

But at last Bill Hassett said, "There is the end of it. He was the last Republican, he was the best man of us all, save perhaps Cathal Brugha, a man I never met."

"Sure Liam Lynch himself was reading the writing on the wall," Paddy O'Beine said. "Not to mention Dev."

The heavy curtains of the two kitchen windows were drawn, and they sat talking by the ruddy glare of the fireplace. There had been a sweep of the road outside the house earlier in the day, a Crossley loaded with riflemen and an armored car.

"What are your thoughts on the matter, Frank?" Hassett said. "Aiken will be in command now, would you not think? Dev will be sending out word to Aiken, and Aiken will find a way of informing us."

"It's all over, lads," Lacy said. "In a day or two, Dev will be telling you as much, and Aiken as well, no doubt."

"All over like that?" Carmody said, and sopped up cabbage-flavored butter from his plate. "Because some hoor of a Free Stater had a lucky shot at a better man than himself?"

"Yes," Lacy said. "All over."

After cups of tea, at Lacy's suggestion, Carmody brought out an unlabeled bottle of whiskey, and poured out generous measures.

It was more than a month before the Free State would accept Republican terms for a cessation of hostilities, although the Republicans brought all offensive operations to a close as of noon of April 30. Free State army and police sweeps continued, Republicans taken "in the field" were shipped to the prison camps, and, in Ennis, three prisoners were executed by firing squad. The final Republican order to cease fire and dump arms was issued on the twenty-fourth of May, and published in the national newspapers.

For the final week, Lacy, Casey and their men had been living in a house westwards of Aghabullogue, keeping their heads low, and trusting that neither Cogley nor Rafferty would order sweeps sent out from Kilpeder.

When some columns in the South were disbanded, there were short, melancholy ceremonies, but Lacy had kept his men busy for a full day and far into the night storing the arms and ammunition, the Lee-Enfields and the Brownings. They were stored in the barn, and bricks and mortar carried in from which, later, a false wall could be built. They worked until after one in the morning, and then fell asleep, some in the house and others in the barn. In the morning, they had tea. Then Lacy talked quietly to them in the farmyard, praised them for their services to the Republic, and sent them on their way. Then he and Casey walked back into the kitchen.

"All over," Casey said, sitting with his hands wrapped around his cup. "As easily as that, as easily as men hauling bricks, and the Republic is dead."

"The war is dead, Joe," Lacy said, "not the Republic. You cannot kill the Republic." But he was not certain of that any longer.

"What is to become of us?" Casey said.

Lacy chose to take the question in practical terms.

"They will take their own sweet time before they let our people out of the prison camps; they will be hostages for our good conduct. But at last they will, and Pat MacCarthy will be back there in Kilpeder at his garage."

"If they give it back to him," Casey said.

"They will of course," Lacy said. "The Free Staters have great respect for the rights of property. It is their only principle, and they cling to it fiercely. You have a fine hand for machinery, Joe, motorcars and Vickers guns and so forth. See when the time comes if Pat cannot have work for you. Pat always had great plans. The future lies with the motorcar, he would say, and he would talk of a chain of garages stretching from here into the midlands—motorcars, lorries, the lot."

Casey looked at him uncertainly. He had not gone a far distance in his schooling, but he had an instinct for language.

" 'Tis all over is what you are telling me," he said. "The war and the Republic and all that."

But Lacy's mind had drifted away from their conversation toward the recollection of what Sean Brady had told him, two weeks before, of his last meeting with Liam Lynch, at Poulacappel, a few miles south of Callan. "The headquarters, Frank," Sean said, "of the Irish Republican Army, and a damned ingenious headquarters it was. Twelve feet wide by thirty feet long, with a roof of thatch and galvanized iron, and no entrance save through the secret door of the cowshed, with three cows tied to it, and for additional safety a jennet tied at the hideout side of the cows."

After Lacy had seen Casey on his way, he went back into the silent farmhouse, took the kettle from the hearth, poured some of the hot water into the teapot, and used the rest of it to shave. There was a small mirror beside the sink, discolored and with a piece broken away from one of the corners. The farmhouse held an oppressive quiet, now that the lads had moved out from it. As he shaved, he looked when he needed to at his reflection, but then out through the small, leaded window toward the brightening May morning. He went through each of the rooms, picking up bits of paper to crumble and throw into the fire.

He walked for most of that day, westwards toward the Derrynasaggarts, along twisting roads whose hedges had already brightened into the colors of the season, past silver freshets, past meadows starred with wildflowers. When he came at last to a stream, quick-moving, which flowed southwards into the Sullane, he paused to study it and then walked along its banks for an hour or so until, unexpectedly, it burrowed itself underground. He slept rough that night and the night following it, eating the bread and the heels of cheese which he had carried away with him, and, early on the morning that followed, he stood upon a tall ridge, with mist beginning to wet the gray boulders into black. Between the boulders, coarse, rank grass, and the budding yellow of gorse. A wind from the west freshened the air, and they seemed alone in the world, himself and the darkening boulders and the wind.

He unbuttoned his jacket, slipped free the strap of his shoulder holster, and took out the Parabellum. Without hesitation, without bothering to think what he was doing, he held the pistol by its long barrel, his hand aware of cold, smooth metal, and flung it on a long, tumbling end-over-end arc, into the valley.

XXXI

JANICE NUGENT, 1934

This spring, three years almost to the week after I came back to Ireland, to make my home with Betty at Coolater, I went up to Dublin to spend the day on business with George Fitzmaurice, our family solicitor, and, as reward, to have dinner with Patrick Prentiss.

George has been our lawyer for as long back as I can remember, ever since Betty and I were children, and Betty claims that she can remember breakfast tables at which Mother would propose some new extravagance, a week in Italy perhaps, and Father would say, in significant tones, "We must ask George Fitzmaurice." He had his offices in Merrion Square, with front windows looking out upon the gardens, in which hawthorns were just blossoming, white and pink, and George himself was hawthorny, pink cheeks and a fringe of white hair and all sorts of hidden prickles.

He said not a word about anything save my train journey from Galway, not until Callan had laid out the appropriate ledgers and folders and things tied up with pink tape and had gone away and come back with a pot of India tea and sugar-encrusted biscuits.

"These are difficult times, Janice," George began, as he always did, "difficult for all of us, but especially for two women, two sisters, on an estate that has been partly sold away." But then he added, as he always did once he had tasted his sugared tea, "You have done wonders, though. First Betty on her own after your father died, and now the two of you. So good that you do have each other. And I think we are all in order, at least for a year or two, who can speak for the years beyond that, save perhaps some fortune-teller."

As he spoke, I imagined him saying the same thing, more or less, every morning and every afternoon, to people more or less like Betty and myself. Save of course for some awful morning when he would tell some unhappy small landowner in Leitrim that things were not in order, that he should take a best offer and clear off, clear out of the country. It reminded me—I put the point last year to Betty, and she agreed entirely—of a "treat" we saw once at Bray: a woman dressed up as a gypsy, bright-colored skirts, earrings, who had a pet jackdaw in her booth with her, and if you put tuppence in the tray, the jackdaw would jump down, catch up a tiny scroll, and there would be your fortune.

George had more to say than the jackdaw, much more, but I understood little of it, mostly it was papers to sign or to bring home to Betty to sign.

After two hours or more, he relented, and rang for fresh tea.

"Dear Janice," he said, "such awful times in which we have been sentenced to live. First Charlie, and then Christopher. I scarcely knew Christopher of course, but Charlie and I were great chums."

Which was not strictly true in either particular. He had never met Christopher, and Charlie had thought him an awful bore. He was the O'Gormans' solicitor, not the Nugents'. And besides, Charlie had suspected him of being a golfer. In George's office, looking out upon flowering hawthorn, there was upon one paneled wall a set of Malton's prints of eighteenth-century Dublin, the Parliament House as it then was and Trinity College and the Four Courts and the Custom House. Scattered beyond these, with a calculated irregularity, some of "Spy's" and "Ape's" caricatures of legal luminaries, solicitors and barristers and judges, black gowns, wigs, red gowns. And, on the opposing walls, bound volumes of statutes, pale tan buckram, a bit of black, a bit of gilt.

"Such awful times," George said again, "such awful luck." As though suddenly compelled, recognizing our long years with one another, remembering his visits in my childhood to Father, who did not consider him a bore, toward some personal utterance. "First Charlie being killed in that awful corner of the world. And then Christopher dying."

"Christopher being killed," I said. "Charlie was killed by the

Turks in 1916, and Christopher was killed in 1922, on the Loughrea road." By the Irish, I added to myself, but you can carry brutal honesty of speech only so far.

"Yes," George Fitzmaurice said, and he straightened papers on his desk, dominated by a handsome, vulgar little onyx elephant. And suddenly I was angry with myself for my secret belittlement of George Fitzmaurice, who was quite splendid in his way. There were George Fitzmaurices scattered across Dublin and Cork City and Limerick, solicitors and physicians and surgeons and civil servants who had had nothing to do, one way or another, with what had been happening in Ireland ten years earlier than this spring day, nothing to do with ambushes or Lewis guns or land mines. For whom the Four Courts and the Custom House were as Malton had etched them with his grave, affectionate instruments, and not what history, our own history, had made of them, blackened and dynamited hulks beside a dirty river.

We completed our labors, George and I, far sooner than we had expected, and I had a chance to walk through the Green and down Grafton Street, across the bridge to Sackville Street, or rather to O'Connell Street as we were now to call it, a walk of an hour or two in Dublin's marvelous spring sunlight upon Portland stone and claret brick, before going back to the hotel for a rest before dinner. At dinner that night, Patrick Prentiss was to tell me that George Fitzmaurice was a very nice chap indeed, a bit dull beyond question but sound, but that George did not stand in need of my sentimental defense. Nice chaps like George Fitzmaurice were doing very well in the new Ireland, as they had in the old.

"Take me, for example," Patrick was to say, with his bantering, nearly constant self-irony. Patrick was now a judge in the High Court, and, as we sat facing each other in Jammet's flattering light, I remarked to myself how well he looked the part, gone gray at the temples but no need for eyeglasses, and the empty right sleeve of the handsomely tailored jacket looking like some discreet, dandyish decoration, and not because the arm had been torn off from him in an ugly, bloody trench. And so, in the afternoon, Dublin had seemed to me, the tulip-stained gardens of the park, and the smart shops along Grafton Street, Tyson's, which catered to what remained of the huntin', shootin' gentry, hacking waistcoats of sunflower yellow, raspberry red, small-check tattersalls gray-and-black-hatched. As though two Special Branch men, in 1921, had not been shot dead directly in front of Tyson's by three gunmen, while two others held at bay the small, frightened after-theater crowd. Now, no doubt, Patrick, a judge of the High Court, sat in white wig, gown black or scarlet concealing the empty sleeve, leaning over the bench, solemn as a judge, in the Four Courts, which once I had seen guarded by gunmen. And which, a few days later, was shelled by other gunmen, but these ones in what had become the uniform of order and law, British brown dyed Free State green.

In the Shelbourne, I bathed and then, in the robe which when new Christopher had so admired, pale orange dragons upon dark blue silk, I stretched out to rest, with a packet of Goldflakes on the table beside me and *Country Life* and *Claudius the God.* I had a cigarette and then lay there a bit, tired from my walk but nowhere near sleep. Then I began to cry. I cried quietly at first, but presently I was sobbing, and then, after a bit, the sobbing stopped. This happens to me these days only once in a great, great while, and yet I am always half-expecting it.

That weekend, the last of our Connemara weekends in Myles Keough's cottage, I told Christopher of how I had felt when I had knelt beside the body of Bowers, the bank inspector or spy or informer or whatever he was, with the blood oozing from his throat and the back of his head out on to the dusty railway platform in Moate. That was on the Thursday night, after Christopher and I had driven across Galway, from Coolater to the cottage at Ballyconneely. We sat together at the window and drank a bottle of good wine, and ate the sandwiches we had brought with us.

Finisterre, I had always thought of Connemara, loving the word, the world's end, beyond Oughterard, beyond Clifden, and then, at last, with Christopher, *finisterre,* beyond history. Beyond table, wineglasses, small streaked window, lay only coral strand and the waters of the Atlantic.

A few miles beyond us, along the coast road, lay Renvyle, or rather, what now remained of it, the western house of Dr. Gogarty, who had waited with Christopher on the North Wall, in drizzling rain, for Collins's body. The house had been burned down by the

Republicans two months earlier, all the books gone, all the paintings, and nothing left, as Gogarty wrote to Myles, "but a charred oak beam quenched in the well beneath the house. And ten tall square towers, chimneys, stand bare on Europe's extreme edge."

It was a season of burnings, that spring of 1923, "the country houses of Ireland," as Elizabeth Fingall put it, "a chain of bonfires stretching across the country." They were often very polite, so Elizabeth wrote me, "kind and helpful and sympathetic. They would call themselves 'the burning party.' Had a festive air, almost. 'We can give you fifteen minutes and we can help you. Will you hurry now!' Often, in panic, foolish things were chosen, stacked on the lawn, but the Romneys and the Chippendale furniture and the old Irish silver had perished." When George Moore's house in Mayo was burned, a lovely house of the old Catholic gentry which Charlie and I had visited once, George off in London of course but his brother the colonel was there, Father's friend. When Moore Hall burned, a huge mass of flames and clouds of sparks like snowflakes, there was nothing left, the caretaker wrote, "except some vestments and the objects from the Altar in the priest's chapel." When Senator Bagwell's house in Clonmel was set afire, one of the two finest private libraries in the country was destroyed; the other was the Tighe house, in Graiguenamanagh, and that went too, a bit later. And between such houses and the Custom House and the Four Courts, it was as though the history of Ireland itself was under attack, subject of paraffin and petrol and Mills bombs.

But much else went too, houses which played no part in the life of the country, and which held no Romneys nor Irish silver, but only bound volumes of *Punch* and tarnished punch bowls, photographs of subalterns and captains grouped together, that sort of thing. Derek and Hazel's house had been one of those, and it was burned down a fortnight before we drove west to Galway.

Betty could see it almost, across the lake, a rim of red, pink, and took the motorcar to see could she help, but there were three or four determined men at the entranceway, determined and ashamed all at once. She turned straight round and drove back to Coolater, to phone the barracks, but the wires had been cut.

Hazel and Derek moved out of the country straight away, to England, but straight away is never immediate, and after the burning, Betty brought them back to us at Coolater, and then telephone calls began, to Goodbody their solicitors in Dublin, and all the rest of it, and Free State officers came round to Coolater to take depositions, and so forth. And for most of that time, Derek sat with Father in our estate office, but Father was no longer of much help, although in his failing state, a weighty, meaty reminder that there had been a past. Derek talked and talked and talked to him; Derek was very shaken, and would never again be quite the person he had been, boisterous and well-meaning and awful.

Hazel, Betty told me, was quite different from Derek and greatly his superior. They arrived in a pony and trap, about four in the morning, carrying with them nothing, entirely nothing, although surely something could have been crammed into the trap, those awful Wedgwoods and the bas-relief of Mount Vesuvius which Derek's grandfather had brought back from his month-before-university. And at five that morning, disdainful of the tea which cooled before her, Hazel sat drinking sherry after sherry. The Free State people asked them whether they distrusted any of the servants, but of course they did not, although Derek, making a brief emergence from the estate office, confided his suspicions of Mary Frances, "that awful embittered little housemaid you fobbed off on us years ago, and then we discharged her." But the Free State officer was a sensible fellow and did not take Derek seriously. "A very nice young fellow," Hazel said, after what must have been her fifth sherry, filled up to the brim of a not-so-tiny glass, "a manly sort of chap."

When Christopher and I were about to drive off to Connemara, we stood by the motorcar, the three of us, to talk about Father. And then, just before we left, Betty leaned into the car toward Christopher, and put her hand on his forearm. I can see the moment so clearly, as I can see all the moments of that weekend, her square, competent hand resting on his tweed jacket. "You be very careful, now, Christopher."

That first night in Ballyconneely, I was thinking of Hazel and Derek, and of the ruins of their quite modest but grandly named house, and yet what I said, quite suddenly and unexpectedly, was how I had felt that day, four years earlier, as I knelt beside Bowers on the railway platform.

It was still full light, with nothing beyond the window save the wide bay, its waters colored by the declining sun.

"That was a legitimate act of war," Christopher said. "He was an informer."

"And what of poor Derek and Hazel," I said, "was that a legitimate act of war?" Perhaps it was. I could almost see the fellows who stood beside the road, shotguns and cloth caps.

Christopher picked up the wine bottle and refilled his glass. "These are all acts of desperation," he said, "the Republicans are beaten and they know it. There are feelers moving out from their side and from ours. It will all be over in a month or two."

"How nice for Derek and Hazel," I said, and turned away from him, to look out at the bay, where, far off, a trawler moved southwards.

He leaned forward across the table to talk with me, and put his hand on my forearm, as Betty, a few hours earlier, had put her hand on his. But I pulled away from him, not angrily, but in a movement of withdrawal, a withdrawal away from men shot down on railway platforms, and houses put to the torch, it did not matter by whom.

Christopher stood up, and without asking me to join him, unlatched the door and walked out onto the strand. And I sat by myself. After a bit, I finished his glass of wine, tasting its coolness in the cooling evening. Then I laid a turf fire and put a kettle on the hob, and threw on a jacket and went outside myself. I set off on my own, needing to be by myself with my quiet anger and sullenness, and hoping that the full, salt-scented air would drive away that memory of blood and dust on the platform at Moate. I walked for the better part of an hour, and when I returned, I sat down on the flat stone outside the cottage door, and at last I could see him walking back to me, walking, as sometimes he did, quickly but with crossed arms. And when he was near enough to hear me, as he walked along the strand in the evening's queer greenish light, I stood up and waved, and called out to him, "Christopher! Christopher!"

I had brought with me for my dinner with Patrick one of my London frocks, a deep lilac, which hung from me in a way I especially liked, and I studied myself in the hotel room mirror, turning this way and that. There were still dinner parties in Galway, and I was fit for them even if Betty disliked them, and the lilac gown had passed the essential test: other women would look at me angrily, because perhaps it *was* cut a bit short, and if I still have smashing legs, that is scarcely my fault, now is it? I have become what people in books call a woman "of a certain age," which has always, even in girlhood, seemed to me a phrase mysterious and fine.

Where would Dublin be without Jammet's? In London or New York it would be quite an ordinary place to eat, but here it always has a sense of the Continental, of being a bit grand, and it does have those lovely small lamps, shaded by pink silk, so flattering to women of a certain age, and those dim, deep mirrors, echoing off each other. But the food, so it seems to me, is not much better than what you get at the Prince of Wales in Athlone. You don't really improve the *tin* soup and the *tick* soup by calling them *potages*.

All round us was the new Ireland, which the fighting had been about, senators and politicians and portrait painters, and their well-mannered wives.

But when I remarked upon this to Patrick, he said, "And judges of the High Court. Don't forget about us. Your snobbishness is incorrigible, Janice. How do you keep it up, out there in Galway?"

"No better place," I said.

"Over there," Patrick said, looking past me to one side, "no, don't turn round, dear, it's rude, over there you will find a member of Mr. De Valera's cabinet, having a quiet dinner with his wife, and ten years ago, he was a man hunted in the hills, desperate in his defense of the Republic." Patrick sipped his *potage*. "Jammet's is a great leveler for those who can afford it."

"It is probably all for the best that you never married, Patrick. Imagine spending all of one's mornings at the breakfast table, listening to your irony."

"At the breakfast table! You should hear me in court. Judges in these islands have a reputation for savage irony, and I wouldn't want to let the side down. And right there, right where Mickey Molloy is sitting, there was sitting two weeks ago General Mulcahy of the Free State army, who had been hunting poor Mickey. Without much success. Mulcahy succeeded Collins as commander-in-chief, but he could not fill his boots. Who could?"

I caught our reflections in a mirror, and marveled at what a handsome couple we made. Pity.

"Two barristers were in my court last month, arguing against each other, who had been battalion commandants against each other. They would clutch their gowns and lean forward, and I imagined that I could see the dried blood under their fingernails."

"Patrick, I asked you out to dinner to put a question. It has to do with dried blood, in a way. A young man named Hennessy keeps coming to see me and asking questions of me. About Christopher. He is writing a small book about Christopher, he says."

"Yes," Patrick said. "I know. He has been on to me as well, and Myles Keough."

"Why Christopher?" I asked. "Of all the chaps who were at work in those years, why Christopher? I ask him, but I cannot understand his explanations. Some writers, you ask them why they are writing whatever it is, and suddenly their mouths are full of hot potatoes. Not that he isn't a nice enough fellow. Very, very serious."

"Serious is the answer," Patrick said, and looked at me across his soup spoon. "Most of the fellows in the movement were rough and ready sorts, like Mickey Molloy having his gammon steak in Jammet's, but Christopher was rather special, like O'Higgins on one side and—oh, like Lacy on the other. And Collins, of course, there will be no end of books about Collins. And De Valera one of these days."

"Christopher was not a Collins," I said decisively, "and still less was he a De Valera."

Patrick looked at me closely, and then shrugged.

"Christopher was a publicist, was he not, Patrick? He worked on the literary side of the movement, did he not? The *Republican Bulletin* and explaining things to foreign journalists and so forth. And of course, he was secretary during the Treaty negotiations, like Childers. Is that not right, Patrick?"

Patrick continued to look at me, then broke his gaze to call over Bernard, our waiter. I waited patiently while Patrick explained about the lamb, and then waited while he gave Bernard a message for the wine waiter. And then I sat there waiting.

"That is what young Mr. Hennessy believes," I said. "He plans to call his book *Ideas and Rebellion*, something silly like that."

"A dreary enough title," Patrick said, "but why do you call it silly?"

"Because you know," I said, "and I know what young Mr. Hennessy does not know, that Christopher was also some kind of intelligence officer for Collins, and that he arranged murders and accidents and ambushes and God knows what else."

We sat looking at each other, and in the silence I could hear phrases floating toward us from other tables, and I could hear the curious hum which crowded restaurants have, not just the voices.

"And why would I know that, Janice?" he said at last.

"Because you were Christopher's closest friend," I said, "and because he would talk to you about things. He told me so, on that last weekend we had, at Myles's cottage, he told me so. You know all about it, Patrick. That general who was shot down in London, and the other general who was murdered in Cork, on his way to a wedding. You know all about that."

"No," he said, "I did not know about the general in London and the one in Cork. I should have guessed, but it never occurred to me. You see, he never told me quite everything."

"We had a long weekend in which to talk," I said. "He set off by himself along the coral strand, and came back when it was almost dark, and sat down beside me outside the cottage. We talked that weekend, or rather, I listened to him, and then I made meals, and once we drove over to Renvyle, and we quarreled, I expect it could be called a quarrel. And we never made love that weekend. Christopher was expected in Dublin on the Monday, and so early on Sunday, we motored back to Coolater, and sometime before noon he left me there with Father and Betty. And I kissed him goodbye, the kind of kiss which says, 'It is all all right, we did not really quarrel.' He was to come back to Coolater, but of course he did not. That was the last time I saw him. We stood together, Betty and I, and we waved to him, the two of us waved."

Patrick has a way of sitting quietly and listening, his face sympathetic to be sure, but quite unreadable. Perhaps that is what made him a clever barrister, and now he is, I am certain, a clever judge. I wanted to say something which would shock him, but I knew that I could not. Instead, I said nothing at all, and at last Patrick had to speak.

"Why?" he asked. "Why then?"

When Bernard served our lamb, I noticed that the kitchen had discreetly and delicately cut Patrick's for him, so that he could manage, despite the empty sleeve. But he paid no attention to food, neither of us did, and the spring lamb grew cold.

Sometimes I have thought that my description, and not, God knows, for the first time, of that awful railway station, blood and hair mixed together, blood and flesh, exploded something within Christopher. But I know that that is not really the explanation.

He had come to believe—so he told me sometime or other over the weekend, nothing that he said was orderly, or arranged in sequence—that Collins had seen in him from the first qualities that could be used, that he could use, had seen them in those early days in 1917, the two of them released from their English prison camps and working in the Exchequer Street office. "You be certain to attend to that, now, Chris," Collins said to him in the public house close to the quays, the smell of spilled porter mingling with oily smells from the river. It had been a test, that first assignment, and Christopher had handled it well, as he had handled, a week later, the rental of the house down the coast which was used later for dealings with foreign arms merchants.

"You understand, do you not," Christopher said to me, "you understand that either a war is fought or it is not, and if it is fought, things are done of which the less said, the better." He told me about Bloody Sunday, and how he had worked out the identity of the British agents, beginning with little more than the word "Cairo," and how they had to be—"eliminated," was his word. "Killed, you mean," I said. "Yes," he said, "killed. They were sent over to smash us," he said, "but we smashed them instead. They sent over other agents after that, tried to build up a second network, but we were on to them."

It was the next morning, the Friday, that he told me about Bloody Sunday, as we walked together along the strand, the air beautifully clean, and the early sky unflawed except for a few frail-seeming clouds. "You do see, do you not?" he would keep saying, as though there were something he expected me to say, and something more than, "Yes, I see."

Once he told me about one of "our" people, who had turned informer, and Christopher and a man named Murphy, Cornelius

Murphy, had met with him in a flat in Gardiner Street, and held their guns on him until he confessed. Then Murphy shot him.

"Not you," I said, in a voice I tried to keep expressionless. "Murphy killed him."

"Yes," he said, reading my tone, "Murphy."

And so it went, he told me bits and pieces, out of order, told me very flatly some of them, but sometimes he would sketch in a scene, like that first drink with Collins in the public house off the quays, and how vividly he recalled the odors. He told me about the bungled killing of the general in London, and of how, with the Civil War about to begin, he had given to Lacy, a Republican commandant, the assignment to eliminate the fellow who would be motoring down to the wedding. As he talked, he conjured for me a room I have never seen, the abovestairs room in a public house off Parnell Square, beyond uncurtained windows the dark night of Dublin.

"They were organizing a pogrom up there," he said, and he looked northwards, beyond clear pale sky, beyond pale mountains, browns, blues. "They had to be shaken up."

"Yes," I said, "I see."

"And *did* you," Patrick Prentiss asked me years later, in Jammet's, "did you see?"

"I don't know," I said, "it was being told so many things at once, and by someone you had been certain you knew, someone with whom you made love, bodies touching, trusting."

"They have their toughies over there," Christopher had said suddenly on the Saturday, "they have their toughies, their Churchills and their Lloyd Georges and Birkenheads, and they rule the world with their toughies. Well, Collins was our toughie, paid them back." But then he shook his head. "You cannot pretend, you know. Now, with Collins gone, they are all pretending to be like him, but all they know how to do is take men out of prison cells and shoot them."

"Or burn down houses," I said.

"Yes," he said, "or burn down houses."

Toward the end of the day, he said, with a kind of shrug, "At the end, at the very end, I don't think that Collins knew what to do, either. I think he went down to West Cork not knowing what to do."

"And now," I said, "you don't know what to do either. Isn't

that it, Christopher?" But he did not answer my question. He looked across the blue, unruffled water.

At the end, we sent back our meals, untouched, and Patrick ordered us coffees and cognacs.

"Poor Janice," he said at last.

"Poor Christopher," I said. "Because I am certain that he was going through a bad patch, as everyone does from time to time, and if he had been able to come back to Coolater at the end of the week, everything would have been fine."

"Yes," Patrick said, and covered my hand with his, an old lover's hand, a judge's hand. "I am certain that it would have been fine."

I had not been talking nearly as long as I imagined, because Jammet's was still full, and after a bit I asked for a second cognac, please, and as I looked about me, at other diners, at Patrick and myself in the oblique, cloudy mirrors, I said, "Tell me about them, Patrick, tell me about the other diners."

But he smiled, and said, "I don't know quite everyone in Dublin, you know. Why do you want to know?"

"I walked across O'Connell Bridge today," I said, "and remembered how it was shelled, and the stories about the GPO in flames and the buildings across from it, and the stories about the man running out from the blazing building to be shot down. And all around were enormous garish electric signs waiting for nightfall, signs for Bovril and milk chocolate and so forth."

Often when I say something like that, I am expected to explain it, but never with Patrick.

I took the afternoon train, and Betty met me at the railway station in the old Morris, which always was dusty, and whose back seat was always a scattering of newspapers and things in burlap sacks. She eyed me as she always did, with a mingling of affection and disapproval, although I was dressed sensibly enough, even by her austere standards, in a suit of oatmeal tweed with a bright paisley scarf tied about my throat. It is as though she knew all about the short lilac frock in my suitcase.

"It all went well?" she asked.

"Of course," I said. "George is a dear, and I have all sorts of things for us both to sign, and other things just for your signature. He says we are all right for another year or so."

"I told you we were," Betty said, "I can do sums just as capably as George Fitzmaurice."

"And then I had dinner with Patrick at Jammet's," I said, "and it was just like old times."

"He can well afford it," she said, "the salaries that the Free State hands out to judges are scandalous, and it will be even worse now that De Valera and his crowd are in power. At least the old crowd had a few miserly instincts."

"Patrick wanted me to stay on a few days," I said. "There is something good on at the Abbey, he says."

"I doubt it," Betty said. "Never anything at the Abbey but old rubbish about peasants and how will they ever keep hold of the farm."

"Like us," I said, and she had the good grace to smile. Betty and I have grown very fond of each other.

There is a narrow place in the road, about five miles before one comes to the turning for Coolater, and very close in fact to the turning for what had been Hazel and Derek's. Sometimes I can drive straight through it without giving it a thought, and then other times I will remember that it is there that Christopher was killed, that spring morning in 1923, about twenty minutes after Betty and I had stood waving to him.

Very early that morning, it seems, the road was safe, but then at some point a milk cart was turned over, and felled trees piled up against it. The Free State officer who came round later said that very possibly it was Christopher they were after, but then later everyone came to agree that what they had had in mind was an ambush of an army convoy which would be moving south from Athenry. There were stories about it everywhere in the neighborhood, and there still are, but not much that is agreed upon. Sean Brady, the Republican commandant, had moved his column up into the Slieve Aughties, and he would have had to move back into our area in the night. He was captured a few weeks later, and held in Gormanstown for a year, and was on the hunger strike there. After his release, he moved to the States, and so far as we know, he has never claimed responsibility for the attack on Christopher's motorcar.

But there is a fellow named Geraghty in the town, a man who lives with his married sister and does casual labor, who was a member of Sean Brady's column, and he has been known to talk in public houses, with enough drink taken. It was the convoy from Athenry that they had in mind, but they recognized Christopher and his car, and decided, almost on the spur of the moment, to have a go at him. But the odd thing, Geraghty says, is that Christopher saw the blockade, and drove straight into it, as if he could smash his way through. And Brady stood behind his rock, hand upraised as if paralyzed, and then someone—"Not me!" Geraghty will say, raising up his own hand—cut loose and began firing. It matters terribly to me that Christopher died and what he may have been thinking as the road twisted and then narrowed, but I am strangely indifferent as to who pulled the trigger or at whose orders.

Even before Father's decline we had sold off some of the best land, but what has always seemed to me a marvel is how Father and Betty and then Betty on her own have kept up the look of things, the poplars on either side of the graveled entranceway, past the gatehouse, which now of course is neatly bricked up, and the lances of the gates sprucely painted, green in Father's day and white in Betty's and mine. To be sure, we still had a gardener and a half, old Spellacy from Father's day and Henry Dixon from down the road, who worked with Spellacy as needed.

Most of this, perhaps all of it, was of Betty's contriving. She was managing most of the estate business in Father's final years, but discreetly, and after he died, she settled down in the estate office. Now she had new ledger books and files and boxes for letters and an American adding machine and a typewriter. When we reached Coolater, she led me there straight away, leaving my case in the hall, from which she had allowed me to drag out the papers which George Fitzmaurice had sent down to her.

As she worked at Father's desk, without looking up from the papers, she pushed her packet of cigarettes toward me, and for twenty minutes or more I sat quietly smoking and watching her. "There," she said, and put down her pen, took one of the cigarettes and smiled. "Yes, indeed, we will be all right for a few years, three at least, as I make it." And for all of the days ahead, her brusqueness would be gone, and she would be my Betty. She told me once, a year or so ago, that when she saw Father begin to fail, it terrified her, not only the thought of Father failing, but the thought of someday losing Coolater, losing the lake, losing the road and the pasturelands and the plantations of trees, the herd. Save for our years at school and that month when Mother had taken her to Rome and Florence, and save for two weeks when Charlie and I had carried her off to Paris, she had known only Coolater.

"It must be awful for Hazel and Derek off there in London," she said to me once, after the burning.

"Nonsense," I said. "I see them every few months, and they are flourishing. Derek was well recompensed by the government for the loss of the house and they sold off the land at a profit, as well you know. 'Best thing that ever happened to us,' Hazel tells me."

"She doesn't mean that," Betty said. "Do you remember, every year when Derek was MFH, they gave the hunt ball? He was wonderful at that, it was the one thing he did well."

"Well," Hazel had said to me once, "I do miss the hunt, but we have a jolly one here, and Derek is happy. He has the hunt and he has his club and he is active in the League of Empire Defenders, doesn't that sound ghastly?"

"But what about you, dear Hazel?" I said. "Surely there are no clubs for women?"

"There is that drawback," she said. We were having tea in the Savoy. "But then, I am still bouncy and beddable. You should have touched a match to Coolater, but it's too late now. There has to be a war."

Now, in the estate office, where Betty had been busy saving Coolater, I smiled, and Betty asked me why and I could not explain. I was very happy being back at Coolater, and never once have I regretted coming home.

We had tea and sandwiches in the drawing room. Never anything dainty about Mrs. Donovan's sandwiches; she was arthritic now, but she had kept the art of thick sandwiches.

"Do you know what I was remembering last night?" Betty asked me. "I expect that thinking about meeting you at the railway station put me in mind of it. Do you remember once, when we were little, and Father was coming in by train from Galway

City and we were let take the pony cart to meet him?" But I did not remember it and it did not matter, I let her voice flow on, a tranquil stream. She was never happier than when we would have tea and thick sandwiches in the late afternoon or early evening, ourselves, or perhaps ourselves and friends, Dr. Riordan and his wife, or Mr. Elliott, the bank manager. Once she had saved Coolater for another month, she would move toward her memories of Coolater years before, verdant and nourishing, Father's boisterous laugh, the hunt in the early russet morning, the two carriages rolling past flowering hedges to Easter-morning Mass, the altars flower-bedecked.

"Yes," I said after a bit, "I do remember that."

"You do not," she said, pouting a bit but not really angry. "You weren't even listening. You have never listened, Janice, not to me, not to Father, not to—to anyone."

"Perhaps not," I said, and, before setting off for a walk, while there was still light, I crossed over to her and kissed her. Her skin was very smooth, unbruised by the winds and bad weathers of the West.

Along the path to the lake, a path badly overgrown, Spellacy could not attend to everything, the hedges and the larches gave to the light an attractive, greenish color. The hedges were so thick and dense that the notion of a grotto occurred to me. But no hedges grew at the water's very edge and its reeds were pale and straight. By pushing past the growths along the other path, I was able at last to reach the keep, where Betty and I had once played. It was like a jagged tooth of history, shoved up among nature's leaves and branches.